THE ENEMY

Desmond Bagley was born in 1923 in Kendal, Westmorland, and brought up in Blackpool. He began his working life, aged 14, in the printing industry and then did a variety of jobs until going into an aircraft factory at the start of the Second World War.

When the war ended he decided to travel to southern Africa, going overland through Europe and the Sahara. He worked en route, reaching South Africa in 1951.

He became a freelance journalist in Johannesburg and wrote his first published novel, *The Golden Keel*, in 1962. In 1964 he returned to England and lived in Totnes for twelve years. He and his wife then moved to Guernsey in the Channel Islands. Here he found the ideal place for combining his writing with his other interests, which included computers, mathematics, military history, and entertaining friends from all over the world.

Desmond Bagley died in April 1983. Two previously unpublished Bagley novels have since been published: the first, *Night of Error*, was published in 1984, the second, *Juggernaut*, in 1985. Both were on the bestseller lists for many weeks.

DESMOND BAGLEY

The Enemy

FONTANA/Collins

First published by William Collins Sons & Co. Ltd 1977
First issued in Fontana Paperbacks 1978
Fifteenth impression March 1990

Printed and bound in Great Britain by
William Collins Sons & Co. Ltd, Glasgow

To all the DASTards

especially

Iwan and Inga
Jan and Anita
Hemming and Annette

We have met the enemy, and he is ours.

OLIVER HAZARD PERRY
Heroic American Commodore

We have met the enemy, and he is us.

WALT KELLY
Subversive Sociological Cartoonist

1

I met Penelope Ashton at a party thrown by Tom Packer. That may be a bit misleading because it wasn't the kind of party that gets thrown very far; no spiked punch or pot, and no wife-swapping or indiscriminate necking in the bedrooms at two in the morning. Just a few people who got together over a civilized dinner with a fair amount of laughter and a hell of a lot of talk. But it did tend to go on and what with Tom's liberal hand with his after-dinner scotches I didn't feel up to driving, so when I left I took a taxi.

Penny Ashton came with Dinah and Mike Huxham; Dinah was Tom's sister. I still haven't worked out whether I was invited as a makeweight for the odd girl or whether she was brought to counterbalance me. At any rate when we sat at table the sexes were even and I was sitting next to her. She was a tall, dark woman, quiet and composed in manner and not very forthcoming. She was no raving beauty, but few women are; Helen of Troy may have launched a thousand ships but no one was going to push the boat out for Penny Ashton, at least not at first sight. Not that she was ugly or anything like that. She had a reasonably good figure and a reasonably good face, and she dressed well. I think the word to describe her would be average. I put her age at about twenty-seven and I wasn't far out. She was twenty-eight.

As was usual with Tom's friends, the talk ranged far and wide; Tom was a rising star in the upper reaches of the medical establishment and he was eclectic in his choice of dining companions and so the talk was good. Penny joined in but she tended to listen rather than talk and her interjections were infrequent. Gradually I became aware that when she did speak her comments were acute, and there was a sardonic cast to her eye when she was listening to something she didn't agree with. I found her spikiness of mind very agreeable.

After dinner the talk went on in the living-room over coffee and brandy. I opted for scotch because brandy doesn't agree with me, a circumstance Tom knew very well because he poured one of his measures big enough to paralyse an elephant and left the jug of iced water convenient to my elbow.

As is common on these occasions, while the dinner-table conversation is general and involves everybody, after dinner the party tended to split into small groups, each pursuing their congenial arguments and riding their hobby-horses hard and on a loose rein. To my mild surprise I found myself opting for a group of two – myself and Penny Ashton. I suppose there were a dozen of us there, but I settled in a corner and monopolized Penny Ashton. Or did she monopolize me? It could have been six of one and half-a-dozen of the other; it usually is in cases like that.

I forget what we talked about at first but gradually our conversation became more personal. I discovered she was a research biologist specializing in genetics and that she worked with Professor Lumsden at University College, London. Genetics is the hottest and most controversial subject in science today and Lumsden was in the forefront of the battle. Anyone working with him would have to be very bright indeed and I was suitably impressed. There was a lot more to Penny Ashton than met the casual eye.

Some time during the evening she asked, 'And what do you do?'

'Oh, I'm someone in the City,' I said lightly.

She got that sardonic look in her eye and said reprovingly, 'Satire doesn't become you.'

'It's true!' I protested. 'Someone's got to make the wheels of commerce turn.' She didn't pursue the subject.

8

Inevitably someone checked his watch and discovered with horror the lateness of the hour, and the party began to break up. Usually the more congenial the party the later the hour, and it was pretty late. Penny said, 'My God – my train!'

'Which station?'

'Victoria.'

'I'll drop you,' I said and stood up, swaying slightly as I felt Tom's scotch. 'From a taxi.'

I borrowed the telephone and rang for a taxi, and then we stood around making party noises until it arrived. As we were driven through the brightly-lit London streets I reflected that it had been a good evening; it had been quite a while since I had felt so good. And it wasn't because of the quality of Tom's booze, either.

I turned to Penny. 'Known the Packers long?'

'A few years. I was at Cambridge with Dinah Huxham – Dinah Packer she was then.'

'Nice people. It's been a good evening.'

'I enjoyed it.'

I said, 'How about repeating it – just the two of us? Say, the theatre and supper afterwards.'

She was silent for a moment, then said, 'All right.' So we fixed a time for the following Wednesday and I felt even better.

She wouldn't let me come into the station with her so I kept the taxi and redirected it to my flat. It was only then I realized I didn't know if she was married or not, and I tried to remember the fingers of her left hand. Then I thought I was a damned fool; I hardly knew the woman so what did it matter if she was married or not? I wasn't going to marry her myself, was I?

On the Wednesday I picked her up at University College at seven-fifteen in the evening and we had a drink at a pub near the theatre before seeing the show. I don't like theatre crush bars; they're too well named. 'Do you always work as late as this?' I asked.

She shook her head. 'It varies. It's not a nine-to-five job, you know. When we're doing something big we could be there all night, but that doesn't happen often. I laboured tonight because I was staying in town.' She smiled. 'It helped me catch up on some of the paperwork.'

'Ah; the paperwork is always with us.'

'You ought to know; your job is all paperwork, isn't it?'

I grinned. 'Yes; shuffling all those fivers around.'

So we saw the show and I took her to supper in Soho and then to Victoria Station. And made another date for the Saturday.

And, as they say, one thing led to another and soon I was squiring her around regularly. We took in more theatres, an opera, a couple of ballets, a special exhibition at the National Gallery, Regent's Park Zoo, something she wanted to see at the Natural History Museum, and a trip down the river to Greenwich. We could have been a couple of Americans doing the tourist bit.

After six weeks of this I think we both thought that things were becoming pretty serious. I, at least, took it seriously enough to go to Cambridge to see my father. He smiled when I told him about Penny, and said, 'You know, Malcolm, you've been worrying me. It's about time you settled down. Do you know anything about the girl's family?'

'Not much,' I admitted. 'From what I can gather he's some sort of minor industrialist. I haven't met him yet.'

'Not that it matters,' said my father. 'I hope we've gone beyond snobberies like that. Have you bedded the girl yet?'

'No,' I said slowly. 'We've come pretty close, though.'

'Um!' he said obscurely, and began to fill his pipe. 'It's been my experience here at the college that the rising generation isn't as swinging and uninhibited as it likes to think it is. Couples don't jump bare-skinned into a bed at the first opportunity – not if they're taking each other seriously and have respect for each other. Is it like that with you?'

I nodded. 'I've had my moments in the past, but somehow it's different with Penny. Anyway, I've known her only a few weeks.'

'You remember Joe Patterson?'

'Yes.' Patterson was head of one of the departments of psychology.

'He reckons the ordinary man is mixed up about the qualities he wants in a permanent partner. He once told me that the average man's ideal wife-to-be is a virgin in the terminal stages of nymphomania. A witticism, but with truth in it.'

'Joe is a cynic.'

'Most wise men are. Anyway, I'd like to see Penny as soon as you can screw up your courage. Your mother would have been happy to see you married; it's a pity about that.'

'How are you getting on, Dad?'

'Oh, I rub along. The chief danger is of becoming a university eccentric; I'm trying to avoid that.'

We talked of family matters for some time and then I went back to London.

It was at this time that Penny made a constructive move. We were in my flat talking over coffee and liqueurs; she had complimented me on the Chinese dinner and I had modestly replied that I had sent out for it myself. It was then that she invited me to her home for the weekend. To meet the family.

11

2

She lived with her father and sister in a country house near Marlow in Buckinghamshire, a short hour's spin from London up the M4. George Ashton was a widower in his mid-fifties who lived with his daughters in a brick-built Queen Anne house of the type you see advertised in a full-page spread in *Country Life*. It had just about everything. There were two tennis courts and one swimming pool; there was a stable block converted into garages filled with expensive bodies on wheels, and there was a stable block that was still a stable block and filled with expensive bodies on legs – one at each corner. It was a Let's-have-tea-on-the-lawn sort of place; The-master-will-see-you-in-the-library sort of place. The good, rich, upper-middle-class life.

George Ashton stood six feet tall and was thatched with a strong growth of iron-grey hair. He was very fit, as I found out on the tennis court. He played an aggressive, hard-driving game and I was hard put to cope with him even though he had a handicap of about twenty-five years. He beat me 5–7, 7–5, 6–3, which shows his stamina was better than mine. I came off the court out of puff but Ashton trotted down to the swimming pool, dived in clothed as he was, and swam a length before going into the house to change.

I flopped down beside Penny. 'Is he always like that?'

'Always,' she assured me.

I groaned. 'I'll be exhausted just watching him.'

Penny's sister, Gillian, was as different from Penny as could be. She was the domestic type and ran the house. I don't mean she acted as lady of the house and merely gave orders. She *ran* it. The Ashtons didn't have much staff;

there were a couple of gardeners and a stable girl, a houseman-cum-chauffeur called Benson, a full-time maid and a daily help who came in for a couple of hours each morning. Not much staff for a house of that size.

Gillian was a couple of years younger than Penny and there was a Martha and Mary relationship between them which struck me as a little odd. Penny didn't do much about the house as far as I could see, apart from keeping her own room tidy, cleaning her own car and grooming her own horse. Gillian was the Martha who did all the drudgery but she didn't seem to mind and appeared to be quite content. Of course, it was a weekend and it might have been different during the week. All the same, I thought Ashton would get a shock should Gillian marry and leave to make a home of her own.

It was a good weekend although I felt a bit awkward at first, conscious of being on show; but I was soon put at ease in that relaxed household. Dinner that evening, cooked by Gillian, was simple and well served, and afterwards we played bridge. I partnered Penny and Ashton partnered Gillian, and soon I found that Gillian and I were the rabbits. Penny played a strong, exact and carefully calculated game, while Ashton played bridge as he played tennis, aggressively and taking chances at times. I observed that the chances he took came off more often than not, but Penny and I came slightly ahead at the end, although it was nip and tuck.

We talked for a while until the girls decided to go to bed, then Ashton suggested a nightcap. The scotch he poured was not in the same class as Tom Packer's but not far short, and we settled down for a talk. Not unexpectedly he wanted to know something about me and was willing to trade information, so I learned how he earned his pennies among other things. He ran a couple of manufacturing firms in Slough producing something abstruse in the chemical line and another which specialized in high-impact plastics. He employed about a thousand men and was the sole owner, which impressed me. There are not too many organizations like that around which are still in the hands of one man.

Then he enquired, very politely, what I did to earn my bread, and I said, 'I'm an analyst.'

He smiled slightly. 'Psycho?'

I grinned. 'No – economic. I'm a junior partner with McCulloch and Ross; we're economic consultants.'

'Yes, I've heard of your crowd. What exactly is it that you do?'

'Advisory work of all sorts – market surveys, spotting opportunities for new products, or new areas for existing products, and so on. Also general economics and financial advice. We do the general dogsbodying for firms which are not big enough to support their own research group. ICI wouldn't need us but a chap like you might.'

He seemed interested in that. 'I've been thinking of going public,' he said. 'I'm not all that old, but one never knows what may happen. I'd like to leave things tidy for the girls.'

'It might be very profitable for you personally,' I said. 'And, as you say, it would tidy up the estate in the event of your death – make the death duties bit less messy.' I thought about it for a minute. 'But I don't know if this is the time to float a new issue. You'd do better to wait for an upturn in the economy.'

'I've not entirely decided yet,' he said. 'But if I do decide to go public then perhaps you can advise me.'

'Of course. It's exactly our line of work.'

He said no more about it and the conversation drifted to other topics. Soon thereafter we went to bed.

Next morning after breakfast – cooked by Gillian – I declined Penny's invitation to go riding with her, the horse being an animal I despise and distrust. So instead we walked where she would have ridden and went over a forested hill along a broad ride, and descended the other side into a sheltered valley where we lunched in a pub on bread, cheese, pickles and beer, and where Penny demonstrated her skill at playing darts with the locals. Then back to the house where we lazed away the rest of the sunny day on the lawn.

I left the house that evening armed with an invitation to return the following weekend, not from Penny but from Ashton. 'Do you play croquet?' he asked.

'No, I don't.'

He smiled. 'Come next weekend and I'll show you how. I'll have Benson set up the hoops during the week.'

So it was that I drove back to London well contented.

I have given the events of that first weekend in some detail in order to convey the atmosphere of the place and the family. Ashton, the minor industrialist, richer than others of his type because he ran his own show; Gillian, his younger daughter, content to be dutifully domestic and to act as hostess and surrogate wife without the sex bit; and Penny the bright elder daughter, carving out a career in science. And she *was* bright; it was only casually that weekend I learned she was an MD although she didn't practise.

And there was the money. The Rolls, the Jensen and the Aston Martin in the garage, the sleek-bodied horses, the manicured lawns, the furnishings of that beautiful house – all these reeked of money and the good life. Not that I envied Ashton – I have a bit of money myself although not in the same class. I mention it only as a fact because it was there.

The only incongruity in the whole scene was Benson, the general factotum, who did not look like anyone's idea of a servant in a rich household. Rather, he looked like a retired pugilist and an unsuccessful one at that. His nose had been broken more than once in my judgement, and his ears were swollen with battering. Also he had a scar on his right cheek. He would have made a good heavy in a Hammer film. His voice clashed unexpectedly with his

15

appearance, being soft and with an educated accent better than Ashton's own. I didn't know what to make of him at all.

Something big was apparently happening in Penny's line of work that week, and she rang to say she would be in the laboratory all Friday night, and would I pick her up on Saturday morning to take her home. When she got into the car outside University College she looked very tired, with dark smudges under her eyes. 'I'm sorry, Malcolm,' she said. 'This won't be much of a weekend for you. I'm going to bed as soon as I get home.'

I was sorry, too, because this was the weekend I intended to ask her to marry me. However, this wasn't the time, so I grinned and said, 'I'm not coming to see you – I'm coming for the croquet.' Not that I knew much about it – just the bit from Alice and an association with vicars and maiden ladies.

Penny smiled, and said, 'I don't suppose I should tell you this, but Daddy says he can measure a man by the way he plays croquet.'

I said, 'What were you doing all night?'

'Working hard.'

'Doing what. Is it a state secret?'

'No secret. We transferred genetic material from a virus to a bacterium.'

'Sounds finicky,' I remarked. 'With success, I hope.'

'We won't know until we test the resulting strain. We should know something in a couple of weeks; this stuff breeds fast. We hope it will breed true.'

What I know about genetics could be measured with an eye-dropper. I said curiously, 'What good does all this do?'

'Cancer research,' she said shortly, and laid her head back, closing her eyes. I left her alone after that.

When we got to the house she went to bed immediately. Other than that the weekend was much the same as before. Until the end, that is – then it changed for the worse. I played tennis with Ashton, then swam in the pool, and we had lunch on the lawn in the shade of a chestnut tree, just the three of us, Ashton, Gillian and me. Penny was still asleep.

After lunch I was introduced to the intricacies of match-play croquet and, by God, there *was* a vicar! Croquet, I found, is not a game for the faint-hearted, and the way the Reverend Hawthorne played made Machiavelli look like a Boy Scout. Fortunately he was on my side, but all his tortuous plotting was of no avail against Gillian and Ashton. Gillian played a surprisingly vicious game. Towards the end, when I discovered it's not a game for gentlemen, I quite enjoyed it.

Penny came down for afternoon tea, refreshed and more animated than she had been, and from then on the weekend took its normal course. Put down baldly on paper, as I have done here, such a life may be considered pointless and boring, but it wasn't really; it was a relief from the stresses of the working week.

Apparently Ashton did not get even that relief because after tea he retired to his study, pleading that he had to attend to paperwork. I commented that Penny had complained of the same problem, and he agreed that putting unnecessary words on paper was the besetting sin of the twentieth century. As he walked away I reflected that Ashton could not have got where he was by idling his time away playing tennis and croquet.

And so the weekend drifted by until it was nearly time for me to leave. It was a pleasant summer Sunday evening. Gillian had gone to church but was expected back at any moment; she was the religious member of the family – neither Ashton nor Penny showed any interest in received religion. Ashton, Penny and I were sitting in lawn chairs arguing a particularly knotty point in scientific ethics which had arisen out of an article in the morning newspaper. Rather, it was Penny and her father doing the arguing; I

17

was contemplating how to get her alone so I could propose to her. Somehow we had never been alone that weekend.

Penny was becoming a little heated when we heard a piercing scream and then another. The three of us froze, Penny in mid-sentence, and Ashton said sharply, 'What the devil was that?'

A third scream came. It was nearer this time and seemed to be coming from the other side of the house. By this time we were on our feet and moving, but then Gillian came into sight, stumbling around the corner of the house, her hands to her face. She screamed again, a bubbling, wordless screech, and collapsed on the lawn.

Ashton got to her first. He bent over her and tried to pull her hands from her face, but Gillian resisted him with all her strength. 'What's the matter?' he yelled, but all he got was a shuddering moan.

Penny said quickly, 'Let me', and gently pulled him away. She bent over Gillian who was now lying on her side curled in a foetal position, her hands still at her face with the fingers extended like claws. The screams had stopped and were replaced by an extended moaning, and once she said, 'My eyes! Oh, my eyes!'

Penny forced her hand to Gillian's face and touched it with her forefinger, rubbing gently. She frowned and put the tip of her finger to her nose, then hastily wiped it on the grass. She turned to her father. 'Take her into the house quickly – into the kitchen.'

She stood up and whirled towards me in one smooth motion. 'Ring for an ambulance. Tell them it's an acid burn.'

Ashton had already scooped up Gillian in his arms as I ran to the house, brushing past Benson as I entered the hall. I picked up the telephone and rang 999 and then watched Ashton carry his daughter through a doorway I had never entered, with Penny close behind him.

A voice said in my ear, 'Emergency services.'

'Ambulance.'

There was a click and another voice said immediately, 'Ambulance service.' I gave him the address and the telephone number. 'And your name, sir?'

'Malcolm Jaggard. It's a bad facial acid burn.'

'Right, sir; we'll be as quick as we can.'

As I put down the phone I was aware that Benson was staring at me with a startled expression. Abruptly he turned on his heel and walked out of the house. I opened the door to the kitchen and saw Gillian stretched on a table with Penny applying something to her face. Her legs were kicking convulsively and she was still moaning. Ashton was standing by and I have never seen on any man's face such an expression of helpless rage. There wasn't much I could do there and I'd only be in the way so I closed the door gently.

Looking through the big window at the far end of the hall, I saw Benson walking along the drive. He stopped and bent down, looking at something not on the drive but on the wide grass verge. I went out to join him and saw what had attracted his attention; a car had turned there, driving on the grass, and it had done so at speed because the immaculate lawn had been chewed up and the wheels had gouged right down to the soil.

Benson said in his unexpctedly gentle voice, 'As I see it, sir, the car came into the grounds and was parked about there, facing the house. When Miss Gillian walked up someone threw acid in her face here.' He pointed to where a few blades of grass were already turning brown. 'Then the car turned on the grass and drove away.'

'But you didn't see it.'

'No, sir.'

I bent and looked at the wheel marks. 'I think this should be protected until the police get here.'

Benson thought for a moment. 'The gardener made some hurdles for the new paddock. I'll get those.'

'That should do it,' I agreed.

I helped him bring them and we covered the marks. I

straightened as I heard the faint hee-haw of an ambulance, becoming louder as it approached. That was quick – under six minutes. I walked back to the house and rang 999 again.

'Emergency services.'

'The police, please.'

Click. 'Police here.'

'I want to report a criminal assault.'

3

They got Gillian into the ambulance very quickly. Penny used her authority as a doctor and went into the ambulance with her, while Ashton followed in a car. I judged he was in no condition to drive and was pleased to see Benson behind the wheel when he left.

Before he went I took him on one side. 'I think you ought to know I've sent for the police.'

He turned a ravaged face towards me and blinked stupidly. 'What's that?' He seemed to have aged ten years in a quarter of an hour.

I repeated what I'd said, and added, 'They'll probably come while you're still at the hospital. I can tell them what they need to know. Don't worry about it. I'll stay here until you get back.'

'Thanks, Malcolm.'

I watched them drive away and then I was alone in the house. The maid lived in, but Sunday was her day off, and now Benson had gone there was no one in the house but me. I went into the living-room, poured myself a drink and lit a cigarette, and sat down to think of just what the hell had happened.

Nothing made sense. Gillian Ashton was a plain, ordinary woman who lived a placid and unadventurous life. She was a homebody who one day might marry an equally unadventurous man who liked his home comforts. Acid-throwing wasn't in that picture; it was something that might happen in Soho or the murkier recesses of the East End of London – it was incongruous in the Buckinghamshire countryside.

I thought about it for a long time and got nowhere.

Presently I heard a car drive up and a few minutes later I was talking to a couple of uniformed policemen. I couldn't tell them much; I knew little about Gillian and not much more about Ashton and, although the policemen were polite, I sensed an increasing dissatisfaction. I showed them the tracks and one of them stayed to guard them while the other used his car radio. When I looked from the window a few minutes later I saw he had moved the police car so he could survey the back of the house.

Twenty minutes later a bigger police gun arrived in the person of a plain clothes man. He talked for a while with the constable in the car, then walked towards the house and I opened the door at his knock. 'Detective-Inspector Honnister,' he said briskly. 'Are you Mr Jaggard?'

'That's right. Won't you come in?'

He walked into the hall and stood looking around. As I closed the door he swung on me. 'Are you alone in the house?'

The constable had been punctilious about his 'sirs' but not Honnister. I said, 'Inspector, I'm going to show you something which I shouldn't but which, in all fairness to yourself, I think you ought to see. I'm quite aware my answers didn't satisfy your constable. I'm alone in Ashton's house, admit to knowing hardly anything about the Ashtons, and he thinks I might run away with the spoons.'

Honnister's eyes crinkled. 'From the look of it there's a lot more to run away with here than spoons. What have you to show me?'

'This.' I dug the card out of the pocket which my tailor builds into all my jackets and gave it to him.

Honnister's eyebrows rose as he looked at it. 'We don't get many of these,' he commented. 'This is only the third I've seen.' He flicked at the plastic with his thumbnail as he compared me with the photograph. 'You'll realize I'll have to test the authenticity of this.'

'Of course. I'm only showing it to you so you don't waste

time on me. You can use this telephone or the one in Ashton's study.'

'Will I get an answer this time on Sunday?'

I smiled. 'We're like the police, Inspector; we never close.'

I showed him into the study and it didn't take long. He came out within five minutes and gave me back the card. 'Well, Mr Jaggard; got any notions on this?'

I shook my head. 'It beats me. I'm not here in a professional capacity, if that's what you mean.' From his shrewd glance I could see he didn't believe me, so I told of my relationship with the Ashtons and all I knew of the attack on Gillian which wasn't much.

He said wryly, 'This is one we'll have to do the hard way, then – starting with those tracks. Thank you for your co-operation, Mr Jaggard. I'd better be getting on with it.'

I went with him to the door. 'One thing, Inspector, you never saw that card.'

He nodded abruptly and left.

Ashton and Penny came back more than two hours later. Penny looked as tired as she had the previous morning, but Ashton had recovered some of his colour and springiness. 'Good of you to stay, Malcolm,' he said. 'Stay a little longer – I want to talk to you. Not now, but later.' His voice was brusque and he spoke with authority; what he had issued was not a request but an order. He strode across the hall and went into the study. The door slammed behind him.

I turned to Penny. 'How's Gillian?'

'Not very good,' she said sombrely. 'It was strong acid, undiluted. Who would do such a barbarous thing?'

'That's what the police want to know.' I told her something of my conversation with Honnister. 'He thinks your father might know something about this. Does he have any enemies?'

'Daddy!' She frowned. 'He's very strong-minded and single-minded, and people like that don't go through life

23

without treading on a few toes. But I can't think he'd make the kind of enemy who would throw acid into his daughter's face.'

Somehow I couldn't, either. God knows some funny things go on in the economic and industrial jungles, but they rarely include acts of gratuitous violence. I turned as Benson came out of the kitchen carrying a tray on which were a jug of water, an unopened bottle of whisky and two glasses. I watched him go into the study then said, 'What about Gillian?'

Penny stared at me. 'Gillian!' She shook her head in disbelief. 'You're not suggesting Gillian could make that kind of enemy? It's preposterous.'

It was certainly unlikely but not as impossible as Penny thought. Quiet homebodies have been known to lead exotic and secret lives, and I wondered if Gillian had done anything else on her shopping trips into Marlow besides buying the odd pound of tea. But I said tactfully, 'Yes, it's unlikely.'

As I helped Penny get together a scratch meal she said, 'I tried to neutralize the acid with a soda solution, and in the ambulance they had better stuff than that. But she's in the intensive care unit at the hospital.'

We had rather an uncomfortable meal, just the two of us because Ashton wouldn't come out of the study, saying he wasn't hungry. An hour later, when I was wondering if he'd forgotten I was there, Benson came into the room. 'Mr Ashton would like to see you, sir.'

'Thank you.' I made my excuses to Penny and went into the study. Ashton was sitting behind a large desk but rose as I entered. I said, 'I can't tell you how sorry I am that this awful thing should have happened.'

He nodded. 'I know, Malcolm.' His hand grasped the whisky bottle which I noted was now only half full. He glanced at the tray, and said, 'Be a good chap and get yourself a clean glass.'

24

'I'd rather not drink any more this evening. I still have to drive back to town.'

He put down the bottle gently and came from behind the desk. 'Sit down,' he said, and thus began one of the weirdest interviews of my life. He paused for a moment. 'How are things with you and Penny?'

I looked at him consideringly. 'Are you asking if my intentions are honourable?'

'More or less. Have you slept with her yet?'

That was direct enough. 'No.' I grinned at him. 'You brought her up too well.'

He grunted. 'Well, what are your intentions – if any?'

'I thought it might be a good idea if I asked her to marry me.'

He didn't seemed displeased at that. 'And have you?'

'Not yet.'

He rubbed the side of his jaw reflectively. 'This job of yours – what sort of income do you make out of it?'

That was a fair question if I was going to marry his daughter. 'Last year it was a fraction over £8000; this year will be better.' Aware that a man like Ashton would regard that as chickenfeed I added, 'And I have private investments which bring in a further £11,000.'

He raised his eyebrows. 'You still work with a private income?'

'That £11,000 is *before* tax,' I said wryly, and shrugged. 'And a man must do something with his life.'

'How old are you?'

'Thirty-four.'

He leaned back in his chair and said musingly, '£8000 a year isn't bad – so far. Any prospects of advancement in the firm?'

'I'm bucking for it.'

He then asked me a couple of questions which were a damned sight more personal than digging into my finances but, again, in the circumstances they were fair and my answers seemed to satisfy him.

He was silent for a while, then he said, 'You could do better by changing your job. I have an opening which is ideal for a man like yourself. Initially you'd have to spend at least one year in Australia getting things off the ground, but that wouldn't hurt a couple of youngsters like you and Penny. The only trouble is that it must be now – almost immediately.'

He was going too fast for me. 'Hold on a moment,' I protested. 'I don't even know if she'll marry me.'

'She will,' he said positively. 'I know my daughter.'

He evidently knew her better than I did because I wasn't nearly so certain. 'Even so,' I said. 'There's Penny to consider. Her work is important to her. I can't see her throwing it up and going to Australia for a year just like that. And that's apart from anything I might think about the advisability of making a change.'

'She could take a sabbatical. Scientists do that all the time.'

'Maybe. Frankly, I'd need to know a lot more about it before making a decision.'

For the first time Ashton showed annoyance. He managed to choke it down and disguise it, but it was there. He thought for a moment, then said in conciliatory tones, 'Well, a decision on that might wait a month. I think you'd better pop the question, Malcolm. I can fix a special licence and you can get married towards the end of the week.' He tried to smile genially but the smile got nowhere near his eyes which still had a hurt look in them. 'I'll give you a house for a dowry – somewhere in the South Midlands, north of London.'

It was a time for plain speaking. 'I think you're going a bit too fast. I don't see the necessity for a special licence. In fact, it's my guess that Penny wouldn't hear of it, even if she does agree to marry me. I rather think she'd like to have Gillian at the wedding.'

Ashton's face crumpled and he seemed to lose what little composure he had. I said evenly, 'It was always in my mind to buy a house when I married. Your offer of a house is very generous, but I think the kind of house it should be – and where it should be – are matters for Penny and me to decide between us.'

He stood up, walked to the desk, and poured himself a drink. With his back to me he said indistinctly, 'You're right, of course. I shouldn't interfere. But will you ask her to marry you – now?'

'Now! Tonight?'

'Yes.'

I stood up. 'Under the circumstances I consider that entirely inappropriate, and I won't do it. Now, if you'll forgive me, I have to go back to town.'

He neither turned nor made an answer. I left him there and closed the study door quietly behind me. I was at a loss to understand his driving insistence that Penny and I should marry quickly. That, and the offer of the job in Australia, had me worried. If this was the way he engaged his staff, not to mention picking a son-in-law, I was surprised how he'd got to where he was.

Penny was telephoning when I entered the hall. She replaced the receiver and said, 'I've been talking to the hospital; they say she's resting easier.'

'Good! I'll be back tomorrow evening and we'll go to see her. It might make her feel better to have someone else around, even a comparative stranger like me.'

'I don't know if that's a good idea,' said Penny, doubtfully. 'She might be . . . well, self-conscious about her appearance.'

'I'll come anyway and we can decide then. I have to go now – it's late.' She saw me to my car and I kissed her and left, wondering what kind of bee was buzzing in Ashton's bonnet.

4

Next morning, when I walked into the office I shared with Larry Godwin, he looked up from the Czechoslovakian trade magazine he was reading and said, 'Harrison wants to see you.' Harrison was our immediate boss.

'Okay.' I walked straight out again and into Harrison's office, sat in the chair before the desk, and said, 'Morning, Joe. Larry said you wanted to see me.'

Harrison was a bit of a stuffed shirt, very keen on formality, protocol and the line of authority. He didn't like me calling him Joe, so I always did it just to needle him. He said stiffly, 'On checking the weekend telephone log I found you had disclosed yourself to a police officer. Why?'

'I was at a house-party over the weekend. There was a nasty incident – one of the daughters of the house had acid thrown in her face. She was taken to hospital and, when the police pitched up, I was alone in the house and they started to get off on the wrong foot. I didn't want them wasting time on me, so I disclosed myself to the officer in charge.'

He shook his head disapprovingly and tried to hold me in what he supposed to be an eagle-like stare. 'His name?'

'Detective-Inspector Honnister. You'll find him at the copshop in Marlow.' Harrison scribbled in his desk book, and I leaned forward. 'What's the matter, Joe? We're *supposed* to co-operate with the police.'

He didn't look up. 'You're not supposed to disclose yourself to all and sundry.'

'He wasn't all and sundry. He was a middle-ranking copper doing his job and getting off to a bad start.'

Harrison raised his head. 'You needn't have done it. He would never seriously suspect you of anything.'

I grinned at him. 'The way you tell it co-operation is a one-way street, Joe. The cops co-operate with us when we need them, but we don't co-operate with them when all they need is a little setting straight.'

'It will be noted in your record,' he said coldly.

'Stuff the record,' I said, and stood up. 'Now, if you'll excuse me I have work to do.' I didn't wait for his permission to leave and went back to my office.

Larry had switched to something in Polish. 'Have a good weekend?'

'A bit fraught. Who's pinched our *Who's Who*?'

He grinned. 'What's the matter? Wouldn't she play?' He fished out *Who's Who* from among the piles of books which cluttered his desk and tossed it to me. Our job called for a lot of reading; when I retired I'd be entitled to a disability pension due to failing eyesight incurred in the line of duty.

I sat at my desk and ran through the 'A's and found that Ashton was not listed. There are not many men running three or more factories employing over a thousand men who are not listed in *Who's Who*. It seemed rather odd. On impulse I took the telephone directory and checked that, and he was not listed there, either. Why should Ashton have an ex-directory number?

I said, 'Know anything about high-impact plastics, Larry?'

'What do you want to know?'

'A chap called Ashton runs a factory in Slough, making the stuff. I could bear to know a little more about him.'

'Haven't heard of him. What's the name of the firm?'

'I don't know.'

'You don't know much. There might be a trade association.'

'Great thinking.' I went to our library and an hour later knew there were more associations of plastic manufacturers

29

than I wotted of – there was even one devoted to high-impact plastics – but none of them had heard of George Ashton. It seemed unnatural.

Gloomily I went back to my office. It's a hard world where a man can't check up on his prospective father-in-law. Ashton, as of that moment, knew a hell of a lot more about me than I knew about him. Larry saw my face and said, 'No luck?'

'The man keeps a bloody low profile.'

He laughed and waved his hand across the room. 'You could ask Nellie.'

I looked at Nellie and grinned. 'Why not?' I said lightly, and sat at the console.

You don't have to cuddle up to a computer to ask it questions – all you need is a terminal, and we called ours Nellie for no reason I've ever been able to determine. If you crossed an oversized typewriter with a television set you'd get something like Nellie, and if you go to Heathrow you'll see dozens of them in the booking hall.

Where the computer actually was no one had bothered to tell me. Knowing the organization that employed me, and knowing a little of what was in the monster's guts, I'd say it was tended by white-coated acolytes in a limestone cavern in Derbyshire, or at the bottom of a Mendip mine-shaft; anywhere reasonably safe from an atomic bomb burst. But, as I say, I didn't really know. My crowd worked strictly on the 'need to know' principle.

I snapped a couple of switches, pushed a button, and was rewarded by a small green question mark on the screen. Another button push made it ask:

IDENTIFICATION?

I identified myself – a bit of a complicated process – and Nellie asked:

CODE?

I answered:

GREEN

30

Nellie thought about that for a millionth of a second, then came up with:

INPUT GREEN CODING

That took about two minutes to put in. We were strict about security and not only did I have to identify myself but I had to know the requisite code for the level of information I wanted.

Nellie said:

INFORMATION REQUIRED?

I replied with:

IDENTITY

MALE

ENGLAND

The lines flicked out as Nellie came back with:

NAME?

I typed in:

ASHTON, GEORGE

It didn't seem to make much difference to Nellie how you put a name in. I'd experimented a bit and whether you put in Percy Bysshe Shelley – Shelley, Percy Bysshe – or even Percy Shelley, Bysshe – didn't seem to matter. Nellie still came up with the right answer, always assuming that Bysshe Shelley, Percy was under our eagle eye. But I always put the surname first because I thought it would be easier on Nellie's overworked little brain.

This time she came up with:

ASHTON, GEORGE – 3 KNOWN

PRESENT ADDRESS – IF KNOWN?

There could have been two hundred George Ashtons in the country or maybe two thousand. It's a common name and not surprising that three should be known to the department. As I typed in the address I reflected that I was being a bit silly about this. I tapped the execute key and Nellie hesitated uncharacteristically. Then I had a shock because the cursor scrolled out:

THIS INFORMATION NOT AVAILABLE ON CODE GREEN

TRY CODE YELLOW

I looked pensively at the screen and tapped out:

HOLD QUERY

Dancing electronically in the guts of a computer was a whole lot of information about one George Ashton, my future father-in-law. And it was secret information because it was in Code Yellow. I had picked up Larry Godwin on a joke and it had backfired on me; I hadn't expected Nellie to find him at all – there was no reason to suppose the department was interested in him. But if he had been found I would have expected him to be listed under Code Green, a not particularly secretive batch of information. Practically anything listed under Code Green could have been picked up by an assiduous reading of the world press. Code Yellow was definitely different.

I dug into the recesses of my mind for the coding of yellow, then addressed myself to Nellie. 'Right, you bitch; try again!' I loaded in the coding which took four minutes, then I typed out:

RELEASE HOLD

Nellie's screen flickered a bit and the cursor spelled out:

THIS INFORMATION NOT AVAILABLE ON CODE YELLOW

TRY CODE RED

I took a deep breath, told Nellie to hold the query, then sat back to think about it. I was cleared for Code Red and I knew the information there was pretty much the same as the code colour – redhot! Who the hell was Ashton, and what was I getting into? I stood up and said to Larry, 'I'll be back in a minute. Don't interfere with Nellie.'

I took a lift which went down into the guts of the building where there lived a race of troglodytes, the guardians of the vaults. I presented my card at a tungsten-steel grille, and said, 'I'd like to check the computer coding for red. I've forgotten the incantation.'

The hard-faced man behind the grille didn't smile. He merely took the card and dropped it into a slot. A machine chewed on it for a moment, tasted it electronically, and liked the flavour but, even so, spat it out. I don't know

32

what would have happened if it hadn't liked the flavour; probably I'd have been struck down by a bolt of lightning. Strange how the real world is catching up with James Bond.

The guard glanced at a small screen. 'Yes, you're cleared for red, Mr Jaggard,' he said, agreeing with the machine. The grille swung open and I passed through, hearing it slam and lock behind me. 'The coding will be brought to you in Room Three.'

Half an hour later I walked into my office, hoping I could remember it all. I found Larry peering at Nellie. 'Do you have red clearance?' I asked.

He shook his head. 'Yellow is my top.'

'Then hop it. Go to the library and study *Playboy* or something elevating like that. I'll give you a ring when I'm finished.'

He didn't argue; he merely nodded and walked out. I sat at the console and loaded Code Red into Nellie and it took nearly ten minutes of doing the right things in the right order. I wasn't entirely joking when I called it an incantation. When faced with Nellie I was always reminded of the medieval sorcerers who sought to conjure up spirits; everything had to be done in the right order and all the right words spoken or the spirit wouldn't appear. We haven't made much progress since then, or not too much. But at least our incantations seem to work and we do get answers from the vasty deep, but whether they're worth anything or not I don't know.

Nellie accepted Code Red or, at least, she didn't hiccough over it.

I keyed in:

RELEASE HOLD

and waited with great interest to see what would come out. The screen flickered again, and Nellie said:

THIS INFORMATION NOT AVAILABLE ON CODE RED
TRY CODE PURPLE

Purple! The colour of royalty and, possibly, of my face at that moment. This was where I was stopped – I was not cleared for Code Purple. I was aware it existed but that's about all. And beyond purple there could have been a whole rainbow of colours visible and invisible, from infra-red to ultra-violet. As I said, we worked on the 'need to know' principle.

I picked up the telephone and rang Larry. 'You can come back now; the secret bit is over.' Then I wiped Nellie's screen clear and sat down to think of what to do next.

5

A couple of hours later I was having a mild ding-dong with Larry. He wasn't a bad chap but his ideals tended to get in the way of his job. His view of the world didn't exactly coincide with things as they are, which can be a bit hampering because a man can make mistakes that way. A spell of field work would have straightened him out but he'd never been given the chance.

My telephone rang and I picked it up. 'Jaggard here.'

It was Harrison. His voice entered my ear like a blast of polar air. 'I want you in my office immediately.'

I put down the phone. 'Joe's in one of his more frigid moods. I wonder how he gets on with his wife.' I went to see what he wanted.

Harrison was a bit more than frigid – he could have been used to liquefy helium. He said chillily, 'What the devil have you been doing with the computer?'

'Nothing much. Has it blown a fuse?'

'What's all this about a man called Ashton?'

I was startled. 'Oh, Christ!' I said. 'Nellie *is* a tattle-tale, isn't she? Too bloody gossipy by half.'

'What's that?'

'Just talking to myself.'

'Well, now you can talk to Ogilvie. He wants to see us both.'

I think I gaped a bit. I'd been with the department for six years and I'd seen Ogilvie precisely that number of times; that's to talk with seriously. I sometimes bumped into him in the lift and he'd exchange pleasantries courteously enough and always asked to be remembered to my father. My monkeying with Nellie must have touched a nerve so sore that the whole firm was going into a spasm.

'Well, don't just stand there,' snapped Harrison. 'He's waiting.'

Waiting with Ogilvie was a short, chubby man who had twinkling eyes, rosy cheeks and a sunny smile. Ogilvie didn't introduce him. He waved Harrison and me into chairs and plunged *in medias res*. 'Now, Malcolm; what's your interest in Ashton?'

I said, 'I'm going to marry his daughter.'

If I'd said I was going to cohabit with the Prince of Wales I couldn't have had a more rewarding reaction. The clouds came over Mr Nameless; his smile disappeared and his eyes looked like gimlets. Ogilvie goggled for a moment, then barked, '*What's that?*'

'I'm going to marry his daughter,' I repeated. 'What's the matter? Is it illegal?'

'No, it's not illegal,' said Ogilvie in a strangled voice. He glanced at Mr Nameless as though uncertain of what to do next. Mr Nameless said, 'What reason did you have for thinking there'd be a file on Ashton?'

'No reason. It was suggested jokingly that I try asking Nellie, so I did. No one was more surprised than I when Ashton popped up.'

I swear Ogilvie thought I was going round the twist. 'Nellie!' he said faintly.

'Sorry, the computer.'

'Was this enquiry in the course of your work?' he asked.

'No,' I said. 'It was personal and private. I'm sorry about that and I apologize for it. But some odd things have been going on around Ashton over the weekend and I wanted to check him out.'

'What sort of things?'

'Someone threw acid into his daughter's face and . . .'

Mr Nameless cut in. 'The girl you intend to marry?'

'No – the younger girl, Gillian. Later on Ashton behaved a bit strangely.'

'I'm not surprised,' said Ogilvie. 'When did this happen?'

'Last night.' I paused. 'I had to disclose myself to a copper, so it came through on the weekend telephone log. Joe and I discussed it this morning.'

Ogilvie switched to Harrison. 'You *knew* about this?'

'Only about the acid. Ashton wasn't mentioned.'

'You didn't ask me,' I said. 'And I didn't know Ashton was so bloody important until Nellie told me afterwards.'

Ogilvie said, 'Now let me get this quite right.' He stared at Harrison. 'A member of your staff in this department reported to you that he'd been involved in police enquiries into an acid-throwing attack, and you didn't even ask who was attacked. Is that it?'

Harrison twitched nervously. Mr Nameless paused in the act of lighting a cigarette and said smoothly, 'I think this is irrelevant. Let us get on with it.'

Ogilvie stabbed Harrison with a glance which told him that he'd hear more later. 'Of course. Do you think this is serious?'

'It could be very serious,' said Mr Nameless. 'But I think we're very lucky. We already have an inside man.' He pointed the cigarette at me just as Leonard Bernstein points his baton at the second violins to tell them to get scraping.

I said, 'Now, hold on a minute. I don't know what this is about, but Ashton is going to be my father-in-law. That's bringing things very close to home. You can't be seriously asking me to . . .'

'You're not being asked,' said Mr Nameless coolly. 'You're being told.'

'The hell with that,' I said roundly.

Momentarily he looked startled, and if ever I thought those eyes had twinkled it was then I changed my mind. He glanced at Ogilvie, and said, 'I know this man has a good record, but right now I fail to see how he achieved it.'

'I've said it once this morning, but I'll say it again,' I said. 'Stuff my record.'

'Be quiet, Malcolm,' said Ogilvie irritably. He turned to Harrison. 'I don't think we need you any more, Joe.'

Harrison's expression managed to mirror simultaneously shock, outrage, curiosity and regret at having to leave. As the door closed behind him Ogilvie said, 'I think a valid point has been made. It's not good for an agent to be emotionally involved. Malcolm, what do you think of Ashton?'

'I like him – what I know of him. He's not an easy man to get to know, but then I haven't had much chance yet; just a couple of weekends' acquaintanceship.'

'A point has been made,' conceded Mr Nameless. He twinkled at me as though we were suddenly bosom friends. 'And in rather unparliamentary language. But the fact remains that Mr Jaggard, here, is on the inside. We can't just toss away that advantage.'

Ogilvie said smoothly, 'I think that Malcolm will investigate the circumstances around Ashton as soon as it is properly explained to him why he should.'

'As to that,' said Mr Nameless, 'you mustn't overstep the limits. You know the problem.'

'I think it can be coped with.'

Mr Nameless stood up. 'Then that's what I'll report.'

When he had gone Ogilvie looked at me for a long moment, then shook his head. 'Malcolm, you really can't go about telling high-ranking civil servants to get stuffed.'

'I didn't,' I said reasonably. 'I told him to stuff my record. I didn't even tell him where to stuff it.'

'The trouble about people like you who have private incomes is that it makes you altogether too bloody independent-minded. Now that, while being an asset to the department, as I told his lordship before you came in, can make things difficult for your colleagues.'

His lordship! I didn't know if Ogilvie was being facetious or not.

He said, 'Will you take things a bit easier in future?'

That wasn't asking too much, so I said, 'Of course.'

'Good. How's your father these days?'

'I think he's a bit lonely now that Mother's dead, but he bears up well. He sends you his regards.'

He nodded and checked his watch. 'Now you'll lunch with me and tell me everything you know about Ashton.'

6

We lunched in a private room above a restaurant at which Ogilvie seemed to be well known. He made me begin right from the beginning, from the time I met Penny, and I ended my tale with the abortive checking out of Ashton and my confrontation with Nellie. It took a long time to tell.

When I had finished we were over the coffee cups. Ogilvie lit a cigar and said, 'All right; you're supposed to be a trained man. Can you put your finger on anything unusual?'

I thought a bit before answering. 'Ashton has a man called Benson. I think there's something peculiar there.'

'Sexually, you mean?'

'Not necessarily. Ashton certainly doesn't strike me as being double-gaited. I mean it's not the normal master-and-servant relationship. When they came back from the hospital last night they were closeted in Ashton's study for an hour and a half, and between them they sank half a bottle of whisky.'

'Um,' said Ogilvie obscurely. 'Anything else?'

'The way he was pressuring me into marrying Penny was bloody strange. I thought at one time he'd bring out the traditional shotgun.' I grinned. 'A Purdy, of course – for formal weddings.'

'You know what I think,' said Ogilvie. 'I think Ashton is scared to death; not on his own behalf but on account of his girls. He seems to think that if he can get your Penny away from him she'll be all right. What do you think?'

'It fits all right,' I said. 'And I don't like one damned bit of it.'

'Poor Ashton. He didn't have the time to polish up a scheme which showed no cracks, and he sprang it on you too baldly. I'll bet he pulled that Australian job out of thin air.'

'Who *is* Ashton?' I asked.

'Sorry; I can't tell you that.' Ogilvie blew a plume of smoke. 'I talked very high-handedly to that chap this morning. I told him you'd take on the job as soon as you knew what was involved, but he knew damned well that I can't tell you a thing. That's what he was objecting to in an oblique way.'

'This is bloody silly,' I said.

'Not really. You'll only be doing what you'd be doing anyway, knowing what you know now.'

'Which is?'

'Bodyguarding the girl. Of course, I'll ask you to body-guard Ashton, too. It's a package deal, you see; one automatically includes the other.'

'And without knowing the reason why?'

'You know the reason why. You'll be guarding Penelope Ashton because you don't want her to get a faceful of sulphuric acid, and that should be reason enough for any tender lover. As for Ashton – well, our friend this morning was right. A commander can't tell his private soldiers his plans when he sends them into battle. He just tells them where to go and they pick up their feet.'

'The analogy is false, and you know it,' I said. 'How can I guard a man if I don't know who or what I'm guarding him against? That's like sending a soldier into battle not only without telling him where the enemy is, but *who* the enemy is.'

'Well, then,' said Ogilvie tranquilly. 'It looks as though you'll have to do it for the sake of my bright blue eyes.'

He had me there and I think he knew it. I had an idea that Mr Nameless, whoever he was, could be quite formi-dable and Ogilvie had defused what might have been a nasty situation that morning. I owed him something for it. Besides, the cunning old devil's eyes were green.

'All right,' I said. 'But it isn't a one-man job.'

'I'm aware of that. Spend this afternoon thinking out your requirements – I want them on my desk early tomorrow morning. Oh, by the way – you don't disclose yourself.'

I opened my mouth and then closed it again slowly before I swore at him. Then I said, 'You must be joking. I have to guard a man without telling him I'm guarding him?'

'I'm sure you'll do it very well,' he said suavely, and rang for the waiter.

'Then you'll be astonished at what I'll need,' I said acidly.

He nodded, then asked curiously, 'Hasn't it disturbed you that you'll be marrying into a rather mysterious family?'

'It's Penny I'm marrying, not Ashton.' I grinned at him. 'Aren't you disturbed for the same reason?'

'Don't think I'm not,' he said seriously, and left me to make of that what I could.

When I got back to the office Larry Godwin looked me up and down critically. 'I was just about to send out a search party. The griffin is that you've been given a real bollock-ing. I was just about to go down to the cellar to see if they really do use thumbscrews.'

'Nothing to it,' I said airily. 'I was given the RSPCA medal for being kind to Joe Harrison – that's all.'

'Very funny,' he said acidly, and flapped open a day-old copy of *Pravda*. 'The only time you'll get a medal is when you come with me when I get my knighthood.' He watched me putting a few things in a bag. 'Going somewhere?'

'I won't be around for a couple of days or so.'

'Lucky devil. I never get out of this bloody office.'

'You will one day,' I said consolingly. 'You have to go to Buck House to get a knighthood.' I leaned against the desk. 'You really should be in Slav Section. Why did you opt for General Duties?'

'I thought it would be more exciting,' he said, and added sourly, 'I was wrong.'

'With you around, the phrase "as happy as Larry" takes on an entirely new meaning.' I thought he was going to throw something at me so I ducked out fast.

I drove to Marlow and found the police station. My name presented to the desk sergeant got me Honnister in jig time. He shared an office with another inspector and when I indicated a desire for privacy Honnister shrugged and said, 'Oh, well; we can use an interview room. It's not as comfortable as here, though.'

'That's all right.'

The other copper closed a file and stood up. 'I'm going,

43

anyway. I don't want to pry into your girlish secrets, Charlie.' He gave me a keen glance as he went out. He'd know me again if he saw me.

Honnister sat at his desk and scowled. 'Secretive crowd, your lot.'

I grinned. 'I don't see you wearing a copper's uniform.'

'I had one of your blokes on the blower this morning – chap by the name of Harrison – threatening me with the Tower of London and unnameable tortures if I talk about you.'

I sat down. 'Joe Harrison is a silly bastard, but he means well.'

'If anyone knows how to keep secrets it's a copper,' said Honnister. 'Especially one in the plain clothes branch. I know enough local secrets to blow Marlow apart. Your chap ought to know that.' He sounded aggrieved.

I cursed Harrison and his ham-fisted approach; if he'd queered my pitch with the local law I'd string him up by the thumbs when I got back. I said, 'Inspector, I told you last night I had no official connection with Ashton. It was true then, but it is no longer true. My people now have a definite interest.'

He grunted. 'I know. I've been asked to make an extra copy of all my reports on the Ashton case. As though I don't have enough to do without producing a lot of bloody bumf for people who won't even give me the time of day without consulting the Official Secrets Act.' His resentment was growing.

I said quickly. 'Oh, hell; you can forget that nonsense – just as long as I can see your file copies.'

'You got authority for that?'

I smiled at him. 'A man has all the authority he can take. I'll carry the can if there's a comeback.'

He stared at me and then his lips curved in amusement. 'You and me will get on all right,' he said. 'What do you want to know?'

'First, how's the girl?'

44

'We haven't been allowed to talk to her so she must be pretty bad. And I need a description. I don't even know the sex of the assailant.'

'So that means no visitors.'

'None except the family. Her sister has been at the hospital most of the day.'

I said, 'I think I might be able to help you there. Suppose I got Penny to ask Gillian for a description. That would do to be going on with until you can ask. her yourself.' He nodded. 'I won't be seeing her until later. Where will you be tonight?'

'Theoretically off duty. But I'll be sinking a couple of pints in the Coach and Horses between nine and ten. I'm meeting someone who might give me a lead on another case. You can ring me there. Doyle, the landlord, knows me.'

'Okay. Now, how have you got on with the acid?'

Honnister shrugged. 'About as far as you'd expect. It's battery acid, and the stuff's too common. There are filling stations all around here, and then it might have come from somewhere else.' He leaned back in his chair. 'To me this has the smell of a London job.'

'Have you seen Ashton?'

'Oh, yes, I've seen Ashton. He says he can think of absolutely no reason why his daughter should be attacked in such a manner. No reason whatsoever. It was like talking to a bloody stone wall.'

'I'll be talking to him myself tonight. Maybe I'll get something.'

'Does he know who – and what – you are?'

'No, he doesn't; and he mustn't find out, either.'

'You blokes lead interesting lives,' said Honnister, and grinned crookedly. 'And you wanting to marry his daughter, too.'

I smiled. 'Where did you get that?'

'Just pieced it together from what you told me last night, and from what one of the uniformed boys picked up when talking over a cuppa with the Ashtons' maid. I told you I hear secrets – and I'm not a bad jack, even though I say it myself.'

'All right,' I said. 'Tell me a few secrets about Ashton.'

'Not known to the police. Not criminally. The CPO had a few words with him.'

'CPO?'

'Crime Prevention Officer. There are a lot of big houses around here full of expensive loot worth nicking. The CPO calls in to check on the burglar-proofing. You'd be surprised how stupid some of these rich twits can be. A man will fill his house with a quarter of a million quids' worth of paintings and antiques and balk at spending a couple of thousand on keeping the stuff safe.'

'How is Ashton's burglar-proofing?'

Honnister grinned. 'It might rate second to the Bank of England,' he conceded.

That interested me. 'Anything more on Ashton?'

'Nothing relevant. But he wasn't the one who was attacked, was he?' He leaned forward. 'Have you thought of the possibility that Gillian Ashton might have been sleeping in the wrong bed? There are two things I think of when I hear of an acid attack on a woman; the first is that it could be a gangland punishment, and the other is that it's one woman taking revenge on another.'

'I've thought of it. Penny discounts it, and I don't go much for it myself. I don't think she's the kind.'

'Maybe, but I've been doing a bit of nosing around. I haven't come up with anything yet, but I can't discount it.'

'Of course you can't.'

I stood up, and Honnister said, 'Don't expect too much too quickly. In fact, don't expect anything at all. I've no great hopes of this case. Anyway, we've not gone twenty-four hours yet.'

That was so, and it surprised me. So much had happened that day that it seemed longer. 'Okay,' I said. 'I'll be in touch tonight.'

8

I drove in the direction of Ashton's house and cruised around slowly, making circuits on the country roads and looking for anything out of the ordinary such as cars parked on the verge with people in them doing nothing in particular. There was nothing like that so after an hour of futility I gave up and drove directly to the house.

The gates were locked but there was a bell-push which I pressed. While I waited I studied the gates in the light of what Honnister had said about Ashton's burglar-proofing. They were of ornamental wrought-iron, about ten feet high, very spiky on top, and hung on two massive stone pillars. They barred an opening in an equally high chain-mesh fence, unobtrusive because concealed by trees, which evidently circled the estate. All very good, but the gates hadn't been closed the day before.

Presently a man came down the drive, dressed in rough country clothes. I hadn't seen him before. He looked at me through the gates and said curtly, 'Yes?'

'My name is Malcolm Jaggard. I'd like to see Mr Ashton.'

'He's not in.'

'Miss Ashton?'

'They're not in, either.'

I tugged thoughtfully at my ear. 'What about Benson?'

He looked at me for a moment, then said, 'I'll see.' He stepped to one side behind one of the stone pillars and I heard a click and the whirr of a telephone dial. There's a phrase for what was happening; it's known as closing the stable door after the horse has gone.

The man came back into sight and wordlessly began to unlock the gate, so I got back into the car and drove up to the house. Benson, in his courtly Boris Karloff manner, ushered me into the living-room, and said, 'I don't expect Miss Penelope will be long, sir. She rang to say she would be back at five.'

'Did she say how Gillian is?'

'No, sir.' He paused, then shook his head slowly. 'This is a bad business, sir. Disgracefully bad.'

'Yes.' I had always been taught that it is bad form to question servants about their masters, but I had no compunction now. Benson had never struck me as being one of your run-of-the-mill servants, least of all at that very moment because, unless he'd developed a fast-growing tumour under his left armpit, he was wearing a gun. 'I see you have a guard on the gate.'

'Yes; that's Willis. I'll give him your name so he will let you in.'

'How is Mr Ashton taking all this?'

'Remarkably well. He went to his office as usual this morning. Would you care for a drink, sir?'

'Thank you. I'll have a scotch.'

He crossed the room, opened a cabinet, and shortly came back with a tray which he put on a small table next to my elbow. 'If you will excuse me, sir.'

'Thank you, Benson.' He was not staying around to be questioned, but even if he had I doubted if I could have got much out of him. He tended to speak in clichés and bland generalities, but whether he thought that way was quite another matter.

I had not long to wait for Penny and was barely half way through the drink when she came into the room. 'Oh, Malcolm; how good to see you. What a blessed man you are.' She looked tired and drawn.

'I said I'd come. How's Gillian?'

'A little better, I think. She's getting over the shock.'

'I'm very glad to hear it. I had a talk with Honnister, the police inspector in charge of the case. He wants to interview her.'

'Oh, Malcolm; she's not ready for that. Not yet.'

She came to me and I took her in my arms. 'Is it that bad?'

She laid her head on my chest for a moment, and then looked up at me. 'I don't think you know how bad this sort of thing is for a woman. Women seem to care more for their appearance than men – I suppose we have to because we're in the man-catching business, most of us. It's not just the physical shock that's hit Gillian; there's the psychological shock, too.'

'Don't think I'm not aware of it,' I said. 'But put yourself in Honnister's place. He's in a jam – he needs a description. Right now he doesn't even know if he's looking for a man or a woman.'

Penny looked startled. 'I hadn't even thought of that. I assumed it would be a man.'

'Honnister hasn't made that assumption. He hasn't made any assumptions at all because he has damn-all to go on. Is Gillian talking to you?'

'A little, this afternoon.' Penny made a wry face. 'I've kept off the subject of acid-throwing.'

'Could you go to the hospital tonight and see what you can get out of her? Honnister is really at his wits' end about this. Your father couldn't help him and he's stuck.'

'I suppose I could try.'

'Better you than Honnister; he might not have your understanding. I'll come with you; not into the ward, but I'll come along.'

'Will eight o'clock be all right for you? Not too late?'

'All my time is at your disposal.' I didn't tell her that was literally true, by courtesy of one Ogilvie and paid for by the taxpayer. 'You look as though you could do with a drink.'

'I could stand a gin and tonic. Bring it into the kitchen, will you? I have to do something about dinner – Daddy will be home soon.'

She went away and I fixed the drink and took it into the

49

kitchen. I offered to help but she laughed, and said, 'You'd just be in the way. Mary is coming down to help.'

'Mary who?'

'The maid – Mary Cope. You find yourself something to do.'

I went away reflecting that what I really wanted to do was to give Ashton's study a good shake-down. But if it's bad form to question the servants I don't know what the devil it would be called to be found searching through your host's private papers in his *sanctum sanctorum*. Moodily I walked out into the garden.

I was knocking croquet balls about on the lawn when Ashton pitched up. There was a worn and honed look about him as though he was being fined down on some spiritual grindstone. His skin had not lost its tan but he looked paler than usual, and there was still that hurt look in his eyes. It was the look of a little boy who had been punished for something he hadn't done; the anguished look of the injustice of the world. It's hard to explain to a small boy that the world isn't necessarily a just place, but Ashton had been around long enough to know it.

I said, 'Penny's in the kitchen, if you want her.'

'I've seen her,' he said shortly.

'She tells me Gillian's better this evening.'

He looked down, kicking the turf with the toe of his shoe. He didn't speak for some time and I began to think he'd misheard me. But then he looked up and said abruptly, 'She's blind.'

'Christ; I'm sorry to hear that.'

He nodded. 'I had a specialist in this afternoon.'

'Does she know? Does Penny know?'

'Neither of them know. I had it kept from them.'

'I can understand not telling Gillian, but why keep it from Penny?'

'Unlike many sisters they've always been very close even though they are so unalike in temperament – perhaps because of it. I think if Penny knew, Gillian would get it out of her, and she couldn't stand the shock now.' He looked me in the eye. 'Don't tell her.'

Now that was all very logical and carefully thought out, and he had just given me a direct order, there was no doubt about that. 'I won't tell her,' I said. 'But she might find out anyway. She's medically trained and nobody's fool.'

'Just so that it comes later rather than sooner,' he said.

I thought I'd better start to earn my pay. 'I saw Honnister this afternoon. He tells me he didn't get much change out of you this morning. Don't you have any idea why Gillian should be attacked?'

'No,' he said colourlessly.

I studied him carefully. His jacket was much better cut than Benson's but no amount of fine tailoring could hide the slight bulge under his arm. 'You haven't had threatening letters or anything like that?'

'Nothing like that,' he said impatiently. 'I'm at a loss to understand it.'

I felt like asking him, 'Then why carry a gun?' My problem was that I didn't know why he was on our files. Men were listed for many reasons and to be listed did not make them villains – far from it. The trouble was that no one would tell me which class Ashton came into, and that made this job damned difficult. Difficult to know how to push at him; difficult to identify the cranny into which to push the wedge that would crack him.

But I tried. I said practically, 'Then the reason must lie somewhere in Gillian's own life. Some crowd she's been mixed up with, perhaps.'

He became instantly angry. 'Nonsense!' he said sharply. 'That's a monstrous suggestion. How could she get mixed up with types like that without me knowing? The type who could do such a dreadful thing?'

I was acting the part of the impartial onlooker. 'Oh, I don't know,' I said judiciously. 'It happens all the time judging by what we read in the newspapers. The police arrest a kid and uncover a whole series of offences, from mainlining on heroin to theft to get the cash to feed the habit. The parents are shocked and plead ignorance; they had no idea that little Johnny or little Mary was involved. I believe them, too.'

He took a deep breath. 'For one thing, Gillian isn't a kid; she's a grown woman of twenty-six. And for another, I know my family very well. You paid me a compliment last night; you said I'd brought up Penny too well. That goes for Gillian, too.' He drove his toe viciously into the turf. 'Would you think that of Penny?'

'No, I don't think I would.'

'Then why should you think it of Gillian? It's bloody ridiculous.'

'Because Penny didn't have acid thrown in her face,' I reminded him. 'Gillian did.'

'This is a nightmare,' he muttered.

'I'm sorry; I didn't mean to hurt you. I hope you'll accept my apology.'

He put his hands to his face, rubbing at closed eyelids. 'Oh, that's all right, Malcolm.' His hand dropped to his side. 'It's just that she was always such a good little girl. Not like Penny; Penny could be difficult at times. She still can. She can be very wilful, as you'll find out if you marry her. But Gillian . . .' He shook his head. 'Gillian was never any trouble at all.'

What Ashton said brought home to me some of the anguish parents must feel when things go wrong with the kids. But I was not so concerned with his agony that I didn't note his reference to *if* I married Penny, not *when* I married her. Evidently the fixation of the previous night had left him.

He disillusioned me immediately. 'Have you given any thought to what we discussed last night?'

'Some.'

'With what conclusion?'

'I'm still pretty much of the same mind,' I said. 'I don't think this is the time to present Penny with new problems, especially if the girls are as close as you say. She's very unhappy, too, you know.'

'I suppose you're right,' he said dispiritedly, and kicked at the grass again. He was doing that shoe no good at all, and it was a pity to treat Lobb's craftsmanship so cavalierly. 'Are you staying to dinner?'

'With your permission,' I said formally. 'I'm taking Penny to the hospital afterwards.'

He nodded. 'Don't tell her about Gillian's eyes. Promise me that.'

'I already have.'

He didn't answer that, but turned on his heel and walked away towards the house. As I watched him go I felt desperately sorry for him. It didn't matter to me then if Nellie had him listed as a hero or a villain; I still felt sorry for him as a simple human being in the deepest of distress.

Penny and I got to the hospital at about half past eight. I didn't go in with her but waited in the car. She was away quite a long time, more than an hour, and I became restive because I had promised to call Honnister. When she came out she said quietly, 'I've got what you wanted.'

I said, 'Will you tell it to Honnister? I have an appointment with him.'

'All right.'

We found Honnister standing at the bar of the Coach and Horses looking broodily into a glass of beer. When we joined him he said, 'My man's been and gone. I've been hanging on waiting for your call.'

'Inspector Honnister – this is Penny Ashton. She has something to tell you.'

He regarded her with gravity. 'Thank you, Miss Ashton. I don't think you need me to tell you that we're doing the best we can on this case, but it's rather difficult, and we appreciate all the help we can get.'

'I understand,' she said.

He turned to me. 'What'll you have?'

'A scotch and . . .' I glanced at Penny.

'A gin and tonic.'

Honnister called to the man behind the bar. 'Monte, a large scotch and a gin and tonic.' He turned and surveyed the room. 'We'd better grab that table before the last-minute crowd comes in.'

I took Penny over to the table and presently Honnister joined us with the drinks. He wasted no time and even before he was seated, he said, 'Well, Miss Ashton, what can you tell me.'

'Gillian says it was a man.'

'Aah!' said Honnister in satisfaction. He had just eliminated a little more than half the population of Britain. 'What sort of man? Young? Old? Anything you tell me will be of value.'

He led her through the story several times and each time elicited a further nugget of information. What it boiled down to was this: Gillian had walked back from church and, coming up the drive towards the house, had seen a car parked with the bonnet open and a man peering at the engine. She thought he was someone who had broken down so she approached with the intention of offering assistance. As she drew near the man turned and smiled at her. He was no one she knew. She was about to speak when he slammed down the bonnet with one hand and simultaneously threw the acid into her face with the other. The man didn't speak at any time; he was about forty, with a sallow complexion and sunken eyes. She did not know the make of car but it was darkish in colour.

'Let's go back a bit,' said Honnister yet again. 'Your sister saw the man looking at the engine with the bonnet open. Did she mention his hands?'

'No, I don't think so. Is it important?'

'It might be,' said Honnister noncommittally. He *was* a good jack; he didn't put his own ideas into the mouth of his witnesses.

Penny frowned, staring at the bubbles rising in her glass,

54

and her lips moved slightly as she rehearsed her thoughts. Suddenly she said, 'That's it, Inspector. Gillian said she walked up and the man turned and smiled at her, then he took his hands out of his jacket pockets.'

'Good!' said Honnister heartily. 'Very good indeed!'

'I don't see the importance,' said Penny.

Honnister turned to me: 'Some cars have a rod on a hinge to hold up the bonnet; others have a spring-loaded gadget. Now, if he had his hands in his pockets he couldn't have been holding the bonnet open manually; and if he took them out of his pockets to close the bonnet and throw the acid at the same time then that bonnet was spring-loaded. He wouldn't have time to unhook a rod. It cuts down considerably on the makes of car we have to look for.' He drained his glass. 'Anything more to tell me?'

'I can think of nothing else, Inspector.'

'You and your sister have done very well,' he said as he stood up. 'Now I have to see a man about a dog.' He grinned at me. 'I really mean that – someone pinched a greyhound.'

Penny said, 'You'll let us know if . . .'

'You'll be first to know when something breaks,' promised Honnister. 'This is one villain I really want to get my hands on.'

As he walked out I said, 'He's a good copper.'

'It seems so,' said Penny. 'I wouldn't have thought of the significance of the way a car bonnet is held open.'

I stared into my glass. I was thinking that if I got hold of that acid-throwing bastard first there wouldn't be much left of him for Honnister to deal with. Presently Penny said, 'I can't say, "A penny for your thoughts", or you might get the wrong idea; but what are you thinking?'

I said it automatically; I said it without moving my mind. I said, 'I'm thinking it would be a good idea if we got married.'

'Malcolm!'

I'm pretty good at detecting nuances but there were too

damn many in that single two-syllable word to cope with. There was something of surprise and something of shock; something, I was afraid, of displeasure and something, I hoped, of delight. All mixed up together.

'Don't *you* think it's a good idea?' I watched her hunt for words. 'But don't say, "This is so sudden!"'

'But it *is* so damned sudden,' she said, and waved her hand at the room. 'Here, of all places.'

'It seems a good pub to me,' I said. 'Does the place matter?'

'I don't suppose it does,' she said quietly. 'But the time – and the timing – does.'

'I suppose I could have picked a better time,' I agreed. 'But it just popped out. I'm not the only one who thinks it's a good idea. Your father does, too; he wanted me to ask you last night.'

'So you two have been discussing me behind my back. I don't know that I like that.'

'Be reasonable. It's traditional – and courteous, too – for a man to inform his prospective father-in-law of his intentions.' I refrained from saying that it had been Ashton who had brought up the subject.

'What would you have done if he had been against it?'

'I'd have asked you just the same,' I said equably. 'I'm marrying you, not your father.'

'You're not marrying anyone – yet.' I was thankful for the saving grace of that final monosyllable. She laid her hand on mine. 'You idiot – I thought you'd never ask.'

'I had it all laid on, but circumstances got in the way.'

'I know.' There was melancholy in her voice. 'Oh, Malcolm; I don't know what to say. I've been so unhappy today, thinking about Gillian, and seeing her in such pain. And then there was that awful task you laid on me tonight of questioning her. I saw it had to be done, so I did it – but I don't like one bit of it. And then there's Daddy – he doesn't say much but I think he's going through hell, and

I'm worried about him. And now you come and give me more problems.'

'I'm sorry, Penny; I truly am. Let's put the question back in the deep freeze for a while. Consider yourself unasked.'

'No,' she said. 'You can't unask a question. In a way that's what my work is all about.' She was silent for a while. I didn't know what she meant by that but I had sense enough to keep my mouth shut. At last she said, 'I will marry you, Malcolm – I'd marry you tomorrow. I'm not one for non-essentials, and I don't want a white wedding with all the trimmings or anything like that. I want to marry you, but it can't be now, and I can't tell you when it will be. We've got to get this matter of Gillian sorted out first.'

I took her hand. 'That's good enough for me.'

She gave me a crooked smile. 'It won't be the usual kind of engagement, I'm afraid, I'm in no mood for romantic frivolities. Later, perhaps; but not now.' She squeezed my hand. 'Do you remember when I asked you to come here and meet Daddy? It was the night we had the Chinese dinner in your flat.'

'I remember.'

'It was a diversion. I had to stop myself from doing something.'

'Doing what, for God's sake?'

'Marching into your bedroom and getting into your bed.' She disengaged her hand and finished her drink. 'And now you'd better take me home before I change my mind and we start behaving badly.'

As I escorted her to the car my heart was like a singing bird and all the other guff poets used to write about. They don't any more; they leave it to the writers of pop songs, which is a pity. I drove her home and stopped the car before the gates, and we had five minutes' worth of love before she got out. She had no key and had to press the button for someone to come.

I said, 'We won't announce the engagement, but I think your father ought to know. It seems to be on his mind.'

'I'll tell him now.'

'Are you going to London tomorrow?'

She shook her head. 'Lumsden has given me a few days off. He's very understanding.'

'I'll pop out to see you.'

'But what about your job?'

I grinned. 'I have an understanding boss, too.'

There was a rattle at the gate and it swung open, pushed by Willis, the dour and unfriendly type who had let me in that afternoon. Penny kissed me and then slipped inside and the gate clanged shut. I stepped up to it, and said to Willis, 'Escort Miss Ashton up to the house, see her safe inside, and make sure the house door is locked.'

He looked at me for a moment in silence, then smiled, and it was like an ice floe breaking up. 'I'll do that, sir.'

9

I was in the office early next morning and first I had an extended chat with Nellie. I had just moved to the typewriter when Larry came in with a pile of newspapers which he dumped on his desk. 'Thought you were out on a job.'

'I am,' I said. 'I'm not here. I'm a figment of your imagination.'

I finished my list and took it in to Ogilvie, and wasted no time in getting down to the bones of it. I said, 'I don't mind fighting with one hand tied behind my back, but I object to having both hands tied. I'll need a list of Ashton's present overt activities and affiliations.'

Ogilvie smiled and pushed a file across the desk. 'I anticipated you.'

In return he got my sheet of paper. 'That's more of what I need.'

He scanned it. 'Six men, six cars, telephone ta . . .' He broke off. 'Who do you think we are – the CIA?'

I looked studiously at the back of my hands. 'Have you ever been in the field, sir?'

'Of course I've . . .' I looked up and found him smiling sheepishly. The smile disappeared as he said irritably, 'I know; you people think we desk-bound types have lost touch. You could be right.' He tapped the paper. 'Justify this.'

'I have to do a twenty-four-hour secret surveillance of three – perhaps four – people. It'll be . . .'

He caught me up on that. 'Which three or four?'

'First Ashton and Penny Ashton. Then Gillian Ashton. Just because she's been attacked once doesn't give her a lifelong exemption. I might be able to arrange with Honnister to have one of his chaps at the hospital if I ask him nicely enough. That'll take some of the load off us.'

'And the fourth?'

'Benson. I pushed the lot of them through the computer until I lost them in Code Purple.'

'Benson, too?' Ogilvie thought about it. 'You know, the computer might be going by the address only. Anyone living there might be classed with Ashton.'

'I thought of that and it won't wash. Mary Cope, the maid, lives in and I put her through as a control. Nellie has never heard of her. If Ashton is so damned important then he's six-man-important.'

'I agree – but you can't keep an eye on four people with six men. I'll let you have eight.' He smiled slightly. 'I must be going soft-headed. If Harrison was handling this he'd cut you down to four.'

I was taken aback but rallied enough to discuss who we were going to use on the operation. I said, 'I'd like to take Laurence Godwin.'

'You think he's ready?'

'Yes. If we don't use him soon he'll go sour on us. I've been keeping an eye on him lately; he's been right more times than he's been wrong, which is not bad going in this trade.'

'Very well.' Ogilvie returned to my list. 'I agree that Ashton's telephones should be tapped. If he's being threatened we want to know about it. I'll have to get authorization from upstairs, though; but I'll be as quick as I can. As for the postal surveillance, that's trickier but I'll see what I can do.' He put his finger down. 'This last item worries me. You'll have to have a damned good reason for wanting a pistol.'

'Benson's carrying a gun in his oxter, and Ashton is carrying another. If they are expecting that sort of action I think we should be prepared.'

'You're sure of this?'

60

'Dead certain. I'd like to know if they have gun permits.'

Ogilvie considered it. 'Under the circumstances, Ashton might. I don't know about Benson. I'll check.' I'd have given a lot to know what those circumstances were but I didn't ask because I knew he wouldn't tell me.

We settled a few more minor details, then Ogilvie said, 'Right, that's it. Round up your boys and brief them. I want a recording made of the briefing, the tape to be given to me personally before you leave. Get on with it, Malcolm.' As I was leaving he added, 'I'll authorize two pistols.'

I went back and gave Larry a list of names. 'Get on the blower. I want those men in my office ten minutes ago.' I paused. 'And put yourself on the bottom of the list.'

His expression was a study in pure delight. 'You mean . . .'

I grinned. 'I mean. Now get busy.' I sat at my desk and opened the file on Ashton. It was very thin. The names and addresses of his firms were given, but his other associations were few, mostly professional men – lawyers, accountants and the like. He was a member of no club, whether social, sporting or intellectual. A millionaire hermit.

The team assembled and I switched on the tape-recorder. The briefing didn't take long. I outlined the problem and then told how we were going to handle it, then allocated jobs and shifts. One pistol would be carried by the man overseeing Ashton, whoever he happened to be at the time; the other I reserved for myself.

I said, 'Now we have radios so we use them. Stay on net and report often so everyone is clued up all the time. Those off-shift to be findable and near a telephone. You might be needed in a hurry.'

Simpson asked, 'Do off-shift men go home?' He'd just got back from his honeymoon.

'No. Everyone books into hotels in or near Marlow.' There was an audible groan. 'As soon as you've done it

61

report which hotel together with its phone number so we can find you. I'm at the Compleat Angler.'

Brent said, 'Living it up on the expense account.'

I grinned, then said soberly, 'I don't think we'll have much time for that on this exercise. I might add that this is an important one. You can judge its importance by the fact that Ogilvie raised the team from six to eight on his own initiative and without me having to needle him. In the light of our staff position that says a lot. So don't lose any of these people – and keep your own heads down. Right; that's all.' I switched off the recorder and rewound the tape.

Larry said, 'You haven't given me a job.'

'You stick with me. I'll be back in a minute – I'm going to see Ogilvie.'

As I walked into his outer office his secretary said, 'I was about to ring you, Mr Jaggard. Mr Ogilvie wants to see you.'

'Thanks.' I went on in, and said, 'Here's the tape of the briefing.'

He was frowning and said directly, 'Did you cancel a request given to Inspector Honnister for copies of his reports on the Ashton case?'

I put the cassette on his desk. 'Yes.'

'Why?'

'Because I thought it was a lot of bull,' I said bluntly. 'It was getting in the way of good relations. What Harrison did was bad enough.'

'Harrison? What did Joe do?'

I related Harrison's flat-footed approach and Honnister's reaction to it, and then his views on providing extra copies of his reports. I added, 'If we're going to ask Honnister to provide a guard at the hospital we need to keep in his good books.'

'Very good thinking,' said Ogilvie heavily. 'But for one thing. This department did not request those copies. It

62

came from elsewhere, and someone has just been chewing my ear off by telephone.'

'Oh,' I said, rather inadequately, and then, 'Who?'

'Need you ask?' said Ogilvie acidly. 'The gentleman you met yesterday is sticking his oar in – which, I might add, he is perfectly entitled to do.' He rubbed his jaw and amended the statement. 'As long as he restricts himself to requests for information and does not initiate any action.'

He pondered for a moment, then said, 'All right, Malcolm, you can go. But don't take any precipitate action without referring back to me.'

'Yes. I'm sorry, sir.'

He waved me away.

10

There was nearly an hour of bureaucracy to get through before Larry and I could drive to Marlow. On the way I gave him the score up to that point, and his reaction was emphatic. 'This is downright stupid! You mean Ogilvie won't tell you what's behind all this?'

'I think his hands are tied,' I said. 'This is real top-level stuff. He has a character from Whitehall like a monkey on his back.'

'You mean Cregar?'

I glanced sideways at Larry. 'Who?'

'Lord Cregar. Short, chubby little chap.'

'Could be. How did you get on to him? Did you bug Ogilvie's office?'

He grinned. 'I went to the loo yesterday and saw him coming out of Ogilvie's room while you were in there.'

I said musingly, 'Ogilvie did refer to him as "his lordship" but I thought he was joking. How did you know he was Cregar?'

'He got divorced last week,' said Larry. 'His photograph was splashed on the middle inside pages of the *Telegraph*.'

I nodded. The *Daily Telegraph* takes a keen interest in the marital ups-and-downs of the upper crust. 'Do you know anything more about him, other than that he's wifeless?'

'Yes,' said Larry. 'He's not womanless – *that* came out very strongly in the court case. But beyond that, nothing.'

We crossed the Thames at Marlow, and I said, 'We'll check the hospital first, then go to the police station and I'll introduce you to a good copper. How good are you at grovelling? I might need a few lessons.'

The hospital car park was full so I put the car illicitly

into a doctor's slot. I saw Jack Brent, who was trailing Penny, so that meant she was in the hospital; he was talking to someone over his radio. I was about to go over to him when someone hailed me, and I turned to find Honnister at my elbow.

He seemed quite cheerful as I introduced Larry. I said, 'I got some wires crossed yesterday. My people didn't ask for reports; the request came from elsewhere.'

He smiled. 'I thought the Super was a bit narky this morning. Not to worry, Mr Jaggard. A man can't do more than his best.'

'Any progress?'

'I think we have the make of car. A witness saw a Hillman Sceptre close to Ashton's place on Saturday afternoon. The driver fits the description of the suspect. A dark blue car and spring-loaded bonnet, so it fits.' He rubbed his hands. 'I'm beginning to think we stand a chance on this one. I want to get this man before Miss Ashton for a firm identification.'

I shook my head. 'You won't get it. She's blind.'

Honnister looked stricken. 'Christ!' he said savagely. 'Wait till I lay my hands on this whoreson!'

'Stand in line. There's a queue.'

'I'm just going up to see her. The doctor says she's fit to talk.'

'Don't tell her she's blind – she doesn't know yet. And don't tell her sister.' I pondered for a moment. 'We have reason to believe another attack may be made on her. Can you put a man in the hospital?'

'That's asking something,' said Honnister. He paused, then asked, 'Do you know what's wrong with the bloody force? Too many chiefs and not enough Indians. If there's a multiple smash on the M4 we'd be hard put to it to find four uniformed men for crowd control. But go into the nick in Slough and you can't toss a pebble in any direction without it ricocheting off three coppers of the rank of chief inspector or higher.' He seemed bitter. 'But I'll see what I can do.'

I said, 'Failing that, give the hospital staff a good briefing. No stranger to get near Gillian Ashton without authority from you, me or the Ashton family. Pitch it to them strongly.'

Brent left his car and joined us and I introduced him to Honnister. 'Everything okay?'

'She's inside now; that's her car over there. But this town is hell on wheels. She went shopping before she came here and led me a devil of a dance. There's nowhere to park – I got two tickets in half an hour.'

'Hell, we can't have that.' I could imagine Penny being abducted while my man argued the toss with a traffic warden. I said to Larry, 'I want CD plates put on all our cars fast.'

'Oh, very tricky!' said Honnister admiringly.

Larry grinned. 'The Foreign Office won't like it.'

'Nothing to do with the Foreign Office,' observed Honnister. 'It's just a convention with no legal significance. A copper once stopped a car with CD plates and found a Cockney driver, so he asked him what CD stood for. The bloke said, "Cake Deliverer". And he was, too.' He shrugged. 'There was nothing he could do about it.' He nudged me. 'Coming in?'

'I'll join you inside.'

Jack Brent waited until Honnister was well out of earshot before saying, 'I thought it best not to talk in front of him, but Ashton and Benson haven't been found.'

'Ashton isn't at his office?'

'No, and he isn't at home, either.'

I thought about it. In the course of his business Ashton might be anywhere in the Home Counties; he might even have gone to London. And there was nothing to say that Benson was a prisoner in the house; he had to go out some time. All the same, I didn't like it.

I said, 'I'm going to the house. Come on, Larry.' I turned

to Brent. 'And you stick close to Penny Ashton. For Christ's sake, don't lose her.'

I drove a little faster than I should on the way to Ashton's place, and when I got there I leaned on the bell-push until Willis arrived wearing an annoyed expression. 'There's no one in,' he said abruptly.

'I want to make sure of that. Let me in.' He hesitated and then opened the gate reluctantly and I drove up to the house.

Larry said, 'He's a surly devil.'

'But reliable, I'd say.' I stopped before the front door, got out, and rang the bell. It was a fair time before the door opened and I was confronted by the maid who looked surprised to see me. 'Oh, Mr Jaggard, Miss Penny's not here. She's at the hospital.'

'I know. Mr Ashton's not in?'

'No, he's out, too.'

'What about Benson?'

'I haven't seen him all morning.'

I said, 'Mind if we come in? I'd like to use the telephone.'

In response she opened the door wider. Larry and I walked into the hall, and I said, 'You're Mary Cope, aren't you?'

'Yes, sir.'

'Have you seen either Mr Ashton or Benson at all today?'

'No, sir.'

'When was the last time you saw them?'

'Well, not really to see,' she said. 'But they were in the study last night; I heard them talking. That would be about nine o'clock. Just before, really, because I was going up to my room to catch the nine o'clock news and I switched on five minutes early.' She paused, wondering if she was right in talking of the doings of the family. After all, I hadn't been around all that long. She said nervously, 'Is this anything to do with what happened to Miss Gillian?'

'It could be.'

'Mr Ashton's bed wasn't slept in,' she volunteered.

I glanced at Larry who raised his eyebrows. 'What about Benson's bed?'

'I haven't looked – but he always makes up his own bed.'

'I see. I'll use the telephone if I may.'

I rang the hospital, asking for Penny, and told the operator she'd be in or near the intensive care unit. It was a long time before she came on the line. 'I hope you haven't waited long,' she said. 'I slipped away for a cup of tea. Gillian's much better, Malcolm; she's talking to Honnister now, and she doesn't mind a bit.'

I said, 'Did you tell your father about us last night?'

'No. He'd gone to bed when I got in.'

'Did you tell him this morning?'

'No. I slept late and he'd gone out when I got up. I expect Mary made breakfast for him.'

I didn't comment on that. 'When did you last see Benson?'

Her voice was suddenly wary. 'What's the matter, Malcolm? What's going on?'

I said, 'Look, Penny, I'm at your house. I'd like you to come home because I want to talk to you about something. I expect Honnister will be at the hospital for quite some time, and there's nothing you can do there.'

'There's something wrong, isn't there?' she said.

'Not really. I'll tell you when I see you.'

'I'm coming now.' She rang off.

I put down the receiver and looked around to see Mary Cope regarding me curiously from the other end of the hall. I jerked my head at Larry and gave him my keys. 'In the special compartment of my car you'll find a file on Ashton. There's a list of cars he owns – on page five, I think. Nip round to the garage and see what's missing. Then go down to the gate and ask Willis what time Ashton and Benson left here.'

He went quickly and I walked into Ashton's study. On his desk were two envelopes; one addressed to Penny and the other to me. I picked up mine and broke the seal.

The note might have been enigmatic to anyone else, but to me it was as clear as crystal. It read:

My dear Malcolm,
You are far too intelligent a man not to have seen what I was driving at in our more recent conversations. You may be acquainted with the French proverb: *Celui qui a trouvé un bon gendre a gagné un fils; mais celui qui en a recontré un mauvais a perdu une fille.*

Marry Penny with my blessing and make her happy – but, for her sake, be a bad son-in-law.
Yours
George Benson.

I sat down heavily and had a queasy feeling in the pit of my stomach because I knew we'd botched the job. I picked up the telephone to ring Ogilvie.

11

I didn't wrap it up for him. 'Our pigeons have flown the coop,' I said baldly.

He was incredulous. 'What! All of them?'

'Just the two cock birds.'

He was silent for a moment, then said slowly, 'My fault, I'm afraid. I ought to have given you your team yesterday. How certain are you?'

'He left me a note.' I read it out.

Ogilvie put the French into English. '"He who has found a good son-in-law has gained a son, but he who has picked up a bad one has lost a daughter." What the hell is that supposed to mean?'

I said, 'It may be my fault that he's cut and run. He tackled me again last evening about marrying Penny, and I gave him another refusal. I think that since he couldn't get her to cut loose from him, he has cut loose from her. If you read the note in that context you'll see what I mean.'

'Um. What was his attitude last evening?'

'He was a walking disaster,' I said flatly.

'How much start have they had?'

I sorted through the details I had picked up, then checked the time. 'I don't know about Benson, but for Ashton say fifteen hours maximum. I might get to know a bit more in the next few minutes.'

'We don't know that he went,' said Ogilvie objectively. 'He might have been taken. That note to you may be a fraud. Either case is serious, of course.'

'I don't think he was taken. The note is too accurately pointed, and this house is well protected.'

70

'Yes, it would be.' Ogilvie knew enough of the background to make a statement like that. 'How's the girl taking it?'

'She doesn't know yet. Ashton left her a note, too. I haven't opened it – I'll let her do that. I'll let you know anything that's relevant.'

'Think she'll tell you?'

'Yes. It's a funny thing, sir, but I did ask her to marry me last night and she accepted. She was going to tell Ashton when she got home but she said he'd gone to bed. I think he'd already left. If he'd waited another couple of hours he might have decided not to go.'

'Yes,' said Ogilvie meditatively. 'But don't blame yourself for that.' I looked up as Larry came into the study. Ogilvie said, 'Did you disclose yourself to her?'

'No.'

There was a pause. 'You take your duties very seriously, don't you, Malcolm?'

'I try to. Hang on a minute.' I looked up at Larry. 'Well?'

'There's an Aston Martin short, and both Benson and Ashton left last night at about half past nine, and didn't come back.'

The Aston Martin was Penny's car. I said to Ogilvie, 'We've got a pretty firm time. They left together at nine-thirty last night, probably in a hired car.' He seemed to be a long time digesting that, so I said, 'What's the next step?'

'There's going to be a row, of course,' he said, not sounding too perturbed. 'But I'll handle that. What you do is to go through that house like a dose of salts. See if you can find anything to indicate where Ashton has gone. Anything you don't understand bring here for evaluation.'

I said, 'That will blow my cover with Penny. I can't search the house without giving her an explanation.'

'I know.'

'Hold on.' I turned to Larry. 'Get on the radio – I want everyone here as soon as possible.'

'Off-shift boys included?'

71

'Yes. And go to the gate to make sure they can get in.'

Before speaking to Ogilvie again I glumly contemplated the explanation I'd have to give Penny. It was a hell of a thing to tell a girl you've just proposed to, and I had the feeling that our relationship was about to alter for the worse.

I pushed it out of my mind, and said, 'Do we bring the police in on this?'

I could almost hear Ogilvie's brains creaking as he thought that one out. At last he said, 'Not at this stage. I'll have to push it upstairs for a ruling. Police security is not too good on this sort of thing – they have too many reporters watching them. How long do you think you'll be there?'

'I don't know. It's a big house and I can see at least one safe from here. If we can't find keys we may have to take extreme measures. I'll give you a ring in an hour. I'll have a better idea by then.'

'I can't hold this for an hour. If you look towards London in fifteen minutes you'll see flames rising from Whitehall. Do your best.' He rang off.

I put down the telephone and looked thoughtfully at the letter addressed to Penny, then crossed to the safe. It had a combination lock and the door didn't open when I turned the handle. I went back to the desk and gave it a quick once-over lightly in the hope of finding something useful immediately. There was nothing. Five minutes later I heard a car draw up outside and, thinking it might be Penny, I went outside.

It was Peter Michaelis, one of the team. He came over with an enquiring look on his face, and I said, 'Stick around.' He had given Larry a lift from the gate, so I called him over. 'Take Ashton's file and start ringing around – his office, factories, every address you find in there. If Ashton is seen he's to ring his home immediately.' I shrugged. 'It won't work but we must cover it.'

'Okay.'

An Aston Martin was coming up the drive so I braced myself. 'Use the telephone in the hall. I want to use the study.'

Larry walked towards the house as Penny's car came to a fast halt, braked hard. She tumbled out, looking uncertainly at Michaelis, then ran towards me. 'I'm being followed,' she said, and whirled around, pointing at the car coming up the drive. 'He followed me into the grounds.'

'It's all right,' I said, as Brent's car stopped. 'I know who he is.'

'What's happening?' she demanded. 'Who are these men?' Her voice caught. 'What's happened to Daddy?'

'As far as I know he's all right.' I took her elbow. 'I want you to come with me.'

I took her into the house and she paused in the hall as she saw Larry at the telephone, then quickened her pace again. We went into the study and I picked up the letter from the desk. 'You'd better read this.'

She looked at me uncertainly before glancing at the superscription. 'It's from Daddy,' she said, and ripped open the envelope. As she read the note she frowned and her face paled. 'But I don't . . . I don't understand. I don't . . .'

'What does he say?'

Wordlessly she handed the letter to me, then walked over to the window and looked out. I watched her for a moment, then bent my head and read:

My dearest Penny,

For reasons I cannot disclose I must go away for a while. The reasons are not disreputable, nor am I a criminal, although that imputation may be made. My affairs are all in order and my absence should not cause you any trouble financially. I have made all the necessary arrangements: for legal advice consult Mr Veasey of Michelmore, Veasey and Templeton; for financial advice go to Mr Howard of Howard and Page. They have been well briefed for this eventuality.

I do not know for how long I shall have to be away. You will be doing me a great service if you make no attempt at all to find me and, above all, I do not wish the police to be brought into this matter if that can be avoided. I assure you again that my reasons for leaving in this manner are purely private and personal. I will come to no harm because my old friend, Benson, will be looking after me.

It would give me the greatest peace of mind if you would marry your Malcolm as soon as is practically possible. I know that you love him and I know that he wants to marry you very much, and I have a great respect for the intelligence and character of the man you have chosen. Please do not let the matter of poor Gillian impede your plans to marry and, on the occasion, please put a notice in *The Times*.

I have the greatest confidence that the two of you will be very happy together, and I am equally sure that you will both look after Gillian. Forgive me for the abrupt manner of my depature but it is in the best interests of all of us.

Your loving father,
George.

I looked up. 'I'm sorry, Penny.'

'But I don't understand,' she cried desolately. 'Oh, Malcolm, what's *happened* to him?'

She came into my arms and I held her close. 'I don't know – but we'll find out.'

She was still for a while, but pushed herself away as two cars arrived in quick succession. She stared from the window at the gathering knot of men. 'Malcolm, who are all those men? Have you told the police? Daddy said not to.'

'No, I haven't told the police,' I said quietly. 'Sit down, Penny; I have a lot to tell you.' She looked at me wonderingly, and hesitated, but sat in the chair behind the desk. I hesitated, too, not knowing where to begin, then thought it best to give it to her straight and fast.

'I work for the firm of McCulloch and Ross, and I've told no lies about what the firm does. It does everything I've said it does, and does it very well, too. Our clients are most satisfied, and they ought to be because of the amount of public money going into their service.'

'What are you getting at?'

'McCulloch and Ross is a cover for a sort of discreet government department dealing mainly with economic and industrial affairs in so far as they impinge on state security.'

'State security! You mean you're some sort of secret agent. A spy?'

I laughed and held up my hands. 'Not a spy. We're not romantic types with double-o numbers and a licence to kill – no nonsense like that.'

'But you were watching and investigating my father like a common spy.' Anger flamed in her. 'And was I just a means to an end? Did you snuggle up to me just to get to know him better?'

I lost the smile fast – this was where the crunch came. 'Christ, no! I didn't know a damned thing about him until yesterday, and I don't know much more now. Believe me when I say it was something I stumbled into by accident.'

She was disbelieving and contemptuous. 'And just what did you *stumble* into?'

'I can't tell you that because I don't know myself.'

She shook her head as though momentarily dizzy. 'That man in the hall – those men outside: are they in your department, too?'

'Yes.'

'Then I'd like to talk to the man in charge.' She stood up. 'I'd like to tell him just what I think of all this. I knew Daddy was under pressure. Now I know where it was coming from.'

I said deliberately, 'You're talking to the man in charge, and you're dead wrong.'

75

That stopped her. She sat down with a bump. '*You* are in charge?'

'That's right.'

'And you don't know what you're doing?' she laughed hysterically.

'I know what I'm doing, but I don't know why. There's a hierarchy of levels, Penny – wheels within wheels. Let me tell you how I got into this.'

So I told her. I told her everything, holding nothing back. I told her about Nellie and the colour codes; I told her about Ogilvie and Lord Cregar. I told her a damned sight more than I ought to have done, and to hell with the Official Secrets Act.

She heard me out, then said thoughtfully, 'Your people aren't very trusting, are they?'

'They're not in the trust business.' I lit a cigarette. 'The pressure didn't come from us, Penny. We threw no acid. We came into it after that, and my brief was to watch over your father and protect him – your father, you and Gillian, and Benson, too, if I thought it necessary.' I walked over to the window and looked at the cars. The gang had all arrived. 'I've not done a very good job so far.'

'It's not your fault that Daddy went away.' Her words hung heavily in the air, and she seemed to take another look at her father. 'That he *ran* away.'

I turned to her. 'Don't start blaming him without knowing what you're blaming him for.'

She said pensively, 'I wonder if he'd still want me to marry you, if he knew what I know now?'

'I'll ask him as soon as I catch up with him,' I said grimly.

'You're not going after him?' She picked up her letter. 'He said . . .'

'I know what he said. I also know he's regarded by my people as a very important man, and he may be going into danger without knowing it. I still have my job to do.'

'But he doesn't want . . .'

I said impatiently, 'What he wants or doesn't want is immaterial.' I plucked the letter from her fingers and scanned it. 'He says he doesn't want you to go looking for him. Well, you won't – I will. He says not to involve the police. Right; they haven't been told. He says, "I will come to no harm because my old friend, Benson, will be looking after me." Good God, Penny, how old is Benson? He must be pushing sixty-five. He's in no position to protect himself, let alone anyone else.'

She started to weep. She didn't sob or make an outcry, but the tears welled in her eyes and ran down her cheeks. She cried silently and helplessly, and she was shivering as though suddenly very cold. I put my arm around her and she clung to me with a fierce grip. One of the worst things that can happen is when a hitherto cosy and secure world falls apart. An icy wind seemed to be blowing through that pleasant panelled study from the greater and more vicious world outside.

'Oh, Malcolm, what am I to do?'

I said very quietly, 'You must do what you think is best. If you trust me you will help me find him, but I wouldn't – I couldn't – blame you if you refuse. I haven't been open with you – I should have told you about this yesterday.'

'But you were under orders.'

'A common plea,' I said. 'All the Nazis made it.'

'Malcolm, don't make it harder for yourself than you have to.' She put my arm aside, stood up, and went to the window. 'What are your men waiting for?'

I took a deep breath. 'For your decision. I want to search the house, and I can't do that without your permission.'

She came back to the desk and read her father's letter again. I said, 'He wrote to me, too,' and produced the letter. 'You can read it if you like.'

She read it, then gave it back to me. 'Bring in your men,' she said tonelessly.

12

We found a number of surprising things in that house but nothing that did us much good, at least, not then. In the basement there was a remarkably well-equipped workshop and chemical laboratory, way beyond amateur standard. There was also a small computer with a variety of input and output peripherals including an X–Y plotter. Still on the plotter was a sketch which had been drawn under computer control; it seemed to be a schematic of a complicated molecule and it made no sense to me, but then I'm no expert. For bigger problems with which the little computer couldn't cope there was a modem and an acoustic coupler so that the little chap could be used as a terminal to control a big computer by way of the post office land lines.

In the workshop was a bench on which a thingamajig was under construction. Whatever it was intended to do it was going to do under computer control because there were no fewer than fifteen integrated-circuit microelectronic chips built into it, and that's a fair amount of computing power. Also coupled into it was a laser, a cathode ray tube, a lot of laboratory glassware and a couple of gadgets I didn't recognize.

I didn't snap any switches or push any of the unlabelled buttons because I didn't know what would happen if I did. Instead I said to Larry, 'Any of Ashton's firms connected with electronics or computers?'

'No, just chemicals and plastics moulding. Some of the chemical processes might be computer-controlled, though.'

I grunted and had the entire basement sealed. The boffins from the department would have to check it out, and I wasn't going to touch anything until they had done so.

78

Penny had the combination for the safe in the study, and I knew by that we were unlikely to find anything of consequence in it. I was right. There was a bit of money, less than £50, which was not much considering Ashton's resources – I suppose it was emergency pocket money. There were some account books on which I wasted some time until I discovered they related to the running of the household, the stables and the cars. All very orderly. There was a whole sheaf of balance sheets headed with the name of the firm of accountants, Howard and Page. A quick glance at the bottom lines told me that George Ashton was doing very nicely, thank you, in spite of the economic recession.

And that was all.

Ashton's own quarters were a bit more productive. He had a suite – bedroom, bathroom, dressing-room and sitting-room which were as clean as a whistle. He seemed to live somewhat spartanly; there was less than the usual amount of junk which a man tends to accumulate and it was all very clean and tidy. There was nothing at all in any of the pockets of the clothes hanging in the wardrobes; whoever did his valeting – Benson probably – did a good job.

But a considerable amount of panel-tapping discovered a tambour which, when slid aside after a complicated procedure involving switching on certain lights in all four rooms thus releasing an electrically-controlled lock, revealed a massive metal door of armour-plated steel. The way I've described that might make you think we were lucky to find it, but it wasn't luck. The boys were good at their jobs.

Not good enough to open that vault door, though. After Simpson had done some architectural measuring with a tape I knew that beyond that door was not merely a safe but a sizeable room, big enough to swing a kitten in, if not a cat. Now, any man who would put a door like that as entrance to a room would be sure to take other precautions.

The walls, floor and ceiling would be very thick concrete, well reinforced with toughened steel, and the whole package would weigh a lot even when empty. It was on the second floor which meant that a special underpinning structure must have been built to support it. I made a note to look up Ashton's architect.

When the vault door was shown to Penny she was as surprised as anyone. She had never suspected its existence.

All this doesn't mean that I was prowling about the house personally knocking on walls. I left that to the boys and only inspected the results when they came in. I supervised the search of Ashton's study in Penny's presence, then settled down to talk to her because I assumed she would know more about her father than anyone else.

'Benson,' I said. 'How long have you known Benson?'

She looked surprised. 'He's always been around.'

'That's a long time. How long is always?'

'Always is always, Malcolm. I can't remember a time when there wasn't Benson.'

'As long as that? Twenty-five or twenty-six years?'

Penny smiled. 'Longer than that. He was with Daddy before I was born.'

'Always is a long time,' I agreed. 'He does the faithful family retainer bit very well, I must say. But he's more than that, isn't he?'

She crinkled her brow. 'I don't know. That's difficult to assess. When a man has been with a family as long as Benson he tends to become regarded as more of a friend than a servant.'

'To the extent that your father would share a bottle of whisky with him?'

'I don't think he ever did that.'

'He did on Sunday night,' I observed. 'Has Benson always been a personal servant to your father?'

She thought for a moment. 'We moved into the house in 1961 – I was twelve then. It was then Benson moved in here as Daddy's valet and dogsbody. Before that we had a house in Slough; just a little one, nothing as grand as this. Benson worked in one of Daddy's factories, but he visited the house quite often – at least once a week.' She smiled. 'He was one of our favourites. He used to bring us sweets – forbidden fruit because Daddy didn't like us to eat too many sweets. Benson used to smuggle them to us.'

'What was Benson doing in the factory?'

'I don't know. I was only a little girl.'

'When did your mother die, Penny?'

'When I was four.'

I thought that was bad luck on Ashton, having to bring up two small daughters. Still, he hadn't made a bad job of it. It seemed he didn't make a bad job of anything. I said, 'Do you know how your father got started? I mean, how did he start in business? Did he have inherited money, for instance?'

She shook her head vigorously. 'Daddy never talked much about his early life but I know he didn't inherit anything because he was an orphan brought up in a foundling home. He was in the army during the war and when he came out he met my grandfather and they set up in business together. They didn't have much money at the time, so my grandfather said before he died. He said Daddy's brains made it a success.'

'What was he in the army?' I asked idly.

'Just a private.'

That surprised me. Ashton would have been twenty-six or twenty-seven when he was demobbed and it was strange that a man of his drive and character should still have been a private soldier. Perhaps his army record would bear looking into.

'Did your father ever carry a gun?'

She misunderstood me. 'He did rough shooting at times, but not often.'

'I don't mean a shotgun. I mean a revolver or automatic pistol.'

'Lord, no! He hasn't got such a thing.'

'Would you know?'

'Of course I would.'

'You didn't know about that strong room upstairs.'

She was silent and bit her lips, then said, 'You think he's armed?'

I was saved from answering that because Larry popped his head around the door. 'Can I have a word, Malcolm?' I nodded and joined him in the hall. He said, 'Gillian Ashton's rooms are clean, nothing there of consequence. I read her diaries; she seems to live a quiet, upper-middle-class life – theatre, ballet, opera and so on. She reads a lot, too.'

'Not any more. Any liaisons?'

'Nothing very strong; a string of men who appeared one at a time and then petered out after a while.' He grinned. 'No mysterious assignations with people referred to by only their initials, nothing like that.'

'What about Penny's rooms? Have you checked there?'

Larry looked at me a bit queerly. 'But I thought . . .'

'I don't care what you thought,' I said evenly. 'Do it.'

'Okay.' He went downstairs again, and I thought that young Larry still had a lot to learn.

I was about to return to the study when Michaelis came through the hall. I said, 'Found anything?'

'Nothing for us. But in an attic there's the damndest thing – the biggest model railway set-up I've seen in my life.'

'Model railway!' I said incredulously.

'It's a real enthusiast's job,' he said. 'I'm a bit keen, myself, but I've never seen anything like this. There must be over a mile of HO-gauge track up there – it's like a bloody spider web. You'd have to do some smart scheduling to keep that lot runing smoothly.'

It was a facet of Ashton I wouldn't have dreamed of, but it didn't have a thing to do with the matter at hand. I dismissed it. 'Where's Jack Brent?'

'Giving the outbuildings a going-over – the garages and stables.'

'Tell him I want to see him when he's finished.' I went back into the study and thought it was time to try to find Ogilvie again. I'd been ringing every hour on the hour but each time he'd been out of the office so I'd passed my stuff on to Harrison. I put my hand out to dial again but the telephone shrilled before I got there.

It was Ogilvie. 'What have you got?' he said abruptly.

'I've passed it all to Harrison. Have you spoken to him?'

'No. As you may have gathered the balloon went up on schedule and I've been busy the last few hours. Give me the gist of it.'

'We've got a bloody big vault here,' I said. 'Not a safe, but a professional bank vault. We'll need experts to open it, and it'll probably take *them* a week.'

'It had better not,' said Ogilvie. 'You'll have them within the hour. What else?'

'I'd like some boffins – electronic and chemical. There's a cellar full of scientific stuff to look at. And you'd better send someone competent in computers.' I grinned. 'And maybe a model railway expert.'

'What's that?' he barked.

'Ashton has a model railway lay-out in his attic. I haven't seen it but I'm told it's quite something.'

'This is no time to be funny,' said Ogilvie acidly. 'What else?'

'Damn all. Nothing of use to us.'

'Keep looking,' he said sharply. 'A man can't live fifteen years in a house and not leave something of his personality lying around. There'll be *some* indication of where he's gone.' He thought for a moment. 'But I want you back here. Put someone else in charge.'

'That'll be Gregory,' I said. 'I still have a few things to wrap up – I'll be back in two hours.' I rang off and said to Penny, 'Well, that's it, love. The boss wants me back.'

She said, 'Just before you went out you said something about Daddy having a gun. What did you mean?'

'He's armed,' I said.

She shook her head disbelievingly but, since so many strange things had occurred that day, she could not combat my statement. 'And will you find him?'

'Oh, we'll find him. What's worrying me is that perhaps someone else is looking for him who will find him first. And the hell of it is we aren't sure, one way or another.'

Brent came in. 'You want me?'

I waved him out and joined him in the hall. As I stripped off my jacket, I said, 'Find anything?'

'Nothing.'

I unhitched the shoulder-holster from under my left armpit. 'Take this; you might need it.' I waited until he'd put it on, then took him into the study. 'Penny, this is Jack Brent; he's your guardian angel from now on. He sticks with you everywhere you go, excepting the loo and the bedroom – and he inspects those first.'

Penny looked at me as though she suspected me of joking. 'Are you serious?'

'You'll have to find a room for Jack – he'll be living here as long as you do.' I turned to Brent. 'Make yourself acquainted with the burglar precautions here, and make sure the damn things work.'

He nodded, and said, 'Sorry about this, Miss Ashton; I have to do as I'm told.'

'Another man under orders,' she said tightly. There were pink anger spots in her cheeks. 'Do you really mean that this man goes everywhere I go?'

'As long as you want to keep your schoolgirl complexion.'

Maybe I was a bit brutal about it, but the force of what I said hit her hard. She went very pale. 'My God, Malcolm. What *is* my father?'

'I don't know; but I'm going to wring it out of Ogilvie if it's the last thing I do.'

Jack Brent gave me a look as though he thought it would

be the last thing I did. Twisting the boss's arm in any organization is not the way to promotion and that indexed pension.

I said, 'I have things to do. I'll see you before I go, Penny.' I went to brief Gregory on the latest developments and to hand over to him. I found him with Simpson going over Benson's quarters which were a bit more opulent than you'd expect of a house servant – a three-roomed suite. Gregory and Simpson had torn the place apart on my instructions because I was particularly interested in Benson. 'Any luck?'

Gregory grunted. 'Not much. There's this.' He pointed to a small can of oil. 'Recommended for gun actions. And we found a single round of ammunition – unfired. It had rolled under the bed and dropped into a crack near the wall.'

It was a 9 mm parabellum round, popular with the military and the police. 'We know he was armed,' I said. 'Now we know what with – not that it helps. Anything else?'

'Not yet.'

I told Gregory the score and then went to check the activities of the rest of the team. I had to find *something* to take to Ogilvie. In the attic I found two of the boys playing trains. 'Oh, Jesus!' I said. 'Cut it out. We're here on business.'

Michaelis grinned. 'This is business – all in the line of duty. If you want this place searched thoroughly we'll have to look inside every engine, carriage and truck in this lay-out. The only way to do it is to bring them to this central control point a trainload at a time.'

I examined the lay-out and saw he had a point. You might have found a more complicated system in an international model engineering exhibition but I doubted it. There were about ten levels of track and a complexity of points and sidings which was baffling, and the whole lot was controlled from a central console which looked like the flight deck of Concorde. Michaelis seemed to have got the hang of it; maybe he was a budding genius.

'How many trucks and carriages are there?'

'We've looked at about three hundred so far,' he said. 'I reckon that's about a quarter. We're lucky there's an automatic coupling and uncoupling system. See those trucks in the siding over there?' He pointed to a spot about eight yards inside the spider's web of rails. 'We'd never be able to get in there without smashing the lot up – so we send an engine in to pull them out. Like this.'

He flicked switches and an engine about five inches long moved into the siding and attached itself to a line of trucks with a slight click. It reversed slowly, drawing out the train of trucks, and Michaelis smiled with pleasure. 'Now the problem is – how do we get it from there to here?'

My God! I thought. What we have to do in the line of duty.

I snorted and left them to it, and went in search of Penny to make my farewells. Somebody said she was in her bedroom. She answered when I tapped on the door, and she was as angry as I'd ever seen her. 'Come in,' she said impatiently, so I did and she slammed the door behind me with a crash, 'Someone has been searching my room.'

'I know. *All* rooms in the house have been searched.'

'On your instructions?'

'Yes.'

'Oh, no! I thought I deserved better of you than that. You were right when you said you people don't deal in trust. Last night you asked me to marry you, and less than twenty-four hours later you show just how much you trust me. What sort of a man are you that you would send someone in here to paw over my things?'

'It's not a question of trusting or not trusting,' I said. 'I do my job the way I was taught.'

'So you go by the book! It's not the kind of book I'd want to read.'

And so we had a flaming row – our first. I got so boiling

mad that in the end I stormed out of the house and jumped into my car. I left a bit of rubber on the drive and got to the office in record time, being lucky not to be picked up by the police for speeding.

I wasn't in the best of moods when I confronted Ogilvie. He said immediately, 'Got anything more?'

I dropped the round of ammunition on his desk. 'Benson has something which shoots these.'

'All right, Malcolm,' he said. 'Let's begin at the beginning.'

So we talked. I told him in detail everything that had happened and we discussed the implications. Or rather, Ogilvie did. I didn't know enough about Ashton to see any implications. At one point in the discussion I said, 'It's obvious that Ashton had been prepared for this a long time. He told Penny that his lawyer and accountant had been well briefed, and he couldn't have done that in a day. I don't know if he expected acid-throwing, but he was certainly ready to jump. Someone has put the frighteners on him.'

Ogilvie made no comment on that. He said. 'You may know – or not know – that there's an inter-departmental committee for organizations like ours which sits to straighten out any demarcation disputes.'

'I don't know, but it sounds a good idea.'

'There was a special meeting called for this afternoon, and I had to talk very hard and very fast. There was considerable opposition.'

'From Lord Cregar?'

Ogilvie's eyebrows rose. 'How did you identify him?'

'He gets his pictures in the papers,' I said sardonically.

'I see. Do you know anything of the early history of this department?'

'Not much.'

He leaned forward and tented his fingers. 'The British way of intelligence and security is rather strange. Over the years we've acquired a reputation for being good at it, good and rather subtle. That is the considered assessment of our American and Russian rivals. They're wrong, of course. What they mistake for subtlety is merely that our right hand hardly ever knows what our left hand is doing.'

He took out a case and offered me a cigarette. 'The politicians are deathly afraid of a centralized intelligence outfit; they don't want anything like the CIA or the KGB because they've seen what happens when such a group becomes too big and too powerful. And so, in the classic way of divide and rule, intelligence work in Britain is broken down among relatively small groups.'

He accepted a light. 'That has its drawbacks, too. It leads to amateurism, rivalry between departments, overlapping functions, the building of empires and private armies, lack of co-operation, a breakdown of the lines of communication – a whole litany of petty vices. And it makes my job damned difficult.'

His tone was a mixture of bitterness and resignation. I said, 'I can imagine.'

'In the early 1950s the risks of industrial espionage became noticeable. We weren't really bothered about one firm stealing secrets from another, and we're still not, unless it affects state security. The whole problem was that our friends to the east have no private firms, so any industrial espionage from that direction was *ipso facto* state inspired, and that we couldn't have. In our inimitable British fashion a new department was set up to cope. This department.'

'I know what we're doing, but I didn't know how we got started.'

Ogilvie drew on his cigarette. 'There's an important point. In an attempt to cut down on duplication of effort, several other departments had to hand over large chunks of their *raison d'être* and were closed down completely. They were only small fry, though. But it all led to jealousy and bad blood which exists in a dilute form to this day. And that's how we inherited the problem of Ashton.'

I said, 'Who did we pinch Ashton from?'

'Lord Cregar's department.' Ogilvie leaned forward. 'This afternoon the Minister came down on our side. Ashton is still our baby and we have to find him. You are still inside man, and that means *you* find him. Any help you need just ask for.'

'That suits me,' I said. 'I want clearance for Code Purple.'

Ogilvie shook his head. 'Not that.'

I blew up. 'For Christ's sake! How can I look for a man when I don't know anything about him? Back in Marlow I had an interesting lecture on trust which has soured me to the belly, and this job has already interfered too much with my private life. Now you either trust me or you don't – and the crunch comes here. I get clearance for Code Purple or my resignation will be on your desk at nine tomorrow morning.'

He said sadly, 'I have warned you about being impetuous. To begin with, I couldn't get you clearance in that time, and even if you did you wouldn't find what you're looking for because Ashton is in Code Black.' His voice was grim. 'And you couldn't be cleared for Code Black inside three months – if ever.'

Code Black sounded as though it was the end of the rainbow and Ashton was the pot of gold. There was a silence which I broke by saying diffidently, 'That's it, then. I'd better go along to my office and type my resignation.'

'Don't be a young fool!' snapped Ogilvie. He drummed on the desk, then said, 'I've come to a decision. If it gets out I could be fired. Wait here.'

He got up and went to an unobtrusive door behind his desk and disappeared. I waited a long time and wondered what I'd done. I knew I'd laid my career on the line. Well, I was prepared for that and with my financial backing I could stand it. Maybe I wouldn't have done it if I had only my pay to depend on. I don't know. And I'd pushed

Ogilvie into doing something he might be sorry for, and that was bad because I liked him.

Presently he opened the door and said, 'Come in here.' I followed him into a small room where there was one of the ubiquitous computer terminals. 'I'm cleared for Code Black,' he said. 'The information on Ashton is coming on line. If you sit there you'll know what you need to know. The computer won't know who is pushing the buttons.' He checked the time. 'I'll be back in two hours.'

I was a bit subdued. 'All right, sir.'

'I want your word,' he said. 'I don't want you roving at random in Code Black. I want to know that you'll stick to Ashton and only to Ashton. There are other matters in Code Black that are better for you not to know – for your own peace of mind.'

I said, 'You can make sure of that just by sitting in here with me.'

He smiled. 'You made a point just now about trust. Either I trust you or I don't, and there's an end to it.'

'You have my word.'

He nodded abruptly and left, closing the door behind him.

I glanced at Nellie who was staring at me with an interrogative bright green question mark, and then glanced around the small room which was really more of a cubicle. On one side of the terminal was a small plotter, very much like the one in Ashton's cellar; on the other side was a line printer.

I sat at the console and reflected that if Ashton was so important and had been around and of interest since before the department had started then there was probably reams of stuff about him in Nellie's guts. This idea was reinforced by the two hours Ogilvie had allowed for reviewing the information, so I switched on the printer, and typed:

OUTPUT MODE – PRINTER

Nellie had an attack of verbal diarrhoea. She came back at me with:

PRINTER OUTPUT NEGATIVED UNDER CODE BLACK
NOTE WELL: NO WRITTEN RECORD TO BE MADE
UNDER CODE BLACK
NOTE WELL: NO TAPE-RECORDED TRANSCRIPTIONS
TO BE MADE UNDER CODE BLACK
NOTE WELL: NO PHOTOGRAPHS TO BE TAKEN OF
THE CRT UNDER CODE BLACK

I sighed and switched off the printer.

I've described before how one juggles with Nellie so there's no point in going into that again. What I haven't said is that Nellie is accommodating; if she's going too fast you can slow her down, and if she's producing something of no interest you can speed her up. You can also skip about in the record, going back to items forgotten or neglected. She's quite a toy.

I did quite a bit of skipping when swanning around in Ashton's life. He'd lived quite a bit.

13

Aleksandr Dmitrovitch Chelyuskin was born to poorish, but respectable parents in the small town of Tesevo-Netyl'skiy, just to the north of Novgorod in Russia. The year was 1919. Both parents were schoolteachers; his mother taught in an infants' school and his father taught mathematics and allied subjects to older boys.

These were the years of revolution, and whether the Whites or the Reds were to come on top had not yet been decided in 1919. Armies of foreigners – British, French, American – were on Russian soil, and it was a time of turmoil and conflagration. Little Aleksandr was very nearly snuffed out just after birth as the waves of war swept over the country. In fact, his elder brother and his two sisters did die during this period as the family was buffeted in the storm; the record did not disclose just how they died.

Eventually, in 1923, the family Chelyuskin came to haven in the town of Aprelevka, just outside Moscow. The family had been reduced to three and, since Aleksandr had been a late child and his mother was now apparently barren, there were to be no more children and he was brought up as an only child. His father found a job teaching mathematics and they settled down to a life of relative security.

Although Dmitri Ivanovitch Chelyuskin was a teacher of mathematics he was not a good mathematician himself in the sense that he produced original work. His role in life was to teach small boys the elements of arithmetic, algebra and geometry, which he did largely by rote, a sarcastic tongue and a heavy hand. But he was good enough at his job to notice that he did not have to tell young Aleksandr anything twice, and when the time came that he found he did not have to tell the boy once and that his son was beginning to ask unanswerable questions it was then that he thought he might have an infant prodigy on his hands.

Aleksandr was about ten years old at the time.

He played chess very well and joined the chess club in Aprelevka where he proceeded to lick the pants off his elders and betters. The elder Chelyuskin forgot about the mathematics and thought of the possibility of having a Grand Master in the family, a great honour in Russia.

One Suslov, a member of the chess club, disagreed. He persuaded Chelyuskin *père* to write to a friend of his in Moscow, a member of the Board of Education. Letters and months passed, and eventually, after a series of supposedly gruelling examinations which Aleksandr went through without so much as a qualm, he was admitted to a Lycée in Moscow at the hitherto unheard-of age of twelve years and ten months. Whether the fact that Suslov had been the undisputed chess champion of Aprelevka until the appearance of Aleksandr had anything to do with that, is not known. At least, Suslov said nothing for the record but went on to win the club championship the following year.

In Britain the left wing decries elitism; in Russia the communists foster it. When a bright youngster is found he is whisked away to a special school where his mind is stretched. He can no longer count on having an easy time walking nonchalantly through the school subjects without effort, coming out on top while his duller brethren work like hell plodding along behind. Aleksandr was subjected to a forced draught of education.

He liked it. He had the cast of mind which loves grappling with the abstruse and difficult, and he found much to his liking in pure mathematics. Now, mathematics at its purest is a game for adults and need have no relationship at all to the real physical world, and the fact that it sometimes does is a bit of luck. The pure mathematician is concerned with the concept of number at its most abstract, and Aleksandr played happily among the abstractions for quite a while. At the age of sixteen he wrote a paper, 'Some Observations on the Relationship between Mathieu Functions and Weierstrass Elliptic Functions.' It consisted of three paragraphs of written text and ten pages of mathematical formulae, and was rather well received. He followed it up with another paper the following year, and that brought him under the eye of Peter Kapitza and led to the second great change in his life.

It was 1936 and Kapitza was the white hope of Russian physics. He was born in Kronstadt and studied in Kronstadt and Petrograd, as it was then. But in 1925 he made a change which was rather odd for a Russian at the time. He went to Cambridge, then the leading university dealing with physics. He became a fellow of Trinity College, and assistant director of research at the Cavendish Laboratory under Rutherford. He was elected a Fellow of the Royal Society in 1929, and managed to pick up about every scientific honour that was not absolutely screwed down except the Nobel Prize which he missed. In 1936 he went back to Russia, supposedly on a sabbatical, and never left again. Stalin is reputed to have lowered the portcullis on him.

This, then, is the man who extended his influence over Aleksandr Chelyuskin. Perhaps he looked at the youth and was reminded of himself at the age of seventeen. At any rate, he diverted Aleksandr from his playground of pure mathematics and showed him that there were real problems to be solved in the world. Kapitza introduced him to theoretical physics.

Physics is an experimental science, and most physicists are good mechanics and have broken fingernails caused by putting bits and pieces of equipment together. But there are a few – a very few – who do nothing but think. They tend to sit around, gazing into space, and their favourite weapons are blackboard and chalk. After a few hours, days or years of thought they diffidently suggest that an experiment should be made.

The realm of the theoretical physicist is the totality of the universe, and there are very few good ones around at any one time. Aleksandr Chelyuskin was one of them.

He studied magnetism and low temperature physics under Peter Kapitza and, applying quantum theory to the earlier work of Kammerlingh Onnes, did important work relating to phase II of liquid helium, and the new field of superconductivity got under way. But this was just one of the many things he thought about. His work was astonishingly wide-ranging and eclectic, and he published profusely. He did not publish everything he thought because he liked to have things wrapped up tidily, but some of his work, reproduced in the record from his notebooks written at this time, clearly anticipated the cosmological theories of Fred Hoyle in the '50s and '60s. Other work from his notebooks included thoughts on the nature of catalytic action and a brief sketch extending these thoughts into the organic field of enzymes.

In 1941 the war came to Russia, but the brain the state had so carefully nurtured was considered too valuable to risk having a bullet put through it, and Chelyuskin never saw a shot fired in anger. For most of the war he sat behind the Urals and thought his thoughts. One of the many things he thought about was the fine structure of metals. The resultant improvement in Russian tank armour was quite noticeable.

In March 1945 he was visited by a high official and told to give careful consideration to the atomic structure of certain rare metals. Stalin had just come back from the Yalta Conference where he had been informed of the existence of the atomic bomb.

In the period immediately following the war Chelyuskin became increasingly dissatisfied, mainly because, although the war was over, he was still constrained to involve himself in weapons research. He did not like what he was doing and deliberately slowed his pace. But a mind cannot stop thinking and he turned to other things than physics – to sociology, for example. In short, he stopped thinking about things and began to think about people.

He looked at the world immediately about him and did not like what he saw. This was the time when Stalin was conducting an extended post-mortem on the mistakes made during the war. Returning Russians who had been taken prisoner were hardly given time to sneeze before being whisked into Siberian camps, and hundreds of former officers mysteriously dropped out of sight. He reflected that continuous purging is as bad for society as it is for a body, and he knew that the infamous army purge of 1936 had so weakened the army that it had contributed largely to the startling defeats at the beginning of the war. And yet the process was continuing.

He was determined, on moral grounds, not to continue with atomic research, and beyond that he was sure he did not want to put such weapons into the hands of a man like Stalin. But he was equally determined not to end up in a forced labour camp as some of his colleagues had done, so he was presented with quite a problem which he solved with characteristic neatness and economy.

He killed himself.

It took him three months to plan his death and he was ruthless in the way he went about it. He needed the body of a man about his own age and with the same physical characteristics. More complicatedly, he needed the body before it had died so that certain surgical and dental work could be done and given time to age. This could not be done on a corpse.

He found what he wanted on a visit to Aprelevka. A boyhood friend of his own age was afflicted with leukaemia and there was much doubt about his survival. Chelyuskin visited the hospital and chatted to his friend, at first in generalities and then, more directly and dangerously, about politics. He was fortunate in that he found his friend to have much the same convictions as himself, and so he was encouraged to ask the crucial question. Would his friend, in the terminal stages of a killing illness, donate his body for Chelyuskin's survival?

The record does not disclose the name of Chelyuskin's friend but, in my opinion, he was a very brave man. Chelyuskin pulled strings and had him transferred to another hospital where he had the co-operation of a doctor. File entries were fudged, papers were lost and bureaucracy was baffled; it was all very efficiently inefficient and ended up with the fact that Chelyuskin's friend was effectively dead as far as anyone knew.

Then the poor man had his leg broken under surgical and aseptic conditions and suffered a considerable amount of dental work. The fracture in the leg corresponded exactly with a similar fracture in Chelyuskin's leg and the dental structure duplicated Chelyuskin's mouth exactly. The bone knitted together, and all he had to do was to wait for his friend to die.

Meanwhile, going through underground channels, he had contacted British Intelligence and requested political asylum. We were only too glad to oblige, even on his terms. To wave a defecting Russian scientist like a flag is not necessarily a good ploy, and we were quite happy to respect his terms of secrecy as long as we got him. The necessary arrangements were made.

It took a long time for Chelyuskin's friend to die. In fact, for a period there was a marked improvement in his condition which must have infuriated my masters. I doubt if it worried Chelyuskin very much. He went about his work as usual, attending the committees which were an increasing and aggravating part of his life, and soldiered on. But his friends did comment that he appeared to be doing his best to drown himself in the vodka bottle.

Seven months later the Russian scientific community was saddened to learn that Academician A. D. Chelyuskin had been burnt to death when his *dacha*, to which he had retired for a short period of relaxation, had caught fire. There was a post-mortem examination and an enquiry. The rumour got around that Chelyuskin had been smoking in bed when in his cups and that vodka added to the flames had not helped him much. That was a story everybody could believe.

A month later Chelyuskin slipped over the Iranian border. Three days later he was in Teheran and the following day he was put down at RAF Northolt by courtesy of Transport Command. He was given an enthusiastic welcome by a select group who turned out to welcome this genius who was then at the ripe age of twenty-eight. There would be a lot of mileage left in him.

The powers-that-be were somewhat baffled by Chelyuskin's comparative youth. They tended to forget that creative abstract thought, especially in mathematics, is a young man's game, and that Einstein had published his Special Theory of Relativity when only nineteen. Even the politicians among them forgot that Pitt was Prime Minister at twenty-four.

They were even more baffled and irritated by Chelyuskin's attitude. He soon made it clear that he was a Russian patriot and no traitor, and that he had no intention of disclosing secrets, atomic or otherwise. He said he had left Russia because he did not want to work on atomics, and that to communicate his knowledge would be to negate the action he had taken. Conversations on atomic theory were barred.

The irritation grew and pressure was applied, but authority found that it could neither bend nor break this man. The more pressure was applied the more stubborn he became, until finally he refused to discuss *any* of his work. Even the ultimate threat did not move him. When told that he could be disclosed to the Russians even at that late stage he merely shrugged and indicated that it was the privilege of the British to do so if they wished, but he thought it would be unworthy of them.

Authority changed its tack. Someone asked him what he wanted to do. Did he want a laboratory put at his disposal, for instance? By now Chelyuskin was wary of the British and their motives. I suppose, in a way, he had been naïve to expect any other treatment, but naïvety in a genius is comparatively normal. He found himself surrounded, not by scientists whom he understood, but by calculating men, the power brokers of Whitehall. Mutual incomprehensibility was total.

He rejected the offer of a laboratory curtly. He saw quite clearly that he was in danger of exchanging one intellectual prison for another. When they asked him again what it was he wanted, he said something interesting. 'I want to live as an ordinary citizen,' he said. 'I want to sink and lose myself in the sea of Western capitalism.'

Authority shrugged its shoulders and gave up. Who could understand these funny foreigners, anyway? A dog-in-the-manger attitude was adopted; if we couldn't get at the man's brain then the Russians didn't have it, either, and that was good enough. He could always be watched and, who knows, he might even declare a dividend in the future.

So Chelyuskin got exactly what he asked for.

An REME soldier called George Ashton had been killed in a traffic accident in Germany. He was twenty-seven and had been brought up in a foundling home. Unmarried and with neither kith nor kin to mourn him, he was the perfect answer. Chelyuskin was flown to Germany, put in the uniform of a private in the British Army, and brought back to England by train and sea, accompanied discreetly at all times. He went through a demobilization centre where he was given a cheap suit, a small amount of back pay and a handshake from a sombre unrecruiting sergeant.

He was also given an honorarium of £2000.

He asked for, and was given, something else before he was cast adrift. Because of the necessity for scientific study he had learned English in his youth and read it fluently. But he never had occasion to speak it, which might have been an advantage when he was put through a six months' total immersion course in conversational English, because he had no bad habits to unlearn. He came out of it with a cultured generalized Home Counties accent, and set out to sink or swim in the capitalist world.

Two thousand pounds may not seem much now, but it was quite a sizeable piece of change back in 1947. Even so, George Ashton knew he must conserve his resources; he put most of it in a bank deposit account, and lived very simply while he explored this strange new world. He was no longer an honoured man, an Academician with a car and a *dacha* at his disposal, and he had to find a way of earning a living. Any position requiring written qualifications was barred to him because he did not have the papers. It was a preposterous situation.

He took a job as a book-keeper in the stores department of a small engineering firm in Luton. This was in the days before computers when book-keeping was done by hand as in the days of Dickens, and a good book-keeper could add a triple column of pounds, shillings and pence in one practised sweep of the eye. But there weren't many of those around and Ashton found himself welcome because, unlike the popular myth, he was an egghead who could add and *always* got his change right. He found the job ridiculously easy if monotonous, and it left him time to think.

He struck up an acquaintanceship with the foreman of the toolroom, a man called John Franklin who was about 50 years of age. They got on very well together and formed the habit of having a drink together in the local pub after work. Presently Ashton was invited *chez* Franklin for Sunday dinner where he met Franklin's wife, Jane, and his daughter, Mary. Mary Franklin was 25 then, and as yet unmarried because her fiancé had been shot down over Dortmund in the final days of the war.

All this time Ashton was being watched. If he was aware of it he gave no sign. Other people were watched, too, and the Franklin family came in for a thorough rummaging on the grounds that those interested in Ashton were *per se* interesting in themselves. Nothing was discovered except the truth; that Jack Franklin was a damned good artisan with his brains in his fingertips, Jane Franklin was a comfortable, maternal woman, and Mary Franklin had suffered a tragedy in her life.

Six months after they met, Ashton and Franklin left the engineering firm to strike out on their own. Ashton put up £1500 and his brains while Franklin contributed £500 and his capable hands. The idea was to set up a small plastics moulding shop; Franklin to make the moulds and the relatively simple machines needed, and Ashton to do the designing and to run the business.

The small firm wobbled along for a while without overmuch success until Ashton, becoming dissatisfied with the moulding powders he was getting from a big chemical company, devised a concoction of his own, patented it, and started another company to make it. After that they never looked back.

Ashton married Mary Franklin and I dare say a member of some department or other was unobtrusively present at the wedding. A year later she gave him a daughter whom they christened Penelope, and two years later another girl whom they called Gillian. Mary Ashton died a couple of years later in 1953, from childbirth complications. The baby died, too.

All his life Ashton kept a low profile. He joined no clubs or trade associations; he steered clear of politics, national or local, although he voted regularly, and generally divided his life between his work and his home. This gave him time to look after his two small girls with the help of a nanny whom he brought into the small suburban house in Slough, where he then lived. From the record he was devoted to them.

About 1953 he must have opened his old notebooks and started to think again. As Chelyuskin he had never published any of his work on catalysts and I suppose he thought it was safe to enter the field. A catalyst is a substance which speeds up the chemical reactions between other substances, sometimes by many thousands of times. They are used extensively in chemical processing, particularly in the oil industry.

Ashton put his old work to good use. He devised a whole series of new catalysts tailored to specialized uses. Some he manufactured and sold himself, others he allowed to be made under licence. All were patented and the money began to roll in. It seemed as though this odd fish was swimming quite well in the capitalist sea.

In 1960 he bought his present house and, after fifteen months of extensive internal remodelling, he moved in with his family. After that nothing much seemed to happen except that he saw the portent of North Sea oil, opened another factory in 1970, took out a lot more patents and became steadily richer. He also extended his interest to those natural catalysts, the enzymes, and presumably the sketchy theory presented in the early notebook became filled out.

After 1962 the record became particularly flat and perfunctory, and I knew why. Authority had lost interest in him and he would exist only in a tickler file to remind someone to give an annual check. It was only when I set the bells jangling by my inadvertent enquiry that someone had woken up.

And that was the life of George Ashton, once Aleksandr Dmitrovitch Chelyuskin – my future father-in-law.

14

What I have set down about Ashton-Chelyuskin is a mere condensation of what was in the computer together with a couple of added minor assumptions used as links to make a sustained narrative. Had I been able to use the printer it would have churned out enough typescript to make a book the size of a family bible. To set down in print the details of a man's life needs a lot of paper. Yet I think I have presented the relevant facts.

When I finished I had a headache. To stare at a cathode ray screen for two and a half hours is not good for the eyes, and I had been smoking heavily so that the little room was very stuffy. It was with relief that I emerged into Ogilvie's office.

He was sitting at his desk reading a book. He looked up and smiled. 'You look as though you need a drink.'

'It would go down very well,' I agreed.

He got up and opened a cabinet from which he took a bottle of whisky and two glasses; then he produced a jug of iced water from a small built-in refrigerator. The perquisites of office. 'What do you think?'

'I think Ashton is one hell of a man. I'm proud to have known him.'

'Anything else?'

'There's one fact that's so damned obvious it may be overlooked.'

'I doubt it,' said Ogilvie, and handed me a glass. 'A lot of good men have checked that file.'

I diluted the whisky and sat down. 'Do you have all of Ashton in there?'

'All that we know is there.'

'Exactly. Now, I've gone through Ashton's work in some detail and it's all in the field of applied science – technology, if you like. All the things he's been doing with catalysts is derived from his earlier unpublished work; there's nothing fundamentally new there. Correct me if I'm wrong.'

'You're quite right, although it took a man with Ashton's brains to do it. We've given our own top chemists photo-copies of those notebooks and their attitude was that the stuff was all right from a theoretical point of view but it didn't seem to lead anywhere. Ashton made it lead some-where and it's made him rich. But, in general, your point is good; it's all derivative of earlier work – even his later interest in enzymes.'

I nodded. 'But Chelyuskin was a theoretician. The point is this – did he stop theorizing and, if not, what the hell has he been thinking about? I can understand why you want that bloody vault opened.'

'You're not too stupid,' said Ogilvie. 'You've hit the nail smack on the head. You're right; you can't stop a man thinking, but what he's been thinking about is difficult to figure. It won't be atomic theory.'

'Why not?'

'We know what he reads; the magazines he subscribes to, the books he buys. We know he's not been keeping up with the scientific literature in any field except catalytic chemis-try, and no one thinks in a vacuum. Atomic theory has made great strides since Ashton came out of Russia. To do any original work a man would have to work hard to keep ahead of the pack – attend seminars and so on. Ashton hasn't been doing it.' He tasted his whisky. 'What would you have done in Ashton's position and with a mind like his?'

'Survival would come first,' I said. 'I'd find a niche in society and look for security. Once I'd got that perhaps I'd start thinking again – theorizing.'

'What about? In your struggle for survival the world of thought has passed you by; you've lost touch. And you

104

daren't try to regain touch, either. So what would you think about?'

'I don't know,' I said slowly. 'Perhaps, with a mind like his, I'd think about things other people haven't been thinking about. A new field.'

'Yes,' said Ogilvie thoughtfully. 'It makes one wonder, doesn't it?'

We sat for a few moments in silence. It was late – the light was ebbing from the summer sky over the City – and I was tired. I sipped the whisky appreciatively and thought about Ashton. Presently Ogilvie asked, 'Did you find anything in the file to give you a clue about where he's gone?'

'Nothing springs to mind. I'd like to sleep on it – let the unconscious have a go.' I finished the whisky. 'Where does Cregar fit into this?'

'It was his crowd Ashton approached when he wanted to leave Russia. Cregar went into Russia himself to get him out. He was a young man then, of course, and not yet Lord Cregar – he was the Honourable James Pallton. Now he heads his department.'

I'd come across the name Pallton in reading the file, but I hadn't connected it with Cregar. I said, 'He mishandled Ashton right from the start. He approached him with all the sensitivity of a fifty-pence whore. First he threatened, then he tried to bribe. He didn't understand the type of man he'd come across, and he put Ashton's back up.'

Ogilvie nodded. 'That's one element in the mixture of his resentment. He always thought he could retrieve Ashton; that's why he was so annoyed when the Ashton case was transferred to us. That's why he's sticking his oar in now.'

'What steps have already been taken to find Ashton?'

'The usual. The Special Branch are on the watch at sea ports and airports, and they're checking passenger lists for the past twenty-four hours. You'd better liaise with Scotland Yard on that tomorrow.'

'I'll do that. And I'll have a go from the other end. There's one thing I'd like to know.'

'What's that?'

'Who threw such a scare into Ashton? Who threw that bloody acid?'

I was overtired that night and couldn't get to sleep. As I tossed restlessly Penny was very much on my mind. It was evident from what she had said that she knew nothing of Ashton in the larval stage, before he changed from Chelyuskin. Her account of his early life fitted that of the REME soldier killed in Germany.

I wondered how it would be with Penny and me. I had been damned insensitive that afternoon. Her room had to be searched, but if anyone had done it then it ought to have been me, preferably in her presence. I didn't blame her for blowing her top and I wondered how I could retrieve the situation. I felt very bad about it.

Most people, when they have had a burglary, are not so much concerned about the articles stolen as about the intrusion into the heart of their lives, the home which is so peculiarly their own. It is the thought that strange hands have been delving among their innermost secrets, rummaging in drawers, opening doors in the private parts of the house – all this is profoundly shocking. I knew all that and ought to have applied it to Penny.

At last I sat up in bed, checked the time, then stretched for the telephone. Although it was late I was going to talk to her. Mary Cope answered my call. 'Malcolm Jaggard here; I'd like to talk to Miss Ashton.'

'Just a moment, sir,' she said. She wasn't away long. 'Miss Ashton isn't in, sir.' There was a hint of nervousness in her voice as though she thought I wouldn't believe her. I didn't, but there was nothing I could do about it.

It was early morning when I finally slept.

* * *

I spent most of the forenoon at Scotland Yard with a Special Branch officer. I had no great hope of success and neither had he but we went through the motions. His crowd had been busy but even so the reports were slow to come in. A lot of people leave from Heathrow in twenty-four hours and that is only one exit from the country.

'Ashton and Benson,' he said morosely, as he ticked off a name. 'Bloody near as bad as Smith and Robinson. Why the hell do people we're interested in never have names like Moneypenny or Gotobed?'

Six Bensons and four Ashtons had left from Heathrow. Half could be eliminated because of sex and the Ashtons were a family of four. But two of the Bensons would have to be followed up; one had gone to Paris and the other to New York. I got busy on the telephone.

Heathrow may be large but it is still only one place and there are other airports, more than the average person realizes. And there were the sea ports of which islanded Britain had a plenitude. It was going to be a long job with nothing but uncertainty guaranteed.

The Special Branch man said philosophically, 'And, of course, they may have left under other names. Getting a spare passport is dead easy.'

'They may not have left at all,' I said. 'Tell your chaps to keep their eyes open.'

I lunched in a commissary at the Yard and then went back prepared for a slogging afternoon. At three o'clock Ogilvie rang me. 'They'll be opening that vault later today. I want you there.'

A drive to Marlow would be a lot more refreshing than checking passenger lists. 'All right.'

'Now, these are my exact instructions. When that door is opened you will be present, and the head of the safe-cracking team. No one else. Is that clear?'

'Perfectly clear.'

'Then you send him out of the room and check the contents. If they are removeable you bring them here under

107

guard. If not, you close and lock the door again, first making sure we can open it again more easily.'

'How long are you staying at the office?'

'All night, if necessary.' He hung up.

So I drove to Marlow and to Ashton's place. I was wearing grooves in that road. Simpson was the gate man and he let me in and I drove up to the house. I met Gregory in the hall. 'Found anything useful?'

He shrugged. 'Not a thing.'

'Where's Miss Ashton?'

'At the hospital. Jack Brent is with her.'

'Good enough.' I went up to Ashton's quarters and found the safe-cracking team at work. I don't know where the department kept its experts when not in use, but they were always available when needed. The chief safe-cracker was a man I'd met before by the name of Frank Lillywhite. 'Afternoon, Frank,' I said. 'How much longer?'

He grunted. 'An hour.' He paused. 'Or two.' There was a longer pause as he did something intricate with a tool he held. 'Or three.'

I grinned. 'Or four. Is this a tricky one?'

'They're all tricky. This is a twenty-four-hour safe, that's all.'

I was curious. 'What do you mean?'

Lillywhite stepped away from the vault door and an underling moved in. 'Safe manufacturers don't sell security – they sell time. Any safe made can be cracked; all the manufacturer guarantees is the length of time needed to crack it. They reckon this is a twenty-four-hour job; I'm going to do it in twenty – with a bit of luck. The tricky part comes in circumventing the booby traps.'

'What booby traps?'

'If I do the wrong thing here, twelve bloody big tungsten steel bars will shoot out all round the door. Then only the maker will be able to open it.'

'Then why didn't we get the maker on the job in the first place?'

108

Lillywhite sighed, and said patiently, 'The whole vault would have to be ripped out and taken to the factory. They've got a bloody big tin-opener there that weighs a thousand tons. Of course the vault wouldn't be good for much after that.'

I contemplated the awful possibility of taking the whole vault out. 'Neither would this house. I'll stop asking silly questions. Don't open the door unless I'm here.'

'Message received and understood.'

I went down to the cellar where I found a couple of studious-looking types being baffled by Ashton's contraption. Their conversation, if you could call it that, was in English, but that's to use the word loosely; it was technical jargon-ridden and way over my head, so I left them to it. Another man was packing tape cassettes into a box ready to take away. I said, 'What are those?'

He indicated the little computer. 'Program and data tapes for this thing. We're taking them to the lab for analysis.'

'You're listing everything, I hope. You'll have to give a receipt to Miss Ashton.' He frowned at that, and I said acidly, 'We're not thieves or burglars, you know. It's only by courtesy of Miss Ashton that we're here at all.' As I left the cellar he was taking cassettes out of the box and stacking them on a table.

An hour and a half later Gregory found me in Ashton's study. 'They'll be opening the vault in about fifteen minutes.'

'Let's go up.'

We left the study and encountered Lord Cregar in the hall; with him was a big man with the build of a heavyweight boxer. Cregar looked brisk and cheerful but his cheerfulness, if not his briskness, evaporated when he saw me. 'Ah, Mr Jaggard,' he said. 'A fine mess has been made of things, I must say.'

I shrugged. 'Events moved faster than we anticipated.'

'No doubt. I understand there's a vault here which is being opened this afternoon. Has it been opened yet?'

I wondered where he'd got his information. 'No.'

'Good. Then I'm in time.'

I said, 'Am I to understand that you wish to be present when the vault is opened?'

'That's correct.'

'I'm sorry,' I said. 'But I'll have to take that under advisement.'

He looked at me thoughtfully. 'Do you know who I am?'

'Yes, my lord.'

'Very well,' he said. 'Make your telephone call.'

I jerked my head at Gregory and we went back into the study. 'There's no need for a call,' I said. 'Ogilvie's instructions were very precise, and they didn't include Cregar.'

'I know that big chap,' said Gregory. 'His name is Martins. A bad chap to tangle with.' He paused. 'Maybe you'd better check with Ogilvie.'

'No. He told me what to do and I'm going to do it.'

'So what if Cregar won't take it? A bout of fisticuffs with a member of the House of Lords could have its repercussions.'

I smiled. 'I doubt of it will come to that. Let's tell his lordship the bad news.'

We went back into the hall to find that Cregar and Martins had vanished. 'They'll be upstairs,' said Gregory.

'Come on.' We ran upstairs and found them in Ashton's room. Cregar was tapping his foot impatiently as I stepped forward and said formally, 'My lord, I regret to inform you that you will not be permitted to be present when the vault is opened.'

Cregar's eyes bulged. 'Did Ogilvie say that?'

'I have not spoken to Mr Ogilvie recently. I am merely following instructions.'

'You take a lot upon yourself,' he commented.

I turned to Lillywhite. 'How much longer, Frank?'

'Give me ten minutes.'

'No – stop work now. Don't start again until I tell you.'

I turned back to Cregar. 'If you would like to speak to Mr Ogilvie yourself you may use the telephone here or in the study.'

Cregar actually smiled. 'You know when to pass the buck. You're quite right; it's better if I speak to Ogilvie. I'll use the study.'

'Show his lordshp where it is,' I said to Gregory, and the three of them left the room.

Lillywhite said, 'What was all that about?'

'A bit of inter-departmental nonsense; nothing to do with humble servants like ourselves. You can carry on, Frank. That vault must be opened come what may.'

He went back to his job and I strolled over to the window and looked down at the drive. Presently Cregar and Martins came out of the house, got into a car, and drove away. Gregory came into the room. 'Cregar was a bit sour when he came out of the study,' he remarked. 'Ogilvie wants to talk to you.'

I walked over and picked up the telephone next to Ashton's bed. 'Jaggard here.'

Ogilvie said quickly: 'On no account must Cregar know what's in that vault. Don't let him pull rank on you – it's got nothing to do with him.'

'He won't,' I said. 'He's gone.'

'Good. When will you open it?'

'Another five minutes.'

'Keep me informed.' He rang off.

Gregory held out a packet of cigarettes and we smoked while Lillywhite and his two assistants fiddled with the door. At last there was a sharp click and Lillywhite said, 'That's it.'

I stood up. 'All right. Everybody out except me and Frank.' I waited until they left then went to the vault. 'Let's get at it.'

'Right.' Lillywhite put his hand to a lever and pulled it down. Nothing happened. 'There you are.'

'You mean it's open now?'

'That's right. Look.' He pulled and the door began to open. It was nearly a foot thick.

'Hold it,' I said quickly. 'Now, can it be locked again and opened easily?'

'Sure. Nothing to it now.'

'That's all I need to know. Sorry, Frank, but I'll have to ask you to leave now.'

He gave a crooked smile. 'If what's in here can't even be seen by a member of the House of Lords it's certainly not for Frank Lillywhite.'

He went out and closed the door emphatically.

I opened the vault.

Ogilvie gaped. 'Empty!'

'As bare as Mother Hubbard's cupboard.' I considered that. 'Except for a layer of fine dust on the floor.'

'You checked all the shelves and cabinets?'

'There were no cabinets. There were no shelves. It was just an empty cube. I didn't even go inside; I just stuck my head in and looked around. Then I closed the door again and had it relocked. I thought I'd better leave it as it was in case you want the forensic chaps to have a look at it. My bet is that it's never been used since it was built fifteen years ago.'

'Well, my God!' Ogilvie stopped then. He seemed at a total loss for words, but he was thinking furiously. I stepped over to the window and looked down into the empty street. It was late and the bowler-hatted tide had receded from the City leaving it deserted except for a few stragglers. There is no other urban area in the world that can look so empty as the City of London.

Ogilvie said thoughtfully, 'So only you, the chief of the safe-opening team, and now me, know about this.'

I turned. 'Even your Chief Burglar doesn't know. I sent Lillywhite out of the room before I opened the vault.'

'So it's only you and me. Damn!'

He swore so explosively that I said, 'What's wrong?'

'It's backfired on me. Cregar will never believe me now when I tell him the truth about that damned vault. I wish now he'd been there.'

Personally I didn't care what Cregar believed or didn't believe. I took a sheet of paper from my wallet, unfolded it, and laid it on the desk. 'This is the new combination for opening the vault. Lillywhite reset it.'

'This is the only copy?'

'Lillywhite must have a record of it.'

Ogilvie wagged his head. 'This will bear a lot of thinking about. In the meantime you carry on looking for Ashton and Benson, and don't forget they might have split up. Made any progress?'

'Only by elimination, if you call that progress.'

'All right,' said Ogilvie tiredly. 'Carry on.' I had my hand on the doorknob when he said, 'Malcolm.'

'Yes.'

'Watch out for Cregar. He makes a bad enemy.'

'I'm not fighting Cregar,' I said. 'He's nothing to do with me. What's between you and him is way over my head.'

'He didn't like the way you stood up to him this afternoon.'

'He didn't show it – he was pleasant enough.'

'That's his way, but he'll only pat you on the back to find a place to stick a knife. Watch him.'

'He is nothing to do with me,' I repeated.

'Maybe,' said Ogilvie. 'But Cregar may not share your view.'

After that nothing happened for a while. The Special Branch investigation petered out with no result although their men at the exits were still keeping a sharp watch in case our pair made a late dash for it. Honnister had nothing to offer. On my third enquiry he said tartly, 'Don't ring us – we'll ring you.'

I spent two and a half days reading every word of the bushel or so of miscellaneous papers Gregory had brought back from Ashton's house – appointment books, financial records, business diaries, letters and so on. As a result of that many enquiries were made but nothing of interest turned up. Ashton's companies were given a thorough going-over with like result.

A week after Ashton's disappearance my team was cut in half. I kept Brent with Penny and Michaelis looked after Gillian, leaving two to do the legwork. I was doing a lot of legwork myself, going sixteen hours a day, running like hell like the Red Queen to stay in the same place. Larry Godwin was back at his desk reading the East European journals. His fling at freedom had been brutally brief.

The boffins had nothing much to report. The computer tapes showed nothing out of the ordinary except some very clever program designing, but what the programs did was nothing special. The prototype whatsit Ashton had been tinkering with caused a flood of speculation which left a thin sediment of hard fact. The consensus of opinion was that it was a pilot plant of a process designed to synthesize insulin; very ingenious and highly patentable but still in an early stage of design. It told me nothing to my purpose.

The day after we opened the empty vault I had telephoned Penny. 'Is this to tell me you've found Daddy?' she asked.

'No, I've nothing to tell you about that. I'm sorry.'

'Then I don't think we've much to talk about, Malcolm,' she said, and rang off before I could get in another word. Right at that moment I didn't know whether we were still engaged or not.

After that I kept in touch with her movements through Brent. She went back to doing her work at University College, London, but tended to use her car more instead of the train. She didn't seem to resent Brent; he was her passenger in her daily journeys to and from London, and she always kept him informed of her proposed movements. He was enjoyng his assignment and thought she was a very nice person. He didn't think she knew he was armed. And, no, she never talked of me.

Gillian was moved to Moorfields Eye Hospital and I went to see her. After checking with Michaelis I had a few words with her doctor, a specialist called Jarvis. 'She's still heavily bandaged,' he said. 'And she'll need cosmetic plastic surgery, but that will be later and in another place. Here we are concerned only with her eyes.'

'What are the odds, Doctor?'

He said carefully, 'There may be a chance of restoring some measure of sight to the left eye. There's no hope for the right eye at all.' He looked straight at me. 'Miss Ashton doesn't know that yet. Please don't tell her.'

'Of course not. Does she know that her father has – er – gone away?'

'She does, and it's not making my job any easier,' said Jarvis waspishly. 'She's very depressed, and between us we have enough problems without having to cope with a psychologically depressed patient. It's most insensitive of the man to go on a business trip at this time.'

So that's what Penny had told Gillian. I suppose it was marginally better than telling her that Daddy had done a bolt. I said, 'Perhaps I can cheer her up.'

'I wish you would,' Jarvis said warmly. 'It would help her quite a lot.'

So I went to talk to Gillian and found her flat on her back on a bed with no pillow and totally faceless because she was bandaged up like Claude Rains in the film, *The Invisible Man*. The nursing sister gently told her I was there, and went away. I steered clear of the reasons she was there, and asked no questions about it. Honnister was probably a better interrogator than I and would have sucked her dry. Instead I stuck to trivialities and told her a couple of funny items I had read in the papers that morning, and brought her up-to-date on the news of the day.

She was very grateful. 'I miss reading the papers. Penny comes in every day and reads to me.'

Brent had told me of that. 'I know.'

'What's gone wrong between you and Penny?'

'Why, nothing,' I said lightly. 'Did she say there was anything wrong?'

'No, but she stopped talking about you, and when I asked, she said she hadn't seen you.'

116

'We've both been busy,' I said.

'I suppose that's it,' said Gillian. 'But it's the way she said it.'

I changed the subject and we chatted some more and when I left I think she was a little better in outlook.

Michaelis found his job boring, which indeed it was. As far as the hospital staff were concerned, he was a policeman set to guard a girl who had been violently attacked once. He sat on a chair outside the ward and spent his time reading paperbacks and magazines.

'I read to Miss Ashton for an hour every afternoon,' he said.

'That's good of you.'

He shrugged. 'Nothing much else to do. There's plenty of time to think on this job, too. I've been thinking about that model railway in Ashton's attic. I've never seen anything to beat it. He was a schedules man, of course.'

'What's that?'

'There's a lot of variety in the people who are interested in model railways. There are the scenic men who are bent on getting all the details right in miniature. I'm one of those. There are the engineering types who insist their stuff should be exact from the engineering aspect; that's expensive. I know a chap who has modelled Paddington Station; and all he's interested in is getting the trains in and out according to the timetable. He's a schedules man like Ashton. The only difference is that Ashton was doing it on a really big scale.'

Hobbies are something that people really do become fanatical about, but Ashton hadn't struck me as the type. Still, I hadn't known that Michaelis was a model railwayman, either. I said, 'How big a scale?'

'Bloody big. I found a stack of schedules up there which made me blink. He could duplicate damn nearly the whole of the British railway system – not all at once, but in sections. He seemed to be specializing in pre-war stuff; he had schedules from the old LMS system, for instance; and the Great Western and the LNER. Now that takes a hell of a lot of juggling, so you know what he'd done?'

Michaelis looked at me expectantly, so I said, 'What?'

'He's installed a scad of microprocessors in that control board. You know – the things that have been called a computer on a chip. He could program his timetables into them.'

That sounded like Ashton, all right; very efficient. But it wasn't helping me to find him. 'Better keep your mind on the job,' I advised. 'We don't want anything happening to the girl.'

Two weeks after Ashton bolted Honnister rang me. Without preamble he said, 'We've got a line on our man.'

'Good. When are you seeing him?' I wanted to be there.

'I'm not,' said Honnister. 'He's not in my parish. He's a London boy so he's the Met's meat. A chap from the Yard will be seeing him tonight; Inspector Crammond. He's expecting you to ring him.'

'I'll do that. What's this character's name, and how did you get on to him?'

'His name is Peter Mayberry, aged about forty-five to fifty, and he lives in Finsbury. Apart from that I know damn-all. Crammond will pick it up from there. Mayberry hired the car for the weekend – not from one of the big hire-car firms, but from a garage in Slough. The bobbies over there came across it as a matter of routine and asked a few questions. The garage owner was bloody annoyed; he said someone had spilled battery acid on the back seat, so that made us perk up a bit.'

I thought about that. 'But would Mayberry give his real name when he hired the car?'

'The bloody fool did,' said Honnister. 'Anyway, he'd have to show his driving licence. This one strikes me as an amateur; I don't think he's a pro. Anyway, Crammond tells me there's a Peter Mayberry living at that address.'

'I'll get on to Crammond immediately. Thanks, Charlie. You've done very well.'

He said earnestly, 'You'll thank me by leaning bloody hard on this bastard.' I was about to ring off, but he chipped in again. 'Seen anything of Ashton lately?'

It was the sort of innocuous question he might be expected to ask, but I thought I knew Honnister better than that by now; he wasn't a man to waste his time on idle chit-chat. 'Not much,' I said. 'Why?'

'I thought he'd like to know. Every time I ring him he's out, and the beat bobby tells me there's been some funny things going on at the house. A lot of coming and going and to-ing and fro-ing.'

'I believe he went away on a business trip. As for the house I wouldn't know – I haven't been there lately.'

'I suppose that's your story and you're sticking to it,' he said. 'Who's going to tell the Ashton sisters – you or me?'

'I will,' I said. 'After I've made sure of Mayberry.'

'All right. Any time you're down this way pop in and see me. We can have another noggin at the Coach and Horses. I'll be very interested in anything you can tell me.' He rang off.

I smiled. I was sure Honnister would be interested. Something funny was going on in his parish which he didn't know about, and it irked him.

I dialled Scotland Yard and got hold of Crammond. 'Oh, yes, Mr Jaggard; it's about this acid-throwing attack. I'll be seeing Mayberry tonight – he doesn't get home until about six-thirty, so his landlady tells us. I suggest you meet me here at six and we'll drive out.'

'That's fine.'

'There's just one thing,' Crammond said. 'Whose jurisdiction applies here – ours or yours?'

I said slowly, 'That depends on what Mayberry says. The acid-throwing is straightforward criminal assault, so as far as that's concerned he's your man and you can have him and welcome. But there are other matters I'm not at liberty

119

to go into, and we might like to question him further before you charge him. Informally, of course.'

'I understand,' said Crammond. 'It's just that it's best to get these things straight first. See you at six, Mr Jaggard.'

Crammond was properly cautious. The police were not very comfortable when mixing with people like us. They knew that some of the things we did, if strictly interpreted, could be construed as law-breaking, and it went against the grain with them to turn a blind eye. Also they tended to think of themselves as the only professionals in the business and looked down on us as amateurs and, in their view, they were not there to help amateurs break the law of the land.

I phoned Ogilvie and told him. All he said was, 'Ah well, we'll see what comes of it.'

I met Crammond as arranged. He was a middling-sized thickset man of nondescript appearance, very useful in a plain clothes officer. We went out to Finsbury in his car, with a uniformed copper in the back seat, and he told me what he knew.

'When Honnister passed the word to us I had Mayberry checked out. That was this morning so he wasn't at home. He lives on the top floor of a house that's been broken up into flats. At least, that's what they call them; most of them are single rooms. His landlady described him as a quiet type – a bit bookish.'

'Married?'

'No. She thinks he never has been, either. He has a job as some kind of clerk working for a City firm. She wasn't too clear about that.'

'He doesn't sound the type,' I complained.

'He does have a police record,' said Crammond.

'That's better.'

'Wait until you hear it. One charge of assaulting a police officer, that's all. I went into it and the charge should never have been brought, even though he was found guilty. He got into a brawl during one of the Aldermaston marches a few years ago and was lugged in with a few others.'

'A protester,' I said thoughtfully. 'Amateur or professional?'

'Amateur, I'd say. He's not on our list of known rabble-rousers and, in any case, he has the wrong job for it. He's not mobile enough. But his appearance fits the description given by Honnister's witness. We'll see. Who does the asking?'

'You do,' I said. 'I'll hang about in the background. He'll think I'm just another copper.'

Mayberry had not arrived home when we got there so his landlady accommodated us in her front parlour. She was plainly curious and said archly, 'Has Mr Mayberry been doing anything naughty?'

'We just want him to help us in our enquiries,' said Crammond blandly. 'Is he a good tenant, Mrs Jackson?'

'He pays his rent regularly, and he's quiet. That's good enough for me.'

'Lived here long?'

'Five years – or is it six?' After much thought she decided it was six.

'Has he any hobbies? What does he do with his spare time?'

'He reads a lot; always got his head in a book. And he's religious – he goes to church twice every Sunday.'

I was depressed. This sounded less and less like our man. 'Did he go to church on the Sunday two weekends ago?' asked Crammond.

'Very likely,' she said. 'But I was away that weekend.' She held her head on one side. 'That sounds like him now.'

Someone walked along the passage outside the room and began to ascend the stairs. We gave him time to get settled then went after him. On the first landing Crammond said to the uniformed man, 'Wait outside the door, Shaw. If he makes a break grab him. It's not likely to happen, but if he is an acid-throwing bastard he can be dangerous.'

I stood behind Crammond as he tapped on Mayberry's door and noted that Shaw was flat against the wall so

121

Mayberry couldn't see him. It's nice to see professionals at work. Mayberry was a man in his late forties and had a sallow complexion as though he did not eat well. His eyes were sunk deep into his skull.

'Mr Peter Mayberry?'

'Yes.'

'We're police officers,' said Crammond pleasantly. 'And we think you can help us. Do you mind if we come in?'

I saw Mayberry's knuckles whiten a little as he gripped the edge of the door. 'How can I help you?'

'Just by answering a few questions. Can we come in?'

'I suppose so.' Mayberry held open the door.

It wasn't much of a place; the carpet was threadbare and the furniture was of painted whitewood and very cheap; but it was clean and tidy. Along one wall was a shelf containing perhaps forty or fifty books; anyone with so many would doubtless be a great reader to Mrs Jackson who probably got through one book a year, if that.

I glanced at the titles. Some were religious and of a decidedly fundamentalist slant; there was a collection of environmental stuff including some pamphlets issued by Friends of the Earth. For the rest they were novels, all classics and none modern. Most of the books were paperbacks.

There were no pictures in the room except for one poster which was stuck on the wall by sticky tape at the corners. It depicted the earth from space, a photograph taken by an astronaut. Printed at the bottom were the words: I'M ALL YOU'VE GOT; LOOK AFTER ME.

Crammond started by saying, 'Can I see your driving licence, Mr Mayberry?'

'I don't have a car.'

'That wasn't what I asked,' said Crammond. 'Your driving licence, please.'

Mayberry had taken off his jacket which was hanging on the back of a chair. He bent down and took his wallet from the inside breast pocket, took out his licence and gave it to

Crammond who examined it gravely and in silence. At last Crammond said approvingly, 'Clean; no endorsements.' He handed it to me.

'I always drive carefully,' said Mayberry.

'I'm sure you do. Do you drive often?'

'I told you – I don't have a car.'

'And I heard you. Do you drive often?'

'Not very. What's all this about?'

'When did you last drive a car?'

Mayberry said, 'Look, if anyone says I've been in an accident they're wrong because I haven't.' He seemed very nervous, but many people are in the presence of authority, even if innocent. It's the villain who brazens it out.

I put the licence on the table and picked up the book Mayberry had been reading. It was on so-called alternative technology and was turned to a chapter telling how to make a digester to produce methane from manure. It seemed an unlikely subject for Finsbury.

Crammond said, 'When did you last drive a car?'

'Oh, I don't know – several months ago.'

'Whose car was it?'

'I forget. It was a long time ago.'

'Whose car do you usually drive?'

There was a pause while Mayberry sorted that one out. 'I don't *usually* drive.' He had begun to sweat.

'Do you ever hire a car?'

'I have.' Mayberry swallowed. 'Yes. I have hired cars.'

'Recently?'

'No.'

'Supposing I said that you hired a car in Slough two weekends ago, what would you say?'

'I'd say you were wrong,' said Mayberry sullenly.

'Yes, you might say that,' said Crammond. 'But would I be wrong, Mr Mayberry?'

Mayberry straightened his shoulders. 'Yes,' he said defiantly.

'Where were you that weekend?'

'Here – as usual. You can ask Mrs Jackson, my landlady.'

Crammond regarded him for a moment in silence. 'But Mrs Jackson was away that weekend, wasn't she? So you were here all weekend. In this room? Didn't you go out?'

'No.'

'Not at all? Not even to church as usual?'

Mayberry was beginning to curl up at the edges. 'I didn't feel well,' he muttered.

'When was the last time you missed church on Sunday, Mr Mayberry?'

'I don't remember.'

'Can you produce one person to testify to your presence here in this room on the whole of that Sunday?'

'How can I? I didn't go out.'

'Didn't you eat?'

'I didn't feel well, I tell you. I wasn't hungry.'

'What about the Saturday? Didn't you go out then?'

'No.'

'And you didn't eat on the Saturday, either?'

Mayberry shifted his feet nervously; the unending stream of questions was getting to him. 'I had some apples.'

'You had some apples,' said Crammond flatly. 'Where and when did you buy the apples?'

'On the Friday afternoon at a supermarket.'

Crammond let that go. He said, 'Mr Mayberry, I suggest that all you've told me is a pack of lies. I suggest that on the Saturday morning you went to Slough by train where you hired a Hillman Sceptre from Joliffe's garage. Mr Joliffe was very upset by the acid damage to the back seat of the car. Where did you buy the acid?'

'I bought no acid.'

'But you hired the car?'

'No.'

'Then how do you account for the fact that the name and address taken from a driving licence – this driving licence – ' Crammond picked it up and waved it under Mayberry's nose – 'is your name and address?'

'I can't account for it. I don't have to account for it. Perhaps someone impersonated me.'

'Why should anyone want to impersonate you, Mr Mayberry?'

'How would I know?'

'I don't think anyone would know,' observed Crammond. 'However, the matter can be settled very easily. We have the fingerprints from the car and they can be compared with yours quite easily. I'm sure you wouldn't mind coming to the station and giving us your prints, sir.'

It was the first I'd heard of fingerprints and I guessed Crammond was bluffing. Mayberry said, 'I'm . . . I'm not coming. Not to the police station.'

'I see,' said Crammond softly. 'Do you regard yourself as a public-spirited citizen?'

'As much as anybody.'

'But you object to coming to the police station.'

'I've had a hard day,' said Mayberry. 'I'm not feeling well. I was about to go to bed when you came in.'

'Oh,' said Crammond, as though illuminated with insight. 'Well, if that's your only objection I have a fingerprint kit in the car. We can settle the matter here and now.'

'You're not taking my fingerprints. I don't have to give them to you. And now I want you to leave.'

'Ah, so that's your true objection.'

'I want you to leave or I'll – ' Mayberry stopped short.

'Send for the police?' said Crammond ironically. 'When did you first meet Miss Ashton?'

'I've never met her,' said Mayberry quickly. Too quickly.

'But you know of her.'

Mayberry took a step backwards and banged into the table. The book fell to the floor. 'I know nobody of that name.'

'Not personally, perhaps – but you do know of her?'

I stopped to pick up the book. A thin pamphlet had fallen from the pages and I glanced at it before putting the book on the table. Mayberry repeated, 'I know nobody of that name.'

The pamphlet was a Parliamentary Report issued by the Stationery Office. Beneath the Royal coat-of-arms was the title: *Report of the Working Party on the Experimental Manipulation of the Genetic Composition of Micro-organisms*.

A whole lot of apparently unrelated facts suddenly slotted into place: Mayberry's fundamentalist religion, his environmental interests, and the work Penny Ashton was doing. I said, 'Mr Mayberry, what do you think of the state of modern biological science?'

Crammond, his mouth opened to ask another question, gaped at me in astonishment. Mayberry jerked his head around to look at me. 'Bad,' he said. 'Very bad.'

'In what way?'

'The biologists are breaking the laws of God,' he said. 'Defiling life itself.'

'In what way?'

'By mixing like with unlike – by creating monsters.' Mayberry's voice rose. '"And God said, 'Let the earth bring forth the living creature after his kind.'" That's what He said – *after his kind*. "Cattle, and creeping thing, and beast of the earth after his kind." *After his kind!* That is on the very first page of the Holy Bible.'

Crammond glanced at me with a mystified expression, and then looked again at Mayberry. 'I'm not sure I know what you mean, sir.'

Mayberry was exalted. 'And God said unto Noah, "Of fowls after their kind" – *after their kind* – "and of cattle after their kind" – *after their kind* – "of every creeping thing of the earth after his kind" – *after his kind* – "two of every sort shall come unto thee, to keep them alive." She's godless; she would destroy God's own work as is set down in the Book.'

I doubted if Crammond knew what Mayberry was saying, but I did. I said, 'How?'

'She would break down the seed which God has made,

126

and mingle one kind with another kind, and so create monsters – chimaeras and abominations.'

I had difficulty in keeping my voice even. 'I take it by "she" you mean Dr Penelope Ashton?'

Crammond's head jerked. Mayberry, still caught up in religious fervour, said thoughtlessly, 'Among others.'

'Such as Professor Lumsden,' I suggested.

'Her master in devilry.'

'If you thought she was doing wrong why didn't you talk to her about it? Perhaps you could have led her to see her error.'

'I wouldn't foul my ears with her voice,' he said contemptuously.

I said, 'Doesn't it say in the Bible that God gave Adam dominion over the fish of the sea, the fowls of the air, and every beast or thing that creeps on the earth? Perhaps she's in the right.'

'The Devil can quote scripture,' said Mayberry, and turned away from me. I felt sick.

Crammond woke up to what was happening. 'Mr Mayberry, are you admitting to having thrown acid into the face of a woman called Ashton?'

Mayberry had a hunted look, conscious of having said too much. 'I haven't said that.'

'You've said enough.' Crammond turned to me. 'I think we have enough to take him.'

I nodded, then said to Mayberry, 'You're a religious man. You go to church every Sunday – twice, so I'm told. Do you think it was a Christian act to throw battery acid into the face of a young woman?'

'I am not responsible to you for my actions,' said Mayberry. 'I am responsible to God.'

Crammond nodded gravely. 'Nevertheless, I believe someone said, "Render unto Caesar the things that are Caesar's." I think you'll have to come along with me, Mr Mayberry.'

'And may God help you,' I said. 'Because you got the

127

wrong girl. You threw the acid in the face of Dr Ashton's sister who was coming back from church.'

Mayberry stared at me. As he had spoken of being responsible to God he had worn a lofty expression but now his face crumpled and horror crept into his eyes. He whispered, 'The wrong . . . wrong . . .' Suddenly he jerked convulsively and screamed at the top of his voice.

'Oh, Christ!' said Crammond as Shaw burst into the room.

Mayberry collapsed to the floor, babbling a string of obscenities in a low and monotonous voice. When Crammond turned to speak to me he was sweating. 'This one's not for the slammer. He'll go to Broadmoor for sure. Do you want any more out of him?'

'Not a thing,' I said. 'Not now.'

Crammond turned to Shaw. 'Phone for an ambulance. Tell them it's religious mania and they might need a restraining jacket.'

16

By the time we'd got Mayberry into an ambulance Ogilvie had left the office and gone home. I didn't bother ringing his home, but I did ring Penny because I thought she ought to know about Mayberry. Mary Cope answered again and said that Penny wasn't in, but this time I pushed it harder. She said Penny had gone to Oxford to attend a lecture and wouldn't be back until late. I rang off, satisfied I wasn't being given another brush-off.

Before seeing Ogilvie next morning I rang Crammond. 'What's new on Mayberry?'

'He's at King's College Hospital – under guard in a private ward.'

'Did he recover?'

'Not so you'd notice. It seems like a complete breakdown to me, but I'm no specialist.'

'A pity. I'll have to talk to him again, you know.'

'You'll have to get through a platoon of assorted doctors first,' warned Crammond. 'It seems he's suffering from everything from ingrowing toenails to psychoceramica.'

'What the hell's that?'

'It means he's a crack-pot,' said Crammond sourly. 'The head-shrinkers are keeping him isolated.'

I thanked him for his help and went to see Ogilvie. I told him about Mayberry and his face was a study in perplexity. 'Are you sure Mayberry isn't pulling a fast one?'

I shook my head. 'He's a nutter. But we've got him, and a psychiatrist will sort him out for us.'

'I'll buy that – for the moment.' Ogilvie shook his head. 'But I wouldn't call psychiatry an exact science. Have you noticed in court cases that for every psychiatrist called for the defence there's another called for the prosecution who'll give an opposing opinion? Still, supposing Mayberry is established as a religious maniac without doubt, there are a few questions which need asking.'

'I know. Why did he pick on Penny – or the girl he thought was Penny? Did he act of his own volition or was he pointed in the right direction and pushed? I'll see he gets filleted as soon as he can be talked to. But you're avoiding the big problem.'

Ogilvie grunted, and ticked points off on his fingers. 'Supposing Mayberry *is* crazy; and supposing he *wasn't* pushed – that he did it off his own bat, and that Penelope Ashton was a more or less random choice among the geneticists. That leaves us up a gum tree, doesn't it?'

'Yes.' I put the big question into words. 'In that case why did Ashton do a bunk?'

I was beginning to develop another headache.

I'd had second thoughts about ringing Penny; it wasn't the sort of thing to tell her on the telephone. But before going to University College I rang Honnister and told him the score. He took it rather badly. His voice rose. 'The wrong girl! The inefficient, crazy bastard picked the wrong girl!' He broke into a stream of profanity.

'I thought you ought to know. I'll keep you informed on future developments.'

I went to University College and was about to enquire at the reception desk when I saw Jack Brent standing at the end of a corridor. I went up to him. 'Any problems?'

'Nary a one.'

'Where's Penny Ashton?'

He jerked his thumb at a door. 'With her boss. That's Lumsden's office.'

I nodded and went in. Penny and Professor Lumsden looked very professional in white laboratory coats, like the chaps who sell toothpaste in TV ads. They were sitting at a desk, drinking coffee and examining papers which looked like computer print-outs. Lumsden was much younger than I expected, not as old as I was; pioneering on the frontiers of science is a young man's game.

Penny looked up. A look of astonishment chased across her face and then she became expressionless, but I noted the tightening of muscles at the angle of her jaw and the firmly compressed lips. I said, 'Good morning, Dr Ashton – Professor Lumsden. Could I have a word with you, Penny?'

'Well?' she said coolly.

I glanced at Lumsden. 'It's official, I'm afraid. In your office, perhaps?'

She said shortly, 'If it is official . . .' and regarded me distrustfully.

'It is,' I said, matching her curtness.

She made her excuses to Lumsden and we left his office. I said to Brent, 'Stick around,' then followed Penny who led me along another corridor and into her office. I looked around. 'Where's the microscope?'

Unsmilingly she said, 'We're working on things you can't see through microscopes. What do you want? Have you found Daddy?'

I shook my head. 'We've found the man who threw the acid.'

'Oh.' She sat on her desk. 'Who is he?'

'A man called Peter Mayberry. Ever heard of him?'

She thought for a moment. 'No, I can't say that I have. What is he?'

'A clerk in a City office – and a religious maniac.'

She frowned, then said questioningly, 'A religious maniac? But what would he have to do with Gillian? She's an Anglican – and you can't get more unmaniacal than that.'

I sat down. 'Brace yourself, Penny. The acid wasn't intended for Gillian. It was intended for you.'

'*For me!*' Her forehead creased and then she shook her

131

head as though she wasn't hearing aright. 'You did say . . . for me?'

'Yes. Are you sure you haven't heard of this man?'

She ignored my question. 'But why would a religious maniac . . . ?' She choked on the words. 'Why me?'

'He seemed to think you are tampering with the laws of God.'

'Oh.' Then: 'Seemed? He's dead?'

'No, but he's not doing much thinking right now. He's gone off into some kind of fugue.'

She shook her head. 'There have been objections to what we've been doing, but they've been scientific. Paul Berg, Brenner, Singer and a few others objected very strongly to . . .' Suddenly it hit her. 'Oh, my God!' she said. 'Poor Gillian!'

She sat rigidly for a moment, her hands clasped together tightly, and then she began to shake, the tremors sweeping across her body. She moaned – a sort of keening sound – and then fell forward across her desk, her head pillowed on her arms. Her shoulders shook convulsively and she sobbed stormily. I located a hand basin in the corner of the office and filled a glass with water and returned quickly to the desk, but there wasn't much I could do until the first shock had abated.

Her sobbing lessened in intensity and I put my arm around her. 'Steady on. Drink this.'

She raised her head, still sobbing, and showed a tear-stained face. 'Oh, Gillian! She'd be . . . all right . . . if I . . . if I hadn't . . .'

'Hush,' I said. 'And stop that. Drink this.'

She gulped down some water, then said, 'Oh, Malcolm; what am I to do?'

'Do? There's nothing to do. You just carry on as usual.'

'Oh, no. How can I do that?'

I said deliberately, 'You can't possibly blame yourself for what happened to Gillian. You'll tear yourself apart if you try. You can't hold yourself responsible for the act of an unbalanced man.'

'Oh, I wish it had been me,' she cried.

'No, you don't,' I said sharply. 'Don't ever say that again.'

'How can I tell her?'

'You don't tell her. Not until she's well – if then.' She began to cry again, and I said, 'Penny, pull yourself together – I need your help.'

'What can *I* do?'

'You can tidy yourself up,' I said. 'Then you can get Lumsden in here, because I want to ask you both some questions.'

She sniffled a bit, then said, 'What sort of questions?'

'You'll hear them when Lumsden comes in. I don't want to go through it all twice. We still don't know why your father went away, but it seemed to be triggered by that acid attack, so we want to find out as much about it as we can.'

She went to the hand basin and washed her face. When she was more presentable she rang Lumsden. I said, 'I'd rather you don't say anything about your father before Lumsden.' She said nothing to that, and sat at the desk.

When Lumsden came in he took one glance at Penny's reddened eyes and white face, then looked at me. 'What's happened here? And who are you?'

'I'm Malcolm Jaggard and I'm a sort of police officer, Professor.' To divert him from asking for my warrant card I added, 'I'm also Penny's fiancé.'

Penny made no objection to that flat statement, but Lumsden showed astonishment. 'Oh, I didn't know . . .'

'A recent development,' I said. 'You know, of course, of the acid attack on Penny's sister.'

'Yes, a most shocking thing.'

I told him about Mayberry and he became very grave. 'This is bad,' he said. 'I'm deeply sorry, Penny.' She nodded without saying anything.

'I want to know if you or anyone in your department has

been threatened – anonymous letters, telephone calls, or anything like that.'

He shrugged. 'There are always the cranks. We tend to ignore them.'

'Perhaps that's a mistake,' I said. 'I'd like some specifics. Do you keep any such letters? If so, I want them.'

'No,' he said regretfully. 'They are usually thrown away. You see . . . er . . . Inspector?'

'Mister.'

'Well, Mr Jaggard, most of the crank letters aren't threatening – they just tend to ramble, that's all.'

'About what?'

'About supposed offences against God. Lots of biblical quotations, usually from *Genesis*. Just what you might expect.'

I said to Penny, 'Have you had any of these letters?'

'A couple,' she said quietly. 'No threats. I threw them away.'

'Any telephone calls? Heavy breathers?'

'One about six months ago. He stopped after a month.'

'What did he say?'

'What Lummy has described. Just what you might expect.'

'Did you get the calls here or at home?'

'Here. The telephone at home is unlisted.'

I turned to Lumsden. 'You've both used the same phrase – "Just what you might expect". What might I expect, Professor Lumsden?'

'Well, in view of our work here . . .' He threw out his hands expressively.

We were still standing. I said, 'Sit down, Professor, and tell me of your work, or about as much as you can without breaking the Official Secrets Act.'

'Breaking the Official Secrets Act! There's no question of that – not here.'

'In that case, you won't object to telling me, will you?'

'I don't suppose so,' he said doubtfully, and sat down.

He was silent for a moment, marshalling his thoughts, and I knew what was happening. He was hunting for unaccustomed simple words to explain complex ideas to an unscientific clod. I said, 'I can understand words of three syllables – even four syllables if they're spoken slowly. Let me help you. The basis of inheritance is the chromosome; inside the chromosome is an acid called DNA. A thing called a gene is the ultimate factor and is very specific; there are distinct genes for producing the different chemicals needed by the organism. The genes can be thought of as being strung along a strand of DNA like beads on a spiral string. At least, that's how I visualize them. That's where I get lost so you'd better go on from there.'

Lumsden smiled. 'Not bad, Mr Jaggard; not bad at all.' He began to talk, at first hesitantly, and then more fluently. He ranged quite widely and sometimes I had to interrupt and bring him back on to the main track. At other times I had him explain what he meant in simpler terms. The basic concepts were rather simple but I gathered that execution in the laboratory was not as easy as all that.

What it boiled down to was this. A strand of DNA contains many thousands of genes, each gene doing its own particular job such as, for instance, controlling the production of cholinesterase, a chemical which mediates electrical action in the nervous system. There are thousands of chemicals like this and each has its own gene.

The molecular biologist had discovered certain enzymes which could cut up a strand of DNA into short lengths, and other enzymes which could weld the short lengths together again. They also found they could weld a short length of DNA on to a bacteriophage, which is a minute organism capable of penetrating the wall of a cell. Once inside, the genes would be uncoupled and incorporated into the DNA of the host cell.

Put like that it sounds rather simple but the implications are fantastic, and Lumsden was very emphatic about this. 'You see, the genes you incorporate into a cell need not

135

come from the same kind of animal. In this laboratory we have bacterial cultures which contain genetic material from mice. Now a bacterium is a bacterium and a mouse is a mammal, but our little chaps are part bacterium and part mammal.'

'Breaking down the seed, mingling one kind with another, creating chimaeras,' I mused.

'I suppose you could put it that way,' said Lumsden.

'I didn't put it that way,' I said. 'Mayberry did.' At that stage I didn't get the point. 'But what's the use of this?'

Lumsden frowned as though I was being thick-witted, as I suppose I was. Penny spoke up. 'Lummy, what about *Rhizobium*?'

His brow cleared. 'Yes, that's a good example.'

He said that although plants need nitrogen for their growth they cannot take it from the air, even though air is 78 per cent nitrogen. They need it in the form of nitrates which, in man-planted cash crops, are usually spread as artificial fertilizer. However, there is a range of plants, notably the legumes – peas, beans and so on – which harbours in its roots the *Rhizobium* bacterium. This organism has the power of transforming atmospheric nitrogen into a form the plant can use.

'Now,' said Lumsden. 'All plants have bacteria in their roots and some are very specific. Supposing we take the *Rhizobium* bacterium, isolate the gene that controls this nitrogen-changing property, and transfer it into a bacterium that is specific to wheat. Then, if it bred true, we'd have self-fertilizing wheat. In these days of world food shortages that seems to me to be a good thing to have around.'

I thought so, too, but Penny said, 'It can be pretty dangerous. You have to be damned sure you've selected the right gene. Some of the *Rhizobium* genes are tumour-causing. If you get one of those you might find the world wheat crop dying of cancer.'

'Yes,' said Lumsden. 'We must be very sure before we let loose our laboratory-changed organisms. There was a

136

hell of a row about that not long ago.' He stood up. 'Well, Mr Jaggard, have you got what you wanted?'

'I think so,' I said. 'But I don't know if it's going to do me a damned bit of good. Thanks for your time, Professor.'

He smiled. 'If you need more information I suggest you ask Penny.' He glanced at her. 'I suggest you take the day off, Penny. You've had a nasty shock – you don't look too well.'

She shivered. 'The thought that there are people in the world who'd want to do that to you is unnerving.'

'I'll take you home,' I said quietly. 'Jack Brent can follow in your car.' She made no objection, and I turned to Lumsden. 'I suggest that any crank letters – no matter how apparently innocuous – should be forwarded to the police. And telephone calls should be reported.'

'I agree,' he said. 'I'll see to it.'

So I took Penny home.

17

My relationship with Penny improved although neither of us referred to marriage. The shock of Mayberry's error had been shattering and I stuck around and helped her pick up the pieces; from then on propinquity did the rest. She was persuaded by Lumsden to stay with her work and her life took a triangular course – her home, her work, and whatever hospital Gillian happened to be in at the time.

Mayberry was thoroughly investigated by a band of psychiatrists and by Mansell, the department's best interrogator, a soft-spoken man who could charm the birds from the trees. They all came to the same conclusion: Mayberry was exactly what he appeared to be – a nut case. 'And a bit of a coward, too,' said Mansell. 'He was going for Lumsden at first, but thought a woman would be easier to handle.'

'Why did he pick on Lumsden's crowd?' I asked.

'A natural choice. Firstly, Lumsden is very well known – he's not as averse to talking to newspaper reporters as a lot of scientists are. He gets his name in the papers. Secondly, he hasn't been reticent about what he's been doing. If you wanted a handy geneticist Lumsden would be the first to spring to mind.'

Mayberry was the deadest of dead ends.

Which caused the problem Ogilvie and I had anticipated. If the acid attack had been fortuitous why should Ashton have bolted? It made no sense.

Once Mayberry had been shaken down the guards were taken from Penny and Gillian, and my legmen were put to other work. Ogilvie had little enough manpower to waste and the team investigating the Ashton case was cut down

138

to one – me, and I wasted a lot of time investigating mistaken identities. Ashton's bolt-hole was well concealed.

And so the weeks – and then the months – went by. Gillian was in and out of hospital and finally was able to live at home, managing on a quarter of her normal eyesight. She and Penny were making plans to go to the United States where she would undergo plastic surgery to repair her ravaged face.

Once, when I persuaded Penny to dine with me, she asked, 'What did you find in that big vault of Daddy's?'

It was the first time she had shown any interest. 'Nothing.'

'You're lying.' There was an edge of anger.

'I've never lied to you, Penny,' I said soberly. 'Never once. My sins have been those of omission, not commission. I may have been guilty of *suppressio veri* but never *suggestio falsi*.'

'Your classical education is showing,' she said tartly, but she smiled as she said it, her anger appeased. 'Strange. Why should Daddy build such a thing and not use it? Perhaps he did and found it too much trouble.'

'As far as we can make out it was never used,' I said. 'All it contained was stale air and a little dust. My boss is baffled and boggled.'

'Oh, Malcolm, I wish I knew why he disappeared. It's been over three months now.'

I made the usual comforting sounds and diverted her attention. Presently she said. 'Do you remember when you told me of what you really do? You mentioned someone called Lord Cregar.'

'That's right.'

'He's been seeing Lumsden.'

That drew my interest. 'Has he? What about?'

She shook her head. 'Lummy didn't say.'

'Was it about Mayberry?'

'Oh, no. The first time he came was before you told us

139

about Mayberry.' She wrinkled her brow. 'It was two or three days after you opened the vault.'

'Not two or three weeks?'

'No – it was a matter of days. Who is Lord Cregar?'

'He's pretty high in government, I believe.' I could have told her that Cregar had smuggled her father out of Russia a quarter of a century earlier, but I didn't. If Ashton had wanted his daughters to know of his Russian past he would have told them, and it wasn't up to me to blow the gaff. Besides, I couldn't blab about anything listed under Code Black; it would be dangerous for me, for Ogilvie and, possibly, Penny herself. I wasn't supposed to know about that.

All the same it was curious that Cregar had been seeing Lumsden before we knew about Mayberry. Was there a connection between Ashton and Lumsden – apart from Penny – that we hadn't spotted?

I caught the eye of a passing waiter and asked for the bill. As I drained my coffee cup I said, 'It's probably not important. Let's go and keep Gillian company.'

Ogilvie sent for me next morning. He took an envelope, extracted a photograph, and tossed it across the desk. 'Who's that?'

He wore a heavy coat and a round fur hat, the type with flaps which can be tied down to cover the ears but which never are. Wherever he was it was snowing; there were white streaks in the picture which was obviously a time exposure.

I said, 'That's George Ashton.'

'No, he isn't,' said Ogilvie. 'His name is Fyodr Koslov, and he lives in Stockholm. He has a servant, an elderly bruiser called Howell Williams.' Another photograph skimmed across the desk.

I took one look at it, and said. 'That be damned for a tale. This is Benson. Where did you get these?'

'I want you to make quite sure,' said Ogilvie. He took a

sheaf of photographs and fanned them out. 'As you know, we had a couple of bad pictures of Ashton and none at all of Benson. You are the only person in the department who can identify them.'

Every one of the photographs showed either Ashton or Benson, and in two of them they were together. 'Positive identification,' I said flatly. 'Ashton and Benson.'

Ogilvie was pleased. 'Some of our associated departments are more co-operative than others,' he remarked. 'I had the pictures of Ashton circulated. These came back from a chap called Henty in Stockholm. He seems to be quite good with a camera.'

'He's very good.' The pictures were unposed – candid camera stuff – and very sharp. 'I hope he's been circumspect. We don't want them to bolt again.'

'You'll go to Stockholm and take up where Henty left off. He has instructions to co-operate.'

I looked out at the bleak London sky and shivered. I didn't fancy Stockholm at that time of year. 'Do I contact Ashton? Tell him about Mayberry and persuade him to come back?'

Ogilvie deliberated. 'No. He's too near Russia. It might startle him to know that British Intelligence is still taking an interest in him – startle him into doing something foolish. He had a low opinion of us thirty years ago which may not have improved. No, you just watch him and find out what the hell he's doing.'

I took the sheet of paper with Henty's address in Stockholm and his telephone number, then said, 'Can you think of any connection between Cregar and Professor Lumsden?' I told him Penny's story.

Ogilvie looked at the ceiling. 'I hear backstairs gossip from time to time. There could be a connection, but it's nothing to do with Ashton. It *can't* have anything to do with Ashton.'

'What is it?'

He abandoned his apparent fascination with the electric

fittings and looked at me. 'Malcolm, you're getting to know too damned much – more than is good for you. However, I'll humour you because, as I say, this is only servants' hall rumour. When this department was set up we took a sizeable chunk from Cregar which diminished his outfit considerably, so he began to empire-build in a different direction. The story is that he's heavily involved in CBW – that would explain any interest he has in Lumsden.'

By God it would! Chemical and bacteriological warfare and what Lumsden was doing fitted together like hand in glove. 'Is he still in security?'

'No, he's executive. He mediates between the Minister and the scientists. Of course, with his experience he also handles the security side.'

I could just imagine Cregar happily contemplating some previously inoffensive microbe now armed for death and destruction by genetic engineering. 'Is he in with the Porton Down crowd?'

'The Ministry of Defence is closing down Porton Down,' said Ogilvie. 'I don't know where Cregar does his juggling with life and death. Microbiology isn't like atomics; you don't need a particle accelerator costing a hundred million and a power plant capable of supplying energy for a fair-sized city. The physcal plant and investment are both relatively small, and Cregar may have a dozen laboratories scattered about for all I know. He doesn't talk about it – not to me.'

I contemplated this, trying to find a link with Ashton, and failed. There was only Penny, and I said so. Ogilvie asked, 'Has Cregar talked to her?'

'No.'

'I told you it can't have anything to do with Ashton,' he said. 'Off you go to Sweden.'

There was something else I wanted to bring up. 'I'd like to know more about Benson. He's probably filed away in Code Black.'

Ogilvie looked at me thoughtfully then, without speaking, got up and went into the room behind his desk. When he came back he was shaking his head. 'You must be mistaken. Benson isn't listed – not even under Code Green.'

'But I took him up as far as Code Purple,' I said. 'Someone is monkeying around with that bloody computer.'

Ogilvie's lips tightened. 'Unlikely,' he said shortly.

'How unlikely?'

'It's not easy to suborn a computer. It would need an expert.'

'Experts are ten a penny – and they can be bought.'

Ogilvie was palpably uneasy. He said slowly, 'We aren't the only department on line with this computer. I've been pressing for our own computer for several years but without success. Some other department . . .' He stopped and sat down.

'Who determines what material is added to the files – or removed?'

'There's an inter-departmental review committee which meets monthly. No one is authorized to add or subtract without its approval.'

'Someone has subtracted Benson,' I said. 'Or, more likely, he's been blocked off. I'll bet someone has added a tiny sub-program which would be difficult to find – if Benson is asked for say there's no one here of that name.'

'Well, it's for me to deal with,' said Ogilvie. 'There's a meeting of the review committee on Friday at which I'll raise a little bit of hell.' He stuck his finger out at me. 'But you know nothing about this. Now, go away. Go to Sweden.'

I got up to leave but paused at the door. 'I'll leave you with a thought. I got into the Ashton case by asking Nellie about Ashton. Two hours later I was on the carpet in your office with you and Cregar asking awkward questions. Did Cregar come to you with it?'

'Yes.'

'In two hours? How did he know who was asking questions about Ashton unless the computer tipped him off? I don't think you have far to look for the chap who is monkeying around with it.'

I left leaving Ogilvie distinctly worried.

18

It was dark and cold in Stockholm at that time of year. All the time I was in Sweden it didn't stop snowing; not heavily most of the time, but there was a continual fall of fine powder from leaden-grey clouds as though God up there was operating a giant flour sifter. I was booked into the Grand, which was warm enough, and after I had made my call to Henty I looked out over the frozen Strömmen to the Royal Palace. Edward VII didn't like Buckingham Palace, and called it 'that damned factory'. It's not on record if he said anything about the Palace in Stockholm, but that afternoon it looked like a dark satanic mill.

There were swans on the Strömmen, walking uneasily on the ice and cuddling in clusters as though to keep warm. One was on an ice floe and drifting towards Riddarfjärden; I watched until it went out of sight under the Ström bridge, then turned away feeling suddenly cold in spite of the central heating. Sweden in winter has that affect on me.

Henty arrived and we swapped credentials. 'We don't have much to do with your mob,' he commented as he handed back my card. He had a raw colonial accent.

'We don't move out of the UK much,' I said. 'Most of our work is counter-espionage. This one is a bit different. If you can take me to George Ashton I'll buy you a case of Foster's.'

Henty blinked. 'Good beer, that. How did you know I'm Australian? I've not been back for twenty years. Must have lost the accent by now.'

I grinned. 'Yes, you've learned to speak English very well. Where's Ashton?'

He went to the window and pointed at the Royal Palace. 'On the other side of that. In Gamla Stan.'

Gamla Stan – the Old Town. A warren of narrow streets threading between ancient buildings and the 'in' place to live in Stockholm. Cabinet ministers live there, and film directors – if they can afford it. The Royal Palace is No. 1, Gamla Stan. I said, 'How did you find him?'

'I got a couple of crummy pictures from London, and the day I got them I walked slam-bang into this character on the Vasabron.' Henty shrugged. 'So it's a coincidence.'

'By the laws of statistics we've got to get lucky some time,' I observed.

'He has a flat just off Västerlånggatan. He's passing himself off as a Russian called Fyodr Koslov – which is a mistake.'

'Why?'

Henty frowned. 'It's a tip-off – enough to make me take the pictures and send them back. There's something about the way he speaks Russian – doesn't sound natural.'

I thought about that. After thirty years of non-use Ashton's Russian would be rusty; it's been known for men to forget completely their native language. 'And Benson is with him in the flat?'

'Benson? Is that who he is? He calls himself Williams here. An older man; looks a bit of a thug. He's definitely British.'

'How can I get a look at them?'

Henty shrugged. 'Go to Gamla Stan and hang around outside the flat until they come out – or go in.'

I shook my head. 'Not good enough. They know me and I don't want to be seen. What's your status here?'

'Low man on the bloody totem,' said Hentry wryly. 'I'm junior partner in an import-export firm. I have a line into the Embassy, but that's for emergency use only. The diplomats here don't like boys like us, they reckon we cause trouble.'

'They could be right,' I said drily. 'Who do I see at the Embassy?'

'A Second Secretary called Cutler. A toffee-nosed bastard.' The iron seemed to have entered Henty's soul.

'What resources can you draw on apart from the Embassy?'

'Resources!' Henty grinned. 'You're looking at the resources – me. I just have a watching brief – we're not geared for action.'

'Then it will have to be the Embassy.'

He coughed, then said, 'Exactly who is Ashton?' I looked at him in silence until he said, 'If it's going to be like that . . .'

'It always is like that, isn't it?'

'I suppose so,' he said despondently. 'But I wish, just for once, that I knew why I'm doing what I'm doing.'

I looked at my watch. 'There's just time to see Cutler. In the meantime you pin down Ashton and Benson. Report to me here or at the Embassy. And there's one very important thing – don't scare them.'

'Okay – but I don't think you'll get very much change out of Cutler.'

I smiled. 'I wouldn't want either you or Cutler to bet on that one.'

The Embassy was on Skarpögatan, and Cutler turned out to be a tall, slim, fair-haired man of about my age, very English and Old School Tie. His mamnner was courteous but rather distant as though his mind was occupied by other, and more important, considerations which a non-diplomat could not possibly understand. This minor Metternich reminded me strongly of a shop assistant in one of the more snob London establishments.

When I gave him my card – the special one – his lips tightened and he said coolly, 'You seem to be off your beat, Mr Jaggard. What can we do for you?' He sounded as though he believed there was nothing he could possibly do for me. I said pleasantly, 'We've mislaid a bit of property and we'd like it back – with your help. But tact is the watchword.' I told him the bare and minimum facts about Ashton and Benson.

When I'd finished he was a shade bewildered. 'But I don't see how . . .' He stopped and began again. 'Look, Mr Jaggard, if this man decides to leave England with his man-servant to come to Sweden and live under an assumed name I don't see what we can do about it. I don't think it's a crime in Swedish law to live under another name; it certainly isn't in England. What exactly is it that you want?'

'A bit of manpower,' I said. 'I want Ashton watched. I want to know what he does and why he does it.'

'That's out of the question,' said Cutler. 'We can't spare men for police work of that nature. I really fail to see what your interest is in the man on the basis of what you've told me.'

'You're not entitled to know more,' I said bluntly. 'But take it from me – Ashton is a hot one.'

'I'm afraid I can't do that,' he said coldly. 'Do you really think we jump when any stranger walks in off the street with an improbable story like this?'

I pointed to my card which was still on the blotter in front of him. 'In spite of that?'

'In spite of that,' he said, but I think he really meant because of it. 'You people amaze me. You think you're James Bonds, the lot of you. Well, I don't think I'm living in the middle of a highly coloured film, even if you do.'

I wasn't going to argue with him. 'May I use your telephone?' He frowned, trying to think of a good reason for denial, so I added, 'I'll pay for the call.'

'That won't be necessary,' he said shortly, and pushed his telephone across the desk.

One of our boffins once asked me what was the biggest machine in the world. After several abortive answers I gave up, and he said. 'The international telephone system. There are 450 million telephones in the world, and 250 million of them are connected by direct dialling – untouched by hand in the exchanges.' We may grouse about the faults of local systems, but in under ninety seconds I was talking to Ogilvie.

I said, 'We have Ashton but there's a small problem. There's only one of Henty, and I can't push in too close myself.'

'Good. Get on to the Embassy for support. We want him watched. Don't approach him yourself.'

'I'm at the Embassy now. No support forthcoming.'

'What's the name of the obstruction?'

'Cutler – Second Secretary.'

'Wait a moment.' There was a clatter and I heard the rustle of papers in distant London. Presently Ogilvie said, 'This will take about half an hour. I'll dynamite the obstruction. For God's sake, don't lose Ashton now.'

'I won't,' I said, and hung up. I stood up and picked my card from Cutler's blotter. 'I'm at the Grand. You can get me there.'

'I can't think of any circumstances in which I should do so,' he said distantly.

I smiled. 'You will.' Suddenly I was tired of him. 'Unless you want to spend the next ten years counting paper clips in Samoa.'

Back at the hotel there was a curt note from Henty: 'Meet me at the Moderna Museet on Skeppsholmen.' I grabbed a taxi and was there in five minutes. Henty was standing outside the main entrance, his hands thrust deep into his pockets and the tip of his nose blue with cold. He jerked his head at the gallery. 'Your man is getting a bit of culture.'

This had to be handled carefully. I didn't want to bump into Ashton face to face. 'Benson there too?'

'Just Ashton.'

'Right. Nip in and locate him – then come back here.'

Henty went inside, no doubt glad to be in the warm. He

149

was back in five minutes. 'He's studying blue period Picassos.' He gave me a plan of the halls and marked the Picasso Gallery.

I went into the Museum, moving carefully. There were not many people in the halls on the cold winter's afternoon, which was a pity because there was no crowd to get lost in. On the other hand there were long unobstructed views. I took out my handkerchief, ready to muffle my face in case of emergency, turned a corner and saw Ashton in the distance. He was contemplating a canvas with interest and, as he turned to move on to the next one, I had a good sight of his face.

To my relief this *was* Ashton. There would have been a blazing row if I had goosed Cutler to no purpose.

19

Cutler jumped like a startled frog. An hour later, when I
was unfreezing my bones in a hot bath and feeling sorry for
Henty who was still tagging Ashton, the telephone rang to
announce that he was waiting in the hotel foyer. 'Ask him
to come up.' I dried myself quickly and put on a dressing-
gown.

He brought two men whom he introduced as Askrigg
and Debenham. He made no apologies for his previous
attitude and neither of us referred to it. All the time I knew
him he maintained his icily well-bred air of disapproval;
that I could stand so long as he did what he was told and
did it fast, and I had no complaints about that. The only
trouble was that he and his people were lacking in
professionalism.

We got down to business immediately. I outlined the
problem, and Askrigg said, 'A full-time surveillance of two
men is a six-man job.'

'At least,' I agreed. 'And that's excluding me and Henty.
Ashton and Benson know me, so I'm out. As for Henty,
he's done enough. He spotted Ashton for us and has been
freezing his balls off ever since keeping an eye on him. I'm
pulling him out for a rest and then he'll be in reserve.'

'Six men,' said Cutler doubtfully. 'Oh, well, I suppose
we can find them. What are we looking for?'

'I want to know everything about them. Where they go,
what they eat, who they see, do they have a routine, what
happens when they break that routine, who they write to –
you name it, I want to know.'

'It seems a lot of fuss over a relatively minor industrialist,'
sniffed Cutler.

I grinned at him, and quoted, '"Yours not to reason why, Yours but to do or die." Which could happen because they're probably armed.'

That brought a moment of silence during which Cutler twitched a bit. In his book diplomacy and guns didn't go together. I said, 'Another thing: I want to have a look inside Ashton's apartment, but we'll check their routine first so we can pick the right moment.'

'Burglary!' said Cutler hollowly. 'The Embassy mustn't be involved in that.'

'It won't be,' I said shortly. 'Leave that to me. All right; let's get organized.'

And so Ashton and Benson were watched, every movement noted. It was both wearisome and frustrating as most operations of this nature are. The two men led an exemplary life. Ashton's was the life of a gentleman of leisure; he visited museums and art galleries, attended the theatre and cinemas, and spent a lot of time in bookshops where he spent heavily, purchasing fiction and non-fiction, the non-fiction being mostly biographies. The books were over a spread of languages, English, German and Russian predominating. And all the time he did not do a stroke of what could reasonably be called work. It was baffling.

Benson was the perfect manservant. He did the household shopping, attended to the laundry and dry-cleaning, and did a spot of cooking on those occasions when Ashton did not eat out. He had found himself a favourite drinking-hole which he attended three or four times a week, an *ölstuga* more intellectual than most because it had a chess circle. Benson would play a couple of games and leave relatively early.

Neither of them wrote or received any letters.

Neither appeared to have any associates other than the small-change encounters of everyday life.

Neither did a single damned thing out of the ordinary

152

with one large and overriding exception. Their very presence in Stockholm was out of the ordinary.

At the beginning of the third week, when their routine had been established, Henty and I cracked the apartment. Ashton had gone to the cinema and Benson was doing his Bobby Fischer bit over a half-litre of Carlsberg and we would have an hour or longer. We searched that flat from top to bottom and did not find much.

The main prize was Ashton's passport. It was of Israeli issue, three years old, and made out in the name of Fyodr Antonovitch Koslov who had been born in Odessa in 1914. I photographed every page, including the blank ones, and put it back where I found it. A secondary catch was the counterfoil stub of a cheque-book. I photographed that thoroughly, too. Ashton was spending money quite freely; his casual expenses were running to nearly £500 a week.

The telephone rang. Henty picked it up and said cautiously, '*Vilket nummer vill ni ha?*' There was a pause. 'Okay.' He put down the receiver. 'Benson's left the pub; he's on his way back.'

I looked around the room. 'Everything in order?'

'I reckon so.'

'Then let's go.' We left the building and sat in Henty's car until Benson arrived. We saw him safely inside, checked his escort, then went away.

Early next morning I gave Cutler the spools and film and requested negatives and two sets of prints. I got them within the hour and spent quite a time checking them before my prearranged telephone call from Ogilvie. It had to be prearranged because he had to have a scrambler compatible with that at the Embassy.

Briefly I summarized the position up to that point, then said, 'Any breakthrough will come by something unusual – an oddity – and there are not many of those. There's the Israeli passport – I'd like to know if that's kosher. I'll send you the photographs in the diplomatic bag.'

'Issued three years ago, you say.'

'That's right. That would be about the time a bank account was opened here in the name of Koslov. The apartment was rented a year later, also in the name of Koslov; it was sublet until four months ago when Ashton moved in. Our friend had everything prepared. I've gone through cheque stubs covering nearly two months. Ashton isn't stinting himself.'

'How is he behaving? Psychologically, I mean.'

'I've seen him only three times, and then at a distance.' I thought for a moment. 'My impression is that he's more relaxed than when I saw him last in England; under less of a strain.' There didn't seem much else to say. 'What do I do now?'

'Carry on,' said Ogilvie succinctly.

I sighed. 'This could go on for weeks – months. What if I tackled him myself? There's no need to blow my cover. I can get myself accredited to an international trade conference that's coming up next week.'

'Don't do that,' said Ogilvie. 'He's sharper than anyone realizes. Just keep watching; something will turn up.'

Yes, Mr Micawber, I thought, but didn't say it. What I said was, 'I'll put the negatives and prints into the diplomatic bag immediately.'

Two more weeks went by and nothing happened. Ashton went on his way serenely, doing nothing in particular. I had another, more extended, look at him and he seemed to be enjoying himself in a left-handed fashion. This was possibly the first holiday he'd ever had free from the cares of the business he had created. Benson pottered about in the shops and markets of Gamla Stan most mornings, doing his none-too-frugal shopping, and we began to build up quite a picture of the culinary tastes of the *ménage* Ashton. It didn't do us one damned bit of good.

Henty went about his own mysterious business into which I didn't enquire too closely. I do know that he was in some form of military intelligence because he left for a week and went north to Lapland where the Swedish Army was holding winter manoeuvres. When he came back I saw him briefly and he said he'd be busy writing a report.

Four days later he came to see me with disturbing information. 'Do you know there'a another crowd in on the act?'

I stared at him. 'What do you mean?'

'I've got a bump of curiosity,' he said. 'Last night, in my copious spare time, I checked to see whether Cutler's boys were up to snuff. Ashton is leading quite a train – our chap follows Ashton and someone else follows him.' I was about to speak but he held up his hand. 'So I checked on Benson and the same is happening there.'

'Cutler's said nothing about this.'

'How would he know?' said Henty scathingly. 'Or any of them. They're amateurs.'

I asked the crucial question. 'Who?'

Henty shrugged. 'My guess is Swedish Intelligence. Those boys are good. They'd be interested in anyone with a Russian name, and even more interested to find out he's under surveillance. They'll have made the connection with the British Embassy by now.'

'Damn!' I said, 'Better not let Cutler know or he'll have diplomatic kittens. I think this is where we join in.'

Next morning, when Ashton took his morning constitutional, we were on the job. Ashton appeared and collected the first segment of his tail who happened to be Askrigg. Henty nudged me and pointed out the stranger who fell in behind. 'That's our joker. I'll cross the road and follow him. You stay on this side and walk parallel, keeping an eye on both of us.'

By God, but Henty was good! I tried to watch both him and the man he was following but Henty was invisible half the time, even though I knew he was there. He bobbed back and forth, letting the distance lengthen and then closing up, disappearing into shop entrances and reappearing in unexpected places and, in general, doing his best not to be there at all. Two or three times he was even in front of the man he was shadowing.

It was one of Ashton's book mornings. He visited two bookshops and spent about three-quarters of an hour in each, then he retired with his plunder to a coffee-house and inspected his purchases over coffee and Danish pastries. It was pretty funny. The coffee-house was on the corner of a block. Askrigg waited outside while, kitty-corner across the street, his follower stamped his feet to keep warm while ostensibly looking into a shop window. The third corner held Henty, doing pretty much the same, while I occupied the fourth corner. My own wait was made risible by the nature of the shop in which I was taking an intent interest. Henty was outside a camera shop. Mine sold frilly lingerie of the type known pungently as passion fashion.

Out came Ashton and the train chugged off again, and he led us back to where we had started, but going home by the Vasabron just to make a variation. So far the whole was a bust, but better times were coming. Our man went into a tobacconist's shop and I followed. As I bought a packet of cigarettes I heard him speaking in low tones on the telephone. I couldn't hear what he said but the intonation was neither English nor Swedish.

He left the shop and walked up the street while I followed on the other side. A hundred yards up the street he crossed, so I did the same; then he reversed direction. He was doing what he hoped was an unobtrusive patrol outside Ashton's flat.

Fifteen minutes later the event we'd waited for – his relief arrived. The two men stood and talked for a few moments, their breath steaming and mingling in the cold air, then my man set off at a smart pace and I followed. He turned the corner which led around the back of the Royal Palace, and when I had him in sight he was dickering with a taxi-driver.

I was figuring out how to say, 'Follow that car!' in Swedish when Henty pulled up alongside in his car. I scrambled in, and Henty said in satisfaction, 'I thought he might do that. We've all had enough walking for the day.' I've said he was good.

So we followed the taxi through Stockholm, which was not particularly difficult, nor did he take us very far. The taxi pulled up outside a building and was paid off, and our man disappeared inside. Henty carried on without slackening speed. 'That does it!' he said expressively.

I twisted in my seat and looked back. 'Why? What is that place?'

'The bloody Russian Embassy.'

20

I expected my report on that to bring action but I didn't expect it to bring Ogilvie. I telephoned him at three in the afternoon and he was in my room just before midnight, and four other men from the department were scattered about the hotel. Ogilvie drained me dry, and I ended up by saying, 'Henty and I did the same this evening with the man following Benson. He went back to a flat on Upplandsgatan. On checking, he proved to be a commercial attaché at the Russian Embassy.'

Ogilvie was uncharacteristically nervous and indecisive. He paced the room as a tiger paces its cage, his hands clasped behind his back; then he sat in a chair with a thump. 'Damn it all to hell!' he said explosively. 'I'm in two minds about this.'

I waited, but Ogilvie did not enlarge on what was on either of his minds, so I said diffidently, 'What's the problem?'

'Look, Ashton hasn't given us what we expected when we sprung him from Russia. Oh, he's done a lot, but in a purely commercial way – not the advanced scientific thought we wanted. So why the hell should we care if he plays silly buggers in Stockholm and attracts the attention of the Russians?'

Looked at in a cold and calculating way that was a good question. Ogilvie said, 'I'd wash my hands of him – let the Russians take him – but for two things. The first is that I don't *know* why he ran, and the hell of it is that the answer might be quite unimportant. It's probably mere intellectual curiosity on my part, and the taxpayer shouldn't be expected to finance that. This operation is costing a packet.'

He stood up and began to pace again. 'The second thing is that I can't get that empty vault out of my mind. Why did he build it if he didn't intend to use it? Have you thought of that, Malcolm?'

'Yes, but I haven't got very far.'

Ogilvie sighed. 'Over the past months I've read and reread Ashton's file until I've become cross-eyed. I've been trying to get into the mind of the man. Did you know it was he who suggested taking over the persona of a dead English soldier?'

'No. I thought it was Cregar's idea.'

'It was Chelyuskin. As I read the file I began to see that he works by misdirection like a conjuror. Look at how he got out of Russia. I'm more and more convinced that the vault is another bit of misdirection.'

'An expensive bit,' I said.

'That wouldn't worry Ashton – he's rolling in money. If he's got something, he's got it somewhere else.'

I was exasperated. 'So why did he build the safe in the first place?'

'To tell whoever opened it that they'd reached the end of the line. That there are no secrets. As I say – misdirection.'

'It's all a bit fanciful,' I said. I was tired because it was late and I'd been working hard all day. Hammering the ice-slippery streets of Stockholm with my feet wasn't my idea of pleasure, and I was past the point of coping with Ogilvie's fantasies about Ashton. I tried to bring him to the point by saying, 'What do we do about Ashton now?' He was the boss and he had to make up his mind.

'How did the Russians get on to Ashton here?'

'How would I know?' I shrugged. 'My guess is that they got wind of a free-spending fellow-countryman unknown to Moscow, so they decided to take a closer look at him. To their surprise they found he's of great interest to British Intelligence. That would make them perk up immediately.'

'Or, being the suspicious lot they are, they may have been keeping tabs on the British Embassy as a matter of routine and been alerted by the unaccustomed activity of Cutler and his mob, who're not the brightest crowd of chaps.' Ogilvie shrugged. 'I don't suppose it matters how they found out; the fact is that they have. They're on to Koslov but have not, I think, made the transition to Ashton – and certainly not to Chelyuskin.'

'That's about it. They'll never get to Chelyuskin. Who'd think of going back thirty years?'

'Their files go back further, and they'll have Chelyuskin's fingerprints. If they ever do a comparison with Koslov's prints they'll know it wasn't Chelyuskin who died in that fire. They'd be interested in that.'

'But is it likely?'

'I don't know.' He scowled in my direction but I don't think he saw me; he was looking through me. 'That Israeli passport is quite genuine,' he said. 'But stolen three years ago. The real Koslov is a Professor of Languages at the University of Tel Aviv. He's there right now, deciphering some scrolls in Aramaic.'

'Do the Israelis know about Koslov? That might be tricky.'

'I shouldn't think so,' he said absently. Then he shook his head irritatedly. 'You don't think much of my theories about Ashton, do you?'

'Not much.'

The scowl deepened. 'Neither do I,' he admitted. 'It's just one big area of uncertainty. Right. We can do one of two things. We can pull out and leave Ashton to sink or swim on his own; or we can get him out ourselves.' Ogilvie looked at me expectantly.

I said, 'That's a policy decision I'm not equipped to make. But I do have a couple of comments. First, any interest the Russians have in Ashton has been exacerbated by ourselves, and I consider we have a responsibility towards him because of that. For the rest – what I've seen of Ashton I've liked and, God willing, I'm going to marry his daughter. I have a personal reason for wanting to get

160

him out which has nothing to do with guessing what he's been doing with his peculiar mind.'

Ogilvie nodded soberly. 'Fair enough. That leaves it up to me. If he really has something and we leave him for the Russians then I'll have made a big mistake. If we bring him out, risking an international incident because of the methods we may have to use, and he has nothing, then I'll have made a big mistake. But the first mistake would be bigger than the second, so the answer is that we bring him out. The decision is made.'

21

Ogilvie had brought with him Brent, Gregory, Michaelis and, to my surprise, Larry Godwin, who looked very chipper because not only had he got away from his desk but he'd gone foreign. We had an early morning conference to discuss the nuts and bolts of the operation.

Earlier I had again tackled Ogilvie. 'Why don't I approach Ashton and tell him the Russians are on to him? That would move him.'

'In which direction?' asked Ogilvie. 'If he thought for one moment that British Intelligence was trying to manipulate him I wouldn't care to predict his actions. He might even think it better to go back to Russia. Homesickness is a Russian neurosis.'

'Even after thirty years?'

Ogilvie shrugged. 'The Russians are a strange people. And have you thought of his attitude to you? He'd immediately jump to wrong conclusions – I won't risk the explosion. No, it will have to be some other way.'

Ogilvie brought the meeting to order and outlined the problem, then looked about expectantly. There was a lengthy pause while everyone thought about it. Gregory said, 'We have to separate him from the Russians before we can do anything at all.'

'Are we to assume he might defect to Russia?' asked Brent.

'Not if we're careful,' said Ogilvie. 'But it's a possibility. My own view is that he might even be scared of the Russians if he knew they were watching him.'

Brent threw one in my direction. 'How good are the Russians here?'

'Not bad at all,' I said. ' A hell of a lot better than Cutler's crowd.'

'Then it's unlikely they'll make a mistake,' he said glumly. 'I thought if he knew the Russians were on to him he might cut and run. That would give us the opportunity for a spoiling action.'

Ogilvie said, 'Malcolm and I have discussed that and decided against it.'

'Wait a minute,' I said, and turned to Larry. 'How good is your conversational Russian?'

'Not bad,' he said modestly.

'It will have to be better than not bad,' I warned. 'You might have to fool a native Russian.' I didn't tell him Ashton *was* a Russian.

He grinned. 'Which regional accent do you want?'

Ogilvie caught on. 'I see,' he said thoughtfully. 'If the Russians don't make a mistake we make it for them. I'll buy that.'

We discussed it for a while, then Michaelis said, 'We'll need a back-up scheme. If we're going to take him out against his will we'll need transport, a safe house and possibly a doctor.'

That led to another long discussion in which plans were hammered out and roles allocated. Kidnapping a man can be complicated. 'What about Benson?' asked Gregory. 'Is he included in the deal?'

'I rather think so,' said Ogilvie. 'I'm becoming interested in Benson. But the primary target is Ashton. If it ever comes to a choice between taking Ashton or Benson, then drop Benson.' He turned to Michaelis. 'How long do you need?'

'If we use Plan Three we don't need a house, and the closed van I can hire inside an hour. But I'll have to go to Helsingborg or Malmo to arrange for the boat and that will take time. Say three days.'

'How long to cross the strait to Denmark?'

'Less than an hour; you can nearly spit across it. But

someone will have to organize a receiving committee in Denmark.'

'I'll do that.' Ogilvie stood up and said with finality, 'Three days, then; and we don't tell Cutler anything about it.'

Three days later the operation began as planned and started well. The situation in Gamla Stan was becoming positively ridiculous: two of Cutler's men were idling away their time in antique shops ready for the emergence of Ashton and Benson and unaware that they were being watched by a couple of Russians who, in their turn, were not aware of being under the surveillance of the department. It could have been a Peter Sellers comedy.

Each of our men was issued with a miniature walkie-talkie with strict instructions to stay off the air unless it was absolutely necessary to pass on the word. We didn't want to alert the Swedes that an undercover operation was under way; if they joined in there'd be so many secret agents in those narrow streets there'd be no room for tourists.

I sat in my car, strategically placed to cover the bridges leading from Gamla Stan to the central city area, and kept a listening watch. Ogilvie stayed in his room in the hotel next to the telephone.

At ten-thirty someone came on the air. 'Bluebird Two. Redbird walking north along Västerlånggatan.' Ashton was coming my way so I twisted in my seat to look for him. Presently he rounded the corner and walked up the road next to the Royal Palace. He passed within ten feet of me, striding out briskly. I watched him until he turned to go over Helgeandsholmen by way of Norrbro, then switched on the car engine. Ahead I saw Larry slide out of his parking place and roll along to turn on to Norrbro. His job was to get ahead of Ashton.

I followed behind, passing Ashton who was already carrying a tail like a comet, crossed Norrbro and did a couple of turns around Gustav Adolfs Torg, making sure that everything was in order. I saw Gregory leave his parking place to make room for Larry; it was important that Larry should be in the right place at the right time. Michaelis was reserving a place further west should Ashton have decided to go into town via the Vasabron. I switched on my transmitter and said to him, 'Bluebird Four to Bluebird Three; you may quit.'

At that point I quit myself because there was nothing left to do – everything now depended on Larry. I drove the short distance to the Grand Hotel, parked the car, and went to Ogilvie's room. He was nervous under his apparent placidity. After a few minutes' chat he said abruptly, 'Do you think Godwin is up to it? He's not very experienced.'

'And he never will be if he's not given the chance.' I smiled. 'He'll be all right. Any moment from now he'll be giving his celebrated imitation of an inexperienced KGB man. From that point of view his inexperience is an asset.'

Time wore on. At twelve-thirty Ogilvie had smörgåsbord sent up to the room. 'We might as well eat. If anything breaks you'll be eating on the run from now on.'

At five to one the telephone rang. Ogilvie handed me a pair of earphones before he picked up the receiver. It was Brent, who said, 'Redbird is lunching at the Opera – so am I and so is everyone else concerned. He's looking a bit jumpy.'

'How did Godwin handle first contact?'

'Redbrid went into that corner bookshop on the Nybroplan. Godwin was standing next to him when he barked his shin on a shelf; Larry swore a blue streak in Russian and Redbird jumped a foot. Then Larry faded out as planned.'

'And then?'

'Redbird wandered around for a bit and then came here. I saw him get settled, then signalled Larry to come in. He took a table right in front of Redbird who looked worried when he saw him. Larry has just had a hell of a row with a waiter in very bad, Russian-accented Swedish – all very noisy. Redbird is definitely becoming uncomfortable.'

'How are the others taking it?'

'The real Russians look bloody surprised. Cutler's chap . . . wait a minute.' After a pause Brent chuckled. 'Cutler's chap is heading for the telephones right now. I think he wants to report that the Russians have arrived. I think I'll let him have this telephone.'

'Stay with it,' said Ogilvie. 'Stick to Ashton.' He replaced the receiver and looked up. 'It's starting.'

'Everything is ready,' I said soothingly. I picked up the telephone and asked the hotel operator to transfer my calls to Ogilvie's room.

We had not long to wait. The telephone rang and I answered. Cutler said, 'Jaggard, there may be an important development.'

'Oh,' I said seriously. 'What's that?'

'My man with Ashton seems to think the Russians are interested.'

'In Ashton?'

'That's right.'

'Oh. That's bad! Where is Ashton now?'

'Lunching at the Opera. Shall I put someone on to the Russian? There may be time.'

Ogilvie had the earphone to his ear and shook his head violently. I grinned, and said, 'I think not. In fact I think you'd better pull out all your men as soon as you can get word to them. You don't want the Russians to know you're on to Ashton, do you?'

'My God, no!' said Cutler quickly. 'We can't have the Embassy involved. I'll do as you say at once.' He rang off, seemingly relieved.

Ogilvie grunted. 'The man's an idiot. He's well out of it.'

'It does clear the field,' I said, and put on my jacket. 'I'm going over to Gamla Stan for the beginning of the second act. If Larry does his stuff we should get a firm reaction from Ashton.' I paused. 'I don't like doing it this way, you know. I'd much prefer we talk to him.'

'I know,' said Ogilvie sombrely. 'But your preferences don't count. Get on with it, Malcolm.'

So I got on with it. I went to Gamla Stan and met Henty in a bar-restaurant in Västerlånggatan, joining him in a snack of herring and aquavit. He had been watching the flat, so I said, 'Where's Benson?'

'Safe at home. His Russian is still with him but Cutler's boy has vanished. Maybe Benson lost him.'

'No. Cutler is no longer with us.' I described what had happened.

Henty grinned. 'Something should break any moment then.' He finished his beer and stood up. 'I'd better get back.'

'I'll come with you.' As we left I said, 'You're our Swedish expert. Supposing Ashton makes a break – how can he do it?'

'By air from Bromma or Arlanda, depending on where he's going. He can also take a train. He doesn't have a car.'

'Not that we know of. He could also leave by sea.'

Henty shook his head. 'At this time of the year I doubt it. There's a lot of ice in the Baltic this year – the Saltsjön was frozen over this morning. It plays hell with their schedules. If I were Ashton I wouldn't risk it; he could get stuck on a ship which didn't move for hours.'

The bone conduction contraption behind my ear came to life. 'Bluebird Two. Redbird by Palace heading for Västerlånggatan and moving fast.' Bluebird Two was Brent.

I said to Henty, 'He's coming now. You go on ahead, spot him and tag that bloody Russian. I don't want Ashton to see me.'

He quickened his pace while I slowed down, strolling from one shop window to the next. Presently there came the news that Ashton was safely back home, and then

Henty came back with Larry Godwin. Both were grinning, and Henty remarked, 'Ashton's in a muck-sweat.'

I said to Larry, 'What happened?'

'I followed Ashton from the Opera – very obviously. He tried to shake me; in fact, he did shake me twice, but Brent was able to steer me back on course.'

Henty chuckled. 'Ashton came along Västerlånggatan doing heel-and-toe as though he was in a walking race, with Godwin trying hard for second place. He went through his doorway like a rabbit going down a hole.'

'Did you speak to him, Larry?'

'Well, towards the end I called out, '*Grazhdaninu* Ashton – *ostanovites!*' as though I wanted him to stop. It just made him go faster.'

I smiled slightly. I doubt if Ashton relished being called 'citizen' in Russian, especially when coupled with his English name. 'The ball is now in Ashton's court, but I doubt he'll move before nightfall. Larry, go and do an ostentatious patrol before Ashton's flat. Be a bit haphazard – reappear at irregular intervals.'

I had a last word with Henty, and then did the rounds, checking that every man was in his place and the Russians were covered. After that I reported by telephone to Ogilvie.

Larry caught up with me in about an hour. 'One of those bloody Russians tackled me,' he said. 'He asked me what the hell I thought I was doing.'

'In Russian?'

'Yes. I asked him for his authority and he referred me to a Comrade Latiev in the Russian Embassy. So I got a bit shirty and told him that Latiev's authority had been superseded, and if Latiev didn't know that himself he was even more stupid than Moscow thought. Then I said I didn't have time to waste and did a quick disappearing act.'

'Not bad,' I said. 'It ought to hold Comrade Latiev for a while. Any reaction from the flat?'

'A curtain did twitch a bit.'

'Okay. Now, if Ashton makes his break I don't want him

to see you – we don't want to panic him more than necessary. Take over Gregory's car, ask him what the score is, and send him to me.'

It was a long wait and a cold wait. The snow came down steadily and, as darkness fell, a raw mist swept over Gamla Stan from the Riddarfjärden, haloing the street lights and cutting down visibility. I spent the time running over and over in my mind the avenues of escape open to Ashton and wondering if my contingency planning was good enough. With Henty there were six of us, surely enough to take out the two Russians and still keep up with Ashton wherever he went. As the mist thickened I thought of the possibility of taking Ashton there and then, but thought better of it. A quiet kidnapping in a major city is hard enough at the best of times and certainly not the subject for improvisation. Better to follow the plan and isolate Ashton.

It happened at ten to nine. Gregory reported Ashton and Benson on Lilla Nygatan moving south, and both had bags. Michaelis chipped in and said that both Russians were also on the move. I summoned up my mental map of Gamla Stan and concluded that our targets were heading for the taxi rank on the Centralbron, so I ordered the cars south ready to follow. More interestingly, on the other side of the Centralbron, in the main city, was Stockholm's Central Railway Station.

Then I ordered Michaelis and Henty, our best strong-arm men, to take the Russians out of the game. They reported that, because of the mist, it was easy and that two Russians would have sore heads the following morning.

After that things became a bit confused. When Ashton and Benson reached the taxi rank they took separate cabs, Benson going over the Centralbron towards the railway station, and Ashton going in the dead opposite direction towards Södermalm. Larry followed Benson, and Brent went after Ashton. I got busy and ordered the rest of the

169

team to assemble at the railway station which seemed the best bet under the circumstances.

At the station I stayed in the car and sent in Henty to find out if Larry was around. He came back with Larry who got into the car, and said, 'Benson bought two tickets for Göteborg.'

They were heading west. From my point of view that was a relief; better west than east. I said, 'When does the train leave?'

Larry checked his watch. 'In a little over half an hour. I bought us four tickets – and I got a timetable.'

I studied the timetable and thought out loud. 'First stop – Södertälje; next stop – Eskilstuna. Right.' I gave a ticket each to Gregory and Henty. 'You two get on that train; spot Ashton and Benson and report back by radio. Then stick with them.'

They went into the station, and Larry said, 'What do we do?'

'You and I lie as low as Br'er Rabbit.' I turned to Michaelis. 'Scout around in the station and see if you can spot Ashton. Make sure he's on that train when it leaves, then come back here.'

He went away and I wondered how Brent was getting on. Presently Gregory radioed in. 'We're on the train – spotted Redbird Two – but no Redbird One.'

We'd lost Ashton. 'Stay with it.'

The time ticked by. At five minutes to train-time I became uneasy, wondering what had happened to Ashton. At two minutes to train-time Brent pitched up. 'I lost him,' he said hollowly.

'Where did he go?'

'He went bloody island-hopping – Södermalm – Lång-holmen – Kungsholmen; that's where I lost him. He seemed to be heading in this general direction at the time so I took a chance and came here.'

'We haven't seen him and he's not on the train so far. Benson is, though; with two tickets to Göteborg.'

'When does it leave?'

I looked over his shoulder and saw Michaelis coming towards the car. He was shaking his head. I said, 'It's just left – and Ashton wasn't on it.'

'Oh, Christ! What do we do now?'

'The only thing we can do – stick with Benson and pray. And this is how we do it. Get yourself a timetable like this one, and check the stops of that train. You and Michaelis take the first stop – that's Södertälje, you check with Gregory and Henty on the train and you team up if Benson gets off. You also report to Ogilvie. In the meantime Larry and I will be heading for the next stop at Eskilstuna – same procedure. And we leapfrog up the line until the train arrives at Göteborg or anything else happens. Got that?'

'Okay.'

'Reporting to Ogilvie is very important because he can keep us all tied in. I'm going to ring him now.'

Ogilvie wasn't at all pleased but he didn't say much – not then. I told him how I was handling it and he just grunted. 'Carry on – and keep me posted.'

I went back to the car, slumped into the passenger's seat, and said to Larry, 'Drive to Eskilstuna – and beat that train.'

22

From Stockholm to Eskilstuna is about 100 kilometres. The firt 40 kilometres are of motorway standard and we were able to make good time, but after that it became more of an ordinary road with opposing traffic and our average speed dropped. It was very dark – a moonless night – but even if there had been a moon it wouldn't have helped because there was a thick layer of cloud from which descended a heavy and continuous fall of snow.

Like all modern Swedish cars ours was well equipped for this kind of weather. The tyres had tungsten-steel studs for traction and the headlights had wipers to clear the encrusting snow, but that didn't mean fast driving and I suppose we didn't average more than 70 KPH and that was a shade fast for the conditions. Neither Larry nor I could be classed as rally drivers, and I was very much afraid the train would be faster. Fortunately, I saw by the map that it had further to go, the track sweeping round in a loop. Also it would stop at Södertälje.

After an hour I told Larry to pull into a filling station where he refuelled while I phoned Ogilvie. When I got back to the car I was smiling, and Larry said, 'Good news?'

'The best. I'll drive.' As we pulled away I said, 'Ashton tried to pull a fast one. When Brent lost him he wasn't on his way to the railway station in Stockholm; he took a taxi ride to the Södertälje station and got on the train there. We've got them both now.'

Thus it was that I was quite happy when we pulled up outside the railway station at Eskilstuna to find the train standing on the platform. I switched on my transmitter, and said, 'Any Bluebirds there? Come in, Bluebirds.'

A voice in my ear. 'Redbird and friend jumped train.'

'What the hell?'

Henty said, 'What do you want me to do?'

'Get off that bloody train and come here. We're parked outside the station.' Even as I spoke the train clanked and began to move slowly. I was beginning to wonder if Henty had made it when I saw him running towards the car. I wound down the side window. 'Get in and tell me what, for Christ's sake, happened.'

Henty got into the back seat. 'The train pulled up at some bloody whistle-stop called Akers-styckebruk, and don't ask me why. Nothing happened until it began to move out, then Ashton and Benson jumped for it. Gregory went after them but it was too late for me – and the way he went he was like to break a leg.'

I got out the road map and studied it. 'Akers-styckebruk! The place isn't even on the map. Have you reported to Ogilvie?'

'No. I was just going to when you called me.'

'Then I suppose I have to.'

I went into the station and rang Stockholm, and Ogilvie said testily, 'What the devil's going on? I've just had a call from Gregory in some God-forsaken place. He's either broken or sprained his ankle and he's lost Ashton. He thinks they've gone to somewhere called Strängnäs.'

Strängnäs was back along the road; we'd skirted around the edges. I said, 'We'll be there in an hour.'

'An hour may be too late,' he snapped. 'But get on with it.'

I ran back to the car. 'Get weaving, Larry – back where we came from.' He moved over into the driving seat and I hadn't closed the door before he took off. I twisted around and said to Henty, 'What can you tell me about Strängnäs? Anything there we ought to know about?'

He snapped his fingers. 'Of course! There's a spur-line going into Strängnäs from Akers-styckebruk – no passenger trains, just the occasional *räslbuss*.'

'What's that?'

'A single coach on the railway – diesel driven.'

'You say it's a spur-line. You mean the rail stops at Strängnäs?'

'It has to, or it would run into Lake Mälaren.'

I contemplated that. 'So it's a dead end.'

'For the railway, but not for cars. There's a road which goes by way of the islands to the north shore of Mälaren. But it's late. I wouldn't bet they'll be able to hire a car at this time of night.'

'True,' I said. 'But step on it, Larry.' I watched the road unwinding out of the darkness against the hypnotic beat of the wipers as they cleared snow from the windscreen. The headlights brightened as Larry operated the light wipers. 'Anything else about Strängnäs?'

'It's not much of a place,' said Henry. 'Population about twelve thousand; a bit of light industry – pharmaceuticals, penicillin, X-ray film – stuff like that. It's also a garrison town for a training regiment, and it's HQ, East Military Command.' His interest sharpened. 'Is Ashton connected with the soldier boys?'

'No,' I said.

Henty persisted. 'You'd tell me if he is? That's my line of country, and I've helped you enough.'

'Definitely not,' I said. 'His interestes aren't military, and neither are mine. We're not poaching on your patch.'

'Just as long as I know.' He seemed satisfied.

We didn't bother going back all the way to Akers-styckebruk; finding Ashton was more important than finding the state of Gregory's ankle. We came to the outskirts of Strängnäs and coasted gently through the snow-covered streets towards the lake edge and the centre of town. A few turns around the town centre proved one thing – there was only one hotel – so we pulled up on the other side of the street from the Hotel Rogge and I sent Henty in to find out the form.

He was away about five minutes and when he came back

174

he said, 'They're both there – booked under the names of Ashton and Williams.'

'So he's reverted,' I said. 'Using his own passport. Koslov has suddenly become too hot.'

'I booked in for the three of us.'

'No; you stay, but Larry and I are going to find Gregory. I'll ring Ogilvie now and ask him to retrieve Brent and Michaelis from wherever the hell they are now – they can have the other two beds here. We'll be back at six tomorrow morning and I want a concentration inside and outside the hotel. Where are Ashton and Benson now?'

'Not in any of the public rooms,' said Henty. 'I'd say they're in bed.'

'Yes, they're getting pretty old for this sort of thing,' I said pensively. 'Come to think of it, so am I.'

Gregory had sensibly waited at the railway station at Akers-styckebruk for someone to pick him up. He said he was stiff, cold, tired, and that his ankle hurt like hell, so we all booked into a hotel. At five the next morning Larry and I were on our way back to Strängnäs, but Gregory was able to sleep in because I decided to send him back to Stockholm. He'd be no good to us because his ankle really was bad, but he had the satisfaction of knowing that, because of him, we'd pinned down Ashton and Benson.

Just before six I parked the car around the corner from the Hotel Rogge, and at six on the button I went on the air. 'Hello,' I said brightly. 'Any Bluebirds awake?'

Henty said disgruntedly into my ear, 'Don't be so bloody cheerful.'

'Did the other two arrive?'

'Yes, at two this morning. They're still asleep.'

'And Redbird and his friend?'

'They're definitely here – I made sure of that – they're asleep, too.' He paused. 'And I wish to Christ I was.'

'Come out here. We're just around the corner on – ' I craned my neck to find a street sign – 'on Källgatan.'

He said nothing but the transmission hum stopped so I switched off. He did not appear for a quarter of an hour so Larry and I made small talk. There was nothing much to say because we'd talked the subject to death already. When Henty did arrive he was newly shaven and looked in reasonably good shape even though his manner was still a little shaggy. 'Morning,' he said shortly, as he got into the car.

I passed a vacuum flask over my shoulder. 'Be gruntled.'

He unscrewed the top and sniffed appreciatively. 'Ah, scotch coffee!' He poured a cupful and was silent for a moment before he said, 'That's better. What's the drill?'

'What time is breakfast?'

'I don't know. Say, from seven o'clock – maybe seven-thirty. These country hotels all differ.'

'I want the three of you in the breakfast room as soon as it opens; you at one table, Michaelis and Brent at another. They are to talk to each other and one of them has to give a running commentary over the air about Ashton and Benson as soon as they come in to beakfast. I want to know exactly how Ashton is acting – and reacting.'

'We can do that,' said Henty. 'But I don't get the reason.'

I said, 'Half way through breakfast I'm going to send Larry in to do a replay of his Russian act.'

'Jesus! You'll give Ashton a heart attack.'

'We've got to keep the pressure on,' I said. 'I don't want to give them time to hire a car, and I want to herd them out of the town pretty early. Where's the closed van Michaelis has been driving?'

Henty pointed across the darkened street. 'In the hotel car park.'

'Good enough. I want him inside it and ready to go as soon as Ashton moves. I want this whole bloody thing cleaned up before eight o'clock if possible. Now you can go in and wake the sleeping beauties.'

When Henty had gone Larry regarded me curiously. 'I know you've been keeping out of sight,' he said. 'But if what you're doing ever comes out you're not going to be popular with the Ashton family.'

'I know,' I said shortly. 'But this is the way Ogilvie wants it done. And I'm making bloody sure I do stay out of sight, not for Ogilvie's reasons but my own.' Christ! I thought. If Penny ever got to know about this she'd never forgive me in a thousand years.

The time passed and we shared the flask of scotch coffee between us. Strängnäs began to wake up and there was movement in the streets, and we occasioned a couple of curious glances from passers-by. I suppose it was strange for a couple of men to be sitting in a parked car so early in the morning so I told Larry to drive into the hotel car park which was more secluded.

The hotel breakfast started at seven-thirty. I knew that because Jack Brent came on the air with a description of the breakfast he was eating. He described the herring and the boiled eggs and the cheese and the coffee and all the trimmings until I began to salivate. He was doing it deliberately, the bastard.

Because I made no response he tired of the game and switched off, but at seven-fifty he said, 'They're here now – Ashton and Benson. Just sitting down – two tables away. Benson looks sour but Ashton seems cheerful enough.'

No one would know Brent was broadcasting; apparently he would be chatting animatedly to Michaelis, but every word was picked up by the throat microphone concealed beneath the knot of his tie. The throat microphone gave a peculiarly dead quality to the broadcast; there was no background noise – no clatter of cutlery or coffee cups to be heard – just Brent's voice and the rasp of his breathing greatly magnified. Even if he spoke in a whisper every word would come across clearly.

I listened to his description and felt increasingly uneasy. Not about Ashton who, according to Brent, seemed fairly relaxed; I was uneasy about myself and my role in this charade. I would have given a lot to be able to walk into the Hotel Rogge, sit down at Ashton's table, and have a down-to-earth chat with him. I was convinced I could get him back to England just by talking to him, but Ogilvie wouldn't have that. He didn't want our cover blown.

I was depressed when I turned to Larry, and said quietly, 'All right. Go in and have your breakfast.' He got out of the car and walked into the hotel.

Brent said, 'Ashton's just poured himself another cup of

coffee. He hasn't lost his appetite, that's for certain. Ho ho! Larry Godwin has just walked in. Ashton hasn't seen him yet, nor has Benson. Larry's talking to the waitress by the door. God, how he's mangling his Swedish – can hear him from here. So can Ashton. He's turned and he's looking at Larry. I can't see his face. He's turned back again and now he's nudging Benson. He's as white as a sheet. The waitress is coming forward with Larry now – showing him to a table. Larry is passing Ashton's table – he turns and speaks to him. Ashton has knocked over his coffee cup. Benson is looking bloody grim; if ever I saw a man capable of murder it's Benson right now. He's no oil painting at the best of times but you should see him now. Ashton wants to get up and leave, but Benson is holding him back.'

I switched channels on my transmitter and Brent's voice abruptly stopped. I said, 'Henty, finish your breakfast and leave. Cover the front of the hotel. Michaelis, same for you, but get in your van and cover the back.'

I reversed out of the hotel car park and drove a little way up Källgatan and parked where I could see the front entrance of the hotel. When I switched back to Brent he was saying '. . . looks pretty shattered and Benson is talking to him urgently. I think he's having a hard job keeping control. You'd think it would be the other way round because Benson is only Ashton's servant. Anyway, that's what it looks like from here – Ashton wants to make a break and Benson is stopping him. Larry isn't doing much – just eating his breakfast – but every now and then he looks across at Ashton and smiles. I don't think Ashton can take much more of it. I'll have to stop now because Michaelis is leaving and I'll look bloody funny talking to myself.'

He stopped speaking and the transmission hum ceased. I keyed my transmitter. 'Larry, when Ashton and Benson leave follow them from behind with Brent.' I saw Henty come out of the hotel and walk across the street. Michaelis came next and walked around to the car park where he disappeared from sight.

Ten minutes later Ashton and Benson appeared, each carrying a bag. They stepped out on to the pavement and Ashton looked up and down the street uncertainly. He said something to Benson who shook his head, and it looked as though there was a difference of opinion. Behind them Larry appeared in the hotel entrance.

I said, 'Larry, go and talk to Ashton. Ask him to follow you. If he agrees, take him to the van and put him in the back.'

'And Benson?'

'Him too – if possible.'

Ashton became aware that Larry was watching him and pulled at Benson's arm. Benson nodded and they began to walk away but stopped at Larry's call. Larry hurried over to them and began talking and, as he did so, Brent came out and stood close to them.

I heard the one-way conversation. Larry talked fast in Russian and twice Ashton nodded, but Benson made interjections, each time accompanied by a headshake, and tried to get Ashton away. At last he succeeded and the pair of them walked off, leaving Larry flat. They were coming straight towards me so I ducked out of sight.

While I was down on the car floor I spoke to Larry. 'What happened?'

'Ashton nearly came, but Benson wouldn't have it. He spoiled it.'

'Did Benson speak Russian?'

'No, English; but he understood my Russian well enough.'

'Where are they now?'

'Going up the street – about thirty yards past your car.'

I emerged from hiding and looked in the mirror. Ashton and Benson were walking away quickly in the direction of the railway station.

After that it all became a little sick because we literally herded them out of town. They found the railway station blocked by Brent, and when they tried to duck back to the town centre they were confronted by Larry and Henty. They soon became aware that they had a quartet of opponents and, twist and turn as they might, they found themselves being driven to the edge of town. And all the time I orchestrated the bizarre dance, manipulating them like puppets. I didn't like myself at all.

At last we got to the main Stockholm-Eskilstuna road and they plunged across, Benson nearly being hit by a speeding car which went by with a wailing blast of horn. There were no more streets or houses on the other side – just an infinity of pine trees. I had Michaelis go back and pick up the van, and sent the other three into the forest while I parked my car before following. It seemed as though the chase was nearly over – you can't be more private than in a Swedish forest.

They made better time over rough country than I would have expected of two elderly men. Ashton had already proved his fitness to me, but I hadn't expected Benson to have the stamina because he was a few years older than Ashton. Once in the trees you couldn't see far and they kept foxing us by changing direction. Twice we lost them; the first time we picked them up by sheer luck, and the second time by finding their abandoned bags. And all the time I was leading from the rear, directing the operation by radio.

We had gone perhaps three kilometres into the forest and the going was becoming rougher. Where the ground was not slippery with snow and ice it was even more slippery with pine needles. The ground rose and fell, not much but enough to take your breath away on the uphill slopes. I paused at the top of one such slope just as Brent said in my ear, 'What the hell was that?'

'What?'

'Listen!'

I listened, trying to control my heavy breathing, and heard a rattle of shots in the distance. They seemed to come from somewhere ahead, deeper in the forest.

'Someone hunting,' said Larry.

Brent said incredulously, 'With a machine-gun!'

'Quiet!' I said. 'Is Ashton spotted?'

'I'm standing looking into a little valley,' said Henty. 'Very few trees. I can see both Ashton and Benson – they're about four hundred yards away.'

'That's all very well, but where the hell are you?'

'Just keep coming ahead,' said Henty. 'It's a long valley – you can't miss it.'

'Everybody move,' I said. Again came the sound of firing, this time a sporadic rattling of badly-spaced single shots. Certainly not a machine-gun as Brent had suggested. It could have been the shoot-out at the OK Corral, and I wondered what was happening. Hunters certainly didn't pop off like that.

I pressed on and presently came to a crest where I looked down into the valley. Henty was right; it was relatively treeless and the snow was thicker. In the distance I saw Ashton and Benson moving very slowly; perhaps they were hampered by the snow, but I thought the chase was telling on them. Henty was at the valley bottom below me, and Brent and Larry were together, bounding down the hill-side, closing in on our quarry from an angle.

Again came firing and, by God, this time it was machine-gun fire, and from more than one machine-gun. Then there came some deeper coughs, followed by thumping explosions. In the distance, not too far ahead, I saw a haze of smoke drifting above the trees on the far side of the valley.

Henty had stopped. He looked back at me and waved, and said over the radio, 'I know what it is. This is an army exercise area. They're having war games.'

'Live ammunition?'

'Sounds like it. Those were mortars.'

I began to run, bouncing and slithering down the slope. When I got to the bottom I saw that Brent and Larry were within fifty yards of Ashton and gaining on him fast.

Ashton switched direction, and I yelled, 'Brent – Larry – fall back!'

They hesitated momentarily but then went on, caught in the lust of the chase. I shouted again. 'Fall back! Don't drive him into the guns.'

They checked, but I ran on. I was going to speak to Ashton myself, regardless of what Ogilvie had said. This was a sick game which had to be stopped before somebody was killed. Ashton was climbing the other side of the valley, heading towards the trees on the crest, but going very slowly. Benson was nowhere to be seen. I ran until I thought my chest would burst, and gained on Ashton.

At last I was close enough, and I shouted, 'Ashton – George Ashton – stop!'

He turned his head and looked back at me as a further burst of firing came, and more explosions of mortar bombs. I took off the fur hat I was wearing and threw it away so that he could get a good look at me. His eyes widened in surprise and he hesitated in his upward climb, then stopped and turned around. Brent and Larry were coming in on my left and Henty on the right.

I was about to call out to him again when there was another single shot, this time from quite close, and Ashton tumbled forward as though he had tripped. I was within ten yards of him and heard him gasp. Then there was another shot and he whirled around and fell and came rolling down the slope towards me to stop at my feet.

I was aware that Henty had passed me and momentarily saw a gun in his fist, then I bent over Ashton. He coughed once and blood trickled from the corner of his mouth. His eyes still held surprise at the sight of me, and he said, 'Mal . . . colm . . . what . . .'

I said, 'Take it easy, George,' and put my hand inside his coat. I felt a warm wetness.

He scrabbled in his pocket for something, and said, 'The . . . the . . .' His hand came up before my face with the fist clenched. 'The . . . the . . .' Then he fell back, his eyes still open and looking at the sky with deeper surprise. A snowflake fell and settled on his left eyeball, but he didn't blink.

In the distance mortars thumped and machine-guns rattled, and there were more single shots, again from quite close. I looked down at Ashton and cursed quietly. Brent crunched over the snow. 'Dead?'

I withdrew my hand and looked at the blood. Before wiping it clean on the snow I said, 'You try his pulse.'

I stood up as Brent knelt and thought of the unholy mess we – *I* – had made of the operation. The snow around Ashton's body was changing colour from white to red. Brent looked up at me. 'Yes, he's dead. From the amount of blood here the aorta must have been cut. That's why he went so fast.'

I had never felt so bad in all my life. We had driven Ashton towards the guns as beaters drive an animal. It was so stupid a thing to do. I didn't feel very human at that moment.

Henty came crunching down the slope, carrying a pistol negligently in his right hand. 'I got him,' he said matter-of-factly.

I could smell the faint reek of cordite as he came closer. 'Got who, for Christ's sake?'

'Benson.'

I stared at him. '*You shot Benson!*'

He looked at me in surprise. 'Well, he shot Ashton, didn't he?'

I was stupefied. 'Did he?'

'Of course he did. I saw him do it.' Henty turned and looked up the slope. 'Maybe you couldn't see him from this angle – but I did.'

I was unable to take it in. '*Benson* shot Ashton!'

'He bloody nearly shot me,' said Henty. 'He took a crack at me as soon as I showed myself up there. And if anyone shoots at me I shoot back.'

It had never occurred to me to ask Henty if he was

armed. Nobody else was on Ogilvie's instructions, but Henty was from another department. I was still gaping at him when there was a grinding rattle from above and a tank pointed its nose over the crest and began to come down into the valley. Its nose was a 105 mm high-velocity tank gun which looked like a 16-incher as the turret swivelled to cover our small group. They wouldn't have bothered to use that, though; the machine-gun in the turret of that Centurion was capable of taking care of us much more economically.

As the tank stopped I dropped to my knees next to Ashton's body. The turret opened and a head popped out, followed by a torso. The officer raised his anti-flash goggles and surveyed us with slightly popping eyes. Henty moved, and the officer barked, '*Stopp!*' With a sigh Henty tossed his pistol aside in the snow.

I opened Ashton's clenched fist to look at what he had taken from his pocket. It was a crumpled railway timetable of the route from Stockholm to Göteborg.

24

I don't know what sort of heat was generated at a higher level but the Swedes never treated me with anything less than politeness – icy politeness. If I had thought about it at all that cold correctitude would have been more frightening than anything else, but I wasn't thinking during that period – I was dead inside and my brains were frozen solid.

The Swedes had found two dead men and four live on army territory. One of the dead men had two passports, one stolen and the other genuine; the other had three passports, all false. The passports of the four live men were all genuine. It was claimed that one of the dead men had shot the other and, in turn, was shot and killed by one of the live men, an Australian living and working in Sweden. He had no permit for a gun.

It was all very messy.

Ogilvie was out of it, of course, and so were Michaelis and Gregory. Michaelis had waited with the van at the road, but when a squad of infantry in full battle order debouched from the forest and systematically began to take my car to pieces he had tactfully departed. He drove back into Strängnäs and rang Ogilvie who pulled him back to Stockholm. And what Ogilvie heard from the Embassy made him decide that the climate of London was more favourable than the chilliness of Stockholm. The three of them were back in London that night and Cutler was saying, 'I told you so.'

The four of us were taken to the army barracks in Strängnäs, HQ the Royal Södermanland Regiment and HQ East Military Command. Here we were searched and eyebrows were lifted at the sight of our communication equipment. No doubt conclusions were duly drawn. We weren't treated badly; they fed us, and if what we ate was representative of army rations then the Swedish Army does a damned sight better than the British Army. But we were not allowed to talk; a stricture reinforced by two hefty Swedes armed with sub-machine guns.

After that I was led into an empty room and, just as I thought the interrogation was about to begin, a civilian arrived and began being nasty to the military. At least, that's the impression I had judging by the rumble of voices from the office next door. Then an army colonel and a civilian came in to see me and, having seen me, went away without saying a word, and I was transferred into a cell in which I spent the next three weeks apart from an hour's exercise each day. During that time I didn't see the others at all, and the Swedes wouldn't give me the time of day, so I ought to have been pretty lonely, but I wasn't. I wasn't anything at all.

I was awakened one morning at three a.m., taken into an ablutions block and told to take a shower. When I came out I found my own clothes – the army fatigues I had been wearing had disappeared. I dressed, checked my wallet and found everything there, and put on my watch. The only things missing were my passport and the radio.

I was marched smartly across the dark and snow-covered parade ground and shown into an office where a man dressed in civilian clothes awaited me. He wasn't a civilian, though, because he said, 'I am Captain Morelius.' He had watchful grey eyes and a gun in a holster under his jacket. 'You will come with me.'

We went outside again to a chauffeur-driven Volvo, and Captain Morelius didn't say another word until we were standing on the apron of Arlanda Airport over three hours later. Then he pointed to a British Airways Trident, and said, 'There is your aircraft, Mr Jaggard. You realize you are no longer welcome in Sweden.' And that is all he said.

We walked to the gangway and he handed a ticket to a

187

steward who took me inside and installed me in a first-class seat. Then they let on the common herd and twenty minutes later we were in the air. I had good service from that steward who must have thought I was a VIP, and I appreciated the first drink I had had for nearly a month.

When we landed at Heathrow I wondered how I was going to get by without a passport; I certainly didn't feel like going into tedious explanations. But Ogilvie was waiting for me and we walked around Passport Control and Customs. Once in his car he asked, 'Are you all right, Malcolm?'

'Yes.' I paused. 'I'm sorry.'

'Not to worry,' he said. 'We'll leave the explanations for later.'

Going into town he talked about everything except what had happened in Sweden. He brought me up-to-date on the news, talked about a new show that had opened, and generally indulged in light chit-chat. When he pulled up outside my flat he said, 'Get some sleep. I'll see you in my office tomorrow.'

I got out of the car. 'Wait! How's Penny?'

'Quite well, I believe. She's in Scotland.'

'Does she know?'

He nodded, took out his wallet, and extracted a newspaper cutting. 'You can keep that,' he said, and put the car into gear and drove away.

I went up to the flat and its very familiarity seemed strange. I stood looking around and then realized I was holding the newspaper cutting. It was from *The Times*, and read:

KILLED IN SWEDEN

Two Englishmen, George Ashton (56) and Howard Greatorex Benson (64) were killed near Strängnäs, Sweden, yesterday when they wandered on to a firing range used by the Swedish army. Both men died instantaneously when they were caught in a shell explosion.

A Swedish army spokesman said that the area was adequately cordoned and that all roads leading into it were signposted. Announcements of the proposed firing of live ammunition were routinely made in the local newspapers and on the radio.

The dateline of the story was five days after Ashton and Benson died.

25

When I walked into my office Larry Godwin was sitting at his desk reading *Pravda* and looking as though he had never left it. He looked up, 'Hello, Malcolm.' He didn't smile and neither did I. We both knew there was nothing to smile about.

'When did you get back?'

'Three days ago – the day after Jack Brent.'

'Henty?'

He shook his head. 'Haven't seen him.'

'How did they treat you?'

'Not bad. I felt a bit isolated, though.'

'Has Ogilvie debriefed you?'

Larry grimaced. 'He emptied me as you'd empty a bottle of beer. I still feel gutted. It'll be your turn now.'

I nodded, picked up the telephone, and told Ogilvie's secretary I was available. Then I sat down to contemplate my future and couldn't see a damned thing in the fog. Larry said, 'Someone knew the right strings to pull. I tell you, I wasn't looking forward to a stretch in a Swedish jail. They'd have put us in their version of Siberia – up in the frozen north.'

'Yes,' I said abstractedly. I wondered what *quid pro quo* the Swedes had claimed for our release and their silence.

Ogilvie called me in twenty minutes later. 'Sit down, Malcolm.' He bent to his intercom. 'No more calls for the rest of the morning, please,' he said ominously, then looked at me. 'I think we have a lot to talk about. How are you feeling?'

I felt he really wanted to know, so I said, 'A bit drained.'

'The Swedes treat you all right?'

'No complaints.'

'Right. Let's get to the crux. Who killed Ashton?'

'Of my own knowledge I don't know. At the time I thought he'd caught a couple from the Swedes – there was a lot of shooting going on. Then Henty told me Benson had shot him.'

'But you didn't see Benson shoot him.'

'That's correct.'

Ogilvie nodded. 'That fits with what Godwin and Brent told me. Now, who killed Benson?'

'Henty said he did it. He said he saw Benson shooting at Ashton so he drew his own gun and went after him. Apparently Benson was at the top of the slope in the trees. He said that Benson shot at him, too, so he shot back and killed him. I didn't even know Henty was armed.'

'Have you thought why Benson should have killed Ashton? It's not the normal thing for an old family retainer to do to his master.'

A humourless thought crossed my mind: in the less inventive early British detective stories it was always the butler who committed the murder. I said, 'I can think of a reason but it doesn't depend on Benson's status as a servant.'

'Well?'

'Henty was coming up on my right, and Brent and Godwin angling in from the left. Ashton was just above, but there was a big boulder screening me from the top of the slope. I didn't see Benson and I don't think he saw me. But he did see Larry, and Larry was a Russian, remember. When Ashton stopped and turned, and showed signs of coming down, then Benson shot him.'

'To prevent him falling into the hands of the Russians. I see.'

I said, 'And that makes him something more than a family servant.'

'Possibly,' said Ogilvie. 'But I've been going into the history of Howard Greatorex Benson and the man is as

191

pure as the driven snow. Born in Exeter in 1912, son of a solicitor; normal schooling but flunked university entrance to his father's disappointment. Did clerical work for a firm in Plymouth and rose to be the boss of a rather small department. Joined the army in 1940 – rose to be a sergeant in the RASC – he was an ideal quarter-master type. Demobilized in 1946, he went to work for Ashton, running the firm's office. There he ran into the Peter Principle; he was all right as long as the firm remained small but, with expansion, it became too much for him. Remember he never rose to be more than a sergeant – he was a small-scale man. So Ashton converted him into a general factotum which would seem to be ideal for Benson. There'd be nothing too big for him to handle, and he was glad to be of service. Ashton probably got his money's worth out of him. He never married. What do you think of all that?'

'Did you get that from the computer?'

'No. The brains are still baffled. They're telling me now Benson can't be in the data bank.'

'They're wrong,' I said flatly. 'He popped up when I asked Nellie.'

Ogilvie looked at me doubtfully, then said, 'But what do you think of his history as I've related it?'

'There's nothing there to say why he should kill Ashton. There's nothing there to say why he should be carrying a gun in the first place. Did he have a pistol permit?'

'No.'

'Have you traced the gun?'

Ogilvie shrugged. 'How can we? The Swedes have it.' He pondered for a moment, then opened a quarto-sized, hard-backed notebook and took the cap off his pen. 'I wanted to go for the main point first, but now you'll tell me, in detail, everything that happened right from the time Ashton and Benson left their flat in Stockholm.'

That took the rest of the morning. At quarter to one Ogilvie recapped his pen. 'That's it, then. Now you can go home.'

'Am I suspended from duty?'

He looked at me from lowered eyebrows. 'There are a few people around who would like to see you fired. Others favour a transfer to the Outer Hebrides so you can counter industrial espionage into the production of Harris Tweed; they're talking about a twenty-year tour of duty. Have you any idea of the trouble this enterprise of ours has caused?'

'I have a good imagination.'

He snorted. 'Have you? Well, imagine how the Swedes felt about it, and imagine their reaction when we began to put on the pressure at a high level. It got up to the Cabinet, you know, and the Ministers aren't at all happy. They're talking about bungling amateurs.'

I opened my mouth to speak, but he held up his hand. 'No, you're not suspended from duty. What you did was under my instruction, and I can't see that you could have done differently given the circumstances. Neither of us expected Benson to kill Ashton, so if anyone carries the can it's me, as head of the department. But this department is now under extreme pressure. There's an inter-departmental meeting tomorrow morning at eleven at which the screws will begin to turn. You will be required to attend. So you will go away now and come back here at ten-fifteen tomorrow, rested and refreshed, and prepared to have a hard time. Do you understand?'

'Yes.'

'And I would be obliged if you do not disclose to the committee that you are aware of the Ashton file in Code Black. We're in enough trouble already.'

I stood up. 'All right, but I'd like to know one thing – what happened to the bodies?'

'Ashton and Benson? They were brought back to England two weeks ago. There was a funeral service in Marlow and they are buried in adjoining graves in the cemetery.'

'How did Penny take it?'

'As you might expect. Both the daughters were hit rather badly. I wasn't there myself, of course, but I was informed of the circumstances. I managed to have word passed to Miss Ashton that you were in America but were expected back in the near future. I thought that advisable.'

Advisable and tactful. 'Thanks,' I said.

'Now go away and prepare your thoughts for tomorrow.' I walked towards the door, and he added, 'And Malcolm: regardless of how the meeting goes, I want you to know there is much still to be explained about the Ashton case – and it will be explained. I am becoming very angry about this.'

As I left I thought that Ogilvie angry might be formidable indeed.

I was left to my own thoughts for a long time while the committee meeting was in progress; it was twelve-fifteen before an usher entered the ante-room and said, 'Will you come this way, Mr Jaggard.' I followed him and was shown into a large, airy room overlooking an inner courtyard somewhere in Westminster.

There was a long, walnut table around which sat a group of men, all well-dressed and well-fed, and all in late middle-age. It could have been the annual meeting of the directors of a City bank but for the fact that one of them wore the uniform of a Commander of the Metropolitgan Police and another was a red-tabbed colonel from the General Staff. Ogilvie twisted in his chair as I entered and indicated I should take the empty seat next to him.

Chairing the meeting was a Cabinet Minister whose politics I didn't agree with and whose personality I had always thought of as vacillating in the extreme. He showed no trace of vacillation that morning, and ran the meeting like a company sergeant-major. He said, 'Mr Jaggard, we have been discussing the recent Swedish operation in which you were involved, and in view of certain differences of opinion Mr Ogilvie has suggested that you appear to answer our questions yourself.'

I nodded, but the colonel snorted. 'Differences of opinion is putting it mildly.'

'That has nothing to do with Mr Jaggard, Colonel Morton,' said the Minister.

'Hasn't it?' Morton addressed me directly. 'Are you aware, young man, that you've lost me my best man in Scandinavia? His cover is blown completely.'

I concluded that Morton was Henty's boss.

The Minister tapped the table with his pen and Morton subsided. 'The questions we shall ask are very simple and we expect clear-cut, unequivocal answers. Is that understood?'

'Yes.'

'Very well. Who killed Ashton?'

'I didn't see who shot him. Henty told me it was Benson.'

There was a stir from lower down the table. 'But you don't know that he did, other than you have been told so.'

I turned and looked at Lord Cregar. 'That is correct. But I have, and still have, no reason to disbelieve Henty. He told me immediately after the event.'

'After he had killed Benson?'

'That's right.'

Cregar regarded me and smiled thinly. 'Now, from what you know of Benson, and I'm assuming you had the man investigated, can you give me one reason why Benson should kill the man he had so faithfully served for thirty years?'

'I can think of no sound reason,' I said.

His lip curled a little contemptuously. 'Can you think of any unsound reasons?'

Ogilvie said tartly, 'Mr Jaggard is not here to answer stupid questions.'

The Minister said sharply, 'We shall do better if the questions are kept simple, as I suggested.'

'Very well,' said Cregar. 'Here is a simple question. Why did you order Henty to kill Benson?'

'I didn't,' I said. 'I didn't even know he was armed. The

195

rest of us weren't; those were Mr Ogilvie's instructions. Henty was in a different department.'

Colonel Morton said, 'You mean Henty acted on his own initiative?'

'I do. It all happened within a matter of, say, twenty seconds. At the time Benson was killed I was trying to help Ashton.'

Morton leaned forward. 'Now, think carefully, Mr Jaggard. My men are not in the habit of leaving bodies carelessly strewn about the landscape. What reason did Henty give for shooting Benson?'

'Self-defence. He said Benson was shooting at him, so he shot back.'

Colonel Morton leaned back and appeared satisfied, but Cregar said to the company at large, 'This man, Benson, seems to be acting more and more out of character. Here we have an old age pensioner behaving like Billy the Kid. I find it unbelievable.'

Ogilvie dipped his fingers into a waistcoat pocket and put something on the table with a click. 'This is a round of 9 mm parabellum found in Benson's room in Marlow. It would fit the pistol found with Benson's body. And we know that the bullet recovered from Ashton's body came from that pistol. We got that from the Swedes.'

'Precisely,' said Cregar. 'All you know is what the Swedes told you. How much is that really worth?'

'Are you suggesting that Benson did not kill Ashton?' asked Morton. There was a note of sourness in his voice.

'I consider it highly unlikely,' said Cregar.

'I don't employ men who are stupid enough to lie to me,' said Morton, in a voice that could cut diamonds. 'Henty said he saw Benson kill Ashton, and I believe him. All the evidence we have heard so far does not contradict that.'

Ogilvie said, 'Unless Lord Cregar is suggesting that my department, Colonel Moreton's department and Swedish Army Intelligence are in a conspiracy to put the blame for

Ashton's death on Benson and so shield the killer.' His voice was filled with incredulity.

The uniformed commander guffawed and Cregar flushed. 'No,' he snapped. 'I'm just trying to get to the bottom of something damned mysterious. Why, for instance, *should* Benson shoot Ashton?'

'He is not here to be asked,' said the Minister coolly. 'I suggest we stop this chasing of hares and address ourselves to Mr Jaggard.'

The Commander leaned forward and talked to me around Ogilvie. 'I'm Pearson – Special Branch. This Swedish operation isn't my bailiwick but I'm interested for professional reasons. As I take it, Mr Ogilvie did not want Ashton to become aware that British Intelligence was taking note of him. Do you know why?'

That was a tricky one because I wasn't supposed to know who Ashton really was. I said, 'I suggest you refer that question to Mr Ogilvie.'

'Quite so,' said the Minister. 'It involves information to which Mr Jaggard is not privy.'

'Very well,' said Pearson. 'At the same time he wanted Ashton out of Sweden because the Russians had become attracted, so he put pressure on Ashton by having a man pretend to be Russian and thus "explode Ashton out of Sweden", as he has put it. What I don't understand is why this kidnapping attempt in Strängnäs was necessary. Why did you try it?'

I said, 'They took tickets from Stockholm to Göteborg. That was all right with me. I intended to shepherd them along and, if they took ship from Göteborg to find out where they were going. The important thing was to get them out from under the Russians in Sweden. But when they gave us the slip and went to Strängnäs it became something more complex than a discreet escort operation. Stronger measures were necessary as sanctioned by Mr Ogilvie.'

'I see,' said Pearson. 'That was the point I misunderstood.'

'I misunderstood something, too,' said Cregar. 'Are we to assume that your instructions precluded the disclosure of yourself to Ashton?'

'Yes.'

'Yet according to what I've been told you did so. We have been informed by Mr Ogilvie this morning that you showed yourself to him. Deliberately. It was only when he saw you that he turned back. Is that not so?'

'That's correct.'

'So you disobeyed orders.'

I said nothing because he hadn't asked a question, and he barked, 'Well, didn't you?'

'Yes.'

'I see. You admit it. Now, with all respect to Colonel Morton's trust in the truthfulness of his staff, I'm not satisfied by the somewhat misty evidence presented here that Benson shot Ashton; but the fact remains that Ashton was shot by someone, and it is highly likely that he was shot *because* he turned back. In other words, he died because you disobeyed an order not to disclose yourself.' His voice was scathing. 'Why did you disobey the order?'

I was seething with rage but managed to keep my voice even. 'The idea was not to kill Ashton but to bring him out alive. At that time he was going into grave danger. There was heavy fire in that part of the forest where he was heading – machine-guns and mortars, together with rifle fire. Just what was going on I didn't know. It seemed imperative to stop him and he did stop and started to come back. That he was shot by Benson came as a complete shock.'

'But *you* don't know he was shot by Benson,' objected Cregar.

The Minister tapped with his pen. 'We have already been over that ground, Lord Cregar.'

'Very well.' Cregar regarded me and said silkily,

'Wouldn't you say that your conduct of this whole operation, right from the beginning, has been characterized by, shall we say, a lack of expertise?'

Ogilvie bristled. 'What Mr Jaggard has done has been on my direct instruction. You have no right or authority to criticize my staff like this. Address your criticisms to me, sir.'

'Very well, I will,' said Cregard. 'Right at the beginning I objected to your putting Jaggard on this case, and all the . . .'

'That's not my recollection,' snapped Ogilvie.

Cregar overrode him '. . . all the events since have proved my point. He let Ashton slip from under his nose at a time when he had free access to Ashton's home. That necessitated the Swedish operation which he has also botched, and botched for good, if I may say so, because Ashton is now dead. As for claiming that all he did was on your direct instructions, you have just heard him admit to disobeying your orders.'

'He used his initiative at a critical time.'

'And with what result? The death of Ashton,' said Cregar devastatingly. 'You have expounded before on the initiative of this man. I wasn't impressed then, and I'm still less impressed now.'

'That will be enough,' said the Minister chillily. 'We will have no more of this. Are there any more questions for Mr Jaggard? Questions that are both simple and relevant, please.' No one spoke, so he said, 'Very well, Mr Jaggard. That will be all.'

Ogilvie said in an undertone, 'Wait for me outside.'

As I walked to the door Cregar was saying, 'Well, that's the end of the Ashton case – after thirty long years. He was a failure, of course; never did come up to expectations. I suggest we drop it and get onto something more productive. I think . . .'

What Cregar thought was cut off by the door closing behind me.

* * *

They came out of committee twenty minutes later. Ogilvie stuck his head into the ante-room. 'Let's have lunch,' he proposed. He didn't seem too depressed at what had happened, but he never did show much emotion.

As we were walking along Whitehall he said, 'What do you think?'

I summoned a hard-fought-for smile. 'I think Cregar doesn't like me.'

'Did you hear what he said as you were leaving?'

'Something about the Ashton case being over, wasn't it?'

'Yes. Ashton is buried and that buries the Ashton case. He's wrong, you know.'

'Why?'

'Because from now on until everything is accounted for and wrapped up you are going to work full time on the Ashton case.' He paused, then said meditatively, 'I wonder what we'll find.'

26

In view of what had been said at the meeting Ogilvie's decision came as a profound surprise. The worst possibility that had come to mind was that I would be fired; drummed out of the department after my special card had been put through the office shredding machine. The best that occurred to me was a downgrading or a sideways promotion. I had the idea that Ogilvie had not been entirely joking when he had spoken of the Hebrides. That he was carrying on with the Ashton case, and putting me in charge, gave me a jolt. I wondered how he was going to make it stick with the Minister.

He told me. 'The Minister won't know a damned thing about it.' He gave me a wintry smile. 'The advantage of organizations like ours is that we really are equipped to work in secret.'

This conversation took place in the privacy of his office. He had refused to speak of the case at all after dropping his bombshell and the luncheon conversation had been innocuous. Back at the office he plunged into the heart of it.

'What I am about to do is unethical and possibly mutinous,' he said. 'But, in this case, I think I'm justified.'

'Why?' I asked directly. If I was going to be involved I wanted to know the true issues.

'Because someone has done a conjuring trick. This department has been deceived and swindled. Who organized the deception is for you to find out – it may have been Ashton himself, for all we know. But I want to know who organized it, and why.'

'Why pick me? As Cregar made plain, I've not done too well up to now.'

Ogilvie raised his eyebrows. 'You think not? You've satisfied me, and I'm the only man who matters. There are several reasons why I've picked you. First, you're the totally unexpected choice. Secondly, you are still the inside man in the Ashton family. Thirdly, I have complete confidence in you.'

I stood up and went to the window. A couple of pigeons were engaged in amorous play on the window ledge but flew away as I approached. I turned and said, 'I'm grateful for your thirdly, but not too happy about your secondly. As you know, I dropped into the middle of the Ashton case sheerly by chance and ever since then my private life has been intolerably disturbed. I have just harried a man to his death and you expect me to be *persona grata* with his daughters?'

'Penelope Ashton doesn't know of your involvement. I made sure of that.'

'That's not the point, and you know it,' I said sharply. 'You're too intelligent a man not to know what I mean. You're asking me to live a lie with the woman I want to marry – if she still wants to marry me, that is.'

'I appreciate the difficulty,' said Ogilvie quietly. 'You mustn't think I don't. But . . .'

'And don't ask me to do it for the good of the department,' I said. 'I hope I have higher loyalties than that.'

Ogilvie quirked his eyebrows. 'Your country, perhaps?'

'Even than that.'

'So you believe with E. M. Forster that if you had to choose between betraying your country and betraying your friend you would hope to have the guts to betray your country. Is that it?'

'I'm not aware that betraying my country comes into this,' I said stiffly.

'Oh, I don't know,' said Ogilvie musingly. 'Betrayal takes many forms. Inaction can be as much betrayal as action, especially for a man who has chosen your work of his own will. If you see a man walking on a bridge which you know

202

to be unsafe, and you do not warn him so that he falls to his death, you are guilty in law of culpable homicide. So with betrayal.'

'Those are mere words,' I said coolly. 'You talk about betrayal of the country when all I see is an interdepartmental squabble in which your *amour propre* has been dented. You loathe Cregar as much as he loathes you.'

Ogilvie looked up. 'How does Cregar come into this? Do you know something definite?'

'He's been trying to poke his nose in, hasn't he? Right from the beginning.'

'Oh, is that all,' said Ogilvie tiredly. 'It's just the nature of the beast. He's a natural scorer of points; it feeds his enormous ego. I wouldn't jump to conclusions about Cregar.' He stood up and faced me. 'But I really am sorry about your opinion of me. I thought I deserved better than that.'

'Oh, Christ!' I said. 'I'm sorry; I didn't really mean that. It's just that this thing with Penny has me all mixed up. The thought of talking to her – lying to her – makes me cringe inside.'

'Unfortunately it goes with the job. We're liars by profession, you and I. We say to the world we work for McCulloch and Ross, economic and industrial consultants, and that's a lie. Do you think my wife and daughters really know what I do? I lie to them every minute of every day merely by existing. At least Penny Ashton knows what you are.'

'Not all of it,' I said bitterly.

'You're not to blame for Ashton's death.'

I raised my voice. 'No? I drove him to it.'

'But you didn't kill him. Who did?'

'Benson did, damn it!'

Ogilvie raised his voice to a shout. 'Then find out why, for God's sake! Don't do it for me, or even for yourself. All her life that girl of yours has been living in the same house

203

as the man who eventually murdered her father. Find out why he did it – you might even be doing it for her sake.'

We both stopped short suddenly and there was silence in the room. I said quietly, 'You might have made your point – at last.'

He sat down. 'You're a hard man to convince. You mean I've done it?'

'I suppose so.'

He sighed. 'Then sit down and listen to me.' I obliged him, and he said, 'You're going to be in disgrace for a while. Everybody will expect that, including the Minister. Some sort of downgrading is indicated, so I'm going to make you a courier. That gives you freedom of action to move around in this country, and even out of it.' He smiled. 'But I'd hesitate about going back to Sweden.'

So would I. Captain Morelius would become positively voluble, even to the extent of speaking three consecutive sentences. And I knew what he'd say.

'We've been making quite a noise in here,' said Ogilvie. 'Had a real shouting match. Well, that will add verisimilitude to an otherwise bald and unconvincing narrative. There's one thing about being in an organization of spies – news gets around fast. You may expect some comments from your colleagues; can you stand that?'

I shrugged. 'I've never worried much about what people think of me.'

'Yes,' he agreed. 'Cregar discovered that when he first met you. All right; you'll have complete autonomy on this job. You'll do it in the way you want to do it, but it will be a solo operation; you'll have all the assistance I can give you short of men. You'll report your results to me and to no one else. And I do expect results.'

He opened a drawer and took out a slim file. 'Now, as for Penny Ashton, I laid some groundwork which will possibly help you. As far as she knows you have been in America for the past few weeks. I hope you didn't write from Sweden.'

'I didn't.'

'Good. She has been tactfully informed that you have been away on some mysterious job that has debarred you from writing to her. Knowing what she thinks she knows about your work it should seem feasible to her. However, you were informed of her father's death through the department, and you sent this cable.'

He passed the slip of paper across the desk. It was a genuine Western Union carbon copy emanating from Los Angeles. The content was trite and conventional, but it would have to do.

Ogilvie said, 'You also arranged for wreaths at the funeral through a Los Angeles flower shop and Interflora. The receipt from the flower shop is in this file together with other bits and pieces which a man might expect to pick up on a visit and still retain. There are theatre ticket stubs for current shows in Los Angeles, some small denomination American bills, book matches from hotels, and so on. Empty your pockets.'

The request took me by surprise and I hesitated. 'Come now,' he said. 'Dump everything on the desk.'

I stripped my pockets. As I took out my wallet Ogilvie delved in the small change I had produced. 'You see,' he said in triumph, and held up a coin. 'A Swedish crown mixed with your English money. It could have been a dead give-away. I'll bet you have a couple of Swedish items in your wallet. Get rid of them.'

He was right. There was a duplicate bar bill from the Grand which had yet to be transferred to my expense account, and a list of pound-kroner exchange rates made when I was trying to keep up with the vagaries of the falling pound sterling. I exchanged them for the Americana, and said, 'You were sure of me, after all.'

'Pretty sure,' he said drily. 'You got back from the States yesterday. Here is your air ticket – you can leave it lying around conspicuously somewhere. Penny Ashton, to the

205

best of my knowledge, is coming back from Scotland tomorrow. You didn't buy any Swedish clothing?'

'No.'

'There are a couple of shirts and some socks in that small case over there. Also some packets of cigarettes. All genuine American. Now, leave here, go back to your office and mope disconsolately. You've just been through the meat grinder and you can still feel the teeth. I expect Harrison will want to see you in about half an hour. Don't try to score any points off him; let him have his little triumph. Remember you're a beaten man, Malcolm – and good luck.'

So I went back to the office and slumped behind my desk. Larry rustled his paper and avoided my eyes, but presently he said, 'I hear you were with the top brass all morning.'

'Yes,' I said shortly.

'Was Cregar there?'

'Yes.'

'Bad?'

'You'll know all about it soon,' I said gloomily. 'I don't think I'll be around here much longer.'

'Oh.' Larry fell silent for a while, then he turned a page and said, 'I'm sorry, Malcolm. It wasn't your fault.'

'Somebody has to get the axe.'

'Mmm. No, what I meant is I'm sorry about you and Penny. It's going to be difficult.'

I smiled at him. 'Thanks, Larry. You're right, but I think I'll make out.'

Ogilvie was right in his prediction. Within the hour Harrison rang and told me to report to his office. I went in trying to appear subdued and for once did not address him as Joe, neither did I sit down.

He kept me standing. 'I understand from Mr Ogilvie that you are leaving this section.'

'I understand so, too.'

'You are to report to Mr Kerr tomorrow.' His eyes glinted with ill-suppressed joy. He had always thought me too big for my britches and now I was demoted to messenger-boy – thus are the mighty fallen. 'This is really very difficult, you know,' he said fretfully. 'I'm afraid I'll have to ask you to clean out your desk before you leave today. There'll be another man coming in, of course.'

'Of course,' I said colourlessly. 'I'll do that.'

'Right,' he said, and paused. I thought for a moment he was going to give me a homily on the subject of mending my ways, but all he said was, 'You may leave, Jaggard.'

I went and cleared out my desk.

27

I trotted in to see Kerr next morning. He was one of several Section heads, but his Section was the only one to make a financial profit because, among other things, it ran the legitimate side of McCulloch and Ross, the bit the public knew about. It made a good profit, too, and so it ought; if it made a loss with all the professional expertise of the other sections behind it then Kerr ought to have been fired. Under Kerr also came several other miscellaneous bits and pieces including the couriers – the messenger-boys.

He seemed somewhat at a loss as to how to deal with me. 'Ah, yes – Jaggard. I think I have something here for you.' He handed me a large, thick envelope, heavily sealed. 'I'm told you know where to deliver that. It appears that . . . er . . . delivery may take some time, so you may be absent for a period.'

'That's so.'

'I see,' he said blankly. 'Will you be needing desk space – an office?'

'No, I don't think so.'

'I'm glad. We're tight for space.' He smiled. 'Glad to have you . . . er . . . with us,' he said uncertainly. I don't know what Ogilvie had told him but evidently he was baffled by my precise status.

In my car I opened the envelope and found £1000 in used fivers. That was thoughtful of Ogilvie but, after all, I could hardly claim expenses in the normal way on this operation. I put the money in the special locker built under the front passenger seat and drove to the police station in Marlow where I asked for Honnister. He came out front to meet me. 'You haven't been around for a while,' he said, almost accusingly. 'I've been trying to get you.'

'I've been in the States for a few weeks. What did you want me for?'

'Oh, just a chat,' he said vaguely. 'You must have been away when Ashton and Benson were killed in Sweden.'

'Yes, but I was told of it.'

'Funny thing, Ashton going away like that.' There was a glint in his eye. 'And then getting messily killed. Makes a man wonder.'

I took out a packet of cigarettes and offered it. 'Wonder what?'

'Well, a man like Ashton makes his pile by working hard and then, when he's still not too old to enjoy it, he suddenly gets dead.' He looked at the packet in my hand. 'No, I don't like American coffin nails. They take good Virginia tobacco, mix it with Turkish, then roast it and toast it and ultra-violet-ray it until it tastes like nothing on God's earth.'

I shrugged. 'Everybody dies. And you can't take it with you, although they tell me Howard Hughes tried.'

'Seen Penelope Ashton?'

'Not yet.' I lit a cigarette although I didn't like them, either. 'I'll be going to the house. I hear she's expected back today. If she's not there I'll see Gillian anyway.'

'And she'll see you,' said Honnister. 'But only barely. I had a talk with Crammond. He tells me Mayberry hasn't been brought to trial, and it's not likely that he will. He's unfit to plead.'

'Yes, I know about that.'

Honnister eyed the desk sergeant and then pushed himself upright from the counter. 'Let's have a noggin,' he proposed. I agreed quickly because it meant he wanted to talk confidentially and I was short of information. On the way to the pub he said, 'You didn't come to chat for old times' sake. What are you after?'

I said, 'When we started investigating we concentrated on Ashton and didn't look too closely at Benson, although at one point it did cross my mind that he might have chucked the acid.'

'Not the act of an old family servant.'

Neither was drilling his master full of holes – but I didn't say that aloud. 'Did you check on him?'

We turned into the Coach and Horses. 'A bit; enough to put him in the clear.' Honnister addressed the landlord. 'Hi, Monte; a large scotch and a pint of Director's.'

'My shout,' I said.

'It's okay – I'm on an expense account.'

I smiled. 'So am I.' I paid for the drinks and we took them to a table. It happened to be the same table at which I'd proposed marriage to Penny; it seemed a lifetime ago. It was early, just before midday, and the pub was quiet. I said, 'I've developed an interest in Benson.'

Honnister sank his nose into his beer. When he came up for air he said, 'There's been something funny going on in the Ashton family. This will have to be tit-for-tat, you know.'

'I'll tell you as much as I'm allowed to.'

He grunted. 'A fat lot of good that'll do me.' He held up his hand. 'All right, I know your lips are sealed and all that bull, and that I'm just a bumbling country copper who doesn't know which end is up – but tell me one thing: was Ashton kidnapped?'

I smiled at Honnister's description of himself which was a downright lie. 'No, he went under his own steam. He specifically asked that the police not be involved.'

'So he thought we might be. That's interesting in itself. And Benson went with him. What do you want to know about him?'

'Anything you can tell me that I don't know already. I'm scraping the bottom of the barrel.'

'Bachelor – never married. Worked for Ashton since the dark ages – butler, valet, handyman, chauffeur – you name it. Age at death, sixty-four, if you can believe *The Times*.'

'Any family – brothers or sisters?'

'No family at all.' Honnister grinned at me. 'As soon as I saw that bit in *The Times* I got busy. The itch in my bump of curiosity was driving me mad. Benson had a bit of money, about fifteen thousand quid, which he left to Dr Barnardo's Homes for Boys.'

'Anything else?' I asked, feeling depressed.

'Ever been in a war?' asked Honnister unexpectedly.

'No.'

'Seen any deaths by violence?'

'A few.'

'So have I, in my professional capacity. I've also seen the results of bombs and shellfire. It was a bit difficult to tell after a pathologist had been at them but I'd say Ashton had been shot in the back twice, and Benson shot through the head from the front. Caught in a shell blast, my arse!'

'You've seen the bodies!'

'I made it my business to – unofficially, of course. I went to the mortuary here. I told you my bump of curiosity was itching.'

'Charlie, you keep that under your bloody hat or you'll find yourself in dead trouble. I really mean that.'

'I told you before I can keep secrets,' he said equably. 'Anyway, Sweden isn't in my parish, so there's nothing I can do about it. If they were killed in Sweden,' he added as an afterthought.

'They were killed in Sweden,' I said. 'That's genuine. And they *were* killed in a Swedish battle practice area while manoeuvres were going on.' I paused. 'Probably *The Times* got the report wrong.'

'In a pig's eye,' said Honnister pointedly.

I shrugged. 'Anyone else here seen the bodies?'

'Not that I know of. The coffins arrived here sealed and complete with death certificates, probably signed by one of your department's tame doctors. Christ, talk about medical ethics! Anyway, they're underground now.'

'Any more about Benson?'

'Not much. He lived a quiet life. He had a woman in Slough but he gave that up about five years ago.'

'What's her name?'

'It won't do you any good,' he said. 'She died of cancer eighteen months ago. Benson paid for her treatment in a private ward – for old times' sake, I suppose. Other than that there's nothing I can tell you. There was nothing much to Benson; he was just a sort of old-maid bachelor with nothing remarkable about him. Except one thing.'

'What was that?'

'His face. He'd taken a hell of a beating at one time or other. Nature didn't make him like that – man did.'

'Yes,' I said. I was bloody tired of coming up against dead ends. I thought about it and decided that my best bet would be to look into Benson's army career but I wasn't sanguine that anything would come of that.

'Another drink?'

'No, thanks, Charlie. I want to see the Ashtons.'

'Give them my regards,' he said.

I drove to the Ashton house and, to my surprise, bumped into Michaelis who was just leaving. Under his arm he carried a loose-leaf ledger about as big as two bibles. 'What the devil are you doing here?'

He grinned. 'Playing puff-puffs. You know I'm interested and Miss Ashton gave me permission to mess about in the attic pretty nearly any time I like. It really is a fascinating set-up.'

I suppose it wasn't too weird that a counter-espionage agent should be nuts on model railways. I indicated the big book. 'What's that?'

'Now this is really interesting,' he said. 'Let me show you.' He rested the book on the bonnet of my car. The leters 'LMS' were inscribed on the leather-bound cover in gilt. 'This is a set of timetables for the old LMS – the London Midland and Scottish railway that was before nationalization. Effectively speaking, the railways were nationalized in 1939 and all the trains were steam in those days.'

He opened the book and I saw column after column of figures. 'Ashton was duplicating the LMS timetable, but I haven't figured out which year he was using so I'm taking this home to check against some old Bradshaws I have. Ashton's system up there in the attic isn't what you'd call standard practice in the model world – most of us can't afford what he'd got. I told you about those microprocessors he can program. These figures give the settings needed to the control panel to duplicate parts of the LMS timetable. He'd also got similar books for other pre-war railway companies – the London and North-Eastern, the Great Western and so on. It's bloody remarkable.'

'Indeed it is,' I said. 'Which Miss Ashton gave you permission?'

'Gillian. I talked to her a lot in hospital, about her father at the beginning, but one thing led to another. She was lonely, you know, being all bandaged up like that. I used to read books and newspapers for her. Anyway, I talked about the model railway and she found I was interested so she said I could come and play.'

'I see.'

'Gillian's a very nice girl,' he said. 'We get on very well.' He paused. 'I don't spend all my time in the attic.'

I studied Michaelis in a new light. It occurred to me that he was unmarried like myself and, if all went well with both of us, I was probably talking to my future brother-in-law. 'Is Gillian home now?'

'Yes – and she's expecting Penny for lunch.' He slammed the ledger closed. 'I heard on the grapevine what's happened to you. I think it's a bloody disgrace. Who the hell was to know . . .'

I interrupted. 'The less said about it the better, even in private. Don't talk about it at all – ever. That way nothing will slip out accidentally.' I consulted my watch. 'If you're

213

so chummy with Gillian I thought you might be staying for lunch.'

He shook his head. 'I don't feel like facing Penny so I made an excuse. You see, Penny hasn't told Gillian about us – the department, I mean. She doesn't know anything about it and that makes it easier. But I haven't seen Penny since we came back from Sweden and I haven't the guts to face her yet – not after what happened. I have a weird feeling she might read my mind.'

'Yes,' I agreed. 'It is bloody difficult.'

'You're more involved than I am,' he said. 'How do you feel about it?'

'Pretty much the same as you, but maybe a bit more so. Well, I'll go in and see Gillian. See you around.'

'Yes,' said Michaelis. 'I hope so.'

28

I had forgotten that Gillian was not very pretty to look at and she came as a renewed shock. Her face was puckered and drawn with scar tissue and her right eyelid was pulled almost closed. The first few moments were not at all easy; there was the double embarrassment of condoling on the death of her father and coping with her dreadful appearance, and I hoped my face did not reflect what I felt. But she put me at my ease, gave me a scotch and had a sherry herself.

Of her father she had little to say beyond expressing a puzzled sadness and a total lack of knowledge of his motives. 'What can I say? There *is* nothing to be said, except that I'm deeply sorry and totally bewildered.'

Of herself she had come to terms with her affliction and was prepared to talk about it. 'Of course, it will be better after the plastic surgery. I'm told the best man for that is in America, and Penny wants me to go over. But my face is not so nice now, and I don't go out much.' She smiled lopsidedly. 'I saw you talking to Peter Michaelis outside. Do you know him?'

I said carefully, 'I met him at the hospital.'

'Oh, yes; you would, of course.' She smiled again, and there was a happy sparkle in her good eye. 'One never thinks of policemen as ordinary human beings – just shadows dashing about on television arresting people. Peter is such a delightful man.'

I agreed that a policeman's lot, etc., 'Must cramp their social lives.'

'He just told me about Mayberry. It appears the man is quite insane. Penny told me about . . . about the mistake.'

'So you know.'

'She waited until I'd been home a few days. I suppose she was right to withhold it until then. I wasn't in any condition to take more shocks. But how awful for her. It took a great deal of straight talking from me to make her carry on with Professor Lumsden.'

'I'm glad you did.'

Gillian looked at me closely. 'There's something wrong between you and Penny, isn't there? I think she's unhappy about it. What is it, Malcolm?'

'I don't know if the trouble altogether concerns me,' I said. 'I rather think she's unhappy about what happened to you, and then to your father.'

'No,' she said pensively. 'She appears to involve you in it, and I don't know why. She won't talk about it, and that's unlike her.' She turned her head to the window as a car drew up. 'Here she is now. You'll stay for lunch, of course.'

'Glad to.'

I was pleased to find that Penny was pleased to see me. 'Oh, Malcolm!' she cried, and hurried to meet me. I met her half way across the room, took her in my arms, and kissed her.

'I was very sorry to hear about your father.'

She looked beyond me to where Gillian sat, and said quietly, 'I want to talk to you about that afterwards.'

I nodded. 'Very well.'

'A sherry,' she said. 'A sherry, to save my life. Lummy and I have talked our throats dry this morning.'

So we had lunch, at which we chatted amiably and kept away from controversial subjects. We discussed Gillian's forthcoming trip to the United States, and Penny asked about my experiences there. 'I was told where you were,' she said obliquely.

Later she said, 'Gillian and I have decided to sell the house. It's much too big for the two of us, so we've decided to set ourselves up in a decent flat in town. Gillian will be closer to the theatres and concert halls, and I won't have to commute to the lab.'

'That sounds sensible,' I said. 'When do you move?'

'I'll be going to America with Gillian,' she said. 'We're selecting some of the best pieces from here and the rest will be auctioned, the antiques at Sotheby's and the rest of the stuff from the house. But we'll be in America then. I couldn't bear to stay and see the place sold up. So I suppose the auction will be in about three weeks. I'm making the final arrangements this afternoon.'

And that would put paid to Michaelis's fun and games with the model railway. I wondered if he was preparing to put in a bid.

After lunch Gillian pleaded tiredness and went to rest in her room, but I rather think she wanted to leave us alone together. Penny and I sat before the blazing fire with a pot of coffee and I could tell she was getting set for a serious discussion. 'Malcolm,' she said, 'what's the truth about Daddy?'

I offered her one of my American cigarettes which she took. 'I don't think anyone will ever know.'

'Did he die the way they said? You must know, being who you are, even though you were in America at the time. You were investigating him, after all.'

'My information is that he was in a Swedish army proving ground where they were using live ammunition when he was killed.'

'And that's the truth?' she said steadily. 'You wouldn't lie to me?'

'That's the truth.' But not the whole truth, Jaggard, you bastard!

She was silent for a while, gazing into the flames. 'I don't understand,' she said at last. 'I don't understand any of it. What was he doing in Sweden?'

'Apparently nothing very much, from what I can gather. He was living quietly in Stockholm with Benson to look after him. He read a lot and went to the occasional concert. A quiet and placid life.'

'How do you know this?'

'The department checked, of course.'

'Of course,' she said colourlessly. 'I'm going to Sweden. I want to find out for myself. Will you come with me?'

That was a poser! I could imagine the expression on the face of the colonel of the Royal Södermanland Regiment if I poked my nose into Strängnäs again. I needed no imagination at all to picture the cold grey eyes of Captain Morelius of Swedish Army Intelligence.

'That may not be easy,' I said. 'I've just been transferred and my time isn't my own.'

'Transferred from your department?'

'No, just within the department, but I may be office-bound from now on. Still, I'll see what I can do.' Which would be precisely nothing. 'Look, Penny, how would it be if I arranged for you to talk with my chief? He can tell you all that's known about your father in Sweden.' And he can tell my damned lies for me, I thought savagely.

She thought about it, then said, 'Very well. But that doesn't mean I'm not going to Sweden.'

'I'll arrange it.' I rose to pour us some more coffee. 'Penny, what's happening to us? I still want to marry you, but every time I get near the subject you edge away. I'm very much in love with you and it's becoming frustrating. Have you turned off?'

She cried, 'Oh, Malcolm, I'm sorry; I really am. Everything turned topsy-turvy so suddenly. First there was Gillian, then Daddy – and then you. I've been going about looking at people I know and wondering if what I think I know is really so. Even Lummy has come under scrutiny – I'm beginning to worry him, I think. He imagines I'm going paranoid.'

'It's not been too easy for me, either,' I said, 'I didn't want to have anything to do with the Ashton case.'

'The Ashton case,' she repeated. 'Is that what they call it?' When I ndoded, she said, 'That takes the humanity out

218

of it, doesn't it? When it's a "case" it's easy to forget the flesh and blood because a case is mostly dockets and paperwork. How would you like to be referred to as the Jaggard case?'

'Not much,' I said sombrely.

Penny took my hand. 'Malcolm, you'll have to give me time. I think – no – I *know* I love you, but I'm still a bit mixed up; and I don't know that I'm too happy about what you do with your life. That's something else which needs thinking about.'

'My God!' I said. 'You make it sound as though I go about eating live babies. I'm just a dreary counter-espionage man specializing in industry and making sure too many secrets don't get pinched.'

'You mean weapons?'

I shook my head. 'Not necessarily. That's not our pigeon – and we're not interested in the latest toothapste additive, either. But if an engineering firm has ploughed a couple of millions into research and come up with something revolutionary, then we don't want some foreign Johnny nicking it and going into competition with a head start. And, don't forget, the foreign Johnnies from the East are state supported.'

'But these things are patented, aren't they?'

'Patents are a dead giveaway. The really big stuff isn't patented, especially in electronics. If you produce a new electronic chip which does the work of eleventy thousand transistors the opposition can put the thing under a microscope and see what you've done, but how the hell you've done it is quite another thing, and our boys aren't telling. They're certainly not going to disclose the process in a published patent.'

'I see,' she said. 'But that means you're just another sort of policeman.'

'Most of the time,' I said. 'Our problem is that the theft of information, as such, is not illegal in this country. Suppose I stole a sheet of paper from your lab, say, and I was caught. I'd be found guilty of the theft of a piece of paper worth one penny, and I'd suffer the appropriate penalty. The fact that written on that paper was some formula worth a million quid wouldn't count.'

Her voice rose. 'But that's silly.'

'I agree,' I said. 'Do you want to hear something really silly? A few years ago a chap was caught tapping a post office line. The only charge they could get him on was the theft of a quantity of electricity, the property of the Postmaster-General. It was about a millionth of a watt.' Penny laughed, and I said, 'Anyway, that's my job, and it doesn't seem all that heinous to me.'

'Nor to me, now you've explained it. But where did Daddy come into this?'

I said, 'You may not realize how important a man your father was. The catalysts he was developing were revolutionizing the economics of the oil industry and helping the economics of the country. When a man like that goes missing we want to know if anyone has been putting pressure on him, and why. Of course, if he's just running away from a shrewish wife then it's his affair, and we drop it. That's happened before.'

'And what conclusions did you come to about Daddy?'

'At first we tied it in with the attack on Gillian,' I said. 'But that's a dead end; we know Mayberry was a loner. As it is, as far as the department could make out, your father was living quietly in Stockholm and apparently taking an extended holiday. There's nothing we could do about that.'

'No,' said Penny. 'We're not yet a police state. What's being done now?'

I shrugged. 'The committee of brains at the top has decided to drop the matter.'

'I see.' She stared into the fire for a long time, then shook her head. 'But you'll have to give me time, Malcolm. Let me go to America. I'd like to get away from here and think. I'd like to . . .'

I held up my hand. 'Point taken – no further argument.

Change of subject. What were you doing in Scotland?' I was damned glad to change the subject; I'd been shaving the truth a bit too finely.

'Oh, that. Acting as adviser in the reconstruction of a laboratory. It's been worrying me because they're only willing to go up to P3 and I'm recommending P4. I was arguing it out with Lumsden this morning and he thinks I'm a bit . . . well, paranoiac about it.'

'You've lost me,' I said. 'What's P3? To say nothing of P4.'

'Oh, I forgot.' She waved her hand at the room. 'I was so used to talking things out here with Daddy that I'd forgotten you're a layman.' She looked at me doubtfully. 'It's a bit technical,' she warned.

'That's all right. Mine is a technical job.'

'I suppose I'd better start with the big row,' she said. 'An American geneticist called Paul Berg . . .'

It seemed that Berg blew the whistle. He thought the geneticists were diddling around with the gene in the same way the physicist had diddled around with the atom in the '20s and '30s, and the potential hazards were even more horrendous. He pointed out some of them.

It seems that the favourite laboratory animal of the geneticists is a bacterium called *Escherichia coli* and it is the most studied organism on earth – more is known about *E.coli* than about any other living thing. It was natural that this creature be used for genetic experimentation.

'There's only one snag about that,' said Penny. '*E.coli* is a natural inhabitant of the human gut, and I don't mean by ones and twos – I mean by the million. So if you start tinkering around with *E.coli* you're doing something potentially dangerous.'

'For example?' I asked.

'You remember Lummy's example of genetic transfer from *Rhizobium* to make an improved wheat. I said we'd have to be careful not to transfer another, more dangerous, gene. Now, consider this. Supposing you incorporated into

221

E.coli, accidentally or on purpose, the gene specifying the male hormone, testosterone. And supposing that strain of *E.coli* escaped from the laboratory and entered the human population. It would inhabit the digestive tracts of women, too, you know. They might start growing beards and stop having babies.'

'Christ!' I said. 'It would be a catastrophe.'

'Berg and some of his concerned friends called an international conference at Asilomar in California in 1975. It was well attended by the world's geneticists but there was much controversy. Gradually a policy was hammered out involving the concept of biological containment. Certain dangerous experiments were to be banned pending the development of a strain of *E.coli* unable to survive outside the laboratory and unable to colonize the human gut. The specification laid down was that the survival rate of the new strain should not be more than one in a thousand million.'

I smiled. 'That sounds like certainty.'

'It's not,' said Penny soberly, 'considering the numbers of *E.coli* around, but it's close. I think that was the most important conference in the history of science. For the first time scientists had got together to police themselves without having restrictions thrust upon them. I think at the back of all our minds was the bad example set by the atomic physicists.'

Fifteen months later the development of the new strain was announced by the University of Alabama. Penny laughed. 'A writer in *New Scientist* put it very well. He called it "the world's first creature designed to choose death over liberty".'

I said slowly, 'The first creature *designed* . . . That's a frightening concept.'

'In a way – but we've been designing creatures for a long time. You don't suppose the modern dairy cow is as nature intended it to be?'

'Maybe, but this strikes me as being qualitatively different. It's one thing to guide evolution and quite another to bypass it.'

'You're right,' she said. 'Sooner or later there'll be some hack or graduate student who will go ahead with a bright idea without taking the time to study the consequences of what he's doing. There'll be a bad mistake made one day – but not if I can help. And that brings us to Scotland.'

'How?'

'What I've just described is biological containment. There's also physical containment to keep the bugs from escaping. Laboratories are classified from P1 to P4. P1 is the standard microbiological lab; P4 is the other extreme – the whole of the lab is under negative air pressure, there are air locks, showers inside and out, changes of clothing, special pressurized suits – all that kind of thing.'

'And you're running into trouble with your recommendations in Scotland?'

'They're upranking an existing P2 lab. In view of what they want to do I'm recommending P4, but they'll only go to P3. The trouble is that a P4 lab is dreadfully expensive, not only in the building, but in the running and maintenance.'

'Are there no statutory regulations?'

'Not in this field; it's too new. If they were working with recognized pathogens then, yes – there are regulations. But they'll be working with good old *E.coli*, a harmless bacterium. You have about a couple of hundred million of them in your digestive tract right now. They'll stay harmless, too, until some fool transfers the wrong gene.' She sighed. 'All we have are guidelines, not laws.'

'Sounds a bit like my job – not enough laws.'

She ruefully agreed, and our talk turned to other things. Just before I left she said, 'Malcolm; I want you to know that I think you're being very patient with me – patient and thoughtful. I'm not the vapouring sort of female, and I usually don't have much trouble in making up my mind; but events have been getting on top of me recently.'

'Not to worry,' I said lightly. 'I can wait.'

'And then there's Gillian,' she said. 'It may have been

223

silly of me but I was worrying about her even before all this happened. She's never been too attractive to men and she looked like turning into an old maid; which would have been a pity because she'd make someone a marvellous wife. But now – ' she shook her head – 'I don't think there's a chance for her with that face.'

'I wouldn't worry about that, either,' I advised. 'Michaelis has a fond eye for her.' I laughed. 'With a bit of luck you'll not have one, but two, spies in the family.'

And with that startling thought I left her.

29

The British weekend being what it is I didn't get to the War Office until Monday. Anyone invading these islands would be advised to begin not earlier than four p.m. on a Friday; he'd have a walkover. I filled in the necessary form at the desk and was escorted by a porter to the wrong office. Two attempts later I found the man I needed, an elderly major called Gardner who was sitting on his bottom awaiting his pension. He heard what I had to say and looked at me with mournful eyes. 'Do you realize the war has been over for thirty years?'

I dislike people who ask self-evident questions. 'Yes, I'm aware of it; and I still want the information.'

He sighed, drew a sheet of paper towards him, and picked up a ball point pen. 'It's not going to be easy. Do you know how many millions of men were in the army? I suppose I'd better have the names.'

'I suppose you had.' I began to see why Gardner was still a grey-haired major. 'George Ashton, private in the Royal Electrical and Mechanical Engineers; demobilized 4 January, 1947.'

'In London?'

'Probably.'

'Could have been at Earl's Court; that was used as a demob centre. The other man?'

'Howard Greatorex Benson, sergeant in the Royal Army Service Corps. I don't know where he was demobilized.'

'Is that all you know of these men?'

'That's it.'

Gardner laid down his pen and looked at me glumly. 'Very well, I'll institute a search. You'd better give me your address or a phone number where I can find you.' He sniffed lugubriously. 'It'll take about a month, I should say.'

'That's not good enough. I need the information a damned sight faster than that.'

He waved a languid hand. 'So many records,' he said weakly. 'Millions of them.'

'Don't you have a system?'

'System? Oh, yes; we have a system – when it works.'

I set out to jolly him along and by a combination of sweet talk, name-dropping and unspoken threats got him out of his chair and into action, if one could dignify his speed by such a name. He stood up, regarding me owlishly, and said, 'You don't suppose we keep five million army records here, do you?'

I smiled. 'Shall we take your car or mine?'

I had what I wanted four hours later. At the time I thought I'd been lucky but later decided that luck had nothing to do with it because it had been planned that way thirty years earlier.

We started with the records of Earl's Court, now an exhibition hall devoted to such things as cars and boats, but then a vast emporium for the processing of soldiers into civilians. There they exchanged their uniforms for civilian clothing from the skin out – underwear, shirt, socks, shoes, suit, overcoat and the inevitable trilby or fedora hat of the 1940s. There was also the equivalent of a bank which took in no money but which lashed it out by the million; the serviceman's gratuity, a small – very small – donation from a grateful nation. At its peak the throughput of Earl's Court was 5000 men a day but by early 1947 it had dropped to a mere 2000.

The ledgers for 4 January were comparatively small; they had coped with only 1897 men – it had been a slack day. Infuriatingly, the ledgers were not listed in alphabetical order but by army number, which meant that every name and page had to be scanned. 'What was the name again?' said Gardner.

'Ashton.'

'Ashton,' he muttered, as he started on the first page of a ledger. 'Ashton . . . Ashton . . . Ashton.' I think he had to repeat the name to himself because he had the attention span of a retarded five-year-old.

I took another ledger and started to check it. It was like reading a war memorial with the difference that these were the survivors; a long list of Anglo-Saxon names with the odd quirky foreigner for spice, and even more boring than checking Heathrow passenger lists. Half an hour later Gardner said, 'What was that name again?'

I sighed. 'Ashton. George Ashton.'

'No – the other one.'

'Benson, Howard Greatorex.'

'He's here,' said Gardner placidly.

'*Benson!*' I went to the other side of the table and leaned over Gardner's shoulder. Sure enough, his finger rested under Benson's name, and the rest of the information fitted. Sergeant H. G. Benson, RASC, had been discharged on the same day, and from the same place, as Private G. Ashton, REME. I didn't think coincidence could stretch that far.

'That's a piece of luck,' said Gardner with smug satisfaction. 'Now we have his army number we shall find his file easily.'

'We haven't got Ashton yet,' I said, and we both applied ourselves to the ledgers. Ashton came up three-quarters of an hour later. Gardner scribbled on a piece of paper and drifted away in his somnambulistic manner to organize the search for the files, while I sat down and began to sort out what we'd found.

I tried to figure out the odds against two specific men in the British Army being demobilized on the same day and from the same place, but the mathematics were too much for me – I couldn't keep count of the zeroes, so I gave up.

It was stretching the long arm a bit too far to suggest that it had happened by chance to two men who subsequently lived together as master and servant for the next quarter of a century. So if it wasn't coincidence it must have been by arrangement.

So who arranged it?

I was still torturing my brain cells when Gardner came back an hour later with the files. There was a sticky moment when I said I wanted to take them away; he clung to them as though I was trying to kidnap his infant children. At last he agreed to accept my receipt and I left in triumph.

I studied the files at home, paying little attention to Ashton's file because it had nothing to do with the Ashton I knew, but I went over Benson's file in detail. His career was exactly as Ogilvie had described. He joined the army in 1940 and after his primary training and square-bashing he was transferred to the RASC and his promotions came pretty quickly at first – to lance-corporal, to corporal, and then to sergeant where he stuck for the rest of the war. All his service was in England and he never went overseas. Most of his duties were concerned with storekeeping, and from the comments of his superiors written in the file, he was quite efficient, although there were a few complaints of lack of initiative and willingness to pass the buck. Not many, but enough to block his further promotion.

His pay-book showed that he was unmarried but was contributing to the upkeep of his mother. The payments ceased in 1943 when she died. From that time until his discharge his savings showed a marked increase. I thought that anyone who could save out of army pay in those days must have lived a quiet life.

His medical record was similarly uneventful. Looked at *en masse* it appeared alarming, but closer inspection revealed just the normal ailments which might plague a man over a period of years. There were a couple of tooth extractions, two periods of hospitalization – one for a bout of influenza

228

and the other when he dropped a six-inch shell on his left foot. Luckily the shell was defused.

My attention was caught by the last entry. Benson had complained of aches in his left arm which had been preliminarily diagnosed as twinges of rheumatism and he had been given the appropriate treatment. He was thirty-three then, and rheumatism seemed a bit odd to me, especially since Benson had a cushy billet for a soldier in wartime. Not for him route marches in the pouring rain or splashing about joyfully in the mud; he worked in a warm office and slept every night in a warm bed.

Evidently the medical officer had thought it odd, too, when the treatment didn't work. In a different coloured ink he had appended a question mark after the previous diag-nosis of rheumatism, and had scribbled beneath, 'Suggest cardiogram.' The amendment was dated 19 December, 1946.

I went back to the general service file where I struck another oddity, because his immediate superior had written as the last entry, 'Suggested date of discharge – 21 March, 1947.' Underneath another hand had written, 'Confirmed', and followed it with an indecipherable signature.

I sat back and wondered why, if it had been suggested and confirmed that Benson should be discharged in March, 1947, he should have been discharged three months earlier. I consulted the medical record again and then rang Tom Packer.

This account started with Tom Packer because it was at his place I first met Penny. I rang him now because he was a doctor and I wanted confirmation of the idea that was burgeoning. If he didn't know what I wanted he'd be certain to know who could tell me.

After a brief exchange of courtesies, I said, 'Tom, I want a bit of free medical advice.'

He chuckled. 'You and the rest of the population. What is it?'

'Supposing a man complains of a pain in his left arm. What would you diagnose?'

'Hell, it could be anything. Have you got such a pain?'

'This is hypothetical.'

'I see. Could be rheumatism. What's the hypothetical age of this hypothetical chap?'

'Thirty-three.'

'Then it's unlikely to be rheumatism if he's lived a normal civilized life. I say unlikely, but it could happen. Did he say pain or ache?'

I consulted the medical file. 'Actually, he said ache.'

'Um. Not much to go on. Doctors usually have real patients to examine, not wraiths of your imagination.'

I said, 'Supposing the man was treated for rheumatism and it didn't work, and then his doctor thought a cardiogram was indicated. What would you think then?'

'How long has the man been treated for rheumatism?'

'Hang on.' I checked the file. 'Three months.'

Tom's breath hissed in my ear. 'I'm inclined to think the doctor should be struck off. Do you mean to say it took him three months to recognize a classic symptom of ischaemia?'

'What's that?'

'Ischaemic heart disease – *angina pectoris*.'

I suddenly felt much happier. 'Would the man survive?'

'That's an imponderable question – very iffy. *If* he's had that ache in his arm for three months and *if* it is ischaemic and *if* he hasn't had treatment for his heart then he'll be in pretty bad shape. His future depends on the life he's been living, whether he smokes a lot, and whether he's been active or sedentary.'

I thought of Sergeant Benson in an army stores office. 'Let's say he's been sedentrary and we'll assume he smokes.'

'Then I wouldn't be surprised to hear he's dropped dead of a coronary one morning. This *is* hypothetical, isn't it? Nobody I know?'

'No one you know,' I assured him. 'But not quite

hypothetical. There was a man in that condition back in 1946. He died about a month ago. What do you think of that?'

'I think that I think I'm surprised, but then, medicine isn't a predictive sport and the damndest things can happen. I wouldn't have thought it likely he'd make old bones.'

'Neither would I,' I said. 'Thanks for your trouble, Tom.'

'You'll get my bill,' he promised, and rang off.

I depressed the telephone rest, rang Penny, and asked her the name of Benson's doctor. She was faintly surprised but gave it to me when I said my boss wanted to tidy up a few loose ends before I was transferred. 'It's just a matter of firm identification.'

The doctor's name was Hutchins and he was a shade reserved. 'Medical files are confidential, you know, Mr Jaggard.'

'I don't want you to break any confidences, Dr Hutchins,' I said. 'But the man is dead after all. All I want to know is when Benson last had a heart attack.'

'Heart attack!' echoed Hutchins in surprise. 'I can certainly tell you all about that. It's no breach of confidentiality on a doctor's part if he says a man is perfectly well. There was absolutely nothing wrong with Benson's heart; it was in better condition than my own, and I'm a much younger man. He was as fit as a flea.'

'Thank you, Doctor,' I said warmly. 'That's all I wanted to know.' As I put down the telephone I thought I'd handled that rather well.

I sat back and checked off all the points.

ITEM: Sergeant Benson was suffering from heart disease at the end of 1946. His condition, according to Tom Packer, was grave enough so that no one would be surprised if he dropped dead.

HYPOTHESIS: Sergeant Benson had died of heart diease some time after 18 December, 1946 and before 4 January, 1947.

231

ITEM: Civilian Benson was discharged at Earl's Court on 4 January, 1947 and subsequently showed no trace of a bad heart condition.

HYPOTHESIS: Civilian Benson was a planted substitute for Sergeant Benson, exactly as Chelyuskin was a substitute for Private Ashton. The method was exactly the same and it happened on the same day and in the same place, so the likelihood of a connection was very high, particularly as Benson worked for Ashton for the rest of his life.

COROLLARY: Because the methods used were identical the likelihood was high that both substitutions were planned by the same mind. But Ogilvie had told me that the idea was Chelyuskin's own. Was Benson another Russian? Had two men been smuggled out?

It all hung together very prettily, but it still didn't tell me who Benson was and why he had shot Ashton.

30

Ogilvie was pleased about all that even though it got us no further into cracking the problem of why Benson should kill Ashton. At least we had seen the common linkage and he was confident that by probing hard enough and long enough we – or rather I – would come up with the truth. All the same he coppered his bet by having me do an intensive investigation into the life of Sergeant Benson before he joined the army. Ogilvie was a belt-and-braces man.

So I spent a long time in the West Country looking at school records in Exeter and work records in Plymouth. At Benson's school I found an old sepia class photograph with Benson in the third row; at least, I was assured it was Benson. The unformed young face of that thirteen-year-old gazing solemnly at the camera told me nothing. Some time in the ensuing years Benson had had his features considerably rearranged.

There were no photographs of an older Benson to be found in Plymouth, but I did talk to a couple of people who knew him before the war. The opinion was that he wasn't a bad chap, reasonably good at his job, but not very ambitious. All according to the record. No, he hadn't been back since the war; he had no family and it was assumed there was nothing for him to go back for.

All this took time and I got back to London just as Penny and Gillian were about to leave for America. I drove them to Heathrow myself and we had a drink in the bar, toasting surgical success. 'How long will you be away?' I asked Gillian. She wore a broad-brimmed straw hat with a scarf tied wimple-fashion and large dark glasses; style coming to the aid of concealment.

'I don't know; it depends how the operations go, I suppose.' She sketched a mock shiver. 'I'm not looking forward to it. But Penny will be back next week.'

Penny said, 'I just want to see Gillian settled and to make sure everything is all right, then I'll be back. Lummy wants to go to Scotland with me.'

'So you undermined his certainty.'

'Perhaps,' she said noncommittally.

'Did you arrange for the auction?'

'It's on Wednesday – viewing day on Tuesday. We already have a flat in town.' She took a notebook and scribbled the address. 'That's where you'll find me when I come back, if I'm not in Scotland.'

Gillian excused herself and wandered in the direction of the ladies' room. I took the opportunity of asking, 'How did you get on with Ogilvie?' I had arranged the meeting with Ogilvie as promised. He hadn't liked it but I'd twisted his arm.

Penny's brow furrowed. 'Well enough, I suppose. He told me pretty much what you have. But there was something . . .'

'Something what?'

'I don't know. It was like speaking in a great empty hall. You expect an echo to come back and you're a bit surprised when there isn't one. There seemed to be something missing when Ogilvie talked. I can't explain it any better than that.'

Penny was right – there was a hell of a lot missing. Her psychic antennae were all a-quiver and she perceived a wrongness but had no way of identifying it. Below the level of consciousness her intelligence was telling her there was something wrong but she didn't have enough facts to prove it.

Ogilvie and I *knew* there was something wrong because

we had more facts, but even we were blocked at that moment.

I saw them into the departure lounge, then went home and proceeded to draw up an elaborate chart containing everything I knew about the Ashton case. Lines (ruled) were drawn to connect the *dramatis personae* and representing factual knowledge; lines (dashed) were drawn representing hypotheses.

The whole silly exercise got me nowhere.

About this time I started to develop an itch in my mind. Perhaps it had been the drawing of the chart with its many connections which started it, but I had something buried within me which wanted to come to the surface. Someone had said something and someone else had said something else, apparently quite unrelated and the little man Hunch who lived in the back of my skull was beginning to turn over in his sleep. I jabbed at him deliberately but he refused to wake up. He would do so in his own good time and with that I had to be content.

On the Tuesday I went to the Ashton house for the public viewing. It was crowded with hard-eyed dealers and hopeful innocents looking for bargains and not finding much because all the good stuff had gone to the London flat or to Sotherby's. Still, there was enough to keep them happy; the accumulated possessions of a happy family life of fifteen years. I could see why Penny didn't want to be there.

I wasn't there to buy anything, nor was I there out of mere curiosity. We had assumed Ashton had hidden something and, although we hadn't found it, that didn't mean it wasn't there. When I say 'we' I really mean Ogilvie, because I didn't wholly go along with him on that. But he could have been right, and I was on hand to see if any suspicious-looking characters were taking an undue interest. Of course, it was as futile an exercise as drawing the chart because the normal dealer looks furtive and suspicious to begin with.

During the morning I bumped into Mary Cope. 'Hello, Mary,' I said, 'Still here, then.'

'Yes, sir. I'm to live in the house until it's been sold. I still have my flat upstairs.' She surveyed the throng of inquisitive folk as they probed among the Ashtons' possessions. 'It's a shame, sir, it really is. Everything was so beautiful before . . . before . . .'

She was on the verge of tears. I said, 'A pity, Mary, but there it is. Any offers for the house yet?'

'Not that I know of, sir.'

'What will you do when it's sold?'

'I'm to go to London when Miss Penny and Miss Gillian come back from America. I don't know that I'll like London, though. Still, perhaps it will grow on me.'

'I'm sure it will.'

She looked up at me. 'I wish I knew what was in God's mind when he does a thing like this to a family like the Ashtons. You couldn't wish for better people, sir.'

God had nothing to do with it, I thought grimly; what happened to the Ashtons had been strictly man-made. But there was nothing I could say to answer such a question of simple faith.

'It's not only Mr Ashton, though,' said Mary wistfully. 'I miss Benson. He was such a funny man – always joking and light-hearted; and he never had a wrong word for anyone. He did make us laugh, sir; and to think that he and Mr Ashton should die like that, and in a foreign country.'

'Did Benson ever talk about himself, Mary?'

'About himself, sir? How do you mean?'

'Did he ever tell anecdotes – stories – about his early life, or when he was in the army?'

She thought about it, then shook her head. 'No, Benson was a man who lived in the present. He'd joke about politicians, and what he'd read in the papers or seen on telly. A real comedian, Benson was; had us in stitches a lot of the time. I used to tell him he should have been on the stage, but he always said he was too old.'

A real comedian! What an epitaph for a man whose last macabre joke was to shoot his master. I said, 'You'd better look sharp, Mary, or some of these people will be stealing the spoons.'

She laughed. 'Not much chance of that, sir. The auctioneer has Securicor men all over the place.' She hesitated. 'Would you like a cup of tea? I can make it in my flat.'

I smiled. 'No, thank you, Mary. I don't think I'll be staying long this morning.'

All the same, I was there next day for the actual auction, and why I was there I didn't really know. Perhaps it was the feeling that with the dispersal of the contents of the house the truth about the Ashton case was slipping away, perhaps to be lost forever. At any rate I was there, impotent with ignorance, but on the spot.

And there, to my surprise, was also Michaelis. I didn't see him until late morning and was only aware of him when he nudged me in the ribs. The auctioneer was nattering about a particularly fine specimen of something or other so we withdrew to Ashton's study, now stripped rather bare. 'What a bloody shame this is,' he said. 'I'm glad Gillian isn't here to see it. Have you heard anything yet?'

'No.'

'Neither have I,' he said broodily. 'I wrote to her but she hasn't replied.'

'She's only been gone four days,' I pointed out gently. 'The postal services weren't that good even in their palmy days.'

He grinned and seemed oddly shy. 'I suppose you think I'm making a damned fool of myself.'

'Not at all,' I said. 'No more than me. I wish you luck.'

'Think I have a chance?'

'I don't see why not. In fact, I think you have everything

237

going for you, so cheer up. What are you doing here anyway?'

'That model railway still interests me. I thought that if it's broken up for sale I might put in a bid or two. Of course, in model railway terms to break up that system would be like cutting up the Mona Lisa and selling bits of it. But it won't be broken up and I won't have a chance. Lucas Hartman is here.'

'Who's he?'

'Oh, everybody in the model railway world knows Hartman. He's a real model railway buff, but he calls it railroad because he's an American. He's also quite rich.'

'And you think he'll buy it as it stands?'

'He's sure to. He's up in the attic gloating over it now.'

'How much do you think it will bring?' I asked curiously.

Michaelis shrugged. 'That's hard to say. It's not exactly standard stuff – there's so much extra built in that it's hard to put a price on it.'

'Have a try.'

'For the rail and rolling stock and normal control instrumentation, all of which is there, it would cost about £15,000 to build from scratch, so let's say it might bring between £7000 and £10,000 at auction. As for the other stuff built in, that's more difficult to assess. I'd say it'll double the price.'

'So you think it will bring somewhere between £15,000 and £20,000.'

'Something like that. Of course, the auctioneer will have a reserve price on it. Any way you look at it, Hartman will get it. He'll outbid the dealers.'

'Ah, well,' I said philosophically. 'It will fall into good hands – someone who appreciates it.'

'I suppose so,' said Michaelis gloomily. 'The bloody thing beat me in the end, you know.'

'What do you mean?'

'Well, you know those schedules I talked about – I showed you one of them.'

'The London, Midland and Scottish, I think it was.'

'That's right. I compared them against old Bradshaws and got nowhere. I even went right back to the mid-1800s and nothing made sense. The system doesn't seem to compare with any normal railway scheduling.'

'Not even when those schedules were clearly labelled "LMS" and so on,' I said slowly.

'They don't fit at any point,' said Michaelis. 'It beats me.'

There was a picture in my mind's eye of Ashton's clenched fist opening to reveal a railway timetable – Stockholm to Göteborg, and it was like a bomb going off in my skull. 'Jesus!'

Michaelis stared at me. 'What's wrong?'

'Come on. We're going to talk to that bloody auctioneer.'

I left the study at a fast stride and went into the crowded hall where the auction was taking place. The autioneer had set up a portable rostrum at the foot of the stairs and, as I elbowed my way through the throng towards it, I took a business card from my wallet. Behind me Michaelis said, 'What's the rush?'

I flattened myself against the wall and scribbled on the card. 'Can't explain now.' I pushed the card at him. 'See the auctioneer gets this.'

Michaelis shrugged and fought his way through to the rostrum where he gave the card to one of the auctioneer's assistants. I walked up the stairs and stood where I could easily be seen. The auctioneer was in mid-spate, selling an eighteen-place Crown Derby dinner service; he took the card which was thrust under his nose, turned it over, looked up at me and nodded, and then continued with hardly a break in his chant.

Michaelis came back. 'What's the panic?'

'We must stop the sale of that railway.'

'I'm all for that,' he said. 'But what's your interest?'

The auctioneer's hammer came down with a sharp crack. 'Sold!'

'It's too complicated to tell you now.' The auctioneer had

handed over to his assistant and was coming towards the stairs. 'It'll have to keep.'

The auctioneer came up the stairs. 'What can I do for you – er – ' He glanced at the card – 'Mr Jaggard.'

'I represent Penelope and Gillian Ashton. The model railway in the attic mustn't be sold.'

He frowned. 'Well, I don't know about that.'

I said, 'Can't we go somewhere a bit more quiet while I explain?'

He nodded and pointed up the stairs, so we went into one of the bedrooms. He said, 'You say you represent the Ashton sisters?'

'That's right.'

'Can you prove that?'

'Not with anything I carry with me. But I can give you written authority if you need it.'

'On your signature?'

'Yes.'

He shook his head. 'Sorry, Mr Jaggard, but that's not good enough. I was engaged by Penelope Ashton to sell the contents of this house. I can't vary that agreement without her authority. If you can give me a letter from her, that's different.'

'She's not easy to get hold of at short notice. She's in the United States.'

'I see. Then there's nothing to be done.' Something in my expression caused him to add quickly, 'Mr Jaggard, I don't know you. Now, I'm a professional man, engaged to conduct this sale. I can't possibly take instructions from any Tom, Dick or Harry who comes here telling me what to do or what not to do. I really don't conduct my business that way. Besides, the railway is one of the plums of the sale. The press is very interested; it makes a nice filler for a columnist.'

'Then what do you suggest? Would you take instruction from Miss Ashton's legal adviser?'

'Her solicitor? Yes, I might do that.' He frowned perplexedly. 'This all appears very odd to me. It seems, from what you say, that Miss Ashton knows nothing about this and it is something you are taking upon yourself. But if I have written instructions from her solicitor, then I'll withdraw the railway.'

'Thank you,' I said. 'I'll get in touch with him. Oh, by the way, what's the reserve price?'

He was affronted. 'I really can't tell you that,' he said coldly. 'And now you must excuse me. There are some important pieces coming up which I must handle myself.'

He turned to walk away, and I said desperately, 'Can you tell me when the railway will come up for sale?'

'Things are going briskly.' He looked at his watch. 'I'd say about three this afternoon.' He walked out.

'A telephone,' I said. 'My kingdom for a telephone.'

'There's one next door in Ashton's bedroom.' Michaelis looked at me a little oddly. 'This sudden interest in model railways doesn't seem kosher to me.'

I had a sudden thought. 'Where are those schedules?'

'In the attic; on a shelf under the control console. There are a dozen.'

'I want you in the attic on the double. Keep an eye on that railway and especially on those schedules. I don't want anything removed and I want note taken of anyone who takes a special interest. Now move.'

I went into Ashton's room and attacked the telephone. For the first time Ogilvie let me down; he wasn't in the office and no one knew where he was or when he'd be back. Neither was he at home. I left messages to say he should ring me at the Ashton house as soon as possible.

There were more frustrations. Mr Veasey of Michelmore, Veasey and Templeton was away in the fastness of Wales talking to a valued but bedridden client. His clerk would not make a decision in the matter, and neither would any of the partners. They did say they would try to get hold of Veasey by telephone and I had to be satisfied with that. I had no great hopes of success – Veasey didn't know me and I had no standing.

I went up to the attic and found Michaelis brooding over the railway. Several small boys were larking about and being chased off by a Securicor guard. 'Any suspects?'

'Only Hartman. He's been checking through those schedules all morning.' He nodded in the direction of the control console. 'There he is.'

Hartman was a broad-shouldered man of less than average height with a shock of white hair and a nut-brown lined face. He looked rather like Einstein might have looked if Einstein had been an American businessman. At that moment he was poring over one of the schedules and frowning.

I said, 'You're sure that *is* Hartman?'

'Oh, yes. I met him three years ago at a Model Railway Exhibition. What the hell are you really up to, Malcolm?'

I looked at the railway. 'You're the expert. Are there any other peculiarities about this other than the schedules?'

Michaelis stared at the spider web of rails. 'It did occur to me that there's an excessive number of sidings and marshalling yards.'

'Yes,' I said thoughtfully. 'There would be.'

'Why would there be?' Michaelis was baffled.

'Ashton was a clever bastard,' I said. 'He wanted to hide something so he stuck it right under our noses. Do you know how a computer works?'

'In a vague sort of way.'

I said, 'Supposing you instruct a computer that A=5. That tells the computer to take that number five and put it in a location marked A. Suppose you gave the instruction C=A+B. That tells the computer to take whatever number is in A, add it to whatever number is in B, and put the result in C.' I jerked my head towards the railway. 'I think that's what this contraption is doing.'

Michaelis gasped. 'A *mechanical* computer!'

'Yes. And those schedules are the programs which run it

242

– but God knows what they're about. Tell me, how many different kinds of rolling stock are there in the system? I'd say ten.'

'You'd be wrong. I counted sixty-three.'

'Hell!' I thought about it a little more. 'No, by God, I'm right! Ten for the numbers 0 to 9; twenty-six for the letters of the alphabet, and the rest for mathematical signs and punctuation. This bloody thing can probably talk English.'

'I think you're nuts,' said Michaelis.

I said, 'When Ashton was shot he couldn't talk but he was trying to tell me something. He pulled something from his pocket and tried to give it to me. It was a railway timetable.'

'That's pretty thin,' said Michaelis. 'Larry had one, too.'

'But why should a man in his last extremity try to give me, of all things, a railway timetable? I think he was trying to tell me something.'

'I can see why you want the sale stopped,' admitted Michaelis. 'It's a nutty idea, but you may be right.'

'I haven't got very far,' I said gloomily. 'Ashton's law firm won't play and Ogilvie's gone missing. I'd better try him again.'

So I did, but with no joy. I tried every place I thought he might be – his clubs, the restaurant he had once taken me to, then back to the office and his home again. No Ogilvie.

At half past two Michaelis sought me out. 'They're about to start bidding on the railway. What are you going to do?'

'Make another call.'

I rang my bank manager, who said, 'And what can I do for you this afternoon, Mr Jaggard?'

'Later today I'm going to write a largish cheque. There won't be enough funds to cover it, either in my current account or in the deposit account. I don't want it to bounce.'

'I see. How much will the cheque be for?'

'Perhaps £20,000.' I thought of Hartman. 'Maybe as much as £25,000. I don't quite know.'

'That's a lot of money, Mr Jaggard.'

I said, 'You know the state of my financial health, and you know I can cover it, not immediately but in a few weeks.'

'In effect, what you're asking for is a bridging loan for, say, a month.'

'That's it.'

'I don't see any difficulty there. We'll accept your cheque, but try to keep it down; and come in tomorrow – we'll need your signature.'

'Thanks.' I put down the telephone knowing that if I was wrong about the railway I was about to lose a lot of money. I couldn't see Ogilvie dipping into the department's funds to buy an elaborate toy, and the only person who might be happy about it would be Michaelis.

I went into the hall to see a small crowd gathered by the rostrum listening to a man talking. Michaelis whispered, 'They've got old Hempson from *Model Railway News* to give a pep-talk. I suppose they think that'll drive up the price.'

Hempson was saying, '. . . core of the system is the most remarkable console I have ever seen, using the ultimate in modern technology. It is this which makes this example of the art unique and it is to be hoped that the system will be sold as a complete unit. It would be a disaster if such a fine example should be broken up. Thank you.'

He stepped down to a low murmur of agreement, and I saw Hartman nodding in approval. The auctioneer stepped up and lifted his gavel. 'Ladies and gentlemen: you have just heard Mr Hempson who is an acknowledged expert, and his opinion counts. So I am about to ask for bids for the complete system. It would be normal to do this on site, as it were, but even in so large a house the attic is not big enough to hold both the exhibit and the crowd gathered here. However, you have all had the opportunity of examining this fine example of the model-maker's art, and on the table over there is a representative collection of the rolling stock.'

He raised his gavel. 'Now what am I bid for the complete system? Who will start the bidding at £20,000?'

There was a sigh – a collective exhalation of breath. 'Come,' said the auctineer cajolingly. 'You just heard Mr Hempson. Who will bid £20,000? No one? Who will bid £18,000?'

He had no takers at that, and gradually his starting price came down until he had a bid of £8000. 'Eight thousand I am bid – who will say nine? Eight-five I am bid – thank you, sir – who will say nine? Nine I am bid – who will say ten?'

Michaelis said, 'The dealers are coming in, but they won't stand a chance. Hartman will freeze them out.'

I had been watching Hartman who hadn't moved a muscle. The bidding crept up by 500s, hesitated at the £13,500 mark, and then went up by 250s to £15,000 where it stuck. 'Fifteen I am bid; fifteen I am bid,' chanted the auctioneer. 'Any advance on fifteen?'

Hartman flicked a finger. 'Sixteen I am bid,' said the auctioneer. 'Sixteen thousand. Any advance on sixteen?' The dealers were frozen out.

I held up a finger. 'Seventeen I am bid. Any advance on seventeen? Eighteen I am bid – and nineteen – and twenty. I have a bid of £20,000. Any advance on twenty?'

There was a growing rustle of interest as Hartman and I battled it out. At £25,000 he hesitated for the first time and raised his bid by £500. Then I knew I had him. I raised a single finger and the auctioneer said, 'Twenty-six and a half – any advance . . . twenty-seven, thank you, sir – twenty-eight I am bid.'

And so it went. Hartman lost his nerve at thirty and gave up. The auctioneer said, 'Any advance on thirty-one? Any advance on thirty-one? Going once,' *Crack!* 'Going twice.' *Crack!* 'Sold to Mr Jaggard for £31,000.'

Crack!

I was now the proud owner of a railway. Maybe it wasn't British Rail but perhaps it might show more profit. I said to Michaelis, 'I wonder if Ogilvie has that much in the petty cash box?'

Hartman came over. 'I guess you wanted that very much, sir.'

'I did.'

'Perhaps you would be so kind as to let me study the layout some time. I am particularly interested in those schedules.'

I said, 'I'm sorry. I acted as agent in this matter. However, if you give me your address I'll pass it to the owner for his decision.'

He nodded. 'I suppose that will have to do.'

Then I was surrounded by pressmen wanting to know who, in his right mind, would pay that much money for a toy. I was rescued by Mary Cope. 'You're wanted on the telephone, Mr Jaggard.'

I made my escape into Ashton's study. It was Ogilvie. 'I understand you wanted me.'

'Yes,' I said, wishing he had rung half an hour earlier. 'The department owes me £31,000 plus bank charges.'

'*What's that?*'

'You now own a model railway.'

His language was unprintable.

31

I saw Ogilvie at his home that night. His welcome was somewhat cool and unenthusiastic and he looked curiously at the big ledger I carried as he ushered me into his study. I dumped it on his desk and sat down. Ogilvie warmed his coat tails at the fire, and said, 'Did you really spend £31,000 on a toy train set?'

I smiled. 'Yes, I did.'

'You're a damned lunatic,' he said. 'And if you think the department will reimburse you, then I'll get the quacks in and have you certified. No bloody model railway can be worth that much.'

'An American called Hartman thought it worth £30,000,' I observed. 'Because that's how much he bid. You haven't seen it. This is no toy you buy your kid for Christmas and assemble on the floor before the living-room fire to watch the chuff-chuff go round in circles. This is big and complex.'

'I don't care how big and complex it is. Where the hell do you think I'm going to put it in the department budget? The accountants would have *me* certified. And what makes you think the department wants it?'

'Because it holds what we've been looking for all the time. It's a computer.' I tapped the ledger. 'And this is the programing for it. One of the programs. There are eleven more which I put in the office vaults.'

I told him how Michaelis had unavailingly tried to sort out the schedules and how I'd made an intuitive jump based on the timetable in Ashton's hand. I said, 'It would be natural these days for a theoretician to use a computer, but

Ashton knew we'd look into all his computer files and programs. So he built his own and disguised it.'

'It's the most improbable idea I've ever heard,' said Ogilvie. 'Michaelis is the train expert. What does he think?'

'He thinks I'm crazy.'

'He's not far wrong.' Ogilvie began to pace the room. 'I tell you what I think. If you're right then the thing is cheap at the price and the department will pay. If you're wrong then it costs *you* £31,000.'

'Plus bank charges.' I shrugged. 'I stuck out my neck, so I'll take the chance.'

'I'll get the computer experts on it tomorrow.' He wagged his head sadly. 'But where are we to put it? If I have it installed in the department offices it'll only accelerate my retirement. Should the Minister hear of it he'll think I've gone senile – well into second childhood.'

'It will need a big room,' I said. 'Best to rent a warehouse.'

'I'll authorize that. You can get on with it. Where is it now?'

'Still in the Ashtons' attic. Michaelis is locked in with it for the night.'

'Enthusiastically playing trains, I suppose.' Ogilvie shook his head in sheer wonderment at the things his staff got up to. He joined me at the desk and tapped the schedule. 'Now tell me what you think this is all about.'

It took four days to dismantle the railway and reassemble it in a warehouse in South London. The computer boys thought my idea hilarious and to them the whole thing was a big giggle, but they went about the job competently enough. Ogilvie gave me Michaelis to assist. The department had never found the need for a model railway technician and Michaelis found himself suddenly elevated into the rank of expert, first class. He quite liked it.

The chief computer man was a systems analyst called Harrington. He took the job more seriously than most of the others but even that was only half-serious. He installed a computer terminal in the warehouse and had it connected to a computer by post office land lines; not the big chap Nellie was hooked up to, but an ordinary commercial time-sharing computer in the City. Then we were ready to go.

About this time I got a letter from Penny. She wrote that Gillian was well and had just had the operation for the first of the skin grafts. She herself was not coming back immediately; Lumsden had suggested that she attend a seminar at Berkeley in California, so she wouldn't be back for a further week or ten days.

I showed the letter to Michaelis and he said he'd had one from Gillian, written just before the operation. 'She seemed a bit blue.'

'Not to worry; probably just pre-operation nerves.'

The itch at the back of my mind was still there, and so the buried connection was nothing to do with the railway. Little man Hunch was sitting up and rubbing his eyes but was still not yet awake. I badly needed to talk to Penny because I thought it was something she had said that had caused the itch. I was sorry she wasn't coming home for that reason among many.

One morning at ten o'clock Harrington opened the LNER schedule. 'The first few pages are concerned with the placement of the engines and the rolling stock,' he said. 'Now, let's get this right if we can. This is silly enough as it is without us putting our own bugs into the system.'

It took over an hour to get everything in the right place – checked and double checked. Harrington said, 'Page eleven to page twenty-three are concerned with the console settings.' He turned to me. 'If there's anything to your idea at all these Roms will have to be analysed to a fare-thee-well.'

'What's a Rom?'

'A read-only module – this row of boxes plugged in here. Your man, Michaelis, calls them microprocessors. They are pre-programed electronic chips – we'll have to analyse what they're programed to do. All right; let's get on with the setting.'

He began to call out numbers and an acolyte pressed buttons and turned knobs. When he had finished he started again from the beginning and another acolyte checked what the first had done. He caught three errors. 'See what I mean,' said Harrington. 'One bug is enough to make a program unworkable.'

'Are you ready to go now?'

'I think so – for the first stage.' He put his hand on the ledger. 'There are over two hundred pages here, so *if* this thing really is a computer and *if* this represents one program, then after a while everything should come to a stop and the console will have to be readjusted for the next part of the program. It's going to take a long time.'

'It will take even longer if we don't start,' I said tartly.

Harrington grinned and leaned over to snap a single switch. Things began to happen. Trains whizzed about the system, twenty or thirty on the move at once. Some travelled faster than others, and once I thought there was going to be a collision as two trains headed simultaneously for a junction; but one slowed just enough to let the other through and then picked up speed again.

Sidings and marshalling yards that had been empty began to fill up as engines pushed in rolling stock and then uncoupled to shoot off somewhere else. I watched one marshalling yard fill up and then begin to empty, the trains being broken up and reassembled into other patterns.

Harrington grunted. 'This is no good; it's too damned busy. Too much happening at once. If this is a computer it isn't working sequentially like an ordinary digital jog; it's working in parallel. It's going to be hell to analyse.'

The system worked busily for nearly two hours. Trains shot back and forth, trucks were pushed here and there, abandoned temporarily and then picked up again in what seemed an arbitrary manner. To me it was bloody monotonous but Michaelis was enthralled and even Harrington appeared to be mildly interested. Then everything came to a dead stop.

Harrington said, 'I'll want a video-camera up there.' He pointed to the ceiling. 'I want to be able to focus on any marshalling yard and record it on tape. And I want it in colour because I have a feeling colour comes into this. And we can slow down a tape for study. Can you fix that?'

'You'll have it tomorrow morning,' I promised. 'But what do you think now?'

'It's an ingenious toy, but there may be something more to it,' he said, noncommittally. 'We have a long way to go yet.'

I didn't spend all my time in the warehouse but went back three days later because Harrington wanted to see me. I found him at a desk flanked by a video-recorder and a TV set. 'We may have something,' he said, and pointed to a collection of miniature rolling stock on the desk. 'There *is* a number characterization.'

I didn't know what he meant by that, and said so. He smiled. 'I'm saying you were right. This railway is a computer. I think that any of this rolling stock which has red trim on it represents a digit.' He picked up a tank car which had ESSO lettered on the side in red. 'This one, for instance, I think represents a zero.'

He put down the tank car and I counted the trucks; there were nine, but one had no red on it. 'Shouldn't there be ten?'

'Eight,' he said. 'This gadget is working in octal instead of decimal. That's no problem – many computers work in octal internally.' He picked up a small black truck. 'And I think this little chap is an octal point – the equivalent of a decimal point.'

'Well, I'm damned! Can I tell Ogilvie?'

Harrington sighed. 'I'd rather you didn't – not yet. We haven't worked out to our satisfaction which number goes with which truck. Apart from that there is a total of sixty-three types of rolling stock; I rather think some of those represent letters of the alphabet to give the system alpha-numeric capability. Identification may be difficult. It should be reasonably easy to work out the numbers; all that it takes is logic. But letters are different. I'll show you what I mean.'

He switched on the video-recorder and the TV set, then punched a button. An empty marshalling yard appeared on the screen, viewed from above. A train came into view and the engine stopped and uncoupled, then trundled off. Another train came in and the same thing happened; and yet again until the marshalling yard was nearly full. Harrington pressed a button and froze the picture.

'This marshalling yard is typical of a dozen in the system, all built to the same specification – to hold a maximum of eighty trucks.' With his pen he pointed out something else. 'And scattered at pretty regular intervals are these blue trucks.'

'Which are?'

Harrington leaned back. 'If I were to talk in normal computer terms – which may be jargon to you – I'd say I was looking at an alphameric character string with a maximum capacity of eighty characters, and the blue trucks represent the spaces between words.' He jabbed his finger at the screen. 'That is saying something to us, but we don't know what.'

I bent down and counted the blue trucks; there were thirteen. 'Thirteen words,' I said.

'Fourteen,' said Harrington. 'There's no blue truck at the end. Now, there are twelve marshalling yards like this, so the system has a capacity of holding at any one time about a hundred and sixty words in plain, straightforward English – about half a typed quarto sheet. I know it's not much, but it keeps changing all the time as the system runs; that's the equivalent of putting a new page in the typewriter and doing some more.' He smiled. 'I don't know who designed this contraption, but maybe it's a new way of writing a novel.'

'So all you have to do is to find out which truck equals which letter.'

'All!' said Harrington hollowly. He picked up a thick sheaf of colour photographs. 'We've been recording the strings as they form and I have a chap on the computer doing a statistical analysis. So far he's making heavy weather of it. But we'll get it, it's just another problem in cryptanalysis. Anyway, I just thought I'd let you know your hare-brained idea turned out to be right, after all.'

'Thanks,' I said, glad not to be £31,000 out of pocket. Plus bank charges.

Two days later Harrington rang me again. 'We've licked the numbers,' he said. 'And we're coming up with mathematical formulae now. But the alphabet is a dead loss. The statistical distribution of the letters is impossible for English, French, German, Spanish and Latin. That's as far as we've gone. It's a bit rum – there are too many letters.'

I thought about that. 'Try Russian; there are thirty-two letters in the Russian alphabet.' And the man who had designed the railway was a Russian, although I didn't say that to Harrington.

'That's a thought. I'll ring you back.'

Four hours later he rang again. 'It's Russian,' he said. 'But we'll need a linguist; we don't know enough about it here.'

'Now is the time to tell Ogilvie. We'll be down there in an hour.'

So I told Ogilvie. He said incredulously, 'You mean that bloody model railway speaks Russian?'

I grinned. 'Why not? It was built by a Russian.'

'You come up with the weirdest things,' he complained.

'I didn't,' I said soberly. 'Ashton did. Now you can make my bank manager happy by paying £35,000 into my account.'

Ogilvie narrowed his eyes. 'It cost you only £31,000.'

'"Thou shalt not muzzle the ox that treadeth the corn",' I quoted. 'It was a risky investment – I reckon I deserve a profit.'

He nodded. 'Very well. But it's going to look damned funny in the books – for one model railway, paid to M. Jaggard, £35,000.'

'Why don't you call it by its real name? A computing system.'

His brow cleared. 'That's it. Now let's take a look at this incredible thing.' We collected Larry Godwin as an interpreter and went to the warehouse.

The first thing I noticed was that the system wasn't running and I asked Harrington why. 'No need,' he said cheerfuly. 'Now we've got the character list sorted out we've duplicated the system in a computer – put it where it really belongs. We weren't running the entire program, you know; just small bits of it. To run through it all would have been impossible.'

I stared at him. 'Why?'

'Well, not really impossible. But look.' He opened the LNER schedule and flipped through. 'Take these five pages here. They contain reiterative loops. I estimate that to run these five pages on the system would take six days, at twenty-four hours a day. To run through the whole program would take about a month and a half – and this is one of the smaller programs. To put all twelve of them through would take about two years.'

He closed the schedule. 'I think the original programs were written on, and for, a real computer, and then transferred on to this system. But don't ask me why. Anyway, now we've put the system back into a computer we're geared to work at the speed of electrons and not on how fast a model railway engine can turn its wheels.'

Ogilvie said, 'Which computer?'

'One in the City; a time-sharing system.'

Ogilvie looked at me. 'Oh, we can't have that. I want

everything you've put into that computer cleared out. We'll put it in our own computer.'

I said quickly, 'I wouldn't do that. I don't trust it. It lost Benson.'

Although Harrington could not know what we were talking about he caught the general drift. 'That's no problem.' He pointed to the railway. 'As a model railway that thing is very elaborate and complex, but as a computer it's relatively simple. There's nothing there that can't be duplicated in the Hewlett-Packard desk-top job I have in my own office. But I'll need a printer to handle Russian characters and, perhaps, a modified keyboard.'

Ogilvie said, 'That's a most satisfactory solution.' He walked over to the railway and looked at it. 'You're right; it is complex. Now show me how it works.'

Harrington smiled. 'I thought you'd ask that. Can you read Russian?'

Ogilvie indicated Larry. 'We've brought an interpreter.'

'I'm going to run through the program from the beginning; it's set up ready. I want you to keep an eye on that marshalling yard there. When it's full you can read it off because I've labelled each truck with the character it represents. I'll stop the system at the right time.'

He switched on and the trains began to scurry about, and the marshalling yard, which was empty, began to fill up. Harrington stopped the system. 'There you are.'

Ogilvie leaned forward and looked. 'All right, Godwin. What does it say?'

Harrington handed Larry a small pair of opera glasses. 'You'll find these useful.'

Larry took them and focused on the trains. His lips moved silently but he said nothing, and Ogilvie demanded impatiently, 'Well?'

'As near as I can make out it says something like this: "First approximation using toroidal Legendre function of the first kind."'

'Well, I'll be damned!' said Ogilvie.

* * *

255

Later, back at the office, I said, 'So they're not going to use the railway.'

'And better not,' said Ogilvie. 'We can't wait two years to find out what this is all about.'

'What will you do with it? According to Harrington it's a pretty simple-minded computer. Without the schedules – the programs – it's just an elaborate rich man's toy.'

'I don't know what to do with it,' said Ogilvie. 'I'll have to think about that.'

'Do me a favour,' I said. 'Give it to Michaelis. It was he who figured those schedules were fakes. It'll make his day.'

32

So Harrington put the programs on tape acceptable to his own computer and the Russian character printer began to spew out yards of Russian text and international figures. When Larry translated the Russian it proved to be oddly uninformative – brief notes on what the computer was doing at the time, but not why it was doing it. I mean, if you read a knitting pattern and find 'knit 2, purl 1', that doesn't tell you if you're knitting a body-belt for a midget or a sweater for your hulking Rugby-playing boy-friend. And that's not really such a good analogy because if you're knitting you know you're knitting, while a computer program could be doing damned nearly anything from analysing the use of the subjunctive in Shakespeare's *Titus Andronicus* to designing a trajectory for a space shot to Pluto. The field was wide open so a selection of assorted boffins was brought in.

All this was beyond me so I left them to it. I had other things on my mind, the principal one being that Penny had cabled me, saying that she was returning and giving her flight number and time of arrival at Heathrow. I felt a lot better immediately because it meant she expected me to meet her, and she wouldn't have done it if her decision had not been in my favour.

When I met her she was tired. She had flown from Los Angeles to New York, stopped for a few hours only to see Gillian, and then flown the Atlantic. She was suffering from jet lag and her stomach and glands were about nine hours out of kilter. I took her to the hotel where I had booked her a room; she appreciated that, not wanting to move into an empty flat with nothing in the refrigerator.

I joined her in a coffee before she retired to her room, and she told me that the operation on Gillian was going well and would I pass that message on to Michaelis. She smiled. 'Gillian particularly wants him to know.'

I grinned. 'We mustn't hinder the marriage of true minds.'

She talked briefly about what she had been doing in California and of a visit to the Harvard School of Medical Studies. 'They're doing good work there with PV40,' she said.

'What's that?'

'A virus – harmless to human beings.' She laughed. 'I keep forgetting you're not acquainted with the field.'

I said nothing to her about the model railway, although she would have to be told eventually. We couldn't just expropriate the knowledge to be found there – whatever it was – although the legal position would seem to be confused. The department had bought it, but whether the information it held came under the Copyright Act or not was something to keep the lawyers happy for years. In any case it was for Ogilvie to make the decision.

But she had just said something that had jerked little man Hunch out of bed and he was yelling his head off. I said, 'Did you talk over your work much with your father?'

'All the time,' she said.

'It doesn't seem a subject that would interest a man primarily versed in catalysts,' I said casually. 'Did he know much about it?'

'Quite a lot,' she said. 'Daddy was a man with a wide range of interests. He made one or two suggestions which really surprised Lummy when they worked in the laboratory.' She finished her coffee. 'I'm for bed. I feel I could sleep the clock around.'

I saw her to the lift, kissed her before she went up, then went back to the office at speed. Ogilvie wasn't in, so I went to see Harrington and found him short-tempered and tending to be querulous. 'The man who put these programs

258

together was either quite mad or a genius. Either way we can't make sense out of them.'

Harrington knew nothing about Ashton and I didn't enlighten him beyond saying, 'I think you can discount insanity. What can you tell me about the programs – as a whole?'

'As a whole?' He frowned. 'Well, they seem to fall into two groups – a group of five and a group of seven. The group of seven is the later group.'

'Later! How do you know?'

'When we put them through the computer the last thing that comes out is a date. The first five seem to be totally unrelated to each other, but the group of seven appear to be linked in some way. They all use the same weird system of mathematics.'

I thought hard for some minutes and made a few calculations. 'Let me guess. The first of the group of seven begins about 1971, and the whole lot covers a period finishing, say, about six months ago.'

'Not bad,' said Harrington. 'You must know something I don't.'

'Yes,' I said. 'I rather think I do.'

I sought Ogilvie again and found he had returned. He took one look at my face, and said. 'You look like the cat that swallowed the canary. Why so smug?'

I grinned and sat down. 'Do you remember the time we had a late night session trying to figure what Ashton would have been working on? We agreed he would keep on theorizing, but we couldn't see what he could theorize about.'

'I remember,' said Ogilvie. 'And I still can't. What's more, neither can Harrington and he's actually working on the material itself.'

'You said he wouldn't be working in atomics because he hadn't kept up with the field.'

'He didn't keep up in any field with the exception of

catalytic chemistry, and there he was mainly reworking his old ideas – nothing new.'

'You're wrong,' I said flatly.

'I don't see what he could have kept up in. We know the books he bought and read, and there was nothing.'

I said softly, 'What about the books Penny bought?'

Ogilvie went quite still. 'What are you getting at?'

'Penny said something just before she went to the States which slipped right past me. We were talking about some of the complications of her work and most of it was over my head. We were in her home at the time, and she said she was so used to talking with her father in that room she'd forgotten I was a layman.'

'The implication being that Ashton wasn't?'

'That's it. It came up again just now and this time it clicked. I've just been talking to Harrington, and he tells me there's a group of seven linked programs. I made an educated guess at the period they covered and I got it right first time. They started when Penny first began her graduate work in genetics. I think Ashton educated himself in genetics alongside his daughter. This morning Penny said he'd made suggestions which surprised Lumsden when they worked in the laboratory. Now, Penny works with Lumsden, one of the top men in the field. Everything he knew and learned she could pass on to Ashton. She read the relevant journals – and so did Ashton; she attended seminars and visited other laboratories – and passed everything back to Ashton. She could have been doing it quite unconsciously, glad to have someone near to her with whom she could discuss her work. He was right in the middle of some of the most exciting developments in science this century, and I'm not discounting atomic physics. What's more likely than that a man like Ashton should think and theorize about genetics?'

'You've made your point,' said Ogilvie. 'But what to do about it?'

'Penny must be brought in, of course.'

He shook his head. 'Not immediately. I can't make that decision off the cuff. The problem lies in the very fact that she *is* Ashton's daughter. She's intelligent enought to ask why her father should have considered it necessary to hide what he's doing, and that, as the Americans say, opens up a can of worms, including his early history and how and why he died. I doubt if the Minister would relish an angry young woman laying siege to his office or, much worse, talking to newspaper reporters. I'll have to ask him for a decision on this one.'

I said, 'You can't possibly suppress a thing like this.'

'Who is talking about suppressing it?' he said irritably. 'I'm merely saying we'll have to use tact in handling it. You'd better leave it with me. You haven't said anything to her about it, have you?'

'No.'

'Good. You've done well on this, Malcolm. You'll get the credit for it when the time comes.'

I wasn't looking for credit, and I had an uneasy feeling that Ogilvie wasn't being quite straight with me. It was the first time I had ever felt that about him, and I didn't like it.

I saw Penny the following afternoon, by arrangement, at University College. As I walked down the corridor towards her office the door of Lumsden's office opened and Cregar came out so that I had to sidestep smartly to avoid barging into him. He looked at me in astonishment and demanded, 'What are you doing here?'

Apart from the fact that it wasn't any of his business, I still felt sore enough at the roasting he had given me at the committee meeting to be inclined to give him a sharp answer. Instead I said, mildly enough, 'Just visiting.'

'That's no answer.'

'Perhaps that's because I neither liked the question nor the way it was put.'

He boggled a bit then said, 'You're aware the Ashton case is closed?'

'Yes.'

'Then I'll have to ask you again – what are you doing here?'

I said deliberately, 'The moon will turn into green cheese the day I have to ask your permission to visit my fiancée.'

'Oh!' he said inadequately. 'I'd forgotten.' I really think it had slipped his memory. Something in his eyes changed; belligerence gave way to speculation. 'Sorry about that. Yes, you're going to marry Dr Ashton, aren't you?'

At that moment I didn't know whether I was or not, but I wouldn't give Cregar that satisfaction. 'Yes, I am.'

'When is the wedding to be?'

'Soon, I hope.'

'Ah, yes.' He lowered his voice. 'A word to the wise. You are aware, of course, that it would be most undesirable if Miss Ashton should ever know what happened in Sweden.'

'Under the circumstances I'm the last person likely to tell her,' I said bitterly.

'Yes. A sad and strange business – very strange. I hope you'll accept my apology for my rather abrupt manner just now. And I hope you'll accept my good wishes for your future married life.'

'Of course – and thank you.'

'And now you must excuse me.' He turned and went back into Lumsden's office.

As I walked up the corridor I speculated on Cregar's immediate assumption that my presence in University College was linked to the Ashton case. Granted that he had genuinely forgotten I was to marry Penny, then what possible link could there be?

I escorted Penny to Fortnum's where she restocked her depleted larder. Most of the order was to be sent, but we took enough so that she could prepare a simple dinner for two. That evening, in the flat, as we started on the soup she said, 'I'm going to Scotland tomorrow.'

'With Lumsden?'

'He's busy and can't come. The extra time I spent in America has thrown our schedule out a bit.'

'When will you be back?'

'I don't think I'll be away as much as a week. Why?'

'There's a new play starting at the Haymarket next Tuesday which I thought you might like to see. Alec Guinness. Shall I book seats?'

She thought for a moment. 'I'll be back by then. Yes, I'd like that. I haven't been in a theatre for God knows how long.'

'Still having trouble in Scotland?'

'It's not really trouble. Just a difference of opinion.'

After dinner she made coffee, and said, 'I know you don't like brandy. There's a bottle of scotch in the cabinet.'

I smiled. 'That's thoughtful of you.'

'But I'll have a brandy.'

I poured the drinks and took them over to the coffee table. She brought in the coffee, and then we sat together on the settee. She poured two black coffees, and said quietly, 'When would you like us to get married, Malcolm?'

That was the night the new carpet became badly coffee-stained, and it was the night we went to bed together for the first time.

It had been quite long enough.

The rest of the week went slowly. Penny went to Scotland and I booked a couple of seats at the Haymarket Theatre. I also made enquiries into exactly how one gets married; it hadn't come up before. I felt pretty good.

Ogilvie was uncommunicative. He wasn't around the office much during the next few days and, even when he was, he didn't want to see me. He asked how I was getting on with the investigation of Benson and made no comment when I said I was stuck. Twice thereafter he refused to see me when I requested an audience. That worried me a little.

I checked with Harrington to find how he was doing and to see if any genetics experts had been brought in – not by asking outright but by tactful skating around the edges. No new boffins were on the job and certainly no biologists of any kind. That worried me, too, and I wondered why Ogilvie was dragging his heels.

Harrington's temper was becoming worse. 'Do you know what I've found?' he asked rhetorically. 'This joker is using Hamiltonian quaternions!' He made it sound like a heinous offence of the worst kind.

'Is that bad?'

He stared at me and echoed, 'Bad! No one, I repeat – *no one* – has used Hamiltonian quaternions since 1915 when tensor analysis was invented. It's like using a pick and shovel when you have a bulldozer available.'

I shrugged. 'If he used these Hamilton's whatsits he'd have a sound reason.'

Harrington stared at a print-out of the computer program with an angry and baffled expression. 'Then I wish I knew what the hell it is.' He went back to work.

And so did I, but my trouble was that I didn't know what to do. Benson was a dead issue – there seemed to be no possible way of getting a line on him. Ogilvie seemed to have lost interest, and since I didn't want to twiddle my thumbs in Kerr's section, I spent a lot of time in my flat catching up on my reading and waiting for Tuesday.

At the weekend I rang Penny hoping she'd be back but got no answer. I spent a stale weekend and on the Monday morning I rang Lumsden and asked if he'd heard from her. 'I spoke to her on Thursday,' he said. 'She hoped to be back in London for the weekend.'

'She wasn't.'

'Well, perhaps she'll be back today. If she comes in is there a message for her?'

'Not really. Just tell her I'll meet her at home at seven tomorrow evening.'

'I'll tell her,' said Lumsden, and rang off.

I went to the office feeling faintly dissatisfied and was lucky to catch Ogilvie at the lift. As we went up I asked bluntly, 'Why haven't you given Harrington a geneticist to work with him?'

'The situation is still under review,' he said blandly.

'I don't think that's good enough.'

He gave me a sideways glance. 'I shouldn't have to remind you that you don't make policy here,' he said sharply. He added in a more placatory tone, 'The truth is that a lot of pressure is being brought to bear on us.'

I was tired of framing my words in a diplomatic mode. 'Who from – and why?' I asked shortly.

'I'm being asked to give up the computer programs to another department.'

'Before being interpreted?'

He nodded. 'The pressure is quite strong. The Minister may accede to the request.'

'Who the devil would want . . . ?' I stopped and remembered something Ogilvie had let drop. 'Don't tell me it's Cregar again?'

265

'Why should you think . . .' He paused and reconsidered. 'Yes, it's Cregar. A persistent devil, isn't he?'

'Jesus!' I said. 'You know how he'll use it. You said he was into bacteriological warfare techniques. If there's anything important in there he'll use it himself and hush it up.'

The lift stopped and someone got in. Ogilvie said, 'I don't think we should discuss this further.' On arrival at our floor he strode away smartly.

Tuesday came and at seven in the evening I was at Penny's flat ringing the bell. There was no answer. I sat in my car outside the building for over an hour but she didn't arrive. She had stood me up without so much as a word. I didn't use the tickets for the show but went home feeling unhappy and depressed. I think even then I had an inkling that there was something terribly wrong. Little bits of a complicated jigsaw were fitting themselves together at the back of my mind but still out of reach of conscious reasoning power. The mental itch was intolerable.

The next morning, as early as was decent, I rang Lumsden again. He answered my questions good-humouredly enough at first, but I think he thought I was being rather a pest. No, Penny had not yet returned. No, he had not spoken to her since Thursday. No, it wasn't at all unusual; her work could be more difficult than she expected.

I said, 'Can you give me her telephone number in Scotland?'

There was a silence at my ear, then Lumsden said, 'Er . . . no – I don't think I can do that.'

'Why? Haven't you got it?'

'I have it, but I'm afraid it isn't available to you.'

I blinked at that curious statement, and filed it away for future reference. 'Then can you ring her and give her a message?'

Lumsden paused again, then said reluctantly, 'I suppose I can do that. What's the message?'

'It'll need an answer. Ask her where she put the letters from her father. I need to know.' As far as I knew that would be perfectly meaningless.

'All right,' he said. 'I'll pass it on.'

'Immediately,' I persisted. 'I'll wait here until you ring me back.' I gave him my number.

When I sorted the morning's post I found a slip from British Road Services; they had tried to deliver a package but to no avail because I was out – would I collect said package from the depot at Paddington? I put the slip in my wallet.

Lumsden rang nearly an hour later. 'She says she doesn't know which particular letters you mean.'

'Does she? That's curious. How did she sound?'

'I didn't speak to her myself; she wasn't available on an outside line. But the message was passed to her.'

I said, 'Professor Lumsden, I'd like you to ring again and speak to her personally this time. I . . .'

He interrupted. 'I'll do no such thing. I haven't the time to waste acting as messenger-boy.' There was a clatter and he was cut off.

I sat for a quarter of an hour wondering if I was making something out of nothing, chasing after insubstantial wisps as a puppy might chase an imaginary rabbit. Then I drove to Paddington to collect the package and was rather shattered to find that it was my own suitcase. Captain Morelius had taken his time in sending my possessions from Sweden.

I put it in the boot of my car and opened it. There seemed to be nothing missing although after such a length of time, I couldn't be sure. What was certain was that Swedish Intelligence would have gone over everything with a microscope. But it gave me an idea. I went into Paddington Station and rang the Ashton house.

Mary Cope answered, and I said, 'This is Malcolm Jaggard. How are you, Mary?'

'I'm very well, sir.'

267

'Mary, has anything arrived at the house from Sweden? Suitcases or anything like that?'

'Why, yes, sir. Two suitcases came on Monday. I've been trying to ring Miss Penny to ask her what to do with them, but she hasn't been at home – I mean in that flat in London.'

'What did you do with them?'

'I put them in a box-room.'

There were traffic jams on the way to Marlow. The congestion on the Hammersmith by-pass drove me to a distraction of impatience, but after that the road was open and I had my foot on the floor as I drove down the M4. The gates of the house stood open. Who would think Mary Cope might need protection?

She answered the door at my ring, and I said immediately, 'Has anyone else asked about those cases?'

'Why, no, sir.'

'Where are they?'

'I'll show you.' She led me upstairs by the main staircase and up another flight and along a corridor. The house was bare and empty and our footsteps echoed. She opened a door. 'I put them in here out of the way.'

I regarded the two suitcases standing in the middle of the empty room, then turned to her and smiled. 'You may congratulate me, Mary. Penny and I are getting married.'

'Oh, I wish you all the best in the world,' she said.

'So I don't think you'll have to stay in London, after all. We'll probably have a house in the country somewhere. Not as big as this one, though.'

'Would you want me to stay?'

'Of course,' I said. 'Now, I'd like to look at this stuff alone. Do you mind?'

She looked at me a shade doubtfully, then made up her mind. So many strange things had happened in that house that one more wouldn't make any difference. She nodded and went out, closing the door behind her.

Both cases were locked. I didn't trouble with lock-picking

but sprung open the catches with a knife. The first case was Ashton's and contained the little he had taken with him on the run from Stockholm. It also contained the clothes he had been wearing; the overcoat, jacket and shirt were torn – but there was no trace of blood. Everything had been cleaned.

It was Benson's case I was really interested in. In this two-cubic-foot space was all we had left of Howard Greatorex Benson, and if I couldn't find anything here then it was probable that the Ashton case would never be truly solved.

I emptied the case and spread everything on the floor. Overcoat, suit, fur hat, underwear, shirt, socks, shoes – everything he had died with. The fur hat had a hole in the back big enough to put my fist through. I gave everything a thorough going-over, aware that Captain Morelius would have done the same, and found nothing – no microfilm, beloved of the thriller writers, no hidden pockets in the clothing, nothing at all out of the usual.

There was a handful of Swedish coins and a slim sheaf of currency in a wallet. Also in the wallet were some stamps, British and Swedish; two newspaper cuttings, both of book reviews in English, and a scribbled shopping-list. Nothing there for me unless smoked salmon, water biscuits and Mocha coffee held a hidden meaning, which I doubted.

I was about to drop the wallet when I saw the silk lining was torn. Closer inspection showed it was not a tear but a cut, probably made by a razor blade. Captain Morelius left nothing to chance at all. I inserted my finger between the lining and the outer case and encountered a piece of paper. Gently I teased it out, then took my find to the window.

It was a letter:

TO WHOM IT MAY CONCERN
Howard Greatorex Benson is the bearer of this letter. Should his *bona fides* be doubted in any way the undersigned should be consulted immediately before further action is taken with regard to the bearer.

Stapled to the letter was a passport-type photograph of Benson, a much younger man than the Benson I remembered but still with the damaged features and the scar on the cheek. He looked to be in his early thirties. Confirmation of this came from the date of the letter – 4 January, 1947. At the bottom of the letter was an address and a telephone number; the address was in Mayfair and the number was in the old style with both letters and digits, long since defunct. The letter was signed by James Pallson.

The itch at the back of my mind was now assuaged, the jigsaw puzzle was almost complete. Although a few minor pieces were missing, enough pieces were assembled to show the picture, and I didn't like what I saw. I scanned the letter again and wondered what Morelius had made of it, then put it into my wallet and went downstairs.

I telephoned Ogilvie but he was out, so after making my farewell to Mary Cope I drove back to London, going immediately to University College. Aware that Lumsden might refuse to see me, I avoided the receptionist and went straight to his office and went in without knocking.

He looked up and frowned in annoyance as he saw me. 'What the devil . . . I won't be badgered like this.'

'Just a few words, Professor.'

'Now look here,' he snapped, 'I have work to do, and I haven't time to play post office between two love-birds.'

I strode to his desk and pushed the telephone towards him. 'Ring Penny.'

'I will not.' He picked up the card I flicked on to the desk, then said, 'I see. Not just a simple policeman, after all. But I can't see this makes any difference.'

I said, 'Where's the laboratory?'

'In Scotland.'

'Where in Scotland?'

'I'm sorry. I'm not at liberty to say.'

'Who runs it?'

He shrugged. 'Some government department, I believe.'

'What's being done there?'

'I really don't know. Something to do with agriculture, so I was told.'

'Who told you?'

'I can't say.'

'Can't or won't?' I held his eye for a moment and he twitched irritably. 'You don't really believe that guff about agriculture, do you? That wouldn't account for the secretive way you're behaving. What's so bloody secret about agricultural research? Cregar told you it was agriculture and you accepted it as a sop to your conscience, but you never really believed it. You're not as naïve as that.'

'We'll leave my conscience to me,' he snapped.

'And you're welcome to it. What's Penny doing there?'

'Giving general technical assistance.'

'Laboratory design for the handling of pathogens,' I suggested.

'That kind of thing.'

'Does she know Cregar is behind it?'

'You're the one who brought up Cregar,' said Lumsden. 'I didn't.'

'What did Cregar do to twist your arm? Did he threaten to cut off your research funds? Or was there a subtly-worded letter from a Cabinet Minister suggesting much the same thing? Co-operate with Cregar or else.' I studied him in silence for a moment. 'That doesn't really matter – but did Penny know of Cregar's involvement?'

'No,' he said sullenly.

'And she didn't know what the laboratory was for, but she was beginning to have suspicions. She had a row with you.'

'You seem to know it all,' said Lumsden tiredly, and shrugged. 'You're right in most of what you say.'

I said, 'Where is she?'

He looked surprised. 'At the laboratory. I thought we'd established that.'

'She was very worried about safety up there, wasn't she?'

'She was being emotioinal about it. And Cregar was pushing Carter hard. He wants results.'

'Who is Carter?'

'The Chief Scientific Officer.'

I pointed to the telephone. 'I'll lay you a hundred pounds to a bent farthing that you won't be able to talk to her.'

He hesitated for a long time before he picked up the telephone and began to dial. Although he was being niggly on secrecy, on security he was lousy. As he dialled I watched his finger and memorized the number. 'Professor Lumsden here. I'd like to speak to Dr Ashton. Yes, I'll hang on.'

He put his hand over the mouthpiece. 'They've gone to call her. They think she's in her room.'

'Don't bet on it.'

Lumsden hung on to the telephone for a long time, then suddenly said, 'Yes? . . . I see . . . the mainland. Well, ask her to ring me as soon as she comes back. I'll be in my office.' He put down the telephone and said dully, 'They say she's gone to the mainland.'

'So it's on an island.'

'Yes.' He looked up and his eyes were haunted. 'They could be right, you know.'

'Not a chance,' I said. 'Something has happened up there. You referred to your conscience; I'll leave you with it. Good day, Professor Lumsden.'

I strode into Ogilvie's outer office, said to his secretary, 'Is the boss in?' and breezed on through without waiting for an answer. There were going to be no more closed doors as far as I was concerned.

Ogilvie was just as annoyed as Lumsden at having his office invaded. 'I didn't send for you,' he said coldly.

'I've cracked Benson,' I said. 'He was Cregar's man.'

Ogilvie's eyes opened wide. 'I don't believe it.'

I tossed the letter before him. 'Signed, sealed and delivered. That was written on the fourth of January, 1947, the day Benson was discharged from the army, and signed by the Honourable James Pallson who is now Lord Cregar. Christ, the man has no honour in him. Do you realize, that when Ashton and Benson skipped to Sweden and Cregar was doing his holier-than-thou bit, he knew where they were all the time. The bastard has been laughing at us.'

Ogilvie shook his head. 'No, it's too incredible.'

'What's so incredible about it? That letter says Benson has been Cregar's man for the past thirty years. I'd say Cregar made a deal with Ashton. Ashton was free to do as he wanted – to sink or swim in the capitalist sea – but only on condition he had a watchdog attached: Benson. And when the reorganization came and Cregar lost responsibility for Ashton he conveniently forgot to tell you about Benson. It also explains why Benson was lost from the computer files.'

Ogilvie drew in his breath. 'It fits,' he admitted. 'But it leaves a lot still to be explained.'

'You'll get your explanation from Cregar,' I said savagely. 'Just before I skin him and nail his hide to the barn door.'

'You'll stay away from Cregar,' he said curtly. 'I'll handle him.'

'That be damned for a tale. You don't understand. Penny Ashton has gone missing and Cregar has something to do with it. It will take more than you to keep me off Cregar's back.'

'What's all this?' He was bewildered.

I told him, then said, 'Do you know where this laboratory is?'

'No.'

I took a card from my wallet and dropped it on the desk. 'A telephone number. The post office won't tell me anything about it because it's unlisted. Do something.'

He glanced at the card but didn't pick it up. He said slowly, 'I don't know . . .'

I cut in. 'I know something. That letter is enough to ruin Cregar, but I can't wait. Don't stop me. Just give me what

I need and I'll give you more than that letter – I'll give you Cregar's head on a platter. But I'm not going to wait too long.'

He looked at me thoughtfully, then picked up the card and the telephone simultaneously. Five minutes later he said two words. 'Cladach Duillich.'

34

Cladach Duillich was a hard place to get to. It was one of the Summer Isles, a scattering of rocks in an indentatiion of the North Minch into Ross and Cromarty. The area is a popular haunt of biological dicers with death. Six miles to the south of Cladach Duillich lies Gruinard Island, uninhabited and uninhabitable. In 1942 the biological warfare boys made a trifling mistake and Gruinard was soaked with anthrax – a hundred years' danger. No wonder the Scots want devolution with that sort of foolishness emanating from the south.

I flew to Dalcross, the airport for Inverness, and there hired a car in which I drove the width of Scotland to Ullapool at the head of Loch Broom. It was a fine day; the sun was shining; the birds singing and the scenery magnificent – all of which left me cold because I was trying to make good speed on a road which is called in Scotland 'Narrow, Class 1 (with passing places)'. I felt with a depressing certainty that time was a commodity which was running out fast.

It was latish in the day when I arrived in Ullapool. Cladach Duillich lay twelve miles further, out in the bay; say a four hour round trip for a local fishing boat. I dickered with a couple of fishermen but none was willing to take me out at that time. The sun was an hour from setting, clouds were building up in the west, and a raw wind blew down the narrow loch, ruffling water which had turned iron grey. I made a tentative deal with a man called Robbie Ferguson to take me out to the island at eight the next morning, weather permitting.

It was not yet the tourist season so I found a room in a

pub quite easily. That evening I sat in the bar listening to the local gossip and putting in a word or two myself, not often but often enough to stake a conversational claim when I decided to do a small quiz on Cladach Duillich.

It was evident that the rising tide of Scottish nationalism was in full rip in the West Highlands. There was talk of English absentee landlords and of 'Scottish' oil and of the ambivalent attitude of the Scottish Labour Party, all uttered in tones of amused and rather tired cynicism as though these people had lost faith in the promises of politicians. There was not much of it, just enough to spice the talk of fishing and the weather, but if I had been a bland habitué of the Westminster corridors of power it would have been enough to scare the hell out of me. Ullapool, it seemed, was further removed from London than Kalgoorlie, Australia.

I finished my half-pint of beer and switched to Scotch, asking the barman which he recommended. The man next to me turned. 'The Talisker's not so bad,' he offered. He was a tall, lean man in his mid-fifties with a craggy face and the soft-set mouth found in Highlanders. He spoke in that soft West Highland accent which is about as far from Harry Lauder as you can get.

'Then that's what I'll have. Will you join me?'

He gave me a speculative look, then smiled. 'I don't see why not. You'll be from the south, I take it. It's early for folk like you.'

I ordered two large Taliskers. 'What sort am I, then?'

'A tourist, maybe?'

'Not a tourist – a journalist.'

'Is it so? Which paper?'

'Any that'll publish me. I'm a freelance. Can you tell me anything about Gruinard Island?'

He chuckled, and shook his head. 'Och, not again? Every year we get someone asking about Gruinard; the Island of Death they used to call it. It's all been written, man; written into the ground. There's nothing new in that.'

276

I shrugged. 'A good story is still a good story to anyone who hasn't heard it. There's a rising generation which thinks of 1942 as being in the Dark Ages. I've met kids who think Hitler was a British general. But perhaps you're right. Anything else of interest around here?'

'What would interest an English newspaper in Ullapool? There's no oil here; that's on the east coast.' He looked into his whisky glass thoughtfully. 'There's the helicopter which comes and goes and no one knowing why. Would that interest you?'

'It might,' I said. 'An oil company chopper?'

'Could be, could be. But it lands on one of the islands. I've seen it myself.'

'Which island?'

'Out in the bay – Cladach Duillich. It's just a wee rock with nothing much on it. I doubt if the oil is there. They put up a few buildings but no drilling rig.'

'Who put up the buildings?'

'They say the government rented the island from an English lord. Wattie Stevenson went over in his boat once, just to pass the time of day, you know, and to say that when the trouble came there'd always be someone in Ullapool to help. But they wouldn't as much as let him set foot on the rock. Not friendly neighbours at all.'

'What sort of trouble was your friend expecting?'

'The weather, you understand. The winter storms are very bad. It's said the waves pass right over Cladach Duillich. That's how it got its name.'

I frowned. 'I don't understand that.'

'Ah, you haven't the Gaelic. Well, long ago there was a fisherman out of Coigach and his boat sank in a storm on the other side of the island out there. So he swam and he swam and he finally got ashore and thought he was safe. But he was drowned all the same, poor man, because the shore was Cladach Duillich. The water came right over. Cladach Duillich in the English would be the Sad Shore.'

If what I thought was correct it was well named. 'Do the people on Cladach Duillich ever come ashore here?'

'Not at all. I haven't seen a one of them. They fly south in the helicopter and no one knows where it goes or where it comes from. Not a penny piece do they spend in Ullapool. Very secret folk they are. There's just one landing place on Cladach Duillich and they've put up a big notice about trespassers and what will be done to them.'

I noticed that his glass was empty and wondered when he'd sunk the whisky. He must have done it when I blinked. I said, 'Have another, Mr . . . er . . .'

'You'll have one with me.' He signalled to the barman, then said, 'My name is Archie Ferguson and it's my brother who'll be taking you out to Cladach Duillich tomorrow morn.' He smiled sardonically at my evident discomfiture, and added, 'But I doubt if you'll set foot there.'

'I'm Malcolm Jaggard,' I said. 'And I think I will.'

'Malcolm's a good Scots name,' said Ferguson. 'I'll drink to your success, anyway; whatever it may be.'

'There's certainly something odd about the place,' I said. 'Do you think it's another Gruinard?'

Ferguson's face altered and for a moment he looked like the wrath of Almighty God. 'It had better not be so,' he said sternly. 'If we thought it was we would take the fire to it.'

I chewed that over together with my dinner, then made a telephone call – to Cladach Duillich. A voice said, 'How can I help you?'

'I'd like to speak to Dr Ashton. My name is Malcolm Jaggard.'

'Just a moment. I'll see if she's available.'

There was a four minute silence, then another voice said, 'I'm sorry, Mr Jaggard, but I'm told Dr Ashton went to the mainland and is not yet back.'

'Where on the mainland?'

There was a pause. 'Where are you speaking from, Mr Jaggard?'

'From London. Why?'

He didn't answer the question. 'She went to Ullapool – that's our local metropolis. She said she'd like to stretch her legs; there's not much scope for walking where we are. And she wanted to shop for a few things. May I ask how you got our number?'

'Dr Ashton gave it to me. When do you expect her back?'

'Oh, I don't know. The weather has closed in, so I don't think she'll be back until tomorrow morning. You could speak to her then.'

'Where would she stay in Ullapool? I don't know the place.'

'I really couldn't say, Mr Jaggard. But she'll be back tomorrow with the boat.'

'I see. May I ask who I'm speaking to?'

'I'm Dr Carter.'

'Thank you, Dr Carter. I'll ring tomorrow.'

As I put down the telephone I reflected that someone was lying – other than myself – and I didn't think it was Archie Ferguson. But to make sure I went into the bar and found him talking to Robbie, his brother. I joined them. 'Excuse me for butting in.'

'That's all right,' said Ferguson. 'I was just talking over with Robbie your chances of getting out to Cladach Duillich the morrow's morn.'

I looked at Robbie. 'Is there any doubt of it?'

'I think there'll be a wee blow,' he siaid. 'The glass is dropping as the weather forecast said. Have you a strong stomach, Mr Jaggard?'

'Strong enough.'

Archie Ferguson laughed. 'You've been talking to them! How?'

'By telephone – how else?'

'Aye,' said Robbie. 'They had the cable laid.' He shook his head. 'Awful expensive.'

'A man there told me a woman came ashore today from Cladach Duillich – here in Ullapool. She's about five feet eight inches, dark hair, age twent . . .'

Robbie interrupted. 'How did she come?'

'By boat.'

'Then she didn't come,' he said positively. 'All the comings and going are by that bluidy helicopter. There's no boat on Cladach Duillich.'

'Are you sure?'

'O' course I'm sure. I pass the place twice a day, most days. You can take my word – there's no boat.'

I had to make sure of it. 'Well, supposing she came anyway. Where would she stay in Ullapool?'

'Ullapool's not all that big,' said Archie. 'If she's here at all we can put our hands on her – in a manner o' speaking, that is. What would be the lassie's name?'

'Ashton – Penelope Ashton.'

'Rest easy, Mr Jaggard. You'll know within the hour.' He smiled genially at his brother. 'Do you not smell something awful romantic, Robbie?'

35

The wind whistled about my ears as I stood on the pier at eight next morning. The sky was slate-grey and so was the loch, stippled with whitecaps whipped up by the wind. Below me Robbie Ferguson's boat pitched violently, the rubber tyre fenders squealing as they were compressed and rubbed on the stone wall. It looked much too fragile to be taken out on such a day, but Robbie seemed unconcerned. He had taken the cover off the engine and was swinging on a crank.

Beside me, Archie Ferguson said, 'So you think the young lady is still on Cladach Duillich?'

'I do.'

He pulled his coat closer about him. 'Maybe we're wrong about the government,' he said. 'Could this be one of those queer religious groups we're importing from America these days? Moonies or some such? I've heard some remarkably funny things about them.'

'No, it's not that.' I looked at my watch. 'Mr Ferguson, could you do me a favour?'

'If I can.'

I estimated times. 'If I'm not back in eight hours – that's by four this afternoon – I want you to get the police and come looking for me.'

He thought about it for a moment. 'No harm in that. What if Robbie comes back and you don't?'

'Same thing applies. They might spin Robbie a yarn, tell him I've decided to stay. They'll be lying, but he's to accept the lie, come back here, and raise the alarm.'

Below, the diesel engine spluttered into life and settled down into a slow and steady thumping. Archie said, 'You know, Malcolm Jaggard, I don't believe you're a journalist at all.'

I took a card from my wallet and gave it to him. 'If I don't come back ring that number. Get hold of a man called Ogilvie and tell him about it.'

He studied the card. 'McCulloch and Ross – and Ogilvie. It seems we Scots have taken over the City of London.' He looked up. 'But you look less like a financier than you do a journalist. What's really going on out there on Cladach Duillich?'

'We spoke about it last night,' I said. 'And you talked of fire.'

A bleakness came over him. 'The government would do that again?'

'Governments are made of men. Some men would do that.'

'Aye, and some men can pay for it.' He looked at me closely. 'Malcolm Jaggard, when you come back you and I are going to have a bit of a talk. And you can tell yon laddies on Cladach Duillich that if you don't come back we'll be bringing the fire to them. A great cleanser is fire.'

'Stay out of it,' I said. 'It's a job for the police.'

'Don't be daft, man. Would the police go against the government? You leave this to me.' He looked down into the boat. 'Away with you; Robbie is waiting. And I'll away and have a talk with a few of my friends.'

I didn't argue with him. I climbed down the iron ladder which was slippery with water and seaweed and tried to time my drop into the boat to coincide with its erratic pitching. I fumbled it but was saved from sprawling full length by Robbie's strong arm.

He looked me up and down, then shook his head. 'You'll freeze, Mr Jaggard.' He turned and rummaged in a locker and brought out a seaman's guernsey. 'This'll keep you warm, and this – ' he gave me a pair of trousers and an anorak, both waterproof – 'this'll keep you dry.'

When I had put them on he said, 'Now sit you down and

be easy.' He went forward, walking as easily in that tossing boat as another man would walk a city pavement. He cast off the forward line, then walked back, seemingly unconcerned that the bow was swinging in a great arc. As he passed the engine he pushed over a lever with his boot, then dexterously cast off the stern line. The throbbing note of the engine deepened and we began to move away from the pier wall. Robbie was standing with the tiller between his knees, looking forward and steering by swaying motions of his body while he coiled the stern line into a neat skein.

The wind strengthened as we got out into the loch and the waves were bigger. The wind was from the north-west and we plunged into the teeth of it. As the bow dipped downwards sheets of spray were blown aft and I appreciated the waterproofing. As it was, I knew I'd be thoroughly drenched by the time we got to Cladach Duillich.

Presently Robbie sat down, controlling the tiller with one booted foot. He pointed, and said, 'The Coigach shore.'

I ducked a lump of spray. 'What sort of man is your brother?'

'Archie?' Robbie thought a bit and then shrugged. 'He's my brother.'

'Would you call him a hot-headed man?'

'Archie hot-headed!' Robbie laughed. 'Why, the man's as cold as an iceberg. I'm the laddie in the family to take the chances. Archie weighs everything in a balance before he does anything. Why do you ask?'

'He was talking about what he'd do if I didn't come back from Cladach Duillich.'

'There's one thing certain about my brother – he does what he says he'll do. He's as reliable as death and taxes.'

That was comforting to know. I didn't know what lay ahead on Cladach Duillich, but I knew I wasn't going to get an easy answer. The knowledge that I had a reliable backstop gave me a warm feeling.

I said, 'If I go missing on that bloody bit of rock you'll

take no for an answer. You'll swallow what they tell you, then go back and see your brother.'

He looked at me curiously. 'Are you expecting to disappear?'

'I wouldn't be surprised.'

He wiped the spray from his face. 'I don't ken what this is about, but Archie seems to like you, and that's enough for me. He's a thinker.'

It was a long haul across Annat Bay towards the Summer Isles. The waves were short and deep, and the pitching was combined with rolling, giving a corkscrew motion which was nauseating. Robbie looked at me and grinned. 'We'd better talk; it'll take your mind off your belly. Look, there's Carn nan Sgeir, with Eilean Dubh beyond. That's Black Island in the English.'

'Where's Cladach Duillich?'

'Away the other side of Eilean Dubh. We've a way to go yet.'

'Why don't they keep a boat there? If I lived on an island it's the first thing I'd think of.'

Robbie chuckled. 'You'll see when we get there – but I'll tell you anyway, just for the talking. There's but one place to land and a chancy place it is. There's no protection for boat or man. You can't just tie up as you can at Ullapool Pier. There'd be no boat when you got back if there was anything of a blow. It would be crushed on the rocks. I won't be waiting there for you, you know.'

'Oh? Where will you be?'

'Lying off somewhere within easy reach. There are more boats wrecked on land than at sea. It's the land that kills boats. I'll be doing a wee bit of fishing.'

I looked at the jumbled sea. 'In this!'

'Och, I'm used to it. You give me a time and I'll be there.'

'I'll tell you now. I want exactly two hours ashore.'

'Two hours you'll get,' he said. 'About the boat they haven't got on Cladach Duillich. When those folk first came they had a boat but it got smashed, so they got another and that was smashed. After they lost the third they began to get the idea. Then they thought that if they could take the boat ashore it would be all right, but it's an awful weary job pulling a boat ashore on Cladach Duillich because there's no beach. So they rigged davits just like on a ship and they could take the boat straight up a cliff and out of the water. Then a wave came one night and took the boat and the davits and they were never seen again. After that they gave up.'

'It sounds a grim place.'

'It is – in bad weather. It won't be too bad today.' I looked at the reeling seas and wondered what Robbie called bad weather. He pointed. 'There it is – Cladach Duillich.'

It was just as Archie Ferguson had described it – a wee bit of rock. There were cliffs all around, not high but precipitous, and the sea boiled white underneath them. Off the island was a scattering of rocks like black fangs and I thought the people on Cladach Duillich had been right when they decided this was no place for a boat.

As we drew nearer Robbie said, 'See that ravine? The landing place is at the bottom.'

There was a narrow crack in the cliff face, at the bottom of which the sea seemed to be calmer – relatively speaking. Robbie swung the tiller over sharply to avoid a rock which slid astern three feet off the port quarter, then he swung hard the other way to avoid another. He grinned. 'This is when you hope the engine doesn't pack in. You'd better get right forrard – you'll have to jump for it, and I won't be able to hold her there long.'

I scrambled forward and stood right in the bows as he brought the boat in. Now I saw that the crack in the rock was wider than at first glance and there was a concrete platform built at the bottom. The engine note changed as Robbie throttled back for the final approach. It was an amazing feat, but in that swirling sea with its cross-currents he brought her in so the bow kissed the concrete with a touch as light as a feather. At his shout I jumped and went sprawling as my feet skidded from under me on the weed-covered surface. When I picked myself up the boat was thirty yards off-shore and moving away fast. Robbie waved and I waved back, and then he applied himself to the task of avoiding rocks.

I looked at my surroundings. The first thing I saw was the notice board Archie Ferguson had mentioned. It was weatherbeaten and the paint was peeling and faded but it was still readable.

GOVERNMENT ESTABLISHMENT
Landing is Absolutely Prohibited
By Order

It did not say who had issued the order.

A path led from the concrete platform up the ravine, so I followed it. It climbed steeply and led to a plateau, sparsely grassed, in the centre of which was a group of buildings. They were low concrete structures which had the appearance of military blockhouses, probably because they were windowless. From what had been said about Cladach Duillich they were the only type of building which could survive there.

I had no more time to study the place because a man was approaching at a run. He slowed as he came closer, and said abruptly, 'Can't you read?'

'I can read.'

'Then clear off.'

'The age of miracles is past, friend. Walking on the water has gone out of fashion. The boat's gone.'

'Well, you can't stay here. What do you want?'

'I want to talk to Dr Carter.'

He seemed slightly taken aback, and I studied him as he thought about it. He was big and he had hard eyes and a stubborn jaw. He said, 'What do you want to talk to Dr Carter about?'

'If Dr Carter wants you to know he'll tell you,' I said pleasantly.

He didn't like that but there wasn't much he could do about it. 'Who are you?'

'Same thing applies. You're out of your depth, friend. Let's go and see Carter.'

'No,' he said curtly. 'You stay here.'

I looked at him coldly. 'Not a chance. I'm wet through and I want to dry out.' I nodded to the buildings. 'Those look as bloody inhospitable as you behave, but I'm willing to bet they're warm and dry inside. Take me to Carter.'

His problem was that he didn't know me or my authority, but I was behaving as though I had a right to be there and making demands. He did as I thought he would and passed the buck. 'All right, follow me. You see Carter and you go nowhere else.'

36

As we walked towards the buildings I looked around at Cladach Duillich. It was not very big – about a third of a mile long and a quarter-mile across. Life had a poor existence on this rock. What grass had managed to gain a roothold was salt resistant marram, growing in crannies where a poor soil had gathered, and even the dandelions were wizened and sickly growths. The seabirds appeared to like it, though; the rocks were white with their droppings and they wheeled overhead screaming at our movements below.

There were three buildings, all identical, and I noted they were connected by enclosed passages. To one side, on a level bit of ground, was a helicopter pad, empty. I was conducted around the corner to one of the buildings and ushered through the doorway, bidden to wait, and then taken through another doorway. I looked back and realized I had gone through an air lock.

We turned sharply left and into a room where a man in a white coat was sitting at a desk and writing on a pad. He was slightly bald, had a thin face and wore bifocals. He looked up and frowned as he saw me, then said to my escort, 'What's this, Max?'

'I found him wandering about loose. He says he wants to see you.'

Carter's attention switched to me. 'Who are you?'

I glanced sideways at Max, and said smoothly, 'Who I am is for your ears only, Dr Carter.'

Carter sniffed. 'More cloak and dagger stuff. All right, Max. I'll take care of this.'

Max nodded and left, and I stripped off the anorak. 'I

hope you don't mind me getting out of this stuff,' I said, as I began to take off the waterproof trousers. 'Too warm for indoors.'

Carter tapped on the desk with his pen. 'All right. Who are you, and what do you want?'

I tossed the trousers aside and sat down. 'I'm Malcolm Jaggard. I've come to see Dr Ashton.'

'Didn't you ring me last night? I told you she wasn't here – she's on the mainland.'

'I know what you told me,' I said evenly. 'You said she'd be back this morning, so I came to see her.'

He gestured. 'You've seen the weather. She wouldn't come over in this.'

'Why not? I did.'

'Well, she hasn't. She's still in Ullapool.'

I shook my head, 'She's not in Ullapool, and she wasn't there last night, either.'

He frowned. 'Look here, when I asked last night you said you were ringing from London.'

'Did I? Must have been force of habit,' I said blandly. 'Does it make a difference where I rang from?'

'Er . . . no.' Carter straightened and squared his shoulders. 'Now, you're not supposed to be here. This establishment is, shall we say, rather hush-hush. If it became known you were here you could be in trouble. Come to that, so could I, so I'll have to ask you to leave.'

'Not without seeing Penny Ashton. She's supposed to be here. Now isn't that a funny thing. I'm where I'm supposed not to be, and she's not where she's supposed to be. How do you account for it?'

'I don't have to account for anything to you.'

'You'll have to account for a lot, Dr Carter, if Penny Ashton doesn't turn up pretty damn quick. How did she get to Ullapool?'

'By boat, of course.'

'But this establishment doesn't have a boat. All journeys are by helicopter.'

He moistened his lips. 'You appear to be taking an unhealthy interest in this place, Mr Jaggard. I warn you that could be dangerous.'

'Are you threatening me, Dr Carter?'

'For any purpose prejudicial to the safety of the State, to approach, inspect or enter any prohibited place, or to – '

'Don't quote the Official Secrets Act at me,' I snapped. 'I probably know it better than you do.'

'I could have you arrested,' he said. 'No warrant is needed.'

'For a simple scientist you appear to know the Act very well,' I observed. 'So you'll know that to arrest me automatically brings in the Director of Public Prosecutions.' I leaned back. 'I doubt if your masters would relish that, seeing that Penny Ashton is missing from here. I told you, you'll have to account for a lot, Dr Carter.'

'But not to you,' he said, and put his hand on the telephone.

'I hope that's to give instructions to have Dr Ashton brought in here.'

A cool and amused voice behind me said, 'But Dr Carter really can't have her brought in here.' I turned my head and saw Cregar standing at the door with Max. Cregar said, 'Doctor, I'll trouble you for the use of your office for a moment. Max, see to Mr Jaggard.'

Carter was palpably relieved and scurried out. Max came over to me and searched me with quick, practised movements. 'No gun.'

'No?' said Cregar. 'Well, that can be rectified if necessary. What could happen to an armed man who breaks into a government establishment, Max?'

'He could get shot,' said Max unemotionally.

'So he could, but that would lead to an official enquiry which might be undesirable. Any other suggestions?'

'There are plenty of cliffs around here,' said Max. 'And the sea's big.'

It was a conversation I could do without. I said, 'Where's Penny Ashton?'

'Oh, she's here – you were quite right about that. You'll see her presently.' Cregar waved his hands as though dismissing a minor problem. 'You're a persistent devil. I almost find it in me to admire you. I could do with a few men of your calibre in my organization. As it is, I'm wondering what to do with you.'

'You'd better not compound your offences,' I said. 'Whatever you do about me, you've already done for yourself. We've linked you with Benson. I wouldn't be surprised if the Minister hasn't already been informed of it.'

The corners of his mouth turned down. 'How could I be linked with Benson? What possible evidence could there be?'

'A letter dated the fourth of January, 1947, carried by Benson and signed by you.'

'A letter,' said Cregar blankly, and looked through me into the past. Comprehension came into his eyes. 'Are you telling me that Benson still carried that damned letter after thirty years?'

'He'd probably forgotten about it – just as you had,' I said. 'It was hidden in the lining of his wallet.'

'A brown calf wallet with a red silk lining?' I nodded and Cregar groaned. 'I gave Benson that wallet thirty years ago. It would seem I tripped myself.'

He bent his head, apparently studying the liverspots on the backs of his hands. 'Where is the letter?' he asked colourlessly.

'The original? Or the twenty photocopies Ogilvie will have already made?'

'I see,' he said softly, and raised his head. 'What were your first thoughts on seeing the letter?'

'I knew you were linked with Ashton because you brought him out of Russia. Now you were linked with Benson, too. I thought of all the odd things that had happened, such as why a gentleman's gentleman should carry a gun, and why you tried to discount the fact he had shot Ashton when we had the meeting on my return from Sweden. It seemed hard to believe he was still your man after thirty years, but I was forced into it.'

Cregar lounged back in his chair and crossed his legs. 'Benson was a good man once, before the Germans got him.'

He paused. 'Of course he wasn't Benson then, he was Jimmy Carlisle and my comrade in British Intelligence during the war. But he lived and died as Benson, so let him remain so. He was captured in a Gestapo round-up in '44 and they sent him to Sachsenhausen, where he stayed until the end of the war. That's where he got his broken nose and his other brutalized features. They beat him with clubs. I'd say they beat his brains out because he was never the same man afterwards.'

He leaned forward, elbows on the desk. 'He was in a mess after the war. He had no family – his father, mother and sister were killed in an air raid – and he had no money apart from a disability pension. His brains were addled and his earning capacity limited. He'd never be any good in our line of work after that, but he deserved well of us, and by 1947 I pulled enough weight to help him, so I offered him the job of shepherd to Chelyuskin – Ashton as he became. It was a sinecure, of course, but he was pathetically grateful. You see, he thought it meant he wasn't finished in his job.'

Cregar took out a packet of cigarettes. 'Are you finding this ancient history interesting?' He held out the packet.

I took a cigarette. 'Very interesting,' I assured him.

'Very well. We switched him into the person of Benson at the same time we switched Chelyuskin to Ashton, then he hung around for a while. When Ashton got going Benson had a job in Ashton's office, and then later he became Ashton's factotum.'

'And Ashton knew what he was?'

'Oh, yes. Benson was the price Ashton had to pay for freedom. I knew that a man with that calibre of mind would not long be content to fiddle around in industry and I wanted to keep tabs on what he was doing.' He smiled. 'Benson was on to quite a good thing. We paid him a retainer and Ashton paid him, too.'

He leaned forward and snapped a gold lighter into flame under my nose. 'When the reorganization came and I lost Ashton to Ogilvie I kept quiet about Benson. In fact, I paid his retainer out of my own pocket. He didn't cost much; the retainer wasn't raised and the erosion in the value of money made Benson dirt cheap. It was an investment for the future which would have paid off but for you.'

I said, 'Did you know Ashton was into genetics?'

'Of course. Benson caught on to that as soon as it started happening. His job was to *know* what Ashton was doing at all times and, being permanently in the house, he could hardly miss. It was an incredible stroke of luck – Ashton becoming interested in genetics, I mean – because after the reorganization I had moved into the biological field myself.' He waved his hand. 'As you have discovered.'

'Ogilvie told me.'

'Ogilvie appears to have told you too much. From what you have let fall he appears to have given you the run of Code Black. Very naughty of him, and something he may regret. I was fortunate enough to be able to put a block on the computer to cover Benson, but evidently it wasn't enough.' He stopped suddenly, and stared at me. 'Even I appear to be telling you too much. You have an ingratiating way with you.'

'I'm a good listener.'

'And I become garrulous as I grow old, a grave failing in a man of our profession.' He looked at his half-smoked cigarette distastefully, stubbed it out, and put his hands flat on the desk. 'I'm at a loss to know how to dispose of you, young Jaggard. Your revelation that Ogilvie has that letter makes my situation most difficult.'

'Yes, he's in a position to blast hell out of you,' I agreed. 'I don't think the Minister will be pleased. I rather think you've put yourself on the retirement list.'

'Very succinctly put. Nevertheless, I will find a way out of the difficulty. I have surmounted difficulties before and I see no reason why I should fail this time. All it takes is applied thought to the study of men's weaknesses.' He slapped his hands together. 'And that is what I must do immediately. Put him somewhere safe, Max.'

I ignored the hand on my shoulder. 'What about Penny Ashton?'

'You will see her in my good time,' said Cregar coldly. 'And only if I think it advisable.'

In my rage I wanted to lash out at him but I couldn't ignore that tightening hand. Max leaned over me. 'No tricks,' he advised. 'I have a gun. You won't see it but it's there.'

So I rose from the chair and went with him. He took me from the office and along a corridor. Because the place was windowless it was almost like being in a submarine; everything was quiet except that the air shivered with the distant rumble of a generator. At the other end of the corridor I saw movement on the other side of a glass partition as a man walked across. He was wearing totally enveloping overalls and his head was hooded.

I had no time to see more because Max stopped and opened a heavy door. 'In there,' he said curtly, so I walked through and he slammed the door, leaving me in total darkness because he had not seen fit to turn on a light. The first thing I did was to explore my prison and arrived at the conclusion that it was an unused refrigerated room. The walls were thick and solid, as was the door, and I soon came to the conclusion that the only way out was to be let out. I sat on the floor in a corner and contemplated possibilities.

It appeared to have been wise to tell Cregar of the letter. Up to then he had primarily been interested in discussing ways and means of transforming me into a corpse safely, but my disclosure that Ogilvie had the letter had put a stopper on that line of thought. But what a ruthless bastard he had turned out to be.

I don't know what makes men like Cregar tick, but there seem to be enough of the bastards around just as there are many Carters eager to help them. Somewhere in the world, I suppose, is the chemist who lovingly mixed a petroleum derivative with a palm oil derivative to produce napthenic acid palmetate, better known as napalm. To do that required a deliberate intellectual effort and a high degree of technical training, and why a man should put his brain to such a use is beyond me. Supervising that chemist would be an American Cregar whose motives are equally baffling, and at the top are the politicians ultimately responsible. Their motive is quite clear, of course: the ruthless grasp of sheer power. But why so many others should be willing to help them is beyond me.

It's hard to know who to blame. Is it the Lumsdens of the world who know what is going on but turn a blind eye, or is it the rest of us who don't know and don't take the trouble to find out? Sometimes I think the world is like a huge ant heap full of insects all busily manufacturing insecticide.

I was in the black room for a long time. The only light came from the luminous dial of my watch which told me of hours ticking away. I was oppressed by the darkness and became claustrophobic and suffered strange fears. I got up and began to walk around the room, keeping to the walls; it was one way of taking exercise. The silence was solid except for the sound of my own movements and a new fear came upon me. What If Cladach Duillich had been abandoned – evacuated? I could stay in that room until the flesh rotted from my bones.

I stopped walking and sat in the corner again. I may have fallen asleep for a while, I don't remember. The hours I spent there are pretty much blanked out in my memory.

But I was aware when the door opened to let in a flood of light as glaring as from arc lamps. I put my hands to my eyes and saw Cregar at the door. He tut-tutted, and said, 'You didn't leave him a light, Max.'

'Must have forgotten,' said Max indifferently.

The light was quite ordinary light shed from fluorescent tubes in the ceiling of the corridor. I got up and went to the door. 'God damn you!' I said to Max.

He stood back a pace and lifted the pistol he held. Cregar said, 'Calm down. It wasn't intentional.' He saw me looking at the pistol. 'That's to warn you not to do anything silly, as well you might. You wanted to see the girl, didn't you? Well, you can see her now. Come with me.'

We walked along the corridor side by side with Max bringing up the rear. Cregar said conversationally, 'You won't see any of the staff because I've had them cleared out of this block. They're scientific types and a bit lily-livered. The sight of guns makes them nervous.'

I said nothing.

We walked a few more paces. 'I think I've found a way of confounding Ogilvie – there'll be no problem there – but that still leaves you. After we've seen Dr Ashton we'll have a talk.' He stopped at a door. 'In here,' he said, and let me precede him.

It was a strange room because one wall was almost entirely glass but the window looked, not upon the outside, but into another room. At first I didn't know what I was looking at, but Cregar said, 'There's Dr Ashton.' He pointed to a bed in the next room.

Penny was in bed, seemingly asleep. Her face was pale and ravaged, she could have been a woman twice her age. Around the bed were various bits of hospital equipment among which I recognized two drip feeds, one of which appeared to contain blood. I said, 'In God's name, what happened?'

Cregar said, almost apologetically, 'We had . . . er . . . an accident here last week in which Dr Ashton was involved. I'm afraid she's rather ill. She's been in a coma for the last two days.' He picked up a microphone and snapped a switch. Dr Ashton, can you hear me?'

His voice came amplified and distorted from a loudspeaker in the next room. Penny made no movement.

I said tightly, 'What's she got?'

'That's rather hard to say. It's something nobody has ever had before. Something new. Carter has been trying to run it down but without much success.'

I was frightened and angry simultaneously. Frightened for Penny and angry at Cregar. 'It's something you brewed up here, isn't it? Something that got loose because you were too tight-fisted to have a P4 laboratory as she wanted.'

'I see that Dr Ashton has been chattering about my business.' Cregar gestured. 'That's not a proper hospital ward of course; it's one of our laboratories. She had to be put somewhere safe.'

'Not safe for her,' I said bitterly. 'Safe for you.'

'Of course,' said Cregar. 'Whatever she's got we can't have spread about. Carter thinks it's most infectious.'

'Is Carter a medical doctor?'

'His degree is in biology not medicine, but he's a very capable man. She's getting the best of attention. We're transfusing whole blood and glucose, as you see.'

I turned to him. 'She should be in a hospital. This amateur lash-up is no good, and you know it. If she dies you'll be a murderer, and so will Carter and everybody else here.'

'You're probably right,' he said indifferently. 'About the hospital, I mean. But it's difficult to see how we could put her in a hospital and still maintain security.' His voice was remote and objective. 'I pride myself on my ability to solve problems but I haven't been able to solve that one.'

'Damn your security!'

'Coming from a man in your profession that smacks of heresy.' Cregar stepped back as he saw my expression, and gestured to Max who lifted the pistol warningly. 'She's having the best attention we can give her. Dr Carter is assiduous in his duties.'

'Carter is using her as a guinea pig and you damned well know it. She must be taken to a hospital – better still, to Porton. They understand high-risk pathogens there.'

'You're in no position to make demands,' he said. 'Come with me.' He turned his back and walked out.

I took a last look at Penny, then followed him with Max close behind. He walked up the corridor and opened a door on the other side. We entered a small vestibule and Cregar waited until Max had closed the outer door before proceeding. 'We do take precautions, in spite of anything you've been told,' he said. 'This is an air lock. The laboratory through there is under low pressure. Do you know why?'

'If there's a leak air goes in and not out.'

He nodded in satisfaction as though I'd passed a test, and opened the inner door. My ears popped as the pressure changed. 'This is Carter's own laboratroy. I'd like to show it to you.'

'Why?'

'You'll see.' He began a tour, behaving for all the world like a guide in one of those model factories where they show you what they're proud of and hide the bad bits. 'This is a centrifuge. You'll notice it's in an air-tight cabinet; that's to prevent anything escaping while it's in operation. No aerosols – microbes floating in the air.'

We passed on, and he indicated an array of glass-fronted cabinets covering one wall. 'The incubating cabinets, each containing its own petri dish and each petri dish isolated. Nothing can escape from there.'

'Something escaped from somewhere.'

He ignored that. 'Each cabinet can be removed in its entirety and the contents transferred elsewhere without coming into contact even with the air in the laboratory.'

I looked into a cabinet at the circular growth of a culture on a petri dish. 'What's the organism?'

'*Escherichia coli*, I believe. It's Carter's favourite.'

298

'The genetically weakened strain.'

Cregar raised his eyebrows. 'You seem well informed for a laymen. I don't know; that's Carter's affair. I'm not the expert.'

I turned to face him. 'What's this all about?'

'I'm trying to show you that we do take all possible precautions. What happened to Dr Ashton was purely accidental – a million to one chance. It's very important to me that you believe that.'

'If you'd listened to her it wouldn't have happened, but I believe you,' I said. 'I don't think you did it on purpose. What's so important about it?'

'I can come to an accommodation with Ogilvie,' he said, 'I'll lose some advantage but not all. That leaves you.'

'Have you spoken with Ogilvie?'

'Yes.'

I felt sick. If Cregar could corrupt Ogilvie I wouldn't want to work with him again. I said steadily, 'What about me?'

'This. I can do a deal with Ogilvie all right, but I don't think I could make it stick if anything happened to you. He always was squeamish. That means you have to be around and able to talk for some time to come which, as you will appreciate, presents me with a problem.'

'How to keep my mouth shut without killing me.'

'Precisely. You are a man like myself – we cut to the heart of a problem. When you appeared in the Ashton case I had you investiaged most thoroughly. To my surprise you had no handle I could get hold of, no peccadilloes to be exploited. You seem to be that rarity, the honest man.'

'I won't take compliments from you, damn it!'

'No compliment, I assure you, just a damnable nuisance. I wanted something to hold over you, something with which to blackmail you. There was nothing. So I have to find something else to close you mouth. I think I've found it.'

'Well?'

'It will mean my giving up more of the advantage I have achieved over the years, but I'll retain the most of it. I'll trade the young lady in the next laboratory for your silence.'

I looked at him with disgust. He had said the solution to his problem would lie in the study of man's weaknesses and he had found mine. He said, 'As soon as you agree, the girl can be taken to hospital, in carefully controlled conditions, of course. Perhaps your suggestion that she be taken to Porton is best. I could arrange that.'

I said, 'What guarantee would you have that I won't talk when she's well? I can't think of anything but no doubt you can.'

'Indeed I can – and I have. In Carter's office there's a document I want you to sign. I should say it's a carefully constructed document which took all my ingenuity to concoct. Quite a literary gem.'

'About what?'

'You'll see. Well, do you agree?'

'I'll need to read it first.'

Cregar smiled. 'Of course you may read it, but I think you'll sign it anyway. It's not much to ask – your signature for the life of your future wife.'

'You sicken me,' I said.

A telephone rang, startlingly loud. Cregar frowned, and said to Max, 'Answer it.' He held out his hand. 'I'll have the pistol. I don't trust him yet.'

Max gave him the gun and walked to the other end of the laboratory. Cregar said, 'Sticks and stones, etcetera. I don't care what you think of me as long as I get my way.'

'Show me what you want me to sign.'

'We'll wait for Max.'

Max talked in monosyllables in a low voice, then hung up and came back. 'Carter's got his knickers in a twist. He says a lot of men are landing. He reckons there are twenty boats out there.'

Cregar frowned. 'Who the hell are they?'

300

'He reckons they're local fishermen.'

'Damned Scots peasants! Go and shoo them away, Max. Put the fear of God into them with the Official Secrets Act. Get rid of them any way you can. Threaten them with the police if you have to.'

'Just threaten or actually send for them?'

'You can send for them if you think the situation warrants it.'

Max nodded towards me. 'That may not be entirely safe.'

'Don't worry about Jaggard,' said Cregar. 'We've reached an agreement.' As Max left he turned to me. 'Is this your doing?'

'How could I start a popular uprising?' I asked. 'They've probably got wind of what you're doing here, and remembering Gruinard, are determined not to let it happen again.'

'Ignorant bastards,' he muttered. 'Max will put them in their place.'

I said, 'I want Penny in hospital fast. How do we get off here?'

'A phone call will bring the helicopter in two hours.'

'You'd better make the call, then.'

He looked down at the floor, rubbing the side of his jaw while he thought about it. It was then I hit him in the belly, knocking the wind out of him. The gun went off and a bullet ricocheted from the wall and there was a smash of glass. I grabbed his wrist as he tried to bring up the gun and chopped him across the neck with the edge of my hand. He sagged to the floor.

When he painfully picked himself up I had the pistol. He glanced at it, then raised his eyes to mine. 'Where do you think this will get you?'

'I don't know about me, but it'll put you in prison.'

'You're a stupid, romantic fool,' he said.

'What's the number to ring for the helicopter?'

He shook his head. 'You don't know how government works, damn it. I'll never go to prison, but you'll be in water so hot you'll wish you'd never heard of Ashton or me.'

I said, 'I don't like hitting old men but I'll hammer hell out of you if I don't get that number.'

He turned his head and froze, then a weird bubbling cry came from him. 'Oh, Christ! Look what you've done!' His hand quivered as he pointed to the wall.

I looked, being careful to step behind him. At first I didn't see it. 'No tricks. What am I supposed to see?'

'The cabinets. Two are broken.' He whirled on me. 'I'm getting out of here.'

Blindly he tried to push past me, ignoring the gun. He was in a frenzy of terror, his face working convulsively. I stiff-armed him but his panic gave him added strength and he got past me and headed for the door. I went after him, reversed the pistol and clubbed him over the head. He went down like a falling tree.

I dragged him away from the door and went back to see the damage. Two of the panes in the incubating cabinets were broken and fragments of the petri dishes were scattered on the floor as were slimy particles of the cultures they had contained.

I whirled round as the door of the laboratory burst open. There stood Archie Ferguson. 'You're right, Mr Jaggard,' he said. 'It's another damned Gruinard.'

'Get out!' I yelled. 'For your life, get out!' He looked at me with startled eyes, and I pointed to the glasss wall at the end of the room. 'Go next door – I'll talk to you there. Move, man!'

The door slammed shut.

37

When I picked up the microphone my hand was shaking almost uncontrollably. I pushed the transmit button and heard a click. 'Can you hear me, Archie?' Ferguson, on the other side of the glass, nodded and spoke but I heard nothing. 'There's a microphone in front of you.'

He looked about him then picked it up. 'What happened here, Malcolm?'

'This place is bloody dangerous. Tell your men not to enter any of the laboratories – especially this one and the one across the corridor. Do that now.'

'I'll have guards on the doors.' He dropped the microphone and left on the run.

I went across to Cregar who was breathing stertorously. His head was twisted in an awkward position so I straightened him out and he breathed easier but showed no signs of coming awake.

'Mr Jaggard – are you there?'

I went back to the window to find Archie and Robbie Ferguson and a third man, one of the biggest I've seen, who was introduced as Wattie Stevenson. Archie said, 'It would seem you have problems. Is the lassie across the corridor the one you looked for?'

'Yes. You haven't been in there, have you?'

'No. I saw her by this arrangement we have here.'

'Good. Keep out of there. What size of an army did you bring? I heard of twenty boats.'

'Who told you that? There's only the six.'

'Have any trouble?'

'Not much. A man has a broken jaw.'

I said, 'How many people are there in this place?'

'Not as many as I would have thought. Maybe a dozen.'

Ogilvie had been right. It didn't take much to run a microbiological laboratory; perhaps half a dozen technical staff and the same number of domestics and bottlewashers. 'Put the lot under arrest. You have my authority for it.'

Archie looked at me speculatively. 'And what authority would that be?' I took out my departmental card and held it against the glass. He said, 'It doesn't mean much to me, but it looks official.'

'It takes you off the hook for invading government property. You did it on my instructions and you're covered. Oh, if you find a character called Max I don't care how roughly he's handled.'

Robbie Ferguson laughed. 'He's the one with the broken jaw. Wattie, here, hit him.'

'Och, it wasna' more than a wee tap,' said Wattie. 'The man has a glass jaw.'

'Wattie won the hammer throwing at the last Highland Games,' said Archie, with a grim smile. 'Besides, it was the man, Max, who sent Wattie away with a flea in his ear when he offered to help. What's to do now?'

'Did you ring Ogilvie as I asked?'

'Aye. He said he already knew about it.'

I nodded. He would have talked with Cregar. 'I want you to ring him again and the call put through to this telephone in here. You'll find a switchboard somewhere.'

'You can't come out?'

'No. You have my permission to listen in when I talk.' There was a groan behind me and I turned to see Cregar stirring. I said, 'Tell your men guarding the laboratories it's just as important that no one comes out. In fact, it's more important. This place being what it is there's probably some guns somewhere. In emergency use them.'

Archie looked grave. 'Is it so fearsome a thing?'

'I don't know,' I said wearily. 'I'm just taking prophylactic measures. Get busy, will you?'

I went back to Cregar, helped him to get up, and sat him

in a chair where he slumped flaccidly. He was dazed and in shock; too old to cope with the rough stuff any more. I said, 'Cregar, can you hear me?' He muttered something indistinguishable, and I slapped his cheek, 'Can you hear me?'

'Yes,' he whispered.

'Don't try to leave. There's a man outside with orders to shoot. Do you understand?'

He looked at me with glazed eyes, and nodded. 'Doesn't matter,' he muttered. 'I'm dead anyway. So are you.'

'We'll all be dead in a hundred years,' I said, and went to look again at the cultures in the broken petri dishes. The stuff looked harmless enough but I was careful not to touch it. Penny had described the elaborate precautions which were taken to prevent the escape of dangerous organisms from laboratories and, according to her, the lab I was now in wasn't up to snuff for what Carter had been doing.

The cultures could have been ordinary *E.coli* and, as such, perfectly harmless. But if they were cultures of *E.coli* which Carter had diddled around with then they could be dangerous in totally unpredictable ways. Cregar wasn't a scientist but he knew what Carter was up to, and the broken dishes had been enough to scare him half to death. From now on no chances would be taken and I hoped there had not been an escape already when Archie had opened the door. I didn't think so – the laboratory had low air pressure and I'd got him out fast.

Twenty minutes later I had Ogilvie on the phone. I wasted no time on politeness and answered none of the questions he shot at me. I said, 'This is a matter for urgency, so get it right the first time. Have you something to write with?'

'I'll record.' I heard a click.

'Cregar's laboratory on Cladach Duillich has run wild. There's one serious case of infection and two suspected. The organism causing it is new to medicine and probably man-made; it's also highly infectious. I don't know if it's a killer but it's highly likely. You'll have to set the alarm ringing and probably Lumsden, Penny's boss, is the best man to do it. Tell him hospitalization for three is needed in P4 – repeat – P4 conditions. He'll know what that means. Tell him I suggest Porton Down, but he might have a better idea.'

'I'll get on to it immediately,' said Ogilvie. 'Who are the three?'

'The serious case is Penny Ashton.'

There was a sharp withdrawal of breath. 'Oh, Christ! I'm sorry, Malcolm.'

I went on, 'The suspected cases are Cregar and myself.'

'For the love of God!' said Ogilvie. 'What's been going on up there?'

I ignored him. 'There's a helicopter pad on Cladach Duillich so Lumsden had better use a chopper. Tell him the man to see here is a Dr Carter. He's the chap who cooked up whatever hellbrew has got loose.'

'I've got that.'

'Then make it quick. I think Penny is dying,' I said bleakly.

38

Cregar and I were in an odd position. Loathing each other beyond all belief, we were condemned to each other's company for an unspecified period. The next few hours were to be extremely uncomfortable, but I tried to make them as comfortable as possible.

Archie Ferguson came back as soon as I had spoken to Ogilvie and the expression on his face was terrifying. He looked like one of the Old Testament prophets might look after inditing one of the more dire chapters of the Bible. 'May their souls rot forever in hell!' he burst out.

'Take it easy,' I said. 'There are practical things to do.' I thought of Ogilvie recording my telephone conversation and it gave me an idea. 'See if you can find a tape-recorder. I'll need it.'

Archie simmered down. 'Aye, I'll see what I can do.'

'And we'll need food in here, but you can give us food once and once only. What you do is this. You open the outer door of the laboratory and put the food on the floor just inside. Tell me when you've closed the door and I'll come out and get it. It can be done once only because I can't risk contamination through the air lock, so you'd better give us enough for three meals. If you can find vacuum flasks for coffee that would be a help.'

Ferguson looked past me. 'Is yon man the Cregar you spoke of?'

'Yes.'

'Then he gets nothing from me.'

'You'll do as I say,' I said sharply. 'We both eat or neither of us eats.'

He took a deep breath, nodded curtly, then laid down

the microphone and went away. Half an hour later he came back. 'Your food's there. I did better than flasks; there's a coffee percolator to make your own.'

'Thanks.' I had another idea. 'Archie, this laboratory is maintained at a lower air pressure than the outside. That means pumps, and pumps mean electricity. Put someone to watch the generator; I don't want it stopping, either by breakdown or lack of fuel. Will you see to that?'

'Aye. It won't stop.'

I went into the air lock and got the food – a pile of sandwiches – and also found a small battery-powered cassette tape-recorder. I put everything on the table next to the telephone. Cregar was apathetic and looked at the sandwiches without interest. I filled the percolator from a tap on one of the benches and got the coffee going. Cregar accepted coffee but he wouldn't eat.

Unobtrusively I switched on the recorder; I wanted Cregar condemned out of his own mouth. I said, 'We've a lot to talk about.'

'Have we?' he said without interest. 'Nothing matters any more.'

'You're not dead yet, and you may not be if Ogilvie does his stuff. When did Benson learn of Ashton's interest in genetics?'

He was silent for a moment, then said, 'Must have been 1971. He saw that Ashton was keeping up with the girl's studies, and then starting to do a lot of work on his own, usually at the weekends – a lot of calculating. He tried to get a look at it, but Ashton kept it locked away.' Cregar brooded. 'Ashton never did like me. I've often wondered if he knew what I was doing.' He waved his hand at the laboratory. 'This, I mean. It's supposed to be secret, but a man with money can usually find out what he wants to know.' He shrugged. 'Anyway, he made damned certain that Benson didn't lay an eye on his work.'

'That empty vault must have come as a shock.'

He nodded. 'Benson knew about the vault but never

managed to get inside. And when Ogilvie told me it was empty I didn't believe him. It was only when he offered to let one of my forensic chaps look at the vault that I accepted that fact.' He looked up. 'You're a clever man. I never thought of the railway. I ought to have done. Ashton wasn't the man to fool about with toy trains.'

Now Cregar had started to talk he positively flowed. I suppose he thought there was no reason to keep his silence. It was a sort of deathbed confession.

I said, 'What I can't understand was how you engineered Mayberry's acid attack – and why. That's the bit that seems senseless.'

'It was senseless,' said Cregar. 'I had nothing to do with it. I didn't even know Mayberry existed until the police tracked him down. Do you remember when you appeared before the inter-departmental committee, Ogilvie said something about you "exploding Ashton out of Stockholm"? Well, I exploded him out of England.'

'How?'

He shrugged. 'Opportunism combined with planning. I'd been wanting to have a dig at Ashton for a long time. I wanted to get him out of that house so I could get into that vault. I thought whatever he had would be ripe. I'd already made preparations – rented the flat and opened the bank account in Stockholm, got the Israeli passport, and so on. All I needed was a trigger. Then along came that maniac, Mayberry – most opportunely. I got Benson to panic Ashton, talking of threats to the other girl, and so on. Benson told him my department couldn't cope with that sort of thing unless Ashton got out, that we were prepared to help and that we had a safe hideaway for him, which of course we had. And after all that the damned vault was empty.'

'But why did Benson kill Ashton?'

'Standing orders from thirty years ago,' said Cregar simply. 'Ashton wasn't to be allowed to go back to the Russians. If there was a chance of him falling into Russian hands Benson was to kill him. Benson had every reason to think you were Russians.'

'Jesus!' I said. 'What sort of man was Benson to kill Ashton after being with him thirty years?'

Cregar gave me a lopsided smile. 'He had gratitude, I suppose; and personal loyalty – to me.'

I remembered my musings in the dark room and, out of curiosity, said, 'Cregar, why did you do all this?'

He looked at me in surprise. 'A man must leave his mark on the world.'

I felt chilled.

There wasn't much I wanted to know after that, but, the dam now broken, Cregar rambled on interminably, and I was glad when the telephone rang. It was Ogilvie. 'There'll be an RAF helicopter on its way with a medical team. Lumsden thinks you're right about Porton and he's made the arrangements.' He paused. 'He also wants me to pass on his apologies – I don't know why.'

'I do. Thank him for me. When will the chopper get here?'

'They're assembling the team now. I'd say six hours. How's Miss Ashton?'

'I don't know,' I said bitterly. 'I can't get to her. She's in a coma. You can tell that to Lumsden, too.'

Ogilvie was inclined to talk but I put him off. I wasn't in the mood for that. Half an hour later the phone rang again and I found Archie Ferguson on the line. 'There's someone called Starkie wants to talk to the man Carter. Shall I let him?'

'Let me talk to Starkie.' The earphone crackled and a deep voice said, 'Richard Starkie here – is that Dr Carter?'

'Malcolm Jaggard here. Who are you?'

'I'm a doctor speaking from Porton Down. Are you one of the infected men?'

'Yes.'

'Any symptoms starting to show?'

'Not yet.'

'If Carter manufactured this bug he'll know more about it than anyone. I need the information.'

'Right,' I said. 'If you don't get satisfaction from him let me know. Are you on the line, Archie?'

'Aye.'

'Let them talk. If Carter wants persuading I'm sure you know what to do.'

They came for us seven hours later, dressed like spacemen in plastic clothing with self-contained breathing apparatus. They put us in plastic envelopes whole and entire, plugged in an air supply and sealed us up. We stopped in the air lock and the envelopes and themselves were drenched with a liquid, then we were carried out to the helicopter where I found Penny already installed in her own envelope. She was still unconscious.

39

A month later I was feeling pretty chipper because Starkie had given me a clean bill of health. 'For three weeks now we've inspected every damned *E.coli* bug that's come out of you and they're all normal. I don't know why you're still lying around here. What do you think this is, a doss house?'

He hadn't always been as cheerful as that. At the beginning I was placed in a sterile room and untouched by human hand for the next two weeks. Everything that was done to me was done by remote control. Later they told me that a team of thirty doctors and nurses was working on me alone.

Penny did better. For her they apparently mobilized the entire medical resources of the United Kingdom, plus sizeable chunks from the United States and the Continent, with a little bit from Australia. The bug she had was different from the one I'd caught, and it was a real frightener. It got the medical world into a dizzy tizzy and, although they were able to cure her, they wanted to make sure that the bug, whatever it was, was completely eradicated. So I came out of Porton Down a month before her.

Starkie once said soberly, 'If she'd have been left another day with the minimal attention she was getting I don't think we could have done it.' That made me think of Carter and I wondered what was being done about him. I never found out.

When I came out of purdah but before I was discharged I went to see her. I couldn't kiss her, or even touch her, but we could speak separated by a pane of glass, and she seemed cheerful enough. I told her something of what had happened, but not everything. Time enough for that when she was better. Then I said, 'I want you out of here pretty damned quick. I want to get married.'

She smiled brilliantly. 'Oh, yes, Malcolm.'

'I can't fix a day because of that bloody man Starkie,' I complained. 'He's likely to keep you in here forever, investigating the contents of your beautiful bowels.'

She said, 'How would you like a double wedding? I had a letter from Gillian in New York. Peter Michaelis flew over and proposed to her. She was lying in bed with her left arm strapped to her right cheek and swaddled in bandages when he asked her. She thought it was very funny.'

'I'll be damned!'

'It will be a little time yet. We all have to get out of our hospitals. Is four months too long to wait?'

'Yes,' I said promptly. 'But I'll wait.'

I didn't ask anyone how Cregar was doing because I didn't care.

On the day I came out of the sterile room Ogilvie came to see me, bearing the obligatory pound of grapes. I received him with some reserve. He asked after my health and I referred him to Starkie, then he said, 'We got the tape cassette after it had been decontaminated. Cregar won't be able to wriggle out of this one.'

I said, 'Had any success with Ashton's computer programs?'

'Oh, my God, they're fantastic. Everyone has claimed the man was a genius and he's proved it.'

'How?'

Ogilvie scratched his head. 'I don't know if I can explain – I'm no scientist – but it seems that Ashton has done for genetics what Einstein did for physics. He analysed the DNA molecule in a theoretical way and came up with a series of rather complicated equations. By applying these you can predict exactly which genes go where and why, and which genetic configurations are possible or not possible. It's a startling breakthrough; it's put genetics on a firm and mathematical grounding.'

'That should make Lumsden happy,' I said.

Ogilvie ate a grape. 'He doesn't know. It's still confidential. It hasn't been released publicly yet.'

'Why not?'

'The Minister seems to feel . . . well, there are reasons why it shouldn't be released yet. Or so he says.'

That saddened me. The bloody politicians with their bloody reasons made me sick to the stomach. The Minister was another Creger. He had found a power lever and wanted to stick to it.

Ogilvie took another grape. 'I asked Starkie when you'd be coming out but he isn't prepared to say. However, when you do I've a new job for you. As you may know, Kerr is retiring in two years. I want to groom you for his job.' Kerr was Ogilvie's second-in-command. He smiled. 'In seven years, when I go, you could be running the department.'

I said bluntly, 'Get lost.'

He was not a man who showed astonishment easily, but he did then. 'What did you say?'

'You heard me. Get lost. You can take Kerr's job and your job and stuff them wherever you like. The Minister's backside might be a good place.'

'What the devil's got into you?' he demanded.

'I'll tell you,' I said. 'You were going to do a deal with Cregar.'

'Who said that?'

'Cregar.'

'And you believed him? The man lies as naturally as he breathes.'

'Yes, I believed him because at that point he had no reason to lie. He did proposition you, didn't he?'

'Well, we talked – yes.'

I nodded. 'That's why you won't get me back in the department. I'm tired of lies and evasions; I'm tired of self-interest masquerading as patriotism. It came to me when Cregar called me an honest man, not as a compliment but

314

as someone to corrupt. I realized then that he was wrong. How could an honest man do what I did to Ashton?'

'I think you're being over-emotional about this,' Ogilvie said stiffly.

'I'm emotional because I'm a man with feelings and not a bloody robot,' I retorted. 'And now you can take your bloody grapes and get the hell out of here.'

He went away moderately unhappy.

40

And they all lived happily ever after. The hero married the principal girl, and second hero got the second girl, and they moved out of the poor woodcutter's cottage into the east wing of the king's palace.

But this is not a fairy tale.

On the day Penny came out of hospital she, Peter Michaelis and I went on a wing-ding in the East End and the three of us became moderately alcoholic and distinctly merry. On the day Gillian arrived back from New York the four of us went on another wing-ding with similar effect. That American plastic surgeon must have been a genius because Gillian's new face was an improvement on the one she had before the acid was thrown. I was very glad for Peter.

The clanging of wedding bells could be heard in the near future. Penny and Gillian were dashing about London denuding the better stores of dresses and frillies for their trousseaux, while I scouted around for a house, introduced it to Penny, and then secured it with a cash deposit against the time the lawyers had finished their expensive wrangling over the deeds. It was all very exhilarating.

Ten days before the wedding I felt it incumbent on me to go back to see Starkie. He heard what I had to say and frowned, then took me into a laboratory where I was subjected to a battery of tests. He told me to go away and return in a week.

On the day I went back I read of Cregar's death in *The Times*. The obituary was sickening. Described as a faithful public servant who had served his country with no thought of self for many years, he was lauded as an example for coming generations to follow. I threw the paper out of the train window and was immediately sorry; that sort of stuff could pollute the countryside very seriously.

Starkie was serious, too, when I saw him, and I said, 'It's bad news.'

'Yes, it is,' he said directly. 'It's cancer.'

It was a blow, but I had half-expected it. 'How long do I have?'

He shrugged. 'Six months to a year, I'd say. Could be longer, but not much.'

I walked to his office window and looked out. I can't remember what I saw there. 'Cregar's dead,' I said. 'Same thing?'

'Yes.'

'How?'

Starkie sighed. 'That damned fool, Carter, was doing shot-gun experiments. That means he was chopping up DNA molecules into short lengths, putting them into *E.coli*, and standing back to see what happened. It's not a bad technique if you know what you're doing and take the proper precautions.'

'He was taking precautions,' I said. 'The stuff got loose because of my own damned foolishness.'

'He wasn't,' snapped Starkie. 'Cregar was putting pressure on him – wanting fast results. He couldn't wait for a consignment of genetically weakened *E.coli* from the States so he used the normal bug. There was no biological containment at all. The stuff went straight into your gut and started to breed happily.'

'To cause cancer?' It didn't seem likely.

'I'll try to explain this as simply as possible,' said Starkie. 'We believe that in the genetic material of all normal cells there are genes which can produce tumour-forming chemicals, but they are normally repressed by other genes. Now, if you do a shotgun experiment and introduce a short length of DNA into *E.coli* you're in danger of introducing a tumour gene without the one that represses it. That's what's

317

happened to you. The *E.coli* in your gut was producing tumour-forming chemicals.'

'But you said the *E.coli* coming out of me was normal,' I objected.

'I know I did, and so it was. One of the most difficult things to do in these experiments is to get a new strain to breed true. They're very unstable. What happened was that this strain began to breed back to normal *E.coli* almost immediately. But it was in your gut long enough to do the damage.'

'I see.' I felt a sudden chill. 'What about Penny?'

'She's all right. That was a different bug entirely. We made sure of that.'

I said, 'Thank you, Dr Starkie. You've been very direct and I appreciate it. What's the next step?'

He rubbed his jaw. 'If you hadn't come to see me I'd have sent for you – on the basis of what happened to Lord Cregar. This is a type of cancer we haven't come across before; at least it hasn't been reported in the literature in this particular form. Cregar went very fast, but that may have been because of his age. Older cellular structures are more susceptible to cancers. I think you have a better chance.'

But not much better, I thought. Starkie spoke in the flat, even tone used by doctors when they want to break the bad news slowly. He scribbled on a sheet of paper. 'Go to this man. He's very good and knows about your case. He'll probably put you on tumour-reducing drugs and, possibly, radiation therapy.' He paused. 'And put your affairs in order as any sensible man should.'

I thanked him again, took the address, and went back to London where I heard another instalment of bad news. Then I told Penny. I had no need to give her Starkie's explanation because she grasped that immediately. It was her job, after all. I said, 'Of course, the marriage is off.'

'Oh, no; Malcolm!'

And so we had another row – which I won. I said, 'I

318

have no objection to living in sin. Come live with me and be my love. I know a place in the south of Ireland where the mountains are green and the sea is blue when the sun shines, which it does quite often, and green when it's cloudy and the rollers come in from the Atlantic. I could do with six months of that if you're with me.'

We went to Ireland immediately after Peter and Gillian were married. It was not the happy occasion one would have wished; the men were sombre and the women weepy, but it had to be gone through.

At one time I thought of suicide; taking the Hemingway out, to perpetrate a bad pun. But then I thought I had a job to do, which was to write an account of the Ashton case, leaving nothing out and making it as truthful as possible, and certainly not putting any cosmetics on my own blemishes. God knows I'm not proud of my own part in it. Penny has read the manuscript; parts of it have amused her, other parts have shattered her. She has typed it all herself.

We live here very simply if you discount the resident medical staff of a doctor and three nurses which Penny insisted upon. The doctor is a mild young American who plays bad chess and the nurses are pretty which Penny doesn't mind. It helps to have a wealthy woman for a mistress. For the first few months I used to go to Dublin once a fortnight where they'd prod and probe and shoot atoms into me. But I stopped that because it wasn't doing any good.

Now time is becoming short. This account and myself are coming to an end. I have written it for publication, partly because I think people ought to know what is done in their names, and partly because the work of Ashton on genetics has not yet been released. It would be a pity if his work, which could do so much good in the right hands, should be withheld and perhaps diverted to malignant uses in the hands of another Cregar. There are many Cregars about in high office.

Whether publication will be possible at all I don't know. The wrath of the Establishment can be mighty and its instruments of suppression strong and subtle. Nevertheless Penny and I have been plotting our campaign to ensure that these words are not lost.

A wise one-legged American, in adapting the words of a naval hero, once said, 'We have met the enemy, and he is us.'

God help you all if he is right.

MICHAEL HARRIS

THE CRUISE

First published in Great Britain in 2012
by The Spectrum Agency, East Sussex.

A catalogue record for this book is available from the British Library.

ISBN 978-0-9572437-0-5

Printed and bound in Great Britain by
CPI Group (UK) Limited, Croydon, CR0 4YY

THE CRUISE
EXTRACTS FROM

I read this book at the seaside where I could see ships passing through the English Channel and became gripped by Michael Harris' graphic description of life aboard a cruise ship. Here was a microcosm of life with its loves and fears, hopes and disappointments paraded before us and resolved through time spent away from home. Altogether a good read.
By Sussexseagull.

I really enjoyed 'The Cruise.' It is a true to life story with interesting characters, ports and good on board descriptions. It makes me want to catch the next ship.
By cruise lover.

Easy reading. One electric moment: a story, told to a claustrophobic, about a giant who threatened a village.
By kettle.

This is a great read for the first-time cruiser, the seasoned voyager and the armchair traveler. In the intimate atmosphere of the cruise ship, personal stories are shared and challenges resolved. The author shows his familiarity with the culture of cruising and a solid grounding in the history of the area.
By AK, San Ramon, Calif.USA.

HORIZON SHIPPING LINE

ms NEPTUNE

Departing 15th September

Sailing from Dover

ITINERARY OF
'MEDITERRANEAN DELIGHTS'
CRUISE

September	Ports of Call	Available tours include to:
Saturday 15th	Depart Dover	
Sunday 16th	At Sea	
Monday 17th	Vigo, Spain	Santiago de Compostella
Tuesday 18th	Lisbon, Portugal	Sintra and Estoril
Wednesday 19th	At Sea	
Thursday 20th	Barcelona, Spain	
Friday 21st	Nice, France	Monte Carlo
Saturday 22nd	Alghero, Sardinia	
Sunday 23rd	Naples, Italy	Capri
Monday 24th	Civitavecchia, Italy	Rome
Tuesday 25th	At Sea	
Wednesday 26th	Gibraltar	
Thursday 27th	At Sea	
Friday 28th	At Sea	
Saturday 29th	Disembark Dover	

**THIS BOOK
IS FOR LYNDA**

**BEAUTY IS BEING
AND
BEAUTY IS EVERYWHERE**

ONE

After having waited ten days it had at last arrived. It was in a shining white envelope bearing the initials *HSL* intricately arranged to form the company's logo. Anne had no difficulty in recognising it among the remaining items of post which were for Vince.

She returned eagerly to the kitchen, where her black coffee awaited, sat down and gazed upon the package which beckoned for her to open. Not wishing to tear any part of the contents she carefully pulled back the adhesive and extracted the brochure.

The cover had been beautifully designed featuring a scene of blue sky and an image of gently moving seas. The words *Horizon Shipping Line* appeared as clouds in bold italics across the sky and a majestic white liner with yellow markings was highlighted as though it was moving towards an unspecified destination. It bore the name NEPTUNE in dark blue. The company operated two vessels, the second bearing the name POSEIDON.

Despite it being a cold, wet day in late April, a warm glow of excitement came across her as she held the brochure in her hands. The cruise was to be their first and would be taken early in September to celebrate their 15th wedding anniversary. She started to slowly turn the pages feeling like Alice entering into adventures in wonderland.

*****

Louise had cooked his favourite meal of roast lamb, roast potatoes, parsnips and spinach followed by baked jam roll with custard. He still had a hearty appetite and had been enjoying every morsel.

"Good job I don't eat like this every day", said Jeff, "I'd be a stone heavier in no time."

"It wouldn't do you any harm to put on some weight," she responded, "You look very thin to me. Are you sure you're eating properly?"

"Stop worrying, Mum. I'm fine and there's certainly no lack of food on the ship."

His father had died from pneumonia when he was 16. Jeff had left school shortly before. He'd always been mad keen on cameras and took photos wherever he went, so it was no surprise to Louise and Mark when he announced that he had enrolled on a two year photography course and would be earning some pocket money at weekends by stacking goods at one of the nearby supermarkets in Dartford.

The shock of his father's death on both Louise and Jeff had been devastating but encouraged by Louise he continued his studies and subsequently passed both end of year exams. He then joined a photographic company that operated a large store in Oxford Street.

Fifteen months passed until the travel bug struck and he started making enquiries as to whether any shipping line vacancies existed. The initial 'we regret' letters began to depress him but this feeling lifted when one morning he received a letter from Horizon Shipping inviting him for an interview. He went to their City offices, was short-listed and attended a second interview two weeks later. Ten days after that was offered a job.

He joined the Neptune in the following January and had now been with the Company for almost sixteen months. Despite having been on board ship for his twenty-first birthday he managed to get a ten-hour pass soon after, when the ship was in Dover, and had made his way home.

"You could do with a break, Mum," he said, "why don't you go away for a couple of weeks with Aunt Marion or your friend Liz?"

"I don't think so, dear. I'm okay. It wouldn't be the same without your Dad."

"I know that," he replied, "but surely you have to get on with your own life now!"

"We'll see," she muttered, "any way your Aunt Marion wouldn't want to go away without your Uncle George and Liz seems to have someone in tow at the moment."

"I knew you'd come up with some excuse or the other so I had a word with my boss who then spoke to the Purser and he's agreed to give you a small outside cabin on a cruise sometime in either late August or September. It has a restricted view but will cost you very little other than your drinks, tips and the price of any tours you choose to take. You can even get your washing done cheap! What do you think of that?"

Louise couldn't believe what he'd said. "Well, I don't know what to say. It sounds lovely but I wonder whether I'll be all right on a ship. I've never been before. Is the sea likely to be rough? I wouldn't want that and......."

Jeff interrupted her. "Mum, I'll leave you to make a big list of all the things that you can enjoy worrying about and when I get back to the ship I'll ask for a cabin to be allocated to you and will let you know the exact dates as soon as poss. Is that okay?"

The remainder of his short visit passed quickly and soon he was getting ready to return.

"You really are a good son." she said, giving him a big hug. "Now don't forget take care of yourself, eat properly and be careful when you go to some of those foreign places."

"'Bye Mum," he replied, "I'll phone you in a few days."

*****

"How did you get on at your meeting with Adrian?" said Alison. They were getting ready to go to the theatre and Jonathan was shaving in the bathroom.

"What was that?" he called out.

"Your meeting with Adrian", she repeated in a louder voice; "I was asking how it went."

"Oh fine. He's going to get his architect and building surveyor to look over the property and prepare a viability study and then he'll send a copy to me. If it looks a goer we'll have another meeting."

"What time have we got to leave?" she asked.

"The play starts at 8. I've booked a cab for 7.15. That should give us plenty of time. It's at the Haymarket.

"By the way, Adrian was telling me that he and his wife went on a cruise last autumn on a ship called The Poseidon. I think he said it was operated by Horizon Cruises or something like that. Anyway they thought it was really good. Apparently they have two ships that one and another called The Neptune and they are both exactly the same size."

3

"I wouldn't want to go on one of these new monsters holding three thousand passengers," commented Alison.

"No, it's nothing like that. He said they only hold about 700 passengers. Why don't you give the agent a call and ask for a brochure."

*****

It was the morning after his outrageous outburst. When she came downstairs from the bedroom he was sitting at the kitchen table having his standard breakfast of toast and orange juice. He rose and slowly came towards her.

"Karen, darling, I'm so sorry, I really am. Please forgive me. I don't know what came over me. It was just that.... well, I suppose it was a bit of a shock, but I know I was wrong and that I over-reacted and I'm really very sorry that I said what I did and called you such terrible names. Oh, please forgive me, Karen. You know I didn't mean it. I really must go now but when I get back this evening I'll take you to Casa Frederick for a lovely dinner. You'd like that won't you?"

She did not respond but simply stared at him as he picked up his brief case, pecked her on the cheek, went out into the hall and finally she heard the front door slam behind him.

She walked into the lounge and flopped into an armchair. Gradually the quiet atmosphere calmed her. Words, words, words, she thought.

David always imagined that any mental or physical abuse could instantly be repaired by a stream of meaningless words – all of which she had heard time and time again during their eight year marriage. She could not believe that over nine years had passed since they first met.

At that time, Karen had been assistant manager of Moretons, a delightful shop in Aylesbury where mainly books were sold and some classical records. As an avid reader she considered herself most fortunate to be earning her living in such a pleasant environment. She had been working there for two years before David appeared on the scene.

Having found the book that he'd wanted and paid for it, he made for the doorway turned at the last moment and said, "Thanks for your help. See you soon."

Two days later he returned.

"I don't really want another book," he said with a smile, "I just popped in to see whether you'd like to meet me after work and have a drink."

The wine bar was within walking distance from the shop. She felt totally relaxed in his company and sensed that this was mutual. He told her that he was twenty-eight, had his own company and worked as a freelance financial broker. She was unsure as to exactly what this might cover but decided not to be too inquisitive. He seemed reluctant to say too much about his past and again Karen was unwilling to pry.

A week passed and he arranged to take her out to dinner during which he told her that his parents had died some years ago, that he was an only child and that his only relations lived in far off lands and he had no contact with them whatsoever.

Shortly after they began to see each other with increasing frequency until they were in each other's company three times during the week and on either the Saturday or Sunday of each weekend. They discovered they had numerous interests in common and seemed to have similar views on many subjects. Karen though undemanding was caring, and despite neither great passion nor fire of uncontrollable lust, a sensitive love gradually developed sufficient for both to realise that they were good together.

The days and evenings when they saw each other were extended with David becoming more attentive and showing a degree of romanticism that had not previously been apparent. Ten months had passed when in the September he agreed to accompany her to Cambridge to meet her parents who would be celebrating their Silver wedding. Both were very polite towards him but Karen could tell that her mother was not enamoured.

Later in that same year they announced their engagement. Her father was concerned that she didn't seem to know much about David or his past, while her mother's comments were simply,

'Are you quite sure about this, darling?' In the October of the following year a quiet wedding took place in Cambridge.

Much to Karen's surprise, David had arranged to take her to the Bahamas for their honeymoon. She was certainly delighted whilst at the same time surprised that he could afford such a trip. It was a long journey involving a change of planes in Miami but finally Nassau was beneath them. After several minutes the aeroplane came to rest at a central bay near the terminal building which was festooned with a large red and white material sign that read 'WELCOME TO NASSAU'.

Within minutes the front and rear doors of the aircraft were opened and the odour of the Caribbean immediately permeated the nasal senses. As they approached the building steel-band music could be heard setting the scene for visitors to the Bahamas who by now had become a straggling line of weary travellers waiting to go through passport control into the baggage area. Inside the Customs Hall there was considerable confusion with officials being mainly interested to know whether arrivals were carrying any drugs or firearms.

On leaving the airport they took a taxi to the Golden Sands Hotel on Cable Beach. They were immediately swathed by considerable heat and humidity that fortunately reduced quickly with blasts of the air-conditioning. Tiredness and jet lag began to take hold and conversation was minimal though they were fascinated by some of the things that they saw as the car proceeded along the bumpy roads in what was for them another world.

Having registered, a bellboy showed them to their second floor room. They were both surprised at the size. It was like a small suite with two double beds, a table with two chairs, two armchairs, a television and a well-stocked mini-bar. The bellboy waited for his expected dollar tip and then left.

Sleep took over for nine hours until they eventually woke feeling completely rested. David drew back the curtains to find a blue sky and rippling sea greeting them. The warmth was in stark contrast to the cold of London twenty- four hours before. The white sanded beach was being sifted and cleaned by some of the hotel staff whilst a few early risers were taking a pre-breakfast dip.

Just before nine they went downstairs to the hotel terrace where a scrumptious buffet was being served. They felt starving and devoured tropical fruits, scrambled eggs with a selection of meats, some cheese, rolls and several cups of coffee.

The remainder of the day was spent at the beach, swimming and generally lazing in the sun. The start of the honeymoon was wonderful and although not over-demonstrative David tried to show an acceptable level of love and charm.

A few days later, as they prepared to go out he suddenly said to her "I wish you wouldn't wear that perfume."

Karen showed surprised. "I thought you liked the smell," she replied, "I've worn it for years and certainly throughout the time we've been together."

"Well I don't," he said abruptly, "Now if you're ready, perhaps we can go."

She didn't comment as they went to the hotel car park to find the Camaro that he had rented for three days. They drove towards the bridge that linked New Providence with Paradise Island where David had reserved a table at a well-known fish restaurant. After the meal they walked over to the casino/theatre/hotel complex and on arrival had a rum punch. He had managed to get two tickets to see the Lido de Paris cabaret, featuring stars from various parts of the world.

When the show ended he took Karen's arm and led her towards the casino that was already bubbling with activity on the roulette, blackjack and dice tables. David placed five dollars on number fourteen at the first roulette table they came to, the wheel spun and within seconds he saw his chip swept away by a swarthy looking croupier wearing dark glasses.

He remained at the table whilst Karen watched him make further bets until he had lost two hundred dollars. At this point she whispered to him, "Don't you think you should stop, David. You've lost quite a bit of money already."

He turned, his eyes glaring at her. "Why don't you mind your own business. It's my money, not yours."

He remained at the table until a further fifty dollars had gone the same way and at this stage said, "Right, let's go."

The following day they drove to Bay Street and strolled round the buzzing Colonial capital visiting the frenetic straw market and numerous shops. All forms of vehicle, many of which were laden with market produce, were causing considerable traffic jams. Men, women and children were swarming all over the roads and pavements with some women carrying personal belongings on their heads. It was a dazzling vista of Bahamian colour coupled with a hubbub of noise and the sounds of steel bands playing Caribbean music.

In the evening they visited a typical tourist restaurant with an enormous courtyard that was tiled with an attractive pattern of mosaics. During the evening local entertainers demonstrated the arts of fire eating and limbo dancing whilst a Nassau band beat out exciting musical rhythms that the waiters moved to as they served customers.

Two days before the honeymoon came to an end David suggested that they should get their first taste of deep-sea fishing. Karen was not over keen since she knew that she'd never been at her best when at sea. Nevertheless she did not wish to spoil the day for David and agreed to go. When they arrived at the quayside two North American holidaymakers were already on board. The captain supplied a picnic lunch and they all commenced eating as the boat moved out of the harbour.

Having sailed for about forty-five minutes, the captain and his mate secured the four amateur fishermen into their individual well-padded chairs. Bait had already been fixed to the lines that were cast off for them. The chase was on. In those dark, trackless deeps another life stirred. The jungle of the ocean waited and they would all hear the shrieking whirr of fishing reels for days to come.

It took nearly an hour before beginner's luck came David's way as he caught and then unassisted hauled in an eleven pound grouper. Each of the Americans caught a red snapper. Karen was the only one to be returning empty handed. As the boat turned towards shore the sea became a little choppy and she began to feel unwell. A member of the crew helped her whilst David merely ignored her discomfort.

They had to be at Nassau airport by four in the afternoon to catch the return flight from Miami. Karen was unable to sleep and frequently looked at her watch. It was now quarter past six. Day was breaking with flimsy shafts of light seeping through the chinks and cracks of the window blinds.

David sat with his eyes shut and, as if watching a film, he replayed in his mind the events of the holiday, the beauty of New Providence and Paradise Island, the deep-sea fishing trip and the straw market. He also began once more to have erotic thoughts of Melanie.

*****

"Hi, darling," said Denise, having instantly recognised Nicola's voice on her mobile phone, despite the crackling interference, "How was Crete? Where are you?"

"Still at the airport," replied Nicola, "but as soon as my case comes off the carousel I'll be on my way home. I should be with about six-thirty. Are you okay? Will you be back from the office by then?"

"I'll make sure I am. I can't wait to see you. 'Bye for now."

Since opening the agency, the agreed plan was to take a three-week skiing holiday together when it was closed over Christmas and New Year, and a separate second vacation during the year.

Nicola usually went somewhere in Greece towards the middle of April. She had a considerable interest in Greek history and mythology and belonged to a society in London that held monthly meetings and arranged cultural tours in both April and October when the weather was still bearable.

Denise was the sun-worshipper and for her it was necessary to crash out in a place in the sun where she would get browner and browner. Generally it was a last minute choice requiring three bikinis and a minimal of clothing to be packed in a very short time.

*****

9

"Of course you can." replied Gilly, "What time will you be arriving?"

"I'll catch the two o'clock from Victoria on Friday and should be at Brighton just before three."

"That's great; I'll ask Richard to meet you at the station."

It had been just a few days earlier when Delia began to feel quite exhausted. She knew that she would be unable to visit Paul for another week and was sure that a long weekend with some sea air and being totally pampered would do her the world of good.

They had been friends of Gilly and Richard for more years than she could remember and ever since Richard had become manager of The Excelsior, they had been told that there would always be a room available for them to stay.

The train arrived on time and as she walked down the platform she could see the slightly over-weight but tall and imposing Richard dressed in a smart grey suit, waving from behind the barrier.

"Welcome to the Sussex Riviera," he said smiling, following it up with a big hug.

"It's so good to see you, Richard." she said "How's Gilly?"

"She's fine, totally immersed in the hotels finances, as usual. She's always been a terrific accounts exec. You'll see her in a few minutes."

The hotel foyer was full of tropical plants and palms and as Delia entered through the swing doors, Gilly was waiting to greet her.

"Oh, I'm so pleased you've come down," she said, as they gave each other a warm embrace.

"I've got a lovely room for you with all mod. cons. facing the sea. You're booked in from today until next Tuesday morning. I couldn't make it any longer since the hotel's completely full for a conference after Monday.

"The room, food and drinks are on the house and if there's anything that you need just ask."

"I can't thank you enough," said Delia, with a few tears showing in her eyes.

"Now none of that, follow me and I'll take you to the room. How's Paul getting on?"

"It's tough for him but this time he's really making a big effort. I'm allowed to call him every day but it breaks my heart just to think about it all."

Her room on the fifth floor was large with a wrought iron balcony running the full width. She had an uninterrupted view of the beach and sea with the Palace Pier to her left and West Pier to her right. The cars beneath appeared as matchbox editions.

On a table by the window was a vase filled with roses attached to which was a card that read, 'Have a great time, Delia, love Gilly and Richard.' On a writing bureau she found a bowl of fruit and a box of Elizabeth Shaw mints.

Once again tears came to her eyes. The shrill ring of the telephone broke her hypnotic gaze.

"Hello, Delia, it's Richard. I hope everything is to your liking?"

"It certainly is. The room is lovely and thank you so much for the flowers and the fruit and the chocolates. I just don't know what to say!"

'It's our pleasure. Would you like to join Gilly and me for dinner this evening?'

'Richard, that's very kind of you but may I take a rain check until to-morrow. I'm feeling extremely tired at the moment and would prefer to have dinner in my room and get an early night.'

"No problem," he responded, "Just call room service. You'll find a menu on the dressing table and have a good night's sleep."

Delia remembered unpacking but when she next looked at her watch it was nearly seven. She realised that she had dozed off in the armchair. She decided to take a shower and then order a salad.

By nine fifteen she was in bed with utter fatigue enveloping her body as she fell into a deep sleep.

*****

"Bob, it's me, Peter."

"You just beat me to it. I guess you've also received a letter this morning from George?"

"That's right, a booking on the Neptune leaving Dover on Saturday 15th September. I've just checked the brochure. It looks terrific. It's a Mediterranean cruise with some smashing port stops."

"Why don't you come over later this afternoon," responded Robert, "we can pop out for some fish and chips."

They were both widowers in their late sixties. When their wives were alive they would often go together to the local dance hall that had at one time been an old training centre for boxers.

Being without their loving partners, the days passed far too slowly until one day Peter had an idea.

"Why don't we try and get ourselves accepted as dance hosts on a ship?"

They found that there was an agent in the centre of Nottingham who might be able to help them. When they arrived at his office they discovered that the owner, George Simpson, was someone that had both known for many years when they had been working for the local insurance company. Before they knew what had happened they had received their first booking on a P & O cruise ship.

And that was the start of a new career and a new life for them both.

*****

Before commencing the next morning's drive, Laura calculated that she was about one hundred and twenty miles from her final destination. She could remember very little of the previous night's dream other than recalling how her mother had come into view and appeared to be watching over her.

She had already driven seven hundred and seventy-seven miles since leaving London. She began to think, lucky seven for gamblers, three sevens make twenty-one, twenty-one today, at one time celebrated as the crossroads into manhood. Perhaps this was now meant to be a major crossroad in her life.

The road to Angers passed through mainly agricultural countryside. She was now at the gateway to the magnificent Loire Valley where, from here and beyond, in a region of so many well-known historical towns and cities, Joan of Arc became the most famous French national heroine of all times.

There was considerable traffic on the main road and Laura decided to take the more scenic route running by the River Loire. The pastel blue of the sky coupled with hints of intermittent threads of white reminded her of fine pieces of Wedgwood glazed with their exquisite cameos. She now had an irresistible urge to reach Asnieres-sur-Vegre as soon as possible.

Frequently disregarding some of the speed limits, she sped through Jumelles and Clefs until reaching La Fleche. Here she took the road that would lead to Sable-sur-Sarthe and thereafter to the last few miles of her journey. Surely now she would be able to solve the all-embracing mystery which had haunted her for months.

This time there was no sudden rainstorm or any sign of inclement weather. The sun continued to shine brightly, lighting up her final path. The River La Vegre lie on the right of the slightly curving road and she could see two men fishing whilst small boats were going up and down the gentle flowing waters. At the tiny village of Le Port de Juigne, a landing stage stood for the hiring of boats.

Laura was relieved to see a signpost indicating that there was only three point three kilometres remaining. Her feelings of anticipation grew as she continued along this countryside route.

A large water tower loomed in the distance and as Laura crossed over a bridge that spanned the rail track she could see cows, sheep and horses. There was nothing of an unwelcome nature here in Asnieres-sur-Vegre.

It was immediately obvious that this was a much larger village than the two previous places she had seen. Weeping willows stood by the river banks waving a greeting to her. At the far end of the village she discovered the Chateau de Moulin-Vieux, and then turned back crossing a twelfth century stone walled bridge, which led into a little square. Laura parked the car and addressed an elderly man who was out walking his two dogs. She spoke to him of a family Flatau.

'Family Flatau.' he repeated, 'I am not sure. The young have left Asnieres. There is nothing here for them any more. Flatau, it is possible. They will have a telephone book at The Auberge Pavillon.'

As Laura walked in the direction of The Pavillon, she came to the Eglise St. Hilaire. Numerous guests were assembling prior to entering the church for a special private service. A war memorial stood in remembrance of those who died in the two World Wars and she noticed that the trees of the church were quite extraordinary having been cut back and then groomed in a rather strange way.

Close to the church was a house where, on the outside wall had been fixed a plaque. Laura laughed and found that she had to read the wording twice, in order to make sure that she'd read it correctly the first time. It bore the inscription "In this house on 26 May 1907 John Wayne was not born."

At The Pavillon Laura was handed a copy of the 'phone book but nobody with the name Flatau was listed. As had happened before, she was directed to the Town Hall. Strolling towards where it stood, she wondered in which of the streets she would find that Monsieur or Madame Flatau lived. She had no doubt that he or she was here somewhere.

The Town Hall was a small building that had recently been re-rendered and where considerable roof repairs were taking place. There was one main office occupied by a man and a woman who were busily working. Laura explained to the man the nature of her visit, whilst the woman continued to be immersed, in what appeared to be, some account books.

The electoral list was produced. Laura felt a numbness creep over her. She swallowed hard and could hear her heart pounding. There was a population of three hundred and eighteen but the name of Flatau was not there.

"C'est pas possible," Laura cried out, "Please check again for me. It cannot be. They have to be here."

Laura assumed that the man must have thought she was going to faint since he quickly brought her a glass of water.

"I'm so sorry Madame, but I cannot help you."

She walked out of the Town Hall feeling totally dejected and started to walk aimlessly away from the building. Within moments, she heard a female voice calling after her.

"Madame, Madame." called the lady from the Mairie, "There was a Madame Flatau here, but she left three years ago."

"Do you know where she went?" asked Laura excitedly.

"Oui, Madame. She moved to a town called La Fleche. It is perhaps forty kilometres from here. Not too far."

"I passed it earlier." commented Laura. "Did you know her well? Do you have her address?"

"Come with me to my house, I'm sure I can help you."

They continued talking as this lady of about sixty years, wearing a black dress with long sleeves and white lace cuffs, led her to her home. It was only two hundred yards from the Town Hall.

"Please, sit down, Madame. You are looking very tired. I will make some coffee."

After ten minutes, she returned with a tray of coffee and a delicious looking brioche full of raisins. She cut a slice for each of them and poured out the coffee. Laura could not believe how heavenly it tasted. She had no doubt that it had been freshly cooked that morning.

"Let me find my glasses, Madame."

Having found them, she went across to the mantelpiece on which there was a pile of letters and other scraps of paper. She commenced rummaging through these until Laura was relieved to hear her pronounce "Ah, je le trouve, I have found it."

She took off her glasses and wrote down the address, 21.Rue Fontaine.

Laura thanked her very much and when leaving turned and said, 'You did not tell me your name, Madame.'

"Sylvie Mercier, and you, Madame"

Warm puffs of wind blew through the car windows as Laura returned to Sable and then took the road to La Fleche. Could the end really be in sight! She felt tremendous excitement as each kilo-meter of the journey passed. She repeated to herself,

"21, Rue Fontaine" and thought, twenty-one - three sevens. These were the numbers that she had been thinking of earlier.

So it was a Madame Flatau. Madame Mercier had not mentioned any Monsieur Flatau, but in her haste she had not asked. What age would she be? What had made her move to La Fleche? The ring had certainly been for a man and Laura began to think that perhaps her mother had once been friendly with this Madame Flatau.

But if that was so, why had she not said so! Maybe Madame Flatau's husband had died and it was he who her mother had known. Soon, very soon and she would know.

Eight miles remained with almost nine hundred miles completed. It had been a long, wearisome drive that she would not wish to repeat. Her emotions had been strung out to the point of exhaustion. She had been to towns and villages bearing the name Asnieres on four occasions and had suffered despair each time, until now, when her hopes were raised to an absolute climax.

She became hypnotised by the road ahead, a road that would lead to Madame Flatau. A hoarding of a big lion glared down at her advertising the Zoo at La Fleche. She remembered that La Fleche, in French, meant *arrow* and how she was being pointed in the direction of the next chapter in her life.

Having driven through the town's industrial area Laura saw a sign 'Centre Ville'. She continued with the river Loir on her right and a monument to Delibes on the opposite side. She stopped at the local tourist office and collected a town map. Rue Fontaine was nearby.

She turned towards Place Henri IV. She was almost there. It was only a matter of one or two minutes. Laura made a silent prayer hoping that Madame Flatau would neither have moved nor be out.

Suddenly, on her left she saw a white street nameplate bearing the words, Rue Fontaine. She slowed to no more than five miles per hour whilst keeping her foot lightly on the brake pedal until she arrived outside a terraced house that had a small, narrow, wooden door on which were brass figures of a two and a one...21.

As she walked up to the front door she felt cold shivers passing through her. Laura pressed the bell and waited. But there was no reply. She tried again with the same result. As she was about to ring for the third time a woman appeared from the house next door.

"Can I help you, Madame?"

"Madame Flatau," said Laura, "I am looking for Madame Flatau."

"She is not here, Madame. She has gone on holiday for seventeen days."

"When did she go?" asked Laura.

"Yesterday, Madame."

"And do you know where she has gone?"

"Oui, Madame. She left for England."

*****

TWO

There could never be any doubt to those who saw them together that they were very much in love. It was as though a certain glow radiated that one does not see too often and they certainly made a handsome couple. Vince was 5'9", slim, clean shaven with a good complexion whilst Anne was a little shorter with mid-length light brown hair and the most engaging of smiles. Both had a friendly personality that made them very popular.

At the time of first meeting they were living in Salisbury with Vince a local private school teacher of Geography, History and the History of Art from 1850, whilst Anne worked for a company dedicated to raising funds for charities.

They were both still single and in their early-30's but on this occasion the magical chemistry of love registered immediately and they were married within six months. Initially, Anne moved in with Vince, who had a delightful flat that was within walking distance of the school and her office.

Their search for a suitable home away from the busy city proved difficult until one Sunday several weeks later they drove out to a popular country restaurant for lunch. When reaching the outskirts of Shaftesbury, they suddenly spotted a 'PRIVATE SALE' notice board outside the most idyllic of thatched cottages, where a lady was watering flowers in the front garden.

Vince stopped the car and asked when it would be convenient for them to return to view the property.

"Why not come in now." she replied.

The next morning Anne telephoned, made an offer that was accepted and ten weeks later they moved in. They were now living twenty miles from Salisbury but the A30 link was a good fast road that prevented commuter problems.

A chorus of birds frequently greeted them and all around were a vast array of wonderful trees and bushes. Apart from the distant noise of the occasional motor vehicle their natural surroundings provided peace and calm.

The garden became a special haven for Anne and her colourful flowers and roses were admired by all. Gradually she added a small ornamental pond, built a rockery in which wild flowers were planted and arranged for a newly seeded lawn to be laid.

During the first two years in the cottage, Anne became pregnant twice, but had a miscarriage each time. She took a pragmatic view concluding that she was not fated for motherhood and the subject became a closed book.

Living in the countryside was a positive delight whilst at the same time they were near enough to many towns and cities where considerable cultural activities could be enjoyed. Their joint income was sufficient to be able to have a good life without going over the top and from time to time they enjoyed vacations in either France or Italy.

They felt sure they were the luckiest people and fortunate to have nothing serious to worry about until….until…..on looking back they were in fact unsure when it had all started!

*****

Jonathan Richards was larger than life and could not fail to make an impression. He was heavyset with broad shoulders and thinning black hair. He had an intelligent face with high cheekbones, was clean-shaven and wore glasses. Though always polite he could be slightly brusque, considerate though prying, serious one moment and capable of making amusing remarks the next.

He was an exciting man to work with continuously having new ideas and constantly exhibiting his entrepreneurial skills. He worked closely with his financial director, Roger Gould, who had been with him for almost twelve years. Roger was forty-three with sharp features and the build of an athlete. His appearance and good speaking voice was such that his presence could never go unnoticed.

He was there to dot the i's and cross the t's on all contracts and other business documents and provide Jonathan with invaluable financial information in relation to the group's projects. He also acted as devil's advocate when considering whether or not 'a new J.R idea' was viable.

Jonathan had accomplished more in his forty-eight years than most men could in ten lifetimes. People, especially women, either loved or hated him, there was no middle course. He had a great sense of humour with a proverbial bark being worse than his bite. He would frequently threaten but never take action against anyone.

His company, Central Property Developments Plc., was well known in the property world with offices in a delightful period house in Chesterfield Street, Mayfair. He never failed to be thrilled by the area and felt as though he was treading the same path as of the many great men who had once resided in that part of London, as Beau Brummell who had dwelt at No.4 Chesterfield Street and Somerset Maughan who had lived at No.6.

Jonathan's marital record was considerable having already been married and divorced three times. The first at age eighteen had lasted six weeks. The second when he was twenty had passed first anniversary but came to an abrupt end one month after. A year later he was joined in matrimony with bride number three and in due course they had three daughters whom he idolised. Their marriage jogged along a very bumpy road for nineteen years until it could go no further.

And now he was with Alison an average height thirty-three year old blonde who when just over twenty, had once been described as being 'a highly attractive and desirable filly who, having been released from her reins - after leaving a Lausanne finishing school – made havoc with every eligible stud that she could find.'

She had lived with Mummy and Daddy – as she called them – in a mansion flat at the wrong end of Kensington. When returning to England she obtained a PA job with a small West End hotel group and soon after, as a result of manipulating her feminine wiles on an unsuspecting guest, managed to obtain a basement flat that was available for rent in King's Road, Chelsea.

Alison then ensured that she went wherever it was that 'the right people' go to be seen and following a series of introductions subsequently became engaged to a man of some wealth who, like Jonathan, was considerably older then she.

After five months the potential groom called off the engagement and was later heard to have said that 'he had escaped just in time from that money-grabbing hard faced bitch.'

Thereafter, she played the field but had no firm offers. Then when twenty eight she met Jonathan who became utterly besotted and spent every possible minute with her. Exotic restaurants, numerous theatre visits and exciting holidays staying in five star hotels all swiftly followed.

Two years later, the bewitched Jonathan married for the fourth time. The 'sloane ranger' who had graduated to a 'sloane princess' was now enthroned. Her prowess at running up expense accounts was instant and on one occasion Jonathan told Roger 'the only time I'm sure that she's not spending money is when she's asleep and even then I wouldn't mind betting that she's dreaming up fresh ways to spend it.'

*****

Karen's net salary was deposited into a joint bank account and was used for almost all household and her personal expenses. David paid out of his office account the rent, utilities and all other expenses of the ground floor/ first floor flat in Aylesbury that they had moved into just before they were married. Although there were no specific grounds for her suspicions she certainly had a feeling that their overall financial situation might not be as good as he had led her to believe.

Her distrust was confirmed when one weekday evening, a few months after they had been married, David was out and whilst she was cleaning the second bedroom she noticed a letter lying on the floor towards the back of his desk. As she picked it up she could not fail to see that it was addressed to him from Barclays Bank, which read –

Dear Mr. Hardwick,

Re: Business Loan Account No.3

I refer to the arrangements made with you in accordance with my facility letter of November last when I agreed to advance you a further loan of £5,000 for the purpose of expanding your business. It was a condition that you would forward quarterly management accounts to me and that you would commence repaying this loan by three- monthly instalments commencing 1st April this year.

Neither of these conditions has been complied with and I must ask you to telephone my secretary and make an appointment to see me next week.

Yours sincerely,

Peter Davis.
Branch Manager

Karen read the letter a second time and placed it on the desk. It then occurred to her that the date of the loan was shortly before they had gone to Nassau.

He arrived home at about 9.30. "Hello David," she called out, "Have you eaten or can I get you something now?"

"I'm okay," he replied, "I'll be with you in a minute." She heard him go into their bedroom and then into the second bedroom.

A few moments went by and he came storming into the living room.

"Have you been reading my letters? Have you been going over my papers?" he shouted. She had never seen him so enraged.

"If you're referring to the Bank letter, David, I found it on the floor at the back of your desk when I was cleaning. I couldn't help but see it and yes I did read it. Perhaps it's as well but please don't accuse me of going over your papers."

"What do you mean, it's as well. My bank finances have nothing to do with you. Just keep your nose out of my affairs. I'm going out for a drink. You'll see me when you see me."

Karen was inwardly shaking and started to cry uncontrollably. She couldn't believe that he would ever talk to her like this or behave in such a manner. She had no doubt that their marriage had not brought the happiness which she had expected and had constantly wondered what else might happen.

It didn't take long before she knew the answer.

Melanie had been the first that she found out about. After her came Erica who was followed by Caroline – and goodness knows how many others.

Karen made a conscious decision never to have children with David and though slightly surprised she found it more than interesting that he never raised the matter at anytime.

She had made her bed…….but what next?

*****

Until she was fourteen, Denise, had thought that her village of two hundred people and seven dogs were the world. She lived in a farmhouse near the Grampian Mountains where her father was the land-manager of a sizeable estate. Life was simple but far from easy. This area had always been formidable with its desolate moorlands, wild and barren hills, fast-flowing rivers and old tiled roofed cottages dotted around the landscape.

The death of the owner brought about the sale of the estate and the end of her father's job. He was fortunate to obtain a new position as an administrator in the offices of Hereford County Council and much to her joy and to that of her mother they moved to a flat on the outskirts of the City.

It was quite beautiful there being close to the Wye Valley and the dramatic gorge of Symonds Yat. Living in an area of orchards and rich grazing pastures with famous Hereford cattle provided a complete contrast to the Grampians and they often visited Hereford Cathedral which over-looked the six-arched stone bridge that spanned the River Wye.

It was there that she found the chained library containing over 1,600 books and the unique 13th Century Mappa Mundi, the map of the world that shows the world as being flat with Jerusalem as being the centre.

Denise continued her education at a nearby school until, when eighteen, she enrolled on a full-time management accounting course at a local college. At the end of two years she was awarded a diploma and obtained a job with a firm of accountants. She had grown into a delightful young lady, slim with long dark hair who was enjoying life to the full, frequently going out on dates but having no desire for any of her suitors to become serious.

Having worked with the accountants for just over a year they suddenly asked whether she'd like the opportunity of transferring to their London office. She could not believe her luck and immediately accepted. Accommodation was made available to her in a spare room in a flat in Queensway where the office manager, Clive Goddard and his wife Tina lived. A few weeks later she took the train to Paddington station where Clive was there to meet her. She and Tina hit it off instantly and in no time became good friends. Tina commented to Clive, "It's like having a sister staying with me."

Denise loved working and living in London and took full advantage of the many galleries, museums and theatres. She made plans to be in Hereford over Christmas but her parents knew that she would have to get back to London by the thirtieth as Clive and Tina had obtained an invitation for her to join them at a New Year's party at the home of one of their major clients in Berkshire.

It was a typically cold December evening when they started their journey in Clive's car. Feathery crystals of snow were lying on the meadows and fields and the trees all around wore a silvery cloak. The traffic had prevented the snow from settling and they reached Ascot in just over an hour. The house stood in five acres of ground and was set well back from the main road. They arrived at the same time as a number of other guests and could hear music being played as they entered the house.

A log-fire burned brightly in the lounge hall where a bar had been set up and waitresses were dispensing drinks and canapés. The party was being held in an enormous drawing room, which appeared to exceed forty feet in length. Most of the furniture had been moved to provide plenty of dancing space on the parquet flooring.

Whilst Clive and Tina were introducing Denise to a group of people she noticed a girl of about her age at the other side of the room. Her short blonde hair and knee-length off-the-shoulder red dress set off by a thin gold chain round her neck disguised her high-spirited tomboy ways.

As the girl smilingly came towards them, Tina whispered, "That's Nicola, the daughter of the house."

Denise could not take her eyes off Nicola and suddenly experienced feelings that she had never felt before.

*****

Delia had married Paul when she was twenty-nine. They had no children. A previous long engagement had been broken off, when she had discovered that her fiancée was still having regular assignations with a past flame. Paul then appeared on the scene. He was a tall, good-looking man aged thirty-four who had the ability to keep her enthralled with his journalistic stories from the past. Five months later they were husband and wife and moved into a detached three-bedroom house in a rural area just outside Dorking.

She worked as a paralegal for a firm of solicitors in their department that dealt with accident claims, many of which related to motor claims arising in France. Their biggest clients were three insurance companies. Her expertise, and in fact the reason why she obtained the job in the first place, was because of her ability to speak fluent French. She dressed very smartly and her blonde hair in a chignon was always well groomed.

The first three years were wonderful until she began to suspect that his drinking habits were becoming excessive. The glass of scotch prior to dinner became two glasses, the half bottle of wine during dinner increased to a full bottle whilst the occasional after dinner brandy turned to three or four.

He refused to acknowledge that his drinking was excessive until one evening he was stopped by the police whilst driving at over ninety miles an hour on the M6. He was found to be three times over the limit and was prosecuted for speeding, dangerous driving, being over the prescribed alcohol limit and having a faulty rear brake light. Apart from monetary fines he was banned from driving for one year.

His work as a freelance representative of International Publications Limited suffered for some time, to the extent that Delia was now the true bread-winner.

She was very much in love with Paul and was pleased that he was now showing signs of reducing his drink intake down to acceptable levels. But the lure of alcohol once again seduced him a few months later when he reverted to his past weaknesses. Delia's life with him was certain only as far as it was surely uncertain, since she never knew how he would be from one day to another or sometimes from one hour to the next.

It was at that time that a wedding invitation had been received and on the morning of the big day Delia was on edge praying that Paul would not throw a wobbly at the last moment.

He started to dress without argument. She had bought a very pretty pastel pink chiffon dress with short sleeves and scooped neckline.

"When did you get that?" he asked.

"Last week, in a sale at a shop near Selfridges. Do you like it?"

"It's all right, mind you, if it had any less material you wouldn't have needed to bother."

He paused and stood staring at her. Her stomach knotted up. He continued in a sneering manner, "Still, I suppose it'll be just great with all your Mayfair and county-county legal friends."

He went from the bedroom into the bathroom and she breathed a sigh of relief until he re-appeared.

"Bloody ties! Who the hell wants to wear a bloody tie in this weather. It's not midday and it's already boiling. It's okay for you to wear sod all, but me....why the hell have I got to wear a tie? I'd be okay if I had a drink."

She trembled as he spoke. She had been sitting at the dressing room table, putting on the final touches of make-up, as she listened to his outburst. As she looked at herself and Paul in the mirror she could see the colour drain from her face until only a ghostly image looked back at her.

She stood up, went over to him, kissed him on the cheek and very quietly suggested "Why don't you leave your tie off for now and put it on when we park at the church? That way you won't get too hot. You certainly look great in that suit. I've always liked seeing you in blue. He's quite the debonair man, my husband."

He looked hard at her for several seconds before commenting, "Oh, all right, but if I'm hot later it's bloody well coming off." and returned to the bathroom.

Each and every day Delia felt as though she was walking on glass, whilst endeavouring to understand him, his pain, his fears and the absolute terror he had of losing her.

The beautiful warm June day had enabled most of the women guests to turn out in the flimsiest of flimsy garments. Seeing this made Delia relax knowing that Paul, now with tie on, when drawing comparisons could not judge her appearance so harshly.

When the ceremony was over everyone left the church and made their way to the home of the bride's parents where a marquee had been erected for a luncheon. Paul immediately obtained champagne cocktails for him and Delia but for the rest of the time he handled himself well.

In due course the wedding reception was over, confetti thrown over the newly weds as they drove off and shortly after the guests commenced their journeys homeward bound.

Delia breathed a deep sigh of relief.

*****

Matt was three-quarters of the way through practising his latest magician's trick when the 'phone rang.

"Damn," he muttered under his breath, thinking every time I'm in the middle of something the 'phone goes.

He dashed into the hall picking up the receiver.

"Hello, Matt Campbell here. Who's that?"

"Good afternoon, Mr. Campbell, it's Bryan Dalton, deputy Entertainments manager of HSL. I see you're scheduled to appear as comedian/magician on the Neptune cruise in mid-September."

"Yes, that's right," responded Matt, "Why, is there a problem?"

"Well in a way there is. Your booking is not affected but unfortunately there are some knew health and safety regulations that have been served on the company that mean we will not be permitted to have both your wife and son and all of your equipment with you in the one cabin as before.

"We have been checking through the reservation schedules and have no other cabin that will be suitable in terms of overall size and we don't have any where else for you to keep your props. during the voyage.

"I'm awfully sorry about this but the only solution is if your five year old son was not travelling with you both. Perhaps you would like to discuss the situation with your wife and call me back in a day or so. Goodbye."

*****

Laura's parents had died when she was only seven years old. They had been on holiday in Hawaii and had taken a helicopter ride along the coast of Maui which suddenly spun out of control and crashed into the waters below. There had been no survivors. She had subsequently lived with and had been brought up by her late mother's sister and her husband in a village near Devizes.

She was an excellent student and had a great passion for the piano. She had been the sole beneficiary of her parent's estates that had been left in trust for her until she reached the age of twenty-five. In the meantime, the trustees had discretionary power to provide all necessary funds from the Trust for her education and maintenance.

As the years passed, she sat for the Associated Board of Royal School of Music examinations, showing considerable ability from Grade 1 through to Grade 8. Her aunt then took her to London for an audition at the Royal Academy of Music in Marylebone Road. She was accepted for a four-year degree course.

And so aged eighteen, an excited, neatly dressed Laura who had auburn-coloured hair with a small fringe, journeyed to

London where initially hostel accommodation had been arranged for her in Camden Town by one of the Academy officers who ensured that all students had somewhere to stay.

The opportunity of being able to hear music in London opened to her like a flower beginning to bud. Concerts, recitals, academy performances and so much more were virtually on offer daily providing time and funds permitted. A year later she left the hostel to share a flat with two other girls, that was also in Camden Town,

She began to realise that only a small percentage of pupils would ever be good enough to reach the top echelon of pianists. Competition was fierce and the work-load severe. Nevertheless, she worked hard and at the end of the four years obtained her degree.

She often returned to Devizes for the weekend enjoying the Wiltshire countryside and taking walks alongside the Kennet and Avon canal. The warm stone of Wiltshire gave her an inner glow that brought pleasure and happiness.

She had begun to supplement her income both as an accompanist and rehearsal pianist and decided that these positions suited her temperament ideally whilst at the same time she would take up piano teaching as a career.

When one of her flat mates decided to return home to Manchester, Laura and the third of the trio, Doreen Langton, who had been studying singing, agreed to share a smaller flat. Contacts in Camden Town proved helpful and a two-bedroom flat was found with a large living room that enabled Laura to buy a piano. Doreen was already receiving engagements that on many occasions took her out of London.

Slowly Laura was able to build up a clientele seeking piano lessons and as her income increased she was able to take advantage of London's offerings. Whenever Doreen was with her visiting art galleries was high on their agenda. From time to time they both had romantic interludes but neither was interested in being other than single at this stage of their careers.

It was on her twenty-fifth birthday that both unexpected and puzzling incidents began to appear that would affect her life considerably.

First, at a celebratory weekend in Devizes she was told of the extent of the trust funds to which she would now be entitled. Although she knew a fund had been created for her benefit it was the amount that surprised her considerably.

Secondly, her aunt handed her a jiffy bag bearing her name c/o the Devizes address. She could feel that there was a small box inside. She shook the envelope but nothing rattled. She took it over to the window but the thickness of the bag prevented her being able to see what the contents might be.

Laura went into the kitchen and with the aid of a small sharp knife slowly opened the bag. Inside was a ring box containing a gentleman's gold signet ring with engraved shoulders and a set stone of reddish-brown colour supported by a closed-in back.

Once more she felt inside the bag and this time found that there was a letter from Edward Wilton, one of the trustees, telling her that he had received instructions to let her have the box when she became twenty-five. She showed the ring to her aunt but she couldn't offer any explanation.

"There's some marking on the inside of the shank but it's so feint that I can't read it," commented Laura, " It's extraordinary but when I held the ring in my hand I felt a cold shiver go down my back."

She had been holding the ring between her fingers as she spoke.

"The stone's a little loose but I'll tell you one thing, it fits me perfectly. I don't understand it."

She and her aunt continued to talk whilst Laura began to replace the ring in the box. As she did so she could feel the lower layer of the box shift very slightly.

"Hold on a moment," she exclaimed, "I've just noticed that the inside layer of the box moves very slightly."

By deft use of her fingernail Laura was able to prise the layer out of the box. When she looked at the reverse side she could see the hardly perceptible lettering which read 'ASNIERES'.

"Does that name mean anything to you?' she asked her aunt.

"Not a thing, I'm not even sure how to pronounce it. It could be the name of a person or the name of a place. I've no idea."

Throughout that day Laura examined and re-examined the jiffy bag, the box, the ring and the layer to which it had been attached. Nothing further was revealed. Mental pictures of the ring and the word Asnieres constantly danced before her eyes as she wondered how and when she would be able to discover the meaning of the ring.

Later that day Laura returned to Camden Town. She slept fitfully seeing the arrival of almost each hour on the hour. At every awakening a vision of the ring and the word Asnieres crept into her mind, as phantoms of the night, teasing, taunting and disturbing sleep. As the silent hands of her luminous bedside clock made their inevitable way towards dawn, Laura struggled to gain rest but it would not come. Her eyes were laden with tiredness, her body ached with fatigue and yet sleep would only comfort her momentarily, until once more she became afflicted by discursive thoughts.

By quarter past six, she could lie in bed no longer. Having showered, dressed and breakfasted she caught an early bus to Regent's Park entering by the Northern gate near the Zoo.

Nature's kaleidoscope of colour was slowly waking and a winged feathery body stirred and fluttered seeking succour whilst nestling in its nest. Ant inhabited pot-holed paths that were foot worn and uneven sloped gently in all directions

She had brought with her the remains of a loaf and now made her way to the boating lake and stood at the edge throwing pieces of bread to the waiting assembly of ducks, geese and swans. An armada of mallards and tufted ducks speedily sailed towards her and the battle began. The older and larger birds seemed to push aside the ducklings and goslings. Laura threw the remaining broken scraps closer to the younger members of this entourage until there was nothing left of the loaf.

As she stepped away from the slopping waters, Laura continued towards the Marylebone High Street exit. She passed a woman who she had noticed had been watching her feed the ducks.

The woman smiled and then in a soft, gentle voice said, "Good morning. Loneliness brings a sense of vulnerability, but do not be anxious for it will pass."

Laura stared at her. She was in her late sixties, dressed in a black and white chequered blouse with a grey skirt and wore full-framed spectacles of almost octagonal shape. She had permanent waved greyish blonde hair off the ears and forehead and from the lope of each ear hung a twisted snake designed gilt earring. A mere touch of lipstick had been applied to her lips. Above all her face was kindness personified.

"Why did you say that?" asked Laura.

"Oh dear, I'm so sorry if I've upset you. Perhaps I shouldn't have said anything. It was just that – well never mind." the woman responded.

"Please, tell me. What were you going to say?"

"It was as you fed the ducks. I suddenly noticed that you were swathed in a green light. Colours can mean so much."

She came closer to Laura.

"You will have great love surrounding you. Don't be frightened of the future. Everything happens for a reason. You are protected."

"Who are you?" asked Laura, speaking very slowly, feeling dumbstruck at the stranger's comments.

"It doesn't matter who I am. Just say I'm a friend. I work considerably in psychic studies. Trust me and believe that what I've told you is truth. I must go now."

"But I don't understand," Laura replied, sounding apprehensive and stressed, "there are so many things happening to me and I don't know why or what they mean - and now you."

"Everything in life gradually becomes clear. Don't fear any of those things. Accept them as being meant and don't fight them. Go with the flow of life. The journey that you're planning will help you. Goodbye."

The woman started to turn away from her.

"Wait, please wait." called out Laura, "What journey? I haven't planned any journey."

"You will and you will be going very soon."

*****

THREE

At first Vince had taken very little notice of what he thought were nothing but isolated events of no great import. First, Anne had started to leave the door ajar when they went into a room. Then, when arriving for dinner at a block of flats in Salisbury, where some friends lived on the third-floor, Anne had said, "Let's not take the lift. I've never really liked lifts and anyway the exercise will do us good."

Sundays were when they would often go out into the countryside and visit places of interest. Anne's love of gardens had motivated her to suggest that they took the car to see those at Stourhead where there was also a lake, temples and many other features.

The site was not very far from where they lived and Vince started off along the A30. Despite the fact that the traffic was not excessive, within minutes, Anne had commented "It's busier than I thought on this road. Maybe we should turn off on to a country road?" It was easy enough for him to do this and he did so without giving the matter another thought.

But the crux of the problem was about to become evident. They had agreed some time before that a vacation to California would be something really special since neither had visited the United States previously. Having spent many winter evenings going through brochures and guide books they settled on an itinerary and Vince made the airline reservations.

About three weeks before departure Anne showed signs of being exceedingly nervous whenever the holiday was mentioned. On more than one occasion she started to tremble, came out in a cold sweat and felt nauseous. Vince kept on asking her what was wrong but each time she just passed over her symptoms as being 'nothing' until finally she burst into tears saying "I can't go, I can't go. You'll have to cancel the American trip. I can't go."

He tried to console her and asked what was wrong.

"I can't face going on the 'plane."

"But we've flown many times before – why not now?"

It was late in the afternoon of the following day that he accompanied her to Dr. Alexander who asked many searching questions before commenting, "I believe you know what's wrong, Anne. Am I right?"

Vince looked on waiting for her to reply but she just sat perfectly still and calm.

"What do you mean, Doctor?"

"Anne is suffering from claustrophobia but let me make it clear that this is not an illness. Basically, it is a fear that Anne has of not always being able to find an easy way of escaping when in an enclosed area. The airplane example that you gave is a perfectly normal one and I have no doubt that should you both look back you will be able to identify this lack of escape route to other situations when Anne has suddenly felt very uncomfortable."

"So what happens now? Will you be giving her pills or some medicine?" asked Vince anxiously.

"It isn't just a matter of taking medication," replied the doctor, "There is no doubt that claustrophobia has an extremely debilitating effect but to a great extent the solution lies in the hands of or, perhaps I should say, the mind of the patient."

He turned to Anne before continuing, "It will be necessary for you to have a strong belief that you can free yourself and overcome these problems. There are many people who have similar difficulties but with conviction and determination you will win through. It will take time but every positive step that you take will be leading you to gradually erasing these fears."

Anne showed signs of being tearful and asked, "So what do I have to do?"

"I'm not an expert in this field but I'd like to recommend that you see a therapist who will be able to discuss everything with you. There is an excellent qualified lady who practises here in Salisbury and should you agree I'll send a letter to her. Leave it a few days then call her secretary to make an appointment."

And so the days and the weeks merged into months and throughout Anne made desperate efforts to improve her reaction to the fears that were triggered whenever conditions arose that caused her panics. She found that the therapist in

Salisbury had showed considerable empathy and after a year or so took her advice and consulted a regression hypnotist but this did not provide any answers to the possible cause of her problems.

There were many periods that she was able to lead a normal life so long as she avoided bringing into play 'the ghouls' as she referred to her difficulties.

One evening Vince was going to be late at school for a parents meeting. "I'll be fine," Anne had told him, "I intend going to bed early."

By her bedside table was a volume on the life of Edward Munch that she had been reading. None of the words of the biography registered, she merely turned the pages to the colour plates of his masterworks. There, were the haunting eyes of the faces in 'Evening on Karl Johan Street', the young girl's encounter with death in 'The Sick Child' and then the most celebrated 'Scream', the same silent scream that she was inwardly experiencing. The book fell from her hands, as the weight of her eyelids could no longer remain open.

She woke with a start, her head thumping and became riddled with anxiety in relation to her fears and by a torrent of thoughts as to how they might affect her marriage.

*****

"Back again already?" said Louise.

Jeff always telephoned her when his ship returned to port and occasionally from a cheap telephone call centre abroad.

"This last cruise was only twelve days." he replied, "How have you been? Got any news for me?"

"Not really, darling, life just goes on although there is one thing that I haven't told you. I've got a part-time job in the local library."

"That's great. How did that come about?"

"Do you remember Mrs. Miller from Stratton Street?"

"Yes."

"Well, I bumped into her a few weeks ago and she mentioned that she and her husband had sold their house and would shortly be moving to Spain. She asked me whether I'd be interested in taking over her job at the library as she knew that they were still looking for someone. I told her I would and last week I went along and met the big-white chief and he gave me the job. I'm really quite excited and it'll give me something of interest to do. I told a little porky by saying that I was expecting to be away in September for a couple of weeks and he said that they'd honour the arrangement."

"I'm really pleased for you. My mum the librarian, eh! And as for the cruise you were right to tell him although I still don't have any definite date for you."

"That's okay. By the way where did you get to on your last trip?"

"It was smashing. It was a Baltic cruise and I managed to get off in Stockholm, Copenhagen and also in St. Petersburg. They often take this route so next time I'll try and get time off in some of the other ports. I've got to go now. Talk to you soon. Carry on reading. 'Bye."

*****

Jonathan and his cousin Donald had always been good friends. Their parents had houses in a suburb of London that were no more than a five minute bus ride away and the two boys had gone to the same school, belonged to the same athletics club and at one time went to the same dances together.

They continued to keep in touch after Donald had married Marjorie and moved to Stroud, despite Jonathan never being enamoured with her. He had rung Jonathan a few days earlier to say they would be near his office on the following Tuesday morning and ask whether it would be convenient for them to call in for a few minutes about ten.

When they arrived Jonathan good not help notice that Marjorie looked as stern as ever having a cold, hard looking face, close-cropped jet black hair and a Modigliani form of neck.

"It's good to see you both," said Jonathan greeting them in his normal friendly manner, "How have you been? It's a while since we've had a chat."

"We're fine thanks, Jonathan, in fact we've decided to emigrate and will be leaving for New Zealand in about a months time."

"You've what?"

"We really have nothing to hold us here. We're both just in our fifties and if we don't make a move now - we never will. You know I've never been particularly successful and I find that running my sandwich bar day by day is dragging me down. Marjorie is still working in advertising and......well there's just no future for us in England and it's time to make the break."

Jonathan could not believe what he was hearing. "But why New Zealand and what will you do there?" he asked.

"Marjorie's sister, Eve, lives there. Her husband has offered me a job in his retail sportswear company and Eve would like Marjorie to help her in the fitness centre that she runs. We'll be fine. Neither of us craves after material things and we'll be able to enjoy a better climate. Anyway, we mustn't keep you. I know you're always very busy. We just thought it would be good to see you again before we go and tell you all about our plans and....."

"Hold on," said Jonathan "I'm off to see a site in Cirencester this morning. Why don't you both come with me, we can then have a bite of lunch and I'll take you on to Stroud."

"That's most kind, Jonathan," responded Marjorie, "but I'm staying overnight with some old friends and won't be going back home until to-morrow morning. You could go Donald it'll give you both time to have a good old chinwag."

Jonathan's fourth marriage was destined to last till death did them part but fate had decreed that he would not make old bones.

It was Donald who had given a statement to the police.

"We were driving through a residential area of Cirencester. Mr. Richards had an appointment to view a property development site. There were two lanes of vehicles on either side of the road. He was in no rush as we'd left London early. He was always a stickler for time. As the road bore to the left a set of traffic lights were ahead with one of those filters for cars turning right. Jonathan was in the inside lane and there was no other car in front of us.

"I remember him slowing down and I noticed that some distance away there was a blue car coming towards the lights on the opposite side of the road. As it approached the driver suddenly swerved, the car veered diagonally across to our side of the road, then without any warning, the other driver straightened up and drove directly towards us."

Jonathan and the driver of the second vehicle were killed instantly. Donald was released from the mangled metal by the Fire Brigade who had to cut him free. He escaped with a series of bruises, lacerations and a broken ankle. A waiting ambulance took him to the local hospital accompanied by a police constable. He gave details of Jonathan's private and office addresses and telephone numbers.

Later a police car was despatched to Jonathan's home to break the news to Alison. An hour later she called Roger Gould. His secretary took the call.

"I have Mrs. Richards on the line for you. She sounds terrible."

Roger then heard the words "Jonathan's dead."

The stark chill voice delivering this mournful two-word message temporarily mesmerised him. She recounted what she had been told by the police. He sat speechless and dumbfounded until quietly and slowly he said "I'll come over straight away."

*****

A number of Karen's friends were aware that she was not happy and could not understand why she stayed with David.

"He's like a spoilt little boy who likes to play with his toys." she would tell them, "Unfortunately his toys are other women and I just ignore it all. There are many times that he can be quite charming and caring and then he becomes almost unbearable. I'm sure that he has some finance problems but he'll never discuss them and I honestly believe that he needs me."

Her days were filled by being in the shop and after a couple of years she registered to take an evening water-colour painting course. She found this new interest exciting and gradually improved considerably. She began to take a sketch book and small tin of paints out with her whenever possible

Karen tried to visit her parents in Cambridge once a month. From time to time she was accompanied by David, but more often than not she went by herself delivering the excuse that he was up to his eyes in work.

Three years later the manager of Moretons retired and she was promoted at an increased salary. Soon after, a second branch was opened and she was then placed in overall charge of both with a small percentage of profits. She decided that to protect her own interests she would keep part of her increased income in a separate account away from David.

It was shortly after their eighth wedding anniversary that veiled shadows began to shroud Karen with further sorrow. In the early part of December, her mother and father were at the annual dinner of the local cricket association. This year he had been asked to give a vote of thanks to the retiring chairman. The toastmaster called his name. He rose from his seat and started to walk towards the top table. Suddenly he stopped, appeared to be faint, held on to a nearby chair and then fell to the floor. He was rushed to hospital and for the next thirty-six hours, remained in intensive care, until he passed away. A week after an autopsy was held, they attended his funeral.

A few days later Karen, her mother and David attended a meeting at the offices of the family solicitor in Cambridge, for the purpose of the reading of her father's will. There was a gift of £5,000 for Karen, a small pecuniary legacy for David and a nominal sum bequeathed to the National Blind Society. The residue of his estate had been left in trust for the benefit of her mother during the remainder of her lifetime and on her demise in trust for Karen for her lifetime. Thereafter the balance was to be divided between any grandchildren who had survived her and if there were none the residue was to go to the same Blind Society. The trustees were authorised to make discretionary payments to the lifetime beneficiaries as they sought fit.

Having left the solicitor's office, David, driving at excessive speeds in absolute silence, dropped his mother-in-law off at her house and headed back towards Aylesbury. The lock gates were then released with a tirade Karen had anticipated.

"You bitch, you f…..g bitch. I should have known that you and your family would be cooking something up against me all these years. I've never been good enough for their precious daughter. Don't try and deny it. The number of times I've heard the whispers behind my back. David this and David that. And now we know. You get all his f…..g money neatly tied up in a brown sack so that David can't touch anything. Wonderful isn't it after all I've done for you."

Karen knew him only too well and tried to placate the situation.

"I hope you don't mean all you're saying, David." she said quietly. "I had no idea what Dad was going to do and in any event it was his decision and nothing to do with me."

"It's everything to do with you. I work my guts out day in and day out and all you do is tart yourself up and trot along to the book shop to earn your monthly pittance as a glorified sales-girl or go out and slop paint and water around pretending to be an artist."

She ignored his comments as he continued driving wildly through Aylesbury narrowly missing a pedestrian crossing the road.

"David, please slow down. We'll have an accident in a minute."

"Oh, so now we give driving instructions! You know it all. A great librarian, a wonder girl artist and now an ace driver"

She felt dreadful. Her stomach was churning and she was relieved when the car came to an abrupt halt outside the flat. She got out, unlocked the front door and went straight up to the bedroom with David following, screaming away.

"Don't like the truth, do we? Oh no. Never mind you just wait. You'll be the loser, I promise you that. Just you wait and see. I'm not going to sit back and let you and your rotten family walk all over me."

"For goodness sake what on earth's got into you." she said. "My pittance as you call it has helped us survive for years and if I recall it was my father who gave you £1,000 to help you change your car. It's about time you faced facts and stopped living in this dream world of yours."

She stopped for a few moments and then in a very cold, deliberate manner, stared at him and continued.

"Do you really think that I don't know what you're up to and how you've been playing around with other women ever since we were married?"

He laughed. "You could always have left me. You're pathetic. Where do you think you'd go, back to Mummy? And who else do you thing would put up with your nonsense? My God, you make me sick."

"Don't push me David otherwise I'll do just that. From now on you're on probation as far as I'm concerned. I'm not prepared to put up with your philandering and lies forever so I suggest you buck up your ideas and make up your mind whether you want me with you or not."

"Damn you." he called out vehemently, as he stormed out of the bedroom and went downstairs. She first heard the front door slam and then the sound of the car being revved up followed by a screech of tyres and he'd gone.

She breathed deeply and much to her surprise she suddenly felt quite relieved and in control of her own life. No longer would he be able to fool himself that he could play around without her knowing. She liked this feeling and the confidence that it was giving her and on going to bed early she fell into a deep sleep until morning.

She had no idea what time David had come home, did not know where he had been and above all didn't care.

*****

"Does he want me to call him back?" answered Stephen.

"Only if you can't do what they've asked." replied his wife, Christine.

Stephen Bond had been selected by HSL to be the art lecturer on board the Neptune cruise in mid-September and there had been a call for him whilst he was teaching at an art college in Oxford where he worked.

"Hello, is that Mrs Bond? It's Bryan Dalton of HSL here. Is it possible to speak to Stephen?"

"He's not here at the moment but I'm expecting him back at about five. Can I get him to ring you?"

"Oh, there's no need for that, but perhaps you'd just give him a message. I wanted to remind him that the cruise in September is one of our 'theme cruises' with art being the designated subject so we'll be having a number of activities for those who may well be interested. Previously I told Stephen that we would want him to give four talks but could you tell him that we would now like him to make five presentations. He need only call me if this is going to be a problem."

"It's no problem to me", commented Stephen, "they can have a half-dozen if they want it."

"I must say I'm really looking forward to this cruise." said Christine, "It sounds super."

*****

Denise had little opportunity to talk to Nicola who appeared to be continuously in demand with most of the people at the party being either family or friends.

The evening passed with the music being played continuously, until midnight was almost upon them. Grains of time had again filtered through the hourglass and at midnight Auld Lang Syne was sung, champagne drunk and everyone celebrated with the traditional hugs, kisses and exchanges of best wishes.

When making their farewells, Denise commented to Nicola, "Tina's told me you have a place in Swiss Cottage. I live with her and Clive in Queensway. What about my giving you a call and we can meet up for a drink or a bite to eat."

"I'd like that," replied Nicola, "Dad's got their number. I'll get it from him and I'll call you next week, but in the meantime a very happy New Year."

She took two steps forward, embraced Denise and gave her a kiss on both cheeks.

She rang the following Thursday and arrangements were made to meet on Saturday evening at a small Greek restaurant off Baker Street. Nicola was already seated when Denise arrived and greeted her warmly. She suggested various Greek dishes that Denise had not eaten before and told her of her love of Greek history and mythology and how she tried to visit the mainland or the Greek Islands whenever she had a holiday.

"It is so exciting being there," she said, "the people are really friendly and the atmosphere resonates with the music of the bouzouki and in the evenings the Greek dancing is wonderful. Did you ever see the film Zorba the Greek? And then there are the Greek ruins and the weather is fabulous and the flowers and blossoms have a fragrance you'll never forget and then......"

She went on and on totally uninterrupted by Denise who was listening with rapt enjoyment, fascinated at Nicola's enthusiasm and unable to take her eyes off her.

"Oh dear," she finally commented, "Sorry, but once I get on to Greece I never seem to be able to stop."

Nicola, at twenty four, was two years older than Denise and worked for an employment agency in Marble Arch which had an excellent clientele.

"I'm in charge of the department that finds personal assistants for the directors of some jolly good companies. Initially I have to find out the exact requirements of the director and subsequently I interview prospective candidates, short list them and arrange for them to attend the company's office for final selection. It's quite fun, really."

The evening passed quickly and they arranged a further rendezvous for the following Wednesday.

Nicola referred to the musical at the Palace Theatre. "Have you seen it?" she asked, "It's supposed to be terrific and I've been given two tickets by one of our clients. Would you like to come with me?"

Their friendship flourished, joint interests expanded and they were both very much at ease with each other at all times. They spoke to one another every day on the telephone and went out two or three times each week. Denise had no doubt that the unspoken special feelings that she had for Nicola were being reciprocated.

At the beginning of April, Nicola's parents were asked whether they would like to use a flat in the second week of May that her mother's sister and husband owned in Palma. They had already made other arrangements but suggested that Nicola might love the opportunity if she could get time off from work.

Nicola invited Denise. They were both able to get a week away from work and with great excitement went off to the airport on what would be the first of many holidays together. The weather was wonderful and they delighted in the different food and drink, the beautiful beaches and the blueness of the azure sea.

They enjoyed walking round the shops of Palma, visited the magnificent Gothic Cathedral and the fourteenth century Bellver Castle. They meandered through the shady, narrow streets of the old town and strolled along the promenade bustling with tourists. During their stay they booked two coach trips to see some other parts of the island including the mountain villages, the northern resorts and the prettiest of all places, Deia.

When the two weeks vacation came to an end they flew back to England bronzed, without a care in the world looking forward to their future together, knowing that they had discovered in each other a partnership of love that they had both been wanting for some time.

*****

"You needn't tell me that you didn't flirt with those bastards. I saw you. They sat leering at you, staring at your tits all evening and you loved it. Which one did you fancy? Well, come on, tell me?"

Delia could not believe the accusations being hurled at her. She and Paul had just returned from the home of friends in Haslemere, who were celebrating their silver wedding. It was almost one-thirty. Up until midnight Paul had limited his drinking but his alcohol intake had then accelerated so that by the time they left he was drunk.

His slurred words continued. "Nothing to say, have you? – No. Nothing to say."

"Paul, please, why are you doing this? You know there's never been anyone other than you. I've always loved you"

He walked over to a cupboard unit in the living room, pulled out a bottle of brandy and poured out the equivalent of a treble into his glass.

As she advanced in his direction, hoping to calm him, the outburst resumed.

"I'll tell you one thing, I'm the only one who's ever going to have you – and what's more – I'm gonna do it now – right now".

He lunged towards her grabbing the front of her dress, tearing it down to her waist, as he fell on to the settee.

"Stop it Paul." she screamed. She went across to the settee to help him get up. He suddenly pulled her towards him. She struggled to release herself and as she was succeeding he pushed her away. She reeled over catching the side of her head on the coffee table.

Two hours passed before she came round.

The following morning Delia telephoned her office to say she was feeling unwell and wouldn't be in.

When he eventually got out of bed, Paul just sat on the bedroom chair as though in a coma. Delia went to find out whether he was all right. He was having fits of crying and she found him holding a brochure that on the front showed a picture of an enormous mansion with the name Charlwood Manor.

"What's that?" asked Delia.

He handed it to her.

"Where did you get it?"

"Bill Godwin gave it to me. He was there for six weeks."

The brochure was of a special drugs/ alcohol abuse rehabilitation centre.

"What's happening to me Delia? Please help me. I have to go there. Please telephone them. I must go there now. I must. I really must. I can't stand all this. What am I doing to you! Oh God, please help me."

"I'll call them immediately but I must tell you one thing, Paul, if anything ever happens again like last night, I promise I'll leave you."

During the afternoon she drove him to Charlwood in Lymington. They had agreed to accept him as a voluntary patient for eight weeks. The resident doctor told her that he would not be allowed any visitors for the first three weeks though she could telephone and speak to him during set hours. She could only leave him with five pounds with any other monies being retained in the reception office.

Delia's external bruising may have begun to heal but internally she was torn apart.

Two days later, wearing dark glasses, she went back to work, and told the girl who had become one of her best friends, "I've tried to make him realise that if he doesn't get treatment we have no chance. I do still love him but I want back the man that I married. Is that too much to ask for?"

"I'm sure it's not," the girl responded thoughtfully, "you cannot be expected to do more than you've already done. You'll just have to wait and see what happens. Let's hope that he is cured and you'll be able to make a fresh start."

Each day about six she called and spoke to Paul. It was obvious that he was undergoing a tough regime at the centre. Withdrawal symptoms had been excruciating, self-analysis was proving to be agonising and not being able to see Delia in the first three weeks of incarceration was highly distressing.

She knew that the success rate at Charlwood was no better than sixty percent but recognised there was no alternate route to take if they were to remain together.

*****

It was just after nine when Laura arrived at the jeweller's shop. The security grids on the windows were being raised as she entered. She pointed out where the stone had become loose and asked if they could re-fix it for her. She was given a repair ticket and told it would be ready in two days.

It was a beautiful day when she returned to collect the ring and Laura felt quite excited at the thought of retrieving it. The owner of the shop was standing behind the counter. He conjured up the mental picture that she had always had of Silas Marner. There were several showcases against the walls on either side of the shop that were full of second-hand items of silver and a considerable collection of necklaces, bracelets and other adornments. It was as an Aladdin's cave containing a hoard of items, each having its own story to tell. Laura presented the ticket and 'Silas' shuffled off behind a curtain at the rear of the shop.

"Unusual ring this." he mumbled, as he re-appeared holding the ring in one hand and the box in the other, "Yes, very unusual. Don't see too many like this nowadays. It's probably, late nineteenth century. I'm not entirely sure, but that's the most likely. Not made here, no, made abroad, somewhere in Europe. I can't say exactly where."

"Have you been able to fix the stone?" asked Laura.

"Oh, yes, no problem. It's a cornelian eighteen-carat gold. We've given it a polish and cleaned it up for you."

"Thanks very much. Are you sure it's eighteen-carat?"

"Am I sure, let me tell you, lady, that I don't need 'A' levels, 'O' levels or spirit levels to know that." responded the jeweller, sounding slightly miffed.

Feeling duly put down, Laura enquired how much the repair had cost and began opening her bag. As the ring was being replaced into the box, she remembered the markings on the inner part of the shank.

"I don't suppose you were able to read the lettering on the ring by any chance?" she asked.

"Indeed I did. It's very feint but under my glass I could clearly make it out."

"Really, that's marvellous. What was it?"

"Flatau. You'll have to excuse the pronunciation but I think it's French, anyway it's spelt F-L-A-T-A-U."

"Does the name mean anything to you?" she asked.

"Why should it mean anything to me? It's a family name. I assumed it must be a name in your family.'

Laura thanked him and left the shop again feeling that events of which she knew nothing were gradually leading her on an unknown path.

Laura called her aunt to tell her what the jeweller had said about the ring.

"I've decided to speak to Edward Wilton and find out whether he can tell me something else about all this. Somebody must know what it's all about and I can't understand why they're not telling me."

A few days after, she arrived for her appointment, at the law offices of Wilton, Lawson & Co., in Lincolns Inn Fields.

Light-hearted conversation passed for a few minutes until Edward became a little more serious.

"I rather expected to hear from you." he said as he began to look a trifle embarrassed.

"It all started a few weeks before your parents had their fatal accident. Your mother told me that there was something she wanted me to do if she were not alive when you became twenty-five.

"She handed to me for safe keeping, a jiffy bag in which, I was told, there was a box containing a ring. I was instructed to send this to you at that time. Your mother told me she felt sure you would then know what to do."

Laura sank back into the chair with a pained expression. She could not believe what Edward had been telling her. He had taken out a handkerchief with which he was touching his brow obviously feeling slightly disturbed.

Laura explained to him how she had discovered the name Asnieres in the box and how the jeweller had been able to detect the name Flatau.

"The jeweller told me he thought it was a family name. I've been so confused that I just don't know what to do."

Edward looked kindly at her and said, "I'm sorry, Laura, but the names don't mean anything to me either. You must believe, what your mother said, that *you will* know what to do. Give it time."

The name 'Flatau' was constantly in her mind, a name that she had never heard mentioned by anybody in her family, but nevertheless, a name that her mother had wanted her to know so that she could.......? Could what?

Having arrived home, she immediately went up to her bedroom and removed the ring from its box. She placed it in the palm of her hand and then put it on the third finger of her right hand. The ring slid along her finger with the same ease as when she had first tried it.

But this time it was different, since, however hard she tried, Laura was unable to remove the ring. She remained in her flat for the remainder of that day and evening almost hypnotised by everything that had happened since her aunt had given to her the bag containing the box with the ring inside.

Whilst asleep during the following three nights, Laura found herself having the same strange dream. She saw herself when a little girl playing in a field of poppies with her mother.

At the end of the field was a wide stream that could be crossed by a light-coloured wooden bridge. On the far side she saw the lady that she had met in Regent's Park. She was beckoning for Laura to come and join her as she stood surrounded with sunflowers that all faced towards Laura as if they were smiling at her and as she looked at the woman she could feel her mother's hand gently touching her back as though she was silently indicating that this was the direction in which she should go.

Laura awoke on the morning of the fourth day having no doubt that she was destined to go to France.

*****

FOUR

The meeting had just commenced in the Board Room on the third floor. It was not a big room but sufficiently large to take a rectangular table and matching chairs that seated twelve people. In all other respects it was simply furnished and could not in any way be considered ostentatious. It was after all the Board Room of Caritas Plc., the company that had been formed over forty years ago with the object of raising funds for children of the third world.

Its executive met promptly at ten on the second Tuesday of each month at which the Chairman or Deputy Chairman, Financial Controller, Legal Adviser, three consultants representing the interests of Africa, Eastern Europe and the Middle East, five fund raising representatives from different areas in the United Kingdom and Anne attended.

Her function was to act as overall coordinator of the various fund raising activities that were continuously taking place. She had been with the company over eighteen years and her undoubted ability and reliability had enabled her to rise within their ranks.

The Chairman announced that Robin Sutton, their legal adviser, had been delayed but should be arriving within ten to fifteen minutes. Anne was sitting on the Chairman's right, preferring to face the large windows. Meetings were always run efficiently with the enthusiasm of the members ensuring that current activities were continuously kept under review and future plans considered carefully.

Robin quietly entered the room shortly after the minutes of the previous meeting had been read and adopted.

"Sorry to be late." he said, as he silently closed the door and found his place at the table.

It must have been about thirty minutes later that he got up and said "Sorry everyone but I must pay a visit. I had some mussels last night, when we went to   Trattoria Pescatore, and I've been dying slowly ever since."

He made for the door and it was only then that Anne realised that he had closed it earlier. He fumbled with the knob but the door wouldn't open.

Anne started to feel beads of perspiration on her forehead. "Let me try," she almost shouted at him, "I don't know why you had to shut the door in the first place. Nobody can hear what we're saying."

Despite considerable efforts being made the door would not open. Robin was feeling more and more uncomfortable with crab-like stomach cramps gripping him, whilst Anne was now almost in a state of terror screaming "Get the door open. I can't stand it closed. Get it open."

The Chairman quickly telephoned his PA and within two minutes someone outside could be heard unscrewing the lock that had become jammed. The door then opened, much to the relief of Robin' who dashed down the corridor, followed by Anne' who almost immediately collapsed on the floor.

The meeting adjourned until noon. Paramedics were called to examine Anne whilst Robin was left to suffer in silence. Within the hour, Anne was confirmed as not having harmed herself in the fall though it was suggested that she should return home for the remainder of the day. A pill was giving to Robin to stop his regular bouts of embarrassment and the Board Room door lock was replaced.

At the same time as the meeting reconvened, Anne was slowly driving home. She had recovered from the panic attack that the shut door had triggered off and a cup of tea made had made her feel much better.

Once home she went to bed, fell asleep and did not wake until two hours later. She had always found the therapeutic value of a warm bath was sheer bliss when troubles had arisen and once again it came to her aid.

Despite it still being afternoon, dark signs of winter were drawing closer. She didn't want to dress again deciding that she would feel far more comfortable cuddled up in her pale pink dressing gown with its designs in pastel yellow.

Anne sat staring out of the bedroom window hoping that Vince would soon be back. There was nothing outside to cheer her. The trees were bare, denuded of leaves and bereft of greenery. Their skeletal form produced a wistful scene of nature's winter with tiny twigs, on the highest of branches, creating a filigree pattern.

She noticed that a few drops of rain were gently appearing on the window until some started to freely run down like tears. She felt sad and distressed and continued to look out into space until the headlights of a car could be seen in the distance.

Vince called her name as he entered the house.

"I'm in the bedroom." she responded.

He found her sitting like a statue still staring out of the window. She slowly turned, rose from the chair, walked towards him, fell into his arms and burst into tears.

"What am I doing to you?" she whispered in a melancholy tone, "Will I ever get better? This has been going on for more than three years."

"You're not doing anything to me. You know I love you more than anything in the world and I always will. Just tell me what's happened."

Anne recounted the events of the day and added, "I can't go on with my job. It's getting too much and I mustn't let them or you down. I'm going to resign."

The following morning she told the Chairman of her decision and also arranged to attend some further sessions with her therapist. On the second Tuesday in February the executive met again. This time the main item on the agenda was a farewell luncheon that had been organised for Anne.

During the remainder of February and March she began to feel more comfortable within herself and found that the freedom of not having to go into the office every day was allowing her time to consider how she could try and cope better with the claustrophobia.

She commenced a daily routine of a long walk to a part of Shaftesbury that overlooked Blackmoor Vale, which Thomas Hardy had referred to in his Wessex novels under the name Shaston. She visited the local park and the lightly planted woods nearby and pottered about in her garden. She started to feel physically stronger and had no doubt that everything she was now doing would help the mental process required.

It was early in April that Vince mentioned their forthcoming fifteenth wedding anniversary.

"I've had an idea how we can celebrate." he said, "Why don't we go on a cruise? We won't have to fly anywhere, we can take a ship from either Southampton or Dover, I can make sure that we have an outside cabin with a balcony and I really don't think you'll have any problems."

Having thought about the suggestion for a few days Anne decided that it sounded wonderful and said she would make some enquiries. Subsequently, she decided that the HSL cruise from Dover in September would be ideal and asked for a copy of their brochure to be sent to her.

*****

Louise and Mark had been married when she was twenty four and they were together for nineteen years when he passed away, always living in the same semi-detached house Throughout that period she had become a great worrier of almost everything regardless of whether worrying was warranted or not. On his death an endowment policy matured that was more than sufficient to pay off the balance of the mortgage.

Mark had been a builder/ decorator in partnership with Frank Collins, a qualified electrician. Work had been plentiful and to quote Louise 'they managed very nicely.' The business was run from a room in their house and after a while Louise began to help considerably by arranging appointments, maintained accounting records and preparing quarterly VAT returns.

Mark had always said, "I don't know what we'd do without her. I couldn't cope with all those bits of paper. We'd have to employ an accountant and goodness knows how much that'd cost." Frank readily agreed.

After Mark died she discovered that apart from her widow's pension, she was entitled to a private pension that he'd taken out for her. There was also some joint savings and a little money that her parents had left her.

"I'm sure I won't starve." she had told some of her closest friends.

Frank found it difficult to cope without Mark and soon asked Louise if she would continue to work as before, but on a proper salary.

She didn't really want to but felt sure that Mark would not have wanted her to let Frank down. Reluctantly she agreed, but after two years she had had enough and asked Frank to find someone to replace her. Three months later she ceased to have anything to do with the firm.

She gradually became a little more independent though continuing to worry was still something she excelled in, with Jeff bearing the brunt of her fixations.

Today she was very happy since he had been able to get some further time off to have lunch with her. As usual she fussed around him the entire time that he was there. When she went into the kitchen to serve the main course he placed an envelope on the table where she would be sitting.

"Here you are," she said gleefully, "another one of your favourites. I hope it'll be okay and not burnt and.......what's in this envelope?"

"Don't know. You better open it."

Inside she found a letter from The Neptune's Hotel Manager addressed to Jeff dated 28th April, two days earlier, offering a cabin for the use of his mother on the 15th September cruise.

*****

Jonathan's funeral would never be forgotten by those who attended. It was time for them to present their loving farewells to a man who had stood high among men and who, himself, would never be forgotten. The number of people paying their respects ran into hundreds. The cemetery car park was quickly filled and numerous streets near the burial grounds were soon full of vehicles.

This ceremony was the second saddest in Roger's life. The first had been six years before when he had buried his beloved Lisa, who had died of Leukaemia, aged thirty two.

Alison called Roger a few days after the funeral saying she would like to come to the office the following Tuesday morning and could he make sure that the company solicitor, Andrew Ackroyd, was present. She arrived promptly at ten-thirty and soon discarded the mantle of a widow speedily announcing her intention to sell Jonathan's group of companies as soon as possible, obviously believing that she now owned all of the shares.

Roger was surprised that Alison was unaware of his own thirty-five percent holding, a similar holding held in a Trust Fund for the benefit of Jonathan's children, a further ten percent held within a staff pension scheme and five percent held by wife number three. This left Allison's inherited shareholding at fifteen percent. She paled when hearing these details and became highly agitated.

"I can't believe what you're telling me.' she exclaimed, "Is all of this correct, Andrew? Why didn't Jonathan tell me? It can't be so."

"It's absolutely right, Allison," replied Andrew, "and as a minority shareholder your shares won't have a high value."

As she left, it occurred to Roger that however besotted Jonathan had been with this lady, he had been far more astute than most people imagined.

The next few weeks involved numerous meetings and negotiations for the buy-out of Alison's shares among the existing shareholders until eventually a deal was struck with her to be paid over a period of five years.

Roger was appointed Managing Director and given a new ten-year service agreement. On the day the parties met to sign the final documents, Roger felt sure that Jonathan was giving an approving nod from his astral home.

It was about four months after that Roger spotted the 'sloane queen' being driven in a Bentley Continental - no doubt by her latest amour!

*****

David arrived home that evening as if absolutely nothing had happened the day before and immediately announced, "I've booked a table at Casa Frederick for eight. Is that okay?"

"No it's not." Karen replied, "I've had a terrible headache all day so you better cancel the booking as I intend having an early night."

Returning home two days later she noticed a large removal van, bearing a Harrow address, being unloaded outside the house at number 42 that was diagonally opposite their flat. There was the usual activity with a multitude of furniture and boxes being taken inside. On one occasion she caught sight of a young woman standing for a brief moment at one of the un-curtained bedroom windows and there was a young boy of about ten or eleven who went in and out of the house attempting to assist the removal men.

On Friday evening, she announced that she would be going to see her mother on Sunday. She did not ask David to accompany her since she had no illusions as to what his response would be.

By the middle of the following week several vans were parked outside number 42. The advertisements on the vehicles made it evident that these were decorators, an electrician and a plumber who were about to transform the property to the new owner's requirements.

The agents 'For Sale' board had been taken down and now some net curtains appeared covering the ground and first floor front windows. Privacy had been exercised. Hanging in the front door porch was a set of wind chimes that made an eerie sound each time a breeze reached this inner area.

As she left home a few days after Karen noticed the young woman from number 42 waving to her. She went across and introduced herself.

"I'm Julie. Sorry I haven't made contact before but it's been like Victoria Station with the builders coming and going and I seem to have done nothing other than make cups of tea all day long."

She had medium length brown hair with some blonde highlights. Karen guessed that they were about the same age and found her sparkling eyes and bubbly personality most engaging.

"Did I notice that you have a little boy?" asked Karen.

"Yes, that's Anthony, the little monster. He's twelve, from my first marriage. I was divorced when he was four. Craig, that's my present husband has been marvellous with him. We've been married five years. I certainly did the right thing when getting rid of number one. What about you?"

"Oh, I seem to have been married forever. It's now nine years. My father died recently so I haven't been the best of company."

"Sorry to hear that. Let me get a little straight then come over for a drink with your husband one night."

"That would be lovely," replied Karen, "Just give me a call if you need any help."

Karen and her mother became considerably closer. The link may have been lost but the chain had strengthened. Her mother was bearing her heartache with silent whispers and during the next three to four weeks Karen spoke to her almost daily and saw her once a week. Sleep was the healer of her body and her mind and gradually Karen could see her begin to rise from her darkened descent.

It had been about two weeks since she'd seen Julie when suddenly, just after she had come back from Moretons, the front door bell rang and there she was.

"Hope I'm not disturbing you but I thought we could fix a date for you to come over. Craig has been working from home today so I've left Anthony with him"

"Come in, it's really nice to see you again," said Karen in a most welcoming voice, "I've only just got back from work and was about to make a cup of tea."

Conversation flowed as though they had been the best of friends for years. Julie told how her she'd often had doubts about her first husband being unfaithful and then caught him out by pure accident. "You'll love this story." she said with a slight giggle.

I went with a really good friend of mine Hilary, to the sales in London. By lunchtime we could hardly stand on our feet. We'd been through umpteen shops in Regent Street, Bond Street and that area generally. There's a little coffee lounge in Piccadilly that we'd been to before and we made straight for it.

When we'd finished and resumed our trek along Piccadilly, Hilary remarked, "Isn't that Tom?"

I couldn't see him until she pointed out that he was walking across the other side of the road, arm in arm with a woman in a black and white outfit. Hilary made some comment that she was probably a client and I said, "Well let's find out, shall we?"

We followed them until they went into the Meridian Hotel when I saw him at the reception desk. He and the lady then went towards the lifts.

I said to Hilary, "Well, do you still think she's a client?"

I went up to one of the receptionists and asked whether a Mr. Tom Saunders had checked in. She looked at their computer and told me that he and his wife had just checked in to Room 314.

I must say that I felt pretty damn dazed and numb. Imagining hanky-panky going on is one thing, but facing the reality is something else. Opposite the bank of elevators were a settee and two chairs. I told Hilary I was going to wait for them to come down.

She thought we should go but I told her I wanted him to know that I knew. I wanted to see his face, when he came down with her from that bedroom and then saw me.

We sat and waited for almost two hours during which time the lifts were going up and down with guests and visitors. Each time the doors of a particular lift opened I could feel my stomach turn and could sense every nerve in my body was at fever pitch.

Then it happened, the doors slid open and there they were. I got up from the settee and walked towards them and said, "Hello Tom. Have you had a good afternoon? I do hope so because we're now absolutely finished. At last it will give me considerable pleasure to get shot of you. Don't bother to come home tonight – you're not wanted. Tomorrow I shall go and see a solicitor."

"And that Karen was the end of Mr. Thomas Saunders", added Julie.

They continued chatting for some time until Julie looked at her watch and jumped up, saying, "I hadn't realised the time. I must go".

It was agreed that Karen and David would go over to their house on Saturday evening for a light supper.

After she had gone Karen began to think back on Julie's story and in particular the way in which she had ended it with the words 'and that was the end of Mr. Thomas Saunders.'

She also recalled what she had recently told David and had little doubt that at some time in the future, when speaking to a friend or a relative or an acquaintance she may well find herself telling her story that would end with the words 'and that was the end of Mr. David Hardwick'

*****

They had only been back from Palma for a few days when Nicola suggested that Denise should move into her flat. They continued working in their usual jobs until, when having dinner one evening Nicola said she had an idea.

"Why don't we open a dating agency?"

"What on earth made you think of that?" asked Denise.

"Well, if you think about it, there are thousands of people seeking partners. You see a tremendous number of newspaper adverts. and there are numerous dating agencies all over England. There are web-sites and television channels geared to lonely people and agencies that arrange dinner parties. It seems as though the demand just goes on and on."

"I'm sure you're right," reflected Denise, "but we'd have to be awfully careful if you're thinking we take out an ad. in one of the daily papers? That could be both very expensive and dangerous. You'd never be sure of the sort of person who'd reply."

"I agree but my idea is we aim for a market where the singles are seeking a serious relationship and not just a one night bonk"

"Where are we going to find them?" asked Denise.

"I thought to keep costs down we simply have some fliers prepared that we can send to friends and suggest they pass them round to people they know. We can also send some to the secretaries of various cultural societies and arrange to advertise in the programmes of their events.

"Then we can try and place notices in the windows of bookshops and selected local newspapers and make use of all our own contacts. I know a number of young company executives and I'm sure you'll be able to come up with names through your accountancy firm."

"I must say you seem to have given it a lot of thought but where will we operate from? They can't come here."

Nicola smiled. "I had a feeling that darling daddy might well be able to come to the rescue. I've had a chat with him and his company has an old property in Paddington that has been let out as offices for years. One of their tenants recently died. He was renting two first floor rooms. Daddy has said that if we want them, he'll let us have them rent free for twelve months, to help us on our way. All we'll have to pay is the lighting and heating and telephone"

"That's fantastic, but if we leave our jobs we're not going to have any income coming in."

"I know. What I thought was, if you keep your job we can see how things go over the first six months. At that stage it'll either have taken off or flopped. If it proves no good then I can always get another job. In the meantime I can work my butt off with organising the fliers, distributing them, placing the ads. and seeing as many people as possible. We can use the office telephone number with an answer machine and should we get some response then appointments can be made and initially I can see people in Paddington."

Denise sat quietly feeling quite amazed at the extent that Nicola had thought through the project.

"You know," she said, "I think it could work. We'll never know unless we give it a whirl and the downside isn't great. If we both put a thousand pounds each into the venture then that should get us through the initial stages. Let's do it."

"You're sure?" exclaimed Nicola.

"Absolutely, but what are we going to call this agency of ours?"

"I really don't know," replied Nicola, "I've thought of lots of names but haven't liked any of them. Perhaps you can come up with a suggestion."

"I've got one," responded Denise, "Let's keep it simple, a name people will remember and one that's really apt. Let's call it The 'EROS' Agency."

During the following week it had been her father's birthday and Denise had told her parents that she'd come up to Hereford for Sunday lunch. It was a beautiful morning with a cloudless sky reflecting the untold shades of green that created the magic of the countryside. Here and there in the patchwork of fields she could see a scarecrow whilst hedgerows, plants and flowers with twigs and sprigs and sprays of coloured leafs all added grace to the panorama.

They were overjoyed to see her and asked all about her job and the shows that she'd seen. They told her all the local gossip and how various friends had wanted to be remembered to her. It was, she thought, the normal stilted conversation that tends to go on between parents and their children as the years pass by, when they gradually find they no longer have very much in common.

It was whilst they were eating lunch that Denise told them she had moved into a flat with Nicola.

"Will you be staying there long?" asked her mother.

"Well I guess so." she responded.

"What's that supposed to mean?" added her father.

"Well we're hoping that it'll be permanent. We're very happy together and it seems very right for both of us."

There was a sudden silence. Neither her mother nor father said a word though Denise noticed from the corner of her eye they were throwing glances at each other. She decided to simply carry on eating and wait for the next comment, despite the fact she feared she would choke on every mouthful.

Finally, her mother said, "Well, I suppose that'll be nice for you dear."

Whilst helping to clear up, Denise's mother commented, "Your father's migraines will be the death of me. They don't get any easier and at times drive him crazy. I feel upset for him but I'm the one that has to live with him and his bad temper.

"I didn't want to tell you but he's also had some chest pains recently and felt really poorly. The Doctor sent him to the hospital for various tests and although there is nothing serious he's been told he should avoid all stress and strain."

Denise could not fail to notice the emphasis that had been placed on the last four words and instantly recognised she was being sent on a guilt trip that only parents can do so expertly. She breathed a sigh of relief when about five-thirty she announced she must get back to London, said her fond farewells, started up the engine of her car and commenced the return journey.

On arriving at Swiss Cottage she saw Nicola waving out of the flat window. She rushed through the front door, embraced her and said, "You've no idea how wonderful it is to be home."

*****

Delia did not wake until seven and noticed the morning newspaper had already been pushed under the bedroom door. She drew back the curtains deriving instant pleasure in being welcomed by the sight of the gently breathing sea opposite. The Brighton front was sparsely dotted with those out for an early morning stroll or jog. On the beach two people were exercising both themselves and their dogs. It was a bright day though some distant clouds appeared distinctly threatening.

Later she ordered natural yoghurt, toast, marmalade and some tea. She felt extremely lazy and idled the following two hours away by reading the paper, bathing and then dressing.

Finally, she was ready to explore Brighton. She walked in the direction of Palace Pier, passing the Brighton Centre, until a little further on she turned into West Street. It was then she noticed a sign pointing to 'The Lanes'. She had heard of them and now made her way in their direction not knowing what to expect.

Delia was astonished to find an array of small shops as she walked along the narrow cobbled alleyways. Externally, most of the properties had been painted in differing colours and revealed a wide array of merchandise ranging from jewellery to gift shops and antiques to boutiques. She passed a public house bearing a plaque proclaiming it was the oldest licensed premises, established in eighteen hundred and sixty-four.

In Market Street and the surrounding area Delia came upon a mass of small restaurants and bistros. It was almost one o'clock and the tantalising aromas coming from these eating-houses made her feel hungry. She discovered an attractive looking trattoria with pale blue walls and a white ceiling. Numerous paintings of Italian scenes had been hung and this touch of Italy in Brighton had been completed with delightful terrazzo tiles.

She ordered Fusili All Arrabbiata and a glass of Valpolicella Zanzi. The pasta was hot and delicious and she finished with a cup of black coffee. Eating on her own had never appealed and she was pleased when two sisters, who lived in Hove, sat at the adjoining table and started to engage her in conversation. It was nearly three when she left the restaurant.

The ominous looking clouds seen earlier had spread considerably. It was now bleak and drear and when reaching the promenade a cold wind convinced her that she would be better off returning to the warmth of the hotel.

Richard noticed her as she went towards the lift.

"Hi, Delia, did you sleep well last night?" he asked.

"It was the best sleep I've had for weeks. Thanks for everything, Richard. I took advantage of the fresh Brighton air this morning and went to The Lanes for the first time. Now, I'm looking forward to having dinner with both you and Gilly this evening."

Delia enjoyed being with them and it gave them a chance to find out from her what had happened with Paul.

By the time they had finished it was nine thirty and she began to feel quite weary. She excused herself and went to her room, trusting that she would have another peaceful night.

*****

"Well, what am I supposed to say?" asked Matt's wife. She was obviously very upset now he had told her of the telephone call that he had received from Bryan Dalton.

"If those are the rules, then that's it. We can't leave Simon with just anybody and you can't afford to turn down the job. Let's face it, we need the money. Not that they pay you a fortune. Quite frankly, although I enjoyed the last cruise I couldn't believe that they had given us such a small cabin with bunk beds for the three of us. It was far from comfortable. I don't understand why they can't find you somewhere to store your equipment when you're not using it. After all they found a space for the illusionists stuff and where are the props. for the dance shows kept?"

He didn't know how to reply and decided agreeing with her would be the best policy.

"You're absolutely right. It's just that I don't want to leave you and Simon for two weeks although as you say we do need the money. Perhaps I can talk to Alan Spencer when I'm on board. Maybe he can do something for us another time."

*****

Laura's initial research took her to the local library where she went through all of their Central London and suburban directories, looking for the name Flatau. None were listed with that name. The jeweller had thought the name to be French but there were plenty of French people who lived in England.

The following morning she returned to the library's travel section to check French towns or villages bearing the name Asnieres. This time her investigation produced a speedy result. She found a copy of the Bordas Guide des Voyages and breathed a sigh of relief when seeing the name listed in the index. Her triumphant mood was short-lived when she then noticed a second, and then a third and finally a fourth entry, all bearing the same name. A temporary simple solution had suddenly become a four-fold problem.

Against each of the listed titles was the word Asnieres appearing in bold face type, followed by smaller italic type to complete the geographical title. She wrote down the names of the four places.

ASNIERES - sous - Bois
ASNIERES - sur - Blour

ASNIERES - sur - Seine

ASNIERES - sur -Vegre

Page and map references followed enabling notes of exact locations to be recorded. She was convinced that if a person named Flatau lived in any one of these places she would now be able to trace him or her. Not until then, would she have complete peace of mind

By the middle of the following week Laura's plans were complete. On the eve of departure she sought sleep in the comfort of her bed but her slumbers were interrupted throughout the night. She thought the telephone had rung yet it was silent, she believed that someone was pressing the front door bell but no one was there and later she dreamed that she was at a fairground standing and watching a carousel with beautifully carved horses painted in bright yellows, reds and greens, moving slowly up and down to the haunting music of a hurdy-gurdy. As each of the horses passed by she could see printed words appearing alternately on their saddles that read

THE RING...FLATAU...ASNIERES...THE RING....FLATAU....ASNIERES........

Her mouth became dry and her legs felt like lead until finally she woke with a jolt. The clock indicated five forty-three when she rose from the bed. Though she had already left a note for Doreen, she remembered to leave a postscript asking her to telephone one of her pupils, who had been on holiday, and cancel his next appointment.

At seven-thirty she left the flat, put her case in the boot, opened the driver's door and simply sat behind the wheel gathering her thoughts. She was excited yet apprehensive, calm but nervous. She was about to face a journey that might exceed nine hundred miles. A journey she was taking alone that would enable her to find......?

Suddenly Laura recalled the French saying 'En y va', turned the key in the engine and shouted, "Yes, let's go."

She drove virtually unaware of anything around her until a chorus of squawking gulls made her realise the sea was near. Having reached Dover, she drove along Marine Parade, flagged by its Victorian terraced houses, until ahead she saw the Channel Port with its sign to 'Eastern Docks'.

The sun shone brightly and Laura could feel the warmth as she took a seat on the outside deck. Slowly the vessel's engines responded to the captain's orders and the ferry sailed towards the harbour exit. Behind her could be seen the chalk white cliffs of Dover curtaining the shore and rising as a buttress. The pulsating throb of the engines stirred the lanes of the sea until within a half-hour the distant outline of the French coast came into view.

The snub-nosed amphibian pointed its way in the direction of the walled harbour of Calais, arriving eighty-five minutes after leaving Dover. Soon the jaws of the ferry opened, disgorging all that had been swallowed before, as the big fish came to rest and within minutes Laura found herself driving on the auto-route leading towards Paris.

Sixty miles from Paris, road works narrowed the motorway route to two lanes, slowing down traffic for nearly two miles. Asnieres-sur-Seine was getting nearer. Close to Charles de Gaulle airport, cypress trees were gently shimmering, reminding her of Monet's landscapes.

Having reached Enghien, Laura suddenly realised she was lost. She asked a bus driver for Asnieres-sur-Seine and was pointed in the direction of Argenteuil and Epinay-sur-Seine. Having followed what she thought were his instructions she again found herself on the wrong road and had to frequently stop to ask the way until, much to her surprise, she entered the Grande Rue Charles de Gaulle and found herself in the centre of Asnieres-sur-Seine.

There was a mixture of old and new shops in the main square, many of which looked drab. Laura continued driving slowly looking for an hotel until she noticed the Hotel Wilson. Having checked in and gone to the room she lay on the bed, shut her eyes and fell asleep for just over an hour. It was almost six and after taking a warm shower she put on fresh clothing and went out to become further acquainted with her surroundings.

By half past seven, Laura felt pangs of hunger and was pleased to come across the Bistrot D'Or. A set meal, for eleven Euros, consisting of melon, turbot in a white wine sauce with rice and spinach, followed by a lemon sorbet, a glass of merlot and a coffee revived her considerably.

She was in bed by ten and though exhausted from her day's travels again found it difficult to sleep. The bed was uncomfortable, the pillows hard and each time that she woke she could hear the noise of passing cars and motorcycles.

Having breakfasted early on croissants and coffee, Laura made her way to the Central Police Station, situated a short distance from the hotel. At the main desk a heavily built Brigadier de Police confronted her.

"Oui, Madame, qu'est-ce que vous voulez?" he asked, wishing to know what it was that she wanted.

Laura decided that this was not the time to speak in French if she could avoid it, despite her reasonable prowess in the language.

"Parlez-vous Anglais, Monsieur?" she enquired.

"A little, how can I help you?"

Laura explained that she was trying to trace a family with the name of Flatau.

"You go to Mairie, Town Hall, Madame." he replied, whilst handing to her a street map.

She arrived at Place de l'Hotel de Ville where the majestic Town Hall stood with wide whitened stairs leading to three sets of double glass entrance doors all with ornate wrought-iron work on the exterior.

Laura asked the receptionist how she could trace the family of Flatau and was directed to the Bureau of Elections where the elector's roll was maintained. The town had a population of almost seventy thousand but the name of Flatau could not be found.

She returned to the hotel car park disappointed but confident her wanderings would lead to whatever it was that her mother intended she should discover.

*****

FIVE

Anne was thrilled as they began to look through the brochure received from HSL.

"I can't believe all the things that are included." said Anne, as she became more and more excited, "Have you read there's a fantastic number of events taking place daily, and then there are shows every night, dancing, a library, a card room – who knows we may be able to play a little bridge again, swimming pools and even a casino. It's incredible."

"It certainly is." responded Vince, "Are you absolutely sure that you'd like to go, providing I can book an outside cabin with a balcony?"

"Oh, yes, I'm sure. It'll be wonderful and I'll get a few pills from Dr. Alexander before we go to keep me calm - should I need them."

"That's fine. Now tell me, have you found a cruise that takes your fancy?"

"Yes, this one here." replied Anne, as she pushed the brochure in front of him. It was titled 'MEDITERRANEAN DELIGHTS'. "It's on the Neptune and, guess what?..... it leaves Dover on 15th September."

"So we would leave on the 15th to celebrate our 15th. Is that what you're trying to tell me?"

"You got it in one," said Anne, "and just take a look at some of the places that we'd be going to Barcelona, Monte Carlo, Rome and Florence. Oh, Vince it would be out of this world. Do you really think that we can afford it?"

"Leave it to me and I'll see what I can do." he said, "By the way, what time is your Aunt Ellen coming tomorrow?"

"I told her you'd pick her up at Salisbury station at noon. She said she was very happy to come by train as she'd like to see some of the countryside. It's over twenty years since I've seen her. I'm sure it's the first time she's been back in England since she emigrated to New Zealand."

"It's a good job she's not coming on Sunday. I read there's going to be repairs to the line."

As Vince began to leave on Saturday morning, he called out to Anne, "How did you say I'd recognise her?"

"She'll be wearing a dark green coat and carrying a brown handbag."

The reunion between aunt and niece could not have been better. They immediately chatted away as though they'd never been apart. Vince found her quite delightful with a tremendous sense of humour and enjoyed hearing some of the stories she recounted of her life in New Zealand.

Whilst having an after lunch coffee, Ellen suddenly asked, "So tell me dear, have you ever had any recurrence of your claustrophobia?"

Vince could see Anne turn white as she stared at Ellen. She slowly responded with her voice reaching a higher pitch after each sentence "Why on earth did you ask that? What do you know about *my* claustrophobia? Who told you? It only started three years or so ago. I've never mentioned it to you. Who told you?"

"Oh dear, I'm so sorry Anne, I'd no intention of upsetting you. I was just hoping that having overcome the problem last time, all had been well."

Anne began to feel anxious and could feel herself shaking very slightly, as though she had a chill. She started to talk louder and breathe heavily "What are you talking about? What do you mean last time? When last time? I wish you'd explain yourself. I just told you it started about three years ago. That was the first time. There wasn't any *last* time."

Vince went to placate her, "Anne darling, let Ellen explain what she means."

"I'm truly sorry I even mentioned the subject. It happened when you were about ten. Your father took you to a special pop concert at Wembley Stadium. I honestly can't recall exactly what occurred, but it had something to do with you being on a train on the way home. I think my brother said there had been some sort of accident, but I can't remember any more details, other than the incident brought about an attack of claustrophobia. You saw several therapists afterwards and by the time you were about twelve, it somehow or the other passed. I'm just very sorry if it has come back."

Anne became very tearful and buried her head in Vince's arm, which he had put round to comfort her.

In a gentle, softly spoken voice he whispered to her, "You know something, Anne, this may be the best news we could have heard. If we can only find out more about this train story we may be able to discover the cause of all your problems."

"But how can we possibly find out," said Anne, "both mum and dad are dead and Aunt Ellen doesn't remember anything else. We'll never find out and I'll never know."

"Don't say that, darling." said Vince. "There has to be a way and we can start to make enquiries next week. I'm sure one way or the other the story of the train will come to light and will help you. I honestly believe this is the reason why your aunt was meant to come here today"

*****

"Well what exactly do you do?" asked Jeff, having made one of his regular calls to her.

"Officially I am a library assistant," replied Louise, "and although it may sound boring to you I can't believe how quickly the days pass. Most of the time I'm dealing with people and their various queries, I issue books out to library members and help them select books and all sorts of other things. I'll tell you more when we next get together. Now you look after yourself and make sure you dress up warm."

"Oh, mum, give me a break. I'm glad you're enjoying yourself. Speak to you soon. 'Bye."

Louise was enjoying herself and was delighted she had decided to have taken the job. She helped shelve the books and gradually became aware of the enormous range of subjects covered. She answered the 'phones so that members could make renewals or reserve computer time on the few PCs they had and generally helped with everything that arose.

The staff had been told a DVD/CD section and an area to stock piano and vocal music would open soon. A children's book department already existed supervised by a qualified assistant. The job had given a fillip to her life and it pleased her to realise she was doing something really useful.

Next door to the library there was a travel agency and the following day she went and obtained one of HSL's brochures so as to read all about her September trip and the ship she would be sailing on.

*****

Taking over the running of 'Central Property Developments Plc.' had not been easy. Roger had received the full support of the staff but working without Jonathan left an enormous void in his life.

They had been so close and had discussed everything together. He found he was working harder than ever with a strong determination to succeed. Being successful without Jonathan would not only be a personal triumph but would also be a thank you to him.

A concentrated work effort was enabling Roger to instigate both an expansion programme within the company and an investigation of other projects. He often worked late and one evening, whilst preparing for a meeting in Bath the following day, he noticed it was almost nine. As he was placing documents in his briefcase, he heard a noise coming from his secretary's office. He moved towards the inter-communicating door, swiftly pulled it back calling out "Who's there?"

Much too his relief it was only one of the two cleaners who came to Chesterfield Street.

"Sorry if I scared yer guvner," she said, "I didn't know you was 'ere. Never mind, you're okay ain't yer?"

"Yes I am. I hadn't realised you came in so late, Gwen."

"Oh, bless yer, sir. Yours ain't me only job. I couldn't last if it was. Still I do like working 'ere. I might tell yer I resigned from one of my other jobs last month. When they asked me why I was leaving, I told 'em I was no longer getting' any job satisfaction. All they did was laugh. I don't know why."

Next morning Roger headed westwards. It was a beautiful day and the shining sun produced touches of warmth. He bathed in the beauty of the scenery that awakened his rural feelings.

Timeless trees displayed guards of honour across the country roads and winding paths until he joined the city roadways.

Immediately his thoughts turned to Lisa. He had been with her to Bath many times. As typical tourists, they would visit everything from the Abbey to the Pump Rooms, from Pulteney Bridge to the Roman Baths and their eyes would feast on the perfect symmetry of the Royal Crescent and The Circus inspired by the Roman Colosseum.

Later that same week Roger went to the rearranged meeting with Martin Willis. Martin had been Bank Manager to the group for many years and had assisted Roger at various stages after Jonathan's death, when additional financing had been required. It had been suggested he went to the Bank about twelve and then stayed for one of their in-house 'special customer' luncheons.

The meeting went well despite Roger finding the lunch a complete drag. Six other male customers wined, dined and smoked until three fifteen. These peacocks exulted in themselves until egotism filled the room. As usual, the conversational agenda consisted of business, cricket, golf and cars. Nothing else seemed to be of any relevance to them.

Roger was content to sit, listen and politely join in from time to time. Why is it, he thought, that men can be so boring. He had often wondered what women saw in such dreary, tedious examples of the male species. Maybe they didn't find out until it was too late.

*****

Karen's weekly escape to her art class had proved to be highly successful but when her tutor suggested she take a foundation course she told him her personal situation made this totally impractical. Some of her work was exhibited in the school's main building and she was selected as one of twelve local resident artists to have two of her paintings shown at an exhibition held at the Aylesbury library. Her work was improving and she started to paint small canvases during the evenings when David was out and at weekends when it did not interfere with any other arrangements.

The art course provided two visits each year, to galleries and exhibitions, enabling students to see and discuss works painted by great artists of the past and present. They had been to the National Gallery, the Tate and the Hayward Gallery and the Royal Academy. Now in their final term, students were bubbling with excitement, since those who were able, could register to go on a two-day trip to Paris, staying overnight at a small pension on the Left Bank area of St. Germain.

When she returned home, Karen decided to broach the subject with David, who seemed to be in a fairly calm frame of mind. He immediately caused an unbelievable rumpus, shouting and raving and hurling his normal flow of invective until disappearing out of the house, his face resembling volcanic fury.

The next evening she made it clear that there had been no need for him to have taken such an attitude and continued by telling him, "I've spoken to the tutor during the day and I've told him I'll be going to Paris with the others." adding, "I'd have thought you'd be quite pleased to be rid of me for a night!"

He didn't say a word.

Their visit to Julie and Craig was very pleasant and Karen was relieved when David displayed considerable charm and didn't in any way become argumentative. She thought it was probably because he found Julie attractive. The fact he took time to talk to Anthony surprised her even more.

The Lucas's were anxious to show them over the house that had now been completely decorated. Generally they had selected pastel shades with the sitting room and dining room painted in a wonderful hue of yellow that gave out a warm glow. The furniture though modern was comfortable with tasteful drapes and net curtains.

This was not just a house but a welcoming home with both silk and fresh flowers, books with colourful jackets begging to be taken off their shelves and read and inexpensive landscape paintings bringing the countryside into the room.

"You certainly have a good eye for colour," commented Karen, "your home is lovely."

"Thank you." replied Julie, "I used to do some oil painting but I haven't the time nowadays."

73

"That's interesting," said Karen, "I go to an art class every week. I prefer water colours. It's a great course and the tutor's marvellous. Perhaps you could come along. It's from seven fifteen to nine thirty every Tuesday"

"Well that's an idea. What do you think, Craig?"

"I don't see why not, after all it doesn't appear to take up too much time." he replied.

"Great, that's it then. I'll come with you next week, if that's okay? I must say I envy you being able to do water colours. I think it's the most difficult medium to use. I've tried umpteen times but I always make a complete hash of my paintings with water running everywhere, so I stick to oils and can cover up my mistakes more easily."

Julie had made a cold meat and salad meal for them and aided by a couple of bottles of wine an enjoyable time was had by all. Craig told them he was a computer programmer and that Julie gave French and Italian lessons from home.

"I'm lucky since I can make appointments with pupils to fit in with my schedule as wife and mother." commented Julie, "I thought I'd lose all my pupils when we moved here but I'm amazed how many have told me they'll be quite happy to drive over here. Fortunately, it's not too far."

As they walked back to their house, David said, "That was a good evening. They're very nice. You'd better invite them back." and then grudgingly added, "So what date are you going to Paris?"

The forty-eight hour excursion took the students back several centuries and Karen was spellbound by all they saw. They visited the Musee D'Orsay, to be greeted by the Impressionists; the Louvre, where the Mona Lisa smiled down upon her; the Orangerie, featuring the genius of Monet and the steel and glass building of the Georges Pompidou National Centre of Art, where Braque, Picasso and artists of the twentieth century awaited.

They walked until numb from the pain of walking, stood until their necks and backs could no longer suffer the strain of looking upwards at any more items of beauty and remained awake until the weight of sleep prevented their seeing anything else.

When she returned home, David was not yet back from work. She went to the bedroom. A glance at the bed revealed that it had not been slept in the night she had been away.

*****

Joanne was one of life's characters. Aged 33, with two children, she had been divorced for three years and currently had a live-in partner, Dean, two years younger than her, who she absolutely adored. Her son was nine and her daughter was seven and Dean had embraced them into his life, without any problem on either side.

She was slim, had long brown hair, wore with-it clothes, that in the warm weather turned the heads of all men passing by and had a tremendous sense of humour. She was also very sensible, down-to-earth and a pragmatist. The expression 'what happens, happens' frequently tripped off her tongue.

She was a manicurist and nail expert working in the town's main beauty salon though from time to time she also gave private manicures from home. Dean was a lorry driver for one of the large supermarket chains driving solely within Bedfordshire.

"It's absurd," she told her best friend Tracey, "if we go during the school holidays to somewhere like Lanzarote, it'll work out about £1,500 more than if we went during term time."

"How much?" responded Tracey, "That's crazy, but won't you get fined if you take the kids out of school during term?"

"Probably, I think it'll be £50 each but even if it's £100 we'll still be in pocket."

"Where does Dean want to take you?" asked Tracey

"That's the next problem. He changes his mind nearly every day. First it was Lanzarote, then it was Tenerife, then it was Majorca. You'll never guess what the latest is?....a Mediterranean cruise. I told him we can't afford it, but he says nowadays, if you make a late booking, you can get really good deals."

"Even so, it can't be that cheap." said Tracey.

"I know and don't think I haven't told him. He maintains you can pick up real bargains on the internet. He also said lots of the cruise ships are owned by the same company – Fiesta or Carnival or something like that – I can't remember, and when it gets close to departure date they want to see bums on seats and cheap tickets suddenly hit the market. Don't ask me, Tracey, I'm just going to wait and see what he does next."

*****

Shortly prior to the end of October, the 'EROS' agency was launched with a bang though initially landing with a gentle thud. The response was much slower than they had anticipated. Only a few clients registered and when told they'd have to wait two to three weeks before being introduced to a member of the opposite sex, they were none too happy.

Nicola told Denise, "At this stage we need this time lag to get sufficient people signed up so as to operate a proper matching system."

Throughout, Nicola remained confident and told Denise, "These things take time and with Christmas soon coming up most people will have already made their arrangements."

"Then I suggest we close over Christmas and New Year and take that cheap skiing holiday we saw advertised in last Sundays Mail." said Denise, "It will do us both the world of good and set us up for the year ahead."

It didn't take long for them to agree and Denise made a booking the following day. A few days before going they decided to drive into Central London to see the Christmas decorations

It was a clear dry night and those who had made a wager on there being a White Christmas were about to lose their money. The decorations in both Oxford Street and Regent Street were again disappointing. They turned into Shaftesbury Avenue and drove towards Waterloo Bridge where Denise parked on the South side. All of the major buildings were lit with the Thames alive with speckled reflections and the occasional small craft gently stirring the waters.

Nicola spotted a hot drinks stand alongside the National Theatre. It was then that they noticed him crouched on the damp embankment steps. He sat shivering, a sorrowful specimen of human loneliness with staring eyes that pierced the dark. His place of rest would be the pavement with a cardboard box as covering. His sole companion was the cold of night.

He did not seek money from them. He just sat and stared. Before anything was said, Nicola took some silver coins from her handbag and placed them by his side. Not a word passed between them, he simply turned his head slowly and looked towards her, his eyes acknowledging her kindness.

The warmth of the coffee helped dispel the chill and melancholy that had overcome them. Having returned to the car they went back over the bridge, down The Strand until they reached Trafalgar Square. High above the lions, stood the enormous Norwegian Christmas tree, closely surveyed by Nelson perched on the top of his column with pigeons flying higher and higher.

Refreshed by their holiday in the Austrian Tyrol, Nicola's EROS efforts were soon rewarded. The numbers of enquiries increased considerably with most being followed up with interviews. By the end of February eighty people had registered at a fee for the ensuing twelve months of one hundred and twenty pounds.

March and April were even more hectic and after the first six months had passed they had no doubt the agency would be a success. Nicola could no longer cope single handed and, as planned, Denise resigned from her job and joined her full-time.

In the second week of May, Nicola said she'd like to take a couple of days off to visit her parents in Ascot. She proposed driving down after they shut the office on Tuesday evening and be back by about midday on Thursday.

As she left she failed to notice there was a dark blue Vauxhall parked at the end of the road with only it's sidelights on. As Nicola moved off in her car the other vehicle followed.

She had been driving as on automatic pilot until she found herself turning into Gunnersbury Lane. The Vauxhall followed keeping an appropriate distance between them. She noticed the other vehicle for the first time when approaching the large roundabout at Hangar Lane. The impending rain was now falling and this together with the darkness and gloom prevented her from being able to see anything clearly other than the blurred facial outline of the driver, a woman with dark hair.

She tried to convince herself she was imagining herself being followed until as she turned on to the A.40, Nicola glanced in her side-mirror only to find the woman still behind her, headlights on full and wiper blades moving slowly from side to side.

She again accelerated, glimpsed in her mirror and once more found the other car was in pursuit. She could feel an uncomfortable dampness on her face and under her armpits and her hands began to get clammy. A large articulated lorry overtook her, causing a deluge of water to hit and cover her windscreen. Momentarily, everything went black. Nicola switched her wiper blades to fast position but gained little respite.

A flash of lightening lit up the sky followed by loud rumblings of thunder. She could feel the car sliding on the rain soaked road. The speedometer showed fifty-five. She felt as though her foot was fastened to the accelerator pedal. She could not move it and then without warning the high beam headlamps of the other vehicle dazzled and almost blinded her.

There were few cars on the road and Nicola was able to move over to the outside lane. The other vehicle also drew out and closed the gap between them, its headlights, still at full beam, brandishing a violent threat. Nicola increased her speed to over seventy and began to sob as she drove. Her eyes were screwed up as she desperately tried to concentrate on the road ahead handicapped by the storm and the glaring light from behind.

Without warning, it was almost upon her, she passed the 'WORKS AHEAD' sign which shortly after was followed with illuminated arrows indicating 'CHANGE LANE' and then, directly in front of her, Nicola saw the barricades, small yellow lamps and a line of striped cones. She veered to the left merging into the inner lane, slowing slightly, as she completed the manoeuvre, her heart pounding with anxiety.

The other vehicle had been too close and unable to take the same diversionary action. It slid uncontrollably forward, crashing through the wooden structures, until hitting parked road machinery, awaiting use the following morning, The Vauxhall soared into the air landing upside down and then burst into flames. Nicola managed to draw to a halt in a lay-by two hundred yards ahead. She sat with her hands frozen to the wheel, unable to make the slightest movement and remained in this same position secured by the seat-belts with the engine turned off.

How he had got there she did not know but standing outside peering through the windscreen was a policeman. The storm had subsided.

Having moved to the side of the car where Nicola was sitting, she heard him call, "Are you able to turn down the window, please, madam?"

Obeying the command, she slowly turned the window handle and looked towards the policeman.

"Are you all right, madam? Do you think anything is broken? Did you fall against the wheel or knock your head in any way? Please do not move. An ambulance is on its way and we'll get you checked over shortly"

Nicola was certain she had not been hurt, but remained in the car as instructed. She was shaking and could only think of the nightmare journey that had just ended.

As the policeman stood guard, ensuring that she did not require any immediate assistance, she turned to him and very slowly asked, "What happened to the other lady? Is she still alive?"

"What other lady would that be, madam?" asked the policeman inquisitively.

"The woman who was driving the vehicle that was following me. I saw it crash, turn upside down and then I saw it on fire."

"I think the shock of the accident has caused you to become a little confused, madam. The driver of the other car wasn't a lady, it was a man."

*****

Delia heard a gentle tapping noise on the bedroom door. She picked up her clock. It was only twenty-five minutes to seven. She thought she'd been dreaming until she suddenly heard the tapping once more, this time accompanied by a female voice calling out 'Delia.'

She dashed out of bed and opened the door very slightly. Richard and Gilly were standing there.

"Hello you two." she said, "Aren't we the early ones. What surprise do you have for me today?"

"Can we come in?" said Gilly, "There's been a call from the doctor of Charlwood Manor. Paul's gone missing. The doctor wants you to call him back."

Having spoken to him, Delia told them Paul had been at the Manor when the main doors were locked at ten thirty the previous night, but found missing when the morning check was made at six this morning. They've searched all of the out-buildings on the grounds but to no avail.

"I must go there." said Delia, expressing great concern. "Could you order me a cab, Richard? I'll be ready to leave in…let's say in a half-hour."

"Don't worry about a cab," he replied, "I'll drive you."

At that time of the morning the traffic was very light and Richard had no difficulty in covering the ninety miles to Lymington by nine.

The doctor saw them immediately greeting them with "I'm really sorry that this has happened, Mrs. Scott. Since speaking to you we believe Paul hid in the small ante-room near the front door, waited for it to be unlocked and then made a run for it. Would you have any idea as to where he may have gone?"

"Well normally I'd have thought he'd have made his way home," said Delia, but without transport, I've no idea and in any event he knew I was spending the weekend with our friends in Brighton. But tell me, what do you think has brought this on? When I spoke to him on the telephone he gave me the impression you were satisfied with his progress."

"That's so," said the doctor, "but you must remember he has travelled through his own journey of darkness and nightmares. Frequently, he has had outbursts indicative of an explosive temper but we expected this and they will pass. His inner turmoil is connected with understanding how he has been dependant on alcohol for so long that he has been ruining his health and putting your marriage in jeopardy.

"I've no doubt by the time he leaves here he will have benefited enormously. He is a good patient and normally sticks to the rules and complies with all we ask of those who come here. You shouldn't worry yourself. The most important thing is that we must find him and find him quickly."

"Thank you," said Delia, "I must say you have made me feel a little easier. Is it possible that I could see his room?"

"Of course, follow me."

All three climbed the two flights of stairs before entering Paul's room. It was simply furnished with a single bed, bedside table, wash-stand, a plain desk, upright wooden chair and a small wardrobe. Delia felt tearful. She noticed there was a note pad and pencil on the desk and a mystery book by the bed.

Looking round the room she noticed a sheet of paper on the floor. It seemed as though it might have been propped up on the pillow and slipped off. She picked it up. It read 'Geshe Will Know'.

"Look at this," she said, "now I know where he is."

They looked at her waiting for an explanation. She turned to the doctor and asked, "Do you have a local telephone book I could look at?"

"Certainly, there's one in the general office."

After she had thumbed her way through part of the book for a minute or two, she gleefully announced, "Got you. This is where he will have gone – to this address in Southampton."

"How can you possibly know that?" asked Richard.

"I'll tell you how." replied Delia, "For some months wherever he has gone he has carried with him a book called 'Transform Your Life'. That's right, isn't it, doctor?"

"Absolutely." he said.

"The book wasn't in the room and will still be with him." continued Delia, "It was written by a renowned teacher of Buddhism whose name is Geshe Kelsang Gyatso and sets out practical advice to transform our mind and our life. This book has undoubtedly been helping Paul to find the real meaning of human life and how to find the source of happiness.

"Geshe is the title given by certain Tibetan monasteries to accomplished Buddhist scholars. In his note he said, 'Geshe will know'. This gave me the clue and in this telephone book I've found that in Southampton there's a Buddhist centre. I have no doubt he'll already have discovered they are holding a meeting today. He'll have decided it would beneficial for him to be there and he'd know you wouldn't have let him go. I'm sure we'll find him there."

"Are you Buddhists?" asked the doctor.

"No," replied Delia, "and you don't have to be, in order to gain considerable knowledge from their philosophical teachings. Richard, can we go and fetch him?"

The meeting was half-way through when they arrived. Paul was sitting in the third row of the seats from the front and did not see them until it was over. He looked tired and pale but appeared to emit a glow of happiness and gave a short wave before walking slowly towards them.

He took Delia into his arms and held her tight for what seemed an age. He then partially released her, kissed her gently on the lips and said "I love you more than anything in this world. Could you please now take me back to Charlwood."

*****

"Who's next? Who's next? That's what I want to know – who's next?" shouted out James whilst asleep.

"Be quiet, James dear, you're dreaming." said Phyllis, as she placed a hand on his shoulder.

Her sympathetic manner seemed to work and the remainder of the night passed peacefully.

When he appeared for breakfast she asked him, "What on earth was all that noise about last night?"

"What noise? What are you talking about?" he replied.

"You kept on calling out in your sleep, 'Who's next? Who's next?'"

James went very quiet, until saying, "Well is it surprising! During the last five weeks, both Graham and Brian have kicked the bucket from cancer and Jason had a massive heart attack. They were all my age group and now all three are six feet under."

"I know. It's not amusing but one has to just carry on and try and enjoy life as much as we can."

"What I want to know," he continued, "is, how many more of these damn cruises are we going to do? I'm now seventy nine and although I don't mind helping you with your art classes on the ships, nothing nowadays is the same as it was. I mean when you look around – talk about cruises for the masses – some of them dress as though they were at a holiday camp in Benidorm.

"And you're not getting any younger. Surely you've also had enough at sixty eight. It's not as though they pay you. Yes, it's been nice going on the cruises for nothing but how many more times do we need to see Warnemunde or Tallinn or Valetta or Cueta or Bergen or that dump Gibraltar? God knows why the Spanish want that place!"

"Let's talk about it later," replied Phyllis, "I really must get dressed and go to the art studio. I said I'd help them prepare for their weekend exhibition."

*****

For some reason or the other she had neither liked nor felt comfortable in Asnieres-sur-Seine and apart from the Town Hall had found nothing likely to leave a lasting impression.

Laura was aware she could either go round the Boulevard Peripherique or endeavour to drive across Paris in order to reach Asnieres-sous-Bois. She decided the former was the lesser of the two evils.

The comparatively short drive to Porte D'Orleans took just over a half-hour and having safely exited, Laura followed the sign A6 Lyons, knowing she would now be on a fast road for some considerable distance.

She stopped at the service area of Nemours to refuel and have a cold drink. All was peaceful in the cafeteria until she noticed a French couple enter with their Yorkshire terrier. Trouble broke out shortly after, when two young women arrived accompanied by their poodle. Without warning gladiatorial battle commenced between these two miniature combatants, The growling and snapping, the barking and yapping became too much and Laura picked up her handbag and returned to the car.

Her journey took her alongside the forest of Fontainebleau and through to Burgundy passing numerous farming communities with farmhouses standing apart with their shuttered windows of autumnal colours.

From the size of Asnieres-sous-Bois on her map, Laura assumed it would be a fairly small place but how small she did not know. And who was it she might find there? It was getting on for two when she first spotted in the distance the magnificent Basilica of the hilltop town of Vezelay and decided to stop for a little lunch.

When leaving Vezelay, Laura commenced a winding descent until reaching the main road and had not driven far before she nearly missed an almost indistinct wooden sign indicating "Asnieres-sous-Bois- 8kms".

The road climbed tortuously. A mass of trees had been cut down and were lying on the roadside. As she entered Les Bois de la Madeleine logs could be seen piled up for use by residents.

The skies suddenly darkened, followed by a heavy outburst of rain that produced a mesh of droplets travelling upwards and sideways on the windscreen. This together with the reflected headlights of the occasional oncoming vehicle, glistening and bouncing off the wet road, disturbed her vision. On either side a ground mist coiled round the sensuous tree trunks, enveloping and devouring them until they were out of sight.

The road continued to twist and turn and Laura began to feel scared. She imagined this terrifying transformation in the weather was an ominous warning, endeavouring to bar her way. She already sensed her visit here would not resolve anything.

As the light of a bulb being switched off, the rains suddenly ceased and the skies brightened and within a further two minutes she had arrived. She slowed, finding it difficult to believe Asnieres-sous-Bois appeared as a deserted village with only a garden gnome to greet her.

Numerous houses were visible but none of the villagers could be seen in the streets. Laura drove up and down what she assumed to be the main road until at last, standing by their front garden gate, she noticed an elderly lady standing with a young girl of eight or nine years.

She stopped the car and walked across to them. They seemed friendly and, speaking in French, Laura enquired as to whether anybody either lived or had lived there with the name Flatau. The lady replied she knew nobody of that name and sent her granddaughter into the house to fetch the latest local directory. The booklet listed the names, addresses and telephone numbers of the entire population of one hundred and forty-eight persons. The name of Flatau did not appear.

Once more Laura felt disheartened having driven a long distance only to find there was nothing here to relieve her concerns. She could not imagine anything would be gained by delaying her departure and returned down the same winding roads she had previously ascended until heading in the direction of the medieval city of Clamecy.

She was amused to pass through a small village called La Pouce, knowing this French word meant thumb. Green fields stretched for vast distances over the Berry plain and Laura sped past at over seventy miles an hour. On this fast road, she was able to cover a distance of thirty miles in a half-hour before coming to the bridge that crossed the River Loire to Bourges.

Another fast road lay straight ahead with the town of Gueret seventy miles away. Laura thought she could be there by seven and although it was not late, she was beginning to tire.

It was seven-fifteen when she drove outside the Hotel Auclair. Accommodation was inexpensive and she took a room at the back of the hotel described as 'plus calme'.

She immediately turned on the bath water, undressed, threw her clothes on the bed and immersed herself whilst the water was still pouring out of the tap. She closed her eyes feeling a wonderful sensation as the heated molecules massaged the pores of her skin. She added more hot water and did not come out of the bath until twenty minutes later.

She was now totally refreshed, felt very hungry and decided to eat in the hotel's restaurant. The menus were enticing and she thoroughly enjoyed a typical French meal accompanied by a half-bottle of Pouilly-Fume.

A wearisome day travelling, coupled with the disappointing visit to Asnieres-sous-Bois and finally three glasses of wine ensured that Laura was able to get a good night's sleep – without worrying about what she would find tomorrow.

*****

SIX

A further consultation took place at Dr. Alexander's surgery early the following week, at which Anne and Vince recounted Ellen's visit and her comment about an incident involving a train when Anne was young.

"I don't recall you having had any such recollection when you saw the regression therapist, Anne." he said.

"No, I didn't," she replied, "but that may have been my fault, I was frightened at the idea of being hypnotised and I believe that I may have hindered his efforts to take me back earlier in my life."

"That's possible," said the Doctor, "although I can't comment with any degree of expertise since it is out of my field. But tell me can you now clearly remember what happened?"

"That's just it. I can't. My Aunt Ellen knew very little, there's nobody alive who can tell me and I find not remembering scary."

"There can be no doubt finding the root cause of phobia problems can assist a patient enormously. I think you should go back to the regression therapist and see whether he can now help you further."

"No, I can't," said Anne, already showing signs of becoming agitated, "I won't be hypnotised."

"But Anne, darling, it could really help you this time." said Vince.

"I won't be hypnotised. I just won't." she replied forcefully.

Dr. Alexander sat thoughtfully and then said, "There is a possible alternative. It is a method used both in the United States and England and is called EFT that stands for Emotional Freedom Techniques. I also understand it has been adopted in some branches of the NHS.

"It is believed to help people recover from some fearful past experience and to help them dispel their problems that have no doubt arisen from the original cause. Hypnotism is not involved. It is a process of tapping fingers on specific points as on the neck and face, areas adopted in acupuncture except here needles are not used.

"I certainly would have thought it worth a try. I've been told of a practitioner in Andover who is said to be very good. Ask my receptionist for his telephone number when you leave. His name is Michael Rawlings."

A week later, Vince drove Anne to Andover. Mr. Rawlings was perfectly charming and immediately put Anne at her ease. He started by asking questions relating to her current health and claustrophobia problems. He also made notes of the various treatments and therapies she had received to date and listened to what had happened when Ellen had visited them.

"I'm quite sure," he said, "that by now you know the cause of phobias is not well understood but it is believed they arise from some unpleasant experience that a person has had at some time during their life.

"In your case it may well be the train journey was the cause of your difficulties but there can be no certainty, since they could relate to an incident that arose even earlier. In the meantime let me tell you something about EFT."

He then explained the general nature of the treatment adding, "EFT works by stimulating energy points – that we call meridians - and as a result placing the mind and body into a state of harmony. It clears emotional blockages and helps to reduce or sometimes take away the pain, when events occur that you find trigger off your current phobia. As with other forms of treatment, there is no guarantee that EFT will provide a cure. What I can tell you is that most patients generally attain some form of relief.

"Once I have told you more about the pressure points, you will be able to tap on them yourself whenever you feel an attack coming on and this should reduce the stress level that you would otherwise have."

"What I don't understand," said Anne, "is why, even now, I can't remember anything about what happened on the train."

"I cannot be sure," he replied, "but the most likely explanation is that you've been able to block it out of your mind completely."

Turning to Vince, he said, "Mr. Rogers, I think it might be better if you would now wait outside whilst I continue this session with your wife."

Having been told to remain seated comfortably in the chair, Anne then noticed that the lights of the room had dimmed and some gentle music portraying the sea lapping on the shore was being played. He walked over to her and said "Now Anne, there's nothing to worry about, I'm just going to tap my fingers on various parts of your face, neck and near your collar bone."

During this procedure, Anne felt totally relaxed and laughed when he commented, "Well, that wasn't so bad, was it?"

She liked and trusted him and did as he asked until after a few minutes she said, "What about the train?"

Dr. Rawlings smiled at her and replied, "Well that's an idea. Shall we give it a try?"

She began to tell him how when she was very young she and her friends all loved pop music.

"Did you ever see any of the famous pop groups?" he asked.

"Only once." she replied.

"And where was that?"

"At Wembley Stadium, my father took me for my birthday when I was nine."

"Did you like going out with your father, Anne?"

"Oh yes. He often took me out for special treats."

"Where were you living at that time?"

"In Islington"

"Did your father drive to Wembley?"

"No, he said that the traffic would be terrible so we went by train."

"Did you enjoy going to Wembley by train?"

"I think so," replied Anne hesitantly, "but it was crowded and I didn't like the tunnels."

"What happened after that?" asked Mr. Rawlings.

"We had to walk a long way before reaching the stadium the stadium. We got there early. It was very exciting and after about half-hour the first of the groups started to play. It was fantastic."

"It certainly sounds as though you and your Dad had a good time, Anne. Is there anything else you'd like to tell me about what happened?

"Well, walking back to the station after the show took ages. The crowds were enormous and daddy told me to make sure I held his hand tight.

"When we got to the station we stood with hundreds of passengers until I saw what looked like the powerfully lit eyes of a gigantic snail with a metal body draw alongside the platform. We couldn't get a seat and daddy again told me to hold him tightly.

"As the train went faster I could see lots of houses and blocks of flats with freshly washed clothes dancing in the garden breezes. The train passed the rail-yards at Neasden and after increasing speed, went on through three or four other stations. I saw rows of terraced houses and dark, dirt-coloured brick buildings.

"Most of the passengers stayed on the train at Finchley Road and as soon as it had started again it entered a brick tunnel. I didn't like it because it was very black and I thought that we might crash into the tunnel walls. Sometimes I could see a red or green signal and then for a few seconds I saw daylight until the train once more was swallowed into the darkness.

"I started to feel scared and asked daddy whether we could get off the train. He said we would very soon. Then the train vibrated violently and stopped. All the lights went out with only one small roof light working. A young child, who had been sitting quietly in a pram by the side of his mother started to scream.

"I told daddy that I was frightened and he tried to calm me. People were pushing and shoving us and I slipped on to the floor but daddy pulled me up again. I remember I started to cry and said I wanted to get out. Many people were nervous and I could hear them coughing and sneezing. It was getting hotter and hotter in the train and one man fainted.

"Suddenly there was a spluttering sound from the engine and the lights started to flicker but then went out again. It was then I lost hold of daddy's hand and I started to shout out for him. A lady caught hold of me and called out to daddy she had me. He pushed through the people until he reached me. I was shaking and crying and screaming to be let out.

"I then heard the engine start up again. The train shuddered once more and then started to move on very slowly. Within seconds it came to a halt and again there was total darkness. I was still crying and I heard the sound of another train passing through a tunnel nearby.

"We were stuck for nearly five minutes until the train started to move and began to glide smoothly along the lines. We then arrived at Baker Street station and I was so pleased to see all the lights. We heard an announcement telling us we must all change as the train was being taken out of service.

"Daddy said we would have to wait for the next train but I started to scream and told him I couldn't go on another train. I think he could tell I was feeling terrible and so he took me out of the station and we took buses for the rest of our journey."

As soon as she had finished telling the story Anne appeared to be quite exhausted. Dr. Rawlings gave her a glass of water and allowed her to sit and rest. He turned off the music and turned the lights up higher.

He smiled at her and said, "Well, I guess we've both learnt something today, Anne. Is that right?"

"Well, yes," she responded, "but what happens now?"

"At this stage, you should go home and I'll give you details of the areas you can tap, when you feel some form of attack about to take place. Telephone, if you need to speak to me, or should you prefer you can always make another appointment.

"Now you have recalled the story of the train, you will be able to focus on this from time to time and see whether you feel it has been the cause of your problems. Remember, I told you it may not have been but at least you now know what happened that day.

"Give me a call in a couple of weeks and let me know how you are getting on."

When they got home there was a letter waiting for Vince. He opened it and then called Anne, "Darling, I've got something to show you."

He handed her the letter. It was confirmation of their booking on the Neptune cruise departing on 15th September in an outside cabin with balcony.

"Oh, Vince, that's marvellous. Thank you so much, I feel better already."

*****

Roger and Lisa had bought a beautiful cottage in Rickmansworth shortly after they were married and Roger had continued living there after her death. He could no longer regard it as a home but it was certainly a welcome bolt-hole that enabled him to relax and forget his day-to-day business problems.

He was beginning to feel exhausted from the tremendous pressures of work that had arisen since Jonathan's death and was pleased he could now crash out for the weekend.

Whilst struggling to read one of the usual mammoth Sunday newspapers he suddenly came across an enticing advertisement of cruises in the Mediterranean. One of these gave details of a cruise on the HSL ship, the Neptune, departing Dover on 15th September.

He then remembered Jonathan had been telling him about this cruise line. Just what I need, he thought, and immediately dialled the number shown and requested a brochure.

*****

Martin and Shirley West lived in the beautiful town of Bradford-on-Avon, situated about eight miles from Bath. Like its neighbour, houses of Bath stone are predominant and it is here medieval pilgrims bound for Glastonbury used to pray in the chapel on its bridge.

They were both in their early sixties, retired and frequently enjoying cruises when Martin was asked to give either destination or entertainment talks. He had the ability of charming his audiences and endeavoured to keep them amused however serious his subject. He always said, it was important to recognise that those listening were on the cruise to have fun and be entertained and they were not wanting academia to be thrust down their throats.

His next booking was to be on the HSL ship, the Neptune, leaving mid-September, a vessel on which they had travelled on two previous occasions. Generally, he would be expected to give a talk on each of the days that the ship was at sea, which in this case was scheduled to be six, but this time he had been told he need only provide five destination talks.

"Have you got all your talks planned for the cruise?" asked Shirley.

"Yes, no problem whatsoever. I'll take the lap-top for the power point presentations in case they don't have one free when I'm about to give a talk."

"What have you been writing?" she asked, "You seem to have been at the PC for hours."

"I've been finishing the article the World Travel magazine editor asked me to write. Don't you remember? It's called 'A day in the life of a Cruise Lecturer'. Would you like to read it?"

Shirley took the article and began to read.

'At last we're out of the Bay of Biscay. I know this to be true, not because the ship sailed across any red tape signifying this achievement, but because the Captain, who insisted in prefacing all of his announcements by telling passengers that 'he was on the bridge' - well, I ask you, where else should he be!

It was a relief to most on board since many had been 'out of sorts' to put it mildly. Personally, though I did not suffer any of the slings and arrows of wind blown and swollen seas, I nevertheless was now far happier knowing that my next lecture would be given when conditions were expected to be calm.

Making a presentation in choppy seas does have its problems. As a result of the ships continuous movements, my normal firm stance is blown off course and frequently those sitting and watching may well believe that I am giving an introduction to the waltz or veleta!

Following the end of each talk I always call for questions, though I normally make it clear I only take simple ones. This usually enables me to leave the auditorium unharmed before a second hand is raised.

I find giving lectures on board ship is quite delightful, since when talks are land based, shortly after presentation I am homeward bound behind the wheel of my car. On a ship there is no escape, enabling discussions with passengers on the content of my talks to continue for some days thereafter - should they so choose.

This has its inherent problems since not all listeners remember what I've said for more than thirty minutes. About a week after giving a presentation on Spanish culture, I was seized upon by one irate gentleman who asked, 'Why did you say that the inquisition was a good thing?' No doubt yet another total misunderstanding arising from a senior moment.

Regardless of whether contracted as a port lecturer or as an entertainment or destination lecturer, officially, to the powers that be, we are considered as crew. Passengers will not normally be aware of this fact. Nevertheless, many will assume that you know all about the vessel, the weather and sea conditions, times of disembarkation, the cost of tours and how much it is likely to cost to have a cheese and ham roll on an island off Croatia.

From time to time I have found it quite extraordinary how some of my associates in the world of lecturing can be so boring. They will stand before their audience droning on and on during their allotted time, normally about forty-five minutes, completely oblivious some have fallen asleep and of those who have managed to keep awake a high proportion have either quietly or sometimes not so quietly walked out.

Lecturers on any subject that you may mention, should always bear in mind that whether young or old, the assembled listeners have an attention span of no more than about fifteen to twenty minutes. As a result a speaker must garnish his or her pearls of wisdom by keeping everyone entertained with either a selection of slides, amusing anecdotes, a short musical excerpt or other aids and above all remain animated at all times.

It is also vital for any good speaker to be aware he may well have competition from the next scheduled activity the cruise director has planned. Should this be a class on water- colour painting or flower arranging or a demonstration on how to make scones it may well attract a few devotees who will be fidgeting with their wrist watches.

The biggest hazard for any speaker arises when the next programmed pursuit is Bingo. Just take my word the mere mention of Bingo is likely to cause an exodus, as though the ship's fire alarms have gone off. Sad though it may be, all speakers know from past experiences on board they haven't got a chance against Bingo.

In the same way packaged holidays became the rage and enabled millions to travel the world at acceptable budget prices, a similar situation has arisen with cruising. We now have 'cruising for the masses', whereby, the market place caters for all pockets and provides varying attractions to suit those expected on board.

There can be little doubt that the expression 'there's none so queer as folk' frequently fits the bill and the wide spectrum of ship travellers will normally provide a series of humdinger comments.

I recently asked one man about his occupation. 'I'm retired', he replied. 'And what did you do before then?' I asked. 'I worked', said he. Then there was the lady who told me that her husband was a very balanced man and added, 'He has a chip on both shoulders'.

Finally, there was Shirley, not Valentine, who thrived on complaining. Well, this must have been the case, since in fourteen days I never heard one positive comment from her. The weather was either too hot or too cold, the vegetarian food was certainly not up to standard, the air-conditioning was too noisy in her cabin, the chocolates left on her pillow each night were not the sort that she would ever buy, the sandwiches at tea-time were always the same and guess what, yes, you have it in one, the time that they scheduled bingo was too early except on other days when it was too late.

As I was about to disembark at the end of the voyage to my horror I suddenly saw Shirley making a beeline for me. There was no place to hide. She smiled, extended out a hand and said 'I'm so pleased to have met you. Wasn't it a wonderful cruise?'

It definitely takes all sorts but that is the wonderful part of our world and there is no doubt that cruising for most is great and provides something for everyone.'

THE END

Shirley appeared to have found the article amusing and commented, "I like it and how true to life. Do you want me to post it for you? I'm going out in about ten minutes."

*****

Deep sadness was again destined to enter Karen's life. She had been in the shop for about an hour when there was a call for her from mother's long-life friend and neighbour, Carole Jennings.

"Is that you Karen? It's me, Carole, Carole Jennings."

"Hello, Carole. Is something wrong with Mum?"

"Well, yes dear. She's had a stroke. They've taken her to the local hospital. I'm going over there now. Will you be able to get over there?"

"Of course, it'll take me some time but I'll be there as soon as possible. I'll give you my mobile number so you can reach me whilst I'm en route."

Mr. Moreton told her to shut the shop leaving a notice it will be re-opening at noon. "I'll come over and handle everything today." he said, "Don't you worry about anything, Karen. Just get over to you mum and I hope you find she's not too bad."

Despite being caught up in a traffic jam between Bedford and St. Neots, Karen arrived at the hospital in just under two hours.

She found Carole sitting by her mother's side. She could barely recognise her mother's face. It was contorted, her dentures had been removed, her hair was matted and she lay on the bed gazing into space. She had aged twenty years in a matter of hours. Seeing Karen had arrived, the Sister had bleeped for the doctor.

'I'm so sorry, Mrs. Hardwick. Your mother's had a severe stroke and is totally paralysed on her right side. She's unable to speak and at the moment there's no telling whether she'll recover. The next few hours are critical"

Karen telephoned David to tell him and prayed that her mother would be taken soon and released from her undoubted torment. He suggested that he'd drive over but she said it wouldn't be necessary.

Karen had always hated hospitals. She disliked the smells and could not bear to look across at other patients. She found herself walking up and down the corridors sensing something was about to happen until suddenly she heard her name being called. She turned and found the ward sister hurrying towards her.

"What's happened?" she asked.

"Your mother's had another stroke. We don't believe she'll survive more than a few minutes."

They both immediately hastened to her mother's bed only to hear the nurse say, "I'm sorry Mrs. Hardwick, but she's gone."

The cold pronouncement of death had struck and reverberated as a hammer blow on an anvil. Tears were gently running down her face as Karen turned away.

It was then she heard the sister say, "She's at peace now, Mrs. Hardwick. Do take another look at her."

For the first time since her mother had been struck down, the distorted features lined with anguish and fear had been smoothed away. Now there was a vision of tranquillity. Now her torment had ended.

And now the umbilical cord had been severed.

Once again Karen called David to tell him and said she'd drive herself home.

When the time came for the funeral both Julie and Craig attended and Julie was very supportive towards Karen throughout her period of mourning. It became obvious that Craig appeared to be having a sobering affect on David but Karen could not be sure as to how long this was likely to last.

"You know what they say about leopards never changing their spots." Karen commented to Julie.

The next few weeks saw all four seeing each other frequently and this gradually helped Karen get over her loss.

One evening Craig said, "We've been thinking it would be nice to get away for a couple of weeks and we've found a

Mediterranean cruise advertised departing in September. It isn't expensive when you start to work out all that's included. Anthony will be back at school by then and can stay with Julie's brother and his wife and we were wondering whether you two would like to come with us."

*****

"Hi, Tracey." said Joanne, having excitedly made a call to her friend, "He's gone and done it."

"Steady on, Jo. Who's gone and done what?"

"Dean. I told you what he was thinking and last night he turned up with tickets for the four of us to go on that Mediterranean cruise. It leaves on 15th September. I just can't believe it. Oh, Tracey, I'm so excited. I'll be able to see Monte Carlo. You'll have to come and help me do some shopping. I'll have to buy some more clothes."

"What will you do about the children and the school?"

"I've decided to tell the truth to the teacher. I can't do otherwise. It wouldn't be fair on the kids and if they fine us then so be it. I shall tell her it'll be of educational value and that I'll give them some school work to do every day."

*****

Having assured the police officer she was perfectly all right, apart from being a little shaken, he wrote down her name, address and other personal details together with some information about EROS. He checked her driving licence and requested sight of her insurance documents. Not having these with her, Nicola was told to produce them at her local police station during the next few days.

"Well, if you're sure you're okay, Miss, I have no reason to stop you from proceeding. I think you said you were on your way to see your parents in Ascot. What would be the address and telephone number there? You'll receive a call in a couple of days from the local station and they may want to interview you further."

"Why would that be?" asked Nicola.

"I imagine you may be able to help us in identifying who was in the other car, Miss. You thought it was a woman but as I've said, in fact it was a man. We'll have to wait until our forensic team examine the body and the car so as to obtain some firm evidence. I'd be surprised if you were followed by someone who didn't know you. That would indeed be rather strange, wouldn't it?"

"I suppose it would," responded Nicola thoughtfully, "but I can't imagine who it could have been or why."

Once in Ascot, Nicola telephoned Denise and told her what had happened.

"Perhaps it was a client who you interviewed? suggested Denise.

This initial suggestion proved to be the answer. The local police sergeant telephoned Nicola two days later and said he needed to come to the office and examine some of their records. When he arrived she handed to him her insurance documents.

"Thank you, Miss. We've found the remains of your business card in the dead man's wallet. His name was Derek Simms. Does that name ring a bell?"

"Yes, it does," replied Nicola, "I remember him well. I interviewed him here. Hold on a minute and I'll get his registration card."

Having retrieved it from the filing cabinet she showed it to the sergeant.

"You'll see he was in his mid-forties and had never been married. He said he had his own consultancy company but was not very forthcoming. He wanted to meet someone over thirty for a serious relationship hoping it might lead to marriage. He was neatly dressed but there was something about him that seemed a little odd although I couldn't put my finger on what it was. I thought he might just be shy.

"I spoke to three of the ladies registered with us and in each case they gave me permission to let him have their telephone number. All three obviously met him but the subsequent feed back I received was they all felt as though he was rather strange and refused to make a second date with him. I decided not to recommend him to anyone else."

"I think that was a very wise move." said the sergeant. "We've been making our own enquiries and it appears he has been admitted into hospital for treatment for schizophrenia on several occasions. I'm not a medical man but I'd guess he blamed you for the lack of interest shown by these women and was intending to harm you when his car crashed. By the way, the reason you thought he was a woman, was because he was wearing a wig."

Nicola did not hear anything further from the police but the incident raised notes of caution with both her and Denise when holding subsequent interviews.

EROS continued to flourish and Nicola's father gave them a three-year lease on the premises. There was no time for Nicola to go to Greece that year and Denise knew she too would have to remain with head down to ensure the success of the agency.

The end of October saw the first anniversary of EROS and when yet another Christmas and New Year arrived they again went skiing, though this time to a rather more fashionable resort in the French Alps.

Life was good. They thoroughly enjoyed running the agency. They loved living together and did not doubt that fate had brought them together.

*****

On the appointed day, eight weeks after Delia had originally driven him there, Paul left Charlwood. He had lost a little weight, looked fitter and for the first time in months his eyes sparkled.

Prior to departure they had a meeting with the senior consultant who said he'd been very pleased with the progress made by Paul. He reiterated this would not be the end of his fight against alcoholism but as a result of his stay at Charlwood he would have a better understanding of the nature of the problem and what steps he had to take in the future.

"It's vital, Paul, you not only join Alcoholics Anonymous but you go to their meetings on a regular basis, probably three times a week. In addition, you should both go to AL ANON, the advisory group for family members of alcoholics."

Delia knew she would have to remain strong for Paul not only to help him overcome his ordeal but also to ensure the survival of their marriage.

Once they were home, Paul found where the nearest A.A. meetings were held and they went to the advisory group. He discovered part of the programme suggested by A.A. was set out in a record of practice known as 'The Twelve Steps.' This had been based on the knowledge gained by some of the original members of the organisation.

He began to realise how A.A. members helped each other by sharing their experiences and by giving assistance to others who had a drinking problem, but were not as yet members of A.A.

They all understood that the hardest initial step a person could take was to openly acknowledge he or she was indeed an alcoholic. Paul would never forget how, at his first meeting, he got up and said "My name is Paul Scott and I'm an alcoholic." A statement that he and all members made repeatedly.

As the weeks passed Paul was able to acknowledge the benefits arising from his going to the A.A. meetings with other men and women who all had the singleness of purpose of avoiding the strong draw of returning to alcohol. Whenever the urge arose it had to be firmly pushed into the background.

Delia had become more confident he would indeed succeed in his fierce battle. He had committed himself and had not touched one drop of drink. The mutual love between them was gaining in depth daily and they were very happy together.

Towards the middle of August she had an idea, made some enquiries and then came up with her suggestion.

"You know, Paul, I really believe it would do us both the world of good if we were to have a holiday."

"How can I?" he replied, "I really need to go to the meetings every week. I honestly don't think I'd be strong enough without them."

"I know," said Delia, "and that's why I'm sure my idea will work. How about if we go on a cruise for two weeks? I've got a number of brochures we can look through. What's important is it seems all cruise ships have regular A.A. meetings for passengers. Apparently, it's shown on their daily programme in such a way very few other passengers realise to what they're referring.

"The girl in the travel agency told me it might read: '4.00p.m. Meet Bill and Bob.' She couldn't remember the exact names they use but she thought it was the same on all ships."

"That's amazing." said Paul. "Providing we can get confirmation that meetings would be taking place, I think I'd like to go."

Delia gave him a big hug whilst saying, "I'm really proud of you, Paul."

*****

Laura did not wake until eight, and was content tiredness and fatigue had taken leave of her eyes and body. She had no reason to rush and after a leisurely breakfast, studied the road map and departed at nine-twenty. She filled up at a nearby Total garage and then headed towards Bellac.

The unbroken clear blue sky accompanied by the gleaming, glow of the sun created an idyllic day making her feel very happy. The scenery was attractive without being outstanding and after reaching La Souterraine she commenced a descent to the Limousin plain.

Seven miles from the far side of Bellac, she arrived at Mezieres-sur-Issoire and knew it was now only eight miles from the third of her four scheduled destinations. Once more she became slightly lost, stopped and asked a weather-beaten farm worker, dressed in blue denims and wearing a flat cap, for Asnieres-sur-Blour. He constantly nibbled at the large French loaf he was carrying, whilst giving her directions towards a church at St. Brabant.

The road was deserted and then it happened again. She had just reached the church when the clouds blackened and there was a loud crack of thunder with lightening, striking in the distance. The torrential rain made it impossible for her to see. She drew into the entranceway of the church and waited until the storm had quelled its appetite.

She could not believe that the weather had turned against her with such ferocity. Was this to be another warning as the one she had received at Asnieres-sous-Bois? Within minutes the angry roar of wind, rain and thunder ceased. Laura reversed out and cautiously continued.

Turning into a narrow bend in the road she found herself behind a tractor slowly idling along. Overtaking was impossible and she was forced to follow this mechanical tortoise until they came to the village - the village that she had been seeking.

When arriving at a nearby Mill, Laura noticed two men working opposite to where she'd parked. The ground was soggy and she found herself tiptoeing through a muddy field to reach them. Though they certainly saw her coming towards them, they remained motionless, observing her in silence.

She greeted them and explained she was looking for someone with the name of Flatau.

"I've lived here all my life," said the older of the two, "but there has never been a family here with that name."

The second nodded in agreement and suggested, "You must go to the Mairie. It's just opposite the church."

Having previously seen the church, Laura returned, stopped outside and looked across to the Town Hall. She entered the tiny building and immediately found herself in a small room containing a table, two chairs and two filing cabinets.

A lady in her late fifties, seated at an old typewriter, looked up showing considerable surprise at seeing Laura. She produced the latest electoral list which showed there was a population of two hundred and sixty-eight, but, as the two workmen had said, there was nobody with the name Flatau.

Returning to the car, Laura noticed a woman coming towards her carrying an umbrella. She wore a scarf over her head, wore a mauve cardigan, chequered overall, brown skirt, heavy brown shoes and a shawl over her shoulders.

Laura assumed the woman intended walking past her - but she didn't. She drew closer and closer until she was standing directly in front of her. She stood looking straight at her face and then uttered the words "Continuer, Madame, continuer. Tout va bien, tout va bien."

Throughout she had remained staring at Laura and, having finished speaking, she side stepped past her and went into the church.

Laura felt a cold chill pass over her. How was it possible that a complete stranger should tell her to continue and that all was well? The woman had no way of knowing what she was doing in the village or what had happened previously both in London and in France. Until the woman had spoken to her, Laura had been disappointed with the negative results of her journey.

The woman's words left such a firm impression they gave her fresh confidence, and now she was certain, the story she was waiting to unfold would take place when she reached Asnieres – sur-Vegre.

*****

SEVEN

Sarum College had been established for over 40 years and throughout that time had maintained an excellent teaching staff enabling a very high standard of education to be achieved. Despite different governments tinkering with examinations, burdening with bureaucracy and endeavouring to bring elements of a 'nanny state' to schools generally, the results obtained by their students, had always ensured Sarum's ranking was in the top ten. The subsequent icing on the cake arose when a high proportion went on to one or other of the best universities in England.

The Board of Governors wasn't scheduled to meet again until the last week of September but having received Vince's telephone request, the Chairman decided he would call his fellow Board members to seek their views.

"Sorry to trouble you, Christopher," he said to the first, "but Vince Rogers has been in touch with me. You'll recall his wife has been suffering from claustrophobia and recently resigned from Caritas. I happen to know their chairman and he told me they've been very sorry to lose her.

"Anyway, it appears she's recently been having further treatment and Vince is desperately keen to take her on vacation since he feels sure it'll help her considerably. He has to be very selective because she's unable to fly and has problems being in a car other than for short periods.

"She's agreed to go on a two-week cruise providing they are in a cabin with a balcony. The problem is the first cruise leaving an English port with these facilities is not until 15th September, when Sarum will have re-commenced.

"He's spoken to the Head and to some of his co-teachers and they've all agreed that with a little juggling they can arrange cover for him. I've also spoken to the Head and he's told me, under normal circumstances he would never agree, but as Vince has been with the college for nearly twenty years, he believes special dispensation could be given on this occasion.

"I must say I rather agree with him but obviously the majority of the Board will have to accept the proposal before we can give him the okay."

Subsequently, there was no need for a majority decision to be taken, since without fail, every member of the Board indicated their approval.

"Well, I guess, it's all steam ahead." Vince said to Anne. He had now received the Board's decision and was thrilled that the college had decided to be so supportive.

Since seeing Mr. Rawlings, Anne had found she'd been able to obtain a degree of relief from the EFT process whenever she found something or the other was about to trigger off the claustrophobic symptoms.

Although she didn't wish to take up further full-time employment she nevertheless began to think it would be a waste should she no longer use her considerable skills.

"One door closes and another opens. Isn't that right?" she commented to Vince.

"Yes, it is. But what are you talking about?"

"When I was in Sherbourne last week I passed by their Citizens Advice Bureau. There was a notice in the window indicating they required volunteers, so I went in and had a chat with the woman who's in charge.

She told me the Bureau offers a free and confidential service of advice and information on a wide range of subjects including money management, employment problems, housing and marriage. Most of the volunteers tend to work two mornings or afternoons weekly and initially one receives some training. It really sounds quite interesting.

"I think you'd be very good there," responded Vince, "and some of the work you did with Caritas would be really useful. See how you feel when we come back from the cruise."

"Speaking of the cruise," said Anne, "I hadn't realised that when the ship makes its first port of call in Vigo it's possible we may be able to visit Santiago de Compostela. I've always wanted to go there, even when in my teens."

Vince looked a little vague and then said, "Oh dear, I think my brain's seizing up. Remind me quick. I ought to know. I am after all a geography teacher – or so they tell me!"

She laughed. "Of course, you know, it was the world-famous place of pilgrimage in the Middle Ages."

"But why are you so keen to go there?"

"I really don't know. In a way, it would be like going to Jerusalem or Rome as the pilgrims did at that time. I've met several people who've been there and they've all said it was an amazing experience."

"Are you expecting it to provide you with some form of help like those who visit Lourdes?"

"No, it's nothing like that. It doesn't even have any religious significance for me. I guess you could call it a personal mission I would like to make during my lifetime."

"Then you shall go to the ball, Cinderella." replied Vince.

"Thank you. You really are a darling.

*****

Daylight had faded and now the noticeable darkness brought night into her living room without being invited. Inwardly she felt happy and had so enjoyed reading about all the places she would be seeing on the cruise. But now, she wished to be alone with her thoughts, comforted by light not night, and so Louise crossed between the front and rear windows, gently drew the curtains and once more felt at ease with herself and her memories.

She returned to the comfort of the armchair she had always been used to sitting in, with the brochure on her lap. Though she had been married to Mark for almost two decades and loved him dearly, there were many times she'd accepted he was a real stick-in-the-mud.

The subject of holidays was always one of those occasions. As far as he was concerned a holiday in one of the three B's – Brighton, Bournemouth or Blackpool - 'was smashing'.

"Why do I need to travel on uncomfortable airplanes to places where the temperature is in the nineties and where the food is no where near as good as you make?" he would say.

Gradually she managed to persuade him to become a little more adventurous. Brighton became Malta, Bournemouth was dropped for Tenerife and Blackpool was changed for the Costa del Sol. There was no enthusiasm and plenty of moans but nevertheless Louise had been thrilled to see places new, be with people from different countries and hear other languages being spoken, despite the fact she had no idea what was being said.

The most exciting trip came when their fifteenth anniversary was drawing near.

"Is there anywhere special you'd like me to take you to?" he'd asked.

That question had been answered by her in seconds and resulted in a four day extended week-end break to Venice. This had always been a dream for Louise and suddenly she found herself transported to the home of the Venetians, crossing the Grand Canal by motor-bus, being sung to by a gondolier, visiting the Doge's Palace, having a coffee in St. Mark's Square and wandering, spell-bound, whilst looking at all of the wonderful shops with their designer clothes, fabrics, glassware and lingerie.

Those four places abroad, had been the extent of their foreign travel in nineteen years and now, in a period of two weeks, she would be seeing more than she could ever imagined.

*****

He was looking out of the window when the car arrived promptly at ten-thirty on the Sunday morning. Charles and Emma had previously cajoled him into going with them to the Cotswolds for lunch at The Bear in Burford. Ever since he and Lisa had moved to Rickmansworth, they had not only been good neighbours but also very good friends, and he felt he couldn't refuse their kind invitation.

Emma was sitting on one of the rear seats and blew a kiss as he opened the front car door to sit next to Charles.

"Wouldn't you prefer to sit up front?" he asked her.

"I'm fine." she replied, "From here I can both hear and keep my eye on the two of you, although, quite frankly, I'm simply looking forward to seeing the scenery of the Cotswold Hills."

Charles headed towards Oxford and then kept on the main road leading to Burford. It was a beautiful day and Roger was pleased this was one of those rare occasions when somebody else was driving. He had always been captivated by the old-world charm and friendliness of this part of England with its mellow-coloured limestone which had been used in many of the picturesque villages.

He was also relieved to find conversation was light, amusing and general. He wanted this to be a relaxing day without having either his work or past memories of Lisa being discussed.

"I've booked the table for one, so we've plenty of time." said Charles, as he drove into The Bear car park.

They decided to take a stroll before lunch and were soon able to spot the impressive spire of the Church of St. John the Baptist. As they walked up the main street to the three-arched bridge over the River Windrush, the little shops on either side reminded Roger of the miniature butcher, baker and sweetshops he'd played with as a child.

"It's all the little villages I like," commented Emma, "with those wonderful names like Stow-on-the-Wold, Moreton-in-Marsh, Upper and Lower Slaughter and, of course. Bourton-on-the-Water."

"I think that's my favourite." said Charles, "The trouble is, at this time of the year there are too many tourists. It's all much nicer to visit in spring or autumn."

During lunch Roger said he was thinking of taking a couple of weeks holiday and told them of the cruise he'd read about on the Neptune.

"Oh, how funny you should mention that ship." said Lisa, "A couple I know from the golf club recently went on one of its voyages. They really enjoyed the trip. They said they've been on a number of cruises and this was one of the best. It's not a big ship and they said the food and entertainment was jolly good. Give it a whirl, Roger, you'll probably have a great time and anyway, I'd have thought you needed a good rest."

On the return journey Roger thought back on Emma's words and having reached home made a note to telephone his travel agent the next morning to make a booking on the 15ᵗʰ September cruise.

*****

Two days later, Karen called to see Julie.

"I really can't make up my mind about going on the cruise." she said, "I've told you what David can be like and I certainly don't wish to find myself embarrassed by any of his antics. I really have put up with them for far too long."

"I can understand that," replied Julie, "but surely, as we'll also be there he's bound to behave himself?"

"I only wish I could be so sure." commented Karen, "He wants us to go with you and hasn't talked about anything else since you made the suggestion."

"I tell you what, let me talk to Craig and make sure he keeps his eye on David. They seem to get on well enough."

That evening Karen discussed the cruise further with David and attempted to read the Riot Act to him.

"I know you want to go," she said, "but should you cause any problems with Julie or Craig or attempt to fool about with any of the passengers, it'll be the last time I'll ever go away anywhere with you again. I really mean it, David, so don't think I'm kidding."

Before leaving for work the next morning, Karen called Julie to confirm that they'd join them on the cruise.

"Would you make the reservations and let me know when you need to have a cheque."

She didn't notice David had smartened himself up considerably on that same morning and assumed his jaunty appearance had resulted from her agreeing to go on the cruise. But once again little did she know.

Douglas and Gail Price had been happily married for over thirty years and, despite never having children, their lives were totally complete. He had an antiques shop in Tunbridge Wells and she was an interior decorator. They would often work together whenever a suitable project arose requiring their joint expertise.

The death of Douglas had been totally unexpected. During a vacation in the Middle East he contracted a virus that severely affected his liver. He saw numerous specialists but none could provide a cure. The virus attack intensified until he began to lose weight at an alarming rate. The end came within a few days, during the middle of one night, whilst in The London Hospital.

As soon as she felt strong enough to deal with their financial affairs, Gail arranged for their accountant, Roy Chambers, to review the status of the antiques business and advise her as to the best course of action to take. As a result of his evaluation, he concluded a further injection of capital would be necessary to ensure future successful trading.

There was too much stock, insufficient sales and her own bank had refused to extend existing facilities. By a series of coincidences, an accountant colleague had told Mr. Chambers of a broker called David Hardwick, who assisted clients in obtaining finance.

David received a telephone call, asking whether he would visit Mrs. Price. He hated driving in South London but having passed through Elephant & Castle, New Cross and Lewisham he was pleased to find the remainder of the journey was on a fast road with little traffic.

The 19th century house stood within a parkland setting outside a small village about eight miles from Tunbridge Wells. David became suitably impressed and even more so when meeting Gail Price. He could smell the light fragrance of her perfume and was captivated by the gentle movement of her body. Her softness and warmth cast their spell over him and he was sure she was the most sensual woman he had ever met.

At the same time he found her to be extremely formal and it did not take long before he recognised she was very capable and had considerable knowledge regarding her late husband's antiques business. Nevertheless, 'what would she know about finance' he thought. David hated clever women and felt sure this could be an opportunity for him to carve out a good deal for himself. He immediately turned on the charm, acted with considerable politeness and never once made a wrong move.

Gail was far from sure about this young man but eventually agreed he should prepare a report setting out his recommendations. David sent this to her ten days later, suggesting they again meet after she had studied the contents.

He had managed to ensure it maximised every penny of commission he could possibly earn by including a mortgage protection plan, an inheritance tax scheme, a pension policy and several other unnecessary proposals to benefit his pocket but not in the interests of Gail Price. In addition, he sent a letter of appointment, requiring her to sign an agreement, whereby she would pay him an introductory commission based on 2 ½% of the amount of finance raised by him.

Today, was the morning for their second meeting. He felt very pleased with himself when, walking into his office. His secretary told him Mrs. Price had called to say she'd been slightly delayed but would be arriving at eleven thirty 'to make final arrangements with David'. He had preened himself ready to win over this lovely widow.

Just after eleven-thirty the inter-com buzzed. "Mr. Price is here." the secretary announced.

Stupid girl he thought, "Show her in." he said.

The door to his office opened, his secretary entered followed by a man in his late fifties. "Mr. Price for you." she again announced

David rose from his desk looking more than surprised at his unknown visitor, who placed a visiting card on the desk. "Guy Simmonds, brother of Gail Price. I assume you are Mr. David Hardwick? May I sit down?"

David began to feel distinctly uncomfortable as Mr. Simmonds opened his brief case and produced David's report.

"I assume you prepared this?" he asked

"That's right." responded David, not knowing what was coming next.

"Yes, I thought it was. Well, I won't keep you long Mr. Hardwick but I must tell you, the last time I saw a report of this nature, containing recommendations similar to those suggested by you, was in the Law Courts. I was prosecuting barrister and the defendant was sentenced to seven years for deception and fraud.

"Mrs. Price has decided not to take this matter any further but I would ask you to bear in mind that ...."

Up until this time the words spoken by Guy Simmonds had been in a quiet voice, enunciating each word clearly and precisely, but now he raised his tone by several decibels.

".........should you make any further contact with her by either letter or telephone I shall return here and knock your bloody head off."

His voice again reverted downwards to a lower range.

"Do we understand each other? I certainly hope so for your sake. Good morning."

He got up from the chair and left David's office. David could not remember anybody ever talking to him in such a manner before. His anger level shot up immediately. He stormed out of his room saying he would be gone for the rest of the day and made for the nearest bar constantly muttering 'What a bitch, what a bitch'

*****

At forty-eight, still single and living in Norwich, Colin had decided he wanted a change of career from art lecturer and had been searching for premises suitable for a restaurant. He had always loved cooking and thought from now on he might as well make some money from it.

He had now found them in Reigate and realised the legal, finance and survey wheels would turn slowly until a date for exchange of contracts had been reached.

He was doodling with some proposed menus when the telephone rang.

"May I speak to Mr. Colin Price?"

"Speaking." replied Colin.

"Good afternoon, Mr. Price, my name's Dalton, Brian Dalton of HSL shipping. We've somewhat of a problem and were wondering whether you might be able to help us out, bearing in mind you've been on our ships previously.

"We had booked one of your colleagues, Stephen Bond, on the Neptune cruise which is scheduled to leave Dover on 15th September. I've just had a telephone call from Mrs. Bond to tell me her husband was admitted into hospital last night and found to have pneumonia."

"Pneumonia!" interrupted Colin, "you don't hear of that happening very often these days, unless to a much older person."

"Quite," said Brian Dalton, "anyway, as you will realise he's not going to make a sufficient recovery before the ship sails and I thought you might be able to take his place. Is this a possibility?"

"Hold on a minute, whilst I get my diary." replied Colin.

It was in fact by the side of the phone but he wanted to give himself a few moments to think. Nothing very much would be happening during the period of the cruise and he could always be reached on his mobile. A freebee holiday at this time wouldn't go amiss and he could do considerable planning whilst on the ship.

He picked up the telephone again, "Sorry for the delay, Mr. Dalton. It looks like I'll be able to help you. Where's the ship going to?"

"It's a Mediterranean art-themed cruise. We would require five talks during the two weeks. Would that be okay?

"Yes, that's perfectly all right."

"Good. Well I'll send you a letter of confirmation during the next day or two but in the meantime, thanks very much for coming to the rescue. 'Bye now."

*****

They sat at a table outside a wine bar, enjoying the warmth of a sunny August day, with a glass of white wine eating a few of the titbits the bar served. Their feet had called time out as Joanne had gone on a shopping spree in Bedford, with her friend Tracey as advisor, prior to the cruise holiday.

"So where's the cruise going?" asked Tracey.

"Well, I told you Monte Carlo, then there's Barcelona and Rome and….and…I can't remember where else, oh yes, Lisbon and I think there are three other places or is it four. Never mind. I'm sure it'll be great.

"I'll tell you one thing," continued Joanne, "going to the South of France is bringing back some memories. When I was seventeen a group of us went to St. Tropez or St. Trop as everyone called it. What a place! Brigitte Bardot territory or it was in the fifties. We had a ball. It was a holiday of very late nights and catching up on sleep during the day.

"When I came home my mother said, *'You don't look very brown. You couldn't have had much of a holiday.'* I just told her the weather was a bit mixed and left it at that – but I nearly creased myself laughing.

"Whilst I was there I managed to get a job in a bar during the following summer. They weren't bothered I didn't speak French but suggested I learned a little before I went back. I kept in touch, making sure they didn't change their mind, but all was well and I went at the beginning of June. I was there for three months. It was fantastic. I didn't want to come home.

"Loads of young people go there during the evenings from the camp sites where they're staying. It's like two places in one. Parts of it are really chic with expensive flats but then you have the areas of denims and loud rock music, short skirts and lots of blondes. It's really go-go, especially for teenagers."

"The nearest I ever got to anything like that was in Benidorm." said Tracey. "It was all right at the beginning but by the time I'd been there ten days I'd had enough. Have you heard anything from the school yet?"

"No. They won't be able to let me know until the new term starts. Well we better push on. Dean won't want to be locked up with the kids all day."

*****

It had been ages since they had seen one and another and arrangements had been made for the four of them to go to an excellent Chinese restaurant in Queensway, near where Tina and Clive lived. Denise and Nicola were the first to arrive and chose a table where they wouldn't all be overheard.

"It's so lovely to see you both." said Tina, "I kept saying to Clive, if I don't hear from those girls soon I'll launch a rocket to Swiss Cottage."

"How's Eros, going?" asked Clive.

"Really well," replied Nicola, "We're working our butts off, but it's taken off and we've got lots of smashing people who have joined our lonely hearts club, though I shouldn't call it that, since most of our members are perfectly genuine but have been unable to find Mr. or Mrs. Right."

"In fact," interjected Denise, "we can spot in a minute those who just want to fool around."

The next ten minutes were spent in virtual silence as each studied the menu.

"Why don't we order a variety of dishes and that way we can all have a little of everything?" suggested Clive.

Whilst waiting for their starters Nicola told Clive they would like his firm to act as their accountants.

"Oh, I don't know about that," he replied in a serious voice, "we'll probably have to take up references!"

"He never changes." commented Tina, "By the way how was your Crete holiday Nicola?"

"It was wonderful." said Nicola, "I've already bored the pants off Denise by telling her everything I saw so I won't go over it again, in case she starts to throw spring rolls at me.

"The weather was perfect and as it's the biggest of the Greek Islands, there is so much to see. The highlight was visiting the four thousand year old Minoan Palace at Knossos. Our Sir Arthur Evans discovered it in eighteen ninety-nine. But apart from the Palace, in the capital Heraklion, there is a magnificent museum that houses the most amazing objet d'arts and other treasures found during the archaeological dig. The jewellery is to die for."

"Okay, Clive." said Tina, "I'm convinced, add it to the list of places to go."

"So do you have any plans to get away, Denise?" asked Clive.

"Well, as a matter of fact, we were talking earlier about where I should go. I'm certainly a sun worshipper but sitting in ninety degrees of August sun in Crete does not appeal. Nicola is trying to convince me into taking a cruise I've had my eye on in mid-September, but I'm rather concerned since it would mean my being away from the office for two weeks."

"Which cruise is that?" asked Tina.

"It's a trip round the Med. which in the main is going to Portugal, Italy, France and Spain. It's a lovely itinerary."

"What ship would you be on?" asked Clive.

"It's called the Neptune. I believe it only holds about seven hundred passengers."

"That's interesting." he commented, "I've a client who in July went on her sister ship, the Poseidon, and told me he and his wife had a great holiday."

"Well, there you are then," interrupted Nicola, "that settles it. You go and make your booking tomorrow morning. I can manage the office for a couple of weeks. I did it before and I shall refuse to discuss the subject again."

*****

The sculptured symmetry of the 11th century cathedral always drew a vast number of visitors, particularly during the summer months. Winchester had been a great city since Roman times and in the reign of Alfred the Great became the capital of England. It was here that King Canute, Izaak Walton and Jane Austen had been buried and where in 1086 the Domesday Book was compiled.

It was the beauty of the city and its history that had originally attracted Rosalind and Andrew to live there some twenty-five years ago and they were still thrilled by the many cultural activities that took place. They had been attending a lunchtime piano recital of music by Bach, Vivaldi and Faure and were now walking towards the gardens near the Cathedral so as to munch the sandwiches she had prepared.

"Did you say we leave on the fifteenth?" she asked.

"Yes, I believe it's a Saturday. We should be able to drive down to Dover without too many delays. Have you bought everything you'll need?"

"Oh, I think so and quite frankly if I've forgotten something, I can buy it whilst we're away. It isn't as though we're going to be in the middle of the desert!"

"I haven't checked my medical supplies as yet," said Andrew, "but normally the ship's surgery is well stocked."

"I only wish you didn't have to wear a uniform when we're on board." commented Rosalind, "As soon passengers see this and find out you're the ships doctor, they start asking questions from having wax in their ears to boils on their bottoms. It is rather tiresome."

"It doesn't really bother me too much," he replied, "and let's face it we do receive the benefit of a jolly good cruise."

*****

Delia had made contact with the Head Office of HSL and obtained confirmation that meetings of Alcoholics Anonymous would be regularly held on the September cruise of the Neptune. She and Paul had previously been studying the various brochures and agreed the mid-September cruise sounded absolutely marvellous.

"We can always leave it until next year if you would prefer." said Delia.

"No, I really would like to go in September so please firm up the booking tomorrow." replied Paul, "Quite frankly I'm thrilled that the ship will be calling in at Naples. It's not that I particularly wish to see Naples but with a bit of luck we should be able to visit Pompeii. It's supposed to be fantastic and I have always wanted to go there. Do you know how the saying 'See Naples and Die' arose?"

"Can't say I do." said Delia.

"Well, in ancient times, the Island of Capri was the holiday retreat for some of the early Roman emperors. Tiberius moved his court there and built a villa overlooking the Gulf of Naples. From this spot, enemies of the emperor were flung to their death, so creating the saying."

When she returned home from her office the following day, she went over to where he was sitting and gave him a warm kiss.

"Right," said Delia, "the cruise is now booked and paid for, I've ordered some currency, made a hair appointment for the day before we leave and I went out lunch-time and bought myself a new bikini. How was that?"

"Well done," said Paul, "and I've got some news for you. I received a letter from IPL this morning together with a cheque. They've accepted the article I wrote "It's a beautiful world, but…..."

"Oh, Paul, that's marvellous. I'm so proud of you."

She dashed into the kitchen, returning with two glasses of tonic water both filled with ice and lemon. Having handed one glass to Paul, she raised her glass towards him saying, "To the Neptune and all who'll be sailing in her."

*****

The house in Berkhamsted had been inherited by James when he was considerably younger. It was a rambling property having five bedrooms, two bathrooms, three reception rooms and a large kitchen. A considerable sum of money would be required to modernise it and for all of the repairs and redecorations to be carried out. Their friends couldn't understand why it was the two of them wanted to rattle around in this barn of a place, but neither James nor Phyllis had any wish to move.

During the summer months they enjoyed the bonus of having a large garden. James loved pottering around with the flowers and shrubs, driving his tractor and feeding the birds who presented themselves daily round the bird bath. Whilst all this activity was taking place, Phyllis was totally content to sit in the sun with easel and paints.

It was on one of these warm summer evenings that James appeared with a chilled bottle of Chablis.

"How about a little tipple?" he asked.

"What a lovely idea." replied Phyllis, "You know James, I've been thinking about what you said the other day and you really are right, my darling. It's time I put a stop to all our running around. How about if I retire when I reach seventy? It's not far away and we've already got quite a number of bookings during the next year or so but I won't accept any more."

"Well that would be marvellous." he said, "By then I'll be in my early eighties and it would be nice to think that we could have some quality time together."

*****

Laura said goodbye to Madame Flatau's neighbour, returned to her car, drove round the next corner, stopped and burst into tears. She could not believe that having driven nine hundred miles, the woman who she craved to meet was herself somewhere in England. *'How could this be happening to her?'* she thought.

At this moment in time her feelings prevented logic coming to the rescue. She wondered whereabouts Madame Flatau was in England. *Was she on vacation? Was she visiting family or friends?* It could be anything – she just had no idea. She felt elated and devastated at the same time. At least she now knew where Madame Flatau lived, but against this would be unable to see her for several weeks.

Her excitement when entering the final stage of the journey had repelled the tiredness of her body but now……now, she yearned for a magic carpet to whisk her home to England. Laura snapped out of her melancholy and once again started the car making her way to the nearest auto-route that would take her to Calais.

She eventually arrived in Camden Town at just after nine in the evening totally exhausted and rather saddened to find Doreen was still away, leaving an empty flat to greet her with nobody there to whom she could tell the story of her expedition.

Just before ten she picked up the telephone and dialled her aunt.

"Hello, Aunt Debra, it's me, Laura. I'm back and feeling very low. May I come and stay with you and uncle for a day or two tomorrow?"

Duly refreshed by a good night's sleep, Laura left a message on Doreen's mobile saying she could be reached at her aunt's home. She took the M4 turning off towards Marlborough and before reaching the Devizes road had a strong urge to visit

Avebury. This would not be for the first time. It had always fascinated her with its Neolithic circle of vast standing stones some of which were supposed to date back to about 3,700 BCE.

Their exact origin unknown, they were frequently referred to as The Mysterious Stone Circles. How they came to be at Avebury was a matter of conjecture but it was thought they were part of a religious temple.

Being at the site made Laura think back on her past and how she had come to be living with her aunt and uncle following the death of her parents and again the name Madame Flatau flashed through her mind. Yet another mystery, she told herself. But this time it was one very personal to her.

They were anxiously awaiting her arrival, saddened on hearing how distressed she was feeling from her telephone call.

They sat silent, spellbound by the tale of her travels in France. Finally, her uncle said, "I think you've done very well and it won't be long before you can speak to this Madame Flatau."

"Speak to her about what?" said Laura, becoming quite distraught, "She's never tried to contact me. What am I supposed to say, *'I'm Laura, I have this ring. What can you tell me about it?'*

"I honestly feel as though I've had a long wasted journey and I wish I'd never gone in the first place. I don't know why I bothered."

"But that's not true, is it?" responded her aunt, "You must never forget why you went to France. It's obvious your mother wanted you to go for a good reason. I'm sure when the time comes and you meet this Madame Flatau, all will become clear. Don't despair. You're young and you should treat the whole affair as an exciting adventure in your life.

"I can see you're very tired and we understand you're anxious, but just relax. We're delighted you're here and can now have a well-earned rest."

"I'm sorry I was such a moan-a-lot yesterday." she told them, when appearing for breakfast, "I didn't mean to be. I suppose it was the fact that the anticipated high-point of my trip suddenly took an about-turn and for a while I just lost heart and began to collapse in a heap. Seeing you both and being able to get it all out of my system has helped no end – as always."

"I've been instructed by your aunt to take you for a long walk whilst she cooks lunch." said her uncle smiling, "Do you think you can put up with me for a couple of hours!"

He took her for a drive to the Savernake Forest with its wonderful avenues of oak and beech where shafts of sunlight seeped through the branches of the trees as they strolled along.

"You've just missed Doreen." said her aunt, when they returned, "She needs to speak to you urgently and will call back in about half-hour."

"I wonder what that's all about." said Laura.

"You'll soon find out, but in the meantime my fish pie is ready and I don't want it spoilt."

"Nobody makes a fish pie like you do." replied Laura.

"Good, now you can both sit down and we can eat."

Two portions had been thoroughly enjoyed by Laura when the telephone rang.

"You take it," said her aunt, "it's probably Doreen."

"How did it go?" Doreen asked.

"Have you got a few hours to spare? I'll tell you the entire saga when we're both back at the flat. I found where Madame Flatau lives but there was one major problem."

"What was that?"

"She'd left to go on holiday and guess where…..to England"

"You're kidding." said Doreen.

"I wish," replied Laura, "but never mind me, my aunt said you needed to get hold of me urgently. What's the problem?"

"Just after you left I had a call from my agent asking me to take a late booking on a cruise. Apparently, the cruise line entertainments executive had suddenly realised that though the original singer had cancelled, I believe her son needed an operation, he had forgotten to get a replacement.

"I agreed to help out but I can't find a suitable accompanist who will also be required to give some solos. That's the problem and so I need a big help from someone I know well. So guess who I thought of?"

"Now who's kidding? I haven't got any pieces prepared and we would need to practice together."

"Don't worry. You won't be performing at the Festival Hall. You'll be fine and we'll have plenty of time to practice on the ship."

"And when, may I ask, is all this scheduled to take place?" asked Laura.

"In four days time, on a ship called the Neptune. It will be leaving from Dover on a Mediterranean cruise. It sounds great and the fees they're paying are pretty good. Will you do it?"

"Oh, why not, I really can do with a holiday and it will take my mind off Madame Flatau for a while."

*****

EIGHT

As The Neptune moved slowly and majestically through the sea towards its destination, the Port of Dover, the hour of midnight struck welcoming the dawning of Saturday 15th September.

Later that day seven hundred names in the liner's reservation records would be registered by security personnel, recorded by the purser's office and entered on dining plans.

These names would be those scheduled to sail on the ship's next voyage, on its cruise titled 'Mediterranean Delights' a journey that would commence when the vessel departed port at six o'clock in the evening on this same day.

Going on a cruise or any other holiday is just like Easter and Christmas when generally everyone has been aware for some time that the event will be taking place but often it is not until the last moment that the mind functions registering the mental process of 'I must buy'—'I must find'---'I must do.'

And so it was with many of the next Neptune passengers.

*****

"It's wonderful you are beginning to feel so much better." commented Vince, "I know car journeys still sometimes upset you so I've had an idea that can make our trip to Dover less stressful. I thought we should treat the drive as part of the holiday as opposed to thinking of it as a tiresome chore…a touch of positive thinking.

"How far is it?" asked Anne.

"Just over two hundred miles, but I suggest we stop after about eighty miles by which time we will have reached Chichester. We can then have a super breakfast at a small café I know near the Cathedral and afterwards visit the Cathedral and see Chagall's stained glass window and have a stroll round the centre of the city.

"Once we're back in the car we can go on for another fifty miles or so to Eastbourne, stop and have coffee at the famous Pavilion Tea Rooms near the sea front and take a breath of sea air until finally we take the last seventy miles to Dover. What do you think?"

"You're an absolute darling. It sounds absolutely perfect. Thanks for being so considerate."

*****

Louise sat re-reading Jeff's instructions:–

'Take the 9.43 train from Rochester to Dover Priory. It's a direct journey and you'll arrive at about 10.45. Then take a cab to the docks. It's possible that two cruise ships may be leaving on the same day so tell the driver you're sailing on The Neptune and he'll take you to the right place.

'When you arrive the baggage staff will take your case to the ship and in due course this will be delivered to your cabin. It may take hours to reach you but <u>don't worry</u> --- it'll get there, eventually!

'When you get to the arrivals desk, tell them you're my mother. They'll be expecting you and someone will show you to the cabin. I'll be working most of the day. New arrivals day is usually a bit of a madhouse with our having to take photos of the guests as they are about to go up the gangway.

'Once you're settled in you can roam around the ship, have a spot of lunch and relax. I'll meet up with you ASAP.'

*****

Having been working in his office until just after eight, Roger's secretary suggested enough was enough and it was time for them both to go home. He had asked her to stay on so he could deal with last minute business matters.

"You're not exactly sailing up the Amazon in a canoe." she said, "I have the ships telephone and fax numbers apart from your mobile number and in the event of a catastrophe I'll send up a red flare."

He laughed, "Okay, okay, you win. I'll keep in touch from time to time. Thanks for staying late. Now off you go and I'll see you in a couple of weeks."

Arriving home he was pleased he had sorted out all the items of clothing he would be taking with him during the previous two evenings. Now they were spread out on the bed in the spare room and he only needed to put them in the suitcase and he would be ready to go. He made himself a sandwich, poured out a gin and tonic with an abundance of ice and a slice of lemon and sat in his favourite armchair. He began to think of Lisa and wished she were still alive and coming with him.

The telephone rang at seven-thirty on Saturday morning. It was Emma.

"Just wanted to make sure that you were up and about and hadn't backed out at the last moment." she said.

"How could I possibly. I've too many caring women bossing me around making sure I get away."

"Well there you are then. Have a great time. We'll be thinking of you and who knows who you'll meet."

"Thank you Emma and goodbye. Say hello to Charles for me. Thanks for ringing."

*****

"How are things?" asked Julie.

"So far so good but I must say I'm still a little concerned all will be okay on the ship." replied Karen. "Are you sure Craig's happy about driving all of us down to Dover?"

"No problem. He's borrowed his brother's estate car and there'll be plenty of room for the four of us and the luggage. Russell will be using our car whilst we're away.

"It'll be better if we go down together. It'll ensure David doesn't start any arguments with you. We took Anthony to my brother and sister-in-law a couple of hours ago. He's just fine. Craig said we should leave about ten in the morning. Will that be all right with you two?"

"Hold on a moment, I'll just have a word with David" She called out to him, "David, Julie's on the phone. Craig suggests we leave at ten tomorrow. Is that okay with you?"

"Great," he responded, "and don't forget to give Julie my love."

"I heard him," said Julie laughing, "see you then."

*****

"How do you think I'll look in this dress on one of the formal nights?" asked Joanne.

Dean glanced across the bedroom. "You'll look terrific, now stop getting so nervous. You've been flitting between one room and another for hours."

"Well it's easy for men to pack their clothes but I've also had to pack for the children. I don't want to leave anything behind they may need and I want to make sure *I'm going to look just right* - after all I've never been on a cruise before. It's not exactly like going to Margate or Yarmouth."

She went over to the mirror and started to examine her hair.

"Perhaps I should have had this cut a little shorter. What do you think?"

Dean went over to where she was standing and slipped his hands round her waist.

"You look wonderful." he said, as his hands started to move towards her breasts.

"Thank you, but you can cut that out straight away. I haven't got time. What are the kids doing?"

"Lucy's watching TV and Oliver's finishing his homework. I'm going to put all of their school work into a separate bag so that we can carry it on board and make sure it doesn't get lost."

"You're an angel." She turned and gave him a long kiss. "I do love you. We're going to have a wonderful holiday. Now let's get finished and who knows what might happen!"

*****

"I wish we were going away together, it would be so much nicer."

"I know," replied Nicola, "but Eros must continue to cast his arrows among would be lovers and we need to make some money to pay our way and be able to afford holidays. What time do you have to leave tomorrow?"

"There's a train leaving Victoria at just after eleven that'll get me into Dover about quarter to one."

"That's great. I'll take you to the station. It won't take any time at all and then I'll go on to the office."

"You sure that's okay?" responded Denise.

"Of course, all I have to do is leave an answer machine message tomorrow evening saying that we'll be closed until eleven on Saturday morning."

"Well that would really be lovely. Bless you."

*****

Not long now." said Paul.

"I know. Isn't it exciting? Are you still feeling relaxed about going?"

"Generally, I'm thrilled but occasionally I get the collywobbles. I must say it makes a big difference knowing I'll still be able to attend some AA meetings."

"You'll be fine." replied Delia, "You've done so well since leaving Charlwood and I'm sure the sun and sea air will do you a power of good."

"It's just that this will be the first time I shall be within constant touching distance of so much alcohol and with so many people who will be drinking during the cruise."

"That's true but you should remember, there will be plenty of passengers who just don't drink and we will simply fall into that category. Let everyone else do what they want to do and we'll do what we choose and, if I may say so, my being with you all day and everyday should help."

"Of course it will." he said, "I'll make it – with your support I can do anything."

"Good." said Delia, "I'm glad that's settled. Now I'm just going to finish off my packing."

When she went into their bedroom she sat on the bed for a few minutes thinking over their conversation. It was going to be tough for Paul and she must make sure they were together as much as possible.

The demon drink would be winking at him and tempting his taste buds daily and he would need to be strong. It had not occurred to her before but this would be a major milestone for him to come through.

*****

"What's wrong, Matt?" asked his wife, "You've been wandering about like a caged lion for days. What's bothering you?"

"Oh, I don't know – nothing really I suppose – and yet – I just don't know. It's nothing to do with you or Simon – it's me – but I can't explain what it is."

"Maybe it's your mid-life crisis!" said Pauline.

"Perhaps it is, after all I'll be forty soon, but I seem to spend most of my life trying to make people laugh – yet there are times when I feel as though I could sit down and cry."

"You'll feel better when you get on board the ship." responded Pauline.

"And that's the other thing – I really don't want to go."

*****

Robert had been in the kitchen polishing his black dance shoes for about five minutes when the telephone rang.

"Hi, it's me, Peter. I've booked a taxi to pick me up at seven thirty. We'll be with you a few minutes later and then go on to the station. The train leaves at eight-seven and is due to arrive in St. Pancras at about ten past ten. Our connection from Victoria leaves at shortly after eleven and we'll be in Dover about quarter to one."

"That sounds fine. By the way, the clasp of my red bow has snapped. I'll have to take my pale blue one instead."

"Okay. I'll make sure I do the same. They really do get quite testy if we don't dress exactly alike."

"I know." replied Robert, "Never mind who cares if that's the way they want it. See you in the morning. 'Bye now."

*****

"I can't find my watch." said Phyllis, "I must have lost it when I went shopping this morning. What's the time?"

"Quarter to six. Have you looked in the bathroom?"

There was a few moments silence followed by her calling out "Yes it's here. What are you doing?"

"I've loaded up the car with all of your painting equipment." replied James, "Now all we need do in the morning is to put the cases in and the bag with our pillows."

"Having the Ford Mondeo gives us so much more room than when we had the Renault." commented Phyllis

"It certainly does and it's great being able to take our own pillows. That should be our new motto 'Have pillows – will travel.' It makes a terrific difference having them with us."

"Wherever you go nowadays, they use those awful rubber pillows." she said, "They're so hard and I wake up in the morning looking as though a steam-roller has gone over my face."

"Well, if there's nothing else for the time being my lovely, I'm going to watch the six o'clock news and as soon as you're ready, I'll take you out for our normal pre-cruise dinner of fish and chips."

*****

"It's such a drag from here to Dover," commented Martin, "but being a Saturday I think we should go via the M4, M25 and then along the M2."

"You're probably right." said Shirley, "It's so much easier when we take a cruise from Southampton but we'll have plenty of time to get down to Dover. Why don't we have some lunch on the way?"

"That's a good idea and it'll break up the journey."

"Have you got all of your talk material ready to take with you?" asked Shirley.

"Yes, they're in the usual bag and I'll take my laptop for the power-point presentations since I can't always rely upon the entertainments staff having one available when I need it."

"What about your portable lectern. Are you taking that as well?"

"Yes, I feel much happier knowing I've got my own equipment. You know the number of times when in the past I've been given a rickety music-stand to use and I've only had to breathe too heavily and it's collapsed in a heap."

"A slight exaggeration," responded Shirley, "but I know what you mean."

*****

Colin kept on thinking that perhaps he had been too hasty in accepting the last minute booking on The Neptune. He had really thought that being away at this stage for two weeks wouldn't interfere in any way with his planned restaurant venture.

Instead of which, from the moment he'd agreed to replace Stephen, all sorts of problems had arisen. First, his solicitors had found that there was a restrictive clause in the lease affecting his trading on Sundays but subsequently the Freeholder had been amicable for that to be amended.

Then the bank wanted a five-year trading forecast supplied to them. He'd spent hours with his accountants putting this together and they'd only managed to get it to him on Thursday afternoon. He'd called and made three changes and they undertook to make these and forward the final statement to his bank manager.

And finally, his intended chef had telephoned him to say he had decided to go and work in a restaurant in France. He immediately rang an ex-girl friend, who ran an employment bureau in Kensington, and she promised to try and find him some suitable applicants whilst he was away.

Whilst packing his mind was like a yo-yo and he kept on silently hearing *'you should have stayed'* followed by *'you can do with the rest'* and a few minutes later a repetition of these mental pin pricks.

Finally, he called out aloud to himself, *'What are you doing? You're going and that's that.'*

And it was and he felt sure he'd have a good time.

*****

Andrew had gone out to fill up the car and have the tyres checked. On his return Ros said, "There's been a call from one of the officers on The Neptune. They want you to report on board by noon."

"What on earth for?" he asked.

"Don't ask me. That was the message and I responded if that was what they required I had no doubt you would be there."

"Hm, what a pain, we'll just have to leave a little earlier."

*****

They had just finished a practice session of over an hour when Doreen said, "You really have an excellent ability to accompany a singer. Not all pianists can do so and I'm amazed at how well we've been able to get everything together. I've no doubt that the cruise audiences will be very content with our performances."

"Well I'm glad you're pleased," replied Laura, "but what about my solo pieces? Do you think they'll be up to standard?"

"From what I've heard, they'll love you. You play beautifully but above all you really must have a good rest on the ship. It's obvious you're thoroughly exhausted from chasing around France. I don't know how you managed to do it – especially on your own."

"I'll tell you something that was very strange." said Laura, "It was as though my mother was with me throughout the journey and I never once felt alone. I must say it was a real body blow when I discovered Madame was in England but at least I know she exists and it seems I shall be meeting her soon. My problem is I keep on asking myself '*Who is she?*' and '*Why do I have to meet her?*' It sometimes really scares me."

Doreen could see how tense and distressed Laura had become. This entire saga had been going on for weeks and Laura had not found time for anything else.

"Just relax as much as you can." said Doreen in a gentle, sympathetic manner, "I'm sure we're really going to enjoy ourselves and you need not worry about meeting Madame Flastau ....."

"Flatau," interrupted Laura, "her name is Flatau – F.L.A.T.A.U."

"Sorry, Madame Flatau, - until we get back all bronzed and buzzing with fresh energy."

*****

NINE

They came by road, they came by rail, they came by car and they came by coach, whilst some, who lived further away in the United Kingdom or abroad, arrived at various airports to be met by HSL transportation, that would then take them to the ship.

By whatever means taken, between eleven in the morning and four in the afternoon hundreds of people of varying ages descended on the dock area at Dover to be greeted by the gleaming white vessel that would be their home for the next fourteen days and nights.

The cruise would be a vacation, an adventure, an introduction to fascinating parts of Europe and for some it would create waves of personal change in their lives.

*****

Louise had woken three times during the night, looked at her watch and seen that it was still far too early to get up. The excitement of shortly beginning the trip of her lifetime was proving too much compared with getting a good night's sleep. Finally at six forty she rose, took a warm bath, made her bed and once more re-checked the clothes she had decided to take with her, being concerned that she had not forgotten anything and then took her case downstairs into the hall.

As the sun came up she began to drift from one room to another ensuring that all of the windows were firmly shut. Each contained objects relating to the past, some, of her years with Mark and others of Jeff, from childhood to manhood. When in the living room she stood before their wedding photo gazed lovingly at it and said, "Well, Mark, what do you think? I can't believe I'm about to go on a cruise. We always said Jeff was a good son – and now this. I'll be thinking of you, my darling."

After having toast and coffee the clock in the kitchen only showed eight-twenty. She was pleased to have arranged for her neighbour's husband to call and take her to the station at nine.

"But your train doesn't leave until nearly quarter to ten." he had said, "You'll be standing around for nearly a half-hour."

"I know," replied Louise, "but I'd rather get there in plenty of time. I'll buy a magazine and have a cup of tea."

The train wasn't crowded and she found a window seat without difficulty, noticing that the window did not seem to have seen a cleaning cloth for weeks. The journey passed quickly and at the scheduled time the train drew alongside the Dover platform.

"May I help you with your case?" asked one of the passengers, who appeared to be just a few years older than Jeff.

"Well that's most kind of you." responded Louise.

"I see from the luggage label you're going on The Neptune." he said.

"Yes, that's right. My son works on the ship and he's managed to get me a cruise. I'm so looking forward to it. I've never been on a cruise before. Do you know the ship?"

"Certainly do, I also work on board. I'm an electrician. What's your son's name?"

"Jeff, Jeff Anderson. He's one of the photographers."

"Yes, I know him. We sometimes manage to go ashore together. How were you intending to get to the ship?"

"Jeff told me I should get a cab from outside the station."

"Don't worry about that. Come with me. One of my mates is meeting this train and he'll give you a lift at the same time. By the way, my name's Harry Dawson."

Having arrived alongside the ship, Harry made sure her case was taken by one of the baggage handlers.

"It will be delivered direct to your cabin." he said, "though it might take some time."

"Yes, that's what Jeff said." she replied.

Now that she was standing by the side the ship, Louise could not believe how big it was and recalled Jeff telling her The Neptune was fairly small compared with some cruise liners.

Harry escorted her into the main departure lounge and introduced her to one of the staff.

"This is Jeff Anderson's mother," he said, "you better look after her."

After her tickets and passport were checked, she was ushered through to security, where a photograph was taken that would automatically register whenever she got on or off the ship. Following the issue of a ship's identity card, a member of crew took her to the cabin on Deck 3, which bore the name 'Venus.'

It was not as small as Jeff had suggested and the port hole didn't have the expected restricted view. The bathroom was certainly tight for space and contained a curtained shower unit. The single bed was up against one wall and a small table with drawers, wardrobe, television and armchair made up the remainder of the furniture.

It's time to investigate, she thought. Apart from the main dining room there was the Ocean Bistro, a cafeteria buffet-styled eating area, the Bacchus Piano Bar and other small lounges where drinks could be purchased, a small casino, the Neptune Theatre, the Trident lounge, a gym, beauty salon, several shops, the tours office, a card/games room, library, internet room and an area where photographs were being displayed. She guessed this would be where Jeff would be working.

Louise also noticed that in about three of four parts of the ship there were pianos and other instruments obviously used for musical entertainment. Two decks above the dining-room she discovered a speciality Italian-style restaurant called 'Ambrosia.' Although she had read the ship's brochure many times, she had not been able to appreciate the full extent of all she was now seeing.

Throughout she admired the ship's furnishings, carpets, lighting and paintings, all of which created a restful atmosphere. Nothing was garish with everything having been selected with considerable taste and a good understanding of complementary colours.

She made her way back to the Ocean Bistro where lunch was now available. Though it was now quarter to one not too many people appeared to have boarded. Strolling through to the sundeck after lunch Louise noticed the small Jacuzzi baths at either side of the pool and when looking over the rail she saw the dockside was swarming with people and noticed Jeff taking photographs from the bottom of the gangway.

An hour sitting in the sun proved most relaxing but not having any suntan cream with her she decided to return to the cabin. Outside the main dining room some passengers had gathered to see the Maitre D' in order to try and change either their seating times or tables.

She was relieved to find that her suitcase had arrived safely and immediately unpacked. She noticed for the first time a leaflet, printed on both sides, entitled 'The Neptune Times'. This was a programme of events for the remainder of the day and indicated a compulsory Life Boat Drill would be taking place at about half past four. Details of dining times were also shown together with a note to the effect that this evening would be 'casual wear'.

A block announcement advertised that at both eight-fifteen and ten-fifteen there would be a show in the theatre titled 'Meet the Crew', to be presented by the Cruise Director, at which the Neptune's Orchestra and Dance Company would be performing.

She decided to stay in the cabin until it was time for the Boat Drill and switched on the television. Some internal information programmes relating to the vessel and to the help available to passengers were showing which she found interesting.

Suddenly, the quietness in the cabin was disturbed by a loud broadcast from the Cruise Director, that would be heard all over the ship, directing all passengers to return to their cabins, collect their life vests and go to their muster stations as shown on the cabin doors.

The statement made it clear that all cabins would be checked by room stewards and every passenger's name would be verified by members of the crew at the muster stations.

The drill did not last too long and Louise was impressed by the efficient manner it was carried out. All passengers were instructed on how to wear the vests with those having a problem immediately receiving personal help.

Once it had finished most passengers went to their cabins to replace the vests. As Louise reached the doors of the lounge she suddenly noticed Jeff standing waiting for her.

"Hi, Mum," he said going towards her and giving her a hug and a kiss, "Well what do you think of The Neptune? Have you had a good time so far?"

"It's lovely," she replied, "and everyone has been so pleasant and helpful. I've a very nice cabin and I was so lucky when I arrived in Dover. I met a friend of yours called Harry Dawson."

"Yes, he saw me during the day and told me what had happened. Sorry, I couldn't get to see you before but as I told you arrivals day is a bit of a madhouse. Let's go and get some tea."

"Gosh, what a spread." she commented, as they entered the Ocean Bistro. "I can't believe all the food they make available. I'll have to watch my weight."

"Don't worry about it." laughed Jeff, "You'll soon adjust without going berserk - as some of the passengers do. How did you get on with the Life Boat Drill?"

"It was amazing," replied Louise, "let's hope that we don't have to do it for real."

"Very unlikely," said Jeff, "nobody's going to hear the words 'Abandon Ship' on this trip, so don't you start worrying about that."

"Even so it must have been terrible on The Titanic." said Louise. "I saw a TV programme recently and they said there were 2,200 passengers and lifeboat space available for only 1,200."

"Absolutely right, Mum." Jeff replied smiling, "Now have another piece of fruit cake."

Louise enjoyed having a leisurely tea break with him until he looked at his watch and said, "Gosh, I must go. I'm due back in five minutes. I'll try and see you later on. Don't forget to see the ship leaving port. It's quite a sight and by the way the Pursers office will be open and you should go along and register your credit card to cover extras and tours. 'Bye now."

It was quarter to six when Louise arrived on pool deck to gain a good position before departure. Even though a vast number of passengers were milling around she managed to find a vantage point that would enable her to see everything that would be taking place.

She leaned on the handrail and could see the entrance to the harbour and the open sea beyond. She recalled part of a poem she had recently read –

'Let us escape the lives that we lead
And journey afar by voyage on the sea.
Let us pretend for two or three weeks
And live in a dream-world of fantasy.'

The gangway had been raised and the captain's voice boomed out over the Tannoy-system confirming all necessary authority regulations had been cleared and the ship would be sailing at six. Louise started to feel the gentle throbbing of the engines and the funnels announced departure was imminent with three blasts of the vessel's horns.

Guy ropes were discarded, tugs were at the ready, the pilot boat could be seen meandering within the general area and this Sinbadian liner began to gently move, no longer to the music of a traditional band of the past but simply being waved away by those standing and watching on dock side.

The passengers were expressing great excitement. This was the moment that they had been waiting for. This was their temporary farewell to England and the start of their holiday. The Neptune slowly approached the wide mouth of the harbour and entered the English Channel, awakening the sleeping sea. She noticed how the previously still water in the swimming pool was now gently moving and lapping the sides.

And suddenly, to everyone's surprise, a group of musicians started to play ably assisted by a very attractive vocalist. Louise ordered a rum-punch, sat listening to this entertainment and suddenly felt tears of joy running down her cheeks.

"Are you okay?" asked a man standing nearby.

"Absolutely," she replied, "from time to time it's a typical woman's reaction when she is experiencing happiness - but thanks for asking. Have you been on this ship before?"

"I certainly have. The name's Matt Campbell. They tell me I'm the magician who also makes people laugh."

"Oh, what fun." said Louise, "I shall look forward to seeing your act. Why don't you take a seat?"

"I'd love to, but I have to dash as all we entertainers, lecturers and so on are attending a cocktail party at six-thirty. The cruise director on this ship always arranges these get-togethers and it really is a good idea. Unfortunately they don't do it on all ships."

"By the way, is this yours?" He had leaned over towards her face and produced from just behind her ear a one-pound coin. "You must make sure you look after you money, you know. See you soon. Have fun. 'Bye."

Having finished her drink, Louise made her way to the Purser's office and nearby saw that the tour office was open. She obtained a copy of the ports of call which had details of the various tours available at each port.

Jeff had told her that all regular paying passengers would have received this information direct from the company before embarkation enabling them to make bookings for tours in advance if they wanted to do so.

"But you needn't worry about it." he had said, "You can get all details when you're on board and there will be plenty of opportunity to reserve tickets for any tour then. When you go to the Tour desk tell whoever's on duty that I'm your son. The tour office manager is Shelley and her assistant is called Lorraine."

Having been allocated a seat in the dining-room for the second sitting at eight-thirty Louise sat in one of the lounges and started to read through the information pack.

There were to be eight ports of call and they were all itemised in date order:-

<u>September</u>

Monday 17th	Vigo, Spain
Tuesday 18th	Lisbon, Portugal
Thursday 20th	Barcelona, Spain
Friday 21st	Nice, France
Saturday 22nd	Alghero, Sardinia
Sunday 23rd	Naples, Italy
Monday 24th	Civitavecchia, Italy
Wednesday 26th	Gibraltar

Against the name of each country was a small picture of the flag of that country and listed below each were the different tours available, being about four or five at each port. Louise had previously discovered that Nice and Civitavecchia were the docks that cruise ships used when disembarking passengers for tours to Monte Carlo and Rome respectively.

A description of each tour was given together with the ticket prices. She was very impressed that a graphic design was shown indicating whether the walking required would be fairly easy, slightly difficult or very tiring. 'Forewarned is forearmed' she thought. Departure times and duration of each tour was also provided.

Having sat and read through the detailed synopsis of the tours her immediate reaction was she'd like to go on all of them but knew she would have to be selective and choose those of particular interest.

A note stated all bookings were sold on a first-come first-served basis and the deadlines operating for each destination would be listed at the Tours Office and in the daily Neptune Times.

On Monday they would be in Vigo and, though a number of the tours from that port sounded very interesting, Louise decided she would be perfectly content to simply disembark and stroll through a foreign city by herself for a few hours.

Again she looked at her watch and decided it was time to get ready for dinner. She noticed that the shops had only opened since the ship had left port. 'More regulations' she thought to herself.

Louise did not want to enter the dining room and be the first at the table to which she had been allocated so she thought she would get ready, then return to the shops, have an initial look around and subsequently go in for dinner.

*****

"It was great seeing the two of you at the cocktail party and knowing you were on this cruise with us." said Martin, "I remember when we were previously together. Wasn't it on The Poseidon? The Baltic cruise, if my memory is still working. As I looked across the room I said to Shirley, look over to your left, there's Phyllis and James. So how have you been?"

"Not too bad," responded James, "There's always something or the other but there's little point in complaining. It doesn't really help and what about you two? Have you been on many cruises recently?"

"We've been okay, thanks. We went on a Caribbean cruise in January and got away from the rotten weather over here. I really enjoy the islands. It's that awful eight-hour flight that puts me off especially nowadays when you have to be at the airport nearly three hours before departure and you're treated like a criminal from the moment you check-in."

"When you go on a long haul with Martin, eight hours is like eight days." interrupted Shirley. "He's so restless, keeps on looking at his watch and continuously reports how much longer it will take before we arrive. It's an absolute blessing with a cruise leaving from England when we need only drive to the port and come aboard."

"Why don't we go into the Bacchus bar and have a drink before dinner?" suggested Phyllis.

"Good idea." said Shirley, "Do you know where you will be sitting for dinner?"

"As a matter of fact the Maitre D' sent us a note just before the cocktail party. It's table 27."

"Wonderful," said Martin, "We're also on that table."

Shirley and Martin were genuinely pleased to have been able to re-establish a friendship so early in the cruise. It wasn't always so easy and they were relieved to know they would be at the same dining table.

Phyllis was quite a character who Martin always said reminded him of Mrs. Tiggy-winkle. She was a lady of short stocky build whose sense of dress in no way compared with her excellent ability to place paints on canvas. She wore many layered frilly skirts with a long jacket hanging down to form yet another layer with no part of this dress-wear blending in any particular colour scheme. Her shoes were more like pixie boots and occasionally a silk scarf was thrown over her shoulders.

Regardless of this, she was delightful and despite the gap in their ages it was obvious she and James adored each other.

Two rounds of drinks later, they made their way into the dining room and were ushered to table twenty-seven where they found three ladies and a man already seated.

"That's what I like," said James with a smile and a wink, "a bevy of beauties surrounding me."

"Take no notice of him," said Phyllis, "he's quite harmless. We're Phyllis and James Mills and this is Shirley and Martin West who we met on a previous cruise. I'm the art instructor for this trip and Martin is the destination speaker – without him we wouldn't know where we're going!"

As they had reached the table, Roger Gould had stood and now introduced himself adding, "I've just met these three charming ladies who, if I remember correctly are, Laura, a pianist and her friend, Doreen, an operatic singer and Denise who has not as yet had time to reveal the nature of her work."

*****

"What was the panic?" asked Ros, as Andrew entered the cabin.

"There's a couple on Deck 5 who are on board with their daughter. She's nearly seventeen and is in an adjoining cabin. As they were coming down to Dover the girl said she wasn't feeling too well and was constantly thirsty. Once they were here they suggested she went to bed for a couple of hours and if she felt better she could join them for dinner.

"It seems she started to feel a little easier so all three started to get ready until they suddenly heard a bang from her cabin. Fortunately the stewardess was just down the hall, opened the door and they found the girl had fainted and was running a high temperature.

"They got her back into bed and I've told her she must stay there until the morning when I'll examine her again. I've given her something that will get the temperature down.

"I don't think it's anything serious. I get the impression she's been studying hard and was waiting for some examination results. I reckon she's been over doing things and is now totally exhausted. I'm sure the fever will reduce during the night but I've given instructions to her parents so that they can keep an eye on her."

"Sounds like she's been burning the candle at both ends." responded Ros. "Well you better get ready quickly so we can get to the dining room - after all you are supposed to be hosting a table."

They managed to arrive just after eighty-thirty when guests were either being shown to their tables or were wandering around looking where they were supposed to be sitting.

Ros, together with Andrew, wearing his white officer's uniform, were shown to table 34. He was pleased to find only one other couple had arrived who introduced themselves as Anne and Vince Rogers. Almost immediately after another couple came along when further introductions indicated they were Delia and Paul Scott.

"Just two to go." said Andrew smiling, "and I think they may be descending upon us right now."

"Good evening," said the gentleman now standing before them, "perhaps I should address you all as Roman citizens bearing in mind the names given to all of the decks. I love the inventiveness."

There is no doubt that some people make an immediate impression the moment they enter a crowded room or an occasion such as now and this was such a man.

He was well-dressed in a smart sports jacket wearing a deep red carnation in his lapel probably in his mid-sixties. He was well built with a round jocular face, thin on top and even though he had spoken but two words the deep resonant tone of his voice was such one could imagine listening to him for hours.

"May I introduce my travelling companion, Liz Thompson, and my name is Henry Arkwright." he had continued, "I trust that we have not delayed you. It seems as though our entire trip to Dover could not have gone less smoothly culminating in a one-hour hold up on the M20 and a long crawl thereafter. Why is it that local authorities take such great delight in organising extensive road works during the summer months? I am sure it is calculated to provide as much inconvenience to as many as possible. It is similar to airline personnel going on strike at Easter or Christmas. No sense of public responsibility, in my view."

He was in no way pompous, possessed an enchanting smile and had a glint in his eye as he had spoken with all at the table simply listening in awe.

"Did you have far to come?" asked Andrew.

"Not really, we both live in the area of Tunbridge Wells," replied Liz, "Although by the time we arrived we felt as though we'd started in Edinburgh.

She seemed to be in her mid-to late-fifties, slightly on the heavy side with reasonably thick blonde hair that had been well cut, looking as though a hair would never fall out of place should she be in a gale force wind.

She was about five-foot six, had a good skin and her sparkling eyes told all.

"I've never been there." commented Ros.

"Its formal name is Royal Tunbridge Wells," said Liz, "but as I live on the outskirts I just say Tunbridge Wells – although some among us who live nearer the centre may well give it the full title"

She had smiled towards Henry as she made this comment.

"It's not a bad place but really had it's heyday among the fashionable people back in the eighteenth century. Like many major towns nowadays, it tends to be rather soulless with not many worthwhile stores to shop at."

When Andrew looked up he saw that the waiter who would be looking after them during the cruise had arrived. Having announced his name, which appeared to have an Eastern European background, he began to take their orders from a menu of considerable choice.

"Thank goodness for that." said Paul, "I'm starving"

It was the wine waiter who then appeared and Paul noticed Delia firmly placing her hand on his knee. The wine list was given to Andrew who suggested that during the trip they took it in turns to order a wine and have it charged to their individual rooms.

"I find that this usually works out to be a pretty fair basis." he said.

"We don't wish to be party poopers," interrupted Delia, "but neither of us drink

— except on special occasions, we prefer to stick to iced water."

'That's fine," said Andrew, "so perhaps we can do the honours between the three of us. Is that okay fellows?"

*****

It was almost twenty minutes to nine as Louise made her way towards the dining room. She began to feel nervous.

"May I help you, madam." said one of the senior personnel.

"Thank you," she replied, "I'm supposed to be at table 45."

"Follow me, please." he said.

When they arrived she found seven other passengers were already seated. Colin immediately rose from his seat that was next to the remaining empty chair.

"Hello," he said, "I'm Colin, come and join me. I was beginning to feel quite lonely."

Louise smiled and introduced herself.

"We four are all friends from Aylesbury," said Craig, "I'll give you all our names and no doubt you'll forget them within minutes. That's what usually happens at a party, isn't it?

"And here, we have Lucy and Joel who have been bold enough to tell us that they are on their honeymoon and rightly have a cabin on Cupid deck."

"Congratulations," said Louise, "I hope you'll both be very happy."

"And I hope we all have a super holiday," said David, "From what I've seen so far it should be more than entertaining."

Karen cringed knowing he had looked over the casino and had already been eyeing up and down some of the women.

*****

During the course of dinner, Paul excused himself and made his way to the gentleman's cloakroom. He had begun to feel the pressure of seeing the others drinking their wine. He splashed his face with cold water, gathered his composure and returned to the dining room. He was seated between Delia and Liz and her fascinating chatter helped him. When dinner was over he left with Delia.

"How are you feeling?" she asked.

"Not too bad. I felt a little pressurised after the main course and that's why I went out to the loo. Some cold water on my face made me feel better but I'd really like to get a breath of fresh air, if that's all right with you?"

They went up to the next deck and strolled outside. It was a beautiful clear evening with very little wind. The light of the moon's rays and beams of the stars dappled the water's surface whilst some way off the gentle waves of the sea revealed reflective tints of white and yellow that could be seen coming from a distant cruise ship.

Delia took Paul's hand saying, "You really did well this evening. I'm so proud of you."

He turned her towards him and kissed her. "How about going to see the show?"

"You sure you're not too tired?"

"Not a bit. I'm looking forward to it."

The Neptune Theatre was delightful with seating on all sides and fronting a large floor stage with beautiful drawn golden coloured curtains temporarily screening where the orchestra would be. All of the front seating was tiered to give maximum view to the audience and throughout there were pale blue small rounded armchairs and three-seat settees.

Having found two excellent seats, Delia said, "I have an idea." as she waved to one of the bar waitresses.

"Two fruit punches, please." she ordered.

"What on earth are you doing?" said Paul, who was beginning to get agitated.

"Trust me. I had a chat earlier with one of the bar staff who told me the fruit punches were very refreshing and did not contain a drop of alcohol. I thought we'd try them now. Should you enjoy it then whilst we're on the cruise and with other people, except at dinner perhaps, you will also be able to order a drink without feeling any embarrassment whatsoever. I reckon it could give you a real psychological boost."

A few minutes later the drinks arrived. "Cheers." said Paul.

He took a few sips announcing, "You know, this is pretty good. You are really amazing. Bless you. It's a great idea."

As the lights in the auditorium dimmed, the orchestra commenced playing, the curtain was drawn back and from the rear of the stage there was an announcement.

"Ladies and Gentlemen, Neptune Show-time is proud to present 'Meet the Crew' and here to introduce tonight's show is your Cruise Director, Alan Spencer."

The orchestra struck up the Louis Armstrong hit number 'When you're Smiling (the whole world smiles at you)' and the Cruise Director appeared, smartly dressed waving at everyone.

His patter was very professional interspersed with a few jokes until he told everyone that this evening's show would not be long since most people would like a reasonably early night after their day of travel.

From that point on, with songs known to almost all the audience being played, he proceeded to introduce the crew starting with his assistant, Sandra Wells, the tour office personnel Shelley and Lorraine and some of the ship's officers including those who worked at the Purser's Desk and the Ship's Doctor.

He then introduced those who would be featured entertainers in the Neptune shows, the well-known comedian/magician, Matt Campbell and Nick Guthrie, singing personality of television. He added that other entertainers would be joining the ship at different ports.

He spoke glowingly of operatic singer, Doreen Longton and her international pianist friend and accompanist, Laura King, and brought on stage the two dance hosts, Robert Mason and Peter Forester.

Finally, there were the Neptune dancers and singers, each of whom appeared as their name was called out –Amy; Danny; Chloe; Luke; Charlotte; Ryan; Jess and Joshua.

"So now, Ladies and Gentlemen," he said, "as all but our dancers and singers leave the stage please give a big welcome to the Neptune orchestra, under the direction of Carlos Alexandre, sit back and enjoy the next thirty minutes of show-time."

A slick presentation of popular music followed with the Neptune chorus performing well. The show ended with the cruise director wishing everyone a great vacation and indicating that a full schedule of events would be in store for them the next day.

Delia and Paul exited to return to their cabin. Both were now feeling quite weary. When they entered the beds had been turned down with a chocolate mint placed on each of their pillows and all of the bathroom towels had been changed for fresh ones.

Delia noticed there was a double-sheeted copy of The Neptune Times lying on the bed dated Sunday 16th September. She glanced at the programme that appeared to commence at seven in the morning and continue past midnight.

"I'm too tired to go through all of this tonight," she said, "but I've noticed one item that will please you – take a look here."

She pointed to -- 4.30 p.m. Friends of Bill meeting....Saturn Club.

"That, my darling, will be your AA meeting".

*****

TEN

During the night, whilst passengers were slumbering, The Neptune became an island – a floating island with 'water, water, everywhere…..'

The sea that has provided a mystical attraction to human beings since creation, the sea that has conjured up images for writers, poets and composers for generations would now provide an array of images to the passengers on their first full day at sea, a day of gently cruising as they would stare out, almost hypnotised, looking at the rippling waves and flamboyant spray of light and dark hues of blue and green.

The sea, according to the beliefs of many, to be the daughter of the Gods, could be calming and therapeutic, though all would be well aware that the mood of the sea could turn and become unfriendly, troubled and even treacherous, as could anyone of those that would watch its every movement.

*****

It had been six-thirty when Vince had woken. He crept quietly across into the bathroom, took a shower and slipped on the shirt and trousers that he had taken with him. Despite trying to quietly open the door so as not to disturb Anne, she was obviously awake and he heard her whisper "Good morning, my darling."

"Did you sleep well?" he asked.

"Like the proverbial log. I think the ship must have lulled me off and I didn't wake until a few moments ago."

"Well that's good. I was so pleased yesterday's journey didn't seem to bother you."

"I'll tell you something odd, Vince." replied Anne, "I felt as though I was being protected on the entire trip here. Don't ask me to explain. It was really quite strange and I can't tell you how thrilled I am we're going to Santiago de Compostela. It's just as well you booked it in advance since I saw a notice at the tour office last night indicating all tickets had been sold. I know I've never been there before yet I keep on thinking that I have been. I really don't understand."

"Well whatever it was that helped you the main thing was you felt okay. I'm going out on to the balcony. Why don't you slip something on and join me."

The sea was very calm. Nothing other than the ocean could be seen for miles ahead and gradually sunrise produced rays of light all around. Initially the sky became tinted with pink and pale crimson until this widened above the horizon as though proclaiming the rising of the sun.

"This has to be one of the most beautiful sunrises I've ever seen." said Anne.

"I guess we'll see some other lovely sights whilst at sea." responded Vince.

"I'd like to go up on deck." said Anne excitedly. "Give me fifteen minutes to have a quick shower and dress and we can go and have a coffee. Don't forget to bring the events programme with you."

Some passengers were already on Pool Deck whilst crew members were making final preparations for the day ahead by ensuring all of the chairs, tables, umbrellas and towels were in place. The deck had been swabbed down earlier and was now drying out.

"It's an amazing programme," commented Anne, "we'd be busy all day if we went to everything."

"Okay, why don't you tell me what you would like to do and we can go from there?"

"Well, at eight we could go on a 'walk a mile' round the ship, at ten there's a Port talk by one of the tour office staff and then at eleven, a talk by the destination speaker entitled 'Cruising Iberia – an introduction to the culture of Spain and Portugal.'

"After lunch, there's a Watercolour Workshop at two and at the same time an Art lecture entitled 'Courbet & Realism' with a recital taking place at four-thirty.

"Apart from all of that we can attend two quizzes, a lecture on and play bridge, see a film, play Bingo or have dance lessons."

"I feel quite exhausted just listening to you." said Vince, "I think I'd prefer to go to the destination talk rather than the Port talk and I'd like to go to the recital. I think that bridge can wait for another day when I feel more rested but what would you like?"

"That's fine by me and I know you'd like to go to the watercolour workshop so why don't you go there at two whilst I just sit and relax." replied Anne.

"You sure?" he said.

"Absolutely, now please take me out for breakfast – I'm starving and I'd prefer to go to the dining-room and be served like a lady. I don't really enjoy all of these help yourself meals and that's what it is here in the Ocean Bistro."

*****

"Morning, Mum. Do you fancy some breakfast? I'll meet you outside the Ocean Bistro in twenty minutes. Will that be okay?"

"That's fine Jeff. I was just dressing. I'll see you soon."

Jeff had already secured a table for the two of them when she arrived.

"You go and get what you want, then when you come back I'll do likewise." he said.

Once they were settled he asked, "How was last night's dinner? Are you with some nice people?"

"It was lovely," Louise replied, "There are two couples that live in the same street in Aylesbury, a honeymoon couple who are delightful and a man called Colin Price. He's the art lecturer and comes from Norfolk."

"Did you see the show?"

"Yes and I also remembered to register my credit card – as my son had instructed." she replied, then, in a whisper, added, "Have you noticed how some people are quite smartly dressed this morning? I wonder why!"

"It's Sunday." he said, "Every Sunday morning at nine there's a non-denominational service held in the Trident lounge."

"That's marvellous. They really think of everything. I thought it might have something to do with the private party that's taking place at four-thirty."

"What party's that?" asked Jeff.

"Louise pulled the programme out of her bag and pointed to '4.30 Friends of Bill meeting...Saturn Club.'

"That's not a party, Mum. That'll be the regular AA meeting they have on board. Apparently all the cruise ships describe it like that so those who wish to go can recognise it will be taking place and not feel any embarrassment.

"So what are you going to do today?" he asked.

"Well I'm not quite sure, but at ten there's a Port talk and at eleven the destination lecturer is speaking about Spain and Portugal. They sound interesting so I'll probably go along to both."

"I meant to have told you if you pop into the library each morning you'll find a daily quiz sheet and a news letter giving all the latest UK news and sports details and before I forget, I've printed out a deck plan for you so you can see where everything is situated. Once you're on a particular deck there are signs pointing in which direction you should go. See you later."

He handed her a sheet of paper which she placed in her bag. Passengers were buzzing to and fro along the buffet areas eagerly inspecting the sumptuous array of breakfast foods. Compared with an ordinary English hotel breakfast, she was amazed at the vast selection of fruits, cereals, egg dishes, pancakes and waffles, ham, bacon, assorted sausages together with mushrooms, tomatoes, baked beans, fried potatoes, fried bread and a wonderful choice of rolls and breads.

Suddenly a voice said, "Would you care for another cup of coffee, Madam?"

"Yes please I think I will."

"And may I get you some Danish pastries, Madam?"

"I think it best if I was to simply have the coffee otherwise I shall be putting on excess weight before the cruise has got very far."

They both laughed and having filled her cup he left her. She opened her bag and took out the sheet which Jeff had given to her and started to read the list which contained the names of so many lovely Greek Gods.

NEPTUNE DECK PLAN

Deck No.	Name	Facilities
10	Apollo	Apollo Lounge and Saturn Club.
9	Hercules	Suites…Beauty Salon…Hairdressers … Gym…Saunas.
8	Jupiter	Suites… 'Ambrosia' Speciality Italian Restaurant… Card Room…Library & Internet room.
7	Pool	Pool/Jacuzzis…Ocean Bistro…Pool Bar…Trident Lounge.
6	Mercury	Dining room…Neptune Theatre and Cinema…Casino…Bacchus Bar.
5	Main	Purser's desk…tour and other offices…cruise sales…photo gallery…shops and cabins.
4	Cupid	Cabins
3	Venus	Cabins

Against 'photo gallery' on Deck 5 he had written 'that's where you'll find me slaving away!!!'

*****

As each hour passed, the joy of basking in the sunshine became like a drug with many finding their eyes closing whilst reading their books or magazines and the subtle world of sleep taking over. The pre-holiday tiredness was allowed to take over. No longer did it have to be resisted. This was the time for relaxation, harmony and peace.

A bird suddenly appeared sitting on one of the hand rails. The passengers were more concerned than the bird was, since no doubt it had been there before. But where had it come from? Land was not evident to the naked eye. The bird slowly walked up and down the rail, resting whenever required, ignoring all those huge humans pointing towards him and making funny sounds. Its sojourn lasted about twenty minutes and suddenly with the slightest of movement the bird flew round the deck, rose into the sky and gradually disappeared. But where was it going to? Nobody seemed to know.

"The soul and the sea are linked." said Henry.

He and Liz had been enjoying a pleasant morning sitting and talking to Andrew and Ros.

"What makes you say that?" asked Ros.

"Well, it's not exactly me saying it. It is more a question of what others have thought, for example, Walt Whitman's poetry often seems to have caught this mood and several composers have produced music leading in a similar direction."

"What music are you referring to?" asked Andrew.

"Well, Vaughan Williams' Sea Symphony and Elgar's Sea Pictures immediately come to mind."

"He may be right," commented Liz, "since I've noticed in a number of shops nowadays you can buy CDs designed to soothe, heal and refresh peoples spirits in time of stress and some of these have actual sounds of the sea."

She then jumped up and said "you'll have to excuse me for a few minutes but I must go to the top deck and book myself in at the hairdressers for Wednesday. I think that's the next day we spend at sea. One of my priorities, you know!"

*****

He was somewhere in his mid-fifties, still slim with receding hair, thin lips and a pale complexion. On the day of arrival he had told the Maitre D' that he would not require a seat in the dining-room preferring to eat in the Ocean Bistro.

His stewardess, of cabin 3098, had noticed that, unlike most other passengers, he had very little luggage with him though everything he had was neatly arranged and all his toilet requisites were lined up like rows of tin soldiers.

She had not seen him on the day the ship disembarked. It was now eleven and she was cleaning the cabin. Only one large and one small towel had been used, again rather unlike most passengers who appeared to take great joy in using every towel made available.

The noise of the Hoover had prevented her hearing the door being opened but when she turned round he was just standing there.

"Good morning," he said, "What is your name?"

"Carla, sir." she replied.

"What a pretty name. Carla, I'm travelling on my own. Perhaps you would be kind enough to look after me during the cruise. Will that be all right?

"Of course, sir, I shan't be more than five minutes. Would you like me to finish now or should I come back?"

"Thank you. You can finish now, Carla. I'll just sit here on the bed."

*****

Joanne had just given him a big hug and said, "I can't tell you how excited I am being on this boat – sorry, I mean ship – I remember it's boats that go on ships and as for the kids, they can't believe it either.

"Is there anything special you wanted to do today? What a programme they have."

"No, I'm fine and really enjoying just relaxing in the sun. We can all get off the ship tomorrow and wander round Vigo. There're certainly some great tours but they're a bit pricey." replied Dean.

"I know and we don't need to go on any of them other than the one to Monte Carlo and I can tell you right now that I'm going to pay for that. I brought some money with me and I've already seen them at the Tour Office."

"That's fantastic." he said, "I was expecting to take you and the kids but instead we'll all go to Rome. Would you like that?"

"Are you sure you can manage?" asked Joanne.

"I just told you, I was going to take you to Monte Carlo but if you're paying for that trip then there's no problem."

Dean suddenly noticed Phyllis and James walking along the deck and pointing to them he said, "Jo, she's over there, on the other side of the pool."

Joanne dashed round to where they were and Dean saw her talking to them. She returned a few minutes later.

"She was really nice and said she'd be delighted for Olly to go to her water colour class."

*****

Louise found both the Port lecture given by Shelley from the Tours Office and the talk by Martin on Spain and Portugal most enjoyable and decided she would take the City tour round Lisbon on Tuesday.

Much to her surprise, when she went to book a ticket and mentioned Jeff being her son, Lorraine, who was then on duty, told her she would be receiving a fifty per cent discount on any tour she booked.

She couldn't believe her luck and spotting Jeff over at the photo gallery immediately went over and told him what had happened.

*****

Roger had not felt in a particularly talkative mood and had gone up to deck nine after hearing Martin's lecture. Despite hundreds of people milling around the ship he had this feeling of loneliness and once again kept thinking of Lisa. He knew it was a passing phase but it was seeing so many couples who appeared so happy together that had brought on this melancholia.

He recalled the words 'girls and boys come out to play.' Is this how it always started, he thought. After an hour he decided to have some lunch and made his way down to Pool deck.

Passengers were busily selecting their food with some piling up their plates to such an extent that it gave the appearance they hadn't eaten for a month. Roger chose various items from the salad bar – despite the fact he wasn't a great salad lover – and then spotted a fruit jelly, a desert that had always been one of his favourites. Lisa had called it nursery food.

As all of the outside tables were already taken he went back into the inside area and again searched for a seat until he heard a voice say, "Would you like to join me?" It was Denise.

"Oh, hello, thank you, I would. It seems I have arrived at a very busy time and most of the seats have been taken. Have you done anything exciting this morning?"

"Not a thing, I simply crashed out on a sun-lounger and hardly moved for three hours. I'm saving myself for the water-colour workshop after lunch and I intend going to the recital at four-thirty. What about you? Have you had an energetic time?"

"Apart from attending the destination lecture I've just sat around by myself. I wasn't feeling too much like company but I'm pleased to be having lunch with you. I must say the lecture was very good and the lecturer was highly amusing. He told a funny story about Columbus.

"He said, *'When Christopher Columbus set sail, he didn't know where he was going. When he got there he didn't know where he was, and when he got back he didn't know where he'd been, and he did it all on borrowed money.'*"

"That is funny." commented Denise.

"I take it you decided to come on the cruise by yourself?" said Roger.

"That's right. I've left my partner to run the shop, as is it said and I guess you're also on you own?"

"Yes. My wife died of leukaemia six years ago." replied Roger, "She was only thirty-two."

"That's terrible. I'm so sorry. Well you'll have to sign up with my partner and I and we'll see whether we can find a lovely lady to introduce you to."

"Why? What do you do?" he asked.

"Nicole, she's my business partner and we also live together, we run a dating agency called 'Eros' in Paddington. We've been quite successful so far. We interview men and women who want to meet someone of the opposite sex, generally with a view to creating a long-term relationship. Then we computerise all of their details, try to match them up and then effect an introduction.

"I daresay that for some they're simply looking for a night out, a bonk and that's it, but our feed back is such they are in the minority. We also organise dinner parties when six of each sex meet up at a restaurant and have a meal together. Some of our clients prefer this to an initial one-to-one meeting since they say they find it's less pressure, but most still want to meet someone without lots of other people around. We also arrange theatre and concert outings, country weekends and visits to stately homes."

"Well, well, it's no wonder you need to collapse in a heap on this cruise and take a rest." responded Roger, "It sounds as though you must be kept extremely busy.

"You could say that but its great fun and we meet some smashing people," said Denise, "but I must fly otherwise I'll be late for the workshop. I'm sure we'll have a chance to chat further another time."

As Denise made her way up to the Apollo Lounge, Karen and Julie and Vince were also preparing to do the same whilst Joanne had already arrived so as to introduce Olly to Phyllis and make sure he would be all right.

"Now don't forget," she said to him, "I'll come back to get you about half past three so you stay here with this lady

"I do hope the Art lectures aren't always going to clash with these workshops," commented Julie to Karen, "I really would like to go to both of them."

"Me too." replied Karen, "Do you know what the fellows are doing this afternoon?"

"Craig told me they intended going to the gym and then play some table tennis. I gather there's some tournament going on. Let's hope it keeps them out of mischief."

*****

At midday, the captain had made his daily announcement of how far the ship had travelled since leaving Dover, its longitude, latitude, the sea and air temperatures and other data.

He had then added, "We shall be docking in Vigo tomorrow morning at seven-thirty and I anticipate that passengers will be able to disembark anytime after eight-thirty once the ship has been cleared by the authorities and I hope you will have a pleasant day in Vigo."

At nine and again now at two, the cruise director, with considerable good humour and friendliness, announced all that was taking place on the ship in the morning and afternoon respectively. He seemed to have endless energy by appearing at each of the lectures for a few minutes, at the morning quiz and going around the decks saying hello to everyone.

"He's at it from morn till night." one of the crew told Roger, "I don't know how he manages."

*****

Anne was delighted Vince had gone to the watercolour workshop. He had always enjoyed painting but work and helping her seemed to have given him little time to place his brushes into the paints.

She creamed herself and then laid out on the sun-bed. She felt a glow of happiness spread over her, shut her eyes and fell asleep. It was not long after that a world of dreams took over and Anne perceived a vast plateau surrounded by mountains. She could feel the heat rising from the sun-drenched dusty arid land.

She then saw a town with many people moving around. They seemed to be speaking in a foreign language that she did not understand and their form of dress was something from centuries ago. She saw the back of a woman wearing a white cap-like hat and a full-length dull mauve-coloured dress that came down to her ankles.

The woman started to walk away from Anne, out of the town and along a road that went on and on into the distance. From time to time the woman stopped at a well to take water and seemed to have some small items of food in the pocket of her dress which she took out to eat.

Evening came and the woman disappeared into a church she had come across. Then it was morning and the same images recurred. Another long walk, another well, another church and yet again the day was over. She did this for four days and on each her pace slowed until finally she reached a bigger town. Just before entering, the woman prostrated herself on the ground and as she rose, for the first time on her journey, turned round and raised her head, making her face clearly visible.

Anne woke up with a start. The face she had seen was her face.

"Are you okay?" asked Vince having returned from the water colour session, "You look as though you've seen a ghost."

"Maybe I have." said Anne, who then told him of the dream.

"I just can't understand it. What do you think?"

"I don't know," he said, "you know how dreams can be quite peculiar at times and then we forget all about them."

"It was when I saw my own face that…..it really scared me."

"Best try and forget it" said Vince, putting his arm around her. "Let's go and have some tea and then listen to the recital."

*****

During the morning, Doreen and Laura had been allocated one and a half hours to practice and now it was almost time for their performance to take place during the next forty-five minutes. They had attracted a good audience of probably eighty passengers and at the appointed time the cruise director appeared and following his introduction they entered, each wearing a long dress.

Doreen had prepared a programme consisting in the main of well-known operatic arias with two lesser played works. She had a beautiful voice that was undoubtedly appreciated as evidenced by the applause received after each item. The regular smile given by Doreen to Laura showed her appreciation of her excellent accompanist.

Half-way through Doreen took a six-minute break whilst Laura continued to entertain with an excellent rendition of Chopin's Polonaise No.6 in A flat major that showed considerable passion of musical poetry. The audience were mesmerised and Laura felt totally uplifted by their acknowledgement of her playing.

Regardless of whether passengers were preparing to take dinner at the first seating at six-thirty or the second seating two hours later there were always scheduled activities taking place that the cruise director trusted would be acceptable to one group of passengers or another. Many who had never cruised before were indeed both surprised and delighted this should be so, as not all wished to constantly attend the evening shows or visit the casino or sit in the Bacchus bar.

Cruising offered different things to different people and as Alan Spencer had always told his staff, '*All ages have to be catered for and a cruise ship only achieves success by not only presenting a wide spectrum of entertainment but by enabling peace and quiet to be sought and found by those seeking just that on their chosen vacation.*'.

Passengers could often be found reading or writing within the restful atmosphere of the library whilst others were able to sit comfortably, with or without a drink, in one of the many lounge areas listening to a pianist or perhaps a harpist or maybe a small chamber music trio at various scheduled times between mid-afternoon and late evening.

The time between five-thirty and seven-thirty had always been a period well loved by Phyllis and James.

Her workshop was then over. James and she would have put away all the painting equipment used and would be ready to relax over the 'happy-hour' cocktail of the day. They were both friendly garrulous individuals and never minded should either one of her pupils or any other guest sat and spoke with them.

Each evening at seven-thirty, they would return to their cabin and be ready an hour later to enter the dining room.

This evening all at their table were in place within a few minutes of the dining room doors opening, when James commented, "Well, apart from Denise and Roger, I guess we've all been singing for our supper today – literally in your case Doreen."

"I thought your recital was terrific," said Roger, addressing the girls, "and I shall very much look forward to the next one."

"Me, too." muttered others at the table.

"Have you known each other long?" continued Roger.

"Yes, for several years now, we both studied at the Royal Academy of Music."

"And do you give recitals together often?"

"Oh, no, very rarely, Doreen is the one who chases around singing. I simply stay at home and give piano lessons." responded Laura with a grin.

"I was booked on this cruise and suddenly found I was without an accompanist," said Doreen, "so Laura came to my rescue - I'm pleased to say."

"I really enjoyed *your* class, Phyllis," said Denise, "who was the little boy? He seemed to be having great fun."

"His mother asked me whether he could be with us. He's only nine but I must say he showed considerable potential. I never like turning kids down since you never can tell how good they may be and at that age a few lessons can make a real difference."

"I was watching him when you gave the demonstration," said Denise, "he was totally fascinated how easy you made it look. Mind you, so was I."

"Practice makes perfect, I suppose", she continued, "I always remember how on one occasion when I went skiing in Austria, the ski instructor gave all of his lessons whilst smoking a pipe. Every time I fell over I felt like throttling him."

"I found your talk on Spain and Portugal interesting, Martin," said Roger "and loved the Columbus joke."

"Thanks, I've always believed whenever anyone gives a talk it should not only be instructive but also amusing. The average person's concentration span is probably no more than about twenty minutes, so a few amusing titbits here and there, hopefully enables the speaker to keep his audience awake."

"Do you enjoy going on all of these cruises with Martin?" asked Doreen turning to Shirley.

"Generally speaking they are fine providing though we don't do too many in any one year. I find two is ideal, otherwise, and I don't mean to sound, blasé, I sometimes find myself getting bored, particularly with not always being able to eat when we want to and the regulations on dress wear."

"I agree," interjected James, "I don't want to eat at six-thirty and I don't want to eat at eight-thirty. I am much happier when we are on board a ship that has open seating. It works a treat and subject to waiting ten or fifteen minutes you can go to the dining room more or less at anytime you like.

"And as for dress wear, it's a pain in the 'you know where'. I'm quite sure formal evenings will be dropped before long except, perhaps, on the very expensive vessels where the passengers obviously want all that glitz and glamour."

Suddenly Phyllis got up appearing highly agitated and started looking under the table and beneath her chair.

"I've lost my watch," she said, "my watch has gone."

James remained totally calm and asked, "When did you last have it?"

"In the bedroom, I remember putting it on before we came down here."

"Have you looked in your bag?"

"Why should it be in my bag?" she said, as she picked it up from the floor opened it and produced the watch, at which James merely shrugged his shoulders and smiled.

"You were pretty cool, James" said Shirley.

"Well, I'll tell you a story. When we were first married and Phyllis announced she had lost something, I hunted high and low looking with her to try and find whatever it was that had been lost. After a while I realised, when she said 'she had lost an article' what she really meant was 'she'd mislaid it' and so I then started to take a rather more laid back attitude."

"I hate you." said Phyllis, lovingly pinching his cheek.

"What's on the agenda for this evening?" asked Denise.

"The theatre show is featuring the television singer Nick Guthrie," said James, "or you can trip the light fantastic with our dance hosts or, providing you are still going strong, there's always the Disco from ten-thirty until the wee hours in the Apollo Lounge."

"Thanks James for that excellent programme. I think I'll give them all a miss."

"Any of you taking tours tomorrow?" asked Phyllis.

"We were thinking of going to Santiago de Compostella," said Laura, "but the tickets had all gone so we've decided to take a leisurely look round Vigo instead. Is there anything you can recommend, Martin?" she asked.

"It's a pleasant town," he replied, "that's got associations with Sir Francis Drake. I'd certainly suggest you visit the Medieval Chapel and also the old quarter which is a very attractive area where you can buy oysters or go and eat them in one of the several nearby bars.

"That's really about it. I've no doubt you will find taking a city tour round Lisbon on Tuesday far more interesting."

It was just after ten when they had all finished their dinner.

"Well, I don't know about all of you good folk but if you will excuse me," said Roger, "I'm going to call it a night. It's been a lovely evening and thank you for your company. I trust you all sleep well and I look forward to seeing you tomorrow."

"He's such a charming man," commented Denise, "he was telling me earlier his wife died of leukaemia six years ago. She was only thirty-two."

"Oh how awful for him." responded Laura, "There's no doubt one has to live for the day."

"When you get to my age," said James, "you really do have to do just that."

"On that cheerful note, I think I shall also go to bed." said Phyllis. "Are you going to join me old man?"

The dining room gradually emptied and whilst many passengers continued to enjoy being entertained a number also made their way to the cabins.

"Vigo, here we come." called out a male voice and the ship continued carving its journey through the sea to that port.

*****

ELEVEN

By seven-thirty a host of people were already up and about. This was to be the first day of port calls, and though, for many, Vigo would not be the most exciting place to visit, nevertheless it would be an opportunity to once more place their feet on terra firma.

The vessel had arrived on time and many passengers had gone to Pool deck and higher in order to observe the intricate manoeuvres undertaken by the captain and his senior officers in berthing the vessel alongside the dock designated by the local officials.

"I have enough problems parking my car," said one early morning joker, "let alone park a thing like this. I don't know how he does it."

Dining room waiters and waitresses were scurrying in and out of the kitchen with the speed of sandpipers providing a constant flow of as many breakfasts as possible within a limited time, for passengers wishing to disembark early. The Ocean Bistro was also full, with dishes being taken on a help-yourself basis and devoured instantly, regardless of the possibility of indigestion being suffered later.

During breakfast, one guest made her way to the Purser's desk to report the loss of her bag the evening before. All details recorded she was advised a full enquiry would be conducted and department heads contacted.

"I'd changed over to an evening bag" she said, "and left my credit cards in the bedroom but I guess there were about eighty Euros, my lipstick/powder case, a hair-brush, handkerchief and my cabin key. Fortunately, my husband had his key so we were able to get back into the room. I told the bar staff in the lounges after I noticed it had gone but they were unable to find it."

"If your key was in the bag then I doubt if it's been found since someone would have been able to make contact with you before now," the member of staff told her, "but we'll see what we can do."

At eight-fifteen an announcement from the cruise director was heard advising everyone the ship had been cleared by Spanish officials and that foot passengers would be able to go ashore from eight-thirty. A warning was given that they must all be back on board by four-thirty as the ship would be leaving the Port of Vigo at five-fifteen.

Those going on tours were reminded to assemble with their tickets in the Trident lounge fifteen minutes before they were scheduled to depart. Here the tour office staff and other crew members were waiting to issue coloured stickers to be placed on clothing for identification whilst on a tour.

Apart from those gathering for the six and a half hour Santiago tour, there were also to be three shorter trips each of two and a half hours, one being the city tour, a second tour, to the historic fishing village of Bayona and the third to the enchanting town of Pontevedra with its historic buildings and attractive arcades and piazzas.

The atmosphere was full of anticipation and excitement. Complete strangers started to talk to each other, '*Have you been to Vigo before?*'...'*Is this your first cruise?*'...'*Where do you live?*'...'*Isn't this a lovely ship?*' and so on.

There were experienced seasoned passengers and those who were about to take their first steps on foreign soil. Many were sitting and, whilst waiting to be called, looked through the travel guides clutched in their hands. Some were carrying bottles of water, a number had cameras and a colourful array of hats and caps of all shapes and sizes could be seen.

By nine-thirty the grand exodus had reduced those remaining on board to but a few, including the man in cabin 3098 who had neither purchased any tour ticket nor had any intention of leaving the vessel.

But a ship does not sleep either by day or night. Whilst passengers enjoy all of the facilities offered to them the crew work non-stop to ensure their every comfort and safety and now was the time for the maintenance crew to carry out certain cleaning and polishing duties that they found difficult to undertake when everyone was on board.

Fresh supplies were taken on board, the lifeboats checked, the pool cleansed, regular painting of parts of the ship was carried out and detailed inspections made of all safety equipment. Coupled with this were all possible steps to safeguard against infections and viruses which had been experienced by cruise ships in the past.

At the foot of the gangway the ship's photographers had their cameras at the ready to snap all as they reached the bottom step. Vigo, Spain's principal transatlantic port and the biggest fishing port in the world was about to welcome its guests and the distant hills could be seen opposite to where the ship was berthed. Passengers were unable to see where the port ended for it continues for several kilometres along the coast.

Vince strode ahead of those making their way to the coach for Santiago so as to secure a front seat where Anne would not experience any problems. He was the first to arrive, handed his ticket to the guide, took the seats with uninterrupted views and waited for Anne to join him along with the other forty members of this party.

When everyone was seated, Maria, the guide, introduced herself, Luis, the driver and the crew member, Callum, who was acting as the ship's escort.

"We are pleased to see all of you here in Vigo," said the guide, "and hope you have a pleasant time on today's visit to Santiago de Compostella."

"I can't believe we're actually on our way." whispered Anne.

Vince took her hand and continued to hold it as the coach exited the port.

"Our route today," said Maria, "will take us through the outskirts of Vigo and then towards the town of Pontevedra, which I think one of the other groups is going to this morning. We will continue along the Rias Bajas and should arrive at Santiago in about one and a half hours. It is about 50 miles or so from here.

"During our drive I will tell you the history of St. James's Way since the eighth century and how the pilgrimage to Santiago has never ceased since the remains of St. James were discovered.

Before I start I would like to refer to two items that some of you have already been asking me about.

"First, the Compestella is a certificate given to pilgrims on completing the Way. None of you will be able to earn this today since you would need to walk a minimum of one hundred kilometres or cycle at least two hundred kilometres.

"The second question has been about the meaning of the scallop symbol that pilgrims wear on their clothing. The scallop shell is frequently found on the shores here in Gallacia and has remained the symbol of the Camino – that is the Way- over many centuries until it seems to have taken on both a mythical and, for some, a metaphorical meaning."

Maria spoke English well and proved to be an excellent guide with a detailed knowledge of Santiago. Her account of the history undoubtedly held the attention of her audience and she never failed to answer the many questions that arose.

"When we get to Santiago," said Maria, "we will be there until two o'clock. This will give you nearly three and a half hours to see the cathedral and other buildings in the city and to have something to eat. On arrival I will walk with you, from where the coach will be parked, to a café in the centre where you can have coffee and there are also toilets. We will stay there for just twenty minutes and then go to the cathedral. After our tour inside, you will be free to do whatever you wish but you must be back at the coach by two."

Traffic was occasionally heavy as Luis drove through a varied landscape with the sun glittering from the rocks and flowering shrubs adding colour to the vista. Anne thought it reminded her of the Scottish Highlands.

As they got nearer to Santiago, Anne leaned forward and told Maria she would like to get off the coach about half-mile from the centre and walk the remaining distance.

I'm not concerned about having coffee," she said, "and if you would just tell me where I can find you I'm sure I'll be with everyone before you leave the café."

Maria spoke to Luis who said he would be able to make a quick stop. Vince was more than surprised at Anne's request but decided not to say anything other than, "You sure you'll be okay?"

"I'll be absolutely fine." Anne replied.

In due course, the coach stopped, Anne alighted and the coach continued with Vince and the remaining members of the tour group, who shortly after, all arrived at the café. Vince stood nearby looking in the direction that Maria had told him Anne would be coming from and waited and waited.

Suddenly he noticed her nearing the Cathedral and seconds later saw her fall on her front. Just as he started to dash over to help her, she got up and waved to him. She had not fallen but, as in the dream sequence that she had related, had simply prostrated on the ground as many of the pilgrims did.

Together with Maria leading the group, they ascended the twenty steps to the entrance of the Cathedral initially coming to the enclosed area of the Portico de la Gloria. Maria directed their attention to a carved pillar showing the Tree of Jesse, from which Jesus sprang.

"It appears," said Maria, "that a long time ago a pilgrim noticed that amidst the carved greenery of the tree, where I am now pointing, there were five hollows in which a human thumb and four fingers could be inserted. Since then it has become a custom for first-time visitors to place their fingers into the spaces and say a prayer."

The tour of the Cathedral continued with Maria explaining the most important aspects, until finally, she again reminded everybody they must be back at the coach by no later than two.

"Are you ready to go now?" Vince asked Anne.

"Would you mind if I have one more look. It is so beautiful."

"That's fine. I'll wait for you at the back." responded Vince.

For him seeing Santiago and its buildings would be like visiting those of any other recommended city, though he also realised that for many, this would be the culmination of a longed for pilgrimage and that nobody, other than the pilgrim him or herself, would be able to explain the innermost feelings experienced of at long last being there in Santiago -in the Cathedral.

It was when he had looked at Anne that he clearly saw how being at Santiago, despite the fact she was not a Catholic, was having a tremendous affect on her. She looked serene as she revisited each area of the Cathedral soaking up every detail, standing before the sculptured carvings and occasionally placing a finger or hand on a column or archway whilst momentarily shutting her eyes.

She soon joined him saying, "I'm ready to go now. Thank you so much, Vince."

Time remained for a further walk round the plaza to see the outside of other buildings and to then take seats at an outdoor café for a cold light beer and sample a range of tapas.

They returned to the coach as instructed and found all other passengers had done likewise and the return journey began. Now, however, the atmosphere was different. Almost all were quiet after what was perhaps a chastened experience. The mountains they passed retained secrets of a human tale linked to religious faith and belief.

Conversation was in a whisper. Anne fell asleep and Vince sat gazing at the road ahead, the road that for some may have been the Way.

*****

It was mid-morning, after most of the passengers had disembarked, that the man in cabin 3098 went to his cabin safe and then left the cabin. He made his way to cabin 4136 on the deck above. The hallway was empty as he knocked on the door. Receiving no reply he placed the card-key into the door-key slot but nothing happened. The door remained shut. He realised that a new key had been issued and the one he held was now defunct.

*****

When returning to the Neptune a crew member was standing at the foot of the gangway, ensuring that all passengers had some hand-sanitizer squeezed into the palm of their hands to be wiped over the hands, similar to the procedure when people went into the dining room areas.

Anne and Vince decided to take afternoon tea in the dining room which was being served a la English tea room style. A selection of finger sandwiches, scones and jam, fruit cake and pastries were all available together with coffee and various blends of tea. A pianist played pleasant, unobtrusive background music creating a tranquil atmosphere, compared with having tea in the Ocean Bistro.

Whilst seated, Ros and Andrew came to their table.

"May we join you?" asked Ros.

"Please do," responded Anne, "though I must say I intend going to the cabin shortly to take a nap before dinner. We've had quite an exhausting day."

After she had left, Vince remained and told of their experiences in Santiago, without going into any details as to Anne's exact reactions.

"Anne certainly enjoyed the trip. She's always wanted to go there and found it absolutely fascinating. I suppose it's the same when someone makes a pilgrimage to Jerusalem or Rome."

"It probably means different things to different people, depending upon their individual life circumstances at any one time." replied Andrew, "Some of my patients have gone to Lourdes and I have no doubt these visits are very much a matter of trusting that the healing energy there may provide a cure or partial cure to a certain medical condition. I really do believe faith, in whatever form, is important in our lives."

"I'm sure you're right." said Vince, "There's usually a time when we all need something to hold on to. I just hope that today's trip will help Anne."

"What makes you say that?" asked Ros, "Does she have a medical problem?"

"Well yes and no." replied Vince, and continued to tell them about her claustrophobia.

"From what you've been telling us," said Andrew, "I wouldn't worry too much. It sounds as though she's already making big strides towards limiting the effects."

Having decided to change the subject Ros asked whether they would be seeing the evening show.

"What exactly is it?" asked Vince, "I haven't looked at the programme."

"It's a revue being presented by the Neptune Company's singers and dancers entitled 'A Life on the Ocean Wave." she replied.

"Well that sound's fun. I'm sure we'll go providing Anne feels up to it, otherwise there's always another night."

"That's for sure," said Andrew, "in any event we'll see you both for dinner."

*****

"If you don't hurry up we'll miss dinner," Joanne told Olly, "and then you won't get to see the show."

Having the children with them meant it was far easier to have dinner either at the first seating or in the Ocean Bistro.

"I'd rather eat then than at eight-thirty- regardless of the kids." she had told Dean. "Eating late means you have to go to the late show and we wouldn't have any time to go dancing or do anything else. I'm really looking forward to going round Lisbon tomorrow, it's supposed to be lovely and.....Olly, give Lucy back her doll or I'll throw you overboard."

Both of the children laughed.

"Come on kids," said Dean, "let's go."

*****

"Good evening, sir," said Carla, "did you have a good day?

"Yes, thank you." he replied.

"Did you go on a tour, sir?" she continued.

"No, I didn't. I prefer to stay on the ship."

"So you won't be taking any trips?" Carla said, sounding rather surprised.

"That's right. They cost a lot of money and everywhere is always so crowded."

"You're right, sir." commented Carla, not wishing to disagree with him.

"Will you be here at the same time every evening, Carla?" he asked.

"That's right, but if it's not convenient just put the 'do not disturb' notice on the door, and I'll come back later."

"Oh, I'm sure that won't be necessary. I always like to be on time for dinner and will be going to the restaurant at about six-thirty. I shall go now, Carla, and I will see you to-morrow. Goodbye."

*****

Conversation had ceased whilst they all studied the dinner menu before placing their order.

"Eating time at the zoo." commented Henry.

"Pardon." said Delia.

"Oh dear, have you never heard the expression?" he said, "When you go to the zoo all of the animals cease their antics as soon as the keeper comes with their food. In the same way, we all went deadly quiet as we considered the nature of tonight's calorie intake. Can you imagine the vast amount of food and drink that comes on board a cruise ship? How many eggs? How many chickens? How much beef, lamb and pork and fish and bread? It's mind blowing."

"Just ignore him." said Liz, "So what did we all do today?"

"Paul and I went into Vigo, had a look around, ate some oysters for lunch and came back to the ship," said Delia, "it was great fun."

It appeared that apart from Anne and Vince, the other four did much the same, without the oyster luncheon.

Between them they were able to tell Anne and Vince about some of the places seen with all agreeing the beauty of the Church of Santa Maria and of its being well worth a visit.

"That leaves you two," said Liz, "What did you get up to – if you don't mind telling us?"

The journey to Santiago and the Cathedral was recounted whilst everyone at the table sat listening with considerable interest. Several questions were asked and the information they had obtained from Maria was passed on.

"I've often wondered what it is that drives one to feel the need of visiting one of those places, other than as a tourist attraction." said Delia.

"The real problem today is that people don't recognise what happiness is and go around believing that it only comes from acquiring material thing or being provided with it by others." responded Henry looking very solemn. "It's all part of the material world syndrome we live in, which, in fact, can be quite destructive. We'd all be better off by being satisfied and accepting what we have and not continuously wanting more.

"Some people just don't know when they're well off even when they get older. You'd think we'd all learn by then but for some reason or the other we don't always and continue stumbling along making the same mistakes, particularly in our relationships with others.

"I recently read something very interesting. It said '*Each and every day we should think* 'today I may die' *since this thought will help us realise the futility of seeking material things whilst at the same time making our life more meaningful by caring about others.*'

"It's not supposed to be morbid. On the contrary, we all know that we're going to die one day. Anyway, since reading this gem, I've been concentrating on this thought each morning."

"And has it helped you in any way?" asked Anne.

"Undoubtedly," he replied laughing, "and Liz will be able to tell you what a splendid fellow I've become."

They had just finished their main courses when Henry said, "Well boys and girls, I hope you will excuse me but I think I better love and leave you for tonight."

As he rose from his chair, he exhibited a pained look and Liz was conscious of light perspiration showing just below his hairline and by the sides of his nose. He blew kisses to all and started to walk away.

"I'll walk you to the lift." said Liz, and then turning to the others added, "Be back in a tic."

It was several minutes later when she returned.

"Is everything all right? Is he okay?" asked Delia.

Liz sat down looking very sad and replied, "As good as it can be."

"What do you mean?" asked Andrew.

174

"He has a rare form of a liver disease. It started some time ago as a result of a visit to the Middle East when he picked up a virus. He has seen some of the top specialists but there's nothing they can do. He has been told that he has less than two years to live.

"He's such a wonderful man. Please don't give any indication that I've told you any of this."

They all sat mute. The words uttered by Liz had hit them as a hammer on an anvil.

"He was right you know" said Paul, "frequently we don't know when we're well off."

*****

The evening's show was obviously popular as witnessed by a virtual full audience now leaving the theatre after the first show and many from the second seating of dinner now lining up waiting to go in for the second showing. The cruise director had again been present and many were repeating a story he had told – *'one of our passengers telephoned the purser's desk on our first evening out of port. She wanted to know how she could get out of her cabin, and added, there are only two doors- one to the toilet and the other says 'do not disturb.'*

*****

Delia and Paul decided to go along to the Trident Lounge where dancing would be taking place until midnight. A five-piece orchestral group was playing accompanied by a young female vocalist wearing a most attractive off-the-shoulder evening dress. She had a delightful voice and her engaging personality helped to create a fun atmosphere not only for those dancing but also for passengers who had come to the lounge simply to sit and watch and listen.

They soon noticed the two dance hosts, Robert and Peter, busily engaged in asking unaccompanied ladies if they would like to dance. Both were dressed in identical outfits even to the colour of their ties. Delia was impressed how light they were on their feet as they whirled passengers through waltzes, quick-steps and rumbas.

She then heard Paul say, "Shall we, Mrs. Scott?" as he now stood in front of her holding out his hand.

"Why not, Mr. Scott." she replied.

As he held her in his arms and they started to dance to a well-known foxtrot, he whispered in her ear, "How long is it since we've done this?"

"I honestly can't remember," responded Delia, "but I'll tell you one thing, it is wonderful being able to do so again."

Cheek-to-cheek they continued for three dances until the music stopped.

As they returned to their table they noticed a lady sitting by herself on an adjoining chair. They all greeted each other and she added, "Am I in your way at all?

"Of course not, my name's Delia and this is my husband Paul."

"And I'm Sophie," replied the woman."

"You travelling alone?" asked Paul.

"Yes, I generally do, nowadays, a merry widow – well at least sometimes. I've been married twice and on both occasions my husband died."

"How awful for you." commented Delia.

"It certainly hasn't been a ball of fun but like everything else in life you have to soldier on. My first husband was an architect who worked for an international firm that had projects in Nigeria. He found himself having to go there from time to time until on one visit there was some political unrest in the city where he was based and road blocks had been set-up.

"I was told by his associate, who had been with him, that, their car was stopped at one of these road-blocks and a Nigerian soldier, pointing a gun through the window, asked for their papers. It seems as though the safety-catch wasn't on and suddenly the gun went off and my husband was killed instantaneously.

"There was an inquest and the verdict was death by accident."

"What a terrible thing to have happened," said Delia, "and what a dreadful shock for you."

"As I said, it wasn't a ball of fun. A few years later I met my second husband. He was about ten years older than me, a real handsome fellow, kept himself very fit, played tennis whenever he could and was a regular at our local gym. He had a company manufacturing ladies swimwear and many other sports accessories. He used to go to the Far East four times a year to buy materials.

"He was on his way back from Thailand when the plane landed at Heathrow. When it was his turn to leave the aircraft he started down the steps, had a massive heart attack, without any prior warning, fell down the stairs and was diagnosed dead."

"I don't know what to say," commented Delia, "how on earth does one cope with something like that?"

"You just do for you have no other choice," said Sophie, "unless you want to curl up and die but believe me there's never going to be a third marriage for me so I content myself with being the merry widow.

"Nowadays I take three cruises a year because I enjoy travelling and have very little hassle with luggage or anything else when going by ship. I'm rarely alone for more than a few minutes since it is so easy to talk to people and I have the added benefit of being able to see the shows and dance whenever I want with the hosts who are always on board to ensure we single ladies don't sit around like wall-flowers. Generally, the dance hosts are very pleasant even though they have to stick to rather strict rules."

"What sort of rules?" asked Paul.

"Well, normally it's one dance only and then change to another passenger but if there aren't too many of us around we can find ourselves getting a second dance, otherwise you wait until they come back to you. Then there must not be any fraternising and they are told to keep six inches away from the woman."

"And I've been assuming that they'd be able to have a ball with all the women." commented Paul.

"You're not too far wrong since, as it said, rules are meant to be broken. You'd be surprised at the way one or other of them disappears at the end of an evening other than to his cabin. In fact, I wouldn't be averse to a little twirl with that one passing us just now." Sophie said laughingly. "Mind you, they're not all the greatest of dancers - but who cares."

They continued talking for some time until Delia and Paul announced they would be calling it a night.

Just before getting into bed Paul said, "That's been quite an evening and it's really made me sit up and take note. It's only when you hear of other people's problems that you realise yours aren't quite so bad. I'm so sorry, Delia, that I've given you such a bad time with my drinking but I really do feel that I'm on the mend and I certainly don't intend taking that slippery road again."

"I know that," said Delia, "and just you remember I have no wish to find myself either a merry widow or divorcee. Sleep well, my darling, we've got an early start tomorrow."

*****

TWELVE

The noise of the ship's engines had woken Colin. He looked at the luminous hands of his travelling clock. It was five-thirty seven – not an hour he normally woke and certainly not a time he usually rose, He turned over hoping to gain some further sleep but his mind was already in overdrive thinking of his restaurant plans.

He remained in bed for a further forty-five minutes, then put on a pair of shorts, shirt and trainers and made his way to the deck indicating six circuits to achieve a mile-run. The gentle early morning warmth signalled the on-coming of a balmy summer's day and he began to look forward to visiting the one place in Portugal
he had not as yet seen.

It was not a large country, virtually half the size of Great Britain, but it was certainly a country of contrasts with its wonderful Manueline architecture and superb hand-painted glazed ceramic tiles that were introduced by the Moors and referred to as Azuleyos. He was always disappointed to find that many tourists failed to see much of the treasures that existed preferring the sun, sea, sand and golf of areas like the Algarve.

Three main tours had been on offer to the cruise passengers. The first was to be of four hours duration, a full-bloodied city tour incorporating all that was best in Lisbon. Then there was the tour of half that length for those who would have had enough after two hours and finally, there was a four hour coastal coach journey featuring the picturesque towns of Sintra, Cascais and Estoril.

Portugal had always been one of his favourite holiday venues and he had visited all of these places more than once and on one occasion, when lecturing on a cruise, had taken a private car to Fatima, that is set in bleak hill country about 85 miles north of Lisbon. Like Lourdes and Santiago de Compostella, it was here in 1917 that this virtually unknown poor village started to become a famous centre of pilgrimage in the Catholic world, following three shepherds claiming that they had seen visions of the Virgin Mary and other phenomenon subsequently taking place.

This time he had reserved a car which he would be collecting near the port about forty-five minutes after the longer-tour buses had left and he was pleased that this extra time would enable him to relax both before and during breakfast.

It was as he began to turn at the bow end of the ship, half-way round his third circuit, that he saw her. *'It can't be.'* he thought, as he brought his jogging to a standstill. He walked slowly towards where she was standing looking out to sea with the gentle breeze caressing her hair, but it was only when he was three paces away and she began to walk further away from him, that he knew for sure it had not been Caroline.

This was not the first time he had imagined she had been close to hand. It had happened when in a theatre and also whilst listening to a concert, though none of these fanciful thoughts had come to mind for some years and he was relieved that time had removed the pain he had felt at the time.

He took a deck-seat nearby and recalled the first time they had met, at a landscape exhibition being presented at Norwich's Castle Museum. It was a delicate Cotman watercolour which had gained their attention.

"It's quite beautiful." she had whispered, as though speaking directly to him.

They walked round the remaining exhibits together. He could not take his eyes off her. She had dark hair, highlighted with a few blonde streaks, possessed a good colour and her face seemed to continuously sparkle as she spoke to him in a soft voice. It had been just after twelve when they reached the exit.

"I don't suppose you'd care to join me for lunch?" he asked.

During their meal she told him she was separated from her husband, who was currently living in Fort Lauderdale where he had a number of friends. They had been married for eighteen years but circumstances, not spelled out, had caused the present rift.

The family home was about forty miles away in Aldeburgh and it appeared that her great love of classical musical had never been enjoyed by her husband, Barry. She played the violin and frequently appeared in local musical events as part of a quartet and regularly attended the Aldeburgh Festival.

Colin had been surprised to learn how none of their interests had ever been mutually compatible with Caroline leaning towards the arts and Barry preferring horse-racing and Formula One car racing, as a result of which he frequently went off with his chums to these events. She loved the sun and sand whilst he adored skiing and the list was endless.

She agreed to meet him the following week when he told her he would take her to The Sainsbury Centre for Visual Arts. The attraction between them grew rapidly until they began to see each other three times a week. An invitation for lunch at her home brought the relationship to a head. Her two children were at university in the North of England ensuring they were alone in the house when he slept over. Although she often went to his home she would never stay the night.

"I can't stay," she would say, "Barry might phone."

He fell crazily in love with her and started to push her into getting a divorce so they could be together but he always knew something was holding her back, which he could not understand and which she never tried to explain.

On one occasion she had told him, *"I'm very fond of Barry."*

He remembered commenting that 'fond of' was a term one used towards a cat or a dog, and asked *'where did love come into their equation?'* but there had been no response.

The affair had lasted five months until one morning she had telephoned him and simply said, *"I've told him I'll take him back but if he ever hits me again then that really will be the end. I shall be flying to Florida the day after tomorrow for a holiday and after we'll be returning to Aldeburgh."*

He recalled how shattered he'd been and how he had tried to persuade her to change her mind – but she wouldn't. Her only comment was to cast out the platitude 'all is fair in love and war.' His immediate reaction was to think he was probably going to be better off without her.

As if stimulated by his thoughts on the past he got up and continued his run round the deck. Others had been in and out of his life without there being a serious relationship though he felt sure one day fate would intervene. Meanwhile he ran and ran and ran losing count of the number of laps he had achieved but knowing that with each circuit the episodes with Caroline and others were in the past and he was going to thoroughly enjoy today.

He decided to take breakfast a little later and avoid the initial rush by passengers taking the early tours. Having showered and dressed he began to read one of the travel guides he had brought with him.

It seemed the royal court of Portugal had for centuries been a place of turbulent intrigue involving power struggles and wars as in other countries throughout Europe. It was the relationship between Alfonso IV and his son in the mid-fourteenth century which began to interest Colin when reading that the King approved the murder of the mistress of his son, who herself was from a noble background.

Their affair had produced four children and Alfonso's son was heartbroken. He immediately led a rebellion and in due course came to the throne as Peter I. He then had the hearts drawn out of the murderers and by so doing became known as Peter the Cruel. The entire story of his love for this woman was subsequently popularised in Portuguese literature.

On leaving his cabin he thought back to Caroline and was pleased that his transient heartbroken experience had not led to anything so bloody.

*****

"Sorry I couldn't have breakfast with you this morning," said Jeff, "we've been preparing for today's tour exit by passengers."

Louise had managed to stop and talk to him for a few moments as she reached the bottom of the gangway. She was very excited at the thought of taking the Lisbon city tour that was scheduled to last for over four hours. She made her way to the coach feeling slightly nervous that she might lose the escort who was at the head of the other passengers.

Having boarded she made her way towards the middle and found two empty seats. Just as she was about to take the window seat she heard a voice say, "Hello, Louise."

She looked behind her and found Lucy and Joel sitting there.

She smiled at them adding, "How nice to see you both. Are you enjoying your honeymoon?"

They chatted for a few minutes until the tour guide came along doing a head count to confirm everyone was present.

A degree of activity between herself and the tour manager, Shelley, followed since it appeared they were one passenger short. Shelley made contact on her walkie-talkie with Lorraine in the Trident Lounge and was told all passengers who had booked to take the tour had checked-in and had been given the appropriate sticker.

Within moments they saw a man of about six-foot wearing baggy fawn trousers and a grey shirt coming towards the coach. He was of big build and initially gave the impression he could well have been employed as a bruiser outside of a club. He was carrying a sizeable camera over his shoulder, held a tour book in one hand and a large bottle of water in the other.

"We'd begun to wonder what happened to you." said Shelley.

Without making any facial response, he merely looked at his wrist-watch and replied in a deep gruff voice, "The tour's supposed to go at eight-thirty. It's now exactly eight-thirty. I don't know why you think I'm late."

He handed his ticket to the guide and stepped on to the coach. As he passed down the aisle he looked at the empty seat next to Louise, looked at her and then passed on to the empty row of seats at the rear. Louise felt relieved. The doors closed, the coach moved on, the usual introductions took place and the city tour was on its way with the guide having the opportunity to give the passengers some basic information about both Portugal and Lisbon.

*****

It was just before nine thirty that Colin, having been processed by the rental office attendant, got behind the wheel of the small car he had hired for the day and made his way in an easterly direction, that would, in about one and a half hours time, bring him to Evora.

He found the landscape of a sun-baked dusty plain far from interesting and was disturbed to find the minimal air-conditioning of the vehicle was far from sufficient as the air temperature gradually increased. After forty minutes he arrived on the outskirts of Vendas Novas and stopped at a roadside café/bar to have a coffee and purchase a bottle of water.

He continued his journey, soon passing the town of Montemor-o-Novo, and despite his discomfort began to get more and more excited at the prospect of reaching Evora, the city of splendid Renaissance buildings with its maze of Moorish alleys and the Royal Church of St. Francis adjoining which was the Chapel of Bones, which for him was the main reason for his visit.

*****

Back on board ship Carla had been carrying out her daily stewardess duties in the cabins scheduled for her to look after. She noticed the 'Please make up cabin' sign was hanging from the doorknob of cabin 3098 and using her pass key entered with all her cleaning materials.

As she was making up the bed she heard a noise coming from the bathroom and the door opening. She turned and screamed out "My God, what do you think you're doing?"

He was standing there stark naked and started to take a step towards her.

"Don't be frightened Carla," he said, "I'm not going to harm you but remember you said you would look after me during the cruise."

"Yes, I did, but not in the way you think."

He took two steps nearer, went to seize her and tore her dress. Carla managed to push him away causing him to slip on to the floor. She managed to pass over him reach the cabin door and ran down the corridor. The incident had upset her considerably and she immediately made her way to the office of the head of housekeeping.

Carla was crying and in a highly nervous state when arriving at the Housekeeper's office where she related the events of the morning and all that had happened previously.

The Housekeeper told her they must now see the Hotel Director. This was not the first time an incident arising on a cruise had to be investigated and the director took a detailed statement from Carla.

Arrangements were made for a photograph to be taken of Carla showing her present state of dress and she was instructed to return to her cabin so that she could rest for a while.

He and the Housekeeper then went to Cabin 3098. The passenger was still there.

"I'm sorry to bother you, sir." said the Hotel Director, "but an official complaint has been made against you by your stewardess for improper behaviour. Do you have any comments to make that may assist my investigation?"

"Well, I suppose it was all rather a misunderstanding. I didn't realise that she would be seeing to the cabin and I was taking a shower when I heard a noise. When I opened the bathroom door she was standing there. I was so surprised that the towel I had round me fell off my body and she just screamed."

"Why would you have been taking a shower at that time of the morning when you had previously placed the card on the door asking that the cabin be made up? And how do you account for the fact that her dress was torn?" continued the Hotel Director.

The more the passenger endeavoured to concoct a story of his version of events the more obvious it became that he was telling a series of lies.

"Are all of the articles in this cabin your property, sir?" asked the Director.

"They certainly are. What are you implying?"

"I'm not implying anything sir, I merely wish to ascertain the overall position for the purpose of making a full report. And what about the cabin safe, do all of the items there belong to you?"

"Yes they do." replied the passenger.

"Then you won't have any objection to opening it for me, will you, sir?"

"Well, the fact is that I haven't been able to find the key."

"Don't worry, there will be a spare one at the purser's desk and I hold a master pass key which you can use."

He passed his master key to the passenger and waited for him to operate the personalised code number and open the safe.

"Would you mind emptying the contents on the bed please sir."

"Slowly various items were taken out."

"I believe you've left an article in there. Please remove that as well sir."

The last item was a ladies hand-bag.

"This does not look as though it belongs to you, sir. Have you an explanation."

"Well, no. I've never seen it before. It must have belonged to a lady who was in this cabin on the last cruise."

"I know whose bag it is," said the Housekeeper becoming quite elated, "It matches the description of the bag reported lost by the lady on Cupid deck."

After the Hotel Director had completed his report he said, "I must ask you to remain in your cabin until I return, sir. I shall now see the Captain to obtain his orders on what action he may wish to take against you.

"I would suggest you pack all of your belongings since it is likely that the Captain may insist on your being put off the ship. If that be the case, you will have to settle any outstanding charges on your account and we will have to make arrangements with you to ensure you have sufficient funds to be able to return from Lisbon to England."

After his meeting with the Captain, the director returned to cabin 3098 when the passenger was told he would have to leave the ship. He was given a copy of the report that had been made against him which included two charges, one of assault on a member of crew and the other theft of a passenger's handbag."

"You can't do this." said the passenger.

"We certainly can, sir. I have prepared a copy of the appropriate authority which you may keep."

The passenger started to read the piece of paper that was handed to him: *If it appears that a passenger has become for any reason unfit to travel or likely to endanger or prejudice the health or safety or*

comfort of him/ herself or anyone else then a duly authorised representative
of the Horizon Shipping Line may arrange for that passenger to be
transferred to another cabin or deal with the passenger as may be considered
necessary including having the passenger removed from the ship and such
passenger shall not be entitled to any refund or compensation."

"I can tell you," continued the director, "that at this stage neither Carla nor the lady in Cabin 4136 intends taking police action. In the event you decide you have been unfairly treated in this matter then you will be at liberty to take legal advice and act accordingly."

He was then accompanied to the Purser's desk to settle his account and on receiving his confirmation that he had sufficient funds to be able to return home he was escorted to the gangway where, after handing in his identification card, he went on his way.

*****

Louise was enjoying every second of the Lisbon tour and felt very relaxed having Lucy and Joel behind her. Whenever a stop was made to see one or other of the highlights all three remained together. They were now half-way and a very special coffee/toilet break was taking place at the most famous cake shop in Portugal known as the Belem Cake Shop, situated near the Tower of Belem.

The passengers were ushered into a room at the rear where, with the drink of their choice, they were served the warm custard tarts with a light crunchy casing made from a recipe that had remained a secret since the mid 1800's.

"These are absolutely wonderful," commented Lucy, "gosh, we're so lucky to be on this cruise."

"Why do you say that?" asked Louise.

"Lucy won it as a prize." said Joel.

"Really, what happened?" asked Louise.

"Well, I still can't believe it. I love listening to Classic FM and on one occasion I called them in connection with a question that they were putting to the listening public but then found I was one of hundreds who had left a message and needless to say I didn't hear anything more.

Then on a Saturday morning about eight weeks before we were going to get married I suddenly received a telephone call and a male voice said he was a Classic FM announcer and that I was live on air. He then said if I answered three questions correctly I would win a holiday cruise for myself and a friend.

"The first two questions were not too bad but I really thought I'd blown it with the third when suddenly I had a touch of inspiration and gave the right answer. The man called me back at the end of the show and asked when it would be suitable for us to leave, giving me a choice of three dates – one of which was on the Neptune for this two weeks – just a few days after our wedding.

"We have a very nice cabin, received travel tickets to and from Dover and were given a booklet of vouchers covering tours on each of the days we're in port."

"That's fantastic," said Louise, "and how wonderful to have a freebie honeymoon. I hope you have a really great time and wish you all the best for the future."

The last person to get back on the coach was the man sitting alone on the rear seat, arriving at the last possible moment as instructed by the tour guide. He had not said one word to any of the other passengers and had not accompanied them to the Belem Cake Shop.

*****

As the cathedral bells struck eleven Colin drove into Evora glancing at a number of its beautifully preserved monuments and buildings, some dating back to the second century, that are protected as a World Heritage site.

Having parked the car, he made his way to the Royal Church and entered the macabre sixteenth century Capela dos Ossos – Chapel of Bones. He felt a slight shiver as he saw how the chancel walls and central pillars were lined with human skulls and other parts of skeletons, all of which were held together by cement.

The chapel was a large room that had been totally constructed with the bones of five thousand monks with skulls forming the window frames and femurs covering the columns.

Once again he felt a cold tremble as he suddenly noticed two complete skeletons hanging from a wall near the ceiling. He had previously read there was a legend existing which indicated they were an adulterous man and his infant son who had been cursed by his wife.

Colin found it difficult to accept how monks could have created this ghoulish chamber because of their wish to be able to contemplate the transient nature of life. At that time there were about forty monastic cemeteries in Evora and they had decided to remove all of the remains into just one consecrated site.

He found the Chapel gruesome yet in a strange way elegant, bizarre but impressive, disturbing though a sight a tourist should see. He could not stay long and on his way out he turned to read the painted message over the door which read, *'Nos ossos que aqui estamos, pelos vossos esperamos.'*

He already knew that this when freely translated said, 'Our bones that are here await yours.'

And on that note Colin continued his tour of Evora and after taking a little lunch commenced his return drive to the ship.

*****

Matt had spent most of the morning getting all of his equipment in place for the two shows scheduled for that evening. It was easier than at other times since he was to be part of a double-bill with Laura who would only be requiring a piano. She was to be on the first half of the evening's entertainment.

Despite the frequency with which he had performed some of his tricks it was imperative that every component part was absolutely in position. The remainder of his act gave the impression of being unrehearsed but in fact he knew exactly what he would be doing at every stage, even when he involved members of the audience.

Finally he would rehearse two songs with the resident band and with a little tap and soft-shoe shuffle end his programme on what he hoped would be a high note.

When he was fully prepared he went off the ship to call Pauline from a nearby phone-box where international calls were reasonably priced.

"Are you all set for tonight?" she asked.

"Just about," he responded, "though I still haven't been able to rehearse with the band. There's always something else that has to come first. It really gets on my tits at times."

"You'll be great as usual." said Pauline. "Do you feel any brighter?"

"Not really and I miss you terribly."

"I miss you too. Call me tomorrow. I've forgotten which port you'll be in?"

"Tomorrow we're at sea but on Thursday we'll be in Barcelona and providing I can drag myself away from the senoritas with their dark flashing eyes I'll call you then. Love you lots. 'Bye for now."

Later in the afternoon he was sunbathing on top deck when a female voice said "Is anyone sitting there?" pointing to the empty adjacent chair.

"No, be my guest." he replied.

As she started to slip off her sun-dress Denise realised who he was.

"Oh, I'm so sorry to have bothered you. Aren't you the magician?"

"I am and you're not bothering me. In fact I'd like the company. I'm about to order a drink. Would you care for one?"

"Well thank you very much. Do you think I could have a rum punch, they're absolutely heavenly and I adore the little decorative umbrellas which are speared into cherries."

"And do you have a name?" asked Matt.

"Oh, I'm so sorry. How rude of me. Yes of course I do. It's Denise."

"And are you enjoying the cruise, Denise?"

"Very much." she replied, "I took the short tour of Lisbon this morning. It's a lovely city and I thought the Monument to the Discoveries was magnificent. Did you go into Lisbon?"

"No, I was sorting out all of my props., for tonight's show and then I went and called my wife."

"Where do you live?" she asked.

"In Epping – but not always in the forest." he responded laughingly.

"What about you?"

"Central London. My partner, Nicola and I share a flat in Swiss Cottage and we run a dating agency."

"That sounds fun," said Matt, "I shall look forward to you telling me more another time. Do come to the show tonight. Even if you don't like magicians I'm sure you'll love listening to Laura who is going to play the piano in the first half."

"I'm sure I'll be there. She sits at the same dining room table as I do. She and her singing friend Doreen are both very nice."

"Good. Then I'll see you later."

"Right and thanks very much for the drink."

"Speak of the devil, just look who's here." said Matt.

"Hello, Laura," said Denise, "I guess you know Matt. I see you're both in tonight's show this evening."

"That's right and I must tell you I'm feeling very nervous. Doreen and I took a bus into the centre of Lisbon this morning but then I had to come back to get some rehearsal time."

"Well I really must go." said Matt, "See you soon, Laura."

"And I must also go." said Laura, "I don't mean to be rude Denise but I'm trying to find Doreen. We'll see you after the late show."

*****

He had watched her swim two lengths of the pool. It wasn't a long pool but nevertheless sufficient. He couldn't take his eyes off her and when she wasn't looking he entered, immediately swimming below the water level until he re-surfaced alongside of her.

"You swim beautifully," he said, "I would love to be able to do the breast stroke with you."

"I suggest you cut out all that crap, David. I know exactly what you would like to do with me and it will never happen." replied Julie.

At this point she pushed his head under the water and swam away in the opposite direction.

Karen, who had throughout been sitting and watching from the other side of the pool, guessed what had happened and chose to say nothing when he returned to sit on the chair next to her.

*****

Once passengers had returned on board at the end of their excursions, it did not take long for stories to circulate about the man who had been in cabin 3098 and his stewardess. Each tale in the whispering game became more and more embroidered. Some said he had attacked her with a knife, others reported she'd been raped whilst their were those who said she'd been bound and gagged in his cabin for over three hours during which time other crew members searched for her.

Whatever the tales they all ended the same, with him being put off to shore on the orders of the captain, the bag belonging to the lady in cabin 4136 being returned and Carla having recovered so as to back on normal duties that evening.

*****

As the four friends made their way towards the dining room David whispered to Julie, "You're wonderful when you're angry." to which she smiled sweetly and replied, "Get lost."

At their table the initial topic of conversation was the tours which they had taken. It was Colin who held them spellbound with the story of his trip to Evora whilst those who had not been were fascinated to hear the story of the Belem Cake Shop.

"I guess we should order some port tonight." suggested David and turning towards Julie and Craig added, "When it becomes mature and of vintage quality it has that dark ruby red colour which glows towards you in a welcoming way waiting to be swirled around your body." Both Karen and Julie cringed.

"We four simply took a bus into Lisbon and returned about midday." said Craig, "It certainly is a lovely city but quite frankly walking around in the heat got a bit much and I for one was delighted to get into the pool and cool down."

"Me too," added Karen, "It gave me an opportunity of catching up on some reading."

"Do you read a lot?" asked Colin.

"Yes, I do. I work in a bookshop and that gives me fantastic access to books both old and new though I must say it is the classics that I still prefer. What upsets me most is when I find young people coming into the shop and buying many of the paperbacks which are so very poorly written. It seems that schools don't seem to encourage their students to read good literature. And as for Shakespeare I believe that most schools don't even include his works in the curriculum. I really don't understand what's going on – perhaps this is part of the reason that our schools are turning out students with very poor grades. Whoops, sorry, but you got me on my hobby-horse"

"I agree with you entirely." responded Colin. "There are times I give special art lectures to schools and I'm appalled at their lack of general art knowledge."

"They're very lucky to have you give them a lecture," said Lucy, "we never had anything like that happen at my school."

"I sometimes watch the programme with Anne Robinson," said Craig – "I can't remember what it's called?"

"The Weakest Link." responded Louise.

"Yes, that's it. It's unbelievable how some of the contestants fail to answer the most basic of questions and as for asking them to deduct nine from eighty-three or something mundane like that, well, without a pocket calculator, they haven't a clue."

"It undoubtedly seems to be a sign of the times." added Julie.

"Never mind," said Colin, "to-night we will be able to enjoy some real culture. I see that Laura King is part of this evening's show followed by the magician, Matt."

"I'm really looking forward to it," commented Karen, "especially Laura's playing."

"It's the magician I want to see," said David, "classical music isn't my scene."

*****

This evening, it was Sandra Wells, the assistant Cruise Director, who acted as MC. Having been introduced by the band leader she told the audience they were to be given a rest tonight from having to hear Alan Spencer's boring jokes. She produced her own brand of repartee and then announced how proud 'The Neptune' was to be able to present Laura King, one of Britain's most exciting pianists.

Laura appeared wearing a long black skirt with a sequined silver top and looked quite radiant. She commenced with Mozart's Sonata No. 8 in A Minor, continued with Mendelssohn's Rondo Capricioso in E and finally, on a slightly lighter note played Madeline Dring's delightful composition 'Blue Air'.

Her programme lasted about thirty-five minutes and was greeted by rapturous applause after which she played an encore of Chopin's impassioned 'Revolutionary Study' in C Minor that was written by him on hearing the news that Warsaw had fallen to the Russians.

By way of complete contrast, Matt held the audience spellbound with his presentation of wonderful magical tricks, with cards, silks and a variety of apparatus of varying size. His performance was interspersed with jokes and finally the Neptune orchestra joined him when he sang and danced to two well rehearsed musical numbers.

The audience had warmed to him immediately and his pleasing personality and ability to relate to them had ensured a successful first show for him on this cruise. He was relieved it was over.

David had made an excuse to avoid seeing Laura play but sidled in alongside where the other three were sitting just before Matt had begun.

He didn't have to say where he had been since Karen had no doubt that it was the fatal attraction of the casino which had once more cast it's spell over him – as it had done at other times since the cruise had commenced.

She also had no doubt that he had lost money since if he had been successful he would certainly have told them. It was like Nassau, all over again.

*****

THIRTEEN

The world of water is the ocean and now on day five of the cruise, the second full day at sea would provide different experiences to different people as the dark curtain of night slowly became dappled with the gentle call of morning and the distant kiss of the ocean and the horizon beyond could be seen.

Being on a cruise ship is not only a vacation but also an escape from the daily events that will have been taking place in the lives of the passengers. Viewing changing clouds and sky, the sunrise and the sunset whilst at sea, is an absolute joy placing all within a peaceful realm of nature, part of the beautiful world that we live in which is only marred and abused by some of the humans who reside in it.

*****

This morning Jeff was once again able to rendezvous with Louise for breakfast and was delighted to hear she had thoroughly enjoyed her trip to Lisbon and the show of the previous evening.

"I am really fortunate to be sitting with some very pleasant people for dinner," she said, "but there is one couple who I have a feeling are having real problems. Still, I have enough to worry about without concerning myself about them."

"Something has cropped up," said Jeff, "which I thought might interest you. It appears that guests have been complaining at the purser's desk that the library is in a mess with books not being stored under their proper headings, causing difficulties in finding those they are looking for. The crew member happened to comment *'it needs someone who knows what they're doing to sort it out once and for all.'*

"I immediately thought of you and told them of your library experience at home. I said I'd ask whether you'd be prepared to straighten it out whilst you're on board. As you know it's not exactly the largest of libraries and I doubt whether it would take all that long and there's certainly no hurry. Should you agree, they don't expect you to do it for nothing and will make sure you are not charged for any of the tours you want to take during the cruise."

"That's terrific," replied Louise, "tell them I'll start today. I hate sitting in the sun all the time doing nothing and that would be fun for me and not having to pay anything for the tours will be wonderful."

"I'm really pleased." said Jeff, "Why don't you come down to the purser's desk with me after we've eaten and you can sort out the arrangements with them direct. I'm quite sure you'll be able to just go in and out whenever you please so long as it doesn't interfere with anything else you want to do during the day."

And this was exactly what was agreed, with Louise being told she could re-arrange the books in anyway she thought fit at any time of the day or evening that it suited her.

*****

The day's activities were beginning but for many not having to go ashore on an early morning tour provided an opportunity for a late leisurely breakfast. Others were still up with the proverbial lark either jogging around the mile-run deck or having a pre-breakfast dip or simply enjoying the restful movement of the gleaming vessel.

This evening would be the first formal night when virtually all passengers would appear dressed in evening attire though some of the men tended to wear a suit and tie either because they did not possess a dinner jacket or alternatively the one they owned no longer fitted them.

The lovely ladies generally made their entrances looking lovelier than ever often being bejewelled accordingly. Not only would this be the first formal evening but, in addition, it would be the night of the Captain's Cocktail party to which all passengers had been invited. The party would be presented twice that evening so that the first-sitting diners would go at the beginning and the late diners would attend the second part of the event.

There was no doubt that these two activities would become a frequent topic of conversation between passengers during the day and were generally looked forward to by most, though, in relation to the party, there were always some who had 'been there, seen it, done it' and had no intention of 'doing it' again.

*****

The choice of taking a cruise for their vacation had so far proved to be an excellent idea and, in the main, Anne had experienced little discomfort during the first few days. It was whilst they were in their cabin that she sometimes could feel the symptoms creeping over her but having a balcony enabled her to step out on to it and obtain considerable relief.

Yesterday she had thoroughly enjoyed taking an open bus with Vince into Lisbon and then walking round the city. In particular, she had loved seeing the Church of St. Roquem with its rich interior beautifully decorated with baroque mosaics, gold gilt and precious marbles.

Tomorrow, when the ship berthed in Barcelona, she was hoping she would be fit enough for them to go ashore, since she was keen to be able to view some of the extraordinary Gaudi architecture.

But, never mind tomorrow, let's live for today she thought, and started to discuss with Vince what he would like to do.

Their programme was soon jointly agreed. At ten they would go along and attend the bridge lecture and follow this up at eleven by listening to the Art lecturer. They both wanted to see the cookery demonstration on Pool deck at noon and after lunch, whilst Vince went along to the Art class she intended listening to the destination speaker. At four thirty they would listen to Doreen's recital and then, as Anne described it, 'I'll get togged up for the night ahead and go out with my handsome husband.'

"It's a good job we're going to find time for lunch and tea." said Vince, "What are we supposed to do if we find we've some spare time?"

"Just you wait and see." Anne replied laughing.

They arrived at the card room about fifteen minutes before the scheduled start, as Anne was anxious to take a seat that was near one of the windows. By ten there were only fifteen people in attendance.

"That's the destination speaker, Martin and his wife Shirley." whispered Vince. "I wonder how good they are."

The instructor, Graham Hyde, having introduced himself and his wife Grace, commenced.

"You should always remember," he said, "bridge is just a game, as I always say, so long as I win." He obviously found this very funny whereas his audience allowed it to pass with barely a snigger. Grace just stood and smiled.

The remaining fifty-five minutes of instruction were given in a monotonous single level tone of voice that made it difficult to stay awake.

They left the room at the same time as Martin and Shirley.

"That has to be the worst bridge lecture I've ever heard. Shirley's learning the game and when we come on a cruise she likes going to the lectures and I go with her to the first she attends.

"I don't think you need bother with any of his others," he said, addressing his remarks to her, "let's just try and play in some of the duplicate games in the afternoons, if we're free."

"I think that's what we'll do." said Anne, "We better rush, we're off to hear the Art lecture. We'll see you later."

"We'll look forward to it." commented Martin, "Colin is very good, he won't send you to sleep."

He was absolutely right as Colin's talk on 'Impressionism' coupled with an array of wonderful photographs, screened on his power-point, had his audience clinging to his every word. He started by explaining that though Impressionism started in the eighteen sixties it was Monet's harbour scene, entitled 'Impressionism, 1873', that gave the name to the work of a group of artists in this field.

He had continued with explaining in simplistic terms the basis of impressionist paintings, particularly in relation to the effect of light and atmosphere. He showed examples of paintings with Monet's Poplars, Haystacks, Water Lilies and Rouen Cathedral, Renoir's The Skiff, Umbrellas and Moulin de la Galette, Pissarro's The Road, Louveciennes and Gare St. Lazare and many by other painters.

When the talk came to an end there was no doubt that Colin would continue to attract numerous art-loving passengers to his other lectures.

"That was terrific," Anne said to Vince, "and so, from one extreme to another, let's go to the cookery demonstration."

This had attracted a vast crowd, most of whom were standing around in their bathing costumes whilst watching three of the ship's chefs producing a main course consisting of magret de canard, pommes dauphinoise and roast parsnips with honey and a dessert of cherry and almond tart with pear sorbet.

The speed with which these dishes were created, amazed all observing the culinary expertise of these chefs, who as top professionals, made their cooking tasks appear to be totally simple.

The duck breasts, skin-side down, were placed in a pre-heated pan until the breasts were dark. The breasts were then turned over and finished in the pre-heated oven for about eight minutes.

After the duck had been sliced for all to see, it was found to be well cooked on the outside and slightly pink in the centre.

All three chefs were demonstrating the various stages of preparing the potatoes, having already placed in their pre-heated portable oven some examples that had been cooking for about thirty-five minutes and required a further twenty-five, to be ready for eating.

The parsnips were prepared in the same twenty-five minute period with the honey being poured lightly over them prior to the last five minutes of cooking.

The various stages required for the tart were also demonstrated, with a large tart, which had been cooking in another portable oven, being taken out and allowed to cool, leaving only the pear sorbet to go on before service.

Samples of these dishes were laid out on a long table for passengers to taste and without exception they all were duly impressed.

"I shall now know what to expect when we get home." said Vince.

"You'll be lucky." replied Anne.

"That's the story of my life," he added, "but I'll tell you one thing I'm starving. Let's go and eat."

Having served themselves at the buffet luncheon they noticed Martin and Shirley sitting at a table for four.

"Come and join us." called Shirley.

They got on very well together and whilst Vince was telling Martin that he taught art from the eighteen-fifties at a school in Salisbury, Anne told Shirley of the claustrophobia problems that she had been experiencing over a period of years.

"Did you hear that, Martin," said Shirley, "Anne has just been telling me she suffers from claustrophobia."

"Really," replied Martin, "Shirley's sister had the same problem a few years ago but nowadays she seems to be absolutely fine. It took some time but gradually she battled against it, received some therapy and all came good. I trust the same thing happens to you."

As they ate, Shirley commented, "Have you noticed that woman over there, the one standing by the water machine? It's quite extraordinary but whenever I see her, during the day or evening, she's always carrying that red file, though I never see her reading it. Rather odd if you ask me."

When Martin announced he must get ready to give his talk Anne told him that she intended being there.

"The programme indicates you'll be speaking about Monte Carlo and Alghero."

"Yes, that's right. I hope you enjoy it. See you soon."

*****

Louise had also been listening to Martins' talk and went up to him at the end offering her congratulations.

"You're very good," she said, "and so animated. I'm sure the other passengers loved it. I shall now look forward to all of your other lectures.

She had only been sunbathing on Mercury deck for about ten minutes when Colin suddenly appeared.

"I thought I'd join you, if that's okay?" he said.

"Of course." replied Louise, feeling delighted with the thought.

As they sat and personal questions were asked, details of each others lives began to flow.

"Of course, I do worry about Jeff but I suppose that's natural."

"Why do you think it's natural?" asked Colin.

"Well, that's the way I am, I've always been a worrier" she responded.

"Let me ask you a question," he continued, "can you give me any one example where your worrying has helped at all?"

"Well, no." Louise replied hesitantly.

"Then can you please explain why you do it? Worrying is pointless. It never helps in fact it makes matters worse, since worrying can make you ill."

"Yes, I know. It's just that - well it's just that I can't help it."

As his story was related to her, she asked, "But how come you intend opening a restaurant? And why in Reigate when you live in Norwich?

As he was about to answer there was an announcement from the cruise director indicating that table tennis and deck quoits tournaments would be starting at three-thirty.

"I was born in Redhill and my father had a restaurant in Reigate which was only a couple of miles away. It was very popular and he worked very hard but, as you can imagine, the unsociable working hours puts a stress on all concerned.

"Unfortunately the biggest strain hit him when I was in my mid-twenties. It was whilst there was a recession. The restaurant trade is always one of the first to suffer. His bank started to pressurise him to reduce the business overdraft and to increase the monthly loan payments that he was making. All of this, when takings were down, did not help him in the slightest.

"It was about four one Monday afternoon, the one day in each week that the restaurant was closed, that he was sitting in our lounge at home reading the paper when my mother heard him call out. She was there in a matter of seconds, but it was too late. He had had an enormous heart attack and had died instantly."

"What a shock for her." commented Louise.

"It certainly was. The bank showed very little sympathy. All they wanted was their money back. The restaurant had to be sold as did the house in which we were living, in order to repay the short-fall. Fortunately there was a surplus arising from the house sale which my mother was able to use to buy a new home.

"Her only family came from Norwich and she decided she would prefer to go back and live there and that's what we did. My mother bought a lovely little bungalow and in due course I rented a flat and subsequently bought a house. I took a three-year art foundation course and gradually found myself having a busy work agenda from teaching and lecturing.

"I'd always enjoyed helping Dad in the restaurant and he and his assistant chef taught me a great deal about cooking. Whilst I was doing the art course I managed to get quite a bit of casual restaurant work which enabled me to make ends meet.

"My constant ambition was to have my own and it was unbelievable when one of the many premises I saw was a now empty property in Reigate that had previously been used as a restaurant. Talk about fate and what's meant to happen happens. I can't tell you how thrilled I am."

"That's an amazing story," said Louise, "but what about your mother."

"She died three years ago and it's only as a result of my being the sole beneficiary of her estate that I can afford the restaurant." responded Colin, "It's like going full circle and there are many times that I have to pinch myself to make sure I'm not dreaming it all."

"Will you be moving permanently to Reigate?" asked Louise.

"Definitely, if not in Reigate somewhere very near by." he replied, "It's a lovely part of England. That's something else which has made me chase around like the proverbial .... fly. I've got my house in Norwich on the market and I'm also looking for one near the restaurant. Never mind, I'm sure it'll all work out okay – I've just got to hang in there, as it is said."

"I don't suppose you've chosen a name for the restaurant?" said Louise.

"Well, as a matter of fact I have."

"May I ask what it is to be?

"Certainly, I'm going to call it 'Maison Pistou'. responded Colin.

"That sounds French," commented Louise, "How did it come about, is it a family name or a place name?"

"Neither actually," he replied, "it's a name which I came across years ago when I regularly visited the South of France. There was this little restaurant in Antibes called Le Pistou that was run by a delightful, very friendly, owner who looked like a garden gnome.

"Various dishes were served some of which were delicious Provencal delicacies, but always, come winter or summer, he had on the menu a wonderful, garlic flavoured vegetable soup, called Le Pistou. The proprietor once told me that it was made from a secret recipe of his grand-mother. I've never forgotten it and thought it would make a great name for the restaurant."

"That's a charming tale." said Louise, "I'm sure it'll be a great success – after all, as you said, it was meant to happen – so it can't possible fail now."

Suddenly, there was the shout of a child from the deck below them on the same side of the ship where they were sitting.

"Mummy, mummy, come quickly, Wendy's fallen in the water."

This was followed almost immediately by an older woman calling out, "There's a child in the sea."

Louise and Colin dashed down the metal stairs leading to the lower deck.

In the short time that it took them to arrive the panic was over. The child's mother was by her side trying to placate her and the other woman, together with a host of passengers who were now looking into the sea, realised that Wendy had been a doll – a fairly big doll – but nevertheless a doll that had been dropped accidentally.

"Time for tea, I believe." said Colin, "Will you join me? I don't know about you but I'd then like to hear Doreen's song recital. She really is very good."

*****

Sandra Wells stepped on to the floor of the Apollo lounge to introduce Doreen and Laura. The lights were dimmed as they appeared. Their considerable passion of musical poetry, with Laura lovingly caressing each accompanying note, produced a dazzling programme which included arias from La Traviata and some songs from the Auvergne. Half-way through, whilst Doreen took a short break, Laura played the Intermezzo in A Minor by Brahms. The euphoric joy of their audience left no doubt as to their popularity..

Apart from Louise and Colin, Roger had also attended. He had become mesmerised with Laura's performance the night before and once again found that he could hardly take his eyes off her.

Henry and Liz had thoroughly enjoyed the singing and playing and went over to speak to Doreen and Laura before they went off stage.

"That was terrific." said Henry, "I never fail to be utterly amazed how a few dots can be placed on a piece of paper and music results. I suppose it's like painting where a few splodges of paint are put on a canvas and where, when writing, a few letters are placed on a piece of paper and suddenly words, sentences, etc., all appear. It's pretty damn marvellous, if you ask me, anyway, thanks again, and good luck to you both."

"Oh look over there, it's Delia and Paul," said Liz, "let's go over to them."

"Well, what did you think of that?" asked Liz.

"Beautiful. I must make sure we try and see their other performances, "replied Delia.

"We really enjoyed your company yesterday" said Henry, "I understand that at one time Estoril was one of the smartest places you could go to in Europe whilst Cascais was just a little fishing village. How things change! "

"And tonight it's party time in our glad rags." commented Liz.

"Don't mention it too enthusiastically," said Delia, "my lovely husband here hates the thought of having to put on his dinner suit – but I'm sure he'll look splendid. Isn't that right, my darling?"

Her comment simply drew a "Huh." from Paul, who, with a smile, then added, "I'll let you know."

*****

As Shirley and Martin were in their cabin getting ready for the evening ahead, he commented, "It really is incongruous that in this day and age, now, in the twenty-first century, an event like the Captain's cocktail party takes place, with passengers getting themselves all dolled up."

"You're right it is incongruous but just remember how the majority of people love it." she responded, "Very few have ever complained to us when we've been on board our many cruises and I think the reason they enjoy it is because we've all read or seen films about cruising in the past which was mainly for the so-called elite and moneyed-members of society and we realised how this type of event was a regular feature and out of the range of the ordinary person.

"But now, cruising is for the masses and it is a wonderful opportunity for everybody to be able to tread in the steps of those who came before and participate in similar social activities and know that they have now actually been there and experienced it for themselves and no longer is it just for the privileged."

When she had finished, Martin, who had sat listening to her with interest, said, "You're absolutely right. I must say that I'd never thought of it in that light."

"Well, whether you have or not, if we're to be ready I need some help with this necklace."

*****

It might have been a reception at the High Commissioner's residence in a colonial capital before independence, it might have been carnival time in a Caribbean city, it might have been a family wedding within the aristocracy but it was none of these – it was simply to be the Captain's cocktail party.

They came dressed in black, they came in blue, they came in white and they came in pink. Dresses were long and dresses were short, dresses had high necks whilst others were daring but whichever it was they presented a delightful picture escorted by their husbands or partners or lovers.

As couples made their way to the entrance to Trident Lounge they were met by the ship's photographers who were at the ready to suggest various poses that could be taken up to hopefully produce a wonderful photograph that might subsequently be purchased and taken home to be proudly shown to family and friends. The process of taking these photographs caused delays and as a result there was a long queue of passengers waiting to be snapped and then admitted to the lounge.

Here to greet them in resplendent white uniforms were the Captain and all of his officers lined up like toy soldiers to shake the hands of their guests whilst in the background a gentle unobtrusive tinkling at a piano could be heard. Mediocre non-vintage champagne was being served together with a selection of canapés. Guests talked to guests until the time came for them to depart from the lounge and make their way to the dining rooms for the next intake of food.

In the meantime, cleaning staff were hovering and polishing the lounge and waiting staff were again making all necessary preparations so as to be ready for the second-sitting diners to appear at the second instalment of the party.

*****

"I love being on cruises." said Graham, the bridge instructor, as he tucked into am enormous plate of food.

He and his wife, Grace, were seated at the same table in the Ocean Bistro as Matt, singer, Nick Guthrie and the two dance hosts.

"How long have you been going on them?" asked Matt.

"This is our third year. Isn't it, Grace?"

"Yes, that's right." she replied.

"Last year we did a cruise of five weeks and next March we're booked for one of six weeks. That's right, isn't Grace?"

"Yes dear."

"I honestly don't know how you can stay on a ship that long." commented Nick.

"Well Peter and I are often on board for long stints." said Robert, "We also enjoy them."

"But surely you must get bored out of your mind trying to help people dance when they don't know their left foot from their right," continued Nick. "And then there's all the chit-chat talk about nothing you have to do to be sociable and I would have thought having to dance with ladies who you would never wish to be with, staying up late at discos and being available at the call of the cruise director is all a bit much. After all, neither of you are exactly young."

"It's the one thing in our lives that gives us a real interest," said Peter, "apart from which when we're on a ship we never lack company, our meals are provided, our rooms are cleaned, bed-linen changed and we don't have to worry about any of the daily chores we'd have at home."

"And I'll tell you something else," added Robert, "the dancing keeps us fit and that is certainly important at our age."

"I suppose all of that's true," said Nick, "it all depends on one's circumstances."

"Well we love the cruises and the foods great," Graham repeated, "Isn't that right, Grace?"

"Yes that's right," responded Grace, "we love cruising. It was so clever of Graham to have got us on the two ships that we go on, mind you, it's the only two that have us and...."

"I told you it's just the start, Grace," said Graham interrupting her and sounding quite hurt, "with a bit of luck we'll be on others."

"Yes I know," she said, "but you won't get on any of the American owned ships since you don't have the qualifications they want."

Graham glared at her but decided not to say anything and simply concentrated on stuffing himself.

"All I know," said Nick, "is that once I've been on board for two weeks I feel as though I can't wait to get off."

"I know what you mean," said Matt, "it's the constant repetition. It's okay for the passengers, they're on holiday, but we're here to work."

"But you get good meals, don't you?" commented Grace.

"I hate buffets," replied Nick, "and that's just about all most of us get. The other lecturers will often get seated in the dining room, but none of us do. There are many times when all I want is egg on chips or a shepherd's pie, not any of that." as he pointed to the buffet service area.

"He's absolutely right. I feel the same way especially when my wife's not on board." said Matt. "You're married aren't you, Nick?"

"Yes, I am with a nineteen year-old daughter at a drama school." he replied. "She's not very good, though she believes she'll be the next Kate Winslett. She occasionally gets some bit parts and gets quite upset if my wife doesn't go to watch her. She'll be lucky to finish up on a third rate circuit staying in boarding houses week after week and maybe finding herself playing in a seaside panto.

"It's a tough life and unless you're really good it's like knocking your head against a brick wall and by the time she actually starts to earn a little money I'll be heading for fifty and still having to provide for her. My wife encourages her, not only because when she was younger, she went through the same scenario and also finished up being a failed actress but now, she hopes to see her wish for success, coming through her daughter.

"So there are times when my household is like a poor man's RADA with two women imagining that this time it will be different, when in fact it won't be. Meanwhile, I'm like a travelling vagabond, singing and strumming my guitar, going wherever my agent can get me a job so as to earn a living. I've got it better than most but on the other hand........."

Nick stopped talking. He suddenly realised how his account of a family of average artists was in fact not only true but rather depressing and he did not wish to add anything else.

Matt could empathise with him and felt his sorrow but in order to cheer him up said, "Well I'll tell you one thing Nick, I'm very much looking forward to the show tonight and seeing this travelling vagabond, who I know only too well is bloody marvellous."

*****

"And now ladies and gentleman," said the announcer, "please give a big welcome to your cruise director, Mr. Alan Spencer who, to the stirring music being played by the orchestra, appeared dressed in a smart lightweight brown suit with white shirt and a yellow tie.

"I'm so pleased to see that none of you tried to get off today, although I believe one 'doll' took an unexpected dive into the sea.

"Of course, being at sea all day means that the crew do receive more complaints than if we're in harbour. I had one this afternoon. This gentleman came up to me and asked *'Does the swimming pool contain seawater or fresh water? I told him it was sea water and explained how it was pumped out of the sea.'* He then replied, *'Just what I thought. That explains why it's so rough in the pool.'*

"But last night was one of the best." the director continued, "Our orchestra leader, Carlos, told me that a lady asked him, *'Do the band live on the ship?'*

"Now I must tell you Carlos is a bit of a joker and obviously could not resist this opportunity."

'No, madam, a helicopter takes them back to land each night.'

"You'll never believe it, but this morning this same lady was at the purser's desk complaining she was being kept awake each night with the noise of the helicopter."

His jokes had gone down well and the atmosphere for the evening was now set as he added, "But now, ladies and gentlemen, it's show-time, and The Neptune is delighted to present for your entertainment 'Harlemania' starring the Neptune Orchestra and our dancers and singers together with the irresistible singer and guitarist, Nick Guthrie."

The show was a great success and very much appreciated by jazz lovers. The programme was a celebration of the small groups that had dominated the New York jazz scene during the nineteen-twenties and –thirties with tributes to Fats Waller, Artie Shaw, Bix Beiderbecke and others.

Nick was in top form and thoroughly enjoying performing within this format of music.

Matt, was thrilled for him and hoped that he too would find the key to his own problems which were making him feel so depressed.

*****

FOURTEEN

Henry, Liz, Andrew and Ros had agreed to meet outside the dining room at seven-thirty in order to take a leisurely breakfast prior to taking the tour to Montserrat, where, located at the top of the four thousand feet mountain, built amid towering peaks, could be found the Monastery of Montserrat, a renowned shrine. It was situated about thirty-six miles from Barcelona requiring a drive round hairpin bends that had been carved through magnificent scenery and was a place where honeymoon couples frequently went seeking the blessing of the Black Virgin.

"I realise that Spain is the third largest country in Europe," said Henry, "but it never fails to amaze me when I think back on its historical and cultural past. If we remember the days of Columbus, the Spanish Armada, the Inquisition and the Spanish Civil War with Franco, there is an immediate picture of days of light and dark that the nation has gone through. I'm not saying such events have not been part of the trials and tribulations of other countries but, somehow or the other, the Spanish scene has always fascinated me."

"I always believed you fellows only thought of dark-eyed senoritas and bullfighting when you were in Spain." commented Liz.

"And what about the abundance of castles in Spain." added Ros, "Isn't that the reason why they have a region named Castile?"

"That's right." agreed Andrew, "As for the bull-fighting, we have to realise the Spanish understand and appreciate all of the nuances existing during each of the individual fights that take place. They don't regard them as being just a blood sport."

"Well I can't bear watching them." said Liz.

"And I wouldn't ever want to go to see one," said Ros, "I'll just stick with all of the lovely music that has come out of Spain."

"Now that's an interesting subject in itself." said Henry, "I bet you'd all have a job telling me the names of any Spanish composer other than Albeniz, Granados, de Falla and Rodrigo."

Their brains started ticking over but none of them could come up with another name.

"I can think of musical compositions geared towards Spain, like Carmen and the Barber of Seville but these are by composers from other countries." commented Ros.

"Exactly my point," said Henry, "and this brings us to us ask, why was it that Spanish music did not continue to mature after the end of the sixteenth century as it did in France, Germany, Italy and England?"

"Have you an answer?" asked Andrew.

"Well it's not my answer but the most powerful explanation is that the blame can be directed to the period of the Inquisition that crushed the creative life of Spain and lasted for nearly four hundred years." replied Henry.

"It's a dreadful thing when the creative spirit and liberty of a human being is put down in such a way." said Ros.

"And it's still going on in some countries." added Andrew.

"Come on, that's enough," said Liz, "we're becoming far too morose on this bright sunny day. Let's go. We've an exciting day ahead."

As they were leaving the dining room they passed a table where Anne and Vince were breakfasting.

"Morning you two," said Liz, "I trust you had a good night? And what are your plans for today?"

"We're going into the centre of Barcelona with Delia and Paul," replied Vince, "It's not far from the ship and we thought we'd share a cab together. And where are you four of to?"

"To the Monastery at Montserrat, you have a great time and we'll see you for dinner."

*****

The most popular of the tours today was 'Barcelona City Highlights' and several coaches had been booked to take passengers. Louise and Colin were on the first coach whereas Roger and les girls, as he referred to them, managed to ensure they were all on the same coach with Roger next to Laura and Denise and Doreen sitting together.

Their guide had a bubbly personality and within minutes gained the attention of all of the passengers. She started by outlining the intended programme of the tour and then explained that the name Barcelona was said to stem from the great Barca family of Carthage, whose family included Hannibal.

Considerable information and statistics followed. She referred to Picasso saying, *'It was here in Barcelona that he began his formal art training and it is believed that his famous Cubist painting Les Demoiselles d'Avignon, was inspired by a brothel located in a part of the Gothic Quarter.'*

As could have been anticipated, some wag asked whether the brothel was being included on the tour.

The four-hour trip included a visit to the Gothic Quarter with its narrow winding streets and fourteenth century Cathedral of Santa Eulalia, which had taken one hundred and fifty years to build and was on the site of a Roman temple dedicated to Hercules.

The guide told how the incredible Gothic style of architecture had began in France in about the middle of the twelfth century and as a result churches had become airy and soaring, with pointed arches and vaults and counter-balancing flying buttresses.

Denise commented how she always felt uncomfortable when seeing the sculpted gargoyles in the form of beasts and grotesque human beings.

The second amazing site was the Sagrada Familia Church – the unfinished masterpiece of the legendary architect, Antoni Gaudi – which he began in eighteen eighty four and was still unfinished.

Here the guide told passengers that it is a complicated structure and that it was only Gaudi's ingenuity that enabled him to create his unusual shapes.

Before the coach returned to the ship, any passengers wishing to stay in the centre of Barcelona, were given the opportunity on the understanding that they would have to find their own way back to the ship and be on board by half-past four. They were also warned that the ship would not wait for them if they were not back by sailing time.

Laura agreed to stay when Roger asked her to join him for lunch.

"I thought it would make a nice change from eating on the ship." he said.

Doreen and Denise decided to return, as did the majority of others.

They immediately went towards La Rambla, the most famous, one mile long pedestrian precinct in Barcelona with outdoor cafes, animal stalls, flowers stalls, newspaper kiosks and street entertainers.

The entire area was buzzing with locals and tourists wearing colourful summer clothing in the heat of the day. They had started in the Place de Catalunya, the most northerly area of La Rambla and were soon able to see the exterior of the Opera House. A cool drink taken at the Café de la Opera refreshed them before they continued their stroll.

Laura was fascinated with everything going on and Roger found her enthusiasm quite delightful. He often thought that too many people were rather blasé in relation to virtually everything they saw and did.

At last they reached the Columbus Statue at the southerly end of the fifth part of La Rambla. He pointed to a little restaurant saying "I think we now deserve a good lunch."

"So do I." replied Laura, "I'm starving."

Having been seated at a window table, Roger asked, "Would you like some Sangria? I think its ideal at this time of day and in this weather."

"I'd love it." replied Laura.

After studying the menu they both ordered the same special dishes of the region starting with pan con tomate (bread rubbed with a cut tomato and garlic and sprinkled with olive oil) followed by sea-bass served with samfaina (tomatoes, peppers and aubergines) and finished with crema Catalina, a kind of crème brulee and then some coffee.

"That was absolutely delicious," said Laura, "Thank you so much, Roger. The next meal is on me."

During lunch Laura had asked him about his work and he told her of his previous working days with Jonathan and his married live with Lisa.

"Two wonderful people," he added, "and yet both were destined to pass on at such early ages. I must say I never expected to be a widower when only thirty seven. But that's life, as it is said. The only problem is when it happens to you twice with people you are so close to you begin to wonder whether you, yourself, had anything to do with it."

"You mustn't think like that," said Laura, placing her hand over his, "you can't blame yourself, that would be foolish and you're bright enough to know better."

"So what about your future business plans?"

"As a matter of fact I have been giving thought to expanding in a new area. One must always be aware that business goes in cycles depending upon economic conditions at any one time. What is good business today can suddenly prove to be undesirable at a later date. I've no desire to have my company take over my life. I'm not a workaholic but it's rather necessary to look to the future with a view to securing ones income and any other benefits that can arise.

"My new idea is to enter into contracts with hotel companies to build hotels for them which they can either run themselves or lease out. By doing this my capital outlay is secured, by taking agreed instalments from the hoteliers as the buildings are erected, they bear any future risk element and I would earn my profit from the building contract."

"That sounds pretty full-proof," said Laura, "It seems that heads you win and tales you win."

"That's it exactly," he responded, "I just have to make sure I have the right building teams available to carry out this type of development.

"But now it's your turn. Apart from knowing you are most attractive and play a mean piano you've told me very little."

"Well, I don't know there's too much to tell." said Laura.

She traced her earlier days through to the years at the Royal Academy of Music to the present time when she mainly taught.

"So how come you're on this cruise?" Roger asked.

Here again the explanation was given about Doreen having asked her to be her accompanist almost at the last minute and she added, "She knew I was feeling very tired and decided some sea air would fit the bill."

"Have you been working too hard?" he asked.

"Well, not exactly, it's rather a long and unbelievable story. I'm sure you'd be bored stiff." she said.

"Try me." said Roger.

During the next thirty minutes Laura told him the complete story of the ring, discovering the name Flatau, the places named Asnieres and her nine hundred mile journey in France.

He did not interrupt her once. Only when she had finished did he say, "That indeed is an unbelievable but amazing story. What do you intend to do next?"

"I'm really not sure," said Laura, "I was told she was holidaying in London for seventeen days so I'm hoping she'll make contact with me after she returns to France. I left my number but if she doesn't call me then I'll call her. One way or the other I'm determined to solve this mystery. It has to have some real relevant meaning for me and I don't believe I can rest until I've found out why it was my mother left me the ring and wanted me to find the family Flatau."

"It's like everything else in life," said Roger, "there are many times some of our experiences initially seem inexplicable until suddenly the reality is revealed. You must remain positive and believe you're doing the right thing and then I've no doubt you'll find the answer."

"Thank you for saying those few words, Roger, they've been most encouraging and thank you once again for the lovely lunch. Perhaps we should now wend our way back to the ship.

When they arrived they were surprised to see a taxi waiting alongside with a crew member placing the suitcase of a lady in the boot and then helping her into the cab which drove off.

"I wonder what that was all about?" commented Laura.

It did not take them long to find out as the incident was being talked about by many of the passengers, one of whom told them the story.

"She had an urgent message telling her she should return home. Apparently, her husband never enjoyed travelling and didn't want to go on this cruise though he had no objections to her going. It seems he was having dinner at the home of their best friends when he suddenly said he had a severe pain in his shoulder and arm, became dizzy and almost fainted. They called an ambulance and after he had been examined he was told he urgently needed to have triple by-pass surgery and it would be carried out today.

"It's a good job he had private health cover. I doubt if he'd have received such speedy attention otherwise.

"One of the officers was advised of the message as soon as it arrived as they couldn't find her on the ship. He made enquiries with the tour office manager who found she had taken the shorter tour of Barcelona and would be back by noon. The tour manager met the coach and told her what had happened."

"Oh, how awful for her." said Laura.

"Absolutely," said the passenger, "anyway it seems that the officer in charge has been marvellous. He arranged for her to speak to her friends in England and organised calls to the hospital whilst the tour manager checked with the airlines and organised a flight for her to get back to Gatwick this evening where her friends will meet her."

"Did her husband have the operation today?" asked Roger.

"Yes he did and she was told it went well and he was currently in intensive care which is normal procedure," said the passenger, continuing with, "It only goes to prove we don't know from one day to another, what's going to happen in our lives. It's best to just get on and enjoy it."

*****

Delia, Paul, Anne and Vince had returned to the ship just before quarter to one. Both couples returned to their cabins agreeing to meet outside the Ocean Bistro in fifteen minutes. They had all enjoyed their visit to the centre of Barcelona and Anne had been delighted to see some of the works of Gaudi.

Delia had become concerned about Paul as he had been edgy all morning.

"I'll be really pleased to go to the AA meeting later this afternoon." he said.

Delia did not want to show any sign of her anxiety and casually replied, "Good, I know you like seeing the other passengers there. I shall properly sit back in the sun and relax after our exhausting walk around the city. What time is the meeting?"

"They obviously don't want to hold it until after the ship has left port so it's not going to be until six – a bit late, but rather late…."

Anne and Paul were already at the Bistro and had taken a table for the four of them.

"I thought it best to take this table, "said Vince, "before those on tours return."

During lunch, Vince said, "So what work do you do, Delia?"

Having explained it in general terms, Vince said, "It sounds fascinating but how does it actually operate?"

"Well, as you know, whenever you use your car you have insurance cover and nowadays this generally covers legal expenses in the event of an accident. My firm is paid by the English Insurance Company, with whom the driver has his or her policy, when a claim needs to be made in relation to an accident that has arisen in France, which was the fault of a French driver.

"The claims normally cover pain and suffering, medical expenses in respect of personal injury and a wide range of other claims that may be justifiable for compensation. The most difficult part of the work arises as the French Insurance Companies are usually very slow in wanting to deal with a claim whereas the policy holder would like to have the matter resolved as soon as possible."

"I can understand that." said Vince. "But how do you manage to agree a sum for medical expenses. I've been told that medical treatment in France is considerably less costly than in England."

"That's another major headache which I think I'd rather forget about whilst on holiday." replied Delia.

"I can well believe that." said Anne, "What about you, Paul, how do you keep yourself out of mischief?"

"I'm a freelance writer and journalist." he replied, and then with a big grin, added, "You'd better be careful otherwise I might write about you."

Once lunch was over, Anne announced she was going back to the cabin to have a rest and Vince said he was going up to the library to get the latest news letter and crossword.

"Okay, we'll see you later." said Delia.

She and Paul went out on to Pool deck and having found two comfortable seats duly dozed off.

About an hour later Delia woke to find that Paul was no longer by her side. She waited for fifteen minutes and then decided she would try and find him. She first went down to their cabin but he wasn't there. She then thought he may have gone to the library to find Vince but again drew a blank.

It was just before she reached the Trident lounge that she spotted him and immediately she could feel her stomach muscles knotting up. He was sitting at the bar of the adjoining cocktail area. In front of him was a glass containing what she could only assume was a large whisky.

He had not seen her and she moved into a position where he would still be unable to see her but she could see him.

He just sat staring down at the glass. Five minutes went by. Occasionally, he picked it up and put it down again. Then he raised the glass towards his mouth, stopped simply to smell the contents and replaced it on the bar.

Each time he picked up the glass, Delia went cold and every time he put it back she breathed a sigh of relief. Once more he took the glass, this time in both hands, and vary carefully swilled the whisky from side to side and once more he placed the glass and its contents back on the bar.

Delia then saw him call over the barman who went further along the bar. She saw him fill a tumbler with orange juice which had been in a jug nearby. Paul picked up the orange juice, made a gesture to the barman indicating he should remove the whisky, went over to a table and started to drink.

She realised he had overcome a tremendous urge to have some alcohol and had no doubt this was the reason why he had been tense throughout the entire day.

She felt proud of him and quickly returned to where they had been sitting took off her robe and went into the pool. As he came along she went up the pool steps, called his name, went over to him and gave him a big hug and kiss.

"What's that for?" Paul asked.

"Because I love you and have decided to keep you – well, for at least another day."

He laughed and kissed her back saying, "And I adore you too."

*****

Denise stood in front of Matt as he was lying in the sun.

"Hello again," she said, "I thought you were great the other evening and you made the audience laugh so much."

"Please sit down, Denise," said Matt, "there's nobody sitting on this next chair. All I need do is to move some of my clothes which I threw on to it."

"Thanks," she replied, "as I was saying you really are a very funny man. I bet you keep your wife well and truly amused."

"Pauline's heard most of my gags time and time again so it has to be a new one before she really laughs. It's being funny that's just the problem."

"What do you mean?" asked Denise.

"It's difficult to explain. You see if someone is an actor or a singer or a performer in many other areas, when you meet them they will generally speak to you in a quite ordinary way and should they have problems from time to time, like all of us, they are able to go on stage and once the adrenaline runs they can immerse themselves into their performance."

"Being a comedian is so different." Matt continued, "For some reason or the other people expect comedians to always be funny but there are countless examples of where some of the most well known comedians have been extremely sad, depressed, lonely individuals. Some have only been able to survive by taking drugs and some have committed suicide.

"Telling jokes is not merely a question of learning a few words – that's the easy part. Countless people can tell a joke and it will flop. Should you ask *'what makes a comedian funny?'* it isn't simply *'because he tells jokes.'* – it's the way in which a joke is told.

"It's the nuances, the pauses, the interjections, the facial expressions and the continuous play-role with an audience. And that is what makes it very difficult if one is to succeed and it's made doubly difficult should a comedian be going through a period in his or her life when doubts arise and soul-searching is taking place in relation to the future."

"You obviously feel you're at the cross-roads and would like to take a different direction in your working career." said Denise, "I often hear similar remarks made to me by some of our clients. It's not easy to advise people and they don't need to hear platitudes but I do believe that, just like the sea we're on, we have the calm and rough patches but somehow or the other a solution presents itself"

"Of that I'm sure," agreed Matt, "and I'm lucky to have Pauline who understands me and is being very supportive. Quite frankly, as you've guessed, I am seriously thinking of giving up my current work and doing something else but it is a question of finding the right niche."

"Well, the good thing is that here on the ship you can hide yourself in the fresh air – until a nosy parker like me comes along – and give yourself time to consider the various alternatives. On that note I'll leave you in peace and will see you soon."

"Thanks for being such a good listener." said Matt, "I shall look out for you."

*****

Roger made sure that he arrived a few minutes early so he could be one of the first to enter the dining room and make his way to his normal table. He was soon able to succeed with his ulterior motive. Doreen and Laura were next to arrive, barely thirty seconds later and he waved them to chairs either side of him. The other five were soon in position.

"So where have all of you youngsters been gallivanting to today?" asked James.

Almost in unison, the reply came back 'Barcelona.'

"Now that is surprising, isn't it Phyllis."

"Stop being daft," she replied, "please excuse him it's a touch of second childhood."

"Never mind," said Doreen, "we still love you James and we'll all tell you whatever you want to know."

"Oh, I don't know about that," said Martin, "I could tell you some terrible stories about this old rogue."

"Now don't you start, Martin," said Shirley, "you're as wicked as he is."

By this time everyone at the table was laughing and stories of the day's events were unfolded.

Roger leaned across to Laura and whispered "I cannot tell you how lovely it was being with you today. I do hope you also enjoyed our being together as I'd very much like to see more of you."

"Well," said Laura with a big grin, "I can hardly jump ship and get away from you so I suppose…(and here she paused momentarily)….. I'll just have to put up with….with your very welcome advances."

He smiled back, delighted to have heard her response and, without any one noticing, touched her hand.

As they were eating, voices could suddenly be heard singing, 'Happy birthday to you, happy birthday to you, happy birthday dear Emily, happy birthday to you.'

At a nearby table they could see the head waiter and five waiters, one of whom was carrying a birthday cake bearing a single candle, singing their greeting whilst the lady herself appeared highly embarrassed by the entire affair.

"I think that's rather nice" said James.

"The trouble with him," commented Phyllis, "is that he's just a rotten old romantic – but he's lovely with it."

*****

As Delia and Paul made their way to the theatre they came across Sophie who had already been to the first show.

"You'll love it, she said, "some of the dancing is great and it's very colourful. It reminded me of when my second husband took me to Seville."

"What are your plans for the rest of the evening?" asked Delia, adding, "You could always come to one of the shows with us or come on one of the tours for that matter."

"That's most kind of you," replied Sophie, "and I really do appreciate the thought but you know once you're on your own, women soon realise a single person should not intrude into Mr. and Mrs. situations. Now you two go off and have fun. As for me, I'm off to dance the light fantastic.

"I told you I've got my eye on one of those dance hosts – even if he doesn't know it!! I only hope he hasn't worn himself out. They sometimes work until two in the morning and they're also expected to be in attendance when the principal dance teachers give their lessons."

Then with a wicked glint in her eye, she added, "Mind you, I can always buy him some Viagra, if I have to."

*****

"And so ladies and gentlemen," continued the cruise director, wearing a wide sombrero, "without any further delay from me, I'm delighted to present to you this evening's show entitled 'A Night in Spain.' So please give a big welcome to Los Barcettas, a magnificent group of Spanish dancers, who came on board this morning, who will be accompanied by the Neptune orchestra, singers and dancers."

Los Barcettas were indeed an excellent group of three men and three women who proceeded to carry out some excellent routines to typical Spanish melodies. During an occasional short break the resident company provided their part of the entertainment to popular songs, well-known to the audience, as Blue Spanish Eyes and Viva Espana.

The grand finale came when the lights were dimmed further and one of the male dancers came to the front of the stage carrying a hand-microphone.

"Buenas noches, senoras y senors. It is now time for Los Barcettas to present to you the world famous Flamenco. It is not just a show to be put on for tourists. It is a display of the true soul of Andalusia. The origin is the 'Canto Jonda' or deep song which describes in ancient poetic phrases the performer's profound emotions. We hope you will like this."

Whilst he had been speaking, a scene of a café had been set up behind the curtain which was now drawn back. At the front was a single chair. A brief introduction from the orchestra provided the entrance music for a man carrying a guitar, who was greeted by applause. He made his way towards the chair, sat and launched into a composition.

The guitarist made his instrument roar and whisper, laugh and sob and in due course, a series of commanding chords were struck and one of the flamenco dancers whirled onto the stage wearing a brilliantly coloured dress, closely fitted with a frilled skirt, a deeply fringed silk shawl and heeled shoes.

As she commenced to dance the others in the group appeared with each of the women in similar clothing though of different colouring whilst the men had close fitting short jacketed suits, wide flat hats and heeled boots.

The songs, guitar accompaniments and the dances were highlighted by hand claps, castanet clacks and a mounting fusillade of heel taps.

The audience were thrilled and frequently joined in with the hand clapping until the final dance brought the show to an end.

"Well," said Alan Spencer, "Were you disappointed?"

A loud 'No' echoed round the theatre.

"And shall I try and get them back to dance and sing one more number."

An even louder 'Yes' boomed out.

The group appeared once more and danced and sang to a beautiful melodic piece of music ending with each dancer going off stage individually, to be finally followed by the guitarist.

*****

"Why didn't they play any tango music?" asked David, as he Karen, Julie and Craig came out of the theatre.

"Because, the tango is the national dance of Argentina, not Spain." replied Julie.

"I'd love to dance the tango with you Julie. Karen doesn't like dancing."

"He never misses a trick." responded Julie, "Why don't you drown him, Karen."

They wished each other good night and as Julie and Craig walked towards the staircase which would take them on to their cabin, Julie said, "I'm so relieved we don't have to endure their problems. David really is a pain."

"He certainly is," said Craig, "but we always knew it wasn't going to be easy taking a holiday with them."

"I know, but we really did it for Karen. She's such a lovely person. I really don't understand how she puts up with all his nonsense."

"I have no doubt," added Craig, "that sooner or later she's going to give him the push."

They had reached the cabin and as they entered Julie said, "Let's forget all about them. All I know is that I had a wonderful day today and I can't tell you how much I'm looking forward to going to Monte Carlo tomorrow."

*****

FIFTEEN

'On 8ᵗʰ *January, in the year twelve hundred and ninety seven, Francois Grimaldi took power of the Monaco fortress and so commenced the seven hundred years of a dynasty.*

'*During that night, a monk appeared at the gates of Monaco. Inconspicuously, Francois Grimaldi was let through. Barely having entered the enclosed grounds, the imposture monk threw himself over the guards.*

'*Apparently few were holding watch, and a full pledged attack was launched as the large Guelf troops, who had been hiding closely behind concealed by the darkness of the night, forced the gates before the guards could react*

'*By his actions, Francois Grimaldi forever engraved the family name on the flanks of Monaco's rock.*

'*I'm sure, as most of you are from England, you will be interested to know that the Grimaldis were part of the Guelf family group from Genoa and had twice been chased away from their city by another major family group called the Ghibellines.*

'*It was this historical saga that lead Shakespeare to write his play* Romeo and Juliet *with Romeo's family belonging to the Guelphs and Juliet's being members of the Ghibellines.*'

It subsequently became evident that this titbit of information was told by all of the guides as they journeyed with coach passengers from Nice to Monte Carlo.

Some of the cruise liners stop in Villefranche and others in Nice for this days sightseeing. Most of those who had booked tours had opted to see the magic of Monte Carlo and once again several coaches were available to cater for them. A further coach would be visiting the towering village of Eze with another bound for Cannes and the walled village of St. Paul de Vence.

This was the day that Joanne had been looking forward to so much and she could hardly sleep the night before. She, Dean and the children were first into the Ocean Bistro for breakfast, first in the lounge to obtain their coach ticket numbers and first again on the coach itself. Karen, David and their friends were on coach No.2 whilst Delia, Paul, Louise and Colin were allotted coach No.3.

Doreen and Laura knew it was most unlikely they would be able to do anything other than have a short walk in Nice later in the day as Doreen was appearing in the show that evening and rehearsals were required. Matt found himself in the same position being on the same bill.

The first week of the cruise had almost passed during which time a number of the passengers had got to know each other even though they were not sitting at the same dining table.

As a result Denise had decided to stroll round Nice with Phyllis and James and were to be accompanied by Anne and Vince, all three of the women wishing to visit the flower-market, whilst Roger had arranged to go with Ros, Andrew, Liz and Henry to the architectural group of buildings known as the Maeght Foundation that overlooks St. Paul.

The Foundation had been conceived as a museum park providing a setting for sculptures by Miro and Giacometti and others, whilst housed inside were paintings by Braque, Kandinsky, Chagall, Matisse and many more wonderful artists.

The Monaco bound coaches took the coastal road close to Europe's bluest sea passing places with the romantic names of Cap Ferrat and Beaulieu and it did not take passengers long to appreciate they were indeed on the French Riviera or Cote d'Azur, as it is called, a name conjured up in a French poem.

One by one the coaches drove into the vast underground car park in the centre of Monte Carlo, the capital of the Principality of Monaco, a sovereign state, of a mere eight square miles. Passengers then followed their guides, who were holding lollipop sticks bearing the number of their respective coach, to the elevators and escalators which took them up to the old city on the hill.

All those from the Neptune had arrived early enough to see the changing of the guard outside the Prince's Palace and would also have time to visit the Cathedral containing the tombs of Prince Rainier and Princess Grace and be able to continue with a guided tour of the narrow streets. Ample free time was also to be available with everyone under strict orders that they must be back in their coaches by no later than half-past three.

Karen over-heard David ask the guide the time the casino opened and was told two o'clock. She was not surprised, as, before having breakfast, she had noticed him open the cabin safe and remove his passport.

Whilst she and the others in Coach 2 commenced walking up the steps to the Cathedral, Craig asked the elderly lady who had been sitting on the opposite side of the aisle to him, whether she thought she would be able to manage as she held a walking stick in each of her hands.

"Oh, yes, I'll be fine, but thank you." she had responded.

He and Julie were not convinced and deliberately walked a short distance behind her. She slowly negotiated each step until three from the top she suddenly fell and slipped back four steps. They rushed towards her seeking to assist but heard the guides voice call, "Please leave her I'm coming."

The guide attended to her quickly and efficiently and said she would take her down the steps and find somewhere for her to rest until the Cathedral tour was over, a suggestion immediately dismissed by the guest.

Much to everyone else's amazement, after being helped up, she again walked step by step until she reached the top and then followed the group round the Cathedral.

Later she told Julie and Craig she was on the cruise with her daughter who, although aware there could be some difficult walking to negotiate, did not wish to go on this tour.

"What a lovely daughter to have" muttered Julie to Craig facetiously.

Once back down the steps the guide told the lady the incident would have to be reported adding she would have to visit the ship's doctor after they had returned. Thereafter, no further problem arose and she seemed to cope magnificently when they walked through the labyrinth of covered alleyways and tiny squares.

Having left the Cathedral, Craig said, "I've come to the conclusion a cruise is not just a holiday it's like a never ending exciting adventure. Each time we go somewhere else it's a wonderful experience of not only being able to see some marvellous sights but one is able to learn so much."

"And just think of all of the remaining places we'll be going to next week." added Julie.

The different groups kept on crossing each other's path enabling chit-chat to take place in relation to what was being seen. Joanne's children had delighted in seeing the palace guards perform their intricate marching manoeuvres when the ceremony of changing the guard took place. They were not quite so impressed with the Cathedral but before they went in, Dean told them all about Grace Kelly, which certainly produced an element of interest.

"Now don't forget everyone," Joanne told the other three, "this is my treat so we can do or have whatever you want." After the Cathedral visit, they told the guide they wanted to go and do their own thing and would be back at the coach as asked.

This was the signal for them to see as much of Monte Carlo as possible subject to the periodic stop for burgers and chips and ice-creams plus on one occasion a wonderful French crepe with the children having theirs with strawberry jam whilst she and Dean had them flambéed with Cointreau.

When they came to the casino Dean did an impersonation of a former well-known English singer who always included in his programme the song, 'I'm the man who broke the bank at Monte Carlo.' The children laughed as he sang and did a little dance. Joanne was also not only amused but delighted that they both got on so well with Dean.

And so their wonderful day continued until it was time to return to the coach.

"That was absolutely great, Joanne, thanks a lot," said Dean, "I hope it didn't cost you too much."

"Nothing I couldn't cope with and I must say it certainly helped when the school agreed not to fine me for taking the kids away. That could have been a hundred pounds down the drain and look what we've all had instead."

Meanwhile, feeling some pangs of hunger coming on, Paul asked Colin whether they fancied having some lunch.

"Normally, we would," Colin replied, "but as time is limited here, Louise said she'd prefer to skip a sit-down lunch and grab a baguette and some coffee as we chase about the place. You go ahead and we'll see you back on the coach."

As Paul and Delia continued walking along he said, "I can't tell you how good it is to be able to wake up each morning and be able to clearly remember the events of the previous day. I owe so much to you for everything you've done to help me."

She squeezed his arm then pointing to a brasserie said "that looks just the job." The waiters were wearing white shirts, black bow ties, dark trousers and pocketed aprons in a dark red, almost crimson colour. The tables all bore check table cloths with blue and white squares. On the table was a semi-cylindrical condiment holder with glass salt and pepper pots and a taller oil and vinegar glass container set between.

The heat of the sun beat down on Paul's forehead. He pulled out a small tube of suntan cream from the pocket of his shirt and smeared some across his nose and cheeks. In the distance they could hear church bells chiming one.

A menu fixe was brought to them together with a carafe of water and a basket of French bread. They selected their meal quickly and started to nibble away at the bread.

"It really is unbelievable how in England restaurants sometimes treat bread or rolls like gold-dust." said Paul, "they give you one piece and then disappear and if you should ask for a second it's as if you've committed a crime. Here in France you can have as much as you like and nobody gives it a second thought."

The atmosphere of the restaurant could only be found in France. Paul sat looking at the faces of the numerous people who were seated for lunch knowing that the manner in which the French clearly demonstrated how much they relished their food was enough to make anyone feel hungry.

Once more the church bells struck. Obviously set on the quarter-hour, he thought. They had thrown dieting to the wind. An enormous tureen arrived with moules frites that were delicious. They were pleased they had scorned a starter. The portion for two was enough for four but neither were bothered and in due course all that was left were the empty shells.

Delia then had a raspberry ice-cream whilst Paul settled on a passion fruit sorbet. The cost of the entire meal together with two black coffees and including service was a pittance compared with meals in England.

"I could just about get a poached egg on toast and a cup of tea at home with the money I've paid here." he said.

At the same time as they had been lunching, Karen, Julie, David and Craig had been eating in a restaurant which David had selected, knowing it was not far from the casino. He frequently looked at his watch and when it showed one-fifty he stood up and announced he'd like to pop over and take a look at the famous casino and would see them at three-thirty. He placed on the table enough Euros to cover their half the bill and within seconds had disappeared.

"He certainly likes to gamble," said Craig, "has he always done so?"

"Always," replied Karen, "even on our honeymoon."

"It sounds as though he may be addicted," commented Julie, "the gambling syndrome can be as serious as alcoholism."

"I know I can't stand much more of his gambling, womanising and tantrums. My problem is I just don't know whether I'm strong enough to make the break."

"It won't be easy," said Craig, "but you can't go on like you are. It's hanging over you like the sword of Damocles and until you make a final decision you won't find any peace."

They were all seated in the coach waiting to make the return journey to Nice. The only outstanding passenger was David, who arrived just after three thirty-five looking annoyed, red-faced and hot and bothered. He apologised to the guide saying he'd lost his way, walked to his seat next to Karen, sat down, shut his eyes and fell asleep.

Once again she had no doubt of the result of his activities. It was simply a question of how much he had lost.

*****

It was almost lunchtime when rehearsals ended in preparation for the evening show and the three leads went to the Ocean Bistro for lunch.

"I'm going to abandon you two lovely ladies." said Matt, "I'm not feeling at my most sociable and I think it would be best if I just go on shore, call my wife and come back to the ship. I hope you'll forgive me."

Doreen and Laura felt very relaxed as they started wandering round Nice.

"I've been looking at a local map," said Laura, "if we walk round to the far side of the harbour we'll come to the Promenade des Anglais and…"

"Promenade des Anglais, what's that?" interrupted Doreen.

"It's the main promenade that goes along the sea-front and has palm trees and flower beds and obtained it's name when Nice became very popular because Queen Victoria frequently stayed here. But I would also like us to go and have tea at the Hotel Negresco. My aunt told me it's absolutely delightful. I gather it really is something out of the past. Probably be a little pricey – but we're not having to pay for much on the ship."

When at the hotel, Doreen turned to Laura and asked, "So tell me more?"

"What do you mean?" replied Laura.

"You know - you and Roger."

"There's nothing to tell. He's a very nice man and we had a lunch together."

"Okay, I'll say no more but my instincts tell me to 'watch this space'" responded Doreen with a grin over her face.

*****

Whereas the dress code for the previous evening had been casual, tonight it was informal. The women wore either dresses or blouses with skirts or trousers whilst the men were supposed to wear a jacket with either shirt and tie or an open-neck sports shirt. Vince and Paul had made the latter choice, Andrew was in his formal naval doctor's uniform whilst fashionable Henry appeared in a smart blue blazer, white shirt, neat maroon coloured tie and light grey trousers.

"I could fall for you, if I didn't know you better." Liz said to him with a laugh.

"And I might join in proceedings, if I didn't know you better." replied Henry, putting his arm round her shoulders and giving her a light peck on the cheek.

"Where did you and Vince go to today?" Liz asked Anne.

"We had a lovely time. We first made for the flower market. It was wonderful and my word what an array of blooms and shrubs. Everything was bursting with colour and life. There was also a flea market with some antique dealers oozing with French charm. It was buzzing with activity with both locals and tourists. Then we had a long walk into the centre of Old Nice and visited La Cathedrale Sainte-Reparate which was built to honour the patron saint of Nice. After that we had lunch and finally went off to the Musee des Beaux-Arts.

"It was really good. It has a marvellous art collection with works by Renoir, Degas, Monet and Picasso. By the time we arrived back on ship my back was numb, my feet felt and looked unrecognisable and I collapsed on my bed and fell asleep. But it had been a really terrific day."

"Another satisfied customer." said Henry, "We too tasted the cultural delicacies of Nice. Is that not right, Andrew?"

"Yes, indeed it is." responded Andrew, and then addressing the others at the table proceeded to tell them of their visit to the Maeght Foundation.

"I must say that Picasso has always intrigued me," said Henry, "apart from his brilliant paintings and sculpture, his personal life was quite something. Did you know his first wife, Olga, was a Russian ballerina? He never seemed to have been happy with her and was extremely promiscuous and was always picking up new girls.

"It was though he was searching for someone very special and he seemed to find her when he was forty-five. She was only seventeen but she was his greatest love for the next nine or ten years. It is said she told a story of what had happened when they first met. Apparently he told her that she had an interesting face and he'd like to do a portrait of her adding '*I'm sure we're going to do great things together. I'm Picasso.*'

"She told him she'd never heard of him so he took her to a book shop and showed her a book that had been written about him.

"How's that for a pick-up line. I really admire him."

"You men," said Ros, "always like little boys who never grow up."

"But we can be so adorable, ma cherie." responded Henry.

*****

Dinner ended and those in the second sitting who chose to do so made their way to the theatre.

The first part of the show was 'Doreen singing Gershwin' and the audience loved listening to the songs many of which were well known to all including I Got Rhythm, The Man I Love, excerpts from Porgy and Bess and others.

She was followed by Matt who again gave a very professional performance that had the audience baffled with his tricks, laughing at his jokes and delighted at his song and dance routine - without knowing how he was really feeling.

*****

When back in their cabin, Karen decided it was time to tell David how annoyed she was with him.

"I'm sick to death of your constant gambling. Every night you're off to the casino and today in Monte Carlo was an absolute embarrassment. I knew we should never have agreed to come on this trip but I really thought you'd behave yourself being with Julie and Craig. We're supposed to be together and you're always disappearing. What do you reckon they're thinking about you?"

"Who cares, you're just too over-sensitive." he replied, "Anyway, what on earth's wrong with a fellow having an occasional flutter?"

"An 'occasional flutter'!" repeated Karen, "Don't make me laugh. If it was an 'occasional flutter' I'd never say a word but it isn't and there's just no stopping you. Goodness knows how much you've been losing."

"And who says I've been losing?" he responded in an angry tone of voice.

"I know you only too well." Continued Karen, "If you'd been winning the whole world would have known about it. How much longer do you think I'm going to put up with all of your nonsense? I've warned you before, David. Don't push me too far."

"Push you too far. You talk such rot. You don't know when you're well off."

"That's your opinion and don't think for one moment I haven't seen you coming-on to Julie. You're absolutely pathetic. Do you really believe she's interested in you? Unlike some of us, she's happily married and does not appreciate a creep like you bothering her."

David's face reddened. He took two steps towards her and for a brief second she thought he was going to hit her until he suddenly turned away saying, "Screw you, I'm going back to the casino." He opened the cabin door then slammed it shut.

Karen began to cry and only wished the cruise was at an end - but she knew she would have to endure a further week. Seven more long days during which time......

*****

SIXTEEN

Islands have a special attraction to those who have been born on an island and lived on an island. Being surrounded by water can be welcoming and healing and being close to the seas that encircle the land mass can be peaceful and comforting.

Today the Neptune was to be in port at the only island it would be visiting on this cruise, Sardinia, the most mountainous island of the Mediterranean. Sea birds were already awake with some swirling round the ship before soaring upwards to the skies above until with a twist and turn they would plunge back towards earthly parts. The vessel had berthed in Alghero by six-thirty and would be leaving at two. Two varying island tours were scheduled with the less adventurous able to visit the capital city.

The daily announcement from Alan Spencer came at seven forty-five, a little earlier than usual, initially hoping that all passengers had enjoyed a good night's sleep.

"It's a beautiful day here in Sardinia," he continued, "with the temperature already registering twenty three degrees. The ship has now been cleared by the authorities and you will be able to go ashore in about fifteen minutes. Please remember that the ship will be sailing at two o'clock so all of you must be back on board by one fifteen.

"This afternoon we have an exciting programme for you with at two o'clock, Martin West, giving an exciting talk which he calls 'Welcome to Italy'. This will be followed at three by our own Shelley Masters who will be giving another of her port lectures and then at four, Colin Price, will be telling all of you art enthusiasts about 'The Post-impressionists.' All three of these talks will be in theatre.

"At two-fifteen, Phyllis and James, will be continuing their series of watercolour workshops in the Apollo lounge and at three dance lessons will be available in the Trident lounge where your hosts Peter and Robert will be ready to tread on your toes (followed by a chuckle).....I didn't mean it boys.

"And then at four-thirty we have one of your favourites – B-I-N-G-O yes Bingo.

"This evening you will have to put your glad rags on at another formal night and this evening's show is called 'Music, music, music' – songs from the shows featuring our own singers, dancers and orchestra.

"What a great day and night ahead and so, as they say somewhere – 'have a good one'."

Anne and Vince had been listening to this broadcast whilst in their cabin.

"I cannot believe that today is the start of the second week." she said, "It's been a fabulous holiday. I'm only sorry that I've probably held you back from seeing some of the places you'd have liked to visit."

"I haven't been bothered in the slightest," he replied, "and after today there's Naples and Rome, and I went to both of those in the dim and distant past, and Gibraltar which we'll be seeing together. The one thing I'm delighted about is that the cruise has done us both the world of good. You seem so much better and I really believe it will be a good idea for you to accept an appointment as a CAB volunteer when we get back home."

*****

Phyllis and James had arranged to go with Shirley and Martin on the Costa Smeralda tour which was scheduled to take them to Porto Cervo.

"At last, at last." said James, as they waited to board the coach.

"At last, what?" asked Phyllis.

"At last we're about to visit somewhere I haven't been to before."

"What can I do with him?" Phyllis asked the other two.

"Just ignore him, is my advice." replied Shirley.

"You've got no chance, James, they're already ganging up on you." commented Martin. "Mind you, we've never been here before, either. Did you know the Aga Khan was caught at sea here in nineteen sixty-five and took refuge along this coast. He fell in love with the island's beauty and was responsible for building Porto Cervo into the resort it is today."

"And I read," James said, "that the revolutionary hero Garibaldi, though being born in Nice, served in the Sardinian navy. How's that for a piece of useless information?"

"Fits in quite nicely with lots of other useless information you come up with." responded Phyllis.

As the coach left Alghero, the guide indicated that a little further north, there was a concentration of prehistoric tombs carved into the hillside with their chambers connected by corridors.

The journey was delightful as they passed through startling rugged landscape and saw some beautiful beaches with white sand and small pieces of pink granite. The waters were clear and countless indentations and promontories could be seen.

Arriving in Porto Cervo they were given an hour under their own steam to see the marina, the shops and anything else that appealed. After wandering around for about thirty minutes they agreed 'coffee called' and settled into four chairs, shaded from the sun by a large colourfully decorated umbrella.

"Have you been enjoying the cruise?" asked Phyllis.

"We, have as it happens," said Shirley, "though it's quite interesting to note how things are always changing nowadays."

"In what way?" James asked.

"Well, first of all it's unbelievable when you speak to passengers and discover the vast differential that often arises between, for example, two couples having the same accommodation on the same deck. There's no doubt that, since so many ships are now owned by one major group, it really has become a 'bum's on seats' policy and I feel very sorry for those who pay the advertised reduced brochure prices and then find last minute bookers have had their cabin prices reduced substantially.

"Then on most ships the shows are nowhere near as good as they used to be with the resident company being used over and over again. There are many times I've found them to be rather amateurish and I doubt if most of them would ever find themselves employed in a West End production."

"I agree with you there," said James, "and I also find the food is not as good as it used to be on some ships. There's always plenty of it but for a lot of passengers it's quality and not quantity that counts."

"That's for sure." agreed Martin, "It's very obvious at the poolside restaurants – in fact, wherever there is buffet-style service."

"That's why we prefer to have breakfast in the dining room." said Phyllis, "I've also noticed the on-board shops have very little to offer and in fact some of the goods are really very poor."

"Nevertheless I still believe cruises provide great value for a holiday when you analyse what is included in the overall price - but how long it lasts is another matter."

"Why do you say that?" asked James.

"I think too many ships have been built and it only needs a recession and the shipping lines are either going to reduce the services they provide or alternatively lower their prices even more. One way or the other something has to give. It'll be interesting to see what happens, but it certainly has become cruising for the masses."

As they began to make their way back to the coach, Shirley turned to Martin and said, "There's that woman with the red book."

"What woman's that?" asked Phyllis.

"Haven't you noticed her, wherever she is, either on or off the ship, she's always carrying that red folder."

"No, I don't think I've seen her before, how odd."

*****

Shortly after two in the afternoon The Neptune slowly pulled away from its berth as locals and dockside workers stood waving at the passengers, whilst a small group of musicians started to play their farewell music. It was a fascinating sight as the buildings became smaller and smaller, with a local church now appearing as though from a Lego construction kit, cars and bicycles looking as if from a match box set, distant people seeming like Lilliputian characters and the background scenery slowly fading.

The Sardinians were now simply continuing their lives since nothing had changed. This was just another day when yet another cruise liner had taken up temporary residence disgorging hundreds of people and then sailing off with them again.

Karen had seen very little of David since the previous evening. In the morning he had been sleeping heavily when she had got out of bed, showered and walked into Alghero with Craig and Julie. She was now looking forward to today's watercolour workshop but decided to first visit the library to see a copy of the news letter.

The only other person there was Louise who was busily re-arranging books of every description.

"You've got your work cut out." commented Karen.

"I know but there's no rush."

"Are you enjoying yourself?" asked Karen.

"I certainly am and who wouldn't, it's marvellous and I've met some lovely people. I volunteered for this job and it's given me the opportunity of going on a number of tours. I work in a library at home. That's really how it came about. Your friend Julie is delightful, isn't she?"

"Yes, she is." said Karen, "I've been working in a book shop for years in Aylesbury. We also sell some classical music. There's something really special about working with books. It's as though they become personal friends. In fact, there are times when I don't really want to see a book sold and taken away by somebody else."

"I understand what you mean," commented Louise, "at least with a library, generally speaking, the books come back to us."

"We'll talk again. It's not always easy over dinner." said Karen, "I must say I think Colin is a real dish. Have you got your eye on him?"

"Well, I wouldn't go that far but as you say he's really very nice and I love listening to his talks."

"That reminds me," said Karen, "I must fly. I'm due at the watercolour workshop any minute now. I'll see you later"

At the same time that Louise and Karen were in the library, Craig had been sitting in the internet room checking emails and dealing with some items of office work when he noticed Roger come into the room.

They hadn't really spoken but simply knew each other by sight.

"Hallo," said Roger, "I'll try not to disturb you."

"Oh, don't worry, I'm almost finished. I just like to keep in touch with things at home whilst I'm away."

"What do you do?" asked Roger.

"I'm a computer programmer," replied Craig, "it gets pretty complicated from time to time but at least I have a partner to talk to when I find myself stuck. You know the expression – two heads are better than one."

"I certainly do. I had a partner but unfortunately he died – killed in a motor accident."

"That must have been awful for you and his family." said Craig.

"It certainly was, but tell me more about your activities."

Craig told him the sort of work he did, the type of companies he acted for and how he and his partner had gradually built up their company over a period of seven years and were now looking for potential situations which would enable them to expand.

Roger appeared more and more interested and asked many searching questions of Craig. He told him of his own business operations and how he too was looking to expand his interests.

"Let me give you one of my cards." said Roger, "Please give me a call when we're all back to the grind. I'd like you to come up and see my offices and have a further chat. I've a feeling you may be able to help us in a number of areas. I can't promise anything but at least I'll give you a good lunch"

"Well thanks very much," replied Craig, "I'll do just that."

*****

"Gosh, you really are getting quite a suntan." observed Delia, "It certainly suits you and reflects the sparkle in your eyes which has re-appeared."

"It's interesting you noticed that – about the eyes – I had thought the same thing and then decided perhaps it was my imagination." replied Paul.

"Not at all," said Delia, "whilst you were having your treatment and before, your eyes had become grey and almost lifeless but that look has now completely disappeared and this trip is certainly doing you a power of good."

"Thanks to you being so supportive." he said, "I wanted to tell you I've had an idea for an article."

"Tell me more." she replied.

"Being at sea has made me think of it and I've decided to call it 'It's a beautiful world but…..'." said Paul.

"It sounds interesting. What are you proposing to write about?"

"I want to take the theme that everything in nature provides us with our beautiful world but frequently it is people and the way in which they make others suffer that represents the 'but' – it is the good and evil syndrome expressed in a different way."

"I shall look forward to reading it." said Delia.

*****

Louise sat fascinated as Colin gave his talk which was dominated by his providing wonderful power-point copies of paintings by Cezanne, Gauguin and Van Gogh.

He had an ability to hold his audience's attention throughout and often told stories of the lives of the painters which explained some of the personal problems and difficulties they had been experiencing at the time of painting a particular subject.

Louise let her mind wander back to the earlier comment made by Karen and thought to herself, *'She's right. He is rather dishy.'*

*****

The penguins and their partners started to appear from five-thirty onwards. Once more this was formal night and many took advantage of the situation by making it very special in their own way. They wanted another photograph for the family back home, it was a time to reminisce over events in the past when they had donned dinner suit and evening dress, it was an excuse to have a glass of champagne and above all it was a chance to once more elevate themselves out of their normal environment.

At dinner the others could all detect the strained atmosphere existing between Karen and David. She decided to try and ignore his petulance and carry on as if nothing had happened.

"I really enjoyed your talk very much indeed." she told Colin, "I've always been fascinated with Van Gogh and not just with his chopping his ear off, although that was horrendous."

"Thank you, so many painters and writers and musicians had very unhappy lives," Colin commented, "with death of family and loved ones or illness bringing untold pain and suffering. I'm surprised they were able to create the amazing works they left to the world."

"Huh." commented David, in a rather supercilious tone.

"You don't agree?" asked Colin, endeavouring to be extremely polite.

"No, I don't agree." said David, rattling out the words as though from an automatic pistol, "Impressionism, post-impressionism, cubism, expressionism, it's all a lot of mumbo-jumbo. All of you art fellows are the same. You pride yourselves in being elitists so that the rest of us can feel ignoramuses.

"It's the same with music critics. They might just as well write their critiques in Chinese. The majority of people haven't a clue what they're trying to say. You all make me sick."

"For God's sake, David, what's got into you?" said Karen, looking totally embarrassed by this unexpected outburst.

"That's okay, Karen." said Colin, again trying to pretend nothing very much had happened, "David's entitled to his opinion, even though it might have been rather excessively expressed. Quite often we tend to be greatly influenced by our teachers who manipulate our minds with some terrible discriminating thoughts that last us most of our lives. Then parents can frequently add to the confusion should they not know any better about a particular subject. Once we reach adulthood we just have to forget all these outside influences and think for ourselves and hopefully decide with a touch of wisdom."

"Well, I've heard enough for one evening." said David, as he got up from his chair and left the dining-room.

Karen excused herself and followed him. Nobody was in any doubt what was likely to follow between them.

"I feel so sorry for her," said Julie, "it was Craig and me who suggested they joined us on the cruise hoping it might make things better between them."

"There's nothing you can do." said Louise, "They are the only two people who can sort out their problems."

Then turning to Lucy and Joel she added, "Most marriages are a great success so just ignore all the antics of this evening."

All at the table concentrated their discussions on the honeymooners finding out how they had met, where they were living and the jobs they did.

Gradually, they all put the previous incident behind them, enjoyed their meal and generally had a good time, though inwardly Julie was still very concerned about Karen.

*****

Joanne, Dean and the kids had all gone to the first showing of 'Music, music, music' and had loved listening to the songs from the shows, some of which they had seen. The children became very excited when numbers from Oliver and the Sound of Music were featured and they were all sorry when the show came to an end.

"You take the children to bed and I'll meet you in the cocktail lounge." said Dean.

Joanne joined him about twenty minutes later and was surprised to find that on the table where he was sitting stood a half-bottle of champagne in an ice-bucket.

"My, my," commented Joanne, "what's all that about?"

"Special occasions warrant champers, is what I've always been told."

"That's as maybe, but as there isn't any special occasion it seems to me you've just found an excuse for us to once again enjoy ourselves."

"Well, you may think it's not special, but I happen to know it is." said Dean.

"Now what are you talking about?" asked Joanne.

"Just this." Dean replied, as he felt into his pocket, pulled out a ring box, opened it, handed it to her and asked, "Will you marry me?"

Joanne sat mesmerized. "I can't believe it." she said.

"Well, will you?"

"Yes, yes and yes again" she said jumping out of her seat onto his lap to give him a big kiss and hug.

People standing nearby began to realise what was happening and started to applaud and offer their congratulations. The cocktail stewardess opened the bottle and poured the champagne.

Dean raised his glass towards Joanne saying, "To us, to the kids and to the remainder of the cruise. I love you to bits my darling."

*****

SEVENTEEN

Joanne could not wait to tell her children of Dean's proposal and to show them the ring he had bought her. They both seemed thrilled and Lucy immediately asked whether that meant she would be stopping her nail and manicure work.

"No, it doesn't," she said, "Dean and I still have to work to pay for all of the things you and Olly need, pay for all the food we have, our clothes and everything else."

Olly did not seem interested in this part of the conversation and simply asked "So what are we going to do today?"

"Today we're in Naples in Italy and we're going out and will have a lot of fun and I will buy you both the biggest ice-cream you've ever had." replied Dean.

"Yippee." they announced in unison.

"We might even see Poppa Piccolino." said Joanne.

"Who's that?" asked Olly.

"Who's that?" repeated Dean, "Well I'll tell you."

And immediately he burst into a short song and dance routine singing:

'All over Italy they know his concertina,
Poppa Piccolino, Poppa Piccolino;
He plays so prettily to ev'ry signorina,
Poppa Piccolino from sunny Italy.'

Both of the children were in fits of laughter until Lucy asked, "What's a sinora?"

"The word is Sig-nor-ina," replied Joanne, "and it means a young lady."

"Right let's go," said Dean, "we must take a look at the Bay of Naples."

*****

Many excursions were scheduled from Naples including one to the Island of Capri. Roger had already asked Laura to go with him and Doreen was quite content to go back on board ship after sightseeing round that part of the city which was close to where it was berthed.

"I'm fine." Doreen had commented, "Don't worry about me. I'm sure you two love birds will have a lovely day."

"Love birds!" responded Laura, "now, now."

"Oh yes, I forgot," said Doreen with a grin, "You're just good friends."

The most popular tour was the one which would be taking passengers to Pompeii and two days previously Karen had made arrangements to go with Liz, Henry, Ros and Andrew since neither David nor Julie or Craig had wanted to go. During his morning greeting, the cruise director had warned it would be very hot on the grounds at Pompeii, as it was sited in an exposed area, and all taking this trip should be well covered and make sure they were using a high factor of sun cream.

Their tour guide was a handsome Italian who oozed charm and immediately made a great fuss of all of the ladies. As the coach continued its journey he told the passengers,

"Pompeii nestles at the foot of Mount Vesuvius and is still a virtually intact 1st century AD Roman town, complete with shops, temples and public buildings. It was the devastating earthquake in 79 AD, coupled with a thunderous cloud of ash and lava exploding from the summit of Mount Vesuvius that caused one of the greatest Italian catastrophes. It was entombed for centuries and it wasn't until 1748 that Pompeii was rediscovered.

When we come to Pompeii, I would like to suggest that as you take your first steps on the grounds you stop for a few moments and let your imagination tell a story. Imagine that the people of those days are all around you dressed in the clothing of that period and imagine the hustle and bustle of them as they carry out their normal business and trading activities.

Imagine them talking to their friends, selling their wares and playing with their children and imagine the soldiers of that time, carrying swords and shields, as they mingle with the crowds.

By imagining all of these things and any others you can think of, you will be creating a living space which may become a reality, as opposed to simply looking at stone and marble relics. Just try it and see if I'm right.'

"He is right you know." Henry whispered to Liz.

On getting off the coach they found many street vendors standing by stalls with an array of goods for sale including numerous books about Pompeii, one of which contained

247

transparent overlays, by way of graphic reconstructions, of the monuments and ancient buildings. Karen was fascinated and immediately bought a copy.

It was indeed very hot and most of the passengers found the walk quite tiring At one point Karen noticed the elderly lady who had fallen over in Monte Carlo, who was struggling to keep up with everybody, as she gingerly took each step with the aid of her walking sticks. Once again her 'darling daughter' was no where to be seen.

This was a trip worth waiting for and Andrew, in particular, was absolutely thrilled. There could be no doubt that all those visiting the site were finding it far better than they ever had thought it would be. They were now able to take a look at everyday Roman life as it had existed at the time of the tragedy.

Just wandering the streets of Pompeii was a fascinating experience with the best preserved villa, Casa dei Vetti, receiving deserved admiration for its atrium, frescoed walls and gardens.

After they had been walking for nearly one and a half hours, Karen and Liz decided to make their way to the entrance area and obtain some cold drinks. The other three continued agreeing to meet them later.

"You have been looking rather preoccupied," Liz said to Karen, "are you okay?"

"Well, yes and no," replied Karen, "yes, in the sense I'm not ill, no, in relation to my marriage."

"Do you want to talk about it?" asked Liz.

Karen felt the empathy passing from Liz and told her the entire story.

"It's just getting worse and although I know I can't go on and on as things are, I'm just uncertain as to what I should do."

"Many of us have been there," said Liz, "including me, and you really have to make up your mind as to whether you are prepared to hang in there or feel it's time to call it a day and move on."

"I'm sure you're right," said Karen, "may I ask what happened with you?"

"I was born in Durham, one of five children. My mother died when I was seven and so my aunt, that's my father's unmarried sister, moved into our house to look after us. It was never the same after that. My aunt was very strict and our best day was always Sunday when dad wasn't working. He gave all of that day to us children and we all loved him for doing so. He had the ability to spontaneously create interesting things for us to do together, whether indoors or out.

"I was married at twenty-eight and moved to Chester where Clifford, my husband, was in partnership. He was a surveyor. We didn't have a very exciting life. Chester was pleasant enough but it tends to be rather boring if you live there all the time. Clifford was eight years older than I, quite a good-looking guy really, but somehow he didn't seem to have many outside interests and turned out to be rather dull.

"He frequently tended to get depressed until after several years his depressions became worse. His doctor gave him pills but they didn't seem to help. About fourteen years ago his mother died and left him a cottage in Wales. Don't misunderstand me, I love Wales, the scenery is gorgeous but this place was in the middle of nowhere, approximately fifteen miles from Llandrindod Wells.

"Holidays had never been high on Clifford's agenda and for the first few years of our marriage, all he wanted to do was to go to Minorca. Have you ever been there?"

"No, I haven't," replied Karen, "is it nice?"

"It's not bad," continued Liz, "and indeed very pleasant round by the port at Mahon but jeepers you can almost see the entire island in under a day and there's very little to do. Clifford liked it so much that he commenced taking a Spanish conversational course at an evening school in Chester.

"Anyway, as I said, along came the cottage and we had four consecutive year's holidays there. I hated it, nothing whatsoever to do, with Clifford not wanting to do a thing. I felt as though I would have been better off at home. I was shopping, cleaning, doing the laundry, ironing and carrying out all of the other usual domestic chores...hardly a picnic! Clifford simply rested then rested some more then read and read some more and then walked and walked some more. In fact all he wanted out of any holiday was to rest, read and walk. He never once lifted a finger to help me.

"When we arrived for the third year, we discovered that a woman artist from Madrid had moved into a similar cottage about quarter of a mile down the road. We were on the usual smiling and nodding acquaintanceship until Clifford commenced trotting out some of his Spanish phrases. One evening she invited us in for drinks and showed us some of her paintings. She was pretty good.

"I thought she was about thirty and resembled the sort of gal who you'd imagine could play the role of Carmen. Bit of a fireball, I guess. Clifford seemed to take to her. You know the way women can tell these things! I was rather surprised. Never thought he had it in him.

"We saw her from time to time and that was that. The following year we had a big set to, since Clifford wanted to go back to the cottage and I didn't. Eventually, we struck a deal. One more year in Wales and the following year he'd take me to France. So off we went.

"And guess what, Senorita Carmen was also there. A further tepid contact was politely made and nothing else. It was in the middle of the second week that Clifford went out on one of his many walks. When it began to get dark and he hadn't returned home, I went outside to look down the lane. There was no sign of him and it then occurred to me that perhaps he'd been nobbled by the senorita, so I decided to walk down the road to her cottage.

"The only light that showed was in the small sitting room at the front of the building. As I went towards the main wooden door I could see them both humping away as if the world was about to come to an end."

"What on earth did you do?" asked Karen excitedly.

"I crept back up the lane and returned to our place and waited for him. It was almost half-hour later when he arrived and told me he'd been for a long walk, forgot the time and found himself a little lost when walking home.

"I remember repeating those words to him 'forgot the time'. I was standing in the kitchen and I just looked at him and said,

'Andrew, do you know what rhymes with fuck?' His face reddened and before he could say anything further I went on, 'Well let me tell you, 'Duck', and with that I threw a frozen duck at him which I'd taken out of the freezer. It caught him on top of his shoulder. He really felt it.

"Me, I got out of the cottage, with a suitcase that I'd already packed, jumped into the car and drove back to Chester."

Karen could not contain herself and burst out laughing.

"I'm sorry," she giggled, "I shouldn't really laugh, but it is rather funny the way that you tell it. You are undoubtedly quite a character compared with me. I suppose I'm just very ordinary."

"Ordinary, ordinary," repeated Liz, "why ordinary? You're far from ordinary. Forget that for a start. You're unique, as we all are."

"Have you been divorced long?" asked Karen.

"Getting on for seven years now - but don't cry for me Argentina. I've been having a ball. I'm convinced when women are encompassed within a long marriage they are not truly known to either their partners or themselves. It's only as you get older you begin to find out who you really are.

"You know the phrase, someone's daughter, someone's wife and someone's mother, then, at about forty you began to wonder "who am I?". You suddenly fear not being a person in your own right. The women I detest most are those who sit at home pretending all is well.

"They are so miserable it just isn't true but they haven't got the spunk to pick up their asses and get out there. They are so f....... scared of treading a path alone they wait for a miracle to happen, and it never does."

Karen had sat intently listening to Liz. She was unable to take in so much in one sitting but believed the sincerity of this woman.

"How do you think divorce has affected you, Liz?' asked Karen.

Liz thought and replied, "I think that one of the difficulties is, there is a loss of status when you become divorced, since you are no longer part of a couple and that in itself shuts many doors.

"Women become so bruised from a previous marriage, that, although they want another serious relationship, it is feared and in consequence as soon as a man gets too close they often turn and run."

"But surely both men and women are hesitant to commit themselves for a second time" retorted Karen.

"That's true, but so many women are insecure." replied Liz, "It is an insecurity that has either been created during childhood or frequently generated by the men they have loved, during either a marriage or long relationship. They are in reality vulnerable and cannot allow that vulnerability to become evident. So they hide – hide some thoughts, hide some emotions and hide their own true selves behind an imaginary barricade or barrier for fear the vulnerability cracks will show, like loose pointing in a brick wall."

Karen was looking sad and started to become tearful. Liz noticed that twice or three times she had placed a hand to her face and eye.

"Get it out of your system, Karen. Don't bottle up your emotions." said Liz, "You cannot expect to become a whole person again within five minutes. It takes time, but stay with it and it will happen."

Karen knew she would look forward to talking further to Liz. They were so different and yet how different were people in reality, she thought.

Suddenly Karen saw the others coming towards them and said, "Thanks so much, Liz. You really have helped me."

"Anytime you want another chat don't be shy, just look out for me." replied Liz, with a smile that seemed to say *'you can do it kid.'*

"I guess you've all had enough" said Liz to the others, as they slumped on to the chairs next to them.

"I must have a drink," said Henry, "non-alcoholic I might add."

Having all been refreshed they made their way back on to the coach. Within minutes all, but one person was on board. Some quickly fell asleep from their exertions on the site. Departure time arrived and at that exact moment 'the bruiser' from other tours arrived, carrying his camera, guide book and large bottle of water. He looked at his watch and muttered "dead on time" and walked through the coach to a seat at the back.

"He's just one of the world's loners," remarked Andrew to Ros, "there are thousands like him. They enjoy life in their own way and rarely do anyone any harm."

*****

David, Julie and Craig had wandered round the same area of Naples as Joanne and Dean but the heat had got to them and they had returned to the ship for an early lunch after which Craig said he was going up to the internet room.

Julie and David went out to the pool deck and found three chairs. Julie placed as much sun cream on herself as she could, then stretched out on the chair lying down on her stomach.

"David," she said, "could you put some cream on my back, please?"

From the moment he touched her she realised how stupid she had been to ask him. Initially all was well as he rubbed the cream into the central part of her back but then he started to reach the bottom half of her two piece and with finger tips only, endeavoured to erotically place some cream in that area.

"Cut it out, David." she said.

"What on earth are you talking about, Julie?" he responded.

"You know damn well. Now give me back the cream and go and sit on your own chair. I've told you before, I'm not in the slightest bit interested in you and I would have thought you would be better employed in behaving yourself for the rest of the cruise and stop upsetting Karen. Equally stop bothering me in this way. I don't like your advances and don't want them."

Craig returned a few minutes later. "Everything okay with you two?" he asked.

"It certainly is." replied Julie.

"Good. Do you fancy some table tennis, David?" said Craig.

As the two of them walked off, Julie muttered under her breath *'What a creep.'*

Laura and Roger had taken the ferry to Capri, from the dock which was near to where the ship was berthed. The waters of the Bay of Naples were like a mill pond reflecting the deep blue of the skies and dappled with the rays of the sun. It did not take long for them to arrive at this tiny island paradise with its lush vegetation and welcoming climate.

There were already a long line of people waiting for the funicular to take them up to the main town set atop limestone cliffs and Roger suggested they should take a taxi instead of waiting around in the heat.

Laura found the town delightful and enjoyed walking along the narrow lanes and in the tiny squares and later taking the footpaths of the island which provided wonderful views of the cliff-edged sea. She was more than comfortable finding Roger had taken her hand and they continued hand in hand or arm in arm for the remainder of the day.

As they returned to the mainland, Roger told her this had been the loveliest day he had been able to enjoy for years. Laura stroked his face placed her warm soft lips on his cheek and then fully responded as he kissed her on the mouth.

"It's been a great day for me too, Roger," she said, "I'm so pleased I've met you."

She again kissed him exhibiting considerable feeling, and added, "I'm pleased it's only you and I who are going to Tarquinia tomorrow. Doreen wanted to go to Rome and has arranged to be there with Denise."

"That's wonderful," he said, "the more time we can have together the better I'll like it."

It had not surprised passengers when they had read in the day's bulletin that this evening was to be casual dress with an Italian theme. The dining staff had placed small Italian flags in holders on each of the tables and larger Italian flags had been installed outside the entrance doors to the theatre. The menus were predominantly of Italian food dishes and many Italian wines were on offer.

As guests appeared prior to dinner, Italian music was being played in the areas where musicians were entertaining. The atmosphere was buzzing with many people thrilled to come out with the few words which existed in their Italian vocabulary.

Jeff and the other photographers were busily taking as many snaps as they could which in due course would be displayed on the various stands in the photo gallery for guests to consider whether or not they wished to buy. He had previously told Louise that one woman had come up to him and asked '*How will I know which is mine?*'

Although many passengers had decided not to join in dress wear for the Italian theme night others had surpassed themselves. A number of men appeared as gondoliers, some women as either signoras or signorinas waving black or white fans and bearing a scarf round their shoulders, their were men who simply wore colourful neckerchiefs, one couple came as Romeo and Juliet – although as one woman commented in a rather sarcastic manner, '*I think she's a bit past it for a fourteen year old Juliet.*' and several men appeared as Italian ice-cream vendors.

When the passengers entered the dining room and saw the way in which it had been decorated their sense of excitement rose further, especially as all of the waiters were also suitably attired. The cruise director and his assistant visited various parts of the ship also dressed appropriately and were thrilled to find so many guests had elected to make this a special evening.

*****

Whilst the ship had been in Naples, another entertainer had come on board, who would remain with the ship until it reached Dover. He was Jake Hammond, aged fifty-seven, who was a comedian and played the saxophone and clarinet. He had been rehearsing during the afternoon with Nick Guthrie as they were sharing the evenings programme.

Matt had been introduced to Jake earlier and after a pre-dinner drink they went to the Ocean Bistro to have dinner together.

"Have you been doing stage work for a long time?" asked Matt.

"Longer than I care to remember," Jake replied, "but I haven't done too many cruises. What about you?"

"I started doing magic when I was a kid and its all gone on from there." replied Matt, "I always wanted to do stage work although I prefer smaller gatherings. I've done quite a lot of cruises but I'm really rather fed up with them and I'm thinking of blowing them out in the future."

"Why's that?" said Jake.

"I'll be forty soon." responded Matt, "I'm married with a son and quite frankly it was all right when my wife accompanied me but now, with so many rules and regulations, she's not able to do so. I find living on a ship for two weeks on my own drives me crazy and I just get very bored. I also feel it's taking away the time I need to pursue other avenues where I can work but still be at home – or certainly for the bulk of the time."

"I can see what you mean." said Jake.

"Are you married?" asked Matt.

"I was married when I was twenty-nine but I've been divorced for some time," Jake replied, then standing up he continued, "I'll be back in a minute, just want to get another pint. Can I get you something?"

Matt declined and began to wonder how much of a drinker Jake was. He had already drunk two pints before dinner and was shortly due on stage.

When Jake returned he immediately continued their conversation from the point where he had left off.

"Ella, my ex, was brought up within the 'me-me-me syndrome'. At first she worked but then decided she would prefer to be a lady of leisure - we couldn't have any kids. She would get up about ten, go off to the gym and then have lunch with one of her girl friends.

"Then she took up tennis and followed this by taking up the tennis pro. Being away so much, I didn't cotton-on to what was going on until one of my friends dropped a couple of hints. I kept my eyes open and one day I told her I had a one-night gig and wouldn't be back until the following mid-morning.

"I came home about midnight, saw the bedroom light was on, caught them at it and that was the end of the marriage. Since then I've been pretending everything is great in my life and I try and put things behind me by making others laugh and probably by drinking too much."

"Well I'm sorry to hear that," said Matt, "I guess life can be a bit of a bummer sometimes."

"It's a matter of che sera, sera matey," Jake replied, "I better go – my audience calls!"

*****

"What a great day we've all had – haven't you? – well, haven't you?" said Alan Spencer.

"Yes." the members of the theatre audience shouted out.

"That's right, and don't forget your lines next time."

"Tonight, ladies and gentlemen you are in for a very special treat. In the second half of the show Nick Guthrie will be back and ready to enchant you with his wonderful singing but, before that, it is going to be my pleasure to introduce you to a gentleman who joined the ship whilst you were all out gallivanting.

"He has been on The Neptune before. We didn't throw him overboard then and I don't think we'll be doing it now. He's an accomplished musician who plays both the saxophone – yes I said saxophone, madam, - and the clarinet but best of all he will undoubtedly have you laughing in the aisles with his great gags and lovely sense of humour.

"Just before I came on stage, he told me that he had received a standing ovation at the last night-club where he appeared. I suppose they didn't have any chairs!

"Sorry Jake, I didn't mean it. Ladies and gentleman, please give a big welcome to Jake Hammond."

Matt had entered the theatre and was standing at the back so as to hear Jake. Neither he nor the audience were disappointed. He was indeed a very funny man, but a very funny man who was far from being a very happy man.

*****

Having seen the show, Craig and David decided to go off for a nightcap. Neither of the girls wanted anything and said they would stay in the lounge.

"How are you?" asked Julie.

"I could be better but I could be worse. I told David on Friday evening that I'm almost at the end of my tether and I asked him how much longer he thought I was going to put up with his nonsense."

"What did he say?" said Julie.

"He stormed out of the cabin and went up to the casino," replied Karen, "and then there was his outburst at dinner yesterday evening. He told me he would apologise to Colin today and I only hope he has. I really have to make up my mind what I want to do. It's either the future with him or without him.

"I had the opportunity of having a long chat with Liz today. She really is smashing and certainly nobody's fool. She has given me some really sensible advice and I know I shall now be able to take a much more positive attitude and sort myself out."

"Good for you." responded Julie, having no intention of mentioning David's behaviour round by the pool. "Oh, here's Craig."

"Where's David?" asked Karen.

Craig became a little embarrassed and then said, "He's popped into the Casino for a few minutes and said he'd see you back in the cabin."

Karen and Julie looked at each other very knowingly.

*****

EIGHTEEN

When we think of Italy it is natural for our minds to turn to Rome.

The rise of Rome, from city-state to empire, is one of history's most gripping epics of war and conquest. The great names of Rome remain with us from birth to death, Caesar, Pompey, Marc Anthony, Cassius, Hadrian, Caligula, Nero and many more.

'*All roads lead to Rome*' – so goes an old saying in praise of the grandeur and importance of a city which claimed for itself the title of 'Caput Mundi' – head of the world. And by the same token, whatever road the visitor takes to reach it, he can be sure what he or she is about to be offered is an opportunity to admire and study an historical, artistic and monumental heritage of universal value. By a strange and uniquely privileged destiny, history conspired to ensure that even after the fall of the Roman Empire, Rome should preserve its role as a cultural and moral centre of the world.

Six different tours were available to passengers, five to Rome and the sixth to Tarquinia, where Etruscan Art could still be seen and admired. Some of the tours to Rome were of shorter duration than others which required a greater degree of fitness and ability to cope with considerable walking.

The most popular tour, entitled 'Classical Rome', would be highlighting the principal sites and this was the one on which Louise had agreed to accompany Colin. There was no doubt that the tours would be tiring and stretch over many long hours, the journey from ship to Rome and return being in excess of three hours. A number of passengers did not wish to be travelling and site seeing in the heat of the day preferring to take a stroll into the town of Civitavecchia with an early return to the ship followed by relaxation.

All the dining areas opened just before seven so those on the early tours could stock up for the day, as camels, with water, prior to crossing the Sahara.

As always the cruise director was up and about and ready to announce his pearls of wisdom for the day ahead.

"Good morning ladies and gentlemen, this is Alan Spencer, your cruise director, trusting you all have a great time here in Rome. Just remember, it has been said *'the Italians invented birth control – they call it 'garlic.'"*

"But seriously folks once again it's going to be hot, so please be prepared, have your sun-creams, take comfortable shoes and ladies, you will require your shoulders and legs to be covered should you be going to St. Peters. Low neck lines are not permitted and please make sure you all have water with you throughout the day.

"I must also warn you to be very careful of the traffic in Rome. It's been said, *'In Milan, traffic lights are instruction, in Rome they are suggestions and in Naples they are Christmas decorations.'*

"I'm sure you're all pleased knowing this evening will again be casual wear, but even after an arduous day this doesn't mean turning up in the dining room wearing pyjamas and dressing gowns.

"I guess that's all from me for the time being. For those staying on board there are a number of activities to keep you out of mischief and tonight our show will be 'Magical Nights at the Movies' featuring the Neptune Orchestra, singers and dancers.

"So take care, have a wonderful day and I'll see you later."

*****

The Trident lounge was teeming with people gathering to collect their numbers for the coaches. This was going to be the busiest of all mornings for the tour staff and other crew members who were on duty to help passengers and make sure they didn't getting lost.

As each group was called to their coach, the escort with lollipop stick lead them down to the gangway and onwards to where the tour bus guide was waiting. Louise was amazed how some passengers always rushed ahead of everyone else to secure the front seats in the coach with those who were older or having a physical disability having no chance.

She and Colin found seats half-way down the coach with Louise preferring to sit by the window.

"My name is Giuseppe," said tour guide and our driver is Stefano. Today we will be very busy and have many things to see. Roma is one of the most exciting places in the world and as Stefano drives us there I will tell you all about it.

"The only thing that is small about Rome, are the four letters that makes up the name. While the works of the Greeks pursued an ideal of pure harmony and beauty, those of the Romans show grandeur and power which you will see by its amphitheatres, basilicas and triumphal arches.

"During our visit we will see the Colosseum, the Vatican City with the famous St. Peters – the largest church in the world, the Roman Forum, the Arch of Constantine, the Fountain of Trevi and other buildings.

"There will be many times we shall get on and off the bus. It has the number 276. Each time, I will tell you exactly when and where to find the bus if you get separated from the group. I suggest you do stay together as it is very easy to get lost in Rome and we won't be able to wait for you. Should you get lost then you must find your own way back to the ship in Civitavecchia.

"So now I'll start to tell you about my lovely city......................."

During the next forty-five minutes Giuseppe gave an excellent talk answering all of the passenger's questions until saying, "We are now about thirty-minutes from Rome so I will be very quiet and you can all have a little rest."

He had a delightful, pleasing personality and a considerable command of English which, when spoken in his Italian accent, accompanied by Italian mannerisms, became quite enchanting.

"Do you realise what a lucky girl you are today?" Colin asked Louise.

"What do you mean?" she asked surprisingly.

"Well you'll have two guides in Rome."

"Why is that?"

"Because during the period that I was on my art foundation course I stayed here for two separate weeks in a small pensione during the school breaks," said Colin, "and I got to know it

261

quite well. Visitors either love being in Rome and cannot wait to return or leave without having any intention of coming back."

"How marvellous you stayed here but why is people think like that?" asked Louise.

"I won't say any more as I don't want to influence you. You can tell me your reactions on the way back." said Colin.

"I've never been to Italy but it has always sounded so exciting." commented Louise, "The language is so musical and I adore hearing Italian songs, especially those sung by Pavarotti."

"Do you like opera?" he asked.

"Well, I don't really know. I've only been three times and there were considerable gaps between."

"What have you seen?"

"The first was La Boheme. A friend of mine told me this should always be the first opera anyone goes to as it has such lovely music and a wonderful love story. She said if I saw anything else it might put me off for life."

"King George V once said, 'My favourite opera is La Boheme because it is the shortest.' said Colin.

She laughed and said, "Well I had wished it would have gone on forever."

"What were the other two?" he asked.

"The next was Madame Butterfly – somebody once told me people sometimes called it 'Madame Flutterby' – and the last one was Tosca."

"Now there's a dramatic opera." commented Colin, "I've seen it many times and it is often recreated in modern times and in modern dress. Once I saw a performance where the head of police was like a German Nazi. It was spine-chilling. There's also a very amusing story about Tosca. Do you remember when she throws herself over the battlements?"

"Yes, I do." replied Louise.

"Well, in this particular production, after she'd jumped she suddenly reappeared in horizontal position. It seems the trampoline which had been erected to break her fall was stronger then suspected, so up she came and down she went."

Louise burst into laughter. She was feeling very relaxed in Colin's company and was thoroughly enjoying his little stories.

The cruise had been a real tonic for her and she felt far more relaxed than anytime since Mark had died.

"And now ladies and gentlemen your rest period is over."

Giuseppe had interrupted individual conversations and was one more in charge of proceedings.

"In a few minutes Stefano will be parking the coach in a special place so I can show you the Colosseum. There will be many other tourists so please keep together and ladies watch your handbags. Stefano will remain on the coach at all times so it is safe to leave any valuables here. I will be counting our numbers as we go in but if anyone loses us please come back to the coach in thirty minutes. As you get out of the coach please make sure you notice exactly where it is parked and please don't be late."

"Is it safe walking round the ruins?" asked Louise.

"Do I hear miss worry pot speaking?" retorted Colin.

"Now you're making fun of me." she said smiling.

As they all stood with the guide inside the Colosseum, Louise stood open-mouthed with astonishment.

"I had no idea it was so vast." she whispered to Colin.

"Just listen to Giuseppi, I'm sure he'll tell you all the facts." responded Colin.

Naturally, Giuseppi was able to do just that, indicating how the structure covered six acres, had three tiers of arches, held nearly seventy thousand people and had been used for games and fights.

He told how the spectators were seated by rank, with the most humble at the top, indicated the four main entrances for the gladiators and told of the special trapdoors through which the wild animals were let in.

"Whenever I come here," commented Colin, "I feel like a mouse."

"Why?" said Louise.

"Well, just look at your height against the size of just one of these concrete building slabs. It makes you realise how small we are, just as a mouse probably feels in our world, when comparing his size with us. It's at such times we can truly realise our minor importance in relation to the world at large despite the fact we have been indoctrinated to believe the contrary."

Louise had looked at him as he had spoken, interested by his expression of thoughts and accepting, that what he had said, made a great deal of sense.

"What sickens me," she said, 'Is the sheer barbarity of what happened here when gladiators were forced to fight to the death killer animals and other gladiators and how people were executed whilst lunch was taking place."

Two passengers were missing when Giuseppi did a head-count on the coach. Five minutes went by until finally, without a word being said by either Giuseppi or them, they boarded and went to their seats.

The coach pulled away and during the next stage Giuseppi pointed out nearby buildings including the Arch of Constantine and the Roman Forum. Throughout he related many interesting stories and imparted further detailed information.

The coach had crossed the River Tiber and had now come to its next scheduled stop. The Vatican City had been reached. This was the sovereign state within the Italian Republic which had been independent since nineteen hundred and twenty nine.

The Vatican City had been a place of pilgrimage for millions over the years and now the passengers would be able to enter the most famous Basilica di San Pietro, the spiritual capital of Roman Catholic faith.

Before they went inside, Giuseppi told of its astounding proportions, the number of columns, altars and statues. He indicated some of the special areas they should look at and in particular spoke of the masterpiece statue by Michelangelo, 'LaPieta'.

"This will be our last stop before lunch." said Giuseppe, "I would like you all to meet back at the bus at two o'clock. Again please do not be late. This will give all of you time to see the Basilica and have some lunch. If you have any questions I will be inside with you or you can ask me when we are back on the bus. Please enjoy your visit."

During the next twenty-five minutes Louise and Colin wandered round St. Peters. Louise found it both breathtaking and yet so large it tended to upset her.

"Is something bothering you?" asked Colin.

"It's too big." she replied, "It's beautiful, its architecture is stunning, the sculptures are wonderful but it's too big. As I've walked round I've seen many people praying or just sitting contemplating but this is not the church in which I could come for solace and comfort. It's too grand. I can barely look up to the top dome without feeling dizzy. Do you understand what I'm trying to say or am I being silly?"

"Not at all," responded Colin, "you're not the first person who has felt that way. I think it best to simply accept it for what it is and leave it like that."

"Yes, you're right but I think I'd like to go now, if that's all right with you."

Having exited they passed close to the Sistine Chapel where a notice indicated it was currently not open to visitors.

"That's where the cardinals meet when electing a new pope and the ceiling and altar wall were painted by Michelangelo." said Colin.

They soon found an outdoor café and ordered lunch. Louise felt quite relieved to be able to sit and rest. It had been quite a morning.

"There's a lovely story about what happened when Oscar Wilde visited here." said Colin, "Apparently he found the Vatican gardens were open only to Bohemian and Portuguese pilgrims. He subsequently told others, *'I at once spoke both languages fluently, explaining that my English dress was a form of penance.'*"

Yet again one of his stories made her laugh.

"I wonder how many other jokes you have stored up to tell unsuspecting ladies." she commented.

"Oh, you'd be surprised," he said, "but some of them only apply to Florence so I thought we might come to Italy together some other time and then I could take you there."

Louise looked at him not being sure how to reply.

"Is that what you thought?" she replied indicating a slight twinkle in her eyes, "I'm not used to this sort of attention, Colin, so please don't rush me. It's not that I don't like being with you but you mustn't make me feel I'm being pushed into a corner."

He smiled, saying, "There's no rush and there'll be no pushing."

As he spoke a fountain of water suddenly appeared a few yards from the café as a broken water pipe released a volume of water from a drain that flowed ever upwards catching many pedestrians totally unaware.

"I don't think this is one of Rome's famous fountains." commented Louise with a wide grin on her face.

The broken water pipe had broken the slightly serious vein their conversation had taken, though Colin felt pleased he had taken the plunge and spoken to her as he had.

It was now time to rendezvous with everyone at the coach. Within two or three minutes of the appointed time all were in their places with the exception of the same couple who had been late previously. They arrived at ten minutes past two and received a pleasant but nevertheless firm reprimand from Giuseppe.

The tour continued with the coach passing slowly when near the Spanish Steps, named as such for a palace that housed the Spanish Embassy.

"Just down the road over there," said Colin pointing past the steps, "is the Via Veneto where Rome's finest hotels are sited and where all the famous film and theatre stars stay."

A little further on, the coach made another stop with passengers being told they should now accompany Giuseppi on a little walk which would take them to the Trevi Fountain and then on to the Pantheon where Stefano would be waiting for them.

"The Trevi Fountain is the most photographed fountain in Rome." Colin told Louise, "Did you ever see the film La Dolce Vita?"

"No, I didn't." she replied.

"Well, it was featured in the film and really became world-famous because of it."

Soon it was in front of them with Neptune riding a shell-shaped chariot drawn by seahorses.

"Isn't that gorgeous?" he said, "Now you mustn't forget to make a wish and toss two coins over your shoulder into the fountain. You will then return to Rome and your wish will come true. Take these two coins for luck."

As promised by Giuseppi, the coach was parked near the Pantheon and was soon on its way to the last stopping place.

"I am sorry we do not have time to show you the Pantheon," said Giuseppi, "but I hope the next time you come to Rome you will go inside. It is bello and is Italy's best-preserved building and was built in the second century by Emperor Hadrian.

"Our last stop today is going to be at the loveliest park in Rome, the Villa Borghese. It is very beautiful and you will be able to see many statues and fountains along the avenues and paths.

"You can stay there for thirty minutes but please be back on the bus in no more than thirty minutes as we have a long drive back to your ship and Stefano does not want to get caught up with the heavy late afternoon Rome traffic."

"So how did you enjoy Rome?" Colin asked.

"I've had a wonderful day. I don't know whether I would want to come back as it is so crowded and noisy everywhere but it has been a great trip."

"You may very well prefer Florence!" said Colin with a boyish smile.

This time all passengers were back on time as Stefano switched on the engine and commenced crossing the city towards the main autostrada back to Civitavecchia.

It was not surprising when a number of passengers soon fell asleep. The day had been long and exciting but also hot and very tiring and they would still have to wait for over an hour and a half before being in their cabins to put their feet up and enjoy a refreshing shower or bath.

When they eventually arrived, Louise turned to Colin saying, "Thank you so much for a really fabulous day. I really did enjoy every part of it. I'll look forward to seeing you for dinner." She gave him a hug and a peck on the cheek and quickly disappeared to her room.

Having returned to her cabin, Louise immediately stripped and took a shower. She felt uncomfortably sticky and wanted to wash her hair and her body before doing anything else.

After wrapping herself in a large fluffy towel she sat at the dressing table and peered into the mirror. She was still the right side of fifty and decided she had worn reasonably well as she probed various parts of her face and neck seeking out tell-tale signs of middle age. Even so she thought she'd better watch herself from now on.

The question then passed through her mind as to why she was now carrying out this self-examination − an exercise she had never bothered with before. Without wishing to acknowledge the reason, the answer was not difficult for her to know, even though she recalled how she had told him not to rush or push her.

*****

With the exception of those who had not been on a tour most diners were feeling rather worn out.

"I suppose at least fifty percent of us will be awake during dinner." said James. "I gather you three girls and you Roger all trundled off to the Eternal City."

"That's right," answered Roger, "and we have aches and pains to prove it. Every picture tells a story - isn't that what they say?"

"I love that expression." said Martin, "I can tell you a little story. Many years ago I attended a philosophy course. We had an excellent tutor and a considerable part of our studies were in relation to Eastern philosophy.

"Well, one day, one of the women asked him a question commencing with the words *'They say.'* He stood listening attentively then walked slowly towards her and with a little smile responded by saying, *'Let's not worry about what they say, until they arrive and then we can ask them.'*"

"Oh, that's wonderful," said Roger, "and how true."

"So what do you think 'they say' about true love, Roger?" asked Doreen, winking across at Laura.

Neither he nor Laura had any doubts as to why Doreen had posed this question.

"Ah, that's not the easiest question to answer, but I suppose in just a few words one could say it is a daily acknowledgement between two parties that they love each other without automatically taking the other for granted." he replied.

"I think that's a super reply." said Denise.

"I agree," said Shirley, "the man or woman who you love has to be both your companion and best friend for a marriage to succeed."

As though pre-arranged, there was a sudden chorus of voices coming from a table on the other side of the room with the well-known wedding anniversary words being sung – '*Oh how we danced on the night we were wed.*' to which James quickly added, '*We danced and we danced 'cause there wasn't a bed.*'

It was the dining room staff again playing their role of greetings singers with one carrying an iced cake bearing a host of candles.

"It looks as though they've stuck by your rules, Roger." said Doreen.

"There's just one thing he forgot." commented James.

"And what's that, Romeo?" said Phyllis.

"We mere mortals, called men, must always remember that, when a woman says a certain thing doesn't matter what she really means is, that it jolly well does."

They all laughed with Phyllis adding, "It's known as a women's prerogative."

"I must say you've been very quiet during this little discourse, Laura." said Martin.

"That's because there are times when silence is golden, Martin." she replied.

After dinner it seemed that none of them intended going to the show, deciding an early night was likely to be more beneficial to prepare for the days and evenings ahead.

*****

Andrew and Ros were sitting on Mercury deck when Louise and Colin came by.

"Come and join us for a nightcap" said Ros.

"Thanks," Colin said, "Is that okay with you Louise?"

"Very much so." she replied.

"Did you have a hectic day?" asked Andrew.

"You could say that. We went on the Classical Rome tour. It was the first time Louise had been there." Colin responded.

"And did you enjoy it?" Ros asked Louise.

"Yes I did although I found everything was just too big for my liking and I really did not feel comfortable in St. Peters."

Having explained her feelings, Andrew said, "I understand what you mean. I've always believed that visiting churches and cathedrals has differing affects on people. The most amazing experience we ever had was in Bethlehem. Do you remember Ros?"

"How could I forget." she said.

"Why, what happened?" asked Louise.

"Well, in the centre of Bethlehem is Manger Square and it is here you find the Church of the Nativity where you can go down a staircase and there at the bottom it is like a small dark cave. This is where it is said Jesus was born. There was a group of women ahead of us from Germany and when we were halfway down the stairs suddenly everyone stopped and a soprano voice from one of these women could be heard singing the first two verses of Silent Night in German.

"You could have heard a pin drop and although this took place many years ago, I can still vividly recollect hearing those words '*Stile Nacht, heilige Nacht, Alles schlaft, einsam wacht.*'

"It was totally beautiful and at the same time quite chilling. So, as I was saying, we can never tell how any religious experience may affect us."

"You're all looking very serious." said a feminine voice.

It was Denise who had been standing looking out to sea on the opposite side of the deck and had now walked across in their direction.

"Not really, we were having a drink and Andrew was recalling one of their travel experiences and now we're about to call it a night." said Martin.

"So am I," said Denise, "but I love taking a last look at the sea before I go to bed each night. This evening I haven't been able to get Lewis Carroll's Walrus and the Carpenter out of my head."

"I can't remember it." said Shirley, "Can you recite it?"

"Not all of it but I'll have a go with the first two verses, -

'THE SUN WAS SHINING ON THE SEA,
SHINING WITH ALL HIS MIGHT:
HE DID HIS VERY BEST TO MAKE
THE BILLOWS SMOOTH AND BRIGHT –
AND THIS WAS ODD, BECAUSE IT WAS
THE MIDDLE OF THE NIGHT.

THE MOON WAS SHINING SULKILY,
BECAUSE SHE THOUGHT THE SUN
HAD GOT NO BUSINESS TO BE THERE
AFTER THE DAY WAS DONE –
'IT'S VERY RUDE OF HIM', SHE SAID,
TO COME AND SPOIL THE FUN!'

"Well done," said Ros, "that's what I call a perfect ending to a perfect day."

They all went down to their respective cabins and as Denise walked to her room she recalled the third verse of the poem -

'THE SEA WAS WET AS WET COULD BE,
THE SANDS WERE DRY AS DRY,
YOU COULD NOT SEE A CLOUD, BECAUSE
NO CLOUD WAS IN THE SKY:
NO BIRDS WERE FLYING OVERHEAD –
THERE WERE NO BIRDS TO FLY'

She began to feel sad and having entered the cabin and with her back leaning on the door she called out in a quiet voice, *'Only four more days Nicola and we'll be back together again.'*

*****

NINETEEN

A day at sea, after a hectic time the day before, can be like the morning after the night before. Today, there was no need for any passenger to be up at the crack of dawn, a leisurely breakfast could be taken at any time desired and everybody could be as busy or as lazy as they chose.

The early morning weather was heavenly and for many the decision to have a restful day to improve their suntan, read a book or just sleep, meant that many chairs were filled before breakfast, though there were still more than enough left for the others. Frequently, conversation brought people round to wondering 'how many more days would there be like this' before they would have to face the reality of cooler, if not decidedly wet and chillier days, back home.

But that was still a few days away and in the meantime the current warm climate would heighten their enjoyment aided by cold drinks, a plunge in the pool, ice-creams and laughter, coupled with any activities which particularly appealed as had been announced by Alan Spencer, when giving details of the morning programme.

The destination lecture at ten by Martin was to be entitled 'On the Rocks' and this was to be followed an hour later with Colin's talk on 'Picasso and friends.' Bridge players could receive a lesson at ten and at noon there was to be a port talk in the Apollo lounge.

"But this morning, we also have something very special for you." the cruise director had said, "At midday our chefs are going to present you with an ice sculpture demonstration on Pool deck. If you've never seen this before you are in for a treat.

"I must tell you we had a similar demo. last week and later that day a man came over to me and asked, '*What happens to the ice sculptures after they have melted?*'

So how would you have answered that, I ask?

"I had another baffling question put to me recently and, as today we are at sea, this will be your great opportunity to provide the answer. A lady asked '*Is there water on both sides of the ship?*'

"You have to remember that you do not need to produce your school examination records when you book a cruise.

"Finally, tonight is not only our last formal night but it is also Gala Night, the very special evening which we schedule once on every cruise. You'll love it and after the scrumptious dinner has been served it will again be show time and tonight you will be entertained by our two funny men, Jake Hammond and Matt Campbell.

The captain will be speaking to you from the bridge at noon and I'll be back after lunch to tell you of the afternoon schedule. So whatever you do, don't leave ship, we've got too many great things for you to enjoy."

*****

Denise having been restless all night, woke early, had breakfast and was comfortably stretched out in the sun by nine.

"I didn't expect to see you at this time of the morning," she said, "it looks as though you're in disguise."

Matt too did not get a good nights sleep and like Denise had ventured on deck far earlier than was normal for him. He was wearing dark glasses and a wide brimmed straw hat

"I probably am," he replied, "but I'm certainly not hiding from you. How have you been? Still enjoying the cruise?"

"I'm fine," she said, "but quite frankly I think I've had enough and shall be pleased to get back home."

"Now you're beginning to see how I sometimes feel," commented Matt, "I told you before not all comedians are happy in their work and it's also quite extraordinary how people react when they learn of some of the tragedies and sadness we experience in our lives. Why, they do this I don't know, we're no different from anyone else. I sometimes think they believe we're super human. Our agents are usually the worst. All they're interested in is their commissions."

"You really are down, aren't you?" said Denise, "Surely it's not always like that?"

"No, of course it isn't, but when one is unsure about what steps to take in relation to the future, it's the uncertainty which hangs about like a dark cloud. I always find it much easier when I can discuss problems with Pauline. She's got a great gift for seeing everything in a clear light and honing in on the important issues."

"Well, you're a very lucky man to have her." said Denise.

"I know that's so and I also know it's nearly ten and I have a rehearsal for tonight's show. See you again. 'Bye."

As she closed her eyes, Denise, started to think of all the people she had met on board the ship. They certainly represented quite a cross-section and she had no doubt some of their personal stories would help her when advising clients of Eros.

*****

Having finished his talk on Gibraltar by quarter to eleven, Martin dashed back to their cabin to take off his 'lecture clothes' and replace them with swimming shorts and light-weight open shirt. As soon as he joined Shirley, he gingerly entered the pool by the steps at the shallow end and whilst walking along the bottom placed himself in a position along the side where he could hold on and not be disturbed by torrents of water coming over him from other swimmers.

He then heard a voice say, "You seem to have negotiated your pool stroll very well. Do I take it you don't swim?"

He looked up and found Vince was standing by his side. "Oh, I swim but I'm not a strong swimmer and have always hated getting water in my eyes. Normally I use goggles but I left them in the cabin and couldn't be bothered to go and get them. Cooling off was top of my agenda and how I did it was unimportant."

"I don't blame you," said Vince, "It's not yet midday and the temperature is rising fast. I must say we've have had some wonderful weather."

"That's for sure." replied Martin, "I'm glad I've seen you. Tell me how's your wife getting on?"

"She's certainly enjoying herself and I believe she's been feeling a little better but there have been many times before when she's given me that impression and then she reverts back. There are good days and then some not so good days and when they're bad she really does suffer. We've tried everything and just trust that in time she will be able to make substantial improvement. Times the great healer, isn't that what they say?"

Martin smiled as he heard these last words.

"As a matter of fact I was going to ask you whether you would have any objection if I could see Anne by herself. There is a story I would like to tell her which may help."

"I've no objection and I don't see why she should. I'll have to ask her but leave it with me and I'll come back to you. Where are you sitting?"

It was about twenty minutes later that Vince reappeared. "Anne says that's fine. Could she meet you in the card room at twelve-thirty, she'd like to see the ice sculpture demonstration at twelve?"

*****

Though Louise had decided she wanted to see the ice sculpture demonstration, first she wanted to make sure she listened to Colin's talk. She knew nothing about cubism and some of the paintings he showed by Picasso and Braque were totally incomprehensible to her. She was much happier when he referred his audience to the paintings of Cezanne, who he said was the father of cubism.

Nevertheless she admired Colin's ability to speak so well and answer the various questions which were put to him at the end.

"Well done," she told him, "that was really interesting and bearing in mind what a lovely day it is you had a good crowd. Would you like to come with me and see the ice sculpture?"

"Give me five minutes to take all my lecture material and the laptop back to my cabin and then change and I'll see you on pool deck."

It was an incredible demonstration with two chefs chipping away at solid blocks of ice until finally one had produced a swan and the other a chicken.

"That was amazing," said Louise, "if I tried to do that, my kitchen would be a mess in two minutes."

*****

Martin was waiting for Anne in the card room and was slightly surprised to find Vince had come along with her.

He stood up as they entered. "Hallo, Anne. I'm so pleased you agreed to see me. Now all we need do is to wave goodbye to Vince for a little while and we can make a start."

Martin then turned to Vince and said, "It really would be better if I saw Anne alone."

"Yes, of course." replied Vince, I'll wait for you in the library, Anne."

Martin placed two chairs opposite each other and told her to sit and make herself comfortable. He could see she was feeling on edge.

He held out his hands and told her to close her eyes and hold his hands.

"I'll tell you when to open your eyes but in the meantime just relax. There's nothing for you to be nervous about. All I am going to do is to tell you a story. That can't hurt you, can it?"

She smiled and started to compose herself. He could feel she was no longer holding his hands so firmly.

"You're doing fine, Anne," he said, "now open your eyes, release my hands and sit back in your chair."

Having seen she was now looking far less strained, he began.

"This is the story of what took place many, many years ago in a small village in a far off country. It was a beautiful village situated on the edge of a forest and all the villagers were very friendly towards each other. They worked together in the fields during the day and socialised with each other in the evenings unless they were at home with their families.

"Living in such peaceful surroundings had brought peace and happiness to all and the elders of the village were always available to help with any problems that arose.

"There was only one road which they could take from the centre of the village and this road lead directly into the forest. One day a giant came along from the far side of the forest and with enormous strides started to walk along the road. Soon he came to the outskirts of the village where he saw many of the inhabitants getting on with their tasks.

"Having seen this he rose to his full height, stepped a little further forward, so that the villagers would be able to see him, and boomed out, *'My name is fear, my name is fear.'*

"Such a loud noise made all the villagers look to see what had happened.

"But again, the giant boomed out the words, *'My name is fear, my name is fear.'*

"By this time, all of the villagers had gathered together in the centre and did not know what to do next. Even the elders were unable to provide a solution. So they all went off to the safety of their homes and it was agreed they would reassemble the following morning.

"The next day they came together but still did not know what to do. It was the first time the villagers had felt concerned and unhappy and it was evident that the peaceful nature of the village was slipping away, until one villager said he would go and confront the giant. Everyone felt very nervous about this and tried to persuade him not to take such a perilous trip but he wouldn't listen to their pleading and with them all watching him, he commenced to slowly walk to where the giant had fallen asleep on the road alongside the village.

"As he got nearer, the giant suddenly woke up and saw the villager coming towards him. So he stood up and once more raised himself to his full height and again boomed out the same words, *'My name is fear, my name is fear.'*

"But the villager did not take any notice and carried on slowly walking towards the giant until they were side by side, when the villager picked up the giant and put him in his pocket."

Anne, remained totally still until tears started to roll down her cheeks.

"I believe you've understood the story." said Martin, "There's no need to cry. Just remember the story. I've told it to many people and all have said it helped them. I trust it will now help you."

She had taken a handkerchief to wipe away the tears.

"Shall we go and find Vince?" he asked.

"Yes, please and thank you so much."

Vince was sitting in the library waiting for her return.

"Are you ready for lunch, Vince?" Anne asked, "Would you like to join us, Martin?"

"No thank you," he replied, "I think I better find my other half and feed the brute. I'll see you soon."

*****

Having thoroughly enjoyed the ice sculpture display, Louise and Colin decided to take lunch in the dining room.

"It's so hot and crowded in the Ocean Bistro we may as well eat in a more pleasant and cooler atmosphere," Colin had suggested.

They found an excellent salad buffet was available together with many hot or cold dishes which could be ordered from the waiting staff.

"This will be ideal," said Louise, "and you're quite right it's so much nicer in here."

"You've been doing a great job in the library," said Colin, "I've been on this ship before and this is the first time I've ever been able to find anything. Let's hope they keep it in order after you leave. You obviously have an interest in books"

"What I've always found interesting," said Louise, "is the amount you can learn about people by looking at the books they have in their homes. It's as though every book tells a story other then the one written."

"It's the same with paintings." continued Colin, "The next time you go to someone's house take a look at the paintings or prints they have on their walls. They also tell you something about your hosts, as music does, but you must admit all of these things can be enjoyed far more when two people can share them together."

Louise looked at him knowing fully well what he was implying. "I realise that, Colin, but I often find that I need my own space."

"I'll tell you one thing Louise, I've heard that expression said many times by women but personally I believe it's a cop out. It's not space people need but closeness and if they find closeness with the right person then that in itself can produce all the space they need."

She sat feeling slightly dumbfounded.

"Well that's told me, hasn't it? I'll tell you one thing Mr. Colin Price you really are quite a guy."

*****

Karen could not believe what she was hearing as she stood washing and tidying herself in the ladies cloakroom. The conversation was between two of the other women.

The first said, "What a dreadful thing to do in the casino of a ship. They must have been watching him, but my husband said there was no doubt he had been switching the chips at the roulette table. He saw him do it and he then argued with the croupier saying the chips had been his."

Karen went cold and only prayed this was not something David had done. She took her comb from her bag and slowly pretended to adjust her hair further.

The second woman then said, "Apparently the croupier called the casino manager and it appears this passenger was being helped by his wife who had been sitting at the same roulette table. They've both been banned from the casino for the rest of the voyage and will be reported to the shipping lines head office."

Karen dropping her bag on the floor held on to the cloakroom basin.

"Are you all right dear?" asked the first woman.

"Yes thank you, I'm fine." replied Karen, "I just came over a little dizzy but it's passed now."

"Well here's your bag, dear," said the second woman having picked it off the floor. "Nothing has fallen out."

Karen left the ladies room relieved David had not been involved in anything so shady, and returned on deck where Julia was sitting.

"Have you thought any more as to what you're going to do?" asked Julie.

"Yes and I've decided I shall get a divorce once we're back home. I shall tell David just before the cruise ends. I can't stand any more of his gambling and chasing after other women and I'm sure it will be better for me to put an end to it now before he really gets himself into hot trouble and drags me into it with him."

"I'm sure you're doing the right thing," said Julie, "and you know if there's anything Craig and I can do to help you only have to say the word."

*****

As they came out of the gym on Hercules deck, Delia noticed the lady with the red folder quietly sitting alone. She was probably in her mid-seventies, a little over-weight with greying hair and with the appearance of someone who would barely be noticed in a crowded room let alone remembered, if it had not been for the folder.

Delia whispered to Paul, "Let's go and say hallo. She looks so lonely."

They casually strolled towards her, looked out to sea near where she was sitting then turned, when Delia said, "It's been a beautiful day. Are you enjoying the cruise?"

"Yes, it's lovely. The cruise has been very nice, thank you. Have you both liked it?"

"Oh yes," said Paul, "I had not been very well before we came on board and it's made me feel much better."

"It's the first time I've been on a cruise for many years but I don't think I'll take another." the woman said, "it's rather strange really but although there are hundreds of people on the ship I feel quite alone."

She had spoken in a quiet, educated voice featuring a slight tremor.

"I've noticed you always have that red folder with you," commented Delia, "are you a writer?"

"Bless you, no dear. That folder is my life."

Paul thought she was about to burst into tears.

"What do you mean? Delia asked.

The woman picked up the folder from her chair and clutched it to her bosom, saying, "In here are photos, newspaper cuttings, letters and many other things that relate to my life. Wherever I go, this folder comes with me since it is me, in the same way as my arms and legs. I could not live without this folder as without it I would have absolutely nothing. I don't expect you to understand but life has only left me with the contents of this folder."

She sat back in her chair and shut her eyes. It was clear that this action was her way of ending a conversation which she did not intend continuing.

*****

Dean had been playing in the pool with the kids whilst Joanne hopefully added another layer to her already excellent suntan.

When he came out, he said, "I've had an idea. I'm fed up driving supermarket lorries every day. It's boring and the number of times I get caught up in heavy traffic nowadays is no fun and very tiring. Then if I arrive late at one destination the pressure is on to get to the next one on time. I think it's time for a change."

"But what will you do?" Joanne asked.

"My car's in good condition and I can register with a car hire company and get daily jobs from them and at the same time do any private trips which come my way. Gradually, I'll build up regular customers who will use me and when I've got enough I can work for myself.

"We both know lots of people who need to be taken to the station or an airport or elsewhere and if I give a good service at a competitive price they will recommend others.

"It's not as though I make a fortune from driving for the supermarket and after a while I've no doubt we'll be better off."

*****

Four-thirty was the scheduled time for another recital by Doreen and Laura which the cruise director had announced earlier. Once again she drew an enthusiastic crowd in the Apollo lounge and presented a balanced programme which satisfied all tastes.

Whilst Doreen took a short break of just over five minutes, Laura played the lilting intermezzo from Schumann's Piano Concerto in A minor. The listener who sat enthralled more than any other was Roger.

*****

Passengers again turned out in their formal clothes, not knowing when the next occasion might arise when they would be able to bring them out of storage. In the meantime they dressed as elegantly as possible and felt a million dollars.

It was Gala Night so why not start the evening with a glass of champagne or a martini or some other alcoholic drink. The lounge bars were crowded with staff working overtime.

When seated, guests were delighted to read the delicacies being put before them as printed on the menu. The starters consisted of either smoked salmon mousse or liver pate or quails egg salad, followed by consommé or lobster bisque or vichyssoise. The main course could be selected from either roast turkey with the usual trimmings, beef Wellington, roast duck or poached sole.

There were many scrumptious desserts with the highlight being Baked Alaska which would be paraded around the dining room by all of the waiters.

Liz said, "The first time I went on a cruise, candles were displayed on the Baked Alaska, which created a glorious effect when the lights of the dining room were dimmed, but nowadays this isn't possible as a result of Health and Safety regulations."

"We're not likely to loose any weight having this meal." said Anne, "I would imagine, Andrew, you'll have a few passengers coming to see you from over-eating tomorrow morning."

"You're probably right," he said, "which reminds me I heard something rather sad today. Do you recall the lady who had to leave the ship and go home after her husband had an emergency triple-bypass?"

"Yes, I remember. Roger and Laura told us about it. She was leaving when they came back from a tour." said Delia.

"Well, her husband died yesterday." said Andrew, "It was just as well she was able to get back to him beforehand."

"How sad for her." said Anne and then, taking Vince's hand, added, "It's certainly true we don't know what's going to happen from one day to the next."

"I have always thought that death is preferable to divorce." said Henry.

"Why do you say that?" asked Paul.

"Death brings finality," said Henry, "whereas divorce can for some be a never ending situation of heartache and despair."

"Don't sound so maudlin." said Liz.

"I was not intending to be" responded Henry, but as the philosopher, Seneca once said *'The whole of life is nothing but a preparation for death.'*"

"Well I suppose that is certainly positive thinking." said Ros.

"And that is exactly the way it has to be." continued Henry, "I can assure you it is both physically and mentally far more exhausting to be negative than to be positive and associating with negative people is certainly counter-productive. My advice to you would be to avoid them as you would any dreaded disease."

As he spoke, Ros observed him with admiration. He was facing adversity with considerable courage and had made up his mind to enjoy whatever time he had left.

The unmistakable voice of Liz interrupted their conversation, "If you're all going to continue to be so miserable, I'll either go out and shoot myself or order another glass of champagne."

The main course had been completed when Henry slowly stood up and announced he was feeling rather weary and should be grateful if they would excuse him so that he may return to his cabin. Liz offered to assist him but he said he would be perfectly all right.

After he'd gone, Liz said she was very worried about him, "He's been in a despondent mood during the last two days despite endeavouring to hide his feelings from others. It's possible that the cruise has been too much for him. I've told him he must get a check up when we get back to England."

*****

"I'm going to take an early night," said Doreen, "the recital this afternoon seems to have made me feel far more tired than usual and after tonight's banquet I have a feeling I'll be asleep in minutes."

"That's fine," replied Laura, "You sleep well and I'll see you in the morning."

She and Roger left the dining room and took the lift up to Apollo deck and found a quiet spot unseen by others, near the Saturn Club.

"Are you sure I can't get you anything to drink?" he asked.

"I'm absolutely positive, Roger, in the same way I have no doubt I've fallen madly in love with you."

He could not believe his ears. He had known for days how he felt about her and now her reciprocating his feelings had made this Gala night into something really special.

He took her into his arms and held her tight. "That's wonderful," he replied, "and I'm sure you know I feel the same towards you. I'm aching to make love to you."

"So what are we waiting for?" said Laura, "Lead on Sir Roger. What did you say your cabin number was?"

*****

TWENTY

"Today will be The Neptune's last port of call until our return to Dover, on Saturday morning," announced Alan Spencer. "Our stay in Gibraltar will be until five-thirty and all passengers must be back on board by quarter to five, unless you want to take a long swim to the Dover channel.

"So here we are, in what is still, a British port with the Union Jack waving its greeting and tonight we'll all be in casual wear coupled with having a British theme night. I'm sure many of you will do us proud with your outfits.

"We will also have a special show for you this evening, when we will be presenting 'The Crew Show'. As you know, our crew come from various parts of the world and once, on every cruise, they put on their own show for your entertainment. You will be amazed at the professionalism shown by some of those taking part. Don't miss their great performance.

"I must admit I'm pleased we're in port today as again I have been put to task by passengers with two tricky questions. The first asked me, '*Can I take a video of the ship leaving port?*' and the second asked, '*Will the ship be docking in the centre of the town?*'

"So as I sit at my desk with a glass of water and a Valium, I wish you all a lovely day with the apes and in the shops."

*****

"The big day has arrived." said James, as he and Phyllis were getting dressed in their cabin, "Once more to the Rock, dear friends, as King Henry might have said, but being a wise man he gave this narrow peninsular a wide berth."

"Each time we arrive here you go on and on," commented Phyllis, "you should be pleased this might be the last time."

"If only that were true, dear heart, I'd pick you up in my arms and give you a wonderful long-lasting kiss." he responded.

"What has got into you?" she said, "You couldn't even lift me two inches above the floor."

"That may be so, but just remember the American composer, Ira Gershwin, forecast *'Gibraltar may tumble'* though it does not seem likely in my life-time."

"That's enough from you, let's go and get some breakfast." said Phyllis.

*****

There wasn't going to be too many things to excite passengers in Gibraltar, other than going on a boat trip to see dolphins in the local waters or taking a tour to the upper rocks, where it was likely the famous Barbary apes would be seen.

When giving her port lecture on Gibraltar, Shelley, had concentrated on the shopping attractions at this duty free haven, whilst Colin had mentioned how those who had died on board Nelson's ship, the Victory, at the Battle of Trafalgar, back in 1805, had been brought to Gibraltar on that vessel and buried in what is known as Trafalgar cemetery, on the edge of the town.

Martin had added, *'It is perhaps amusing to know that Nelson's body was shipped back to England, preserved in a barrel of rum.'*

Once breakfast was over, Matt, Robert, Peter, James and Phyllis with Louise and Colin all disembarked and together made their way to Main Street which they knew would be lined with shops, restaurants and pubs. Being a group of seven was rather awkward when going in and out of shops, so they soon agreed to split up into pairs, with the exception of Matt who stayed with Robert and Peter, and meet up an hour later for coffee at a bar which they had just noticed.

Whilst the other two went into a men's wear store, Matt went off to call Pauline.

"Are you and Simon okay?" he asked, "I've had plenty of time to do a lot of thinking since I've been away and I wanted to tell you I've made up my mind this is going to be my last cruise. I really can't do another one without you and quite frankly I don't want to do any more even if you could come."

"Are you sure, Matt?" said Pauline.

"Definitely, I just don't want to earn a living from being on ships. I'm sure I can get plenty of work and be at home with the two of you."

"Well, I won't pretend I'm sorry." she responded, "I was just anxious for you alone to make the decision."

"You're an angel," said Matt, "I've missed you so much and I can't wait to get home."

"How's the weather?" she asked.

"It's still pretty good. We're in Gib. and will be leaving at about half-past five." said Matt, "I'll call you from Dover. I love you very much, you know."

"And I love you very much also. Now you take care and don't worry about anything. It'll all work out fine."

Armed with various shopping bags, the seven found two tables which they put together, ordered their coffee and told of their purchases.

"Parts of this island are going to pot." said James.

"Here we go," retorted Phyllis, "more complaints are coming up."

"Not at all," he continued, "but did you notice those three small houses which had corrugated iron roofing. I haven't seen anything like that for years."

"That reminds me of a story I must tell you." said Robert, "I had an aunt and uncle who lived in Bristol and a few years after the war they asked my parents if I'd like to stay with them for a week and be with my cousin, Jack.

"My parents agreed and I went off a month later. I had a lovely holiday and they were very nice to me and fortunately Jack and I got on very well. On the night before I was due to go home, my uncle told us he had tickets to take us all to the Hippodrome theatre, which was right in the centre.

"During that week they had an American artiste, called Lena Horne, heading a variety bill. She was a famous black singer who was not only beautiful but had a magical voice.

"Towards the end of her performance, she announced she would sing one of the songs she had made famous called Stormy Weather and as she did so the heavens opened and we could hear the thunder and lightning.

"What made it worse was the fact that during the war, the theatre had received a direct hit from a bombing raid and it had been necessary to replace the roof with corrugated iron sheeting.

"So you can image, Lena Horne, singing Stormy Weather with torrential rain clattering on the roof."

"That's a fabulous story." said James.

The morning passed but by midday they'd all had enough and made their way back to the ship.

"I just rang Pauline to tell her I'm not going to do any more cruises." Matt told James and Phyllis.

"You've done the right thing, Matt. It's not a good idea for you to be on the seven seas whilst she's in Epping. She's a lovely lady and she needs you to be near home not thousands of miles away."

*****

Anne and Vince were also surveying the shops and as they walked along Anne saw Martin standing outside a ladies lingerie shop.

"Is Shirley buying up the shop?" she asked.

"I doubt it, but after one quick peep inside, I said I'd wait here for her."

"I'll pop in and say hallo." said Anne.

As she disappeared, Vince said, "I'm sure you'd like to know that last night, Anne had her best sleep for ages, so thanks once again."

"Well I'm really pleased to hear that." said Martin.

"She said she'll be with you in five minutes," said Anne.

"I'll believe that when it happens." said Martin.

"We'll see you later, Martin." said Vince."

As they continued their stroll, Anne suggested to Vince he should try to become a speaker on board a ship. "After all you also have a considerable knowledge of art like Colin has."

"I don't think it would suit me," he replied, "and I certainly wouldn't want to enter any commitment of that nature at the moment. Perhaps after I've retired we can give it some thought."

He knew only too well that so long as she continued to have her problems, nothing of that nature could be contemplated.

"You're right," she said, "We'll have a lot more free time when you do retire."

"I tell you what I can do I'll have a word with Colin and find out how he went about getting registered."

"That's a very good idea. You do that." she agreed.

Vince was relieved he'd got over this minor hurdle without making her feel any sense of guilt.

*****

Though he felt a little better when first getting up, Henry told Liz he would be happy for her to go down to the shops but he would remain on deck.

When Andrew saw him later in the morning, he noticed Henry was reading 'Don Quixote.'

"Gosh," said Andrew, "I haven't read that book since I left university. It's wonderful, isn't it?"

"Yes it is. I've read it three times during my lifetime," replied Henry, "but recently I thought perhaps I should read it one more time. I'm nearly at the end."

"I think Liz has been my Dulcinea in the story and now our hero will soon be on his deathbed when, if you recall, he confesses the folly of his past adventures."

"I won't disturb you further," said Andrew, "We'll see you both for dinner."

As Andrew walked away he felt a little concerned at the way Henry had spoken. He recollected him saying he would read the book 'one more time.' and had felt a slight shudder go down his back, when Henry had spoken of being 'nearly at the end' and of Don Quixote, soon being 'on his deathbed.' Was Henry trying to say something or was he imagining double meanings that didn't exist!

He put these thoughts out of his head and continued his search for Ros.

*****

Almost on the dot of five-thirty, The Neptune slowly moved ahead preparing to turn away from Gibraltar. Laura and Doreen were on top deck watching with Laura recalling the events of the previous night when she was on top deck with Roger.

"The vacation's drawing to an end." commented Doreen.

Aided by its propellers, the Neptune would be pushing through the deep waters that lay ahead. Here it would find a sea that was expected to be calm but even if some unexpected adverse movements took place, the ships stabilizers would ensure that the majority of passengers would not experience discomfort.

Being the world's biggest inland sea, the Mediterranean did not have the same characteristics of an open ocean, with steep seas only occurring in the event of very strong winds. But after leaving Gibraltar, the Bay of Biscay would have to be treated with great respect.

As all ancient mariners had discovered, the seas and oceans of the world could be tame but could also be wild. Seafarers had frequently put their lives in peril, in order to achieve mercantile contact and commerce with those living in different countries or on other continents.

They sailed being uncertain of what the result of their voyages would be or the effect it would have on them as human beings, travelling in close proximity with others, hearing of their life's experiences, listening to their advice and having time, away from activities on shore, to give thought to their own future.

The Neptune was now entering the final phase of this journey. Perhaps once more, the mythical Gods of sea and sky would watch over the passengers, listen to their highs and lows and silently breathe out thoughts to help those still undecided as to the next steps to take, at this the crossroads of their life, so as to make their cruise truly memorable.

*****

In the same way that table decorations and other areas had flown Italian flags this evening the Union Jack was to be seen everywhere and first-sitting diners, who had already appeared from their cabins, were showing considerable ingenuity in respect of their chosen British theme clothing.

Many used flags for scarves or shirts, some were dressed as costers, two ladies appeared as Nell Gwyn, one couple, who had obviously prepared before coming on board, came dresses as a pearly king and queen and a host of others entered into the spirit of the evening with many men wearing bowler or boaters.

The dining staff had also donned dress suitable for the occasion with some having fun moustaches and beards that added to the all round jollity being enjoyed. Jeff and the photographic staff were once more taking as many photos as possible to hopefully boost the takings of the cruise.

The menu for the evening was predominantly English food. The choice of starters being Potato and egg salad, Smoked mackerel mousse, Potted shrimps and Melon cocktail. Three soups were available, Scotch broth, Mulligatawny or brown Windsor and the main courses were Roast beef with Yorkshire pudding and the usual trimmings, Lancashire hot-pot, Cod and chips, Chicken and mushroom pie or a Vegetable salad

Finally, the desserts, which were finding more appeal with the men than the women, included Jam roly-poly, Treacle pudding, Rice pudding, Stuffed baked apple and Sherry trifle together with the usual ice-creams and sorbet.

It was all a great success and Joanne's children had a ball, never having seen anything like this before.

*****

It was twenty past seven when the cabin telephone rang. Ros picked up the receiver to hear a very anxious Liz say, "Sorry to bother you but I need to speak to Andrew."

Within three minutes Andrew was in Henry's cabin where he was lying unconscious.

"I came to call for him before we went up to the lounge," said Liz, "but he didn't answer the door. I've always had his spare key so I was able to let myself in and found him like that. I 'phoned you immediately."

Andrew had already been examining Henry.

"It's not good news," he announced, "we're going to have to get him off the ship. He needs to have an emergency operation."

"Oh, my God," exclaimed Liz, "what's happened?"

"You told us he had a rare liver disease, well it seems to me he's got a liver abscess from an infection in the large intestine. It's called amoebiases. This is why he has a high fever and there's tenderness over the liver.

"He has undoubtedly had pain in the upper right corner of the abdomen which probably caused him to pass out. The abscess must be drained as soon as possible, since if it isn't it could be fatal."

"But how can he have an operation now we've left Gibraltar?" asked Liz.

"I'll have to speak to the captain and tell him what's happened. The next decision is his but as we've been cruising for over two hours I doubt whether he will want to turn the ship back. The alternative is to use the services of an emergency helicopter and although it could be very expensive it's fortunate we're not all that far from land."

"Don't worry about the expense." instructed Liz, "I know Henry has full medical insurance cover and anything over and above can be met by him, it's not as though he's poor."

"You stay here and apply some cold compresses so as to try and keep the fever down. He'll come round shortly and I'll leave you to tell him what's happened but don't make it sound too serious. I'll have a word with the senior medical officer and the captain and I'll call you in a few minutes. In the meantime I'll arrange for the nurse to come here and give him an injection which will make him feel a little more comfortable."

Andrew and the senior M.O. made their way to see the captain. Although the ship had only covered a distance of about sixty miles it was not going to be practical to return to Gibraltar. The radio officer was instructed to make contact with the Coast Guard controller and, subject to receiving an undertaking from the captain that all costs would be met, communication was made with the helicopter rescue centre.

Having been given the ships co-ordinates, the helicopter took off and in under an hour had reached The Neptune. Henry was secured to a stretcher and taken to top deck where the helicopter was hovering. The stretcher was then fixed to the external winching system which had been lowered and hoisted up to the helicopter door.

Liz had said she wanted to go with him and so a basket was lowered into which she was able to sit, secure herself and then be hoisted up.

The rescue was over with the helicopter making its way to the main hospital in Gibraltar which had been placed on alert for the emergency operation that was to be carried out.

The arrival and departure of the helicopter had brought many passengers out on deck to view an exercise not often seen.

Andrew and Ros had continued watching from the time the whirring blades had first increased speed until the air transport had vanished from sight.

"Do you think he'll be all right?" asked Ros.

"It's difficult to tell. The operation will be taking place without there having been too much delay and it's likely he'll come through okay. The problem is, he already has a liver disease and this incident is likely to aggravate his condition. I just doubt he'll ever be fit enough to take another cruise."

"What will happen to all their clothes?" asked Ros.

"The M.O. will keep in touch with the hospital and arrangements will be made for their belongings to be packed. When the ship lands in Dover, their cases will be transported to the address Liz gives them. I guess she'll stay with him in Gibraltar until he's able to go home."

*****

The incident immediately became the main topic of conversation, particularly with those who had met and spoken to Henry during the cruise.

Louise and Colin were very upset as was Karen who had enormously enjoyed the company of both Liz and Henry when they had visited Pompeii together.

All who had been with him at dinner each evening could not believe what had happened when told by Andrew. He also mentioned Henry's remarks about Don Quixote.

"It was as though he had a premonition something was going to happen" said Andrew.

The night of the British theme had become slightly marred but, as always, life goes on, as did 'Meet the Crew' in the theatre, introduced as usual by the cruise director – with a difference.

This evening he appeared wearing a grey morning suit with carnation, a grey top hat and carried a cane, as though he was attending an Ascot race meeting. Then much to the surprise of the audience he sang *'Get me to the Church on time'* from My Fair Lady. Nobody had realised what a good singing voice he had and how adept he was at dancing.

This was a sensational introduction to a show which was greeted enthusiastically by the audience. Each and every performer was excellent and the singing and dancing to music from other countries provided considerable interest.

Once again The Neptune had provided passengers with a highly entertaining evening.

*****

"I don't want to be late tonight." Laura told Roger and Doreen, as they came away from the theatre. It's my recital tomorrow afternoon and I shall need time to practice."

"Have you decided what you're going to play?" asked Doreen.

"I think it best if I play a mixed bag mainly of Chopin and Debussy. It always seems to go down well."

"I'm really looking forward to listening to you." said Roger, "Do you ever play special requests?"

"Sometimes," replied Laura, "why do you have one?"

"As a matter of fact I do." said Roger beaming, "I'd like you to play Elgar's Chanson d'Amour."

Laura blushed slightly, whilst Doreen turned to her saying, "I think that would be very apt. Don't you, Laura?"

*****

TWENTY ONE

Sleep had been kind to them and both Laura and Doreen had woken feeling refreshed and alert.

They made their way to the dining room where the normal hubbub of passengers could be heard only disrupted from time to time by the cruise director's announcements.

Most of the activities were similar to those which had regularly taken place during the two week period. The special items consisted of Colin's lecture at eleven, his subject being 'Meet Leonardo da Vinci', Laura's recital at four-thirty, information that the show that evening would feature Nick, Jake and Matt and details of a midnight buffet which would be taking place on Pool deck with a reminder that dress would be 'informal'.

Before finishing Alan Spencer told his listening public how a lady had come up to him the previous evening and asked *'Does the lift go from the back of the ship to the front?'* I asked her how long she had been on board and she ensured me since we left Dover!

He had also reminded passengers how at twelve-thirty there would be the final of the horse-racing in the Trident lounge *'when prizes will be doubled and I will be your commentator'*.

"How can anybody go to a midnight buffet after all the food we eat at dinner?" said Laura.

"I've no idea, I know I couldn't."

Just as they were finishing their coffee, a call over the Tannoy came from the Purser's office. Suddenly Laura went ashen.

"What's wrong?" asked Doreen, "Are you unwell?"

"I'm fine it's just that I think my mind played a trick on me. I'm sure it's nothing."

A few minutes later they both clearly heard the repeated call, *'Will Madame Claudine Flatau in Main deck cabin 5296, please report to the Purser's office.'*

Laura sat frozen to her chair as an Egyptian sphinx. She was unable to move her jaws and her eyes stared ahead but failed to register Doreen, who was sitting opposite.

Doreen became concerned as Laura barely seemed to be breathing. Her eyelids had dropped, her arms, with both hands flat down on the table, remained motionless and with her head drooping slightly her mouth remained an immoveable open aperture.

"Laura," whispered Doreen, "Are you sure you're all right?"

There was no response. Now she was really worried. *'Perhaps she'd had a stroke',* she thought.

She asked the waiter to quickly bring a glass of water. She took it to Laura and held it to her lips. She was relieved when Laura opened her eyes, sipped some of the water and started to move her hands.

"I cannot believe what we heard." said Laura, "There can only be one Madame Claudine Flatau. I made a journey of over nine hundred miles in France, returned to England, joined you on this cruise and suddenly we find she's on board the same ship. It is too incredulous for words. I don't think I'll ever be able to believe anything anymore."

"You must not say that," said Doreen, "I'm sure it's no coincidence she's here. It's meant to be, in the same way as your entire journey was meant and now at long last the two of you will meet. Now you'll be able to talk to her and find out for yourself who she is and why you had to make the journey you did."

"Perhaps I should go to the Purser's desk." said Laura, "She may be there."

"I'll come with you."

At the desk they were told Madame Flatau had been but had left about five minutes ago.

Laura turned to Doreen saying, "I'm going to her cabin. Would you mind if I go alone?"

"Of course not," replied Doreen, "Good luck. I trust all goes well. I'll wait for you outside the Bistro."

Laura walked slowly up the staircase to Main deck, her stomach feeling knotted in desperate anticipation. She found the cabin and for a few moments stood staring at the door number 5296 until, having plucked up courage, she knocked gently, took one step back and waited.

A woman in her late-forties came to the door.

"Madame Flatau?" asked Laura.

"Oui, madame."

"My name is Laura, Laura……"

Before Laura could say another word, the woman interrupted and said "Mon Dieu, Laura, c'est toi" and then, changing into English, "At last, Laura, it's you."

A look of utter amazement and disbelief showed in Madame Flatau's face and Laura sensed that tears were forming in her eyes. She wore a dark blue pleated skirt with a white blouse, to which was attached a cameo brooch which looked very old. She had mid-brown hair, cut in a sophisticated urchin look. Her face was small of good complexion, and overall she presented herself neatly and attractively.

"Come in, come in.' she said, "Please, excuse my manners."

Her English was very good though a French accent was continuously present. She closed the cabin door and led Laura into the bedroom area.

They both sat looking at each other.

"I cannot believe what is happening." said Madame Flatau. She sounded as totally amazed as Laura had done earlier.

"Forgive me, but I hardly know what to say." she said, "We cannot stay seated in this little room. Why don't we go upstairs to the Apollo lounge and have some coffee. Would you like that?"

"Yes, I think it's a good idea," replied Laura, "and I know it'll be quiet there for some time."

When in the lounge, they sat facing each other in a corner of the room so as not to be disturbed.

"I cannot believe it," said Madame Flatau, "how did you find me?"

"I heard your name being called out over the speaker system, Madame, saying you were wanted at the Purser's desk" replied Laura, "Your cabin number was mentioned."

"Yes I know, but you have been looking for me before now. I spoke to my neighbour in France and she said you had been to my home. That is what I meant when I asked how did you find me? And please stop calling me Madame my name is Claudine."

Laura began to recount her journey of nine hundred miles from Dover, her visits to the various places called Asnieres until finally meeting Sylvie Mercier who gave her Claudine's address in La Fleche.

Claudine sat listening intently and in silence until Laura had finished. She never once interrupted the flow of her story until at the end she looked down at Laura's hand and commented, "That must be the ring?"

Laura looked surprised.

"You know about this ring?" she said questioningly.

'Mais oui, pour sur. Certainly.' responded Claudine.

"I believe you know more than I do about a number of things." said Laura.

"But how can that be possible?" retorted Claudine, expressing some surprise, "Did not your mother give you the ring?"

Laura began to tell how her mother and father had died when she was seven and how she had been brought up by her aunt and uncle. She then explained how it was their family solicitor who had sent it to her on her twenty-fifth birthday, in accordance with her mother's instructions.

"The box containing the ring showed the name Asnieres and the ring had the name Flatau inscribed. I realised the ring and the names were connected and knew I would never be satisfied until I had gone to France to discover their meaning.

"You must help me, Madame, pardon, Claudine. It is obvious that there is so much I need to be told and for me to uncover.

"I feel as though I've become lost, as in a maze, knowing there is a way out but not being able to find the exit.

"I sometimes have a dreadful sensation of not belonging and yet I know this is not true. It may sound ridiculous, but I have reached a point where I don't know who I am and need to find myself."

By the time she had finished Laura felt quite emotional and placed her handkerchief to her eyes.

Claudine looked across to her smiled reassuringly and whispered, "I promise all will soon become clear. Have you time to talk more with me?"

Laura looked at her watch. Realising she was soon to rehearse in the lounge, she explained the nature of her work and the reason why she was on the ship.

"In a few minutes I have been allotted one hour to be able to practice. Is it possible we could meet again after lunch"

"But of course." said Claudine, "Shall we come here again, say at two."

"No, that will not be possible." replied Laura, "At two o'clock they have a watercolour class here. There is a small room near the library that nobody ever seems to use. Let's meet there."

"That will be good. I will see you then."

Before starting to play, Laura returned to the Bistro to find Doreen and told her all that had taken place so far.

"What's she like?" asked Doreen.

"She's very nice. I've agreed to meet her again at two." said Laura, "When you see Roger could you suggest the three of us have lunch at twelve-thirty. Let's go to the dining room. It will be quieter to talk. I'll meet you both there."

*****

Whilst the unexpected meeting had been taking place between Laura and Claudine, Colin had presented his last talk on the life of Leonardo da Vinci.

Not one of the audience, which included Louise, did not know of his Mona Lisa but as the lecture continued the fact he worked as an architect, engineer and set designer, organising elaborate festivals for the Court of the French King, Francois I, began to fascinate all.

Colin had brought with him for viewing on screen, many examples of the incredible inventions of da Vinci in the field of civil and military engineering, mechanics, optics, hydraulics and aeronautics.

"The man was undoubtedly a genius." he said, "Just think for a moment. It was da Vinci who created the first tank, the first automobile, the swing bridge, the paddle boat, the flying machine, the helicopter, the parachute and many others.

"He died in fifteen nineteen at age sixty-seven, having accomplished more in his lifetime than most of us could achieve in fifty lifetimes."

At the end of his talk, Colin was surprised but very pleased when so many of the passengers came over and congratulated him for an excellent morning and told him how much they had enjoyed all of his other talks during the cruise.

Louise, who had been standing by his side, found herself feeling quite proud.

*****

When Matt saw Denise he informed her of his decision and how he had told Pauline this was to be his last cruise.

"What did she say?" asked Denise.

"She was very pleased but had not wanted to influence me in any way."

"She sounds both a very lovely and very sensible lady." said Denise. "You're on stage tonight, aren't you?"

"That's right, but it's a triple bill and Nick and Jake will also be performing." replied Matt, "As this will be my last cruise ship appearance I'd really appreciate your being there. You've been so kind to me and such a great listener. You've helped me considerably."

"I promise I'll come," said Denise and when you've finished I'll treat you to a celebration drink."

She kissed him on both cheeks and then added, "You may be lucky having Pauline as a wife but I'll tell you something, she's fortunate to have such a lovely man as her husband. I'll see you later."

*****

It was two and Laura and Claudine arrived simultaneously at the agreed meeting point.

"You have told me so much about yourself and your journey but I have not told you anything about myself." said Claudine, "I was born in Paris. My father was made redundant at age fifty-eight, when the company he worked for was taken over. He decided to retire and he and my step-mother moved to

Asnieres-sur-Vegre. As you have seen, it is a delightful place and we enjoyed living there. I was twenty-eight at the time and a little later I moved to Angers to take up a teacher's training course.

"I met Louis Buron when I was thirty-one and we married soon after. He was the headmaster of a school in Laval. I obtained a position teaching five and six year olds. I found this most enjoyable and rewarding. Louis had always been over-weight and smoked too much. I was always trying to stop him but he didn't take any notice. We were unable to have any children but teaching little ones filled this gap for me. One afternoon, I received a telephone call from the assistant head-master to tell me that Louis had suffered a heart attack and was dead. We had only been married nine years."

"Oh, Claudine, I'm so sorry." said Laura.

"These things happen but eventually we realise we have to carry on with our lives. The grieving time is different for everybody but in the end it is important to recognise that to live in the past, can be compared with placing yourself in a darkened room with neither a window nor door available. There is no possibility for any light to come through and no way to find an opening to a new life.

"Life must be lived to the full and when it calls out we must grasp it to ourselves, embrace it, nourish it and let it bring all the joys it holds."

Claudine reached into her handbag and produced two photographs.

"This was my father," she said, "he was a lovely man, very caring and knowledgeable. He died three years ago when he was seventy-four. I returned to Asnieres for a little while before his death but afterwards I decided to move to La Fleche. This was my step-mother. She died a year after my father at age seventy-six."

Claudine replaced the two photographs and then pulled out a third.

"And this was Louis." she whispered in a reverential tone.

As she was replacing the third of the photographs, Laura asked, "Why do you still use the name of Flatau?"

"I kept the name after marriage because it was easier when I was teaching. Now, I do not teach full-time I only help at a nearby school, should one of the teachers be unwell. I also do a little work with children who have special needs."

They continued talking until it was nearly half past three. Laura found herself feeling very comfortable in Claudine's company and was surprised how, after only their second meeting, they were both able to confide in each other with considerable ease.

"This is not the best of days for us to have met like this." said Laura, "As I told you I am giving a recital at half past four and I must now go back to my cabin to rest and change. Would you like to have dinner with me this evening?"

"That would be lovely," replied Claudine, "but as all the dining room tables are full, we better go to the Ocean Bistro. Shall we meet at eight?"

"That's fine by me. Goodbye for now or perhaps I should say au revoir."

*****

Louise and Colin had joined Ros and Andrew for tea.

"Is there any news of Henry?" asked Louise.

"No, not yet." replied Andrew, "It's possible we may not here anything before the end of the cruise. After the operation he's likely to have been placed in intensive care for two or three days. Liz gave me her home telephone number so I'll call her when she's back in England."

"If, I give you my number perhaps you would also telephone me." said Louise, "I really would like to know what happened."

Tea, when taken in the dining room, was a far more formal affair with small sandwiches, scones and jam, fruit cake and pastries.

"I love this sort of tea." commented Colin, "It's like going out into the country and stopping off at a little tea-room. The only thing that's missing is a toasted teacake."

"I agree," said Ros, "when I was a little girl my parents would take us out for a ride on a Sunday afternoon and we'd do just that. My favourite was the small sponge cakes which were covered with icing."

Andrew was holding a finger cucumber sandwich in his hand when he turned to Ros and said, "Do you remember that night at Evelyn's house?"

"Could I ever forget." replied Ros.

"This sounds as though a story is about to be told," said Colin.

"Well, what happened was, one day we were invited by Evelyn, whose husband had died some years before, to go to her house for dinner at seven-thirty on the following Saturday. We'd no doubt it was for dinner as another couple, who we've known for years, were also asked but as they had a previous invitation they had to decline. She did, however, speak to Ros and referred to the fact the invite had definitely been for dinner.

"We arrived at just after seven-thirty and were given a drink but became slightly concerned when, by eight, nobody else showed. Fortunately, Evelyn said she would pop upstairs, to see if her kids were all right, and after she'd gone, Ros made a beeline for the kitchen only to discover that nothing was cooking.

"When I heard this, I wasn't very amused. I'd been working all day and was starving. Anyway Evelyn returned muttering, '*I wonder where they've got to!*' and with that went into the hall and we heard her making a call.

"When she came back, she said, '*The four of them have just finished dinner and should be here in about twenty minutes*'.

"At about quarter to nine they duly arrived. More drinks were served and then we were asked whether we'd like tea or coffee. Evelyn wheeled in a trolley with lots of sandwiches – just like this one – together with a coffee gateau and some chocolate biscuits.

"I might tell you, I hate coffee gateau.

"Never mind, I thought, I'll be able to launch into the sandwiches and biscuits and stem the pangs of hunger.

"Small plates were handed round, followed by the sandwiches. I placed three on my plate but realised they were all very cold. When I picked one up it was obvious they were still frozen so with the plate in one hand and a frozen sandwich in the other, I tapped the sandwich on the plate whilst saying, '*I think there's something wrong with this sandwich.*"

"Oh, I can't believe it, so what did you do? " Louise asked."

"I had some tea and a couple of chocolate biscuits and then feigned a terrible headache and we left. When we arrived back home, Ros cooked some poached eggs on toast with sausages and baked beans.

"The following morning, Evelyn, telephoned to find out if I was okay and told Ros she'd forgotten to take the sandwiches out of the freezer early enough in the day."

"It takes all sorts." said Colin.

*****

Laura's recital was once again received with acclamation. She had her biggest audience of the cruise and the assistant cruise director announced that would make every effort to get Laura back on another cruise.

When she'd completed her main programme she indicated she would be pleased to play an encore, which was by way of a special request, and, as asked for by Roger, played Chanson d'amour.

Roger beamed and when taking a final bow Laura noticed Claudine sitting towards the back of the room. She motioned for her to come forward taking the opportunity to introduce her to both Doreen and Roger as 'a friend of mine from France.'

*****

Once more they met. The Bistro was not over-crowded and they found a table where it seemed they were not likely to be disturbed.

"This morning you told me everything would become clear." said Laura, "I hope you are now going to be able to explain."

"Laura, I have a letter for you." said Claudine, "I didn't want to give it you before your recital. It is from my father. I am sure this is the moment you should read it."

Laura took the envelope and held it seeing on the outside just one word "Laura".

"But, why should your father have written to me?' she asked.

"Please read the letter. I think it will answer a number of the questions that have been causing you such great concern." responded Claudine.

Laura slowly opened the envelope and took out several sheets of close hand-written sheets of paper that had been written in English.

Chere Laura,

'As I begin to put my pen to these pieces of paper, I am sure this will be the most difficult letter I have ever written. I know your mother has sadly passed on, though I have no doubt she will always be watching over you. I need you to know it is your mother who has left it to me, to write this letter and tell you our story.

'My name is Jules Flatau and I was born in a suburb of Paris. I was Company Secretary to an industrial pharmaceutical company and when I was twenty-seven I married my first wife, Simone. She was six years younger than me and her family also came from Paris. She was very beautiful and we were very happy together. After we had been married for three years, Simone became pregnant. We were both very excited and then Simone was told she would be having twins.

'I suppose that fate had said this was not to be for us. Instead of much joy we also had great sadness enter our lives. Two girls were born but the second was dead at birth. Simone was devastated even though Claudine was fit and well. I did not know what to do. I did everything possible to help this woman who I loved very much. Nothing I did helped her condition and I had to arrange for my unmarried sister to move in with us to help Simone look after Claudine.

'Eight years later Simone had a complete mental breakdown from which she was never to recover. I talked many times with her family until it reached a stage where it was becoming impossible for me to look after her. During the next two years she was admitted several times into a hospital as an out patient. Finally it was decided by her doctor she should go into a home where she would receive daily medication and nursing care. By now she had to be fed, bathed and dressed.

'At first I visited her three, sometimes four times a week. She never knew I was there. I would sit and hold her hand and die a little more each time I saw her. I found I could not stand the pain of making so many visits. Soon I only went once a week at the weekend. It was self-torture every time and I

only thank God, Simone did not know what was happening. She died when she was only forty-seven years old.

'It was two years before when I met your mother. She was just twenty-seven and told me she would like to work and live in Paris. She was unmarried and wanted to be able to travel in France and Italy. I cannot remember exactly but I think she stayed with a far cousin, (is that what you say?) who had married a Frenchman and had moved from England many years before. I met Frances, your mother, at a little party of a mutual friend.

'Despite our age difference there was an instant attraction between us and I started to see her many times. She did not go to Italy but stayed in Paris. Whenever possible we visited other places together and would go into the countryside. From the very beginning I told your mother about Simone. Three weeks before she was to go home we went away on a holiday to a beautiful place in Suisse Normande. Perhaps you know it?

'It was a magical trip and I experienced happiness I had not known for so many years. At the same time we were both sad knowing our being together must soon come to an end.

'A few days before leaving Paris, your mother became concerned because she thought she might be pregnant. She knew I would have married her but understood this was impossible. She had great strength of mind and kept on telling me there would be no problems. She was so pleased she would be having our child and over and over again told me she would never do anything to harm the baby. After she returned to England we spoke to each other all the time. Soon she confirmed she was pregnant.'

Laura stopped reading. She could hardly breathe, whilst her throat and mouth had dried as sandpaper. She took a handkerchief from her bag, blew her nose and looked up at Claudine. Neither spoke, as Laura resumed, whilst Claudine sat watching her read, knowing the content of the letter.

'A few weeks later, Frances told me she intended marrying someone called Jeffrey King. She said they had known each other for many years and that he had always wanted to marry her. She told me having a baby did not bother him and he had promised he would always think of the child as if he was the real father.

'I do not need to tell you, Laura, you were that baby. I wanted to be there with you more than anything in the world, but it was impossible. A few

weeks later I sent a ring to your mother. It had been in my family for many years and I wanted Frances to give it you, at a time when she thought right.

'Your mother begged me to stay out of your lives. I promised since I was sure she was doing the right thing. I never told her but I did break this promise many times but it did no harm to anybody. Twice or maybe three times in a year I had to be in England and when this happened I would secretly come down to where you lived so I could see you from a distance. I could do nothing else. I had given my word.

'I re-married eighteen months after Simone died. My second wife is Nadia and Claudine is your half-sister.

Laura put down the letter and again looked at Claudine.

"Do you know what your father has written in this letter?" she asked.

"Yes, I do." replied Claudine, in a very quiet voice.

"So you have known for many years you had a half-sister in England?"

"Yes, I have, but Laura, Let me say that….."

"Please don't say anything at the moment." interrupted Laura, "Let me first finish reading the letter. I have often thought that in France, there was a part of my life which I did not know about, but this, well, I never imagined reading anything like this."

"I understand." said Claudine, smiling at Laura, as once more she continued.

'After I retired we went to live in Asnieres-sur –Vegre. Claudine has also had to endure sadness in her life but should you ever meet her, she can explain for herself.

'Ma chere, Laura. I am now seventy-four and I do not think I shall be here much longer. If you find yourself reading this letter then you will know I have passed on. It has always been my greatest wish to be able to sit by your side and explain all that you will be reading. But, if it is not meant to be, then that is how it must be.

'I want you to know that throughout your life, you have never been far from my thoughts.

'I do not know what more to say to you but be sure what you have read is the truth. Believe it and live the rest of your life knowing this truth and also knowing that my love for you was present at all times. I do not seek your forgiveness only your understanding.'

The letter was simply signed, *Jules*.

Laura placed the letter in her lap and sat completely silent and immobile.

She remained like this for two or three minutes, during which time Claudine sat staring across at her, hoping that she was all right but not daring to guess how she would react having read the words of their father.

Laura rose slowly from her chair and turning to Claudine said, 'Claudine, would you mind if I do not stay any longer for dinner. I am feeling rather bewildered and I need time to think. I will call you in your cabin tomorrow morning."

Having left the Bistro, Laura once more made her way to Apollo deck and stood looking out whilst holding on to the railings. The sky had darkened leaving a blood orange coloured sun glowing bright waiting to be extinguished by the sea below. Clouds appeared to dance like ballerinas on the far horizon to a backcloth of yellow and red daubed between shafts of darkened blue.

Laura knew the dimming lights were bringing this day to an end, a day which had revealed to her a previously unknown part of her life. She now had to give considerable thought to everything she had heard and read before the light of tomorrow morning came. Only then would she be able to decide the next steps which she must take between her and Claudine.

*****

"This evening is the penultimate show which we have for you," said Alan Spencer, "and I am proud to be able to introduce three wonderful artists who you've all seen before but are well worth seeing over and over again."

First, Nick Guthrie appeared and for the next twenty-five minutes sang a series of popular songs together with the Neptune singers and dancers supporting him. He was followed by Jake Hammond who once more entertained on saxophone and clarinet and told jokes non-stop in between.

They were both well liked by the cruise audience and to end the show was a further appearance of Matt Campbell who commenced by saying, "What a relief, the other two didn't sing any of my songs or tell any of my gags and as they can't do magic – I'm safe."

He surpassed himself with a magic show he had specially prepared to include many of the very best he could perform. The audience were in fits of laughter when he brought some on stage to assist him and then unmercifully pulled their legs.

His allotted time was almost over when he went to the front of the stage with a hand-microphone and told everybody he had an announcement to make.

"I've decided this will be the last show I shall be doing on any cruise ship. All comedians and magicians try to make you laugh and smile at every given opportunity but I've no doubt that some of you will realise it's not always easy to play the role of the clown, especially when we have personal problems weighing us down. You've been a great audience and before I leave you I would like to sing the opening verses of one more song. It comes from that wonderful show 'Chicago' and is called 'Mr. Cellophane'.

The lights dimmed, everyone in the theatre stopped talking and the orchestra commenced playing the opening bars of this poignant song until Matt started to sing.

If someone stood up in a crowd,
And raised his voice up way out loud,
And waved his arm and shook his leg,
You'd notice 'em.
If someone in the movie show,
Yelled, "Fire in the second row,
This place is a powder keg!"
You'd notice 'em.
And even without clucking like a hen,
Everyone gets noticed now and then,
Unless of course that person it should be
Invisible, inconsequential, me.
Cellophane, Mr. Cellophane,
Should have been my name, Mr. Cellophane,
'Cause you can look right through me,
Walk right by me,
And never know I'm there.

I tell you, Cellophane,
Should have been my name, Mr. Cellophane,
'Cause you can look right through me,
Walk right by me,
And never know I'm there.

As he started to sing the last lines of the chorus, Matt made his way towards the curtain and went off stage with a wave.

For a few seconds the audience remained silent until suddenly there was tumultuous applause.

Matt returned on three different occasions to acknowledge their ovation trying to avoid showing the tears in his eyes.

On his final bow he suddenly saw Denise standing and clapping him. Their eyes met and she placed both hands to her lips and blew him a kiss.

*****

TWENTY TWO

The last day of any cruise is always pretty hectic for the crew generally and for those working behind the Purser's desk in particular, where passengers tend to appear throughout the day to deal with various matters which they wish to arrange before disembarkation.

Currency changing, checking of bills for extras and confirming return flight or train times are but some of the enquiries, apart from collecting passports, left at the desk since coming on board, obtaining extra baggage labels and seeking advice on tipping arrangements, that were notified to all passengers both before the cruise and in the previous days newsletter. The most frequent of questions usually relate to the time luggage has to be left outside cabin doors that evening despite full details having been given the day before.

*****

As Doreen was still asleep when Laura woke, she pulled the curtains open very slightly so as to be able to once again read the letter from her real father.

She took it from her bag and re-read it twice. It was quite incredible that only now she had discovered another man had been her father and that here was a woman, who was her half-sister.

She rubbed her eyes feeling as though none of this had really happened and that it was all a dream. How do people respond in weird circumstances like this, she thought? How was she supposed to behave? She was confused and unsettled, and yet certain events from the past were now beginning to make sense.

She could now understand the surprising affinity she had always felt towards France and the natural flair and ability she had shown at school in learning the French language.

The contents of the letter had been all too much for one person to absorb in a single sitting. Her initial reaction had been to wonder why her mother had not told her everything before she had died or told her aunt to tell her before now.

But now she understood why her mother had said nothing to her. How could she possibly know how Laura might react or what she might think of her if she were to tell of her past indiscretions? Perhaps her own daughter would have felt shame at her mother's impropriety and disgusted she had never been given a chance to meet her biological father.

Doreen woke a few minutes later and Laura showed her the letter.

"Wow," said Doreen, "that's incredible. What did you say?"

"I didn't know what to say. I couldn't carry on just sitting there having dinner, so I excused myself and having taken a breath of fresh air, I came down to the cabin and collapsed in a heap. I felt totally exhausted and must have slept like a log."

"You were certainly fast asleep when I came to bed." said Doreen, "So what's on the agenda today between the two of you?"

"I told her I'd 'phone her this morning. I'd rather have breakfast with you and Roger and meet her later."

"Well, why not give her a call now and fix a time. She's bound to be waiting to hear from you. Suggest ten in the Apollo. It'll give you time to talk to us and think a little more."

Claudine had been perfectly amenable to this suggestion and at ten greeted Laura in a typically French manner with a kiss on both cheeks.

Conversation was kept at a light level as though they were fencing with foil or epee in an effort to find out each other's interests, weaknesses and strengths. As anticipated, it was not surprising to either one of them that eventually the subject of their blood relationship would arise. Claudine had been both sensitive and clever enough to allow Laura to make the pace and when the time came, Laura found herself speaking very slowly and thoughtfully.

"The man I've known, all my life, to be my father will forever remain in my memory, as my father. It was he, together with my mother, who brought me up, cared for me, looked after me and showed me nothing but love and although I now know he was not my natural father, this cannot make any difference.

"I have no doubt, Claudine, that Jules was a very decent, honest and honourable man. This is good, since it means that I've had two fathers both of whom possessed these fine qualities.

"You have known about me about me for a very long time. It was only yesterday that I discovered your existence and I think we should start on the basis of becoming good friends. I certainly hope this will happen. Then, I think it's very possible the sisterly affection we should have between us will flourish. Perhaps, it will be the same as when a boy and girl first meet. They start by being friends and as time goes by their feelings for each other become deeper.

"There is, however, one thing I should like you to agree to."

"Tell me what it is and I'll try to help." replied Claudine.

"I would like to go back to Asnieres with you and visit the graves of our father and your mother."

Claudine felt emotionally moved as she listened to the words uttered by Laura. She rose from her seat, went towards her and held her close.

"Thank you, Laura. This would be a great pleasure for me and when you come we could go and stay at a cottage in Honfleur, on the coast of Normandy. Our father's parents owned it. They left it to him and he left it to me. It is about two hundred and fifty kilometres from La Fleche. In July and August the cottage is rented but at other times it is empty.

"I had planned to go in October for a week but I thought we should go together. Maybe we owe this to ourselves. It will help us to relax and get to know each other. I'm sure our father would have liked us to do this and the cottage will be a perfect place to stay. What do you think? Is it good, my idea?"

"It sounds perfect. I think you're right," replied Laura, "it would be very sad if we couldn't find one week to try and make up for over twenty five lost years.'

Claudine began to relate and re-live some of the wonderful times she and Louis had enjoyed together. The love and affection she had felt for him was obvious and at no time did she sound embittered at his having been taken from her.

"Have you been interested in anyone since Louis died?" asked Laura.

"Not really, I've been introduced to several men who have all been very pleasant but I've never yet been able to experience the feeling when you know you have met someone very special. You cannot put there, that which is not there.

"Women have the ability to give so much love but to be with the right person there has to be passion and depth of feeling which takes over completely. It happens when you know the other person is the most important being in your life and you equally know you are the most important one in his life."

Laura refrained from comment, knowing the words spoken by Claudine contained considerable meaning in relation to herself. Never once had she been placed first other than by her direct family. Perhaps it was because she had not experienced the strength of love that Claudine was describing.

"What about you?" asked Claudine, "Have you met anyone, yet?"

"Not until this cruise," replied Laura, "and then Roger came along, which reminds me I mustn't leave him and Doreen any longer this morning. Come with me and we'll join them."

"I think it better if you go and meet them," responded Claudine, "there are some things I need to do and I want to get my packing out of the way before this evening. Do you think we could all have dinner together?"

"I'm sure we can. I'll have a word with one of the other couples and with some gentle reorganising it should be fine. Let's meet in the lounge bar at about quarter to eight."

*****

It was the first day since the cruise began that the weather was not particularly pleasant. The sun only managed to peep out occasionally behind grey cheerless clouds. A wind had produced a slight movement on the sea which, although insufficient to bother most people, had already been felt by Joanne,

Dean noticed that she was wearing a wrist band which he had not seen before.

"Where did you get that?" he asked.

315

"From one of the shops." she replied, "I don't like being at sea when it gets choppy and this is supposed to help."

"What does it do?" he said.

"It's a special band with small balls that rest on what is called an acupressure point and it relieves any feeling of motion sickness." explained Joanne.

"And has it?" he asked.

"As a matter of fact, it has. I was beginning to feel slightly queasy but since I put it on I've been fine."

"If the weather doesn't improve," said Dean, "I thought we'd take the kids to the theatre at four-thirty. There's a comic adventure film showing which should be just right for them."

"That seems a good idea and it'll stop them driving us crazy." replied Joanne, "What a holiday we've had. Wait until they get back to school and tell the other kids and the teachers what they've been doing and where they've been."

"And just wait until they go round telling everybody, 'my mum's getting married.'" commented Dean.

"I know and I'm very happy and very excited." said Joanne.

Other passengers were also a little unsure as to how best to pass the day. Sitting outside on one of the decks would require wearing warmer clothing and was not likely to be too agreeable and Anne and Vince had decided to enter a special bridge tournament being organised by Graham Hyde.

"It'll be better than just sitting around doing nothing." said Anne.

*****

Delia and Paul had arranged to have lunch in the dining room with Shirley and Martin. Having arrived a little early they sat on one of the sofas nearby.

"It's been absolutely amazing that I've been able to go to so many AA meetings whilst we've been on board." said Paul, "It's helped me appreciate how much they really help especially when I've talked to some of the men and women who've been going for years."

"They've certainly done you a power of good. You're like the Paul I first met and loved many years ago." replied Delia.

"The important thing is I now feel far more confident and I don't even think of having a drink. Yes, occasionally I feel as though I would like to have one but I don't believe this is any different from someone who has given up smoking after being a forty-a-day man. And that's where AA is helping so much."

"Well I'm thrilled we have our marriage back on track and I'm sure you'll soon put together many more articles for International Publications."

"Here they are." announced Paul, having spotted Shirley leading the way.

"I don't think much of today's weather." she said.

"I know," said Delia agreeing, "but we can't really complain, we've had two weeks when it's been really lovely."

"I could spend all year round in the sun." said Martin.

"Would you ever consider buying a place abroad?" asked Paul.

"Ah, that's another ball game altogether. I doubt it very much. First, I don't want the hassle or expense, should anything go wrong – and I gather from friends who have a second property, there's always something, requiring them to put their hands into their pockets. Then you have to be very careful with income tax and inheritance tax regulations, otherwise you can be in real trouble.

"But most of all once you've got a holiday home you'd probably feel obliged to keep on going down to it. That may suit some but I prefer getting a change of scenery when I go away and wouldn't want to be at the same place over and over again."

"I agree," Delia said, "and I wouldn't want to find that whenever I went on holiday I was cleaning, ironing and cooking, as I do at home. I prefer to have other people looking after me and making the beds and serving up my meals without my having to go shopping and do all those chores."

"Mind you, it can be rather nice being away from hotels." said Shirley, "I wouldn't mind renting a cottage or a villa providing a cleaner came in once a week and we had no responsibilities."

"I'd go along with that," agreed Paul, "when you rent you get the best of both worlds."

"By the way," said Martin, "you may not know it, but you lucky people will have to put up with our company for dinner this evening. We'll be making your table up to eight again."

"How's that come about?" asked Delia.

"It's a rather complicated story which you would do best to ask Laura about, but she asked us whether we would agree to move so that a French friend of hers could join her on this our last night."

"It really is an amazing tale." said Shirley, "It seems this 'French friend' is in fact her half-sister and they only met yesterday for the first time."

"Now that could really make a great story," commented Paul.

*****

The final of the dancing competition began promptly at two in the theatre with the judges being Alan Spencer and Sandra Wells together with Matt. There were four contestants left out of an original entry of seventeen and now each pair had to dance a waltz, quickstep and a rumba.

All of the entrants had dressed smartly with the winners to receive a credit of £100 on their cabin account.

The four contestants would be dancing simultaneously to the music of the Neptune orchestra.

Both Robert and Peter had qualified with their respective partners whilst the other two were married couples who danced regularly together.

A large number of passengers had come to watch and cheer on their respective favourites.

It was Peter dancing with Sophie who were certainly the best turned out but there was little to choose between any of them after the waltz. The quickstep created a gap with Peter and Sophie and one of the married couples providing the most exciting series of steps to the music of a Glenn Miller favourite, 'In the Mood'. Finally, there was the rumba with the orchestra playing the beautiful song 'Sway'.

The rhythmic movements of Peter and Sophie impressed the audience considerably and when individual pairs came before the judges it was they who received the most applause. Their selection as winners gained unanimous approval

"You danced beautifully," Peter told her.

"You just wait until you see me sway when you come to my house." she replied.

They had very much enjoyed being in each other's company ever since she first saw him and like two teenagers had, whenever possible, disappeared from view and sneaked into her cabin.

They'd now agreed he would spend a long weekend with her two weeks after they returned home from the cruise.

*****

"As the weather's so poor I think I'll pop into the casino for a while." said David, having found Karen sitting reading in the library.

"Let's go outside for a minute," she whispered, not wishing to disturb anyone else, "I need to talk to you."

They walked out of the library to the same small room where Laura and Claudine had previously met.

"Before you throw your money away yet again, David, I've something to tell you. I've made up my mind that once we're back home I intend divorcing you." Karen announced.

She had spoken these words slowly and without any emotion and then continued, "I shall use our family solicitor and he will no doubt get in touch with you. I want you to leave home as soon as possible early next week. I'm sure it'll be better for both of us and I'm sure you'll have no problem in being able to stay with one of your lady friends."

David stood staring at her, his face thunderous.

"You're going to divorce me!" he shouted, "I'll believe that when I see it. Don't make me laugh. You'd never be able to manage without me. You're absolutely pathetic. We'll talk about this later."

"There's nothing to talk about, David. The days of talking are over. I'm not prepared to stay with you any longer. I'm sorry you don't believe me, but now I've told you don't be surprised when it happens."

Karen turned, walked out of the room and returned to the library leaving a seething David trying to cool down.

*****

The voice of Alan Spencer was once again heard.

"Sorry about the weather today folks but I did produce the goodies for you up to now. Anyway, I'd just like to remind you Bingo players that at four-thirty we've the final games of this cruise with a carry-over pot of seven hundred pounds that must be won today.

"Also, Phyllis has asked me to announce that the works of her pupils are all on display for you to see. I've had a preview and believe me they are great. So go and have a look.

"Our show tonight is titled 'We'll Meet Again" – and I don't care if that's a cliché. It will star all of your favourites and will provide you with a night to remember.

"But, but, but – please don't forget all your luggage must be outside your cabin for collection by no later than eleven-thirty – that's eleven-thirty TONIGHT – in case you thought otherwise. See you later."

*****

"It's occurred to me," said Colin, "that when we arrive back in Dover I could give you a lift home."

"But surely that would take you miles out of your way?" replied Louise.

"Not at all, I've got to take the A2 to join up with the M25, so it'll be no problem whatsoever."

"Well, if you're really sure that would be marvellous," said Louise, "and I'm sure Jeff will be delighted."

"Good, well that's settled then." said Colin.

"I suppose once you get home you'll be up to your ears planning the opening of your restaurant" said Louise.

She'd been thinking a great deal about him and had realised how fortunate she had been to have met him. He really was very special.

"That's right," Colin replied, "but at least I've been able to have a good holiday before returning to the daily grind," and then, with a cheeky smile, added, "and I suppose meeting you hasn't been too bad either!"

"You stinker," she said, "As a matter of fact, I thought, providing it was not putting you out too much, perhaps the next time you go to Reigate you might like to stay a day or two where I live. I shouldn't think it would take you too long."

"Do you mean to say they have hotels in Rochester where a lad like me might get a room?" he responded in a joking fashion.

"Well, yes, but perhaps you might prefer to stay at my house. I do have a spare room in which I'm sure you'd be comfortable."

He couldn't resist a little laugh and replied, "I think that's an excellent idea. Just make sure you air the sheets before I arrive!"

*****

Once more they met, both displaying punctuality, and ordered a glass of cold white French wine.

"Doreen and Roger will be joining us shortly and everything's arranged for us to be at the same table for dinner." said Laura.

"Thank you," said Claudine, "that really will be very nice and make my last evening on board the ship a positive delight. But Laura, you are looking very sad. Is something wrong?"

"I don't really know." replied Laura, "I've been remembering my mother. The more I think of her relationship with our father, the sadder I become. It must have been so painful for them both. I cannot understand how she must have felt during all those years. Yesterday, you talked of a depth of love. I'm sure my mother must have borne a very special love for Jules throughout her life."

Claudine took Laura's hand.

"I'm sure that's so, just as it was for him." she said, "It was the way it had to be. Everything that happens to us is part of life's drama and has to be played out, whether it brings sadness or joy. You must be emotionally drained with all that you have now discovered."

"That's for sure," responded Laura, "the ring seems to have turned my life upside down. Usually when a young woman receives a ring it gives her considerable pleasure. The ring I received placed a halo of discomfort over me despite the fact I knew this could not have been my mother's intention."

At that moment Doreen and Roger arrived.

"You two are looking very serious," said Doreen, "I hope nothing's wrong."

"It's just me being very tired," replied Laura, "We've been talking about everything that has happened since we met. Being with you on this cruise, Doreen, has not only enabled me to solve the mystery I have been living with for so long, by finding I have a half-sister, but fate has also brought Roger into my life and there's no doubt, Roger, I've fallen very much in love with you."

Doreen gave her a hug and said, "I'm so happy for all three of you and I can't wait to see what happens next, but, in the meantime should you know of another man like Roger here, please point him in my direction."

They all laughed and went into dinner when Laura introduced Claudine to Denise, Phyllis and James, simply saying, "This is my half-sister. She was born and lives in France."

Nobody was surprised as during the past two days word had got around and all three were thrilled to meet Claudine personally.

"I bet you never thought you'd have a concert pianist in the family." commented James.

"That's very true," replied Claudine, "and I'm very proud of her. She plays beautifully."

"Oh, I must tell you all some news." said Phyllis, "Guess who won the Bingo jackpot today. Well, you won't guess so I'll tell you – it was our honeymoon couple, Lucy and Joel. I spoke to them a few minutes ago and she said *'I've hit the jackpot three times without being to the casino once. First, I got Joel and then I won the tickets for this cruise and now the Bingo.'*

"What a great start to their marriage." said Denise.

"Absolutely," said Phyllis, "I can't tell you how excited she was."

Just as she finished a waiter appeared carrying seven glasses of champagne and commenced distributing them round the table.

"Where did these come from?" asked James.

"I understand that a Mr. Roger Gould ordered them, sir." replied the waiter.

A series of comments came from all the others indicating their surprise, delight and thanks.

"It's my pleasure," said Roger, "and is my way of saying thank you to all of you for having been such good fellow companions. I believe we've all had a jolly good holiday and I've thoroughly enjoyed being out and about with some of you."

"Your very good health, Roger," said James, "and good luck with any future plans you may have – isn't that right Laura?"

"James, stop it, just mind your own business." said Phyllis, "I told all of you when we first met he's impossible and you've been able to see it for yourselves."

"Not at all, said Denise, "I think you're like a lovely pussy cat, James."

"What good taste and judgement you have, my dear." responded James.

He raised his glass by way of a toast to all and added, "I've one last suggestion to make, which is, after dinner we all go and see the show together on this final evening. Now all those in favour say 'aye'."

A unanimous 'aye' resounded round the table with passengers seated nearby wondering what all the laughter was about.

*****

They managed to find a group of comfortable seats just behind the front row slightly to the side of the stage.

A roll of drums was heard and then, coming from either side of the wings, Alan Spencer and Sandra Wells appeared, made their way to the microphone at centre stage and commenced singing a duet of Irving Berlin's song 'There's no business like show business' from the musical 'Annie Get Your Gun'.

They then jointly compered the show taking it in turns to introduce the acts. The Neptune orchestra with the Neptune singers and dancers were all on top form and accompanied the leads whenever required. Jake and Nick thoroughly entertained the audience and a big cheer went up when Matt was called to the stage.

It was Alan who interrupted the show for a few moments, saying he had an important announcement to make and told everyone he'd just received an email from the hospital in Gibraltar, and had learned that Henry Arkwright was no longer in intensive care and was expected to make a good recovery. Alan continued by commenting he'd felt sure a number of cruise passengers who had met and got to know him would wish to know of this latest medical bulletin.

"And now ladies and gentlemen," continued Alan, "very shortly the entire cast will be appearing for the final number of the show – yes, you've guessed it "We'll Meet Again" – but before they do, I've spotted two people in the audience who I know you'd want to see up here with them. They have entertained you magnificently, so please give a big hand to Doreen Langton and Laura King."

One of the theatre lights swung over to where they were seated, whilst both began to look rather embarrassed. Knowing what Alan had intended saying, Sandra had already made her way over to them to ensure she would be able to lead them on to the stage.

The entire audience joined in the singing, at the end of which Alan asked that they stay in their seats until the cast had passed through the theatre. The object of this soon became very clear, as lined up on either side of both of the exits were members of the orchestra, the dancers, the singers, Jake, Nick and Matt, Doreen, Laura, Alan and Sandra and some other members of the crew.

All were gathered to say their farewells to the passengers and wish them a safe journey home.

The final goodbyes between the people themselves took place as addresses and telephone numbers were exchanged with the stated intention of use at a future date, though most knew this was not likely to happen.

Last drinks were taken by others, whilst some simply made their swift departures, conscious of having a strenuous day's travel ahead, following disembarkation.

Gradually the numbers declined considerably with the exception of a number of younger people still enjoying the draw of the disco and not being too concerned as to the time.

Luggage was being removed speedily but quietly by the crew with the precision of a mass production line, only interrupting their duties to say 'good-night' to the last trickle of guests, who, hand in hand or arm in arm, were slowly strolling towards their cabins occasionally stealing the warmth of a romantic kiss.

Last emails had been sent, the photo gallery had closed and final accounts were being prepared to be pushed under cabin doors for inspection by passengers when waking in the morning.

Last minute packing of items to be taken off the ship by hand was taking place until the moment came when cabin lights were turned off for the last time by passengers on this Mediterranean cruise, to allow the call of sleep to take over for the remaining hours that were left.

There would be many who were looking forward to arriving in Dover and returning home so as to be able to resume their normal activities, of either a business or social nature, whilst for others the last evening had been tinged with sadness.

Some did not want to find themselves once more immersed in a series of personal problems, which they had been able to put behind them for two weeks and others were not relishing the thought of returning to a lonely existence, living by themselves, away from family and not having any special friend.

And there were those who would be reflecting upon how the cruise had brought them to a point of making decisions which would influence the rest of their life.

TWENTY THREE

As The Neptune moved slowly and majestically through the sea towards its destination, the Port of Dover, the hour of midnight struck welcoming the dawning of Saturday 29th September.

Later that day seven hundred names in the liner's reservation records would be registered by security personnel, recorded by the purser's office and entered on dining plans.

These names would be those scheduled to sail on the ship's next voyage, on its cruise titled 'Baltic Highlights' a journey that would commence when the vessel departed port at six o'clock in the evening on this same day.

Going on a cruise or any other holiday is just like Easter and Christmas when generally everyone has been aware for some time that the event will be taking place but often it is not until the last moment that the mind functions registering the mental process of '*I must buy*'—'*I must find*'---'*I must do.*'

And so it would be with many of the next Neptune passengers.

*****

TWENTY FOUR

FIVE WEEKS LATER.

Delia was sitting in their living room listening to the six o'clock news on Radio 4. The first items had included the latest bulletin covering armed forces activities in Afghanistan, a report on last month's inflation figures coupled with comments from the BBC economics correspondent and an interview with the newly appointed Minister of Education.

It was the next item which made her sit bolt upright as the news reader announced,

'A disruption took place early this afternoon on the Central Line, when a woman, clutching a red file, threw herself in front of a train at Queensway station. Police have stated she is thought to have been about seventy and enquiries as to her identity are being made. Normal service was resumed just before three

'And now for the weather forecast............'

She could not believe what she'd heard, got out of her chair, made her way into their hall and when standing at the foot of the stairs called up, "Paul, can you come down. I've something to tell you."

*****

CRUISE NOTES

CRUISE NOTES

BROC RHYFEL

MARTIN DAVIS

y Lolfa

Dymunaf ddiolch i Alun Jones, Nia Peris a holl staff y Lolfa am eu cyfraniad proffesiynol arferol wrth lunio'r gyfrol hon a hefyd i'm gwraig Siân am ei hysbrydoliaeth a'i chefnogaeth ddiwyro.

Argraffiad cyntaf: 2014
© Hawlfraint Martin Davis a'r Lolfa Cyf., 2014

Dychmygol yw holl gymeriadau'r nofel hon

Cynllun y clawr: Matthew Tyson

Rhif Llyfr Rhyngwladol: 978 1 84771 879 2

Dymuna'r cyhoeddwyr gydnabod cymorth ariannol
Cyngor Llyfrau Cymru

Cyhoeddwyd ac argraffwyd yng Nghymru
ar bapur o goedwigoedd cynaladwy gan
Y Lolfa Cyf., Talybont, Ceredigion SY24 5HE
e-bost ylolfa@ylolfa.com
gwefan www.ylolfa.com
ffôn 01970 832 304
ffacs 01970 832 782